Praise for RaeAnne Thayne

"Seamless, graceful, gritty and big-hearted as only RaeAnne Thayne can do. I couldn't put it down."
—Kristan Higgins, #1 *New York Times* bestselling author, on *15 Summers Later*

"RaeAnne Thayne will capture your heart with her beautiful, touching stories."
—Robyn Carr, #1 *New York Times* bestselling author of the Virgin River series

"[Thayne's] books are wonderfully romantic, feel-good reads that end with me sighing over the last pages."
—Debbie Macomber, #1 *New York Times* bestselling author

Dear Reader,

What an honor it is to be part of Harlequin's 75th anniversary celebration. No other publisher has so consistently been focused on stories of people opening their hearts to love, despite all the many obstacles they may face. For decades, Harlequin has been gracing bookshelves around the world with enchanting stories filled with swoon-worthy heroes and captivating heroines. I'm delighted to play a small part in remembering all the things that make Harlequin books so special—the promise of love, the thrill of unexpected twists and the satisfaction of happily-ever-after.

The anniversary celebration seemed a perfect chance for me to finish off my Women of Brambleberry House series. Through the six books in the series, I have come to adore this rambling old house by the seashore. Returning to it feels like coming home for me and I hope my readers feel the same. I have loved revisiting old friends and making new ones!

Thank you for being part of this incredible journey, and here's to many more years of shared stories, cherished moments and the enduring power of love.

All my very best,

RaeAnne

A BEACH HOUSE BEGINNING

NEW YORK TIMES BESTSELLING AUTHOR
RaeAnne Thayne

FREE STORY BY
MICHELLE LINDO-RICE

H Harlequin
SPECIAL RELEASE

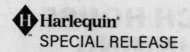

Harlequin®
SPECIAL RELEASE

ISBN-13: 978-1-335-00745-2

A Beach House Beginning
First published in 2024. This edition published in 2024.
Copyright © 2024 by RaeAnne Thayne LLC

A Beauty in the Beast
First published in 2024. This edition published in 2024.
Copyright © 2024 by Michelle Lindo-Rice

For questions and comments about the quality of this book, please contact us at CustomerService@Harlequin.com.

TM and ® are trademarks of Harlequin Enterprises ULC.

 Harlequin Enterprises ULC
22 Adelaide St. West, 41st Floor
Toronto, Ontario M5H 4E3, Canada
www.Harlequin.com

Printed in U.S.A.

CONTENTS

New York Times bestselling author **RaeAnne Thayne** finds inspiration in the beautiful northern Utah mountains, where she lives with her family. Her books have won numerous honors, including six RITA® Award nominations from Romance Writers of America and Career Achievement and Romance Pioneer Awards from *RT Book Reviews*. She loves to hear from readers and can be reached through her website at raeannethayne.com.

Also by RaeAnne Thayne

The Cafe at Beach End
All Is Bright
Summer at the Cape
Sleigh Bells Ring
The Path to Sunshine Cove
Christmas at Holiday House
The Sea Glass Cottage
Coming Home for Christmas
The Cliff House
Season of Wonder
A Beach House Beginning

Visit her Author Profile page
at Harlequin.com for more titles.

A BEACH HOUSE BEGINNING

RaeAnne Thayne

To all the hundreds of people at Harlequin who work with such passion and heart to get our books into the hands of our amazing readers. Thank you!

Chapter One

"Jenna? Are you still there?"

Jenna Haynes slowly lowered herself to one of the kitchen chairs of her apartment on the second floor of Brambleberry House. Her cell phone nearly slipped from fingers that suddenly trembled.

"I...yes. I'm here." Her voice sounded hollow, thready.

"I know this must be coming as a shock to you." Angela Terry, the prosecuting attorney who had worked on the Oregon part of her case, spoke in a low, calming voice. "Believe me, we were all stunned, too. I never expected this. I'm sorry to call you so early but I wanted to reach out to you as soon as we heard the news."

"Thank you. I appreciate that."

"Seriously, what a shock. It's so hard to believe, when Barker was only halfway through his sentence. Who expects a guy in the prime of his life to go to sleep in his cell one night and never wake up? You know what they say. Karma drives a big bus and she knows everybody's address."

Jenna didn't know how to answer, still trying to process the stunning news that the man she had feared for three years was truly gone.

On the heels of her shock came an overwhelming relief. A man was dead. She couldn't forget that. Still, the man had made her life a nightmare for a long time.

"You're…you're positive he's dead?"

"The warden called me to confirm it himself, as soon as the medical examiner determined it was from natural causes. An aneurysm."

"An aneurysm? Seriously?"

"That's what the warden said. Who knows, Barker might have had a brain anomaly all along. What else would cause a decorated police officer to go off the rails like he did and spend years stalking, threatening and finally attacking you and others?"

Jenna fought down an instinctive shiver as the terrifying events of two years earlier crawled out from the lockbox of memories where she tried to store them for safekeeping.

Dead. The boogeyman who had haunted her nightmares for so long was gone.

She still couldn't quite believe it, even hearing it from a woman she trusted and admired, a woman who had fought hard to make sure Aaron Barker would remain behind bars for the maximum allowable sentence, which had been entirely too short a time as far as Jenna was concerned.

Jenna didn't know how she was supposed to feel,

now that she knew he couldn't get out in a few years to pick up where he left off.

"I hope I didn't wake you, but I wanted you to know as soon as possible."

The concern in her voice warmed Jenna. Angela had been an unending source of calm and comfort, even during the most stressful of times during the trial.

"No. I'm glad you called. I appreciate it."

Slowly, her brain seemed to reengage and she remembered the polite niceties she owed this woman who had fought with such fierce determination for her.

"You didn't wake me," she assured Angela. "I have school this morning."

"Oh good. I was hoping I didn't catch you while you were sleeping in on your first day of summer vacation or something."

"One more week for that," Jenna answered. "I'm just fixing breakfast for Addie."

"How is my little buddy? Tell her we need to get together soon for a *Mario Kart* rematch. No way can I let a seven-year-old get the better of me."

"Eight. She turned eight last month."

"Already? Dang. I can't believe I missed her birthday. I'll have to send her something."

"You don't have to do that, Angela. You've done so much already for us. I can never thank you enough for everything. I mean that."

"Well, we still need to get together and catch up. It's been too long."

"Yes. I would love that. I'll only be working part-time at the gift shop this summer so my schedule is much more flexible than during the school year."

"We'll do it. We can have Rosa join us. I'll set up a text string and we can work out details."

"Thank you for telling me about Aaron."

"I know you had been worrying about his possible release next year," the other woman said, her voice gentle. "I hope that knowing he can't ever bother you again goes a little way toward taking a weight off your heart."

"It does. I can't even tell you how much."

They spoke for a few more moments before ending the call with promises to make plans later in the summer.

Jenna set her phone on the table slowly, released a heavy sigh and then covered her face with her hands.

Dead.

She didn't quite know how to react.

Since the arrest and conviction eighteen months ago of the man who had tormented her for years, she had been bracing herself for the moment when he might be released, when she might have to pick up her daughter again and flee.

She had hated the idea of it.

Brambleberry House, this beautiful rambling beach house on the dramatic coastline of northern Oregon, had become a haven for them. She had finally begun to rebuild her life here, to feel safe again and…happy.

Lurking at the edge of her consciousness, though, like the dark, far-off blur of an impending storm, was the grim realization that someday she might have to leave everything once more and start again somewhere else.

Now she didn't have to.

She wiped away tears she hadn't even realized were coursing down her cheeks.

He was gone. They were free.

"What's wrong, Mom?"

She turned to find her daughter in the doorway, wearing shorts, a ruffled T-shirt and a frown.

Jenna gave a laugh and reached for Addie, pulling her into a tight hug.

"Nothing's wrong. Everything is terrific. Really terrific."

Her perceptive child wasn't fooled. She eased away, narrowing her gaze. "What's going on?"

Jenna didn't want to talk about Aaron Barker. She didn't want Addie to have to think about the man who had threatened them both, who had completely upended their lives simply because he couldn't have what he wanted.

"Nothing." She gave a reassuring smile. "I'm just happy, that's all. It's a beautiful day, school will be out next week and summer is right around the corner. Now hurry and finish your breakfast so we can get to school. I could use your help carrying the cupcakes for my class."

Addie still didn't look convinced. Sometimes she seemed far too wise for her eight years on the earth. Apparently she decided not to push the matter.

"Can I have one of the cupcakes? You said I could when we were frosting them last night."

The cupcakes were a treat for her class, a reward for everyone meeting their reading goals for the year.

Jenna pointed to the counter, at a covered container near the microwave. "I've got two there for us. I was going to save them for dessert later tonight after dinner, but I suddenly feel like celebrating. Let's have a cupcake."

Addie's eyes widened with shock and then delight.

She reached for the container and pulled out one of the chocolate cupcakes, biting into it quickly as if afraid Jenna would change her mind.

"You still have to eat your egg bites and your cantaloupe," Jenna warned.

"I don't care. Cupcakes for breakfast is the best idea ever."

She couldn't disagree, Jenna thought as she finished hers, as well as her own healthier breakfast. Still, the call was at the forefront of her thoughts as she hurried through the rest of her preparations for the school day.

Twenty minutes later, she juggled her laptop bag, a box of cupcakes and a stack of math papers she had graded the evening before.

She couldn't help humming a song as she walked out of her apartment, Addie right behind her.

A man stood on the landing outside her apartment, hand on the banister. He was big, dark, muscular, wearing a leather jacket and carrying a motorcycle helmet under his arm.

For one ridiculous moment, her heart skipped a beat, as it always did when she saw her new upstairs neighbor. Her song died and she immediately felt foolish.

"Morning," he said, voice gruff.

"Um. Hi."

"You've got your arms full. Can I help you carry something?"

"No. I've got it," she said, her voice more clipped than she intended.

His eyes darkened slightly at her abrupt tone. Something flickered in his expression, something hard and dangerous, but he merely nodded and gestured for them to go ahead of him down the stairs.

Did he guess she was afraid of him? Jenna had tried to hide it, but she strongly suspected she hadn't been very successful.

"Come on, Addie."

Her daughter, who seemed to have none of Jenna's instinctive fear of big, tough, ruthless-looking men with more ink than charm, smiled and waved at him.

"Bye, Mr. Calhoun. I hope you have a happy day."

He looked nonplussed. "Thanks. Same to you."

Jenna led their little procession down the central staircase of Brambleberry House, which featured private entrances to the three apartments, one on each floor.

As she hurried outside, she couldn't help wondering again what Rosa Galvez Townsend had been thinking to rent the space to this man.

She had heard the rumors about Wes Calhoun. He had a daughter who attended her school, and while Brielle was a grade older and wasn't in Jenna's class, the girl's teacher was one of Jenna's closest friends.

Teachers gossip as much as, if not more than, other populations. As soon as Wes Calhoun rode into town on his motorcycle, leather jacket, tattoos and all, Jenna had learned he was an ex-con only released a few months earlier from prison in the Chicago area.

Learning he would be her new upstairs neighbor had been unsettling and upsetting.

Rosa—who functioned as landlady for her aunt Anna and Anna's friend Sage, owners of the house—assured her he was a friend of Wyatt, Rosa's husband, and perfectly harmless. He had been wrongfully convicted three years earlier and had been completely cleared, his record expunged.

That didn't set her mind at ease. At all. She would have found the man intimidating even if she hadn't known he was only a few months out of prison.

She hurried Addie to her small SUV, loaded the cupcakes into the cargo area and made sure Addie was safely belted into the back.

As she slid behind the wheel, Jenna watched Wes climb onto his sleek, black, death trap of a motorcycle parked beside her and fasten his helmet.

While he started up the bike, he didn't go anywhere, just waited, boots on the driveway. He was waiting for her, she realized.

Aware of his gaze on her, steely and unflinching, she turned the key in the ignition.

Instead of purring to life, the car only gave an ominous click.

She tried it a second time, with the same results, then a third.

No. Oh no. This wasn't happening. She was already running late.

Normally she and Addie could ride bikes the mile and a half to the school, but not when she had two dozen cupcakes to deliver!

Hoping against hope, she tried it a few more times, with the same futile click.

"What's wrong?" Addie asked.

"I'm not sure. The car isn't starting, for some reason."

A sudden knock at her window made her jump. Without power, she couldn't lower the window, so she opened the door a crack.

"Having trouble?" Wes Calhoun looked at her with concern.

She wanted to tell him no, that she was a strong, independent woman who could handle her own problems. But what she knew about cars could probably fit inside one spark plug. If cars even had spark plugs anymore, which she suspected they didn't.

"You could say that. It won't start. I'm not getting anything but clicks."

"Sounds like it might be your battery. Do you know how old it is?"

"No. I bought the car used two years ago. It was three years old then. I have no idea how old the battery is. I do know I haven't replaced it."

"Pop the hood and I'll take a look at it."

"You don't have to do that. I can call road service."

He gave her a long look. "You seemed in a hurry this morning. Do you have time to wait for road service? If it's your battery, I can give you a jump and get you on the road in only a few minutes."

She glanced at her watch. The phone call with Angela had thrown off her whole morning schedule. She was already going to be late, without adding in a potentially long wait for road service.

"Thank you. I would appreciate a jump, if you don't mind. Can you jump a car with a motorcycle, though?"

"I don't know. I've never tried. I was talking about my truck."

He had an old blue pickup truck, she knew. He drove that on the frequent days of rain along the Oregon Coast.

"Right."

"Let's take a look first under the hood. Can you pop it for me?"

She fumbled beneath the steering wheel to find the right lever that would release the hood, then climbed out just as Wes was taking off his leather jacket and setting it on the seat of his motorcycle.

The plain black T-shirt he wore underneath showed off muscular biceps and the tattoos that adorned them.

As he bent over the engine, worn jeans hugging his behind, his T-shirt rode up slightly, revealing a few inches of his muscular back. Her stomach tingled and Jenna swallowed and looked away, appalled at herself for having an instinctive reaction to a man who left her so jumpy.

"Yep. Looks like you need a new battery. I'll give you a quick jump so you can make it to work. If you want, I can pick up another battery and put it in for you this evening."

Jenna tried not to gape at him. Why was he being so nice to her, when she hadn't exactly thrown out the welcome mat for him?

"I...that would be very kind. Thank you."

"Give me a second to pull my truck around."

"What's wrong with the car? Is it broken?" Addie asked from the back seat after Wes moved to his pickup truck and climbed inside, then started doing multiple-point turns to put it in position for jumper cables to reach her battery from his.

"The battery is dead. Our nice neighbor Mr. Calhoun is going to try to help us get it started."

"I can't be late today. I have to give my book report first thing."

"Hopefully we can still make it in time," she answered, as Wes turned off his truck and released the hood latch, then climbed out, rummaged behind the seats for some jumper cables and started hooking things up.

"What do I need to do?" she asked, feeling awkward

and clueless. She had needed to have a vehicle jumped a few times before, early in her marriage, but Ryan had always taken care of those kind of things for her. She should have paid more attention to the process.

"Nothing yet. I'll tell you when to try starting it again."

He hooked up the cables, then fired up his truck before coming back to her car. "Okay. Let's give it a go and see what happens."

Mentally crossing her fingers, she pushed the ignition button. To her vast relief, the engine turned for a second or two, then burst into life.

"Yay!" Addie exclaimed. "Does that mean we don't have to walk to school?"

"We would have found a ride somehow," Jenna assured her. "But it looks like we've been rescued, thanks to Mr. Calhoun."

"Thanks, Mr. Calhoun. I have to give a report this morning on a book about bees and didn't want to be late."

"You're very welcome. You can call me Wes, by the way. You don't have to call me Mr. Calhoun."

Her daughter beamed at him, unfazed by that hard, unsmiling face. "Thanks, Wes."

"You can as well," he said to Jenna. Their gazes met and she couldn't help noticing how long his dark eyelashes were, an odd contrast to the hard planes of his features.

"Thank you, Wes," she forced herself to say. "I really appreciate the help."

"It was no problem. I'll grab a battery for you today. Do you have jumper cables, in case your car doesn't start after you're done at school today?"

She was relieved she could answer in the affirmative. "Yes. I have an emergency kit in back with flares, a flashlight and a blanket, along with a few tools and jumper cables."

"Good. With any luck, you might not need them."

"Thanks again for all your help."

He shrugged. "It's the kind of thing neighbors do for each other, right?"

His words filled her with guilt. She hadn't been very neighborly in the two weeks since he had moved in. She hadn't taken any goodies over to welcome him and did little more than nod politely in passing.

Was he being ironic? Had he noticed how she went out of her way to avoid him whenever possible?

She hoped he didn't notice how her face flushed with heat as she mustered a smile that faded quickly as she backed out of the driveway and turned in the direction of school.

Wes watched his pretty neighbor maneuver her little blue SUV onto the road toward the elementary school.

When he was certain her vehicle wasn't going to conk out on the road, he returned his pickup to its customary spot and climbed back onto his Harley.

It might be easier to take the truck today but he was in the mood for a bike ride, which was just about the only thing that could do anything at all to calm his restlessness.

That was an odd turn for his morning to take, but he was happy to help out, even if Jenna Haynes looked at him out of those big blue eyes like she was afraid he was about to drag her by her hair up the stairs to his apartment and lock her in his sex dungeon.

He might have found her skittishness a little amusing if he hadn't spent the past three years in company with people capable of that and so much worse.

It still burned under his skin how she and others considered him. An ex-con. Not an innocent man wrongfully convicted because of a betrayal but someone who had probably been exactly where he belonged. Even if he hadn't done the particular crime that had put him behind bars, he was no doubt guilty of *something*, right?

He hated it, that pearl-clutching, self-righteous, condemnatory attitude he had encountered since his release. After two months on the outside, he was still trying to adjust to the knowledge that his slate would never be wiped completely clean, no matter how many neighborly things he did.

He couldn't be bothered by what Jenna Haynes thought of him. What anybody thought of him. He had clung to sanity in prison by remembering that he was not the man others saw when they looked at him.

He lifted his face to the sun for just a moment before shoving on his helmet. He couldn't get enough of feeling the warmth of it on his face or smelling air scented with spring and the sea.

Clutch your pearls all you want, Ms. Haynes, he thought. *I'm alive and free. That's enough for today.*

He drove his bike through light traffic to Cannon Beach Car and Bike Repair, the garage where he had been lucky to find a job after showing up in town with mainly his bike, his truck and the small settlement he had received from the state of Illinois.

He had just parked the bike and was taking off his helmet when a tall, dark-haired and very pregnant woman climbed out of a silver sedan and hurried over to him.

Wes sighed and braced himself, not at all in the mood to have a confrontation with his ex-wife that morning. Though they had a generally friendly relationship, he couldn't imagine why she would show up unless she was mad about something. Not when she could have called or texted for anything benign.

"There you are," Lacey exclaimed. "I thought you started work at eight."

He looked at his watch that read eight oh five. "I had a neighbor with a dead battery. It took me a minute to get the car started. What's up? Have you been waiting for me? You could have called."

"I know. But I had to run next door anyway to pick up something at the hardware store after I dropped off Brielle at school, so I figured I would stop here first to talk to you while I was out."

He really hoped she wasn't about to tell him her husband had been transferred again, after only being moved here a year ago to become manager of a chain department store in a nearby town.

Wes liked it here in Cannon Beach. He liked running on the beach in the mornings and sitting in the gardens of Brambleberry House in the evenings to watch the sun slide into the water.

He liked his job, too. He had worked in a neighbor-hood auto mechanic shop all through high school and summers during college and definitely knew his way around an engine, motorcycle or car.

Did he want to do it forever? No. As much as he had admired and respected the neighbor who had employed him—and all those who worked with their hands—Wes didn't think working as a mechanic was his destiny. He still didn't know what he wanted to do as he worked toward rebuilding the life that had been taken from him. But for now he had found a good place, working with honest, hardworking people who cared about treating their customers right.

It paid the bills and was challenging enough not to bore him, but not overwhelming as he tried to ease back into outside life.

"What's going on?"

He could see his boss, Carlos Gutierrez, and his brother Paco watching them through the small front window of the shop.

"You know you don't always have to cut to the chase, right?" Lacey looked exasperated. "We're not having a quick conversation between prison bars anymore. A little small talk would be fine. You could say, *Hi, Lacey. How are you? How's the house? How's the baby?*"

Wes worked to keep his expression neutral. He might have agreed with her, except their marriage hadn't exactly been filled with small talk, even before his arrest.

"How are you feeling?" he asked. He had learned a long time ago it was best to try humoring her whenever possible.

Lacey was a devoted, loving mother to their daughter and he still considered her a dear friend. If circumstances had been different, he would have tried like hell to keep their marriage together.

Still, he couldn't help being more than a little grateful her sometimes volatile moods were another man's problems these days.

"I'm good. Huge. I can't believe I still have ten weeks to go before the baby comes."

They had been divorced for two and a half years. She had remarried her childhood sweetheart a year almost to the day their divorce had been finalized and was now expecting a son with Ron Summers.

Wes was happy for her. When he had little to do but think about his life, it hadn't taken long for Wes to recognize that his marriage to Lacey had been a mistake from start to finish. He had been twenty-one, about to head off overseas with the Army and she had been eighteen and desperate to escape an unhappy home life, with an abusive father and neglectful mother.

They hadn't been a good fit for each other. He could see that now, though both of them had spent years trying to deny the inevitable.

One good thing had come out of it. One amazing thing, actually. His nine-year-old daughter, Brielle. She was his heart, his purpose, his everything.

"That's actually why I'm here. Ron has the chance to take a last-minute trip to Costa Rica for work. He'll be gone ten days and he wants me to go with him, if I can swing it. This is my last chance to travel for a while, at least until the baby is older."

"Sounds like fun," he said, trying to figure out where he came in and why she had accosted him at his workplace to deliver the news.

"The problem is that I can't take Brie. She doesn't have a passport and there's no way to get one for her in time."

Ah. Now things were beginning to make sense.

"Is there any chance she could come stay with you while we're gone?"

A host of complications ran through his head, starting with the building just beyond her. The Gutierrez brothers had been good to him. He couldn't just leave them in the lurch to facilitate his ex-wife's travel plans.

He worked full-time and would have to arrange childcare. Brielle was nine going on eighteen and likely thought she was fully capable of being on her own while he worked all day. Wes definitely didn't agree. But he couldn't bring her down here to the garage with him all day, either.

He would figure that part out later. How could he turn down the chance to spend as much time as possible with his daughter, considering all the years he had missed?

"Sure. Of course. I would love to have her."

Lacey's face lit up with happiness, reminding him with painful clarity that it had been a long time since they had been able to make each other happy.

"Oh, that's amazing. Thank you! Brie will be so excited when I tell her. The alternative was staying with my friend Shandy and she has that five-year-old who can be a real pistol. Brielle will much prefer staying with her dad."

He could only hope he was up to the task. "When do you leave?" Wes asked.

"Next Friday. The last day of school."

It would have been easier if she were leaving during the school year, when he would only need to arrange after-school care until his shift was over, but he would figure things out.

He couldn't say no. He had moved to Cannon Beach, following Lacey and her new family, in order to nurture his relationship with Brielle. He couldn't miss what seemed to be a glorious opportunity to be with her.

"No problem. We'll have a great time."

"You're the best. Seriously. Thanks, Wes."

She stood on tiptoe and kissed his cheek, and as

her mouth brushed his cheek, Wes couldn't help wishing that things could have worked out differently between them.

He couldn't honestly say he regretted the end of a marriage that had been troubled from the beginning. He did regret that the decisions made by the adults in Brielle's life complicated things for her, forcing her to now split her time between them.

"You do remember that today is Guest Lunch at the school, right? Brie said you were planning to go. If you're not, I'm sure Ron could swing by on his lunch break."

He really tried not to feel competitive with his daughter's stepfather, who seemed overall like a good guy, if a little on the superficial side.

"I'll be there," he answered, hoping the day wouldn't be inordinately busy at the shop.

The Gutierrez brothers were great to work with, but an employer could only be so understanding.

As he watched his ex-wife drive away, the second time he had been caught in the wake of a woman's taillights that morning, he was reminded of Jenna Haynes and her car trouble.

If he were swinging by the school anyway for lunch, he might as well take a car battery with him and fix Jenna Haynes's car. It was an easy ten-minute job, and that way she wouldn't have to worry about the possibility of it not starting after school.

He told himself the little burst of excitement was only the anticipation of doing a nice, neighborly deed. It had nothing to do with the knowledge that he would inevitably see Jenna again.

Chapter Two

"Stay in line, class. Remember, hands to yourself."

Jenna did her best to steer her class of twenty-three third-grade students—including three with special learning needs and Individualized Education Programs—into the lunchroom with a minimum of distractions.

The day that had started out with such stunning news from Angela had quickly spiraled. Her dead battery had only been the beginning.

As soon as she reached the school, she discovered both of her paraprofessionals, who helped with reading and math, as well as giving extra attention to those who struggled most, had called in for personal leave. One was pregnant and had bad morning sickness and the other one had to travel out of town at the last minute to be with a dying relative.

Jenna completely understood they both had excellent

reasons to be gone. Unfortunately, that left her to handle the entire class by herself, and her third-grade students were so jacked up over the approaching summer vacation—or maybe from the sugar in her cupcakes—that none of them seemed able to focus.

One more week, she told herself. One more week and then she would have the entire summer to herself.

The previous summer, she had taken classes all summer to finish her master's degree, as well as working nearly full-time at Rosa's gift shop, By-the-Wind.

She didn't feel as if she had enjoyed any summer vacation at all.

She wasn't going to make that mistake again this year. Though she still had two more classes to go before earning her master's degree, she had decided to hold off until after the summer, and she had told Rosa she couldn't work as many hours at the gift shop.

Addie was growing up and Jenna wanted to spend as much time as possible with her daughter while Addie still seemed to like being with her.

"Don't want spaghetti." The sudden strident shout from one of her students, Cody Andrews, drew looks from several students in the cafeteria. Some of the adult guests having lunch with their students also gave the boy the side-eye.

Jenna felt immediately on the defensive. Cody, who had been diagnosed with autism, was an eager, funny, bright student, but sometimes crowds could set him off and trigger negative behaviors.

He had seemed to have a particularly difficult morning, maybe because Monica, the aide he loved dearly, wasn't there.

"Do you want to get pizza from the à la carte line?" she asked him, her voice low and calming.

"No. I don't like pizza." That was news to her, since his favorite food was usually pizza and he could eat it five days a week without fuss.

"What about chicken tenders?"

He appeared to consider that for a long moment, his blond head tilted and his brow furrowed. Finally he nodded. "Okay. I like tenders."

The lunchroom was crowded with parents and friends of the students who had come for their monthly Lunch with a Guest activity.

She strongly suspected another of the reasons for Cody's outburst might have something to do with that. His parents were recently divorced and his father, who used to come have lunch with him every month, had moved two towns over.

Normally she didn't eat with the students, preferring to grab a quick bite at her desk while they were out at recess, unless she was on playground duty. But because Cody was being so clingy, she had decided to bring her sack lunch to the table. Now he slid in next to her with his tray of nuggets.

She waved to a few of the parents, then pulled out her sandwich just as she felt the presence of someone behind her.

She turned and was astonished to discover her up-stairs neighbor standing beside his daughter, Brielle. He was holding a tray that carried both their lunches.

"Hello."

In boots, jeans and the same black T-shirt he had been wearing earlier in the day, he looked big and tough and intimidating. Completely out of place in an elementary school lunchroom.

He should moonlight as a bouncer at a biker bar, since nobody would dare mess with him.

"Hi, Mrs. Haynes. This is my dad." Brielle, his daughter, beamed with pride.

"I know. I've met him. We're neighbors."

"This is his very first time coming to one of the Lunch with a Guest days."

She forced a smile. "Welcome. I hope you enjoy yourself."

"So far so good. It's pizza. What could go wrong with pizza?"

He obviously had not tried the school pizza yet, which could double as a paperweight in a pinch.

Jenna was disconcerted when Wes pointed to an empty spot down the row from her. "Is it all right if we sit here? There doesn't seem to be room with Brielle's class."

It was always a tight squeeze in the small lunchroom when each student brought a guest. Parents ended up finding spots wherever they could. She gestured to the empty spot. "Go ahead."

She was fiercely aware of him as she finished her sandwich.

"I have a dog," Cody suddenly announced. "Her name is Jojo, and she's white and brown with white ears and a brown tail. Do you want to see?"

Jenna realized with some alarm that the boy was talking to Wes in particular, unfazed by his intimidating appearance.

"Um. Sure."

Cody pulled out the small four-by-six photo album

he carried with him all the time in the front pocket of his hoodie, a sort of talisman. He opened it and thrust it into Wes's face, far too close for comfort.

"Wow. She's very pretty," Wes answered.

"Does she do any tricks?" Brielle asked, genuine curiosity in her voice as she peered around her father's muscular arm to see the photograph.

"She comes when I call her and she sits and she can roll over."

"I wish we had a dog," Brielle said, a hint of sadness in her voice. "We have a cat, though, and it's the best cat in the whole world."

Jenna thought the interaction would end there, as Cody could be quiet and withdrawn with strangers. She was surprised when the boy turned the page of his well-worn photo album to show other things that were important to him in his life. His bedroom. His bicycle. His father, who had walked out the previous year.

She might have expected Wes to turn his attention back to his daughter. That was the reason he had come to lunch, after all, to spend time with Brielle. Instead, he seemed to go out of his way to include the boy in their conversation.

She couldn't help being touched by and grateful for his efforts, especially because it allowed her a chance to interact with some of the other students who did not have a guest with them for various reasons.

As soon as the children finished lunch, they were each quick to return their trays to the cafeteria and rush outside for recess.

Brielle seemed to take her time over the meal, probably to spend more time with her father. Cody was the last to linger at the table, apparently enjoying his new friends too much to leave.

When he left to go out to recess, watched over by the playground aides, Jenna rose as well.

"I brought over a battery for your car," Wes said abruptly. "I can switch it out for you before I head back to the garage. I thought that might be better so you don't have to worry about needing a jump again after school is out."

This man was full of surprises. "Really? You would do that on your lunch hour?"

He shrugged. "It's no trouble. Will take me less than ten minutes. Brie can help me. She loves to work on cars, don't you?"

His daughter beamed. "Yep."

"I will need your car keys, though."

"They're in my classroom. I'm about to head back there, if you don't mind following me."

"Not a problem."

He and his daughter walked with her, Brielle chattering happily with her father. She didn't seem to mind his monosyllabic responses.

As they made their way through the halls, Jenna couldn't help but be aware of Wes. She was a little surprised to realize she had lost some of her nervousness around him. It was very difficult to remain afraid of a man who could show such kindness to a young boy who could sometimes struggle in social situations.

"Thank you for helping with Cody. He's having a pretty tough time right now. Guest days are sometimes hard on him. You helped distract him."

"I didn't do much. We just talked about his dog."

She wanted to tell him the conversation obviously

meant much more to the boy, who was deeply missing his father, but she didn't want to get into Cody's personal problems with him, especially not with Brielle there.

"The distraction was exactly what he needed. Thank you."

Wes didn't quite smile, but she thought his usual stern expression seemed to soften a little. "Glad I could help. About those keys…"

"Yes. I'll get them."

She opened her classroom and headed for the closet where she kept her personal effects. After digging through her purse, she pulled out her key chain with her car fob.

"Here you go," she said.

He held his hand out and she dropped the keys into it, grateful she didn't have to touch him for the handover.

"Thanks. I'll bring them back when I'm done."

"Do you need my help out there?"

"No. We got it."

"Thank you."

The words seemed inadequate but she did not know what else to say. As soon as Wes and Brielle walked out the side door closest to the faculty parking lot, her friend Kim Baker rushed out of her classroom across the hall, where she taught fifth grade.

"Who is that?" Kim asked, eyes wide. "I must know immediately."

"My neighbor."

"*That's* the serial killer?"

Jenna winced, feeling guilty that she had confided in her dear friend after she found out Wes had recently been released from prison.

"He's not a serial killer. I never said he was. He was

in prison for property crimes. Fraud, extortion, theft. But Anna and Rosa assure me he was exonerated."

"There you go, then. You should be fine."

"Especially since I have nothing to steal."

"You and me both, honey. We're teachers." Kim looked in the direction Wes had gone. "I have to say, I wouldn't mind having that man on top of me."

"Kim!" she exclaimed.

"Living upstairs," her friend said with a wink. "What did you think I meant?"

She rolled her eyes. "You're a happily married woman. Not to mention soon to be a grandmother."

Kim was only in her midforties but had married and started a family young. Her daughter was following in her footsteps, married and pregnant by twenty-two.

"I am all those things, but I'm not dead. And he is way hotter than you let on, you sly thing."

Jenna could feel her face flush. She hadn't told Kim much about Wes.

"I am curious about why your sexy new neighbor is stopping by in the middle of the day to talk to you. Is there something you're not telling me?"

"No!" she exclaimed quickly. "Nothing like what you're thinking. He jumped me this morning."

"Go on," Kim said, eyes wide with exaggerated lasciviousness.

Jenna let out an exasperated laugh. "My car died, I mean. He jumped my battery. He offered to fix it tonight, but since he was coming by the school today to see his daughter for lunch, he offered to fix it now."

To her vast relief, this information was enough for Kim to drop the double entendres. "That is really nice of him."

"Yes. It is."

"And you're sure that's all?"

"Yes," she said, more forcefully this time. "He's been very kind. That's all."

Kim made a face and reached for Jenna's hand, her features suddenly serious.

"I'm only saying this as your friend, but I can't think of anyone else who deserves to have their battery jumped by a sexy guy. And if he's kind and thoughtful, all the better."

The genuine concern in her voice touched Jenna, even if she didn't agree with the sentiment. She was deeply grateful for the many friendships she had made since coming to Cannon Beach. The people of this community had truly embraced her and welcomed her and Addison into their midst.

She still could not quite believe she was now free to stay here as long as she wanted.

"I appreciate the sweet sentiment, Kim, but I'm fine. Completely fine. I have everything I need. A great apartment, a job I love, Addie. It's more than enough. I don't need a man in my life."

And especially one who intimidated her as much as Wes Calhoun.

Kim did not look convinced, but before her friend could argue, Wes returned to Jenna's classroom, on his own this time instead of with his daughter.

He set Jenna's keys on the edge of her desk. "Here you go. She's running great now. Started right up. Looks like you're due for an oil change, though. You're going to want to get on that."

"I will. Thanks. What do I owe you for the battery?"

He looked reluctant to give a number but finally did, something that seemed far less than she was expecting.

"What about labor?"

"Nothing. There was really no labor involved."

She wanted to argue but couldn't figure out how in a gracious way. "Thank you, then," she finally said. "I'm very grateful."

She would have said more, but the bell rang in that moment and children began to swarm back into the classroom from the playground.

"Glad I could help," he answered. "I'll let you get back to your students."

"I'll settle up with you this evening, if that's okay."

Again she had the impression he wanted to tell her not to worry about it, but he finally nodded. "Sounds good. See you later."

Two students approached her desk to ask a question about the field trip they were taking on Monday to the aquarium in Lincoln City. By the time she answered them, Wes had slipped away.

Chapter Three

"I love, love, *love* pizza night!"

Wes smiled at Brielle, her face covered in flour and a little drip of tomato sauce on her nose. She wore an apron that matched the black one he wore on the rare occasions he cooked. Those occasions mostly consisted of Friday nights, when Brielle came over for her weekend visitation. Their tradition had become centered around pizza night, where they would spend an hour or so making their own pizzas and then would watch a show of her choosing.

The few days he had the chance to spend with Brielle were the highlight of his week. Even when they didn't do anything more exciting than hanging out at his apartment and playing board games, Wes found himself happier than he believed possible three months earlier.

This moment—in his warm kitchen with rain pattering down outside and his daughter giggling at the kitchen table as she made a face on her pizza with pepperoni—seemed worlds away from his life the past three years.

Rich and sweet and filled with joy.

He had been given a second chance and didn't want to waste a minute of it.

"Only one more week of school. Can you believe it?"

Brielle shook her head. "No. And I also can't believe I'm going to be in fifth grade next year. I hope I get Mrs. Baker. She's super funny."

He had met the woman the day before when he had returned Jenna's key to her classroom, he remembered.

While he was thinking about things that seemed far away from prison life, Jenna Haynes was the epitome.

She was lovely as a spring morning, her life worlds away from the darkness and ugliness he had been forced to wallow through in prison.

As lovely as he found her, he would be wise to remember they likely had nothing in common. He was darkness to her light, hard and jaded and cynical in contrast to her sweet innocence.

And she was terrified of him. He couldn't forget that part.

"Looks like we made too much dough. What are we going to do with it?"

"We can make another pizza!" Brielle said with a grin.

"We can do that, but that means we're going to have a lot of leftovers to eat the rest of the weekend."

"We could invite someone over," she suggested. "What about Mrs. Haynes and Addison? I can't believe they lived downstairs all this time and I never knew until today."

He hadn't exactly been holding out on Brielle. He simply hadn't thought to tell her before now about his neighbors.

He had only been in Brambleberry House for two weeks, after spending his first several weeks in the area paying a ridiculous amount for a tiny studio with a short-term lease, until he had found this place available. This was only his daughter's second weekend staying here with him. She had been delighted when he mentioned the other building tenants.

"Mrs. Haynes is super nice. I don't have her but my friend Reina does, and she really likes her," Brie had said when he told her.

"What about her daughter? Do you know her?"

"She's only in third grade, but we have the same recess so we play soccer sometimes. She's super fast. And she's funny!"

A good sense of humor seemed to be the barometer by which Brielle judged everyone. He couldn't disagree.

"So can we take them our extra pizza?" she asked now.

He was trying to come up with a good excuse to refuse when his doorbell rang.

Wes frowned, instantly on alert. Prison had given him a strong dislike of surprises. He wasn't expecting anybody, but maybe Lacey had forgotten to send something with Brielle for her overnight stay. Vitamins or extra socks or something.

"I'll get it," Brie sang out, rushing toward the door.

Wes hated that his life experience made him constantly brace for trouble.

He followed Brie, ready to yank her back to safety if necessary as she opened the door.

It wasn't trouble. At least not the sort he had become used to. His neighbor and her daughter stood on the landing to his apartment.

"Hi, Mrs. Haynes. Hi, Addie," Brielle said.

"Hi, Brielle." Addie beamed at his daughter.

The two girls looked very different. Addie had blue eyes and blond curls while Brie had long straight dark hair, which she usually wore in a ponytail or braid.

"It smells delicious in here," Addie exclaimed, giving a dramatic, exaggerated sniff. "What are you making?"

"Pizza." Brie grinned. "We make the dough and everything. My dad is the best pizza maker. He learned from my grandpa, who died when my dad was a kid. Isn't that sad?"

"My dad died when I was a kid, too. I was only four."

"I'm sorry." Brielle hugged the other girl, which seemed to touch Jenna.

So Addison's father had died. He had wondered if the man was still in the picture somewhere.

He gave Jenna a look of sympathy, which she met with a strained smile.

"Pizza is a great skill," she said. "We brought you dessert, then. Sugar cookies."

Brielle's features lit up. "Wow. Thanks! I love cookies."

"Here you go," Addie said, handing over a plate covered in pastel-frosted flower cutout cookies that looked like spring.

"You didn't have to do that," Wes said.

She had already paid him for the battery, a check in an envelope she had left tucked in the door frame of his apartment. He was more than a little embarrassed that he had noticed the envelope smelled of strawberries and cream, like Jenna.

"It's the least I can do to thank you for all your help with my car yesterday. I know cookies are poor recompense for giving up part of your lunch hour, but I didn't know what else you might enjoy."

"Home-baked cookies are always a treat. I don't get them very often."

"Well, I hope you enjoy them."

"How is the car running?"

"Great. Everything has been perfect."

"I'm glad."

They stood awkwardly for a moment as he fought the urge to brush the pad of his thumb over that slight tinge of pink rising on her cheekbone.

Brielle saved him from doing something so foolish. "Hey, Dad. Can Addie and her mom stay for dinner? You said we had too much pizza to eat ourselves."

The awkward level had now ratcheted up to a ten.

"I'm sure they have other dinner plans," he said quickly.

"We don't," Addie said. "Pizza would be great!"

"We were going to heat up some soup from the freezer, remember?" Jenna said, not meeting Wes's gaze. "We were just saying how soup is just the thing for a stormy night."

As if on cue, lightning arced through the sky, followed by a sharp crack of thunder that made both girls shriek in surprise, then giggle at each other for their shared reaction.

"I like soup, Mom, but I would rather have pizza," Addie said. "It smells soooo good, doesn't it?"

"We really do have more than enough dough and toppings," Wes said. "We were just trying to figure out what we were going to do with it when you knocked on the door. It was perfect timing."

Another bolt of lightning flashed outside and rain began to pelt the window.

It was beyond comforting to be here inside this warm apartment in the big, rambling house by the sea.

"It does smell good," she admitted.

"And tastes even better," he said, not bothering with false modesty. He had very few skills in the kitchen and was justifiably proud of his pizza dough, a recipe his father had perfected over the years before he died.

"All right," she finally said. "If you're sure we won't be imposing on your time with your daughter."

"Not at all," he assured her. "We were just about to put the toppings on, if you want to come and choose what you want."

She followed him to the kitchen of his apartment, which Wes had considered a decent size. He wasn't sure exactly how it seemed to shrink with the addition of another child and a small woman.

"How can I help?" Jenna asked.

How long had it been since he had shared a meal with a woman besides his daughter? He honestly couldn't remember.

"You could throw together the salad, if you don't mind. I've already rinsed the lettuce and it just needs to be tossed."

"I can do that."

She crossed to the sink and washed her hands then went to work ripping leaves from the romaine and green lettuce heads he had purchased earlier that day before picking up Brielle from her mother's.

"What do you like on your pizza?"

"I'm not picky. What do you usually have?"

"Brie is a big fan of plain cheese and pepperoni. I typically go for margherita, with crushed San Marzano tomatoes, fresh mozzarella, basil and a splash of olive oil."

Her eyes had widened during his geek-out about pizza and she gave a surprised laugh. "That sounds really delicious. Addie will probably be happy with the pepperoni as well."

"Perfect. So two margherita and two pepperoni. I can only cook two at a time on my pizza steel so let's do the girls' first. They don't take long."

"Okay."

While he formed another ball of dough into pizza crust for Addie, then enlisted the girls' help to add the sauce, mozzarella and pepperoni, Jenna began slicing cucumbers and tomatoes to add to the salad.

This was nice, he thought as the girls went to work setting the table. He had bought a kitchen-in-a-box set of plates and silverware and serving utensils that supposedly contained everything a person needed to set up a basic kitchen. Now he wished he had sprung for something nicer.

Once the girls' pizzas were in the oven, he went to work with the other two balls of dough, expertly shaping them and adding the toppings. Jenna watched him work, her expression interested.

"You really do know what you're doing."

He gave a rueful smile. "I'm kind of a pizza geek. My

dad spent a year working in Italy at a pizza place during a gap year of college and he taught me a few secrets."

"Brie said you were only a child when he died."

He didn't like remembering the pain of that time. "Ten. He moved from making pizza to opening his own restaurant in the little town outside Denver where he grew up. One night after closing, a couple of drifters broke in, thinking the place was empty. They shot my dad and took off with what was left in the cash register after he'd already made the deposit for the night. Thirty bucks in change."

"Oh. I'm so sorry."

The soft sympathy in her voice, in her expression, seemed to seep through him and he wanted to bask in it.

Embarrassed, he quickly changed the subject as he ripped a couple of basil leaves off the plant he bought at the supermarket.

"I can't get enough of smelling fresh basil," he said as he sprinkled the herb atop the two margherita pizzas. "Sometimes I want to just bury my face in it. Amazing, the things you never realize you missed."

Oh wow. He was just full of brilliant conversation. First he dropped his father's long-ago murder into the conversation, then he started gushing about herbs. He wouldn't be surprised if she scooped up her daughter and went rushing back downstairs, away from the weirdo with a basil fetish.

Instead, she was looking at him again with that same soft compassion. "How long were you…in prison?"

"Three years, two months and five days."

He didn't look at her as he turned on the oven light to check the girls' pizzas.

It didn't matter that he had been cleared of any wrongdoing. The damage was done. He would never get that time back and his reputation would never fully recover.

Guilty or not, he had spent more than a thousand days in prison. Had seen things he couldn't unsee. Cruelty between inmates, intimidation and abuse by guards, people treated more like cattle than human beings until they gradually began to lose their humanity altogether.

He was a different person than he'd been the day he had been arrested.

"I'm not sure what should be the appropriate response to that," she admitted after a moment. "*I'm sorry* doesn't feel at all adequate."

He shrugged. "It happened. It's done. I'm still trying to figure out what comes next."

He wasn't sorry to change the subject again. "Looks like these are ready to come out."

He pulled out the two pizzas, happy to see the crust bubbly with air pockets, then slid the other two into the oven.

"These other pizzas will only take a few minutes. Since the girls' pizzas have to cool down first before they can eat them without burning their tongues, why don't we start with the salad and vegetables?"

He had already prepared a relish plate as it was the only way he could persuade his daughter to eat a few vegetables.

The next few moments were busy finding beverages for everyone and taking the girls' pizzas to the table.

Soon, his timer went off to remove the other pizzas from the oven. He was delighted by the surprise and pleasure on Jenna's expression.

"That looks absolutely delicious."

"I hope it tastes even better."

The girls chattered away about school around mouthfuls of pizza, while he and Jenna worked on their salads. Finally, she picked up her first piece of pizza. He felt silly, but couldn't help holding his breath until she took a bite. The sound of delight she made was gratifying.

"Wow," she exclaimed. "That is really delicious. The flavors come together so perfectly. I'm afraid I might never be happy with pizza delivery again."

"That's the problem with making your own pizza. If you do it right, it kind of ruins you for anything else."

He couldn't help staring at her mouth as it lifted into a slight smile. What would it be like to have her give him a full-fledged smile? Even better, a laugh?

He shouldn't be wondering about that, Wes chided himself. He and Jenna Haynes were simply neighbors, though he wanted to think maybe after the past few days, she would no longer watch him out of those nervous eyes, like he was a mountain lion crouched to pounce on her at any moment.

Her life felt so surreal sometimes, the reality often more bizarre than anything her imagination could conjure up.

A few weeks ago, Jenna would never have believed she would find herself having dinner with her intimidating new neighbor and his daughter.

Or that she would enjoy it so much.

The pizza was delicious, probably the best she'd ever had. And though Wes Calhoun seemed to be going out of his way to be friendly, she still sensed a wary reserve in him.

He seemed to measure each word as carefully as he probably did the flour in his father's pizza dough recipe.

Did he ever completely let down his guard? She doubted it.

She was fine with that. She had to be, since she had her own protective barriers firmly in place.

"Thank you," she finally said, after she had eaten every single bite of her personal-sized pizza. "That was truly delicious."

"It was super good," Addison agreed. "Mom, you should take lessons from Brie's dad on how to make pizza."

She raised an eyebrow. "Should I?"

"You make good pizza," her daughter quickly said. "But Mr. Calhoun makes *really* good pizza."

"He truly does."

"I'm happy to teach you all I know. Which should take maybe five minutes. It's all about not skimping on the quality of your ingredients and putting a little advance thought into it."

"I'll keep that in mind. Thank you again for sharing your pizza night with us."

"You're welcome to come back again the next time we make it," Wes said. "Every Friday night is pizza night. We might even have to do it more than once a week. Brielle is going to be with me full-time for the first few weeks after school gets out, and I don't have that many other specialties. I expect we will have the chance to enjoy a lot of pizza."

"My mom is going to Costa Rica," Brie said. "I think she should take me, but she says she can't because I don't have a passport."

"You'll get another chance to go on a trip with your mom and stepdad," Wes assured his daughter. "Meantime, you get to hang out with me and do all kinds of fun things."

"We can definitely plan some times for you two to hang out while you're staying at Brambleberry House with your dad. It will be great for Addie to have someone her age here."

"My friend Logan used to live downstairs on the first floor, but he moved away with his dad *forever* ago."

"I know Logan. He's nice."

"He is," Addie agreed. Suddenly her eyes widened with excitement. "And guess what? As soon as school is out, we're getting a dog! I've been begging and begging for one, and Mom finally said we can go to the shelter next week to find a rescue."

"Lucky!" Brielle exclaimed. "I always wanted a dog. We just have a cat. What kind are you getting?"

Addie shrugged. "I don't know. We haven't picked it yet. Whichever one needs a home most, I guess."

Jenna did her best to ignore the misgivings she still felt about taking on a pet. She knew full well how much responsibility it would be, adding a dog to their family. But now that she knew for certain they wouldn't have to pack up and disappear again, as she had feared for so long that they would have to do when Aaron Barker was released from prison, she could no longer think of any more excuses.

Addie had been through so much in her short life. Losing her dad. Having to uproot her life and escape here to Cannon Beach. Living for more than two years with a jumpy, scared-of-her-own-shadow mother.

Agreeing to her daughter's relentless pleas to add a dog into their lives felt like the least Jenna could do for her.

"You're so lucky!" Brielle exclaimed. "Can I play with him or her?"

"Anytime you want," Addie said. "You could even help me take him for a walk, if you want. Dogs need a lot of exercise. That's what my mom says."

"Your mom is right," Wes said. "The happiest, healthiest dogs get exercise at least a few times a day."

He sounded like an expert. She really hoped so, since she had no idea what she was doing. Maybe he could give her advice.

While the girls chattered more about what kind of dog was best, Jenna turned again to Wes.

"Thank you again for the pizza, though I just realized that I owe you even more now."

"How's that?"

"First you kindly go out of your way to change my car battery, then you make us the best pizza ever. All I've done in return is bake you a batch of cookies."

"They were delicious cookies, though. I'm sure between Brie and me, they will be gone by morning."

"Cookies hardly compare. You make it tough for a woman to clear her debt to you."

He gazed down at her, something in his expression suddenly that made her cheeks feel hot.

He blinked it away and returned to a polite smile. "You don't owe me anything in return. Cookies are more than enough."

She did not necessarily agree, but couldn't immediately think of anything she could do to repay him for his kindness. She would have to give it some thought.

"Come on, Addie. It's almost bedtime."

Her daughter predictably groaned but headed for the stairs. "See you later," she called to Brielle.

"Good night." Jenna gave one last smile as she followed her daughter down the stairs.

On the positive side, she suddenly realized, the evening together had gone a long way toward reducing her fear of Wes. It was tough to be nervous around a man who obviously adored his daughter and who found such simple pleasure in the smell of fresh basil.

Chapter Four

"This is the one, Mom. He's perfect. We have to get him."

Jenna looked at the floppy tan puppy in her daughter's lap, all paws and ears and big, soulful eyes. She was watching firsthand the process of two creatures falling in love. The dog couldn't seem to keep his eyes off Addie and her daughter was clearly already long gone.

"He's the cutest dog ever. The very best dog. Please, Mom!"

She had envisioned them leaving the shelter with a small older dog. A Chihuahua or a little Yorkie, some kind of petite, well-trained lapdog who didn't bark or chew or make messes all over the floor.

"He was one of a litter of six mini goldendoodles that were found abandoned down near Manzanita."

The shelter volunteer helping them, a woman in her forties with a name tag that read Pam, gave the dog an affectionate pat. "We've adopted out all but him. You could call Theo here the last man standing, I guess."

"Hi, buddy. Hi."

The clever dog licked Addison's cheek, completely sealing the deal, as if he knew exactly which of them really held the power in this situation.

Jenna was suddenly quite certain there was no possible way on earth she would be able to get out of here now without taking along this dog, who literally met none of the qualities on her own personal wish list.

Her daughter clearly loved him. That was the most important thing, she reminded herself. Jenna would simply just have to figure out how to readjust her own expectations.

"How old is he?" she asked Pam.

"We can't say for sure," the shelter worker said. "The vet thinks maybe three to four months? They were weaned puppies when they were found and he's been here a month. That's just an estimate, though."

"Why would anybody abandon a litter of puppies?" Addie looked horrified, her arms tightening around the dog as if to protect him.

Because people can be selfish and cruel sometimes.

She didn't want her daughter to learn that lesson yet, so Jenna only shook her head sadly. "Who knows?"

"I wish I understood it," Pam said. "I can't comprehend how anyone could think a litter of puppies would be better off there, in the middle of a forest, than here at our shelter. It makes no sense to me."

"Me neither." Addie hugged Theo, her cheek pressed against the dog's fur. "Nobody's going to leave you anywhere now, Theo. I promise. You're coming home with us. You'll love our house. We even have a ghost!"

Pam looked startled. "A ghost?"

Jenna gave a rueful smile. "We live in an old beach house. Brambleberry House? You might know it."

"Oh yes. That wonderful place on the edge of town."

She nodded. "Some of the previous residents are convinced we have a benevolent spirit who watches over all those who live in the apartments."

She still wasn't convinced and found it amusing that her friends Rosa and Melissa spoke about Abigail as if she were an old friend, though she had died more than a decade before either woman had lived in the house.

"A ghost!" Pam looked enthralled. "Oh, that's lovely. How about that, Theo? Want to live in a house with a ghost?"

The dog's tongue lolled out and he actually looked enthusiastic, but that could have been more evidence of his growing adoration for the girl holding him.

"Is he trained at all?" Jenna hated to ask but needed to know what challenges she might be facing.

"He's getting there. He's not a hundred percent but he is very smart, and it shouldn't take him long to learn how to follow some basic commands, as soon as he adjusts to the routine of your house."

"I can't wait!" Addie's eyes glowed. "I'm going to teach him to sit, to roll over, to shake hands and to catch a ball in the air like my friend Logan's dog can do."

"Those all sound great but first things first," Jenna said. "We need to start with teaching him not to go to the bathroom inside the house. After that, we can work on the other commands."

"We can provide you with some great websites and other resources that give good training advice," Pam said. "We can also connect you with a few places locally that offer puppy training classes."

"That would be very helpful," Jenna said, again trying to push down her misgivings. She could handle this. She certainly had done harder things in her life than train a puppy.

"So have you decided for sure?" Pam asked.

Jenna gestured to her daughter and the dog. "I think these two have decided for me."

"Oh great. And since you've already been approved for adoption, you can take him home with you today, if you'd like. We do have a few forms for you to fill out. Addison, would you bring Theo with you to my office?"

"Yes!" she exclaimed. Pam provided a leash from a hook on the wall and Addie attached it to the dog's collar, then proudly walked with him down the hall to a small office decorated with pictures of dogs and cats and their happy new humans.

A half hour and several signatures later, they walked out of the shelter with their new family member padding happily beside them.

All her misgivings came flooding back as she loaded Addie and Theo into the car. What had she done? She went through days when she felt as if she could barely take care of herself and her child. Adding another living creature to her responsibilities suddenly felt overwhelming.

"Can I go show Mr. and Mrs. Anderson downstairs? Theo also has to meet Sophie. Do you think they'll be friends?"

The retired couple who lived in the first-floor apartment of Brambleberry House had a very cute—and very spoiled—toy poodle.

"I'm sure they will be great friends." She hoped, anyway. "The Andersons left this week for their trip, remember? They left Sophie with their friend in Portland."

"Oh right."

"We're going to have to pick up some supplies before we can take Theo home. Toys and food and a crate."

She probably should have purchased all that in advance before taking home the dog, but she had been so busy wrapping up end-of-year school details, she hadn't thought that far ahead.

"Can we take him into the store?" Addie asked. "I don't want to leave him alone in the car."

"No," she agreed. "We shouldn't do that. I know they let dogs into the pet store. We'll go there."

They parked at the pet store and headed inside, after stopping long enough for Theo to raise his leg on a fire hydrant conveniently placed near the door.

It didn't take long to fill a shopping cart for the puppy. At this rate Theo would be as spoiled as Sophie, she thought.

They had nearly finished finding everything on the quick list they had made before coming inside when Addie suddenly exclaimed with delight. "Mr. Calhoun! Hi, Mr. Calhoun!"

Jenna whirled around and found her upstairs neighbor walking through the pet store with a bag of cat food.

"Oh. Hi."

She hadn't seen Wes since pizza night, nearly a week earlier, except for a few brief waves of greeting in passing. She had somehow forgotten how big and tough and intimidating he looked.

And gorgeous.

She hadn't forgotten that part.

She could feel her face heat and hoped he didn't notice.

"Wow." He looked down at the gangly dog. "Looks like you've got a new friend."

"This is Theo. He's the best dog ever. And he's our very own dog now! He gets to come home with us."

"That's very cool. Hi, Theo. Nice to meet you." Wes crouched to the same level of the dog and reached out a hand, which Theo investigated with a sniff followed by vigorous tail wagging.

"I think he likes you," Addie said, beaming.

"Hey, bud." He scratched the dog's ears and under his chin, which seemed to earn him Theo's instant adoration.

"I didn't know you had a cat," Jenna said, gesturing to the food bag.

"I don't." He straightened. "But we've got a couple of strays that hang out at the shop. They're good mousers but I still like to leave a little food for them. Plus I guess I'll be cat-sitting for a couple weeks as Brie is bringing along Murphy when she comes to stay with me."

"That's nice of you."

He shrugged. "If I have to take a bad-tempered elderly cat as part of the package in order to hang out with my daughter, it's worth the sacrifice."

He looked back at the dog. "You say his name is Leo?"

"Theo," Addison corrected. "The nice lady at the shelter said his real name is Theodore because he looks like a teddy bear but they didn't want to call him Teddy so they call him Theo."

"Nice name."

"I hope he doesn't bother everyone at Brambleberry

House," Jenna said. "The shelter said he's not one to bark a lot."

"He'll be great, I'm sure. I'm not worried. I hardly ever hear the neighbors' little poodle."

She decided not to point out that Sophie lived two floors below him and had been gone for a week, where Theo would be just downstairs one flight all the time.

"Fingers crossed," she said.

He glanced into their cart. "Looks like you have everything you need to take the dog home."

"And then some, right? I'm afraid we've gone overboard."

"You can never have too many tennis balls when it comes to dogs. I can help you load your supplies into your car after you check out."

She was a tough, independent woman who had been forced by circumstance to learn how to stand on her own two feet. Still, it was nice to have the option to lean on someone once in a while.

"That would be really helpful. Thank you."

As he only had one item, he checked out first, then waited while she did the same. The final tally made her gulp. Having a pet was not a cheap undertaking.

When her items were bagged and she had paid for them, all three of them walked outside.

"When is Brielle coming to stay with you?"

"Tomorrow night."

"How exciting. I bet it's going to be wonderful to have her there."

"Sure. It should be great."

She thought she picked up a note of hesitation in his voice, but she didn't have a chance to ask him about it before they reached her SUV.

She popped the cargo gate and he helped her load all their supplies into the back, including the heavy bag of puppy food.

"Thank you. I really appreciate your help."

"My pleasure."

He gave a smile, or as close to one as he seemed to offer. It wasn't really much of a smile, mostly just a small lifting of his mouth, but it still made her toes tingle.

"I guess we will see you."

"Yes. Leave the dog food by your car and I can carry it upstairs for you."

She could manage, but it seemed ungracious to refuse. "Thank you. I appreciate that."

"See you later, Addison. Bye, Theo."

Addie waved and Theo wagged his tail with delight.

After she made sure Addie had her seat belt on, Jenna drove away, wondering how on earth she had shifted from fear to this wary fascination in such a short time.

Wes had never smoked but some nights, he really longed for a cigarette.

He knew there were guys in prison who had picked up smoking there as a way to relax and beat the boredom. He had preferred other methods. Working out, reading. Studying.

He had taken Spanish lessons in prison as well as a couple of community college history and rudimentary law classes. He also volunteered for a couple of service programs.

Anything he could do not to sit in his cell and feel sorry for himself and angry at the world.

Now he had the freedom to do whatever he wanted, whenever he wanted. Maybe that was why he felt so…

restless. He still didn't quite know what to do with that freedom.

He thought the hour run he had taken earlier might ease this edgy discontent. It hadn't, nor had the long, pulsing, delicious shower after.

He ached for something but wasn't sure what.

After changing channels a dozen times, picking up his book, then putting it back down, scrolling on his phone through news stories he didn't really care about, he decided to take a ride on his bike down the coast. Maybe a little sea air on his face would calm him.

He walked down the two floors of Brambleberry House, sensing, as he sometimes did, the faint, barely perceptible smell of flowers on the stairs.

Rosa Galvez Townsend, who had rented him the apartment, had told him there were rumors that a benevolent spirit walked the halls of the house, the ghost of a longtime owner of the house, Abigail Dandridge.

She had died with no direct heirs and had left the house to two friends and tenants of hers.

She apparently had loved the house so much she had not wanted to leave.

He remembered staring in disbelief at the woman, who had given him an embarrassed sort of laugh. "You do not have to believe it. Most people don't. But I felt like it was only fair to warn you about the rumors before you move in."

A hint of flowers on the stairs was not exactly a convincing argument. Even if there had been a real ghost, how could he pass up a beautiful apartment in a rambling old house on the seashore? He had no problem putting up with the random scent of flowers and the occasional waft of cold air that seemed to come out of nowhere.

As he walked outside, the night smelled of lilacs and lavender, with a salty tang from the Pacific fifty yards away.

And he was not alone in the Brambleberry House gardens, he realized. Jenna stood in the grass, holding the leash of her gangly new puppy.

She spotted him coming onto the porch and waved.

"Hello. Don't mind us. This is about our tenth trip outside this evening. We're working on potty training. I'm not quite sure Theo understands the concept completely yet, so I imagine we'll be coming out frequently to reinforce. So much for my relaxing summer vacation, right?"

She smiled, a white flash in the moonlight, and his entire body seemed to tighten.

"He'll figure it out," he said. "Consistency is the key to training puppies."

She moved closer, and he could smell the scent of her, an intoxicating mix of strawberries and vanilla and sunshine.

"You sound like you have some experience in that area. Have you trained many dogs?"

For a brief moment, he debated how much to tell her and finally decided there was no good reason to withhold the information.

"I was part of a canine training initiative in prison. We did the initial basic training with puppies that might eventually become service dogs. I was lucky enough to have three great puppies during my time. All of them eventually graduated and are working as trained service animals now."

"That sounds like a wonderful program."

The dogs had truly been lifesavers to him, bringing peace and comfort and purpose during those dark years.

"It was a good fit. You have a bunch of people with nothing but time on their hands. That's what dogs need most, especially in the beginning."

He missed those puppies. He had given his heart to each of the three dogs he had worked with in prison and had been gutted when it was time to pass them on for the next phase of their training.

Now that he was on the outside, Wes had been thinking about getting a dog of his own, though he wasn't sure he was ready to start over with another pet.

He supposed some part of him still worried things might change in a heartbeat, that something could happen to throw his life back into chaos. He didn't know what that might be, but didn't want to take any chances that he might not be ready for that kind of complication and commitment.

That was the main reason he was working as a mechanic at the Gutierrez brothers' shop. He was good at it, for one thing, but he also needed something fairly straightforward to do right now while he tried to figure out the rest of his life.

Before his arrest, he had been running a highly successful security company in Chicago with thirty employees and multimillion-dollar contracts.

All of that had disappeared in a blink. The company. His life savings. And most of his trust in humanity, Wes had to admit.

He wasn't sure he had the bandwidth right now to start over and rebuild everything from scratch.

He knew he had to start somewhere, but he had no idea where the hell that somewhere might be.

He wasn't about to spill his angst all over Jenna Haynes. If she knew the tangled morass of his brain, she would probably be more afraid of him than she had been when he first moved in.

She didn't seem as afraid of him now.

He found that awareness both exhilarating and vaguely terrifying.

Some part of him wanted to warn her she had every right to be afraid. Around her, he felt like the proverbial Big Bad Wolf. He wanted to swallow up a sweet thing like Jenna Haynes in one delicious bite.

"I could use any pointers you have with Theo here," she said before he could tell her any of those things. "This is my first time training a dog. My first time being responsible for any pet, actually."

He raised an eyebrow. "You didn't have a dog growing up?"

"No. Believe me, I wanted a dog desperately but it never quite worked out."

"Why not?"

"I grew up with a single mom, with no dad in the picture," she said after a slight hesitation. "I don't even have a name, since he took off before I was born and my mom didn't like to talk about it. Mom always worked two jobs to support us, and she didn't think it would be fair to have a pet when we weren't home very often to take care of him. Also, money was invariably tight so she could never quite justify the cost of pet food or vet bills when she was working so hard just to take care of us."

"Is that one of the reasons you gave in to Addie's

pleas, even though you're nervous about taking on a dog? Because, like most parents, you want to give her what you always wanted but never had?"

Her gaze sharpened at his insight. "Yes. That's exactly why. Good guess, Dr. Calhoun. I must say, I feel a little called out right now."

He gave a short laugh. "I'm not all that brilliant. I only understand it because I'm the same way. I told you my dad died when I was ten. I missed him fiercely when I was a teenager, so I'm determined to be as present as possible in Brie's life. To the point of being obnoxious about it."

Wes paused, then added, "What about after you married? Why didn't you get a dog then?"

"Multiple reasons, I suppose. We wanted one but our first apartment didn't allow pets. We moved into our first home after we had been married two years, but I was pregnant at the time and we decided to wait a bit until adding a pet into the mix, on top of first-time home ownership and new parenthood."

"Sounds sensible."

"Sometimes I wish we hadn't been so sensible. I only had six years with Ryan. We should have done all the crazy things we dreamed about. Flown to Paris. Quit our jobs and lived on the beach in Mexico for a time. Gotten a puppy. Or a half dozen puppies."

Life's cruelties never ceased to infuriate him. A sweet woman like Jenna deserved to have a long and happy life with the man she loved. "How did your husband die?"

"Cancer. Melanoma. He was only thirty."

"That's tough."

"Yes. Addie was barely three when he was diagnosed. He died a year later. It was a very painful time."

"I'm sorry," he said, the words feeling painfully inadequate.

"Thank you. But I've learned since Ryan died that everybody has something, you know? I don't have the monopoly on pain."

He knew so many people who could take a lesson from her, who considered themselves permanent victims of whatever hardship that came their way and refused to accept that someone else might be struggling, too.

"What about you?" she asked, obviously eager to change the subject. "Did you have dogs when you were growing up?"

He nodded. "When I was young, we lived on the small hobby farm where my dad grew up and there were always dogs around. We didn't really have house pets but we always had horses and dogs and chickens."

"Oh, that sounds lovely."

"It was a pretty good childhood, for the most part. Then my dad died and my mom couldn't keep up with things. She sold the restaurant and the farm and we moved to the Chicago area to be closer to her family."

How differently might his life have turned out if his father had not died? Wes probably would have stayed in the Denver area. He might even still be there.

Instead, they had moved to Chicago, where he had struggled in school and became friends with people who hadn't always had his best interests at heart.

Wes had been involved in a few scrapes during his teen years and had even served a brief stint in youth corrections.

He might have continued on that path, except he had one teacher who had given him the straight truth about the dead-end direction he was headed. For some reason, Wes had listened.

He had determined to change his life. He had enlisted in the Army, where he had worked first as a mechanic and then as a military police officer. He had met and married Lacey while he was still in the service and taken her first to Germany and then to Japan.

Even before he got out, he and a buddy had decided to start a security business. Hard work and determination had turned their fledgling enterprise into a success beyond his wildest dreams.

And then everything had changed.

"Were you going somewhere?" Jenna asked.

It took him a moment to realize she was referring to his leathers and helmet. He suddenly didn't feel like taking a ride anymore. He wanted to stay here with her in this moonlit garden and enjoy the sound of the waves and the scent of a lovely woman beside him.

That was a dangerous road. He would be much better off climbing on his bike and riding off into the night.

"I was going to take a ride. Nowhere special. I do that sometimes. It's cliché, I know, but I like to feel the wind on my face."

"I've seen you leave at odd hours and wondered where you go."

He wasn't sure how he felt to know she had watched him from her window as he sped off into the night, trying to outrace demons that always seemed to be racing right behind him.

"How long ago did you lose your husband?"

"It's been four years now. I can hardly believe it's

been that long. It feels like only yesterday. Addie has spent half her life without her father. She hardly remembers him, which I find so sad. Ryan was a wonderful father and adored her from the moment she was born."

"She won't completely forget. Ryan is part of her, just as she is part of him."

"You're right. I see him sometimes in the way she loves to read every sign we pass on the road or tilts her head when she's studying something she doesn't quite understand."

"He lives on in her."

"Yes."

She was pensive for a moment, then smiled. "I'm sorry I kept you from your ride. Thanks for the encouragement with Theo. Don't be surprised if I become annoying and bring you all my many questions."

"You shouldn't expect veterinarian-level answers," he warned. "I spent a year training puppies. That's the extent of my knowledge."

"That gives you a year more experience than I have."

Her smile flashed in the moonlight, and he had to curl his hands around his helmet to keep from crossing the space between them and reaching for her.

"I'm happy to help with whatever I can do."

"Thank you. Good night. Enjoy your ride. And I apologize in advance if Theo and I make too much noise going in and out at all hours."

"Don't worry about that. I can't hear anything up on the third floor except the wind."

"Are you sure you're not hearing Abigail? If you smell freesia, that's supposed to be her."

He raised an eyebrow. "Do you really buy into all the ghost stuff?"

She shrugged with a rueful smile. "Originally I was skeptical when we moved into Brambleberry House. Since then, I don't know. I'm less skeptical, I guess. I hope that doesn't make me sound too out-there. I don't usually believe in that sort of thing, but for some reason living in Brambleberry House leaves you open to all kinds of ideas you might once have thought were unlikely, bordering on ridiculous."

"I'm surprised there wasn't a ghost clause in my rental agreement."

"Did you read all the fine print? There might have been. I don't know. It's been more than two years since I signed my agreement, and to be honest with you, when I moved in, I didn't care if there were a *dozen* ghosts living here. Addie and I just needed a safe place, which we certainly found here in Cannon Beach."

He frowned. A safe place? Why? What had threatened them? Her words did certainly explain her general air of unease, especially around him.

Was she still running? Somehow, he didn't think so.

Even in the short time he had known her, she seemed calmer than she had in the beginning, when he first moved into the apartment. Maybe that was only because she had come to know him a little.

He wanted to press her, but she certainly looked as if she regretted saying anything at all.

"I hadn't realized how late it is," she said quickly, confirming his suspicion. "I should go back in with Addie. Thank you again."

"You're welcome. Good night."

He gave the dog one last pat. "Good night, Theo. Be good."

"Considering he's already chewed up one of my flip-flops and a pair of Addie's socks, I think we're past that."

"He'll outgrow the chewing. Get him a couple of nonrawhide bones he can chomp on. Or you can freeze some wet puppy food in one of those sturdy chew toys you bought at the pet store and give him that. When he's outside, of course, where he can keep the mess in the grass."

"I'll keep that in mind. Thanks. Come on, Theo."

With that, she hurried back inside the house, leaving the scent of her, strawberries and cream, floating on the breeze. Along with lilacs and…was that the smell of freesia? He wasn't sure he even knew what that was and didn't know how to find out. Maybe he would have to make a trip to the garden center to see if they had any of the flowers so he could do a scent test.

The concept made him roll his eyes at himself. Was he really buying the idea that the house might be haunted?

It didn't matter. He was staying put, no matter how many ghosts the house might hold.

Jenna hurried up the steps to her apartment and closed the door behind her. Theo plopped down immediately, as if their trek out to the garden had completely sapped him of all energy.

She could only hope.

"You had better sleep all night now," she said sternly. "I don't feel like going out there at 2:00 a.m."

The puppy yawned, stretched and closed his eyes, right at her feet.

"Nope." She scooped him up. "You need to sleep in your crate."

She set him in the large crate the shelter had suggested. Theo seemed completely comfortable in the space. He immediately curled up on the soft blankets she had folded into the corner.

She could only hope she would sleep as well, but something told her she might be up for a while, remembering that conversation with Wes.

Had she really blurted out that she believed in ghosts?

The encounter played back through her mind, and she suddenly realized something that had been haunting the edges of her subconscious since he moved in.

Wes Calhoun was lonely.

She did not know why she had that impression, but she was suddenly convinced of it. He had come out of the house with a glower she wasn't even sure he was aware of. Nor did she think he realized how that glower had lifted when he spotted her and Theo.

Poor man. He had moved to Cannon Beach to be closer to his daughter and likely knew few people except those he worked with and his ex-wife and her new husband.

She understood where he was coming from. She had certainly felt alone when she first moved to town, though she had had Rosa, her dear friend from college.

Rosa had convinced her to come here in an effort to escape the numbing terror she had lived with for months because of Aaron Barker.

She thought she had fled far enough away so that she and Addie would be safe here in Cannon Beach. Aaron had no idea one of her dearest friends lived here. She knew she hadn't mentioned Rosa during any of their three dates, before she broke things off when his obsessive control began to manifest itself.

She had been wrong about being safe here in Oregon.

By a cruel twist of fate, an accident, really, he had discovered where she had fled and had followed her here, with horrifying consequences.

She pushed the darkness away. She could not let him intrude further in her life. She had already given him far more than he deserved. He was gone now. She was safe, at least physically.

She had attended counseling after Aaron had ultimately been arrested. She had worked through much of her trauma from the long months of relentless anxiety. She had come far, especially if she could chat with a big, dangerous man in a moonlit garden beside the sea.

She hadn't been completely comfortable, but she suspected that might have to do with her growing awareness of him as more than simply her neighbor.

The man seemed in dire need of a friend, someone he could turn to when the nights seemed long and empty.

She wasn't sure she could be that person, nor could she completely understand why she suddenly wanted to try.

Chapter Five

Why, oh why, did she always end up having to carry her groceries into the apartment during a fierce downpour?

Was she a victim of poor planning or merely fickle weather?

When she had set off for the grocery store that Saturday morning after dropping Addie off at a birthday party, the sun had been shining and the birds had been singing. Yes, she knew a storm lurked on the horizon. She couldn't miss those dark clouds gathering offshore. But she hadn't expected it to hit so quickly or with such ferocious fury.

Now she sat in her car in the driveway of Brambleberry House, waiting for the weather to cooperate and the rain to slow at least enough that she could carry a few bags inside without becoming completely drenched.

She also had to let out Theo, whom she had left in his crate inside her apartment.

She had just about decided to run for it anyway when a sudden knock on her window startled her. She gasped at the unexpected sound and momentary fear pulsed through her as she saw the large, hulking shape of a man standing outside the door.

He shouted something she couldn't quite hear over the noise of the storm. Lightning flashed nearby, followed almost immediately by thunder. So close!

The instant she recognized Wes standing outside her car with a large umbrella, her instinctive panic eased.

She opened her door just a crack. Even in the small space, rain poured in.

"Do you need help? I saw you pull in from upstairs. When you didn't go into the house, I was worried something might be wrong."

"Yes, something's wrong. We're in the middle of a hurricane, in case you didn't notice."

He chuckled, a deep, pleasing sound that drifted to her even over the tumult of the storm.

"This is not a storm. I've been in actual hurricanes when I was in the Army stationed in Florida. This is only a little squall."

"It's still enough to soak my groceries. I don't feel like eating soggy bread for a week. I was waiting for it to let up a little."

"Makes sense. You could do that, if you want to. Or I brought you out an extra umbrella. You can run up to the porch with it and I'll grab your groceries."

"Thank you. I usually keep a few in my car, but Addie and I both used one last time we had a big rain and I think I left them inside the apartment."

"Open the back of your car and head inside. I'll grab as many groceries as I can."

"I can grab a few bags, too."

Why had she picked today to do the big grocery shopping, her monthly trip when she stocked up on the necessities they used most?

Oh yes. She remembered. Because as much as she adored her daughter, shopping with Addie usually took twice as long. Her daughter liked to look at every book on the racks, every possible cookie at the bakery and each little item in the tempting little toy section.

She scooped as many bags as she could carry in one hand while juggling the umbrella in the other and hurried up to the porch, where she quickly entered the security code on the front door.

Wes was close behind her. He didn't bother with the umbrella, she noted. He simply sprinted inside so the reusable shopping bags filled with groceries didn't have much time at all to become drenched.

"Is that everything? I can go back out."

He held up both hands, where she saw he had at least three shopping bags in each. "This is everything. One question. Are you planning for the apocalypse?"

She shook her head. "I'm on a teacher's salary and only get paid once a month. When I grocery shop, I try to buy in bulk and freeze food to make it last."

She supposed she hadn't ever really lost the fear that she would never have enough to provide for her daughter, which she knew was a lingering worry from her insecure childhood.

"Thank you for bringing it in and helping me keep everything dry. I can take it up the stairs from here."

He gave her a look that showed he clearly took offense at her suggestion. "I've got it. I haven't had a chance to go on my run today, since I had to take Brielle shopping for a friend's birthday present, so I'll count this as my workout for the day."

He hefted the bags high, which made her smile. The gloomy day suddenly felt much brighter. "Brielle must be at Carly Lewis's birthday party, too."

"Apparently it's the social event of the weekend."

"Of the whole month, according to Addie. She was thrilled to be invited to an older girl's party."

"I can imagine." He made it up the stairs without a sign that carrying the heavy bags was any exertion at all.

"So Brielle's mom has left the country?" she asked as she opened her apartment door for him.

"Yep. I'm flying solo. It's a little daunting to know I'm alone right now in the parent department. Lacey is now two thousand miles away. If I had a problem, I know I could always reach out to her, but it's more than a little intimidating to realize I'm on my own."

"You'll be fine."

"I hope so. The prospect of two weeks of being on my own with Brie gives me even more respect for single parents like you, who do this alone all the time."

She smiled as she started putting groceries away. "I'm lucky. Addie is easy."

"So far. The girls haven't hit their teens yet."

She groaned, not wanting to think about how fast her child seemed to be growing up.

From his crate, Theo whined to be let out. She winced. She was a terrible dog mom. She should have done that first thing. "Oh shoot. I'd better take him outside. He's been in his crate for an hour while I went shopping."

"Why don't I take care of that and you can keep putting away your vast quantities of vegetables?"

"That would be great, actually."

"I'll take him out to the fenced area of the garden. That way we won't need the leash, especially since I don't expect he'll be that crazy about hanging out in the rain, either."

"We call that the dog yard, since that's where the Andersons put their little Sophie."

The entire Brambleberry House property had a wrought-iron fence surrounding it, but it was open in front for the driveway. The completely fenced area adjacent to the house was the perfect size for Theo.

She had just finished finding room in her refrigerator for the rotisserie chicken she planned to shred and use in multiple recipes when she heard a sharp rap on her apartment door.

She hurried to open it for Wes and Theo, both of them drenched.

"Oh my! What happened to the umbrella?"

"It broke in the wind ten seconds after I walked outside."

"You're soaked. Let me find you a towel."

She grabbed two—one for Wes and one for Theo.

"Thanks," he said as Jenna picked up her dripping dog and began rubbing him briskly with the towel, trying not to notice how Wes's blue T-shirt clung to every hard muscle of his chest.

He dried off his hair, not seeming to care that the towel left the ends tousled and sticking up in random directions.

He looked as if he had just climbed out of the shower.

Her shower.

She swallowed and turned her attention back to the dog. She did *not* want to go there, even in her imagination.

"You seem to know what you're doing in the kitchen."

"You mean because I bought a little of everything at the grocery store?"

"Yes. Plus I think you have some things there I've never even heard of."

"I like to cook. I don't have a lot of time during the school year so summer gives me a good chance to experiment and try some new recipes."

"I should do that. I'm sure Brielle will quickly get tired of eating pizza or going down to the taco truck on the beach."

"Who could ever get tired of that? We love pizza and tacos."

His mouth lifted into a slight smile that made her suddenly aware that they were alone here in her apartment, without either of their girls.

And she was suddenly aware that he was an extremely attractive man.

"We should grab tacos together sometime while I have Brielle with me full-time."

She swallowed, her mind racing. Was he asking her out? Panic raced through her. She wasn't ready. Not to date again, to allow herself to be vulnerable again. She wasn't sure she would ever be ready.

Just before she would have made some excuse, common sense reasserted itself. He was not asking her out on a date. He was suggesting that, as two single parents, they share a meal together with their children.

She swallowed. "That would be good."

"How about midweek? That's when I get really tired of coming up with something to cook."

"We could probably make that work."

"Great. I'll be in touch."

She remembered suddenly the loneliness she had sensed in the garden, when they had talked in the moonlight.

Wes had been incredibly helpful to her on several occasions. The least she could do was repay the favor, even if it meant stepping outside her comfort zone.

She hesitated, then plunged forward. "I could also show you how I make a few of my basic recipes. I'm far from an expert but I do have a few specialties and I'm always happy to share. It would be the least I can do, after everything you've done to help me the past few weeks."

"You don't owe me anything. But I'm sure Brielle and I would both appreciate a few new recipes to add to the mix."

"We're having lasagna tonight," she said, then went on before she could change her mind. "I have a good recipe for an easy roll-up lasagna that's delicious and Addie never even notices the spinach I slip in. You and Brielle are welcome to join us, if you don't have plans. Consider it my way of paying you back for pizza the other night and also for sacrificing your comfort for my groceries. We could say around seven."

If he was surprised at her invitation, he hid it well. "That would be great. Thank you. I was trying to figure out what to fix for dinner."

"That's one of the hardest things about being a parent. I hate the idea of having to make that decision every single day for the rest of my life until Addie goes to college."

"I hear that."

"On the other hand, I try to remember to be grateful that I'm not like my mother and I've never had to worry that my child will go hungry."

"That's a good way of looking at things."

He gazed down at her, that half smile playing around his mouth. She shivered at the intense light in his eyes and had to hope he didn't notice.

The moment seemed to stretch out between them, soft and seductive.

What would she do if he kissed her right now? Would she be afraid and pull away? Or would she sink into his arms, surrender to the heat simmering between them?

She didn't have the chance to find out. He didn't kiss her. Instead, he broke the connection between them, a small muscle flaring in his jaw.

"I should go change into dry clothes so I can pick up Brielle."

She glanced at the clock on the mantel, an odd combination of relief and disappointment coursing through her.

"Oh, you're right. I can't believe it's that late. There's no reason for both of us to go. I can pick up the girls, if you want."

He nodded, a little tersely. "Okay. That works. I guess we'll see you at seven, then."

She wasn't quite sure what happened next. She only intended to walk him to the door. One moment they were moving together in that direction and then suddenly Jen thought she caught the vague scent of freesias swirling in the air. At the same time the puppy moved across her path. She caught herself just in time from tripping over him but the awkward movement left her unbalanced.

She was going to trip anyway, she realized in a split second. She reached out instinctively, blindly, to brace herself, and her hand encountered damp cotton covering warm, solid muscle.

"Whoa," he exclaimed. "Careful."

His arms came around her and held her upright. She stared up at him, this man whose intimidating looks concealed emotions she suspected ran deep.

All of him was hard, dangerous, except his mouth. That was soft, mobile. Enticing.

She stared at his mouth, just inches from her own.

She wasn't afraid of him kissing her. She *wanted* him to.

The realization left her more off-balance than stumbling over a puppy.

She wanted to wrap her arms around him and taste and explore that mouth that often looked so stern.

She held her breath, waiting, aching. For a long moment, they gazed at each other, the only sound in her apartment their combined breathing.

Before she could do something foolish like reach up and instigate the kiss, take what she suddenly wanted, Jenna came to her senses.

No. She couldn't do that. She was not in the market for a relationship, and she was certainly not in the market for a relationship with a hard, dangerous man like Wes Calhoun.

She quickly stepped away, pulling her hands together so that he did not see them trembling. "Thank you. I'm not quite sure what happened there. Maybe there is something slippery on the floor."

If she didn't know better, she would almost think Theo had tried to trip her on purpose. She could not say that, of course. It sounded ridiculous. Anyway, why would her sweet puppy do such a thing?

That muscle flexed in his jaw again. "I'm glad you didn't fall," he said.

"So am I. Thanks for catching me. I really don't need any broken bones to start out the summer."

"Watch out for wandering puppies."

"I'll do that. I'll let Carly's mom know I'm taking Brielle home, but she might want to text you to make sure it's okay."

"Sounds good. Thanks. I guess I'll see you tonight, then."

Anticipation curled through her, sharply sweet. "Yes. See you then."

By then, she would try to have a much better hold on this burgeoning attraction to a man she knew she shouldn't want.

He had to stop doing this.

Wes hurried up the steps toward his apartment, for the first time feeling the chill of his damp clothing.

He was a glutton for punishment. Jenna Haynes was not the woman for him. He knew that. She was sweet, warm, nurturing. Innocent.

They couldn't have been more different. He possessed exactly none of those qualities.

That didn't stop him from wanting her anyway.

Some part of him had responded instinctively when she stumbled. He had reached for her and had wanted to pull her tightly against him and keep her safe from any harm.

He had almost kissed her. The urge had almost over-whelmed him.

Fortunately, he came to his senses in time, seconds before he would have pressed his mouth to hers.

Kissing her, unleashing his hunger, would have changed everything.

They were forging a fragile friendship, one he was beginning to cherish. He liked talking with her. She was smart, funny, kind.

While he might yearn for much more than a friend-ship, he knew it was impossible between them. He had to get over it.

She seemed to have lost her outright fear of him, but that didn't make her less wary. She jumped if he acci-dentally touched her and she still watched him as if not sure how he would react to any given situation.

Why was she so nervous? Okay, yes, he looked tough. He could see himself in the mirror every morning when he shaved. He knew he appeared intimidating and fierce. He had put on muscle in prison, not really as protection or defense but mainly as a distraction.

He might have hoped Jenna would know him enough by now to understand he would not hurt her—or any woman, for that matter.

Maybe her unease didn't have anything to do with him.

If she had not spoken of her husband in such affec-tionate terms, he might have thought she had been a victim of domestic abuse. That could still be the case, though somehow he doubted it.

Her secrets were her own, he reminded himself. Ev-eryone had them and if Jenna was not interested in shar-ing hers, he could not fault her for that.

She seemed willing to be friends. She had invited him and Brielle to dinner, after all, and had agreed to take their girls out for tacos some other time during the week.

Could Wes put away his growing attraction for her and be content with only a friendship?

What choice did he have?

He liked being with her. Maybe in time she would trust him enough and would begin to relax a little more in his presence.

He had very few friends here in Cannon Beach. He didn't want to lose this one, even if that meant shoving down his growing attraction for her.

Chapter Six

Later that evening, Wes sat at Jenna's dining table, feeling distinctly uncomfortable.

The food was delicious, pasta in a creamy spinach and tomato sauce with a tossed salad and fluffy breadsticks.

The conversation was fine, too, with the girls chattering away and carrying most of it.

Still, he was aware of a vague feeling of unease.

This felt entirely too domestic, the kind of warm, enjoyable scene that he had dreamed about through all the long months he spent on the inside.

His own marriage had never been this cozy. He and Lacey had been a bad combination from the start. She had been so young, not at all ready for marriage but eager to escape her difficult family.

He had liked her more than most of the women he'd dated. When she had become pregnant about four months after they started dating, despite their use of protection, they both decided marriage was the best course of action.

She had lost the baby a week after their wedding at the county clerk's office in North Carolina, where he had been stationed at the time.

He had once cared about her. Or told himself he had, anyway. Having Brielle two years later had been a joy for both of them, going a long way toward erasing much of the pain of that first miscarriage. But somewhere along the way they had both realized they weren't a good fit and had been talking about ending the marriage before he had ever been arrested.

He knew he had been a lousy husband and blamed himself for the breakdown of their marriage.

He had been a workaholic, completely focused on building up his business. At the time, he told himself he was doing everything for Lacey and Brielle. Lacey had begged him to slow down, to spend more time with them, to help her out more around the house and with their child.

He had made empty promises, again and again, but he hadn't changed.

In prison, he had finally acknowledged to himself that he had always held part of himself back from the marriage. He had never let himself be vulnerable with Lacey, had never truly opened his heart to her.

He had seen how devastated his mother had been after his father's murder, and maybe some part of him had internalized that and prevented him from completely letting down his guard.

Even if he had, he wasn't sure they ever could have healed all that had been withered because of neglect.

By then, Lacey had already reconnected with her

childhood sweetheart. She was now very happily re-married, expecting another child with her new husband.

She had found in Ron Summers all that Wes hadn't been able to give her.

When he saw how happy they were together, Wes had decided he had been the problem all along, as he suspected. He sucked at marriage, apparently. Maybe he should just stick with being the best possible father to Brielle to make up for lost time and leave domestic bliss to others more suited to it.

This, though. This felt so comfortable here in Jenna's apartment, easy and natural and soothing. Rain clicked against the windows and the puppy snored at the girls' feet. As she listened to the girls' steady conversation, Jenna smiled with a warmth that made something in him ache with cravings he thought he had buried long ago.

"That lasagna was delicious, Mrs. Haynes," Brielle said.

"We did a good job on it, didn't we? Thanks for helping me. All of you. We have so much left over—you can take some home and put it in the freezer for another day."

"Good idea."

Dinner prep with her had been a delight as she showed the girls with calm patience how to make the sauce and then layer the ricotta and spinach sauce on the noodles before rolling it up into pinwheels on the pan.

"You did most of the work with dinner," he said now to her. "We can clean up."

"We left the kitchen a mess, though."

"We don't mind the work, do we, girls?"

The girls looked as if they minded very much but

they didn't argue, simply went to work clearing away the table and carrying the dishes to the sink.

The cleanup did not take as long as Jenna seemed to think it would. After they had finished, Brielle and Addie asked if they could play a new board game Jenna had recently purchased.

He couldn't come up with an excuse, since he had nothing else planned for the evening with his daughter and it was too early for bedtime.

The game was fun and challenging and much giggling ensued as they tried to figure out the rules.

"Looks like Theo needs to go out," Jenna said after the second round. "You three keep playing. I'll take him out."

"It's still raining, though," Addie pointed out.

"Yes. We live in Oregon. It tends to do that. But unfortunately for us, dogs still need to go outside occasionally, especially when they're being trained."

"I can take him," Wes offered.

"You're the one who told me how important consistency is in puppy training, remember? I need to reinforce the training. I don't mind."

He rose from the table, undeterred. "Can I come with you anyway? After all those carbs, I could use a stretch."

He wasn't lying. For reasons he wasn't ready to explore, his muscles felt tightly coiled. She hesitated briefly then nodded. "Will you girls be okay in here? We'll just be outside for a few moments."

Addison rolled her eyes. "I'm eight and Brie is nine. We're fine. Can we play *Mario Kart*?"

"Fine with me. We won't be long."

The girls were already moving to the sofa and pulling out the game controllers as Jenna reached for her raincoat. Wes took the coat from her and held it out, manners drilled into him by his mother coming to the fore.

"You don't have a raincoat?" she asked as they headed for the door.

He shrugged. "I have one but it's upstairs. I'll be fine. I'll stay on the back porch."

He would actually welcome a little rain right now to cool his skin and his overheated imagination, though he didn't share that information with her.

She picked up a small towel he assumed was for wiping down the wet dog and handed Wes an umbrella from a container by the door. When she opened the door, Theo trotted happily down the stairs to lead the way.

The rain had slowed to a drizzle, he saw when they walked outside to the rear of the house and the dog yard. The moon even peeked out from behind the clouds to cast a pale light onto the shrubs and flowers.

She inhaled deeply as she walked down the steps with the gangly puppy still leading the way. "Oh, I love that smell. Don't you?"

He drew in night air scented with rain and flowers and the sea.

"It's nice," he had to agree.

"When I was a kid, we lived in one apartment building that had a very small playground with a patch of grass no bigger than one of the flower gardens here. I still loved to go out every time it started to rain and stand on that little patch of grass to sniff the air. My friends all thought I was weird."

"I don't think you're weird."

Funny, warm, appealing. Definitely not weird.

"Since I've moved to Cannon Beach, I've decided everything smells even more delicious here, when you add in the ocean and all the pine and cedar trees around, plus the Brambleberry House flowers. It's magical, isn't it?"

She was magical. Wes found her sweet and refreshing and unforgettable. How was any man supposed to resist her, especially a man who had known far too little sweetness recently?

He could not disagree about the air. It was intoxicating. Something told him he would never be able to smell this particular combination of scents, rain and flowers and the ocean, without thinking of this night and this woman.

"The first night after my release, we had a rainstorm. I stood outside my motel for at least an hour and just relished the rain on my face."

It was an admission Wes suspected he could not tell anyone else on earth. Somehow he knew Jenna would understand.

She said nothing for a long moment, attention fixed on the dog, who was currently sniffing the base of a Japanese maple. Finally she turned to face him, eyes solemn and her features sad.

"Why were you in prison, Wes?"

The question seemed to come out of nowhere, like a sudden unprovoked attack from his six that left him momentarily breathless.

He owed her an answer.

He wanted to tell her all of it. At the same time, he wanted to pretend it had never happened.

"I trusted the wrong person," he finally said. The words sounded naive and unbelievable, even to him. Was it any wonder a jury of his peers had not believed them either?

He wished he didn't have to talk about this. He

wanted to stand in this delicious-smelling garden and enjoy the simple pleasure of talking to a lovely woman. But the past was part of him now, an inescapable imprint on his personal story, and he suddenly wanted her to know.

"I told you I served two tours in the Army as an MP. Military policeman. When I got out, I got a job providing private corporate security. After a year or two of that, I ended up starting a company doing the same thing with a good friend, another MP I served with. Anthony Morris."

Even mentioning Tony's name left a bitter taste in his mouth, pushing away the remaining sweetness of the boysenberry pie they'd had for dessert.

"Tony was my best friend in the service. I thought I knew him. I trusted him. But unfortunately, the man I thought I knew didn't exist. He said all the right words about honor and integrity but lived a completely different reality. Somehow he managed to conceal it from me and our clients, smiling to our faces while filling his pockets with anything he could find."

"He was dirty?"

"To the core. The whole reason he wanted to start Mor-Cal Security was to use our clients, people who trusted us, as his personal booty chest. He didn't steal just a few things, either. The extent of it was staggering. He stole something from every single client. Large or small. Trade secrets. Account information. Personnel records. Even loose change. Whatever he could pocket or sell to the highest bidder. He was an equal opportunity thief."

That helpless rage swept over him again. "And I was stupid enough to hand him the keys. Literally and physically. I never imagined he would betray our clients like that. Betray *me* like that. I didn't believe him capable."

Maybe he deserved to go to prison for being so unbelievably stupid. But if everyone who trusted the wrong person ended up in prison, there would be no room for the actual criminals.

"People can be capable of all sorts of things we never imagine."

Her tone was tight, resigned, making him wonder who could possibly betray someone like Jenna.

"You are right, unfortunately. If I had given it any thought at all, I would have figured a guy whose life you saved in the middle of a firefight is not going to screw you over a few years later."

Her features softened with compassion. "Oh, Wes. I'm sorry."

Her compassion seeped into all the cold places, taking away a little of the chill from the memories. "I should have suspected something was up, but he handled all the finances. He was the brains, I was the muscle. I was just glad I could help my mom and my sister out a little and buy a nice house for Lacey and Brie, after they put up with years of base housing."

"When did you start to suspect?"

He sighed, remembering the bitter shock. "When I was arrested for grand theft. I denied everything, of course. I thought the feds had made the whole thing up. Tony would explain everything, I told them. Then I discovered Tony had fled to South America, leaving me swinging in the wind. Everything traced back to me. He had cleverly covered his tracks and created a false trail that led straight to my door. From the outside, it looked as if I had planned and orchestrated everything and that he had escaped only to protect himself from me when he uncovered the truth."

"Oh no."

"Right. Tony had completely set me up and I was too naive to see what was happening."

"You must have been in shock when you figured out what was really happening."

"You could say that. He was the closest thing I had to a brother, you know?"

She placed a comforting hand on his arm and he gazed down at her fingers, small and pale in the moonlight. Did she feel this pull between them, the same magnetic force of the moon directing the tides?

"Is he still on the run?"

He shook his head with a grim satisfaction. "A couple of my Army buddies went down and found him about a year ago. They dragged him back to face the consequences. He eventually ended up coming clean and admitted I wasn't involved. The prosecutors didn't buy it, but my attorneys fought like hell to find the evidence to exonerate me. Which is how I can be standing here today enjoying a rainy evening with you."

"So in the end Tony did the right thing?"

"Only because he was backed into a corner and had no choice. Don't paint a rosy picture of him, Jenna. He was a bastard who only admitted the truth after he was caught, in hopes that it might mean a lighter sentence for himself. He was only too happy to let me rot in prison for something I didn't do."

The bitterness in his voice made Jenna want to wrap her arms around him and hold him close to ease some of the vast pain of betrayal.

"I'm so sorry that happened," she murmured. "But at least you learned you had good friends you could count on."

He somehow managed a rusty laugh. "Are you always such an optimist, Mrs. Haynes?"

"Oh, no," she assured him. "Far from it. I've just learned the value of good friends over the years. I would have been lost without them."

He gave her a searching look, and she wondered how much truth she had revealed with her words. She wanted to tell him what had happened with Aaron but now wasn't the time, after he had unburdened himself about something much darker from his own history.

She couldn't think of anything else to say and realized they had been standing for a long moment, gazing at each other silently.

He was an extraordinarily good-looking man. Once a woman could see beyond his intimidating size and fierce features, she began to notice other things. The softness of his mouth. The firm line of his jaw. Those intense blue eyes fringed with long dark eyelashes.

She felt hot, suddenly, as if she had stood too long in front of the little electric fireplace in her bedroom.

"The rain has stopped."

He blinked and looked around. "Yes."

"When I'm going through hard times, I try to remind myself that, just like a rainstorm, nothing lasts forever. Pain and betrayal eventually begin to fade."

"Has your grief for your husband faded?"

He seemed genuinely interested, so she didn't answer with the trite response she might have otherwise. "I don't know if it will ever fade completely. But it has... mellowed over the years. I no longer feel devastated every time I think of Ryan. I now can remember the good times as well as the bad. We had several wonderful years together and I will always treasure them. And he gave me the greatest gift of all, Addie."

"He was a lucky man."

Something in his voice, some odd, yearning note, drew her gaze. He was looking down at her with an expression that made her catch her breath.

He wanted to kiss her.

She recognized the hunger deep in her soul because she shared it. It seemed so odd—so wrong—to be talking about her husband to a man who was completely unlike him but who made her ache with awareness.

"I should…" She pointed vaguely to the house, to the door. The girls were waiting upstairs, she reminded herself.

"Yes," he answered.

He didn't look away, though, merely continued watching her. She drew in a ragged breath, intending to call to the dog, but the words died in her throat.

When she tried to analyze it later, she wasn't sure which of them moved first. One moment, they were staring at each other in the garden, the next, they were reaching for each other.

His mouth was cool and tasted of berries but the rest of him was warm. Deliciously warm.

He kissed her with a raw hunger that took her breath away. His mouth moved over hers as if he wanted to memorize every dip, every curve.

Her arms rested against his chest and it took her a moment to realize he was shaking slightly. Not from cold. From hunger.

Jenna found something incredibly powerful and also

deeply terrifying to know this man could tremble with desire because of *her*.

The rain started up again, just a cool mist that landed in her hair. She didn't care. She wanted to stand here forever and go on pretending the rest of the world didn't exist.

He was the first to pull away. She wasn't sure what brought him back to his senses. One moment, his mouth was tangled with hers, the next, he had eased away and gazed down, his breathing ragged and his expression dazed.

"I'm sorry, Jenna. I didn't mean to do that. I've been telling myself all evening that kissing you would be a mistake."

All evening? He had been thinking about kissing her *all evening*? She didn't know what to think, what to say.

"Yes. You're right. It was a mistake."

As soon as she said the word, she thought she saw a flicker of something in his gaze reflecting from the landscaping lights, something that looked almost like... hurt.

He had been the one to say the words first and she could not disagree. They were completely wrong for each other. She was finding herself increasingly drawn to the man. But she knew nothing could ever come of it.

"Let's just blame the moonlight. It's lovely out here, especially after the rain. It's hard not to be...carried away by the moment."

She couldn't look at him as she spoke, hoping he didn't see remnants of her desire on her features.

"We should go in. The...the girls."

Without another word, she scooped up Theo, grabbed the towel off the porch swing and let herself into a house that suddenly, oddly, felt colder than the garden had, almost disapproving.

Jenna hurried up the flight of stairs to her apartment, drying the confused dog as she went.

With each step, she wondered what she had been thinking to kiss him with so much...passion.

That wasn't her.

Or maybe it was.

It was a disconcerting thought.

Maybe there were parts of herself she had never had occasion to explore before, needs and desires that had always seemed warm and comfortable and...*muted* during her marriage to Ryan.

Maybe she was like that ocean out there. On a calm afternoon at low tide, only tiny waves licked at the sand. When conditions aligned, though, and storms blew in, the ocean could be mighty and powerful. Terrifying.

She sensed this thing between her and Wes would be like that—wild, passionate, fierce.

And that she would quickly find herself in over her head.

The rain began in earnest again as Wes watched Jenna hurry into the rambling old Victorian house. Drops slid down his collar, soaking him quickly. But he ignored it, too busy cursing himself for letting his base instincts take over.

After he had kissed her, she had almost looked *afraid*. Did she think he would hurt her?

He had completely screwed up everything.

Why had he kissed her?

He should have simply tamped down his attraction to her, as he had been doing for a long time now.

Maybe he had wondered on some level if kissing her could prove to her he was absolutely no threat to her.

How ridiculous. If he had given her a mild, restrained sort of kiss, that might have been the case, but he had kissed her as if she were his last meal.

Why was she so afraid? She had said something earlier that evening that might have been a clue. He closed his eyes as more rain slithered down his collar.

Who had hurt her? And where was the bastard now, so Wes could make him sorry?

He let out a breath. Her reasons for being jittery around him didn't matter. Nor did it matter if she was actually afraid of *him* or simply of any man.

He had done nothing to ease that fear. By kissing her, giving in to the heat and the hunger, he had only provided her with more reason to be nervous in his company.

How could he help himself? He was finding Jenna increasingly difficult to resist.

It wasn't simply a physical attraction to her, a hunger that kept him up at night and left him aching and empty.

He was quickly developing a thing for her.

Wes curled his hands into fists.

Could he be any more pathetic? He was falling for a woman he couldn't have.

Jenna Haynes was soft and gentle and kind, all the things that no longer fit into his world.

Wes let out a breath, chilled and damp, though he had moved to the porch, out of the drizzle.

As difficult as he knew he would find it, he had to go back up the stairs to Jenna's apartment, for Brielle if nothing else.

He had to forget about that kiss, about his aching

hunger for her and about his growing feelings he knew were doomed to remain unreciprocated.

As he made his way up the stairs, he had the strange feeling that the house responded to his turmoil somehow.

He shook his head at his own foolishness. It was a *house*, for heaven's sake. Four walls, a foundation, a roof. It didn't have feelings and certainly couldn't offer sympathy.

When he reached her apartment, his knock was answered almost immediately by Brielle.

"There you are. Did you get lost out in the rain?" his daughter teased.

Yeah. Something like that.

"It's a pretty night. I was just enjoying it."

Jenna sat in an easy chair, watching the girls playing *Mario Kart*. She had Theo on her lap, almost like a shield.

When her gaze met his, the uneasy apprehension in her expression hit him like a blow coming out of nowhere in the exercise yard.

What did she think? That he was going to rush into the room and kiss her again?

"We're almost done with this race, Dad. Do you want to play?"

"We should head off, kiddo. It's getting late and we have to get ready for camp on Monday."

Jenna's daughter lit up. "Hey, I'm going to camp Monday, too. Are you going to science camp?"

Brielle nodded. "My mom signed me up before she even knew she was going to be out of town. I hope it's not lame."

Addison gave her a look of astonishment. "Science

camp is not lame at all! It's way fun. I went last year and we always did cool things. Experiments and kayaking and bird-watching and stuff."

"I really do think you'll have a wonderful time," Jenna assured his daughter with that warm smile she seemed to give to everyone but him. "Addie loved it last year. She couldn't stop talking about it. She's been looking forward to it all year."

"I hope so. I'm happy you'll be there. At least I'll have one friend," Brielle said.

"You'll have lots of friends," Addie said breezily. "A lot of the kids from school went last year and I'm sure they'll go again. But we can totally be camp buddies!"

"Definitely!" Brielle said with a grin. Wes thought again how grateful he was that his daughter seemed happy and well-adjusted, despite the divorce and his incarceration.

She was a curious child who was kind to others and made friends easily.

"If you want, I'm happy to take Brielle to camp Monday and I can pick her up again as well. And she's more than welcome to hang out here after camp, until you're done with work."

"That's a lot to ask of you for two weeks."

"Not at all. I know how hard it is to be a single parent, trying to coordinate schedules. I don't mind at all."

He had been trying to figure out how he was going to manage things. He had already talked to the Gutierrez brothers, who were willing to be flexible with his schedule, but Wes hated to take advantage after they already had been so good to him.

At the same time, he needed to stay away from Jenna so he could work on getting rid of these inconvenient feelings he was developing for her. Arranging his life so he was guaranteed to see her at least twice a day probably wasn't the solution.

What choice did he have, though? All his efforts to find someone to stay with Brielle for the hour between camp and the end of his shift had come to naught.

"That would actually be really helpful, unless I can find someone else tomorrow. I was trying to figure out how to squeeze in everything. I was planning to go in late and come home early to work around her schedule."

"You don't have to try. I'm more than happy to help."

"Thank you."

She still hadn't met his gaze directly, he realized, except for that first brief moment.

"Thank you also for dinner," he said. "I definitely need the lasagna recipe to add to my rotation."

"No problem. I can share it with you, if you want to give me your email."

She handed him a notebook and he quickly wrote down the email address he rarely used.

"I'll send it later tonight."

"Thanks. I'll watch for it. Let's go, Brie. Looks like the race is over."

His daughter sighed, clearly reluctant to leave her new best friend.

"Bye, Addie. Maybe I'll see you tomorrow."

"For sure on Monday."

The girls hugged as if they were each heading off on different long sea voyages, and Wes had to hide a smile. He caught Jenna's gaze, finally, and saw that she was smiling, too.

She quickly shifted her gaze back to the dog in her lap, leaving Wes feeling slightly bereft.

Bad enough that he had kissed her, when he had every intention of keeping his attraction to her bottled up.

He really hoped he hadn't completely ruined a friendship he was beginning to cherish.

Chapter Seven

"What time will Brielle be here?" Addy asked for what seemed like the hundredth time that morning.

Jenna sipped her tea, frustrated with herself for the butterflies jumping around in her stomach. She had awakened filled with a mix of anticipation and nervousness about seeing Wes that morning when he brought his daughter down the stairs.

She could not stop thinking about the kiss the other night.

The memory of it seemed seared into her subconscious. Every time she closed her eyes, she recalled the heat of his body next to hers, the strength of his muscles beneath her fingers.

She had wanted more than a kiss.

At some point in the early hours of the morning, she had finally admitted that to herself. For the first time since Ryan's death, she had ached for a man's touch.

For Wes's touch.

Despite two tortured nights of wondering what it might be like, she knew anything more than a heated kiss between them was impossible.

She was the problem.

It was easy enough to tell herself she wasn't ready yet. But Ryan had been gone for four years. While some part of her would always grieve for the future they had dreamed about, she had determined years ago that she couldn't spend the rest of her life aching for something she could never recapture.

She had decided to move on three years ago, when she had first accepted a date with Aaron Barker.

That decision had turned out to be a disastrous one, upending her entire life.

She was only now beginning to put the pieces back together.

She might be fiercely drawn to Wes Calhoun and felt great sympathy for what he had endured, spending three years in prison, wrongly convicted for another man's crimes, but Jenna couldn't picture a future with him.

Wes was rough, hard, dangerous. He rode a motorcycle, ran for miles on the beach, was built like a professional athlete.

What did she have to offer a man like that? Her hobbies included knitting and reading the occasional cozy mystery, not riding on the back of a Harley.

She sighed, more depressed than she had any right to be.

Wes was a very nice man and someday he would find the perfect woman for him. Jenna was more sorry than she would have expected that she couldn't be that perfect woman.

The doorbell suddenly chimed through their unit, distracting her from her thoughts.

Her pulse fluttered like the butterflies in her stomach.

"They're here!" Addie exclaimed, rushing to the door. She flung it open before Jenna could tell her daughter to give her a moment to compose herself.

And there he was.

Everything inside her seemed to sigh as he reached down to greet Theo, who rushed to be the first one to say hello.

Yes, Wes Calhoun was big and hard and dangerous. But his eyes were warm, and the genuine smile he gave both her puppy and her daughter touched something deep inside.

"Good morning, Addison."

"Hi, Mr. Calhoun. Hi, Brielle."

Addie reached a hand to the other girl and tugged her into the apartment, already chattering about what might be in store for them that day.

Jenna had to say something to him, she told herself. She couldn't stand here all day simply gazing at the man.

"Good morning," she said, forcing a smile to hide her sudden shyness.

"Morning. Sorry we're a little late. We misplaced a tennis shoe."

"I think the Brambleberry House ghost hid it from us," Brielle said from the sofa, where she and Addie were now sitting, heads together, petting Theo. "I swear, I looked in that closet four times before we finally found it, right in front of us."

"But our ghost usually doesn't tease," Addie said, her

voice perfectly serious. "I don't know why she would hide your shoe."

Brielle shrugged. "Who knows? Maybe she doesn't want me to go to day camp."

"Or maybe," her father said mildly, "you didn't look hard enough in the closet and your shoe was there all along."

"I did look, though," his daughter insisted.

"Well, you found it and you're here now," Jenna said with a smile. "Did you pack a lunch? If not, I made an extra PB&J."

Wes handed over an insulated lunch bag. "This one is turkey and cheese, along with some carrots and grapes and a small bag of chips."

"Sounds delicious."

"I'm still figuring out the sack lunch thing," he admitted.

"You seem to be doing great."

"I guess I should find my own tennis shoes," Addie said.

"Yes. You should," Jenna said. She had only been reminding her daughter to finish getting ready for the past half hour.

"Maybe the ghost hid my shoes, too," Addie said, looking thrilled at the possibility. "Maybe the ghost doesn't want either one of us to go to science camp. Maybe she doesn't like science."

"Before you start spreading any unfounded conspiracy theories about our poor Abigail, go look in your closet," Jenna said.

"You can come help me find them," Addie said to Brielle. "Four eyes are better than two. That's what my mom always says, anyway."

"Okay," the other girl said cheerfully. The two of

them hurried, Theo close on their heels, toward Addie's bedroom door, decorated with drawings of unicorns and flower gardens, along with the occasional bloodthirsty, jagged-toothed dinosaur.

Their departure left her alone with Wes, she suddenly realized.

There was no reason for things to be awkward between them, she told herself. Yes, they had shared a kiss, but they had dealt with it after it happened. Surely they could go back to being friends now, right?

"She's a great kid," Jenna said.

"Yeah. I really lucked out in the kid department. Even with the divorce and all the mess of the past three years, Brielle is great. I thank heaven for it every day."

"Children can be fairly resilient. After my husband died, I was so worried about how it would impact Addie, but she seems to be doing okay, so far."

She couldn't resist knocking on the intricate woodwork of the door frame, which earned her a smile from him.

She did not tell him that while she certainly had worried about Addie losing her father at a young age, she had also stressed about how her daughter internalized their summer two years earlier when they had fled to Cannon Beach. They had been forced to use assumed names, to change their hair color, to be cautious about everyone who came into their tight circle.

She didn't want to share that with Wes, though. That was in the past and she refused to let Aaron Barker take up any more space in her present or her future.

"It's a nice day so we'll probably walk the three blocks to the community center where the camp is based. Is that okay with you? I'm multitasking and walking Theo in hopes of wearing him out so I can get some things done around here today."

"Sounds like a plan. Thanks again."

"The forecast calls for more rain this afternoon, so I'll probably drive to the center to pick them up after day camp."

"I'll be here soon as I can after work."

"No rush. The girls are getting along great and I don't mind having Brielle here at all."

"Thanks. I really appreciate it. I'm definitely going to owe you dinner."

She shook her head. "You don't. This is what friends do for each other, Wes."

His gaze met hers in a searching look that left her slightly breathless.

"I was worried you might not want anything to do with me and Brielle after that kiss the other night."

She studied him, surprised by the note of uncertainty in his voice. Was it possible that he had been left as disconcerted as she was by their kiss?

"Don't be silly. It was only a kiss." She knew that was a vast understatement. It had been much more than that for her. The words *stunning* and *earthshaking* seemed more appropriate. "It shouldn't have happened and we both agree it won't happen again. But it's no big deal."

He didn't answer immediately. "I'll try to keep my hands to myself but I'm very attracted to you and…it's been a long time for me."

His hands had shaken when he touched her, she suddenly remembered. The memory made her toes curl.

"Same here," she admitted. "I guess it's a good thing neither of us is in the market for a quick fling."

"I don't know. I could probably be persuaded."

Her gaze flew to his. Though his tone was sober, there was a sparkle in his gaze, a little devilish glint that made her give a startled laugh.

"So could I, truth be told," she admitted. "But it's not a good idea, right? We're neighbors. Our daughters are friends. I would hate for things to become messy and awkward between us."

After a long moment, he sighed. "I know you're right. But I don't have to like it. It was a really amazing kiss."

She could not disagree.

The girls came out of the room before she could answer.

"Guess what?" Brielle exclaimed. "We found Addie's shoes right away. I guess it was only my shoe that Abigail hid."

"Whew. Good thing." He smiled again at his daughter with so much warmth and affection, Jenna's toes curled again.

"I've got to go. I'll see you all later."

Brielle gave her father a brilliant smile. "Bye, Dad. I'll see you tonight."

"Have fun at camp. Learn all you can about science so you can teach me stuff."

"Okay. But you already know lots of stuff."

"I'm always willing to learn more."

Before he left the apartment, Wes sent Jenna a look that had her wondering exactly what kind of things he knew…and regretting that she would never have the chance to find out.

After she walked the girls to the community center and checked them both into their day camp, Jenna decided that morning was too beautiful to go straight home.

On impulse, she decided to head down to the beach with Theo and walk home along the seashore.

She and Addie had already discovered the dog loved the water. After his initial hesitation, Theo had become a big fan, dancing through the little waves and sniffing every sand mound and seaweed tendril along the beach.

The morning was cool and lovely as they walked along the hard-packed sand close to the water's edge. They certainly weren't alone on Cannon Beach, but it was far from crowded, like it could be on a July afternoon.

A couple of teenagers flew colorful trick kites on the sand and a few hardy souls played in the water, though she considered it still too cold for comfort.

Sometimes Jenna still had to pinch herself to make sure she really was lucky enough to live here, beside the Pacific.

She loved the ocean and found it both invigorating and, conversely, calming.

She wasn't sure if she could ever return to her home state of Utah. While she loved the mountains there, Oregon had mountains, too, whenever she might need a fix.

Utah held plenty of sad memories. She had lost her husband there, had worked to rebuild her life, then had fled, abandoning everything because of one selfish man who didn't know the meaning of the word *no*.

Here in Cannon Beach, she had found peace. Had it been perfect? No. But she had found friends and a community here. Everyone here had been kind to her from the moment she moved into Brambleberry House.

They had nearly reached the beach below Brambleberry House when she spotted a familiar figure moving toward them from the opposite direction with a beautiful Irish setter pacing protectively beside her.

"Rosa!" she called as they approached. "Hello! How are you, darling? And how are you, Fiona?"

"Jenna, my friend. Hello."

Rosa's serene features lit up with happiness. Her friend was round and lovely, her pregnancy giving her a graceful beauty that Jenna loved to see.

"Who is this little sweetheart?" Rosa asked with a smile.

"This is Theo. He's a rescue dog we picked up last week at the shelter. I've been promising Addie we would get a dog forever. I finally ran out of excuses."

"He is beautiful. I am so happy for you and Addie. She must be thrilled."

"They adore each other," Jenna said. "It's been really sweet to see. How are you feeling? Do you need to sit down? There's a bench over there. Let's stop for a minute and visit. We haven't had the chance to talk in forever."

After a moment's consideration, Rosa nodded and made her way to the bench, where she lowered herself down, still graceful despite her advanced stage of pregnancy.

"I am trying to stay active like my doctor says I must do, but it is not easy at this stage. Every day, moving becomes a little harder."

"I remember too well. I was in my first year of teaching when I was pregnant with Addie. Before she was born, I was so miserable. I wasn't sure I would be able to survive it."

"I am the same. I am ready to turn over the store to Carol."

Their mutual friend Carol Hardesty worked full-time

at Rosa's gift shop as the assistant manager. She was competent and efficient but didn't have Rosa's business sense or her creative approach to retail management.

"I'm happy to take a few extra hours during the summer if you need me to," Jenna said. "I can go to three days a week during the busy summer season, if that would help."

Rosa made a face. "It is not necessary. We talked about this. You need to slow down, now that you are done with your school classes. You should take time to enjoy your summer a little bit instead of always working, working, working."

This was the first year of her life that she had decided to take an actual summer break. She still worked twelve to sixteen hours a week at the gift shop, but compared to previous summers, when she had worked full-time and taken extra classes so she could accelerate her advanced degree, that seemed like a breeze.

She knew she would love having time to catch up on projects as well as plan ahead for the next school year.

"I don't mind working, working, working if it will help you out," she said to her friend, to whom she owed so much.

"We will be fine. Do not worry. I have other workers who need the extra hours. You enjoy being with your daughter."

She looked around. "Where is our Addie?"

"Science camp. I am just heading home after walking her and Brielle Calhoun there."

"Brielle. This is Wes's daughter."

"That's right."

"How are you getting along with my new tenant?" Rosa asked.

Jenna remembered the heat of his mouth on hers, the scent of flowers and pine surrounding them as they kissed. She did not meet Rosa's gaze. They had been friends since being paired together as college roommates and Rosa knew her too well. Would she be able to tell the situation had become…complicated?

"He was nice enough to change my car battery a few weeks ago when I had trouble. His daughter is staying with him full-time for the next few weeks while her mother is out of town, so I'm helping out with some gap babysitting."

"That is very neighborly of you. I am sure Wes appreciates your help."

"He seems grateful."

"He is very handsome, do you not think?"

Jenna gave a casual shrug she suspected did not fool Rosa for a moment. "I don't know. I hadn't really noticed. He's just the neighbor who lives upstairs."

Rosa made a disbelieving sound. "I do not believe you. How can any woman not notice a man like that? I am very happily married to my Wyatt and so huge I cannot see my toes right now. And still I would notice someone like Wes Calhoun."

Jenna could feel herself flush. For a moment, she was tempted to confide in her old friend about that kiss two nights earlier and the heated dreams that had left her aching and alone in her bed.

In the old days, they used to wake each other up in their dorm room after dates to talk long into the night. She had told Rosa everything, though she suspected her friend had not ever been entirely truthful with her.

But they were not college students now. She was a grown woman, a respected educator, with an eight-year-old daughter. It seemed undignified, somehow, to dish with her landlady about the gorgeous guy who lived upstairs—even if that landlady was her dearest friend.

On the other hand, she could really use some advice.

She gazed at the dogs, now digging in the sand, probably on the hunt for a crab or some other poor creature.

"Okay," she admitted. "I noticed."

"Ha. I knew it!" Rosa looked inordinately pleased with herself. "I told Wyatt I thought maybe it would be good for you to have such a handsome man living upstairs from you. You spend too much time alone."

Jenna frowned. "Seriously? You were trying to matchmake when you rented the apartment to Wes?"

Her friend tried, and failed, to look innocent. "I would not say matchmake. Maybe just give you a little, what is the word, *nudge*."

Jenna gave Rosa an exasperated look. "I don't need a nudge. And I certainly don't need someone to matchmake for me, especially not with a man like Wes Calhoun."

Now it was Rosa's turn to frown. "How do you mean, a man like Wes Calhoun? What is wrong with him?"

She sighed. "Nothing is wrong with him. As I said, he seems very nice. He's a good father and clearly loves his child. He has been very kind. He has even given me a few training tips for Theo, who adores him."

Rosa laughed. "See? There you go. Dogs are very wise. They see into the heart of a person. If you find Theo does not like a man, that is when you should be nervous about him."

She wasn't sure she was ready to let a dog vet the men in her life. On the other hand, she also wasn't sure she could trust her own instincts about men, considering what happened with Aaron Barker.

"I don't believe that's scientifically proven, Rosa."

Her friend made a dismissive gesture. "Maybe not science. But I have seen it myself. I would never have considered dating anyone if Fiona did not approve. The men she did not like always proved to be someone I did not like, either."

"But do I really have to base my dating decisions on the opinion of a puppy whose favorite thing in the world seems to be sniffing the behind of any other dog who comes along?"

Rosa laughed. "Fine. You may have a point. What does our Abigail think of him?"

Jenna rolled her eyes at Rosa's mention of the woman believed to haunt Brambleberry House. "I don't know. I'll have to ask her. So far, she hasn't seemed inclined to discuss the matter with me."

"She will let you know if she approves." Rosa smiled, then suddenly winced and rubbed at her protruding abdomen.

Jenna didn't miss the gesture. "Everything okay?"

"Yes. Fine. I am having a few twinges, that is all. For the most part, this has been an easy pregnancy, though Wyatt is nervous enough for both of us."

Jenna adored Rosa's husband, Wyatt, who had temporarily lived downstairs from them when Rosa lived on the third floor. Wyatt was a police detective and she considered him one of the good guys, especially after he had worked so hard to make sure Aaron Barker received a lengthy prison sentence.

They sat for a moment on the beach overlooking the

sea. Finally Rosa sighed. "This is so lovely but I should probably go. I have an appointment in a short time."

Jenna hugged her friend. "Take it easy on yourself. And remember that I'm more than willing to help out if you need me to take additional hours at the store."

"I will remember. Thank you, my dear."

Rosa whistled to Fiona, who returned to her side, then the two continued on their walk while Jenna did the same with Theo, heading up the beach toward home.

Chapter Eight

She had come to enjoy this last trip outside before bedtime each night for her and Theo.

With her daughter asleep in her room, Jenna would take the dog down the staircase and out the back door to the fenced dog yard.

In the moonlight, with the murmuring sound of the ocean not far off and the random peeps and calls of the various night creatures who lived nearby, she found it peaceful. Almost meditative.

Once, she had been afraid of the night. Those were the hours when she felt most vulnerable, at risk from a boogeyman whose name she knew all too well.

Since Aaron Barker had been arrested, Jenna worked hard to overcome her fear of nighttime. She wouldn't let him take that from her forever.

Okay, she still walked outside with pepper spray in

her pocket. She could be brave and cautious at the same time, couldn't she?

On impulse, tonight she had brought along Theo's leash as well as her phone, where she had a security camera linked up in the living area of the apartment so she could hear if Addie woke for a glass of water. She decided to walk the dog down the beach a short way, only to the water's edge directly west of the house.

As she watched the moonlight dance on the waves, she released a breath, all the pent-up frustrations and concerns of the day floating away on the tide.

She had worked that day at Rosa's gift shop, and her shift had been unusually stressful from start to finish.

The day had started with her catching a shoplifter, her least favorite thing. Worse, the person who had slipped into her purse a handcrafted necklace valued at several hundred dollars turned out to be someone she knew, the aunt of one of her students.

It hadn't been the woman's first offense and not even her first shoplifting incident at By-the-Wind, so Rosa had no choice but to call the police, who had arrested the woman, angry and protesting all the way.

The event had put a pall over her whole day. After her shift and before she had to go pick up the girls from their fourth day at science camp, Jenna had gone to the grocery store to purchase a few things she had forgotten in Saturday's epic shopping trip and had ended up dropping and breaking an entire bottle of pasta sauce.

She had insisted on helping the store employee clean up the mess. As a result, she had been late picking up the girls and had rushed up to the community center to find them waiting on the curb for her.

She hadn't even had the chance to talk to Wes that

afternoon when he came to pick up his daughter, as Brielle had rushed away with a hurried thank-you as soon as she saw her father's motorcycle pull into the driveway, eager to tell him about all the things she had learned that day.

Jenna told herself it was for the best. She was thinking about the man entirely too much anyway. It didn't help that for the past four days she had seen him in the morning when he dropped off Brielle and then again in the afternoon when he picked her up.

Each time she saw him, Jenna's awareness of the man only seemed to intensify.

What was she going to do about it?

She sighed. Exactly nothing. She planned to remain friendly with him and keep a safe distance.

"Are you ready to head back?" she asked Theo after a few more moments.

The dog turned its head, tail wagging. At odd moments, she almost felt as if he understood exactly what she was saying. As far as dogs went, Theo seemed unusually intuitive.

Sure. And maybe during those odd moments when he seemed to be staring at nothing in the corner, he was really communing with the Brambleberry House ghost.

She shook her head at herself. He was a great dog but he wasn't some kind of canine medium to the other side.

"Come on, Theo. Good boy."

The dog trotted beside her, already well-behaved on the leash. So far, he was fitting into their little family as if he had been there forever.

She keyed in the password to the locked beach gate and made her way through the garden, pausing occasionally to sniff the lavender and the climbing roses over one of the trellises.

She again felt so fortunate to be living amidst such beauty. Not only were the gardens of the house spectacular, but the view was beyond compare. On stormy nights, she loved watching the clouds roll over the water and seeing the waves churn.

Tonight was calm, though, only a light breeze, lush with the smell of flowers and pine and sea, to send the leaves shivering.

She was nearly to the house when the dark shape of a man stepped down from the porch.

She let out an instinctive shriek and reached for her pepper spray.

"Easy, Jenna," a low voice said. "Easy. It's me. Wes. I didn't mean to alarm you. I had no idea you were out here or I would have given you some kind of warning."

Her chest felt tight and shaky and it took her a moment to catch her breath again. With her heart pounding, she slipped the pepper spray back into her pocket.

"Hello. You startled me."

"I can tell. I'm sorry. Are you okay?"

Heat soaked her face and her skin felt tight and itchy with embarrassment. "Yes. Fine. I was surprised, that's all."

"Are you sure that's all?" He stepped down from the porch and moved closer to her. Jenna fought the urge to back away.

"What do you mean?"

"When I first moved in, I thought something about me was causing you to be so jittery."

She sighed, embarrassed all over again. "It's not you," she whispered. Or at least not *completely* him.

He peered down at her in the moonlight. "I think I'm beginning to figure that out."

He reached out and laid a hand on her arm. She didn't feel threat from him. She felt…comfort.

"Why are you so nervous, Jen? Did someone hurt you?"

His voice was gentle, like a cottonwood fluff floating on the breeze. He sounded concerned, not nosy or intrusive, as if he genuinely wanted to know so that he could figure out a way to help her.

"It's a very long story," she said.

He sat down on the bench there in the garden surrounded by rhododendron, iris, rosebushes. He gestured to the spot beside him, not demanding, only inviting her to share if she wanted to, offering a listening ear.

She wanted to tell him, suddenly.

She did not like to talk about what had happened to her two years earlier, especially nights like tonight when the fear and emotional distress seemed so raw and close.

Yet somehow, she wanted to tell Wes.

After a moment, she lowered herself to the bench beside him, strangely aware of the hard slats of the bench beneath her, the sweetly scented night breeze, the soft knit fabric of her sweater.

"I told you a little about my husband and how he died."

"Yes. I'm sorry again for that."

"I loved Ryan dearly. Together we created the family that neither of us had before. He was a kind man. Not perfect, but perfect for me, if that makes sense."

She glanced at Wes in time to see a muscle twitch in his jaw. "He sounds great," he said.

"He was. I was devastated by his death. So was Addie.

I didn't expect to ever date again. But a year after he died, friends pushed me to try online dating. I didn't think I was ready for anything serious, but they persuaded me that I didn't have to marry a man just because I went out on a date with him. It would be good practice, they told me, and would help me figure out what I might be looking for if I ever wanted to let someone else into my heart."

She picked at the cuff of her sweater, unable to meet his gaze. "I didn't want to date anyone. At the same time, I was beginning to feel terribly lonely. I taught all day and then was alone with Addie all evening. I missed adult conversation, especially because Ryan had been sick for so long and hadn't really been a partner for that last year. I thought maybe dating again would distract me from how much I still missed my husband."

"I'm going to assume something went south," he said, his voice low.

She sighed. "You could say that."

She leaned back on the bench, finding an odd sort of strength from Wes's company. How strange, that this dangerous man could make her feel so very safe.

"I met a few guys who seemed nice enough. We went out for coffee or a meal, but things never progressed beyond that. I figured that was enough, then I made one more match on my profile. A man from a nearby town. Aaron Barker."

She couldn't seem to say the name without her whole body tensing. Did Wes notice?

"Aaron seemed very nice on the surface. He was charming and kind. We went for coffee and had a lovely conversation. For the first time, I was tempted to go on a second date with someone. We went to lunch one

afternoon. It was pleasant. Enjoyable, even. We talked
on the phone a few times and met a few nights later,
for dinner this time. After dinner, he walked me to my
car and…kissed me."

At this rate, she was going to unravel her sweater,
so she forced her fretting fingers to relax.

"It was too soon for me. I got into my car and drove
away. Before I could make it home, I had to pull over
and be sick."

"Not a good reaction for a first kiss."

She remembered, suddenly, how she had reacted
after Wes had kissed her. She had certainly not been
sick. She had been achy and hungry and wanted more.

"He called me that night to check that I made it home
safely and I…tried to break things off. I explained that
I wasn't ready to date yet, that it had been a mistake for
me to create a profile on the dating website and that I
should not have let my friends push me into it. I tried
to be as kind as possible and assure Aaron that he had
done nothing wrong. I told him I liked him but that it
wouldn't be fair to date him when my own emotions
were still so tangled up with my late husband."

"I'm guessing he didn't take it well."

She shook her head. "He refused to listen to anything I said. It was almost as if he didn't hear me. He
kept talking about how we clicked and he knew for sure
that I felt it as well. I tried to let him down as gently
as possible, but he would not listen. Not that night and
not the next night when he called me again. He started
to became…forceful."

He grew rigid beside her. "Oh, Jenna."

"Not that. He didn't…sexually assault me or anything. He just refused to accept that I didn't want a re-

lationship with him. He would write me love notes, send flowers to me at work, text me endlessly at any time of the day or night. I finally blocked his number, but he would get another number and start all over again. I changed my phone number and my email, but he always seemed to figure out how to connect with me."

"Did you talk to the police?"

"He was the police," she said simply. "He was a patrol officer for a small department in a nearby Utah town. His uncle was the police chief and he wouldn't listen to any of my complaints. Not only that, but Aaron specialized in cybercrime, which made him a tech whiz. He could infiltrate all my social media, my contact info, even my private school email address. I couldn't escape him. This went on for weeks, until I was completely terrified."

"I can imagine."

"And then he went after Addie."

"How?"

The single clipped word contained both shock and hard fury. It should have frightened her, coming from such a fierce man, but somehow only made her want to lean against him and let this man protect her from the world.

"She was in kindergarten and he picked her up from school early one day. I hadn't said anything to my coworkers about what was going on with me. I guess I was too embarrassed. So when he showed his badge to the kindergarten teacher—who was elderly and should have retired years earlier—and told her we were old friends and that he wanted to take Addie to visit her father's grave and pick up a birthday present for me, she didn't blink an eye."

"I hope she was fired," he said, without a note of sympathy in his voice.

"She was retiring that year anyway, so it was all swept under the carpet. Anyway, he returned her to me about an hour after school was out. He kept her just long enough to terrify me and make it clear that he could get to either of us anytime he wanted. I knew I had to leave. He wasn't going to let up. If anything, he was escalating."

"Sounds like it."

"That very day, I happened to get a phone call from my dear friend Rosa."

"Rosa? As in Rosa our landlady?"

"One and the same. We were college roommates. Somehow in the middle of our conversation, I ended up spilling the entire ugly story to her. For so long, I had carried the burden by myself. It felt so good to tell someone else."

"Rosa was a good choice."

"Yes. Her father was in law enforcement so she wasn't naive. She knew what could happen if I didn't take action. She insisted I come to stay with her. She set me up in my apartment, got me a job at her gift shop and basically helped me begin the process of putting my life back together."

"Good for you."

"I can't explain how wonderful it felt to finally start believing I was safe. I really thought Addie and I could make a new start here. I was even thinking about try-ing to get an Oregon teaching certificate."

Her voice trailed off and she once more gripped her hands together in her lap.

"I take it that didn't happen as seamlessly as you had hoped."

His gentle tone soothed her somehow. The memories were still hard, but they seemed slightly less hard through sharing them.

"Addie and I had a few good months here. We were finally starting to feel safe. And then Aaron found me."

"How?"

"A fluke, really. Apparently someone from his little Utah town came to the coast on vacation and spotted me working at the gift shop. I should have expected it. Many people from other western states come here to enjoy the Oregon Coast. It was my bad luck that one of his friends who had seen a picture of me decided to come to Cannon Beach."

"Did Barker try to come after you?"

She nodded with a shiver she couldn't restrain. The events of that afternoon, here in this very garden, suddenly felt closer than they had since she testified at his sentencing hearing.

"Aaron couldn't understand why I had fled. But he magnanimously told me he was ready to forgive everything as long as I came back with him. When I tried to flee, he…attacked me and especially Rosa, when she tried to protect me. She was so brave. Though she and her dog were both hurt, they still managed to distract him long enough for me and Addie to escape into the house and call 911. I'll never be able to repay her for her courage. She showed far more grit than I did. I was petrified."

"Understandable, after everything you had been through. What happened to Barker? Was he caught?"

"Yes. Rosa hit him with a rock and stunned him. He was still coming to when Wyatt and the other police officers arrived. He was arrested and charged with multiple assault and attempted kidnapping charges. He pleaded not guilty, of course. He would never admit he did anything wrong, but he was convicted and sentenced to serve five years in the state prison system."

"Five years. Hardly seems like enough for what he put you through."

"He was sentenced to five years but was scheduled for a parole hearing in December."

His gaze narrowed. "Was?"

Wes, she had previously noticed, didn't miss much. "Yes. He…he died unexpectedly in prison a few weeks ago. Natural causes. An aneurysm, according to the autopsy."

"Wow. No kidding?"

She nodded. "I finally feel like I can breathe again, you know? For the first time in two years, I can think about the future. In many ways, I feel as if I've been living in suspended animation. Trapped by events beyond my control. I was ready to go into hiding again as soon as he left prison. Now I don't have to. I can stay here in Cannon Beach. We can make this area our forever home. It's liberating."

He looked down at Theo, sleeping at their feet. "Is that what led you to adding a dog to your family?"

She nodded. "I've been in survival mode for so long. It really feels as if Addie and I have been in a constant state of turmoil since Ryan died. We're finally in a good place now. Addie has wanted a dog forever and this seemed like a small thing to do for her, after everything she has endured."

"He seems like a good dog."

"We got lucky. He's really well-behaved and eager to learn."

He petted the dog, and she couldn't seem to stop watching those big, calloused hands.

"So now you know the entire grim story. I don't... trust easily. For obvious reasons."

"Understandable."

"It's easy to fall into the victim mentality. But I don't want to live the rest of my life that way. That is giving Aaron entirely too much power over me. I would rather not have to think about him another moment."

"I'm sorry I dredged up all the bad memories by asking what happened."

She shook her head. "I wanted to tell you. I consider you a friend, and friends share things about their lives with each other, right?"

"I suppose that's true."

"You were honest with me about what happened to you. I should have been honest in return. I suppose I'm a little ashamed that it has affected me so much, when there are others who have been through much worse things. Like you, for instance, convicted for something you didn't do."

"My mom used to tell me not to compare my troubles to anyone else's. I wouldn't want theirs and they wouldn't want mine."

She smiled. "Well, thank you for the sympathetic ear. I'm glad I told you."

"So am I. It only reinforced to me how amazing you are."

She blinked, disconcerted by his words. "Me? I'm not amazing. I told you how terrified I was when Aaron found me. I couldn't think straight. Two years later, I'm still scared of far too many things. I even scream at shadows, as you saw clearly tonight."

"And yet you are inherently kind to your students, to your customers at the gift shop and to random strange men who live upstairs."

He took her hand in his and smiled down at her. Something sparked in his gaze, something warm and glittery, and his throat moved as he swallowed hard.

"Wes."

That was all she said. All she could manage. His gaze met hers and she was unbearably moved when he lifted her hand to his mouth and gently kissed her fingers.

She wanted to kiss him.

An aching hunger bloomed to life, like the rosebushes bursting with color on a June morning.

She looked at his mouth, breathless as she waited for him.

He lowered his mouth and she leaned toward him, heart pounding. At the last moment, he froze, his expression suddenly tormented.

He wouldn't kiss her, she realized. Not only because of what she had told him but because she had been clear that she didn't want more than a friendship with him.

If she were wise, she would count her blessings, gather her dog and rush inside.

She didn't feel very wise right now. Before she could think through the ramifications, she leaned forward, bridging the last few inches between them, and kissed him.

It was as if she had unleashed the storm. He kissed her back with a fierce intensity that pushed every coherent thought out of her head.

Still, she sensed he was holding back. She could feel it in his leashed strength, in the tight control he was keeping over himself.

She wanted that wildness, suddenly. Would this man ever let himself lose control?

She tightened her arms around his neck and tangled her mouth with his, wanting the delicious kiss to go on and on.

thing but how much he wanted this woman in his arms, in his bed.

His hand slid from her back to one hip. He wanted to touch those curves she pressed against him.

He was inches from his goal when she made that soft, sexy sound again.

The sound seemed to yank him back to his senses. What the hell was he doing? He had told himself he couldn't do this again. He wanted her too much, though his kissing her again only showed him how very much he was beginning to care for her.

Beyond that, she had just shared with him her harrowing ordeal. She had been tormented, stalked, terrified by a man who couldn't take no for an answer.

Even though she had made it clear she wasn't interested in anything with him, here he was mauling her in the garden of Brambleberry House, like he was some sort of high school kid making out with a girl behind the bleachers of the football stadium.

He jerked away, disgusted with himself.

She looked small and delicate, lovely as tiny violets springing across the grass in May.

He had spent three years feeling dehumanized, marginalized, discarded.

But he never felt as barbaric as he did right now, taking in the sight of Jenna Haynes staring up at him with huge eyes.

"I'm so sorry. I don't know what came over me."

She blinked a few times and drew in a deep breath. "Why are you apologizing?"

"Because I had no right to kiss you like a starving man who had just been snatched off the streets and plunked down at a table in the middle of a feast."

Chapter Nine

He was in so much trouble.

As flames of desire licked through him, Wes tried his best to hold on to whatever semblance of control he could manage to dredge up out of the depths of his subconscious.

Jenna tasted so damn good. Like chocolate and cherries and this perfect summer night.

She made a soft, breathy sound deep in her throat and her arms seemed to tighten around him.

He could feel his control slip away, inch by painful inch. All he wanted to do was kiss her, taste her, make love to her.

He traced a hand beneath her sweater, to the warm, luscious skin there. She shivered and arched against his hand, pressing her curves into his chest.

He was aching with need, his brain empty of every-

She made a small, strangled kind of sound. "It was only a kiss, Wes. You didn't attack me or anything. In fact, as I recall, I started things."

He closed his eyes, remembering that heart-stopping moment when she had spanned the distance between them and pressed her mouth to his.

Something told him he would be reliving that moment for a long, long time.

"Maybe," he finally said. "But I took things too far. I shouldn't have, especially after everything you told me about what you've been through. I promise, it won't happen again."

She gazed at him, and he watched as she seemed to regain her composure with every passing second.

She nodded and pressed her lips together, those delicious lips he could have explored all night long.

"Okay," she said. She rose and let out a long breath. "Good night, then. Thanks again for...for listening to me."

She grabbed Theo's leash and the two of them walked into the house, leaving him alone to curse and ache and want.

Jenna walked back up the stairs to her apartment on knees that felt weak, somehow.

She still couldn't quite wrap her head around the realization that she had instigated another kiss with Wes Calhoun.

Hadn't she learned her lesson the first time?

She wanted to blame it on the moonlight or the peaceful garden or the simple release of sharing her story with him finally.

She suspected the real reason for her behavior had

nothing to do with that. It had more to do with the man himself.

When Wes first moved into Brambleberry House, she had considered him the very last man in Cannon Beach she might come to trust, someone with whom she had nothing in common.

What an illuminating example of how very wrong first impressions could be. These past few weeks of coming to know him better—of seeing his gentleness with Theo, with his own daughter and with hers—had given her a picture of a kind man beneath the gruff, intimidating exterior.

She respected and admired him more than any other man she had met in a very long time.

What was she going to do about it?

As she reached her apartment, she let herself and Theo inside, where she took off the puppy's leash and harness. The dog rushed to his water bowl, and Jenna closed the door behind her, listening to the small, comforting noises of the apartment settling around her.

Nothing.

That was exactly what she planned to do about this attraction to Wes. They had kissed again and it had been amazing, but now she had to go back to her regular life and try to forget those few stirring moments in the garden had ever happened.

The idea depressed her, even though she knew she had no other option.

They were attracted to each other. She couldn't deny that. The heat they generated could have ignited a dozen beach fires.

Why not give in to it? They were both unattached adults. What would be the harm in finding a secluded spot in the garden, maybe the pergola or one of the padded benches in a dark corner, and surrendering to the attraction between them?

Because she would end up with a broken heart.

She was not a woman who could handle a casual fling. She had seen her mother's heart broken too many times by men who would move in and out of their lives.

She was a forever kind of woman. She knew that about herself and suspected it wouldn't take much for her to fall in love with Wes.

Then what?

Try as she might, she couldn't picture a future with Wes. She again couldn't imagine she could provide anything that a man like him might be looking for in a woman.

Someone adventurous. Audacious. Brave.

She wasn't any of those things. Eventually Wes would figure that out and grow tired of her.

She couldn't go through the pain of loving someone again and inevitably losing him.

Better to stop things now, before either of their hearts were involved. Before she could make a fool of herself over him and destroy a friendship she was coming to cherish.

Theo went to stand by the door of his crate, ready for bed. She opened it for him and watched him curl up on the soft blankets, then headed for her solitary bed.

Chapter Ten

Somehow, she and Wes managed to maintain a cordial relationship over the next week while she helped fill in the gaps of Brielle's care, between his work schedule and the girls' science camp schedule.

He was friendly enough when he would drop his daughter at Jenna's apartment in the morning, a half hour before she had to take the girls to camp.

He would chat with Jenna about her upcoming day and would ask questions of Addie about camp and what other activities she was doing that summer.

A few mornings when he had extra time, he even offered to take Theo outside to the garden so that Jenna could focus on finishing up breakfast and getting ready for her shift at the gift shop, on the days she worked.

In the evenings, the routine was reversed. He would come to pick up his daughter about an hour after camp finished for the day. He never lingered long but took time to chat a little about the day and their respective plans for the evening.

Despite her lingering tumult over the kisses they had shared—and the secret part of her that undeniably wanted more—she quite enjoyed the routine they had fallen into. She sensed he did as well.

Everything changed on the morning of the girls' last day of science camp.

The morning started like all the others. She and Addie both got up early to walk the dog on the beach as the morning mist hung heavy on the shore and the gulls swooped to scavenge for juicy treasure along the detritus left from high tide.

She wasn't quite sure what happened. One moment, they were enjoying the morning, the next, the dog stopped to sniff directly in front of Jenna and she got tangled in his leash.

She could feel herself topple and reached a hand out to brace herself. Under normal circumstances, she would have been fine, simply annoyed at her own clumsiness. She landed on soft sand, after all.

Something in the sand wasn't soft, though. She felt a slicing pain as her palm caught on something jagged buried in the sand. A piece of shell or driftwood, perhaps, or maybe even a shard of glass left by some unknown beach visitor.

She gasped at the pain and immediately rolled to her side, clutching her hand.

Addie looked down at her, wide-eyed. "What happened? Are you okay?"

"I'm fine," she lied.

She pulled her hand away and saw she had a nasty cut about four inches running right through her life line, between her right thumb and forefinger. "I'm afraid I'm bleeding, though," she admitted to her daughter.

She could only be glad she had been the one to fall and not Addie.

"Oh no! How did you cut yourself?"

"I'm not sure. Something sharp in the sand. I should find whatever it was so it doesn't hurt someone else."

"I can look."

"I'll do it," she said quickly, with visions of Addie being cut as well. "I don't want you to hurt yourself, too. Why don't you keep walking Theo down the beach a little more, and I'll dig around and see if I can figure out what it was."

Addie looked undecided but after a moment, her daughter obeyed. She and the dog headed away from Jenna a short distance.

Her hand was now bleeding copiously, which was one of the reasons she had sent Addie away. She didn't have anything with her to stop the bleeding so she grabbed a corner of her T-shirt and ripped, feeling a pang as she did.

This had been one of Ryan's T-shirts that she had packed away after he died. She wore them as sleep shirts and to work out.

She still had several of his shirts left, including three that she had sewn into pillows for Addie's room. Still, losing this one stung worse than her cut, like slicing one more thread between her and her past.

She quickly wrapped the strip of cloth around her hand, hoping to stop the worst of the bleeding, then dug through the deep sand there until she found the culprit, a shell from what looked like a Dungeness crab, with a broken, jagged edge.

She tossed it into one of the garbage cans set at intervals along the beach, then caught up with Addie.

"Mom, you need a real bandage," her daughter said, taking in the makeshift bandage that was also now covered in blood.

Jenna strongly suspected she needed stitches, but she didn't want to worry Addie. A trip to the doctor or urgent care clinic could wait until after she dropped off the girls at day camp. Meantime, she would do some rudimentary first aid back at their apartment to staunch the bleeding.

They reached the second floor landing to their apartment just as Wes came down the stairs from the third floor, chatting with Brielle.

He stopped on the stairs halfway to the landing and stared at her.

"Good Lord. What happened to you?"

He looked gorgeous, she couldn't help but notice, in worn jeans, work boots and a T-shirt that stretched over his hard muscles.

She, on the other hand, looked like she had gone a few rounds with an angry badger. She had tried to hold her arm above her heart to slow the blood flow. As a result, blood had dripped through her makeshift bandage to streak down her arm.

"I'm fine. It's nothing. I stumbled while we were walking. When I reached out to catch myself, I landed on a broken shell with a sharp edge in the sand."

"That looks like it really hurt," Brielle exclaimed.

"It looks worse than it is."

"My mom didn't cry at all. She's tough."

Addie's admiring tone made Jenna feel about a thousand feet tall. She only hoped her daughter still looked up to her after she reached the difficult teenage years, just on the horizon.

"Let me take a look at it," Wes said, holding out a hand.

She didn't want to show him, though she wasn't sure if that was embarrassment at her own clumsiness or hesitation to have him touch her again, given the heat that flared between them at any given moment.

"You don't have time," she protested. "We're late returning from our walk. You'll be late for work. Don't worry about me. I'm fine."

"I have time for this," he said, in a tone that brooked no argument.

When her gaze met his, the implacable hardness there told her she had no choice. He intended to look at her hand. She should be grateful for his concern, not frustrated by his stubbornness.

With a resigned sigh, she unlocked her apartment and opened the door for all of them to follow her inside.

Theo, who had caused the whole disaster, trotted into the house, planted himself on his haunches and grinned at the four of them, clearly delighted to have his favorite people all together.

"Addie, will you clean up the breakfast dishes and load the dishwasher?"

"Okay." Her daughter headed for the kitchen, Brielle right behind her.

"I'll help," her friend said.

Meanwhile, Wes pointed toward Addie's bathroom, the closest to the living room. "Let's start by rinsing it to get the sand and blood off so we can see what we're up against."

She followed him to the bathroom, wondering why she had never noticed how small the room was.

"I don't want to get blood all over you."

"By the end of the day, I usually have oil and brake fluid and any manner of other things all over me. This is nothing."

He turned on the water while he unwound the scrap of T-shirt from her palm. She winced as the fabric caught in her jagged wound.

"Sorry."

"It's not your fault I'm so clumsy. I still don't know quite how I tripped. I think I got tangled in the leash and caught myself before I could fall on Theo."

"Bad luck that you would land right on a broken shell."

"Yes. Out of the entire beach filled with soft, forgiving sand where I could have fallen, I had to choose that very spot."

She shook her head, trying at the same time to catch her breath as he gently held her hand this way and that under the stream of warm water.

He smelled so good. He was obviously just out of the shower and smelled like a combination of laundry soap and some outdoorsy kind of male shampoo.

He was warm, too. After their chilly walk along the beach, she couldn't help wishing she could snuggle up against him to draw some of his heat back inside her.

"How bad is it, Dr. Calhoun?"

"I'm afraid you're going to need stitches. It's not long, but it's pretty deep. You said you landed on a broken shell? When was your last tetanus shot?"

She thought back to her most recent medical history and remembered getting one around the time that Ryan had died, when she had scraped herself on a nail trying to plant some flowers in the small fenced yard of their apartment.

"I should be good in that regard."

"Do you want me to take the girls to day camp and then run you to the urgent care clinic? I can call my bosses and let them know an emergency has come up."

She was very tempted to lean on him, to let him take over. It was very hard to ignore the allure of that broad chest, those strong shoulders.

She was tough, she reminded herself. She could handle this, even though her hand throbbed with pain, which was also giving her a headache.

"I should be all right. If you could just help me wrap it better, that would be really great. It's my right hand and I'm right-handed, so I don't think I will be able to do a very good job with my left hand."

"You got it."

Using her first-aid kit after she showed it to him, he applied antibacterial ointment with a gentleness that made her shiver.

She could only hope he didn't notice as he rooted through the kit to find the largest bandage she had.

"This should hold you for a little while, until you can have someone take a look. You should definitely take care of it sooner rather than later."

"Thank you."

Bending low over her hand, he applied the bandage to her palm, pressing carefully around the edges to ensure the wound was protected as much as possible.

"I wish I could do more."

"You've done enough. I'll be fine. I'll call my primary care doctor right now and see if I can get in this morning to have Dr. Sanderson take a look."

"You see Eli Sanderson?"

"Yes. Do you know him?"

"I knew him in the military, only peripherally. But we have friends in common. He and his wife invited me to dinner when I first moved to town. They were very kind."

"Melissa actually lived here in Brambleberry House before I did. We've become friends through Rosa, who is her good friend."

"She's the one who convinced Rosa to rent me an apartment when I was looking."

"I'm glad she did," Jenna said.

His gaze met hers and the moment seemed to stretch between them, taut and fragile, like the thread of a spider's web, gleaming with morning dew.

Something sparked in his expression as he looked down at her, something hot and glittery that left her a little dizzy.

Maybe she had lost more blood than she thought, she told herself. Or maybe it was simply a result of being in such close proximity to Wes Calhoun.

He was the first to look away.

"That should do it. Are you certain you don't want me to take you to urgent care? I feel wrong leaving you in your hour of need."

"No. Definitely not. I'm fine. Thank you, though. You've been very kind."

"Right. That's what I've been," he said, his voice gruff.

She sensed he wanted to say more, but Addie and Brielle came to check on her and the moment was gone.

After she had been treated at Eli's office, Jenna returned to the house to let Theo out, then moved him to the fenced dog yard, placing his open crate in the shade under the covered porch, along with plenty of water and food.

When she was certain the puppy was settled and comfortable, she drove to the By-the-Wind gift shop for her noon shift.

The morning fog had blown away, as it usually did during the summer, leaving the day sunny and mild. She parked as close as she could manage. She would have been better off walking, judging by the number of vehicles clogging the downtown area.

The tourist season was in full force. From here, she could see the wide, long Cannon Beach stretching north for miles. It was dotted with umbrellas, bikes, swimmers and the occasional kite.

The crowds of visitors descending every summer could be a nuisance but so much of the Cannon Beach economy depended on them that she couldn't be too upset.

Crowds were a small price to pay for the sheer delight in living in such magnificent surroundings. And if the masses of people became too overwhelming, she could always take a drive down the coast and find an isolated beach somewhere or she could hike into the hills east of town and find a beautiful mountain river wending its way to the ocean.

That was the beauty of the Oregon Coast. It was long, vast and certainly not overpopulated.

She let herself into the employee entrance of the store just as Rosa was coming out.

"What is this?" her friend cried, looking aghast at her bandage. "What have you done to yourself?"

"It's nothing. Just a bit of bad luck. I fell on the beach this morning when I was walking with Theo and Addison and managed to land on a broken shell. I'm fine. Eli gave me only five stitches and some local anesthetic so I can't feel a thing right now."

"Oh, you poor thing. You must go home and rest your hand. I can work for you instead."

Jenna rolled her eyes at this very pregnant woman trying to be protective of her over a little scratch.

"Absolutely not. Please don't worry about me. The bandage is annoying but it should not stop me from doing anything."

"I am sorry this happened to you. Did Addie help you with your bandage?"

She held up her bandaged hand. "Dr. Sanderson and his staff get the credit for this one. But Wes helped me with the initial triage."

Rosa gave her a side glance. "Did he? I told you, he is a good man."

Jenna was beginning to agree. Whenever she remembered the tender way he cared for her injury, she felt warmth seep through her.

She did not tell her friend that Wes was not only a good man. He was definitely a good kisser.

"Do not worry about me," she said again to Rosa. "I'll be just fine. Go and put your feet up."

Rosa sighed. "Wyatt will probably come with his police car and drag me home if I don't rest. If not him, Carrie and Bella will do it."

Carrie was the sister of Rosa's husband and Bella was Carrie's daughter. Both of them adored Rosa and were even more protective of her than Jenna was.

"Good. You should listen to them. I'll see you later."

She hugged Rosa and hurried into the gift shop, grateful again for good friends.

Chapter Eleven

On his lunch hour, Wes decided to eat his brown-bag lunch while he walked three blocks downtown to find a birthday present for his sister, who lived in a little town in Idaho called Pine Gulch, on the west slope of the Tetons.

He had a single destination in mind, the gift shop owned by his landlady, Rosa. It was the logical choice, he told himself. By-the-Wind carried unique local products that represented the best artists and craftspeople in the area. His sister would love something handmade, especially something he had specifically picked for her.

As he walked toward the store, he reminded himself there was little chance he would bump into Jenna, though he knew she worked part-time at By-the-Wind during the summer.

Logic did nothing to stop the little buzz of anticipation as he made his way through town.

The sidewalks were busy, but it wasn't the kind of crowd he had been warned to expect in summer. Mostly families were browsing for beach toys or T-shirts or fudge.

He still could not believe he lived in this busy little beach community on the Oregon Coast, that he was working as a mechanic, of all things, and enjoying all of it.

Life had a funny way of taking a guy on adventures he never could have imagined.

Four years ago, he thought he had his life completely figured out. He had loved the hard work of making the security company a success. While his marriage definitely had its ups and downs, he was trying hard to make that a success as well.

He thought he would continue on that same path and eventually attain everything he wanted.

His life hadn't gone exactly as planned. Three years behind bars had a way of derailing an entire future.

Wes had always been a planner, goal oriented and ambitious. Now he tried to focus on the moment. The smell of ice-cream cones from the parlor he passed, the sound of children laughing as they watched someone making saltwater taffy at another shop, the hum of conversation between shoppers. All of it was underlined by the constant song of the sea, which gave him more comfort than he ever could have guessed.

When he finally reached By-the-Wind, he pushed open the door and immediately felt out of place.

Wes didn't consider himself sexist but this didn't really feel like the kind of store that catered to a guy like him. It was filled with scented candles, wind chimes, floral-patterned shopping bags and rows of handcrafted jewelry.

He was the only man in the store, he couldn't help but notice. A trio of older ladies were looking at carved lighthouse figures while a couple of teenagers spun a rotating rack of silver earrings.

What would his sister like here?

He had no idea. While he and Maggie had always been close as children, separated by only a few years, as adults, their paths had diverged. After his arrest and especially after his conviction, Wes had tried to build in more distance between them. Maggie's husband was a small-town lawyer with state political ambitions. He didn't need to be associated with someone who had been convicted on multiple felony charges.

Maggie had tried to stay in touch but he had discouraged contact. She hadn't given up, no matter how tough he made it on her.

He was scouring through some decorative ceramic vases when he saw Jenna emerge from a back room. She did an almost comical double take when she spotted him. He again felt large and ungainly in this store filled with delicate items.

"Hi." She smiled. "This is a surprise."

"For me, too. I wasn't expecting to see you. I figured even if you were scheduled to work, you would have taken time off because of your injury."

She held up her heavily bandaged hand. "Good news. They didn't have to amputate. I only needed a few stitches. Five, but who is counting?"

"Whew." He managed a smile. "Does it still hurt?"

"The local anesthetic they used to put in the stitches has worn off so it's throbbing a bit, but it's not too bad."

"Good. That's good."

Silence descended between them and he didn't want to do anything but stare at her. That wasn't creepy or anything, right?

Around Jenna, he experienced a strange paradox of emotions, both fierce awareness as well as an odd sort of peace.

"Was there something I could help you find?" she asked after a moment.

"Um. Yes. I'm looking for a birthday present for my sister."

"You have a sister?"

She seemed genuinely surprised, and he realized he hadn't mentioned his family much to her, other than to tell her about his father's death.

"Yes. Maggie is three years younger than I am. An artist and writer. She lives in Idaho with her husband and their two kids."

"Wow. Okay. Um, what are her tastes? Does she collect anything? You said she is an artist?"

"Yes. She paints. But I know she also collects pottery. I was looking at your vases here."

"They are very nice. Do you know what kind of pottery she collects?"

He felt stupid for his ignorance. Again, he wished he had not come, that he had simply picked out something for Maggie online.

Had his subconscious led him here, in the random hope that he might find himself in this very situation, speaking with the woman who fascinated him so much? He did not want to admit it, but the truth was becoming increasingly difficult to ignore.

Jenna Haynes was becoming a vital part of his life.

He didn't want to think about how bereft he would feel when his daughter returned to her mother and stepfather's home and he had no more excuse to see Jenna at least twice a day.

He turned his attention back to the problem at hand, finding a gift for his sister. "To be honest, I am not at all sure what to get her. I don't know what she likes. Maggie and I haven't talked much for the past few years. Only a couple of times since I was arrested, actually."

"Why? Did she believe you were guilty?" she asked with a frown. He could almost see her mind working, possibly condemning his sister. He couldn't have that.

"I tried to keep Maggie and her family away from all the ugliness," he said quickly. "She had enough on her plate, with new twins and her husband opening his law practice. She didn't need to be dragged down by worry."

"You don't think she worried about you, whether you were in regular communication or not?"

"Probably," he admitted. In truth, he hadn't wanted the baby sister he adored to see what a mess his life had become.

"We've texted and emailed back and forth a few times since I was released. I was going to swing by and visit on my way to Oregon but it didn't quite work out."

She studied him and he had a feeling she saw right through his excuses and explanations.

"A birthday gift is a lovely way to reconnect," she finally said, her tone gentle. "Though perhaps the best thing you could give Maggie for her birthday would be a video call from her brother and niece so she can catch up on your life."

That was not a bad idea. Because his contact with the outside world had been limited while he had been incarcerated, he had lost the habit of remembering he could pick up the phone at any time now.

"Maybe I can do both. Send her a gift and also catch up over the phone."

She smiled. "That works. I can't help you with the phone call, but let's try to find something wonderful to send her. We have one section of pottery created by local artists. Would you like to take a look?"

"Definitely. I would love to give her something that represents the Oregon Coast."

He looked at the offerings on the shelves she indicated and was immediately drawn to a small, delicate bowl the same iridescent colors found on the inside of an abalone shell. It was even shaped a little like a shell.

"That is beautiful," he said, holding it up to admire the colors.

Her gaze softened. "That is by one of my favorite local artists. She is eighty years old, a real character who lives alone on an isolated stretch near Heceta Head and throws pots every day. You should meet her on one of her visits to town."

"I would like that," he said. He had never been one for art galleries or museums when he was younger but his time in prison had given him a true appreciation for those who could create beauty no matter their situation.

"This one works for me. That was easy. I might even make it back before my lunch hour is over."

"I can wrap it up for you. If you would like to pick out a birthday card while you're here and write a message, we can even ship for you. We have some nice original birthday cards as well as some all-occasion."

While it would certainly take a weight off him not to have to deal with the inconvenience of mailing, he suddenly caught sight of that glaring white bandage on her hand.

"I don't think you should be wrapping up anything right now, with your bum hand. Just slip it in a bag and I can take it home. Brie can help me deal with it tonight."

She made a face. "I appreciate your concern, Wes, but I'm really fine. I've already packaged things for other shoppers today and didn't drop a single thing. If I have trouble, someone else here can handle that part of it."

She was a difficult woman to win an argument against.

"Thank you, I guess. Though I don't feel good about it."

She laughed. "Sorry about that."

He wanted to gaze at her for whatever time was left of his lunch hour but forced himself to head to the cards, where he finally found a lovely hand-painted card he knew Maggie would appreciate as much as the bowl.

Jenna handed him a pen from behind the counter and after a moment's reflection, he wrote a quick message wishing her the happiest of birthdays and expressing his love. It seemed inadequate but he couldn't think of anything else to say.

When he finished the card and slipped it into the envelope, he handed over his credit card and Jenna ran it through.

It sometimes struck him how amazing it was to be able to walk into a store and purchase whatever he wanted. For three years, he had been limited by the prison commissary and what friends on the outside could provide him.

All of his pre-arrest personal assets had been restored to him following the acquittal, along with a healthy settlement for wrongful prosecution. He had plenty of money right now. He couldn't work forever fixing motorcycles. He knew that, but he wasn't in any hurry to change the status quo.

After years of the grind to build his company, then the stress and helplessness of the past three years, Wes found he enjoyed the work he was doing.

He liked taking something broken and repairing it to be as good as new...and sometimes better.

Maybe he would open his own shop somewhere, though probably not. He didn't feel right about going into competition with Paco and Carlos, after they had been so good to him.

"Thank you," Jenna said, handing him the receipt. "I'll try to get this wrapped up and shipped today. It should go out tomorrow at the latest. That's our guarantee. She should receive it within a week. Will that work?"

"It should. Her birthday isn't for a few more weeks. Thank you for your help."

"My pleasure."

He needed to return to work but he was loath to leave her.

"Why don't you let me take care of dinner for us and the girls tonight?" he said on impulse, gesturing to her hand. "It's the least I can do, after all you've done to help me out with Brie this week."

"It has really been no trouble," she protested.

"You keep saying that, but surely it's been a *little* trouble. You've got a sore hand and don't need to be rushing around tonight trying to fix dinner."

She gave a quick laugh that sounded prettier than any of the wind chimes in this charming little store ever could.

"You seem to have this idea that my hand has been grievously wounded. It's only a few stitches. I am really fine."

"Okay, let's take the hand completely out of it. For two weeks, you have stepped up to bail me out with my daughter. I would love the chance to repay you in some small way. Why don't we celebrate the last day of the girls' camp and my last day with Brielle full-time? We could explore one of the nearby state parks, if you have a favorite."

"Have you visited Oswald West State Park? It's just south of town. It has lots of tide pools and trails through the forest that look like something out of *Lord of the Rings*. Addie loves it. It also has a picnic area close to the beach."

"I have not been there. That sounds perfect. The girls can show us everything they learned at camp and, bonus, Theo can get some exercise."

"That is actually not a bad idea," she said after a moment's thought. "It sounds really fun."

He felt a ridiculous sense of accomplishment. "Great. I'm done working today at four. I can pick up some picnic supplies. We can take my truck and load the back with whatever we might need."

"That sounds great. I'm off by three, in time to get the girls."

"Let's plan to leave about five. That will give us several hours before dark to enjoy the scenery."

"Perfect. We'll be ready."

He wanted to stay and talk to her more, but he had already taken too long and needed to return to the bike he was working on.

Besides that, the store had begun to fill with more

customers, and he realized he had been completely monopolizing Jenna's time for the past fifteen minutes.

"Thanks again for your help. I'll see you this evening," he said.

"Great."

That buzz of anticipation carried him toward the door. Before he reached it, he spotted a few women with familiar features whom he knew he had seen around town before. He nodded to them but didn't miss the way the mouth of one of the women tightened. If she had been wearing long skirts, he had a feeling she would have brushed them out of his way with a dramatic sweep.

He wouldn't let it ruin his mood, he decided. Not when he had a fun evening ahead with Jenna and their respective daughters.

Chapter Twelve

As Wes made his way to the exit, Jenna released the breath she hadn't realized she had been holding and tried not to stare at his narrow hips or his broad shoulders in that snug T-shirt.

Seeing him in this setting, surrounded by lovely, fragile objects, only seemed to reinforce his contrasting masculinity.

She finished packaging up the lovely bowl for his sister, catching only bits and pieces of the conversation around her until she heard the word Brambleberry House.

Two women were looking at a collection of handmade jewelry close to the counter, local women she knew vaguely but who weren't close acquaintances.

Donna Martin was a former teacher with a reputation at the elementary school for having been rigid and cold to her students during her time there. She had retired before Jenna took a job at the school, and Jenna knew there were few students or parents who were sorry when she left.

She had always struck Jenna as being thoroughly unpleasant.

Her companion, Susan Lakewood, was tall, almost gaunt, a woman who volunteered at the library as well as managed a string of rental properties on the other side of town. When she wasn't in Donna's company, she could be quite pleasant.

The two had also apparently noticed how out of place Wes seemed in the store. It took Jenna a moment to realize they were talking about him.

"I don't know what Rosa was thinking, to let his type move into that house. Abigail would be rolling in her grave," Donna muttered.

"He has always been very nice in our few interactions."

"He's a criminal! I heard it on good authority that he hasn't even been out of prison four months. It's outrageous that someone like that is allowed to live in Cannon Beach at all, let alone in such a nice place as Brambleberry House."

"I don't know," Susan said in a timid sort of voice. "He seems polite enough when he comes into the library with his daughter. She likes to read the Magic Tree House books."

Donna made a derisive sound. "Doesn't matter how polite he is. You can't change the facts. He looks like a man who just got out of prison, doesn't he? I would be afraid to have him living anywhere close to me. Who knows what he did?"

Jenna frowned, her palm suddenly throbbing worse

than ever with the itch to slap the woman, though she knew she never would.

She did not want to have any sort of confrontation with Donna, who had a reputation for being vindictive to anyone who crossed her. At the same time, she would not stand by and let the woman malign a good man who had done nothing wrong and didn't deserve her disdain.

Under normal circumstances, Jenna would never confront a customer at all, but somehow she sensed Rosa would back her a hundred percent if she were here.

"Can I help you two find something?" she asked loudly.

Susan, at least, had the decency to blush.

"We're just looking," she said quickly.

"Let me know if I can help," she said. Before she could move away to help someone else, she lowered her voice. "For the record, Wes Calhoun was wrongfully convicted and has been exonerated of all charges. He is a loving father and a hardworking employee who is trying to rebuild his life here in Cannon Beach so that he can be closer to his daughter. Don't you find that admirable? There are so many men out there who are only too willing to abandon their children after a divorce. I'm sure as a former educator, Donna, you saw evidence of that as well with your students. What a tough situation that can be on children."

"It's outrageous. Parents don't care about the harm they're doing to their children. All they care about is having what they want."

She let the woman ramble on for a few moments, then finally gave a polite smile.

"Yes. That's why it's so refreshing to see a man like

Wes Calhoun, who is trying his best to be a positive influence in his child's life. Don't you agree?"

"Very refreshing," Susan said.

Donna still wore a sour frown. "He still looks like he just held up a bank somewhere."

"It's a good thing most people don't judge others wholly on their appearance but on their behavior, isn't it?"

She walked away before either woman could answer.

She was shaking a little but told herself it was simply a reaction to the pain shot wearing off.

"What was Donna going on about?" Carol Hardesty asked after the two women quickly bustled out of the store.

Jenna sighed, wishing she had handled things a different way. She would have liked to tell Donna she was a sanctimonious cow.

"Donna was bad-mouthing my neighbor. Wes Calhoun. I was gently trying to set her straight."

"Oooh. He's Lacey Summers's ex-husband, right?"

"That's right."

"Who would walk away from a guy like that?" Carol asked, shaking her head in disbelief. "I don't care if he was in prison. He's the sort of guy worth waiting for on the outside, you know?"

Yes. Jenna understood completely.

"He was innocent," she muttered. "He was cleared of all wrongdoing. That's what bugs me. It doesn't seem fair for people like Donna to treat him like some kind of criminal when he didn't do anything wrong."

"I wouldn't listen to anything she has to say. That woman is perpetually unhappy. She finds fault in everyone."

"It just bothers me. Wes is a wonderful father and a really good man."

Carol shrugged. "Here's the thing about Donna. If you don't fit the mold of what she considers acceptable, nothing else matters. You'll never measure up to her expectations. Some of us figured out a long time ago that it's not worth even trying."

Jenna knew Carol was right. What bothered her most about the encounter was that Jenna had been exactly like Donna. She had judged Wes as scary and intimidating when he first moved into Brambleberry House.

She cringed when she remembered that day he had jumped her car, when she had reacted to him out of fear and nerves.

Since then she had learned he was a kind man who made delicious pizza for his daughter, who loved his sister, who savored the smell of basil leaves and the Brambleberry House gardens after a rain.

And who kissed her until she forgot all the reasons why they weren't right for each other.

The girls were chattering with excitement when she picked them up after their last day of camp.

"That was the most fun *ever*," Brielle said as she slid into the back seat, her cheeks a little sunburned and her bucket hat hanging down her back.

"Yeah. It was so fun," Addie agreed. "I'm sad it's over. I wish we could go to science camp all summer long!"

"Wouldn't that be fun?" Jenna said. "But then you would miss soccer camp and art camp."

"I guess."

"How's your hand, Mrs. Haynes?" Brielle asked as

Jenna turned her vehicle toward Brambleberry House. "Did you have to get a hundred stitches?"

"Not a hundred, no. Only five."

"Do you have to wear a cast?" Addie asked, peering around the seat to see.

"Only a bandage." She held up her right hand for the girls.

"I've never had stitches," Brielle said. "Does it hurt when the needle goes into your skin? I always thought it would be so weird."

"No. They give you a shot first that numbs your skin. You're right. It is a weird feeling. You can tell when they're tugging the stitches. But it wasn't bad."

"I'm really sorry you were hurt, Mom," Addie said. "Me and Brie can take care of Theo if you want. We can even take him out late tonight so you don't have to do it."

Her daughter's thoughtfulness touched her. "Thank you. I might need your help a little more than usual for the next few days."

"Maybe we can cook dinner tonight," Brielle suggested. "I know how to make nachos."

"Actually, your dad thought you might like to go on a picnic at the beach tonight for dinner, since it was your last day at camp today. Plus you'll be going back home tomorrow."

"Oh, that's right," Addie said, her voice disappointed.

"I totally forgot my mom and Ron were coming home tomorrow." Brielle seemed disappointed at the prospect of leaving Brambleberry House.

"It's not like you won't come back and will never see us again. You stay with your dad like every weekend," Addie reminded her.

Brielle's features brightened. "Oh yeah. We can totally hang out when I come stay with him."

For the remainder of the short drive, the girls chattered about their favorite part of science camp and what they planned to do the next week when they didn't have camp. When they pulled up to the house, the first thing Jenna saw was Wes's motorcycle. His daughter spied it as well.

"Dad's home from work already. Yay! Can we leave now for the picnic?"

"I'm afraid I will need some time to take care of Theo, change out of my work clothes and gather a few things," Jenna said, trying to ignore the little buzz of anticipation she felt at knowing she would be spending the evening with Wes and his daughter. "I'm sure your dad could use a little time as well."

They started for the house when the door opened and Wes walked out, arms loaded with blankets and lawn chairs.

Her little buzz became a full-on tremor.

"Oh. Hi. You're home," he said. His face seemed to light up when he spotted them. For his daughter, she told herself. Certainly not for her.

For a moment, she let her imagination wander, wondering what it might be like to have his hard features glow with welcome like that for her.

"There's my girl."

"Hi, Dad." Brielle launched herself at her father, who managed to set down the lawn chairs and blankets in time to catch her.

Jenna found the affection between the two of them sweetly touching, even as it made her ache a little for her fatherless child, who watched their joy-filled reunion with a little glint of envy in her expression.

How Wes must have missed his daughter during those three years he had been incarcerated. When children were young, even a few months' development could mean fundamental changes in maturity, communication and social skills. Jenna couldn't imagine how much Brielle had changed in the three years they were separated.

He lifted his gaze from his daughter to Jenna and something in his expression warmed her to her toes.

"Hi. I'm sorry I wasn't home half an hour earlier or I could have picked up the girls so you didn't have to."

"It's no problem. I was planning on it."

"How's your hand? Were you okay to drive?"

In truth, her hand was throbbing more now than it had since the initial injury but she didn't want to tell him, for fear he would suggest canceling the outing.

She didn't want to disappoint the girls. At least that's what she tried to tell herself was her motive for ignoring the pain.

"It's fine. I'm a little bit sore but not bad."

"Are you sure you're up for a picnic? If you're not, we can do it another day."

She shook her head. "We're all looking forward to it. Aren't we, girls?"

Brielle and Addie both nodded with enthusiasm.

"Give me a few moments and I'll be ready," she told him. "I have to change and take care of Theo."

"Take as long as you need."

The only trouble was, she had no idea how long it would take her to figure out how to protect her heart so she didn't completely fall for Wes Calhoun.

Chapter Thirteen

Could this really be his life or merely some delicious dream he didn't want to end?

Throughout the afternoon and evening Wes spent with Jenna and their respective daughters at the beautiful state park south of Cannon Beach, he had to stop more than once to soak in the moment.

It was a perfect summer evening, in company with his daughter, whom he loved more than anything else in the world, as well as the lovely Jenna Haynes and her daughter.

Only months earlier, he would have been standing in the chow line waiting for his bologna sandwich and pudding cup. If he was lucky.

Now he was sitting on a blanket a few dozen yards from the Pacific Ocean, watching the sky light up with color as the sun began its slow descent into the horizon.

The air was filled with the sound of the girls' laughter as a cute puppy with gangly legs loped around with enthusiasm, trying to catch the tennis ball they chucked between them.

Across from Wes on the blanket, watching the girls with a soft smile, was the warm, beautiful woman who was becoming increasingly important to him.

He wanted to bottle up this moment, to take it out when life felt hard or when he gave in to his occasional bouts of self-pity at all that had been taken from him by someone he had trusted.

"What a beautiful evening." Jenna gave a contented sort of sigh. "Thank you so much for suggesting this. It was exactly what I needed."

"Tough day? I mean, besides the stitches in your hand?"

She looked back at the girls. "Not really. It was busy, but no worse than usual for a Friday. I did have to deal with some…unpleasant customers, but I handled it the best way I could."

"That's always tough, isn't it? That was the hardest part for me of running a business. I tend to be impatient with people who are rude and demanding. It's hard not to want to respond in kind."

"What do you do?"

"Usually just try to remind myself that everybody has a bad day once in a while and I have no idea what they might be going through outside of this momentary interaction. Don't get me wrong. As you know probably too well, there are some garbage people in the world."

"Like your partner who set you up."

"He heads the list."

He didn't like thinking about Anthony Morris for even a moment longer than necessary.

"I doubt I'll ever be able to forgive him for trying to pin his crimes on me."

"And getting away with it for years," she pointed out.

"Right. But even with Tony, I try to remember that he is now behind bars, where he belongs, paying for what he did. I, on the other hand, am currently sitting on a spectacular beach watching the sunset with a beautiful woman."

He hadn't meant to add that part but had to admit he enjoyed seeing the wash of pink across her cheekbones.

She gazed at him for a long moment, then quickly looked away.

"Not so close to the water," she called to the girls, who changed direction and returned to the blanket, with Theo leading the way.

The dog plopped onto the blanket, tongue panting.

"Oh. You're a thirsty guy, aren't you? That's what happens when you play so hard," Jenna said to the puppy.

Working around her injured hand, she opened her own water bottle and poured some into the dog's bowl they had brought. Theo lapped at it gratefully, which made the girls giggle.

"I'm thirsty, too," Brie declared. "Can I have another root beer?"

"I'm thirsty, too," Addie said.

"We have plenty of water but only one root beer left," he answered.

He had picked up a four-pack of craft root beer bottled by one of the local breweries. He and the girls each had enjoyed one but Jenna declared she was happy with water.

The girls studied the sole remaining bottle, clearly understanding the dilemma. Only one of them could have it. But which one?

"It's okay," Brielle said after a moment. "You have it."

Addie shook her head. "No. You have it."

"How about this," Jenna suggested. "You can share it. I can pour half the bottle into one of your empty water bottles."

"Good idea," Brie said, clearly thrilled with the solution.

"My water bottle is empty," Addie said, tipping it for the last drop to be sure.

"Why don't you let me do that?" Wes held out a hand to take the root beer bottle. "We don't want you to splash soda all over your bandages."

Jenna made a face but handed over the root beer bottle and Addie's water bottle.

Wes moved a few steps away from the blanket in case of fizzing and opened the bottle of root beer, carefully pouring out half into the water bottle.

As he returned to the blanket and handed the soda bottle to Brie and the pink water bottle to Addie, Wes couldn't help thinking about the time one of the guys in his block, a particularly nasty guy named Victor, had shivved a guy at lunch over a peanut butter cookie.

He remembered the scream and the blood and the shouting guards as if it happened that morning.

Would memories of that dark time always taint his future happiness? He didn't want it to. He wanted to be able to completely put it behind him, but he wasn't sure that would ever be possible.

He could not pretend it had never happened. Those

three years were part of him, just like the time he had spent in the Army and the years of his childhood when he had lived on that breathtaking Colorado farm.

He had to hope that eventually moments like these, pure and perfect, would overwhelm the darkness.

"Thank you for everything," Jenna said as the girls sipped at their respective root beers. "This was so fun going tide pooling with you girls and having you show us all the creatures you learned about at camp."

That had been one of Wes's favorite parts of the evening. Jenna had orders from the doctor to keep her hand dry, so Wes had set up a beach chair for her on the sand just above the surf. She watched, the dog at her side, while he and the girls scrambled carefully over the rocks looking at starfish, sea urchins and anemones of every color.

Addie and Brie used Wes's cell phone to snap pictures of what they found for Jenna, so she could enjoy the experience, too.

While he had set up their picnic dinner of fried chicken, pasta salad and kettle chips, Jenna had scrolled through the photos, asking the girls questions about their discoveries.

After dinner, the girls had begged to take a walk on one of the lush trails around the state park. With the girls racing ahead, he and Jenna had walked together, chatting about places they had visited and bucket list destinations they would like to see.

Finally, they had returned here to watch the sunset.

"We should probably head back soon," Jenna told the girls as they finished their soda.

"I wish we could stay here all night," Addie said,

lying back on the blanket and gazing up at the few pale stars beginning to appear.

"I'm afraid there's no camping allowed at this park," Jenna said. "But maybe one weekend this summer we could borrow a tent from Rosa and Wyatt and camp at one of the other places along the coast."

"Can we come?" Brie asked.

Wes gave an inward wince at his daughter's forwardness.

"That would be so fun!" Addie exclaimed. "Can we go camping together, Mom?"

That lovely pink rose on her cheeks as she sent Wes a quick look. "I'm not sure Rosa and Wyatt have a tent that would fit the four of us."

"We could bring our own tent!" Brie said. "You have one, don't you, Dad? If not, Mom and Ron do."

"I do have a tent. But maybe Jenna and Addie wanted to have their own trip together."

"It would be so fun to have you come, wouldn't it, Mom?"

Jenna lifted her gaze to his again. Heat surged between them. "Sure," she finally said. "We can probably make that work. We'll have to see."

He would love nothing more than spending a weekend camping with Jenna and their daughters. He had visions of talking by the fire until the early hours of the morning, gazing up at the stars, kissing her again until they were both shaking with need...

Wes sighed. He would be smarter to come up with excuses to stay away from Jenna, instead of letting his mind run wild, imagining mythical future outings together.

Though he didn't want this particular evening to end,

he turned his energy toward loading up his pickup truck with all the things they had brought and making sure they carried away everything from their picnic site.

"Dad, can we stop and have gelato before we go home?" Brielle asked him when they were all finally loaded into the truck and he was about to drive out of the parking area.

His gaze met Jenna's and she shrugged. "Fine with me. I love gelato."

Wes pulled out onto the road back to Cannon Beach, feeling as if he had been handed a reprieve.

Maybe Jenna didn't want the evening to end, either.

After driving back to Cannon Beach, he parked down the street from the small storefront selling gelato in at least two dozen varieties, handmade on the premises.

He and Brielle had discovered the place shortly after he arrived in Cannon Beach, and stopping here occasionally had become something of a ritual for them.

The night was lovely and pleasant, not too warm and not cold enough for a jacket. The streets of downtown were bustling with visitors but the line at the gelato shop moved quickly.

After they ordered and received their gelato—chocolate chip for him and the girls and butter pecan for Jenna—they found an empty picnic table outside the shop and sat down, licking at their cones and people watching.

This was another moment he would store in his memory bank. The girls giggling about something, Theo lapping the ground of any drips from the cones, and Jenna pretty and soft in the lamplight as she tapped her sandal along with the live music coming out of the restaurant next door.

"This has been a perfect evening," she said as she worked to finish off the final few licks of her cone. "Thank you so much for suggesting it."

"Yeah," Addie said. "Thanks. It was really fun."

"Can we do it again the next time I come to stay with you?" Brielle asked him. "Maybe we could go to another beach and try tide pooling there."

"Sure."

He wasn't sure whether Jenna wanted to spend any more time with him, but Wes figured he could always take his daughter on his own.

Same for the camping trip. As much as he would enjoy going with Jenna and Addie, he and Brie could still have a great time, the two of them.

"Looks like somebody is pooped." Jenna gestured to Theo, who had plopped down at her feet and didn't look like he wanted to move.

"He's not the only one. I think I know two girls who are going to drop the moment they get home."

"I'm not tired," Addison insisted.

"Me neither," Brielle said.

"Well, Theo certainly is," Jenna answered.

"Because he's still a baby and babies sleep all the time," Brielle informed her. "That's what my mom says, anyway."

"They do sleep a lot," Jenna said. "All except Addie." She smiled at her daughter. "You were up and down all night long and didn't sleep through the night until you were eight or nine months old. Your dad used to say you were afraid you were going to miss something. You were an early adopter of FOMO."

"What about me, Dad?"

Through his own choices, Wes had missed so much after Brie had been born, too busy trying to build the company. At least his time in prison had helped him realize that any success he earned professionally could be gone in an instant. This. This was the important thing. Family. Friends.

Love.

He didn't want to go there. Yes, he was developing feelings for Jenna but he certainly wasn't falling in love with her. That would be completely self-destructive of him.

"You are *still* afraid you're going to miss something," he said, focusing back on his daughter. "It's one of the things I love most about you."

She rolled her eyes at him. "I can't help it if all the good stuff happens after I go to bed!"

After they finished their gelato, he helped all three of them back into his pickup and drove the short distance back to Brambleberry House.

"Thank you again," Jenna said when he pulled into the driveway. "That was the most enjoyable evening I have had in a long time."

"Same for me," he admitted, his voice somewhat gruff.

"We can help you carry things back inside."

"I've got it. Don't worry."

"Okay. Well, um, have a good night."

He pushed down a hundred things he wanted to say. Especially *Can I carry you to my bed after the girls are asleep and keep you there all night long?*

"Thanks," he finally managed. "If you need help with Theo after Addie goes to sleep, let me know."

All evening, the girls had been taking turns holding

the dog's leash so Jenna didn't have to risk reinjuring her wounded hand.

She nodded. "If I need help, I'll call. But I'm sure we'll be fine."

Before she headed toward the house, she shocked him one last time that day by reaching up and brushing her lips against his cheek.

It was all he could do not to turn his mouth to meet hers and devour her. Desire for her seemed to have become a steady beat through his veins.

"Good night," she murmured, then hurried into the house, leaving him to watch after her and ache.

Chapter Fourteen

She couldn't sleep.

Jenna opened one eye and glared at the clock on the nightstand. It was after 1:00 a.m. and she had been tossing and turning for an hour.

She was so tired but her mind couldn't seem to shut down. While she wasn't scheduled to work at the store the next day, Saturday, she had a packed agenda anyway. She and her friend Kim were cohosting the Brambleberry Book Group, consisting of twenty friends who gathered monthly, taking turns to be in charge.

She thought it would be fun to have dinner in the garden, shaded by the trees and the pergola. Kim was handling the meal, street tacos and taco salad catered by their favorite Mexican food place in town.

While Jenna was only baking a couple dozen cookies, she had plenty of other things to do. Cleaning off the lawn chairs. Setting up tables. Picking up the margarita mix.

She flipped her pillow over to the cool side, punched it with her good hand a few times for more fluff and rolled over.

She needed sleep so she could take on her chores the next day. But sleep still seemed a long way off. Instead, she couldn't seem to stop rehashing the evening spent with Wes and his daughter.

What was wrong with her?

She knew the answer to that, even before she asked it of herself.

She was lonely.

She wanted someone to hold her, to touch her, to cherish her and make her feel wanted.

And not any someone. She wanted Wes Calhoun.

Her mind kept replaying the hot, hungry look in his eyes when she had kissed his cheek several hours earlier.

He shared her attraction, which made it even harder for her to continue resisting him.

What was she going to do about Wes? She was developing feelings for the man, even though she knew anything between them was completely impossible.

Not feelings, she told herself. She couldn't be coming to care for him. They were friends. That was all.

Even as the thought popped into her mind, it rang hollow. Friends didn't make each other yearn. Friends didn't think about each other all the time. Friends didn't kiss each other until they were achy with need.

Wes made it so blasted hard to resist him. That evening with the girls had been magical. Even with her hand aching, she had loved spending time with him and his daughter. He had teased the girls, made them laugh, protected them.

Jenna sighed, turning over again before she finally sat up and pulled off her duvet. She had struggled so much with insomnia during the worst of Aaron's assault on her peace of mind that she was all too familiar with how it worked for her.

She likely had no chance of falling asleep anytime soon, not until she climbed out of bed and tried to do something else to distract herself and calm her mind for an hour or so.

Reading worked best for her, especially if it was something dry and uninteresting. While she focused on something else, all the worries keeping her awake either receded or sorted themselves out.

She had the perfect title in the living room, one of the recommended reading texts left over from her master's program. She had only made it through about a third of the book, despite months of trying.

When she walked out to the kitchen, Theo greeted her with a tail thump inside his crate.

She could also take the dog out for a quick walk through the garden before she settled in to read. The flowers and shrubs laid out in the Brambleberry House landscaping never failed to soothe her, especially in the moonlight.

For a long time, all her instincts had told her to hide behind triple-locked doors and away from any open windows. Going outside by herself after dark would have been out of the question.

Maybe if she still lived in Utah, that might have been the case. As irrational as it might seem, she felt safe here in Cannon Beach.

Yes, bad things happened here. Bad things had happened to *her* here. Aaron had terrorized her and had physically hurt her dear friend and the wonderful Fiona.

Every time she remembered that awful time two summers ago, she felt a little nauseated and had to fight the urge to stay inside where she knew she would be safe.

All the more reason to go outside, she decided. She didn't want to be a person who cowered.

Without taking more time to think about it, she slid into her garden shoes, pulled a hoodie on over her pajama top and went to the dog's crate.

"I know you were all settled for the night, but would you like to go out one more time?"

Theo thumped his tail on the floor, which made her smile. What a joy the dog had been, even in only the short weeks he had been part of their family. She had almost forgotten what their life had been like without him.

Theo jumped from his crate and stretched in a good imitation of a yoga pose, then followed her eagerly out the door as she made her way quietly downstairs.

The house was hushed in these early hours of the morning. She didn't know whether Wes was asleep up on the third floor but the ground floor apartment was empty. The Andersons, the lovely older couple who lived there, were expected home the following week. The retired pair had gone on an extended trip through Europe, including a long cruise, and their weekly email updates filled Jenna with no small degree of envy.

Maybe she should take Addie on a cruise. She could plan it around fall break. They didn't have to go to Europe. Instead, they could stick close to home and take one of the cruises that traveled the Pacific coastline.

The idea was deeply appealing. Four or five days when she didn't have to make all the decisions in life, where someone else would feed them, entertain them, show them beautiful parts of the world.

Still, she couldn't ignore one inescapable truth.

If she was lonely in Cannon Beach, she was going to be every bit as lonely on a cruise, if not more so, surrounded by couples and families having fun together.

How would she ever meet someone new? Jenna wondered as she reached the bottom step. Her job as an elementary teacher didn't bring many unattached men into her life. She didn't socialize much, except with her female friends and other teachers. She would certainly never dare try a dating app again, though she knew several friends who swore by them and had found deep and lasting relationships that way.

Jenna sighed as she pushed open the exterior door to the front of the house.

She didn't want to meet a man, anyway.

Especially a man who wasn't Wes Calhoun.

She pushed away the thought, focusing instead on the fresh, sweet night air, thick with the scent of roses and lavender. She inhaled deeply, feeling tension in her muscles instantly begin to ease.

This was her home. She didn't need to leave Brambleberry House, unless things grew too uncomfortable between her and Wes.

Yet another reason to try putting things back on a safer footing.

Theo lifted his leg on a tuft of grass, then followed after her as she walked through the garden toward the pergola overlooking the water. Jenna wanted to take one more look to see how many tables would fit in the small structure.

Before they reached it, Theo's tail began to wag and he gave a little yip of greeting, her first signs that she wasn't alone in the garden.

Inside the pergola, Wes wore a headlamp to light his task, which seemed to be tightening a screw on one of the wooden lawn chairs. Three other chairs were upside down, apparently waiting their turn.

He must have heard Theo's doggy greeting because he shifted in their direction, the headlamp aimed up at the sky like a beacon, forever guiding her toward him.

"What are you doing out here?" she asked when they approached.

"I noticed the chairs all felt a little wobbly so I thought it wouldn't hurt to reinforce them before one fell apart."

"In the dark, at one in the morning?"

"Is it that late? I hadn't noticed. What about you? What brings you out? I thought everybody was settled for the night. The house seemed quiet."

"I couldn't sleep so I got up to read for a bit. And as soon as I walked out into the living room, I realized Theo would see me and decide he needed to go out."

"It's a beautiful night, isn't it?"

She lifted her face up to the glitter of stars overhead, endless and lovely.

"It really is."

"Everybody told me to be prepared for gray skies and rain when I moved to Oregon. We've had a few of those, but it seems like we have far more sunny days than not."

"You came at a great time of year. Our winters can be cold and stormy."

"I'm looking forward to watching the storms roll in."

Jenna loved the drama of sitting in front of her bay window as the sea turned dark and frothy. "You might get your wish earlier than later," she told him. "A summer storm is supposed to hit tomorrow night. Tonight, I guess. Around ten or so. I just hope it holds off until later than that as I'm having my book club out here tomorrow evening."

"That sounds fun."

"What's not to love about it? Good friends talking about books, eating food and enjoying adult beverages."

He nodded to the overturned furniture in front of him. "Good thing I had a wild hare to fix the chairs, then. I would hate for one of your book club friends to sit down, only to have the whole thing fall apart."

"Yes. Great timing. Can I help you with anything here?"

"I'm nearly done. You could hold the flashlight for me, if you'd like. I've got the headlamp, but every time I turn my head, I can't see what I'm doing."

She picked up the flashlight he indicated, perched on one of the chairs he had apparently already tightened, and aimed it at the chair in front of him. Theo spent a moment sniffing around the pergola, then found a spot to curl up on atop one of the chair cushions.

A subtle intimacy seemed to curl around them, here in the quiet of the garden. Was this the reason she had been drawn outside? Had some part of her suspected he might be out here, the part of her that couldn't seem to stay away from this man?

She didn't want to think so.

"What time are you expecting Brielle's mom to return?"

"Their plane lands in Portland around noon, so a few hours after that."

"I'm sure Brie has missed her."

"They've talked on the phone nearly every day, but yeah. They're very close. Lacey is a great mom."

"That's good of you to say. I've heard other divorced parents who aren't nearly as complimentary of their exes."

He made a sound that was somewhere between a grunt and a sigh. "We're much better friends now than we ever were when we were married."

"Has it been hard for you, seeing Lacey go on with her life?" He must have loved her once, dreamed of a future with her.

This time the sound he made definitely sounded like a laugh. "Not one tiny bit. She deserves to be happy. Lacey had to carry a lot after I went to prison. She really stepped up. I can never repay her for that."

"How did you meet her?"

She wasn't only making conversation. She genuinely wanted to know, Jenna thought, as he turned that chair over and moved to work on another one. She followed with the flashlight, taking a seat on the chair he had just fixed.

"Friend of a friend. I was stationed in North Carolina and she came down from Michigan to visit a friend in the area, who happened to be dating one of my buddies. We went on a couple of double dates and then just sort of…fell into a relationship."

He was quiet, his muscles flexing as he tightened the screws on the underside of the chair. "She was desperate to escape a tough family life, and I was getting ready to head overseas after a transfer to Germany. We decided to tie the knot before I left so she could come with me. Not an uncommon story in the military."

"How long were you in Germany?"

While he worked, he talked about his military service and some of the experiences he'd had, not only there but during a short stint in the Middle East, protecting the base and being fired on by militants.

As they talked and she came to understand him a little, Jenna was aware of a grim realization.

She was doing a lousy job of resisting him.

In fact, quite the opposite.

She was falling for him.

The truth washed over her, and for an instant, she wobbled the flashlight in her shock. He looked over and she quickly corrected it.

Oh no. What had she done?

This wasn't simply an attraction. She was falling in love with him.

He definitely didn't feel the same way. Yes, he was attracted to her, but that was it. He had given her no indication that his feelings might run deeper.

Oh, what a mess.

They lived in the same house. Yes, they had different apartments, but it was impossible to avoid the other Brambleberry House tenants. How would she be able to live one floor below him? Could she possibly return to merely being friends when she was beginning to realize how very much more she wanted?

She didn't want to move out. She loved this house and so did Addie. But how could she stay here and keep her feelings to herself, when she saw him day after day and when their daughters were becoming such close friends?

"What's wrong?" he asked. She looked up to find him watching her, an expression of concern on his face.

She couldn't tell him any of the thoughts racing through her head. He wouldn't want to hear that his foolish neighbor was getting all kinds of inappropriate ideas about him.

She pasted on a smile, hoping the darkness would conceal her sudden distress. "Nothing. Everything's fine," she lied.

"Are you sure? You were frowning like you just spotted a skunk walking through the lilac bushes."

"Oh, I hope not! Don't you think Theo would alert us to any wandering creatures making their way through the yard?"

"Him?"

He pointed to the dog, curled up on the cushion and snoring softly.

She was grateful to turn the subject. "He's not turning into the greatest watchdog, is he? On the plus side, he's the most mellow dog ever and loves everybody. Not an aggressive bone in his body."

"I'm sure he still has enough protective instincts to watch out for you and Addie if the need arises. Dogs are amazing like that."

They talked about some of the dogs he had worked with in prison and the two great dogs he'd had when he was young, before his father died.

Jenna wasn't at all tired, though she knew she would pay the price the next day. She would be lucky to stay awake until book club.

She knew she should go inside, to figure out what she was going to do next, but she couldn't seem to make herself move.

After she had been outside about a half hour, he set the last chair upright and took off his headlamp, switching it off. "There you go. That's the last one."

She handed him the flashlight. He aimed it downward, though didn't shut it off.

"Thank you for doing that. I'm sure my book club members will appreciate chairs that don't fall apart in the middle of dinner."

"Always a good thing, right?"

She managed a smile, and as he gazed down at her, sparkling awareness seemed to shiver to life between them.

Jenna wanted him to kiss her, even though she knew it would only leave her wanting more. She saw him swallow and had the most inappropriate urge to press her mouth to the strong column of his neck.

"I should..." She pointed to the house.

In the light cast from the flashlight, his expression seemed remote, hard. "Probably a good idea." His voice suddenly seemed abrupt and she wondered what she had done.

"Are you staying out a little longer?"

"Yeah."

"Are you sure? It has to be nearly two."

"I'll get there eventually."

Though she knew she needed to go inside, she was reluctant to leave him out here by himself.

They gazed at each other for a long moment as the night air seemed to sigh around them.

"Do you want to know the real reason I came out here?" he asked, his voice low and his features in shadow.

She shook her head, suddenly unable to find her voice.

"I had to do something physical to keep myself distracted from wanting something I can't have."

Her breath seemed to catch at the intensity of his words, the raw emotion there.

"What's that?" she finally asked, her voice barely above a whisper.

"I think you know, Jenna. You. You are what I want."

Heat rushed from her brain to pool in her belly, her thighs.

She swallowed, not sure how to answer him, finally settling on the truth.

"That's the reason I couldn't sleep, either. I keep remembering...kissing you."

He made a low sound, raw and hungry, and then the flashlight tumbled to the ground, pitching them into darkness as he reached for her.

When he kissed her, everything inside her seemed to sigh a welcome. She had wanted him to kiss her again for days. Forever, it seemed.

The reality was far better than any of her memories, and she was lost in the magic of his touch.

They kissed for a long time, tasting and exploring while the dog snored softly and the night breeze stirred the flowers around them.

She was only vaguely aware of Wes lowering down to one of the pergola chairs and pulling her with him onto his lap, where she seemed to fit perfectly. She felt a fleeting moment of gratitude that he had reinforced the chairs. How mortifying if one clattered apart underneath them.

The thought made her smile a little and he eased his mouth away.

"What's so funny?"

"I hope you knew what you were doing when you tightened the screws or we might be in for an unpleasant surprise."

His mouth lifted with a smile that left her breathless. "I wouldn't care. I would still want to kiss you amid the rubble of a dozen chairs."

She shivered at the intensity of his expression, the heat of him surrounding her.

"You're cold," he murmured.

She shook her head, though reality was beginning to push through the haze of desire.

What were they doing? What was *she* doing? A few more moments out here and she would have completely surrendered.

Though it was painfully hard, she slid off his lap. "I should never have come out here. I'm sorry. We... we can't do this."

He froze for a long second, heat and desire mixing with confusion in his gaze. "Why not?" he asked on a growl.

She released a long breath. "We both know where it would lead. Where would we go? Your apartment? We can't because Brielle is inside. My apartment? Addie."

He gazed at her, his breathing ragged.

"Even if the girls weren't inside, you know it wouldn't be a good idea," she said, hating herself for what she had to do.

"Right now, it feels like a damn good idea."

The fierce hunger in his voice thrummed through her.

He rose as well and in the darkness, she could only make out his profile. "You should know, this isn't just physical for me, though that's certainly a factor. I think about you all the time, Jenna. When I'm not with you, I want to be. When I *am* with you, I want to savor every second of it until I get the chance to spend time with you again."

A torrent of emotions poured through her at his words. Tenderness, joy, heat, need.

She wanted to lean into his words, to grab them and treasure them against her heart.

This seemed so very different from the love she and Ryan had shared. Their relationship had been like hot cocoa on a cold winter night. Warm, comforting, sustaining.

This thing between her and Wes was something else entirely.

More like cocoa with a heavy dash of hot sauce.

As much as she longed to consume every drop, a cold fear seemed to spread from her stomach outward, like frost blooms on the window.

She had fought so hard to be in a good place. Wes threatened to ruin all of that peace and calm.

She already had feelings for him. If she gave in to this heat between them, she would fall irrevocably in love and would end up bruised and broken.

But what if she didn't? a little voice whispered. What if they were able to work through all their differences and find happiness together?

It would be amazing. She had no doubt.

I think about you all the time, Jenna. When I'm not with you, I want to be. When I am with you, I want to savor every second of it until I get the chance to spend time with you again.

His words seemed seared into her heart. Was it possible he could be falling in love with her, too?

No. She couldn't believe it. His world was tattoos

and motorcycles, while hers was book clubs and parent-teacher conferences. This heat would pass, like the storms that blew through Cannon Beach. After it was gone, what would they possibly have between them?

"I can't," she whispered, despising herself for giving in to the fear but unable to face the alternative.

"Because I've been in prison."

At his flat, emotionless tone, she stared at him, wishing she could see better in the darkness, could grab the flashlight from the ground and aim it at him so she could read his expression.

"No. That has nothing to do with it. Do you want the truth? Okay. I'm afraid, Wes. There it is. Four years ago, my husband died and left me devastated, then just as I was beginning to come back to life, I became tangled up with the wrong man and ended up in another version of hell. I'm finally beginning to figure things out again. I can't… I don't want to mess that up. Not for me and not for Addie."

"Why would this mess everything up?"

She sighed, moving away. "I love living here in Brambleberry House. So does Addie. I don't want to leave. But what if we give in to this heat between us and something goes wrong? How would I possibly be able to stay here?"

He was quiet for a long moment. When he spoke, his voice was low. "But what if everything between us goes *right*?"

His kisses certainly felt right to her. And she loved being with him and could spend all night talking to him out here in the pergola.

For a moment, she was tempted. So very tempted.

But she had ignored her instincts once with Aaron

by going on a second date with him. She couldn't take that kind of risk again when she had so much at stake.

She didn't for a moment think Wes would hurt her intentionally. But she was already half in love with the man. If they gave in to this desire between them, how would she possibly protect what was left of her heart?

"I'm sorry," she said again. Despising herself, she grabbed a confused Theo and hurried back to the house.

After Jenna left so abruptly, Wes stayed in the pergola, staring at the night sky peeking through the open slat roof.

If this was love, he didn't want it. This ache in his chest, in his bones. In his heart.

He couldn't blame Jenna for not wanting to further explore the attraction between them and pursue a relationship.

How could he?

Wes wasn't exactly a prize. She had talked about her baggage, but he had so much he needed a damn cargo tanker to carry it all.

He sighed, frustrated all over again at the circumstances of his life that had led him here.

Would he change it if he could?

It was a stunning thought.

If he hadn't been arrested, he probably wouldn't be here in Cannon Beach, living upstairs from her.

He looked at the house, cold and dark now where it was usually so warm and filled with life.

She was right. How would they both be able to remain here, with these raw, unfulfilled emotions between them? He would find it excruciating to live one floor above her, to be so close to her but know she would remain forever out of reach.

Even now he wanted to march up those stairs, break down her door and pull her into his arms.

How could he stay here?

She had said she didn't want to move. He didn't want to leave Brambleberry House, either. The house was warm and comfortable, and the view and proximity to the water would be hard to beat somewhere else within his price range.

He would have an easier time moving, though. He had brought very little with him, and it would be simple enough to pack it up into his truck and find somewhere else to live.

It made the most sense. She had been here for years. This was her daughter's home. If they found the situation completely untenable, he would have to start looking for another place. He didn't know where he would go, only that he had to stay in town. He had been separated from Brie for long enough. He wouldn't do it again.

Would anywhere else along the coast be far enough to help him get over Jenna?

He wasn't sure.

What choice did he have? Whatever her reasons, she had made it clear she didn't want things to move forward.

His only option was to try like hell to put away his feelings, to focus on Brie and the future and rebuilding his life.

Chapter Fifteen

The encounter with Wes in the early hours haunted Jenna the rest of the day as she prepped for the book group meeting.

She had been looking forward to the meeting with her friends all week, but now she wasn't certain she would be able to get through it.

She was exhausted, for one thing, after returning to her house to toss and turn again in her bed until she had finally fallen into a fitful sleep.

She also wasn't in a cheerful mood. She had snapped at Addie when she complained about having to do her chores, then had to apologize. She explained that she was having a cranky morning and shouldn't have snapped…but that Addie still had to do her chores.

The rest of the day was busy as she cleaned her apartment, went to the grocery store and had Addie help her make cookies.

She didn't see Wes all day and tried to tell herself she was relieved, not disappointed.

Finally, an hour before the party, as she was covering the tables with linen cloths, she spotted his pickup truck pulling into its usual parking spot.

He climbed out, paused a moment as if trying to make up his mind, then approached her.

"Hi."

"Hello." She tried a smile, even as she felt a sharp pang of longing. "Did Brielle go back to her mom's?"

He nodded. "Yes. I took her there this afternoon. We went to a matinee this morning of a movie she's been wanting to see. Sort of our last hurrah together."

"It must have been tough to say goodbye."

"I won't say dropping her off with her mother becomes any easier with practice. But I'm slowly beginning to accept that I can see her anytime I want and she'll be here again in a week, not every few months when Lacey could arrange a prison visit."

"You're a good father, Wes."

He made a face as if he disagreed but didn't argue with her. "What time does your party start?"

She glanced at her watch. "Another hour. People should be arriving around seven. I've got a babysitter coming for Addie in about a half hour. Rosa's niece Bella is great with her and Rosa's stepson is coming to play, too."

He glanced out to sea, where she could see a rim of dark clouds on the horizon. "Forecasters are saying the storm should hold off until later. Maybe ten or eleven."

"We should be done by then."

"Good to know. I'll be sure to stay out of your way. I might take my bike for a drive down the coast."

She knew that was one of his outlets when he was particularly restless. Was she the cause of his current tumult? She didn't like thinking it.

"You don't have to stay away. In fact, you're welcome to join us at book group, if you'd like."

"I don't think I would quite fit in with your crowd."

She thought of her group, mostly women but a few men, too. "You might. We're open to everyone willing to read the featured book and offer insight."

He gestured to the tables and chairs. "Can I help you set things up? It can't be comfortable, with your injured hand."

She didn't want to feel beholden to him for even one more thing, especially with these currents seething between them. But she had to admit she had been struggling all day to work around her stupid bandage.

"Would you mind carrying out some of the folding chairs from the shed? That would be very helpful."

"No problem. How many?"

"All of them. I think there are about a dozen there. That should give us enough, with the furniture you fixed last night."

As soon as she said the words, conjuring up memories that hadn't been far from her mind all day, her face felt hot. He gazed at her for a long moment, and she knew he was remembering their intense embrace as well.

"Sure. No problem."

He headed toward the shed at the bottom of the garden and returned with three chairs in each hand. He set them up, then returned to the shed for the rest, finishing in about two minutes when the job would have taken her at least ten.

He set them up where she indicated, at the folding tables she had already brought out with Addie's help.

"They're pretty dusty. I gather they haven't been used much lately."

She nodded. "When Rosa still lived here, she liked to have gatherings, but I'm afraid I'm not as social as she is. The Andersons do often have friends over to grill, but a few at a time, not enough that would require them to pull out the extra chairs."

"I can clean them off for you."

She started to protest that he didn't need to do that, then swallowed her words. She was running out of time and still needed to bring down a few more items for the party from her apartment. This was also a good test as to whether they could set aside their feelings and be friendly enough to both stay here at the house.

"I've got a few cleaning supplies stored under the serving table there."

He nodded and went to work without another word. For some reason, his simple thoughtfulness made her eyes burn with tears.

Wes was a good man. Any woman smart enough to build a relationship with him should consider herself very lucky.

She wanted to be that woman, suddenly, with a fierce intensity that brought a lump to her throat.

She swallowed it down quickly. "I've got to run upstairs for a few more things. Thank you so much for your help. I'll save you some cookies."

"This is the kind of thing friends do for each other, right?"

Was that a shadow of bitterness in his voice? She

couldn't quite tell…and her daughter's excited shriek distracted her from trying to figure it out.

"Hi, Logan! You're here!"

She looked up to see Rosa walking toward them, along with Bella and Rosa's stepson, Logan, who had become fast friends with Addie when he and his father temporarily lived in Brambleberry House after a fire at their own home.

"Hi, Addie." Logan beamed at her. "Where's your dog? I can't wait to meet him! I wanted to bring Hank, but my dad said he should stay home since a book party might not be the best time to see if he and your new puppy get along."

"Theo likes everybody," Addie said. "Don't you, buddy?"

In answer, their new puppy licked at Logan, who giggled.

Rosa gave Wes a curious look as he continued wiping off the chairs. "I do hope you're joining us for book group."

"Not me. Sorry. I don't even know what book you're reading."

She told him and he shook his head. "Haven't read that one, thought I did read the author's last book."

"You should come next month," she said with a warm smile.

"By then, we'll have a new baby." Wyatt's teenage niece Bella beamed at Rosa.

"Are you sure you'll be okay with these three?" Jenna asked, pointing to the children and the dog, who were chasing each other around the part of the yard not currently set up with tables.

"We'll be great," Bella answered. "We'll go for a long walk on the beach and build sandcastles and tire everybody out, then come back and watch a movie. I can't wait to hang with them."

Bella was a sweet girl who looked enough like Rosa to be her sister.

Another car pulled in behind Rosa's. Kim, Jenna saw, with the food.

She hurried over to help carry the catering trays to the tables. By the time she returned to the pergola, Wes had disappeared.

"It was nice of Wes to help you set up for the party," Rosa said sometime later, after the book club gathering was in full swing.

Jenna knew she shouldn't feel this little pang in her heart just at the mention of his name. "Yes. He's been very kind."

"I wish he had stayed for the book group. He could have made more friends."

"Too bad he didn't," Kim said. "Maybe we can talk him into helping us move some tables or something later. All those muscles. *Mmm.*"

Jenna fought down a little spurt of annoyance with her friend, which she knew was completely unreasonable. Kim was extremely happily married and was only teasing about Wes. That didn't stop Jenna from feeling protective of him.

She had no right to feel that way. He wasn't hers. She had made sure of that.

She forced a smile. "I think Wes is making himself scarce on purpose tonight. He said doesn't want to get in the way of our fun."

"Are you talking about Wes Calhoun? I heard from Lacey that her ex was living here."

Jenna looked over at Erin Lawson, a yoga instructor

who always recommended motivational self-improvement books when it was her turn to host book group.

"Yes. He lives in the third-floor apartment," Jenna said, her tone guarded. "Do you know him?"

"Not personally, no." Erin looked at the house. "My friend Jewel is friends with Lacey and she told her about him. I just think you're really brave to live in this big house alone with an ex-con, especially with the Andersons still out of town."

Jenna frowned. "Wes is an excellent neighbor. And he was cleared of all charges."

Erin shrugged. "Innocent or not. Prison changes people. My sister's husband went away for a white-collar thing. He spent a year inside and came out a completely different man. And not in a good way, either. I just don't know if I could do it. I admire you."

Jenna had to bite down a sharp retort. First, she was the least brave woman she knew. Second, she had absolutely no reason to be afraid of Wes.

He would never hurt her. He would rather go back to prison than do that. She suddenly knew that with absolute conviction.

How horrible for him, that some people would always judge him for circumstances completely beyond his control.

She opened her mouth to say as much, but Erin had turned away to talk to someone else and the conversation turned away from Wes, much to her relief.

She tried to focus on the conversation and her friends instead of Wes, though she noted she was not the only woman who watched him when he came out of the house sometime later, started up his bike and rode off into the evening sun.

Chapter Sixteen

"That was a terrific book group," Kim said as she carried the last of the folding chairs back to the shed.

"It was fun, wasn't it?" Jenna said, smothering a yawn.

"And the best part is, we don't have to host it again for a whole year."

She smiled. "At least we made it through the book discussion before the storm hit."

"Barely." Kim gestured out to sea, where dark clouds gathered. Lightning arced over the water and she could hear the distant answering thunder.

"I'd better get home. Thanks for hosting. This was a lovely spot for the party."

Her friend hugged her and hurried to her car as the first few drops of rain hit.

Jenna carried the last few serving dishes into the house, worried about Wes. She had seen him leave the house and ride away on his bike during the first hour of the party and he had yet to return.

She hoped he wasn't caught out in the rain. She had heard raindrops could feel like tiny bullets to a motorcyclist.

Her hand throbbed as she made her way up the stairs to her apartment. She needed some ibuprofen and her bed.

She pushed open the door to her quiet apartment. Bella had left a half hour ago with Logan and Rosa, leaving Addie fast asleep in her bed. Jenna had checked on her fifteen minutes earlier when she had carried a load of items upstairs.

She spotted the empty crate as soon as she walked into the kitchen. Oh shoot. On that earlier trip up to the apartment, she had taken Theo back down with her to let him out for the night one last time and then got so busy talking with Kim and cleaning up the final debris from the party that she completely forgot him in the small fenced dog yard.

She made her way back down the stairs and out the back porch.

"Theo? Come on, bud."

She waited for the puppy to come bounding over to her. When he didn't, she frowned. "Theo? Come."

Still nothing.

The storm was moving closer, she saw. A flash of lightning illuminated the yard, revealing no sign of the dog.

She moved down the steps. Where could he be?

When she reached the back of the dog yard, which accessed the beach gate, everything inside her turned cold. The gate was ajar slightly, with just enough room for a puppy to squeeze through.

A few of her guests who lived close had opted to walk home via the beach. She could only guess that one of them must not have closed the gate completely.

Theo was gone.

A storm was coming, her daughter was alone in the house and their small, defenseless puppy was lost somewhere on the beach.

This was her fault. She should have checked to make sure the beach gate was closed before she ever let Theo out into the yard.

Anything could happen to him out there. She couldn't bear thinking about the hazards to a small puppy.

She had to find him, no matter if she had to search all night.

She turned and raced back into her apartment for her phone and a flashlight, tossing extra batteries in her pocket just in case, then hurried back downstairs.

Her fatigue, the ache in her hand and the ache in her heart were all forgotten for now as she focused on finding Theo.

After a long bike ride down to Pacific City and back, Wes hoped he might be tired enough to sleep.

Instead, his mind still raced, his heart still ached and now he was damp and cold from the rain that had caught him about fifteen miles from home.

The party was apparently over, he saw as he pulled into the driveway. The only other vehicles he could see were his pickup truck and Jenna's small SUV.

He looked up to the second floor, where he saw only a dim light on.

Just as he was climbing off his bike, the front door flung open and Jenna raced down the porch toward him wearing a raincoat and carrying a flashlight.

"Oh, thank heavens you're here," she said, her voice frantic. "I am so glad I heard your bike. I need your help."

"What's wrong?" he asked instantly, forgetting all about his wet clothing or the chill beginning to seep in.

"It's Theo. Somehow he wandered off through the beach gate." Her voice bordered on hysteria. "I'm just about to go look for him. Can you help me?"

"Of course." He didn't hesitate for a second. "I've got a flashlight and my headlamp in my pickup. Let me grab them."

He unlocked the truck and found the lights immediately. On impulse, he also threw in a couple of road flares. They might come in handy.

He shut the truck door as another flash of lightning rippled through the night, still distant but moving closer.

"What about Addie?" he asked suddenly. "You can't leave her for long. Why don't you stay with her and I'll go look."

She shook her head vigorously. "I called my friend Kim and she is on her way back to stay with Addie in case she wakes. She should be here in a few minutes. She knows the code to get in the house and I left my apartment unlocked. It's my fault. I should have been more careful and made sure the gate was shut after some of my guests left that way."

Ah. That explained how Theo had managed his escape.

"How long do you think he's been gone?"

"Maybe fifteen or twenty minutes. I don't think it can be longer than that."

A dog could move quickly in that amount of time.

As they hurried toward the beach, he wondered how they were supposed to spot a little tan-colored dog in the sand in the dark, in the middle of a storm.

He didn't want to be the voice of doom by raising the worry. Maybe the dog hadn't gone far. Maybe he would hear them calling him.

"I think we should split up," Jenna said, once they left Brambleberry House property. "Why don't you go north and I'll go south?"

He wasn't thrilled with the idea of separating from her, though it did make the most sense. They could cover twice the ground that way.

"Here. Take a flare. If you find him, light it so I know to come back. I should see it from far down the beach."

"Okay. And you'll do the same, right?"

In another flash of distant lightning, her features looked pale and frightened. He wanted to pull her against him, to keep her warm and safe from the storm, but he knew this wasn't the time for that.

"We'll find him, Jenna. I promise."

"I hope so. Addie has lost enough. She'll be devastated if something happens to him."

"We don't have long. As soon as that storm hits in earnest, we have to find shelter. Puppy or not. I'm sorry."

"I know."

"It's moving this way. We've maybe only got fifteen minutes before we'll have to head back. There's no safe shelter on the beach."

"Let's pray we find him soon then."

She raced toward the water, scanning the sand with the beam of her flashlight and calling the dog's name.

Still reluctant to leave her alone, he headed off in the opposite direction.

He had been looking for perhaps ten minutes. When he turned around, he could see her light still bobbing across the sand, though it was growing dimmer.

He called the dog but it was hard to hear anything with the waves beginning to crash and the wind blowing hard.

Lightning split the sky again, closer this time. In that instant of light, he thought he saw movement in the waves about ten yards from shore, a tiny dark head.

He thought at first it might be a seal or a sea turtle, then wondered if he had imagined it. He aimed his powerful flashlight in that direction. In a second flash of lightning, he realized it wasn't a sea creature, it was a small dog, swimming furiously for all he was worth toward shore and being tossed back again and again by the waves.

"I see him," he shouted, though he knew even as he did, she wouldn't be able to hear him.

Without another thought, he lit his flare, hoping she could see it, then kicked off his boots, yanked off his leather jacket and waded into the cold waters of the Pacific.

He had hoped he might be able to walk to the puppy, but the waves were too intense. They almost knocked him over twice. Finally he dived over the next one as lightning illuminated the water and his path to the puppy. The thunder that followed only a few seconds later confirmed the storm was moving closer.

The puppy was tiring. He could tell. The next wave

went over its head and it didn't pop up again for a long moment. With a fierce burst of energy, Wes swam the last few yards to the dog and scooped him under one arm, then began the journey back to shore.

When he was a few yards from shore, he stood up and fought his way through the waves to the sand as Jenna came running down the beach.

She gasped, trying to catch her breath. "Was he in the water? I saw your flare and then you jumped in and I was so scared. Did you find him? Is he…?"

He hadn't even had the chance to assess Theo's condition. He held the puppy up and felt vast relief when Theo gave a weak-sounding whine.

Jenna, her breath still coming harshly from her run down the beach, reached for Theo and hugged him tightly. "Oh, you poor thing. I'm so glad you're safe. Don't do that again. You scared me so much!"

The labradoodle licked her cheek and rested his wet head against her chest.

Wes couldn't help thinking he would like to do the same thing, just pull her into his arms and bask in her heat.

They couldn't stay here, though. Not with that storm moving ever closer.

He scooped up his boots and his jacket, not bothering to put them on now.

"We have to get back to the house. The lightning is too close."

"Are you okay? I can't believe you did that!"

"I'm fine," he said as they quickly raced back toward the house. "He wasn't that far out. I wouldn't have seen him if he'd been even a little farther out. I didn't think I would have to swim but the waves were stronger than I was expecting, which might be what happened to him. I can carry him. He's soaked, so he has to weigh twice as much as usual."

"I've got him," she said, racing along beside him.

The rain hit hard as they made it the final hundred yards to the Brambleberry House beach gate.

He opened it and together they ran to the back porch.

"Is he okay?" he asked.

"He seems to be." Jenna set the dog down. He sat on his haunches, looking far more alert in the glow from the porch light, but he didn't seem to want to leave her side.

"Wes, thank you," Jenna said as thunder rumbled just beyond the safety of the porch. "I don't know what I would have done if you hadn't been here. You have come to my rescue more times than I can count."

"I'm glad I made it back from my ride in time to help you."

"So am I. Oh, Wes. Thank you."

She wrapped her arms around him and he held her tightly. She was shaking, he realized.

"Let's get you inside. You're freezing."

She shook her head. "I'm a little cold but I'm not the one who went for a dip in the Pacific. I was so scared when you jumped into the water. Terrified. I have never felt so helpless. I could do nothing while you risked your life for my daughter's dog."

"He's a sweet little guy. I didn't want something to happen to him. Not if I could help."

She made a sound halfway between a laugh and a sob. "I can't believe you risked your life for a puppy. I'm so glad you did, but I feel sick when I think of all the things that could have happened to you. To both of you. An undertow. A rogue wave. Or a shark, for heaven's sake."

"Nothing happened," he said, his voice gruff. "I'm here. Just a little wet, but I was wet anyway from my ride."

"Thank you. I can never thank you enough."

When she placed her warm hands on either side of his face and pressed her mouth to his, she completely shattered him.

He closed his eyes and held himself still as she kissed him with a tenderness that made him yearn for more. Finally, he couldn't bear it another moment and he stepped away.

"You're killing me, Jenna. I can't do this anymore. There isn't enough pavement in Oregon for me to ride away how much I want to have you right here in my arms."

Without looking at her or waiting for an answer, he turned around and hurried into the house, already trying to figure out how soon he could move out so he could start the process of trying to get over her.

Jenna watched him go, her heart beating hard. She had been about to tell him she was falling in love with him. What might have happened if she had spoken sooner?

She hadn't. Once more, she had let her fear control her.

At her feet, the still-bedraggled puppy whimpered and she pushed away her angst to focus on his needs for now.

She carried him into the house, where Kim was waiting.

"You found him. Oh, I'm so glad. Where was he?"

"I didn't find him. Wes did. He somehow had gone into the water and then couldn't swim back out. Wes went in after him."

"Is he okay?"

She grabbed the microfiber towel she used to dry him and rubbed him vigorously. He was warm and alert, his eyes bright as he looked over at Kim. After a moment, the puppy wriggled to be let down, and Jenna set him on the floor again, where he trotted to his water bowl and drank it empty. Poor thing, surrounded by all that salt water he couldn't drink. There was a metaphor in that, she was fairly certain, but she couldn't put her finger on it.

She filled his bowl again, not caring that it meant she would have to take him out to do his business again in an hour.

After taking a few more sips, the puppy ate a little of his chow, then padded to his crate, where he curled up on the blankets and went immediately to sleep.

Kim, watching all of this, smiled. "Looks like he's fine. Exhausted, but fine."

"Thank you for coming back to stay with Addie."

"Glad to do it. I haven't even been here twenty minutes."

"Well, thank you. I had no idea how long it might take to find him."

"And you and Wes would have looked all night, wouldn't you?"

Jenna gave a little laugh. "Yes. Wes was going to make me stop if the lightning got too close, but as soon as the storm passed, we would have gone back out."

She knew she wouldn't have stopped looking and suddenly had no doubt that Wes would have been right there at her side.

He was a man she could count on. A man any woman could rely upon to help her through the storms of life. He would do anything for a woman he loved.

She closed her eyes as the realization filled her with a peaceful assurance. She wanted to be that woman, sharing troubles and joys and life with him.

The last of her fear, any lingering doubts, seemed to shrivel away. She wanted to be with Wes. The differences between them didn't matter. They had many more things in common.

"He's a good guy, isn't he?" Kim said, as if reading Jenna's thoughts.

"The very best," she answered.

"You should probably tell him you're in love with him. A guy deserves to know, don't you think? Especially after he risked his life for your dog."

"Yes. Probably." Jenna could feel her face heat.

"Want me to stay with Addie a little longer while you do? I can even stay all night, ahem, if necessary. I don't mind sleeping on the sofa."

Jenna could only shake her head. "Not necessary. I need to change into some dry clothes, then I'll go talk to him. Thank you again."

"Anytime. Though I hope your little buddy over there learns to stay put after his little adventure."

Kim let herself out while Jenna hurried to change into dry clothes. What did a woman wear when she was about to put her heart on the line? She had no idea, so she settled on a pair of yoga pants and a soft sweater that always gave her comfort.

After checking on her sleeping daughter and puppy, she opened her door, drawing on all her courage to make her way up the stairs to his apartment.

As she went, she thought she smelled flowers on the stairs. Was Abigail there, giving her strength? It was a comforting idea, though she still wasn't sure she was buying the whole ghost thing.

At his door, she lingered for a long moment. What if he was asleep already?

He wasn't. She was suddenly sure of it.

There isn't enough pavement in Oregon for me to ride away how much I want to have you right here in my arms.

She shivered, took a deep breath and knocked softly, then waited what felt like an eternity for him to open the door.

He had changed into dry clothes, too. Had possibly showered. His hair was damp and sticking up and he smelled clean and masculine and wonderful.

"Is something wrong?" he asked, his voice so remote she had to pause, some of her uncertainty fluttering back.

No. She wouldn't give in to it. This man had risked his life to save a puppy from drowning in the Pacific in the middle of a lightning storm.

She could certainly take a chance and tell him how she felt.

"Yes. Something is wrong," she murmured.

"What?"

"I need to tell you something. May I…come in?"

He appeared reluctant but finally opened the door further. She walked into the apartment, so different now than it had been when Rosa lived here. It was comfortable and clean, though fairly utilitarian and sparsely decorated. Rosa had taken all her personal things when she moved out to marry Wyatt.

Now that she was here, she didn't know where to start. Doubt began to creep back in but she firmly pushed it away and faced him.

"When my husband died, I told myself I was done with love. I didn't need or want the vulnerability and pain that went hand in hand with it. Then everything happened with Aaron, which only reinforced that relationships were far too messy."

She let out a breath and realized her hands were shaking. She curled them into fists and hoped he didn't notice.

"I told myself I was happy on my own. I had Addie and my students. A life here in Cannon Beach. I didn't need anything else."

She met his gaze but couldn't read anything in his features that looked as if they had been carved from a block of wood.

"And then you moved in and...everything changed. You kissed me. You made me feel cherished. You reminded me that I'm still a woman. A woman who...who apparently can still fall in love."

He gazed at her, still expressionless except for his eyes, which suddenly blazed with emotion.

"Are you?"

"In love? Yes. I'm afraid so. I didn't want to be, but you rode into my life and changed everything."

The last word barely emerged when he crossed the space between them in a blink, pulled her tightly into his arms and kissed her with a humbling mix of ferocity and tenderness.

"Oh, Jenna," he said against her mouth a long moment later. "I love you. I think I have from the moment I moved in, when you were terrified of me."

"Not you," she assured him, kissing the corner of his

mouth, arms around him as tightly as she could manage. "It was never you. It was the image of who I thought you were."

"An ex-con."

"A big, intimidating man who rode a motorcycle and had tattoos."

"I'm still that guy," he pointed out.

"No. You're so much more." She kissed him again, loving the feel of his arms around her and the knowledge that she was exactly where she wanted to be. Where she needed to be.

Where she belonged.

"You're so much more," she repeated. "You're a loving father. A loyal friend. A man willing to drop everything to come to the rescue of a fourteen-pound puppy."

She paused and kissed him again, her mouth slow and lingering. "And you're the man I love with all my heart."

He gave a low sound, picked her up as if she weighed nothing and carried her to the sofa.

"You are the most amazing woman I've ever known," he said, his voice low and rough. "We both know I don't deserve you, but I don't care. I swear to you, Jenna, that I will spend the rest of my life trying to be the man you need."

His mouth brushed hers with a tenderness and care that made her eyes burn.

"You already are," she whispered.

She loved this man deeply. This was right between them.

No. Better than right. It was perfect.

* * * * *

A Q&A with RaeAnne Thayne

What or who inspired you to write?
My mom was a huge reader, inspiring me and my siblings to become readers as well. She is also the one who first urged me to take a journalism class in high school. I ended up becoming the editor of my high school newspaper and falling in love with the power of storytelling.

What is your daily writing routine?
I feel extraordinarily fortunate to have an office outside my home. For my writing routine, I commute through the backyard to my office, usually with my canine writing companion Millie. I spend a few minutes refilling my water bottle, posting to social media and clearing out the most urgent emails before I disconnect from the internet and dive into my current work-in-progress. I have found that writing sprints work best for me. I set a timer for fifty minutes then take a ten-minute break

to walk around my office, let the dog out, etc. I write very rough first drafts using a combination of writing and dictation. I like to finish that first draft completely before I start over and polish the rough draft through the second, third (and sometimes fourth!) drafts.

Who are your favorite authors?
I have far too many to list and I discover new favorites all the time. For pleasure and sheer escape, I mostly read historical romances. I enjoy listening to audiobooks, mostly suspense, self-help and memoirs. I can say that the author who first introduced me to the wonderful world of romance novels was Jude Deveraux, more than forty years ago. I had the pleasure of meeting her a few years ago at an event we both attended and it was a highlight of my career (and life!) to tell her how very much she has influenced me.

Where do your story ideas come from?
Ideas come from anywhere I can find them! Back in the days when I was a newspaper reporter and editor, I could find a dozen stories a day through reading the news wire. Things have become a little more challenging as my writing has matured. I still read newspapers and magazines voraciously and if I read something that sparks a little interest, I keep it in a file on my phone. When I'm looking for a new story idea, I peruse that idea file until something clicks. Often I end up combining two or three ideas for each book.

Do you have a favorite travel destination?
We love the canyons and deserts of my home state, Utah, and spend a great deal of time in southern Utah.

I really love traveling anywhere, though. Travel widens the world and provides an endless well of inspiration.

What is your most treasured possession?
Ooh, that's a tough one. I don't know if I have one thing I treasure above all else. If my house caught fire, I would make sure my family (and dog) were safe, then would probably try to rescue all our boxes of family photos.

What is your favorite movie?
I really love *Pride & Prejudice* with Keira Knightley and Matthew Macfadyen. I rewatch my favorite parts frequently.

When did you read your first Harlequin romance? Do you remember its title?
I do not remember the title but I'm sure it was around age twelve or thirteen. My mother loved to read romance novels so I would take them out of her room and read them. When I was in high school, I was fortunate enough to have a best friend whose older sister subscribed to all the Harlequin Presents. She would let me borrow one at a time and I devoured them!

How did you meet your current love?
My husband and I have been married thirty-seven years. We met as college students when we were both working at the university newspaper. He is also a writer, though enjoys photography much more than agonizing over every word of prose.

What characteristic do you most value in your friends?
Kindness, empathy and a good sense of humor.

How did you celebrate or treat yourself when you got your first book deal?
The evening I sold my first two books, we went to Red Lobster. LOL. At the time we had zero money, a five-year-old daughter and a mortgage and couldn't afford anything fancier! I remember looking around the restaurant and thinking my life was about to change forever.

Will you share your favorite reader response?
I had one reader who emailed to tell me my books saved her marriage. She and her husband read my books aloud to each other, which helps remind them each of the power of love and kindness. I can't ask for more than that!

What are your favorite character names?
After more than seventy books, I have used every character name I ever loved and then some. When I'm coming up with character names, I love finding sites that list the most popular names by year. It's fun to go through and figure out what names were popular when my characters were born.

Other than author, what job would you like to have?
I have been a writer for most of my adult life (after ten years as a journalist, I sold my first book twenty-eight years ago) and I love what I do. I really can't imagine doing anything else!

Michelle Lindo-Rice is an Emma Award winner and a Vivian Award finalist. She enjoys reading and crafting fiction across genres. Originally from Jamaica, West Indies, she has earned degrees from New York University; SUNY at Stony Brook; Teachers College, Columbia University; and Argosy University; and has been an educator for over twenty years.

She also writes inspirational stories as Zoey Marie Jackson. You can reach her online at michellelindorice.com or on Facebook.

Also by Michelle Lindo-Rice

Harlequin Special Edition

The Valentine's Do-Over
A Beauty in the Beast

Seven Brides for Seven Brothers

Rivals at Love Creek
Cinderella's Last Stand
Twenty-Eight Dates

Visit the Author Profile page
at Harlequin.com for more titles.

A BEAUTY IN THE BEAST

Michelle Lindo-Rice

For my son, Jordan Rice. May you find the woman of your heart, the one who will love you as you are and who you will love freely in return.

Thank you to my editor, Gail, Katixa and the team at Harlequin who support my vision, as well as my agent, Latoya, and my sister, Sobi.

Chapter One

When Eden Tempest woke up that morning on the first day of May and heard nothing but birds chirping outside her window, she was all smiles. She wrapped her long tresses in a bun, slapped on sunscreen, donned a long-sleeved shirt, shorts, rain boots and a wide-brimmed hat before bounding down the stairs to eat a breakfast bar and gulp down a glass of orange juice. She grabbed her gardening tools and gloves.

"It's barely six a.m.," her grandmother Susan called out from her bedroom just behind the kitchen. "Where are you going?"

"The sun is finally out and I've got to go check on my rosebushes," she yelled back.

"I'll be out in a few."

"Okay, Grams."

It sounded like her grandmother was still in bed,

which wasn't like the energetic sixty-nine-year-old. Usually Grams would have had biscuits, gravy and eggs ready and would be getting started on dinner or heading out to the farmers market to purchase fresh produce. But Grams had spent most of the evening before cracking walnuts to make her famous black walnut cake. So, Eden suspected that task had tuckered out the older woman.

Eden ventured through the back door in the kitchen, the screen door swishing shut behind her. She stood still when she saw a family of deer munching by an overgrown thicket and bowed trees near the fence. A bee buzzed by her ear. She tilted her head and swatted at it, her movement causing the deer to flee into the woods nearby.

She tugged her hat low on her face and surveyed the one acre of land, surrounded by the iron fence bent like an elderly person with a hump. There was a dilapidated shed in the right corner, the slats gray and covered in moss, as well as an old gazebo where her grandmother used to host weddings or social gatherings for the town of Blue Hen, Delaware. She could still see the ladies and girls twirling in their bright summer dresses, and the men in casual wear milling about the yard, talking and laughing and eating from the spread on the table in the center of the yard. The last event had been thirteen years ago for Eden's sixteenth birthday. The day her life and her grandmother's changed…forever.

That's why she didn't celebrate birthdays.

Her eyes misted. She dipped her head and turned to look at the once-majestic two-story, seven-bedroom bed-and-breakfast, with the paint chipped and blackened with soot. The gutters needed cleaning and the vines had claimed a lot of the room. No wonder the people of Blue Hen called their house haunted, especially after... Nope. It was best for her psyche if she stopped thinking about it. It took some effort, but she shrugged off the gargantuan memories and stomped through high grass and weeds to the best-kept area in the backyard: her rose garden.

She inhaled, appreciating the smell of fresh rain and the heat of the sun. It had rained for three days and she feared her rosebushes had been overwatered. They weren't due to bloom until June, right on time for the yearly rose festival. Eden prided herself on having the most fragrant and beautiful roses in town. Every year, for the past ten years, her roses had won first prize at the Blue Hen Rose Fest and this year would be no different. Hopefully. If the rain hadn't caused irreparable damage.

Carefully, she lifted the bushes and squatted low to inspect the roots. There was no evidence of rotting, a common result of overwatering. Eden exhaled, her shoulders slumping. She steadied herself to keep from falling on her butt. Wearing tan-colored shorts might not have been the right choice, seeing as how the earth was damp and wet. Next, she checked the leaves to see if they had yellowed or were spotted. She saw nothing but green. *Yes!*

She stood and wiped her hands on her shorts before grabbing the small bench she kept by the back door and started her pruning. She snipped and shaped and removed dead tissue; doting on her roses, ignoring the sun rays on her back and the sweat pouring from every crevice of her body. By the time she was finished, her boots and hands were covered in mud, three hours had passed and her skin was the shade of bronze.

She needed a tall, cold glass of water. And a shower.

Stepping back, Eden stood to take in the results of her labor, wiping her hands on her shorts. Beautiful. She pumped her fists. All this would be worth it when her grandmother came home with the first-prize trophy to put with the others on the mantel.

Speaking of her grandmother… Eden raced back into the house and tugged off her boots.

"Grams!" she yelled, but all was quiet. Her grandmother was nowhere about, and it was close to nine thirty. That was odd.

She washed her hands in one of the deep double sinks and helped herself to a tall glass of water then scuttled into her grandmother's room to find Grams nestled under the covers.

Eden heard a moan. "Are you all right?"

"My tummy hurts," Grams said, her body curled, her voice weak.

"Should I call Dr. Goodwin?" Eden crept closer. Her grandmother's face was beaded with sweat.

"No, it was probably the ice cream I ate last night." Grams was seriously lactose intolerant but that didn't stop her from indulging in the treat.

"Let me get you some tea," Eden offered, her heart beating fast in her chest. She couldn't remember when she had ever seen her grandmother bedridden. Grams must have eaten the entire pint. Unless it something more serious. Eden put on the kettle using the front burner that worked. The right one had stopped working about a year ago. The walls, painted buttercup yellow, the matching checkered curtains—slightly tattered— and the worn appliances could use an upgrade. Grams hadn't changed anything in close to fourteen years. It was like the house had been frozen in time since her parents' passing.

Opening the cupboard, Eden searched for a mug that wasn't chipped then dug into the drawer next to the stove for a spoon. She rifled through the different kinds of teas in a jar on the countertop—chamomile, Earl Grey, lemon—until she found a bag of ginger-and-honey. *Please let this solve whatever ails Grams.*

Eden lifted the lid of the cake stand where her grandmother stored freshly baked scones then placed one on a plate. Eden chose a large orange from the fruit basket on the tiled counter, her gaze falling on the oversize wall calendar and the big *X* on the date.

June 26. Her thirtieth birthday.

Her stomach knotted, and her hands shook as she cut into the orange and rested the slices on the plate. "It's just another day," she said, voice shaky. She drew deep, long breaths. "You'll be all right." Eden needed to make a tele-appointment with her therapist, who she used to see weekly until she had transitioned to an as-needed basis.

The kettle whistled and she poured the ginger-and-honey tea into the cup, the spoon making a light *clink* as she stirred. She gathered a wooden lap tray and placed the tea, the orange slices and some crackers on it, before making her way to the back room, rattling along the way and set it on the nightstand. Grams appeared to be sleeping. Eden touched her grandmother's forehead and gasped. Fever. Hot, roasting fever.

This was definitely not lactose intolerance.

She tried to shake Grams awake but the older woman was pretty lethargic. Panic raced through Eden's body. Her grandmother wouldn't approve but she called Dr.

Goodwin from their landline since she didn't own a cell phone. What was the point? She never went anywhere. Eden did, however, have the most up-to-date computer. But that was because she needed it to teach her online courses for Blue Hen College. Eden taught English literature and composition courses to college freshmen and sophomores.

Twenty minutes later, she opened the front door, making sure to keep her neck semihidden, and the doctor went in to check on Grams. Eden used that time to shower, wash her hair and slip into a blue long-sleeved baby doll dress. She put on her hat and hurried down the stairs just in time to hear the bedroom door creak open.

In a flash, Eden was by his side. "Is Grams all right?"

He shook his head, his tone grim. "She's been doing too much. I'm putting her on bed rest for now."

Bed rest? "What's wrong?" she asked, wringing her hands.

"You'll have to talk with your grandmother about that," he said, marching toward the door.

"Wait," Eden called out. "Is it me? Did I somehow cause this?"

"No, my child. She's almost seventy. Some things happen with age. Talk to her."

"Okay, I will. I can't lose her," she whispered. "She's all I have."

Dr. Goodwin, the town physician, and the only one besides her grandmother who she trusted, gave Eden a look of compassion. "This house is too big for the both of you to manage by yourselves. You should think of hiring some help."

Eden stepped back and lifted a hand. She watched the exact moment his eyes took in her scars and shoved her hands in the pockets of her dress. "No one will want to work in the haunted house, and I—I can't be seen like this. I'm gossip fodder."

"Dear, there's more to you than what's on the outside," the doctor said. "There's a whole world out there for you to enjoy."

"I won't be ridiculed or be made into the town laughingstock again." She shuddered, remembering how she had been taunted and teased when she had ventured into town after the fire.

"That was almost thirteen years ago. Things are different now. Even you're different," he urged. "You're not the same person you were all those nights ago. It's time you forgive yourself." Every time the doctor came to visit, he urged Eden to step out of her self-imposed cocoon. This house had become her haven since that fateful day. She never left, a prisoner of her past and fears.

"People don't change," she said, walking over to hold open the door. "And as for forgiving myself…" She shook her head, unable to continue from the heartache and guilt.

"Think about it. You don't want to end up alone, filled with regret for what you didn't do or should have done." After giving her a pat on her cheek, the doctor departed.

Eden trudged into the room to talk with her grandmother. Grams was now sitting up and sipping the tea. Grams's mother had been Chinese and her Jamaican father had been biracial, mixed with Black so Grams had inherited her mother's tiny frame and her father's olive color. Grams got a kick out people always trying to figure out her race. She would quip *I belong to the human race* every time they asked. Eden's mother had looked a lot like Grams while Eden had inherited her own father's height. Eden's father had been from Louisiana, and she had inherited his red curly hair, his cognac-colored eyes and skin the color of sun-kissed sand. She felt like a giant next to Grams, standing at five-feet-eleven to Grams's five-feet-two. Grams would often say Eden had legs for days and beauty for a lifetime, which was why she had been crowned Junior Prom Queen at her high school. But that was history, a lifetime ago,

"Come sit here next to me, baby," Grams said, putting the cup down and patting the bed. Her long black hair hung to her shoulders and she looked frail.

Eden complied. "What's going on, Grams?" she asked, her lips quivering. "What aren't you telling me?"

"I'm not well. I…" She averted her eyes. "Dr. Goodwin ran some tests. We aren't sure what's wrong but I've got to take it easy."

"How long have you been feeling like this?" Eden asked, scooting close, inhaling the powder-and-lavender scent her grandmother always wore.

"I've known for a while but I didn't want to scare you." Grams wiped her eyes. "I've got a good amount of matured certificates of deposits and most of your parents' death benefits saved but I'm worried about how you're going to maintain this property long-term. I think it's time we consider selling this place so you can have those funds when I'm gone."

Eden touched her chest. "No. No. We can't sell. This has been in our family for decades. That's out of the question. Besides, I make good money teaching online."

"That's not enough to cover your living expenses. If you don't want to sell, then we've got to get the bed-and-breakfast going again. It would mean so much to me to restore this house as one of the best places to visit in town." Grams's voice wobbled. "You don't know how much it hurts to have the neighborhood kids call this place haunted."

Every Halloween, they had their house egged or papered.

Though her insides quaked at the thought of strangers traipsing through their home, Eden nodded. "After all you have done for me, how can I say no?" She gave a little laugh. "I just don't want to repulse the guests."

Her grandmother lifted the hat off Eden's face and ran her fingers down the scar leading from Eden's neck down to her left arm and hands. Eden sat still, clenching her jaw.

"You don't see what I see," Grams whispered. "You're beautiful, inside and out. I wish you would believe me when I tell you that."

Eden looked down at her hands and changed the subject. "The roses are going to be magnificent this year."

"They aren't the only thing that's magnificent. In time, my dear, I hope you'll truly see how valuable, how priceless you are." With a sigh, her grandmother drew Eden into her arms and kissed the top of her head. For someone who was burning up not too long ago, Grams felt cool. Odd. Maybe Dr. Goodwin had given her something. "Now let's get back to the house. We need to put an ad in the town paper, hire a handyman of sorts... Maybe you can make a flyer."

All she could do was nod, watching Grams's flashing eyes as she went on about her plans for the bed-and-breakfast. Eden didn't have the heart to tell her that no one would come. Because no one wanted to work for the girl they called the town monster.

Chapter Two

Even a beast deserved a second chance. But his producers didn't think so. His fans didn't think so. And his rumored married lover didn't think so, either.

Mason Powers sat the computer desk off the living-room area and read the email from his agent for the fourth time then bunched his fists. His television show, *Powers Property Rescue*, based in Columbus, Ohio, had been put on hiatus—which was code for canceled—while they worked out his severance pay.

The sad thing was, he was solely to blame.

He had let the fame and the fortune swell his head. Now he was hiding out from everyone at his agent's home in Blue Hen since the scandal broke. Who lived in Delaware? But he couldn't complain because no one, especially his estranged brother, wanted to have anything to do with him—and though Mason had good reason, he couldn't blame Max.

The chair scraped the floor when he stood and with every step the wood creaked. However, the plumbing and structure in the home was sound. Plus, all the appliances worked. He walked to the window. There was nothing but woods and cornfields for miles with the odd house here and there.

Ugh. He had only been there a week, but Mason had to get out and talk to someone. He couldn't stand his own company at the moment. All he had done was watch the video circling the internet of him giving one of the workers from his show a serious put-down before firing him. All because the man had selected the wrong tile for their home renovation. That's right. Mason admitted his behavior had been ghastly but that didn't mean someone should have photoshopped him into a fire-breathing dragon. The internet was ruthless. And he was a joke.

Before he was jobless, Mason was a sought-after home renovator, handling both the interior and exterior redesign, until he had been dubbed The Ogre of Ohio. His weekly show had been sitting pretty at the number three spot on cable television but had since plummeted into oblivion right along with his job prospects.

Everyone had left him.

Except for his agent, Lydia.

His supposed girlfriend had blocked him on social media and on her cell phone. Not that he minded. The media had made more of their relationship than what was true.

He stormed over to the table, stuck his cap on his head and grabbed the keys to his four-wheel drive pickup before starting up the engine. He backed out of the driveway with force, loving how the gravel spewed in his wake down the long driveway. *Whew*. Mason took a deep breath and decelerated once he was out on the main road, if one could call the narrow strip of pavement that. He remembered passing a deli and a department store a couple miles back and headed in that direction. Three miles later, all he saw was land. He must have made a wrong turn. Since there was no one else around, Mason decided to execute a U-turn. The minute he did that, he heard a loud *pop*.

Pop. Squish. Pop. Squish.

The sounds of his right front tire losing air.

Mason inched onto the curb and cut the engine. He dug into his jeans pocket for his cell phone but there was no service. Slamming a hand on the steering wheel, he shoved the door open with enough force that it swung on its hinges. Then he stomped over to investigate the damage before kicking the hubcap. There was a deep gash, which meant he was stuck here.

Clamping his jaw, he had no choice but to start walking. It was high noon and it was hot. His fury escalated with each step. A half mile down the road, he stopped by a rickety fence, bent low enough that he wondered why the owners hadn't just ripped it out. Then he looked at the house about an eighth of a mile from the gate. It was an odd shade of green. No. It looked like it might have been a light gray before all the moss and dried-up vines covered the house. And the lawn! The lawn had to be about eighteen inches high. If it weren't for the 1970s pickup in the yard, he would have thought the property had been abandoned. He wiped a hand on his jeans. It probably should be condemned and it was an echo of the desolation he felt.

The numbers on the mailbox said 345 and the street

sign said Middle of Nowhere. This couldn't be real. Someone in this town had a ridiculous sense of humor.

Slowly, he made his way up the extended driveway, half-expecting a ghoul or some relative of the Addams Family to jump out at him. But he hoped they had a restroom, so he didn't have to whizz on the side of the road. The closer he got, the more he saw that needed fixing.

On the porch, there was a huge sign on a couch the color of lizard green that said Middle of Nowhere Bed-and-Breakfast. He rolled his eyes. *Really?*

Running up the three steps to the porch, Mason then pressed the doorbell several times before deciding to rap on the door. He cupped his face and peered into the window. Someone was in there. Someone hovered close.

"Hello? Can you please let me in?" he asked.

"Go—go away," a voice said from the other side of the door. "We don't want your business and I've already found Jesus. He was never lost."

Mason cracked up. "I'm not selling anything. I broke down a couple miles back and I really have to use the bathroom. I rang the doorbell…"

"It doesn't work."

Figures. He was not surprised.

After a brief moment, the door cracked open and all he could see was a single suspicious eye trained on him. Mason lifted his hands. "Please, I don't have service around here and I need to get a new tire."

"Eden, let the poor man inside," another voice called out.

"Yes, Eden, please let me in," Mason echoed.

She opened the door and spun away before could get a good look at his rescuer. He stepped across the threshold and gasped. It was like he had stepped back in time. The furnishings and decorations were outdated. He would bet some of the art and decor was from the early eighties. He tilted his head. The foundation appeared to be secure but this place needed some serious TLC. It wasn't dirty. In fact, he could see the glasses sparkling in the wall unit nearby. It was that they were... dated. Definitely not antique, which would be considered chic.

This place needed an overhaul.

"Well, are you going to stand there gazing or are you going to go handle your business?"

Mason jumped. "I'm sorry. I was just taking it all in."

An older woman stood leaning against the wall and crooked her head. Her eyes shone and her smile seemed friendly. "Came to see the haunted house for yourself, huh?"

"What? I don't know what you mean." He shook his head. He had better get out of here. "Where is your restroom, please?"

She pointed to the left. "You can see your way out when you're done." With that she shuffled off in the opposite direction. The younger woman had also ventured off, though he felt eyes on him. She was probably lurking close by to make sure he didn't take anything. With a shrug, Mason walked down the narrow hallway and opened the first door he found. Luckily, it was a half bath smaller than a linen closet. He dipped his head, shut the door and clamped a hand over his mouth.

Pink. Frilly, pink curtains with a matching toilet seat cover. If he were on his show, he would be feigning outrage and ripping these off and tossing them out on the lawn.

He relieved himself and washed his hands before

bending down to peer into the mirror made to accommodate someone of a much shorter stature. Goodness. This place needed…him. It could be magnificent.

Drying his hands with a paper towel placed on top of the toilet cistern, Mason then opened the door and returned to the living-room area. Wow. No one was around. They really were going to let a stranger roam their house at will. Unbothered. Unconcerned. Unheard of in this day and time.

"The exit is to your right," someone said from the staircase. Curious, Mason advanced and held onto the banister. "What are you doing?" Her voice sounded shaky, unsure.

"I just wanted to say thank you," he said. "I'm new here in town." He could see her shadow as she lurked by the turn. Talk about shy. Skittish.

He placed a foot on the step.

"Where are you going?" she asked, sounding fearful.

"Sorry." He took off his cap and ran his fingers through his damp coils. "Do you think I could have some water?"

A hand pointed in no specific direction. "Go help yourself in the kitchen. It's just past the living room. Have a scone. You must be hungry."

"All right, thank you." Mason followed her directions, feeling slightly uneasy. This has got to be the weirdest encounter he had ever had. And in his line of work—well, former line of work—Mason had met some folks with strange quirks. He entered the kitchen and saw three beautiful scones beckoning to him from under a glass cake stand.

His stomach growled. He hadn't eaten anything but a banana that morning. Mouth watering, Mason walked toward the counter. He felt like he was living a real-life version of a thriller film and the drawn blinds and dark interior added to the overall mystique. If he ate one of the desserts, would he pass out and wake up bound and gagged?

Then he chuckled. His imagination was putting in overtime. But it sort of felt like the place was enchanted. Mason took out his cell phone, relieved to see he had bars. He made a quick call to get a tow truck. Mason bit into one of the tastiest, fluffiest treats he had ever had. He groaned.

"Delicious, isn't it?"

Once again, he jumped, this time fumbling to keep the treat from falling to the floor. The elderly woman had returned. "Yes, very," he said, taking another bite. "I didn't hear you approach."

Her lips quirked. He suspected she quite enjoyed spooking him out. She picked up a leg. "It's the socks."

"Grams, you need to be in bed." From the corner of his eye, Mason saw a wide-brimmed hat and half of a body.

"Nonsense," Grams said, walking to the refrigerator. He noticed she was moving slow and was hunched over. "We have to entertain our visitor. Don't get much of them for the past thirteen years. Well, none, actually. Not since the fire." She took out a jug of lemonade and fetched a glass. Coming over to hand it to him, she said, "And such a handsome one at that. What's your name, sugar?"

"Mason," he said, mouth full of food. "Mason Powers."

"He's new in town," the younger woman added. Her voice was light, airy, melodic.

"Yes, I realize that," Grams said, all smiles. "You can call me Susan and my granddaughter's name is Eden." Then she grabbed her stomach and screeched as if she were in pain. "I'd better get back into bed. Come back soon, okay?"

He nodded. "I will, Ms. Susan." He sure as heck wouldn't.

The other woman scuttled over, keeping her head bent under that ginormous hat, and helped her grandmother out of the room. Finished with the snack, he took a taste of the most scrumptious, tart-yet-sweet-at-the-same-time lemonade he had ever had. De-li-cious.

Well, if this place was enchanted and he was stuck here for life, he would be happy with the food. Mason decided to grab another scone and leaned against the counter to savor the treat. His eyes fell on a small stack of letter-size posters. The words *Help Wanted* caught his attention. He picked it up.

It looked like they were seeking a contractor.

"What are you doing?" a voice boomed.

Startled, the paper fell from his hands to the floor. What was up with people sneaking up on him? It was the young lady who refused to give her name. "I see you're looking someone to restore your bed-and-breakfast back to its former glory," he said, quoting the words on the flyer.

She folded her hands. "And what's it to you?"

"Turns out, you're in luck. I'm well qualified, over-qualified actually, but I'll take the job. I specialize in home makeovers." Mason doubted she had ever watched his show.

"You're hired," he heard Ms. Susan yell from the back room.

Eden rolled her eyes but didn't refute her grand-mother. He could see that she wanted to though. Badly.

Mason popped the scone into his mouth, wiped his hands on his jeans and stuck out his hand. "I can start tomorrow."

She drew to her full height and whipped her hat off her head, her eyes glaring, challenging him. He was struck by her beauty and those incredible eyes. Then he saw the scar on her neck and his heart twisted. Mason wondered what had happened to her. He took a step toward her.

Eden lifted a hand, her eyes daring. "Are you sure you want to work here for the town's beast?"

Ah… He knew a thing about being a beast. But it was obvious: her scars were on the outside. His were deeper, darker. She stood, chest heaving, proud, defiant and…vulnerable. He reached out to touch her but before he made contact, she shirked away from him. She bent over to retrieve her hat, placing it just so, so that it hid her face and neck.

"I can start tomorrow," he repeated, gently. "Now I'm sure fate brought me here."

"Suit yourself. Stay out of my way," she snarled and stomped out of the room.

Oh but he had no intention of doing that. Mason intended to be in her way. Very much in her way.

Chapter Three

She had looked him up on his website. He was legit. And, she was guessing, expensive.

"We can't afford him, Grams. He's in the big leagues and won't be satisfied with the small-town life," she said to her grandmother the next morning as she stood by the doorjamb of Grams's bedroom with a huge amount of glee. That was her first argument. The second she wouldn't bring up unless she had to.

Eden didn't know what it was about the tall, lean man with skin the color of ebony, warm brown eyes, and those black, luscious coils that made her insides jump like grasshoppers. Um, she did know, using words like *luscious* to describe his hair. He was sexy, attractive, and the worst part was, he knew it.

No way could she chance that beautiful specimen looking at her with…with repulsion. That's why she planned on staying out of his way if Mason was about to be a fixture in their house. Having him there for hours on end meant she would have to quarantine in her room. The thought of that made her grit her teeth. Although she occupied the largest of the four suites on the second floor, she didn't relish not having free rein of the house.

"Let's hear him out first," Grams whispered, huddling further under her blanket. "I have money saved up for this." Eden shoved down her concerns for her grandmother's welfare. She had checked on Grams multiple times through the night until Grams had told her she was all right and to quit her fussing.

"I can put up the flyers tonight and see if we get someone else," Eden said instead, stepping inside. She wasn't about to go out when everyone was about and the thought of doing so caused her heart to hammer and her palms to sweat.

Grams pinned sharp eyes on Eden. "You said yourself no one would want to work here. I thought you would be relieved that we've found someone without trying. Someone who showed up on our doorstep at the right time." Then Grams's eyes went wide and she placed a hand over her mouth. "You like him?"

Eden backtracked. Leave it to her grandmother to pinpoint her real dilemma. "I—I— No, of course not. What's there to like?" His eyes, his smile, those hands, those lips.

"Oh, plenty. Plenty, my child. My eyes work just fine." Grams sat up and Eden clenched her fists to keep from helping.

"It's my body that has a mind of its own," she huffed, out of breath.

"Yes, I can see that." Eden inched her way inside,

deciding not to continue that conversation track around Mason's good looks. Thankfully, her grandmother didn't either. Besides, if she had thought about him till the wee hours of the night, and if she took extra care with her clothing choice this morning, she would never admit it.

What she would talk about was the other disturbing news she had learned about their new contractor. She cleared her throat. "Grams, I think you need to know that Mason isn't as charming as he appears. He got fired from his television show because, and I quote, he is the Ogre of Ohio. He mistreated his employees and there's a clip of his bad behavior all over the internet."

"Pshaw. That's nothing but gossip. You should know better than anyone that you can't believe everything you hear. How many lies have been told about us through town?"

Shame coursed through her. "But this is different. They have an actual video of his misbehaving."

Her grandmother raised a brow. "Everyone deserves a second chance, don't you agree?"

Yes, how she had yearned for one. How she had ached for her friends to treat her with kindness, instead of looking at her in horror. Eden knew that look on Grams's face. Nothing would change her mind. Eden lifted a hand. "All right. All right. I'll leave it alone, but I plan to keep my eyes on him."

"Yes, I think that's what you need to do," Grams said with a chuckle.

Eden rolled her eyes. "That's not what I—" She flashed a hand. "Ugh, forget it. Do you want me to make you some tea and bring you something to eat?" It was now close to six and she had to check on her roses but she needed to make sure Grams ate first. Eden would eat after she was finished in the garden. Then she would log online to meet with her freshman Composition classes to review before their final the following week.

Grams yawned. "No, I'm good. I just need some rest. I think chopping those walnuts the other day did me in." Um, that wouldn't cause a fever or her being bed-ridden but Eden wouldn't argue. "Ugh. I'm supposed to make some black walnut cakes for Doc and Kyle." Kyle worked for Vic's Grocers, the main supermarket in Blue Hen, as their delivery boy.

"I am going to order a couple bags of walnuts from Vic's, so you don't have to deal with those anymore."

The fact that Vic's was housed on a farm meant they often had a great supply of fresh fruit and veggies and Eden planned to get some watermelons, corn, and a couple bags of cherries. Corn was a must. No one had been happier than Eden when Vic's had finally caught up with the rest of the world and opened up for online shopping and delivery. Now Grams wouldn't have to drive all the way into town on her own, schlepping bags. Eden made sure to stay out of sight during the drop-off. But with Grams being sick, she would put in a request for Kyle to drop the bags and go. The young man would gladly comply as he tended to spray dust from speeding when he vacated their yard.

Grams closed her eyes. "All right. Whatever you think is best."

Those words gave her pause. Her Grams never gave in that easy. "Are you okay, Grams?"

"Yes," she said, nodding, her voice slightly weaker than it had been moments before. "Maybe I'll take you up on that tea after all."

"Sure thing." Eden rushed to prepare the brew, tugging her lower lip through her teeth. After getting her grandmother situated with breakfast and her antibiotics, Eden went outside. Surprisingly, the earth felt moist under her boots. Then she recalled the light pinging of raindrops she had heard while checking on Grams and sighed. If this rain kept up, the Rose Fest might not happen this year. She sloshed through the small puddles and squatted near the bush before letting out a gasp.

The leaves near the root of the bush had holes in them.

Rose slugs.

So much for the coffee grounds, and they were out of coffee beans. Eden rushed inside to get a spray bottle, water and vinegar. Seconds later, chest heaving, she realized there was no vinegar. She slapped her forehead. She had used the last of it the week before. She trounced up the stairs to see if she could add it to her online order, but it was too late. Dashing back down the steps, Eden eyed the truck keys on the key ring by the front door. She could borrow the keys and rush into town. It was early enough that her chances of seeing anyone were slim. Maybe she could order and get curbside delivery. Either way she needed to get moving before she had no leaves left.

Eden grabbed the keys between her hands and opened the front door, then froze. Her legs stayed rooted to the ground and her stomach felt hollow. She couldn't do it. She couldn't leave her self-imposed exile, not even for her beloved roses.

She shut the door and bunched her fists. She was going to spray them with the water hose and remove the slugs one by one if she had to. Eden hated touching the slick critters but what choice did she have? Swinging around, she stomped toward the back of the house. Just before she walked through the door, the house phone rang.

She scurried over to answer just in case it was the doctor calling. But it wasn't Dr. Goodwin's voice she heard. It was the one who made her stomach quiver.

"Hello, I was calling to see if you needed anything. I have to stop at the department store before coming there," Mason said. "You all live a good distance away, so I thought I'd ask."

She squinted at the phone, feeling suspicious for no reason at his impeccable timing, when this was of course a coincidence. It was on the tip of her tongue to tell Mason she didn't need anything and hang up, but her roses gave her pause. "Y-yes. I could use a bottle of vinegar, some baking soda and some coffee beans for my rose garden. I—I'll pay you back when you get here." Then with a quick thank you, she hung up the phone. Touching her chest, she drew deep breaths. Just talking to him had raised her heart rate. How was she going to survive having him around?

The phone rang again.

She fluttered her lashes. If that was him again…

It was the head of the English department, Dr. Loft. "Eden? We need to talk. One of your students, Naomi Bush, has lodged a complaint against you for biased grading. She says you gave her a lower grade over another student for the same assignment."

Biased grading? Eden gripped the phone before placing it closer to her ear. "I don't understand. I use a rubric for grading, and I go over all the expectations plus I offer extended office hours. Naomi never took me up on it. In fact, she has missed the last two classes." Sweat lined her brow. In her three years of working for them, she had never had any complaints. Anger whirled in her chest, but she couldn't let her temper get the best of her.

"I understand and I know how much you do for your students, but she is adamant that this is the case and is demanding a regrade. She is sending me both papers to look over to prove her case. Let's set a meeting for the three of us can discuss everything. How about you come in next week?"

Panic lined her stomach like rocks on the ocean. "C-can we set something up online instead?" That way Eden could go on camera and still hide in the shadows. She had the perfect vantage point in her room.

"I really think you should come in person, my dear."

"I—I..." She inhaled and raked her teeth across her bottom lip. "I have a lot going on here. Please can we meet online next week? I have a few days after the finals before I need to submit final grades so we can meet anytime after then."

There was a brief pause before Dr. Loft agreed. "I'll send you the login information. Look out for my email."

Relief curved her shoulders. "Great. I'll wait to hear from you."

"While I have you on the phone, I'd like for us to have a conversation on another matter," Dr. Loft said, raising Eden's anxiety levels all over again. But this time, she had an idea what this was about. The college had been pressuring her to accept a full tenure position but that would mean taking on face-to-face courses and she didn't do...in person. Though her therapist urged her to do so, constantly told her, she wasn't ready.

"Sure. We can talk after Naomi," she said, when Dr. Loft brought up that very issue.

"Okay. That will work. Look out for the invite."

Eden hung up the phone. Her eyes fell on one of the flyers advertising for the position and she curled her fists. She dipped her head to her chest. If her job forced her to come in person, she would have to quit. She didn't have the level of confidence to overcome the looks of disgust and the derision when the students saw her scars, learned her past. It looked like they were going to need Mason after all. And she hated needing anyone, having learned the only person she could depend on was herself…and Grams.

A small sliver of jealousy coursed through her. Mason had been called a beast, like she had been. But the difference was, he appeared to be…trying. He had grabbed this opportunity at a job. A do-over. While she was stuck here in the past.

No.

She was at a good place now in the present. It had taken her years to achieve this kind of…self-acceptance. She saw no reason to change that status quo. But it appeared as if she might not have a choice.

Chapter Four

Mason stalked down the aisle, the owner of the department store on his heels.

"Are you sure you know that you're going to the Middle of Nowhere?" Calvin asked. "No one goes out there unless they have to. Besides Doc and Vic's son, Kyle, nobody enters that property. It's creepy."

"I'm sure." Praying for patience, Mason pushed the cart with enough force to cause the wheels to rattle. The space was too small for them to be side by side, but Calvin sure was trying. Stopping midway, Mason raised his arm above the shorter man's head to grab crowbars, hammers, sledgehammers and other tools and such. His cart was already half-full. When he had been escorted off the set, Mason hadn't been able to take any of the tools with him, so he had to settle with what was in this store.

Although, one benefit was that he was supporting this local business.

"You know that place is haunted? Overrun with rodents and bug infestations."

Mason didn't bother to answer. Instead, he made his way to the next aisle to grab safety gear. It had been a minute since he had had to shop for his own tools and he was actually enjoying it, despite his undesired and unnecessary companion.

When he first entered the store, Calvin had been starstruck and Mason had obliged him with a few pictures, especially since Mason had needed to put up his own help wanted signs. All had been well until Mason had shared his intended destination. For the past ten minutes, Calvin had been determined to dissuade him from going back to the Middle of Nowhere Bed-and-Breakfast. But what the other man didn't know was Mason needed—and wanted—this job. He wasn't a man who liked to sit idle for days on end. That's how he had been for thirty-three years and he didn't see that changing, ever. Mason loved the long hours and seeing a house everyone believed should be demolished restored and made even better. Once he had gotten his tire mended, Mason had gone home to work on some preliminary sketches on his iPad to go over with Eden and Ms. Susan.

Thinking about Eden—something he had done too much of since he had met her—made him realize he didn't want to forget to get the items she requested. "Where can I find vinegar?" he asked the owner.

"On the other side of the store," Calvin replied. "By the cooking oil."

With a nod, Mason went to search for it, grabbing the

coffee beans on the way. Another customer had called out to Calvin for assistance, for which Mason was more than grateful. He didn't want to hear any negative talk about Eden and Ms. Susan.

Not when they had given him a job. A fresh start.

For the first time in months, he had something else to do than troll social media to see what was being said about him. The brouhaha probably would have died down if his supposed girlfriend, Steffie, hadn't kept it going. As soon as the scandal broke, she had made sure to tout on social media that he had pursued her. Which was a lie but great fodder for her reality TV stint. The higher her ratings climbed, the more she added to the story. The more dirt she threw his way, the more innocent she appeared. Never mind that Mason hadn't known Steffie was estranged from her husband when they met. Or that they'd never had an intimate relationship but were in the getting-to-know-you phase. And she neglected to mention that he had broken things off as soon as her spouse contacted him and asked Mason to kindly leave his wife alone. No one cared about the truth. Apparently, her husband didn't either, because the last he checked, they had reconciled. Well, good for them.

Lesson learned. Money brought out bad behavior.

He could definitely testify to that. That's why he hadn't refuted the rumors. Mason knew all too well how success was an aphrodisiac and how it came with a certain level of power that made one feel invulnerable, untouchable.

Until you weren't.

Briefly, he wondered if he should disclose the ghastly details of his show and firing to Eden and Ms. Susan.

With his celebrity status, it would only be a matter of time before they found out from somebody in town. Although, they appeared to be somewhat reclusive... Naw. He would tell them. That's the man that he was. If they decided to fire him, he'd be disappointed, but he would understand.

After grabbing the box of baking soda, Mason made his way to the checkout line, avoiding eye contact with the other patrons. Seeing a cowboy hat on a rack near the register, Mason plopped it on his head and tugged it low.

Right as he finished paying for his goods, his agent, Lydia Silverstein, called.

"How goes it?" she asked, her voice husky from years of smoking. Even though she had quit that habit, Lydia tended to have a cigarette in her mouth. Said she loved the feel of it. There was a huge crack of thunder. The skies had darkened a bit.

"It's going. I got a job, actually," he said, surprised at the enthusiasm in his voice.

"Oh?" Lydia sounded intrigued. He supposed it was because he hadn't provided the usual dejected response. The cart cling-clanged the entire way to his truck.

"Yes, I'm renovating the town's supposed haunted mansion." He opened the bed of his pickup and began putting his purchases inside.

"Say what? Tell me more."

He chuckled. "Yeah, the owner of the department store swore he has seen at least ten ghosts on the property at Halloween." Then he gave her the rundown of how he had gotten lost, ended up on the property and left with employment.

"I love it." She cackled. "How about I see if I can

string a crew together to record your shenanigans? I'm almost positive I could get this picked up. You could make a comeback. Plus, I don't know if you realize it, but your getting stranded up in a grand house in a deserted part of town screams *Beauty and the Beast* to me. Producers will eat this up."

The excitement in her voice was a siren, the thought of regaining his former television glory, a lure. He would be lying if he wasn't tempted. But then he pictured Ms. Susan's trusting face. And Eden's flash of daring when she had whipped off her hat and challenged him to see her as a beast. He thought about her scars and how she hid her beauty, her vulnerability. And those remarkable eyes. Eyes that had filled his sleep the night before. Nope. Mason couldn't exploit them like that, couldn't think of the hurt he could cause Eden by agreeing to this venture.

"Well?" Lydia asked. He could picture her tapping her pen, looking through her old-fashioned Rolodex and thinking of who she could call.

"I'll pass," he said.

"Has all that fresh air gotten to your head? Just a day or two ago you were all about clawing your way back to the top brick by brick if you had to. Your words, not mine. Remember?"

Mason tossed the hat in the back, slammed the door closed and returned the cart to one of the designated areas. "Lydia, I'm not doing it. I haven't lost my ambition, I just hate…hurting people." The truth of his words grounded him. He had done enough wrong to his family, to his former employees and here was his chance to do something right. "We'll think of something else."

"Humph…"

He knew that tone. She wasn't going to drop this idea. "Lydia, I'm serious. Get me a new publicist and strategize."

"Got it." She disconnected the call but Mason wasn't bothered. Lydia was old enough to be his mother but she worked for him. Not the other way around.

Mason felt a plop hit his nose and looked upward. There was a gray streak across the horizon. Another plop hit his cheek and he bustled to his truck. He'd better get going to the Middle of Nowhere before the rain started. Not that it mattered with what he had planned for today. Today was all about going over his specs with Ms. Susan, hearing her vision, and then working out a timeline and budget. He was also going to have to hire someone to assist. He could use a crew of five but if others in the town shared Calvin's superstition, he couldn't see that happening.

More drops of rain on his windshield made him get a move on. He sent Ms. Susan a text.

On my way.

Fortunately, he was able to find his way back to the bed-and-breakfast without getting lost, using the tow truck driver's explicit directions. Just as he pulled up, the rain ceased and sunshine peeked through the clouds. To his left, he could see the rose bushes lined up in neat rows. Now he knew that had to be Eden's handiwork.

Mason rapped on the door, then picked up the bags and his iPad just as Ms. Susan answered his text message. Give me about twenty minutes. Eden will let you inside. His heart galloped in his chest and Mason knew that had nothing to do with the task at hand and everything to do with the young woman inside. She opened the door a crack, then stepped aside to let him in with a grunt for a greeting. Then she headed toward the kitchen.

He followed behind. "Where should I put the stuff you wanted?" he asked, hoping she would pin those gorgeous eyes on him. Mason wasn't sure why he was fascinated by her after one meeting when he could call a number of women who would be delighted if he showed any interest.

"On the counter is fine," she whispered, her voice barely above a decibel.

Then she sniffled.

After resting the bag on the counter, Mason went over to where she stood, with her back turned and her arms wrapped around her. "Are you all right?" She was once again dressed in a high collar blouse with long sleeves and a pair of tan shorts. He gave her toned, tanned legs an appreciative glance. And wouldn't he love to run his fingers through those strands. He had caught a glimpse of her hair before she stuffed it under her hat.

Mason sighed. This sudden infatuation had him feeling like he was nineteen instead of a man, fully grown. He should be able to control this attraction. Fortunately, Eden had no clue how fascinating he found her. He placed a tentative hand on her shoulder, expecting her to shrug him off. "What's wrong?" he asked, his hand tingling from contact. She tensed but she didn't rebuff him, although she had yet to answer. Dang it, if his heart didn't skip a little.

Then she faced him and wrung her fingers. The desolation etched on her face gave him pause. Bravely, he lifted her chin with his index finger. "What's got you all in your feelings?" To Mason, at that moment, she appeared as delicate, as lovely, as the roses she was trying to cultivate in her garden.

For a second, she leaned into his palm and he stood still, afraid to scare her off like a deer in the forest. Then she drew in a shaky breath and tilted her head away from him. "Don't touch me. You don't know me like that." Ah... here were the prickly thorns. She was probably upset with herself for showing any sign of weakness.

He lifted a hand. "I'm sorry. I just saw that you had been crying and I just wanted to help."

Her lips curled. "The only help I need from you is the kind you get paid to do." She jammed a hand in her pocket and pulled out a ten-dollar bill and thrust it toward him. "This should more than cover the cost of the items you picked up for me." She placed her tongue between her teeth and muttered a begrudging *thank you* before stalking over to the counter and digging into the bag. Then she reached for an empty spray bottle and poured vinegar inside before adding water.

Everything about her body language said she didn't want to be bothered with anyone—especially him. Normally, Mason would back off because he had a tankful of pride in his chest. But something compelled him to continue the conversation. "What are you going to do with them?" He went to stand by her side, all up in her space, loving the scent of apples and—he sniffed—champagne? Whatever that concoction was, it smelled heavenly. Too bad he couldn't say the same regarding the attitude of the woman wearing it.

"If you must know, I'm using this as a repellent for the rose slugs who decided to attack my rose bushes overnight. I was plucking away at them when the rain started pouring." She shook up her concoction and put on a pair of gardening gloves. "But this will zap them in no time." Her face held a wicked glee that made his lips quirk.

"Can I watch?" Mason asked.

Those cognac eyes slid his way. "Don't you have things to do?"

"Yes, but your grandmother texted that she needed twenty minutes, so…" He reached for his phone to show her the text message.

Eden pursed her lips. "I suppose I could use your help. The slugs are chomping away on my leaves." Then she went to get another spray bottle to make another bottle of repellant.

Mason was not a fan of the slimy creatures, but he wasn't about to make that known. Instead, he said, "I'm happy to go slugging with you."

She shook her head. "You can't resist, can you?" She did not sound amused.

"What?"

"Flirting? I've seen videos of you online with a woman on each arm." So, she had been checking him out. Interesting. He placed a hand on his chin. And was that a hint of jealousy he detected? But before he could mull on that or explain that had been a publicity stunt, Eden continued. "And, I see how you left Steffie Newman heartbroken." Her tone held contempt. "Going after a married woman is just…abhorrent. Beastly."

That stung. "You don't know me at all to judge me like that," Mason shot back through clenched teeth. "You have no right to pass judgment when you don't have all the facts." His chest heaved. Oh, he was in full spar-mode, but instead of a frosty comeback, she swung around, grabbed her hat and headed outside the kitchen, the screen door slamming behind her. Oh no, they weren't ending things like that. He grabbed the spray bottle and stormed after her.

She was spraying the slugs on the grass, having placed the baking soda on her stool. They were fat and green and squirmy.

"You owe me an apology," he said. She shrugged. Oh, so it was like that? Fine. He sought out slugs on the leaves and pumped twice.

"No!" she called out, coming over to touch his arm. "What are you doing? You will damage the rosebush if you spray vinegar on it."

"How was I supposed to know that?" he snapped, feeling bad for possibly ruining her roses. "You didn't give me any directions." The spray bottle hung loosely in his arms.

Eden lifted her shoulders and took a deep breath. Then she addressed him in a somewhat friendlier tone. "You're right. I'm sorry. For judging you and for expecting you, an amateur, to know what to do with these pests. I should have given you instructions."

His brows rose. "What? Can you repeat that?" Mason made a show of taking out his cell phone to hit record. "I have to have this on playback."

She chuckled and gave his arm a playful shove. "I'm not that bad, am I?" Before he could respond, she stopped him. "Don't answer that." She exhaled and held out a hand. "Can we start over?" Eden asked. "I'm not used to handsome strangers all up in my space." His chest puffed. Handsome? But before he could bask in that compliment, she continued. "I received a tough phone call earlier and it put me on edge." She swallowed. "I'm sorry for taking it out on you."

"Apology accepted," he said, with a wave. "Yes, we can definitely start over." He held out a hand. "I'm Mason Powers, retired Ogre of Ohio. Pleased to meet you."

She giggled. Her laughter was like light and airy piano keys. "I'm Eden Tempest, Beast from the Middle of Nowhere. Happy to make your acquaintance." She slipped off her gardening gloves.

They shook hands and shared a smile.

Her hands felt small and delicate in his.

Gosh, she was beautiful when she sulked. But when she smiled like this, she was radiant. Breathtaking, actually. Mason's feet drew closer following his will. He saw her pupils narrow from newfound awareness. She fiddled with her collar and a red hue spread across her cheeks. If that wasn't the most adorable thing he had ever seen. A true sign of her innocence.

And an even bigger indication of why he should leave her alone.

Mason put some space between them, ruing the question in her eyes, particularly since he knew she would be insulted by his answer. Which was that he was afraid of corrupting her. He touched her curls, moving in the slight breeze. "Why did that phone call upset you?" he asked gently.

She licked her lips. "I don't want to talk about that now." Eden placed a hand on his chest then removed it quickly. "Do you?"

Nope. No. Not at all. His little beauty might be a minx in disguise. Oh what an intriguing discovery that would be if that were true. But he couldn't forget that she was indirectly his boss. Well, her grandmother was but he knew better than to muddle the waters.

His cell phone buzzed with another text from Ms. Susan. Can we do this tomorrow?

Sure, he texted back. I can email my plans if you'd like. Mason had spent a good number of hours working out the concrete details of all his recommendations for the interior and exterior as well as a projection of the costs and labor. It was an enormous feat, but she should be exultant with the end results.

Perfect. Ms. Susan included her email address.

Mason cleared this throat and glanced at Eden. "Seems like my schedule has opened up for the rest of the afternoon." He raised the bottle. "Should we get to spraying?"

"What? Argh." It took a beat but then her mouth formed an O and she cupped her cheeks. "Y-yes. The slugs." She scurried back over to the rosebushes, all business. "You can pluck them off the leaves and I will zap them with the vinegar."

"Erm. How about I zap and you pluck?" He suppressed a shudder before offering a logical excuse. "I don't have gloves."

She looked like she was about to call his bluff but then she pressed her lips together, like she was hiding a smile. "You got it." She sped off to tackle the bugs.

Watching her, Mason smiled. From her determined look, those slugs didn't stand a chance. He shoved his hands in his jeans pocket and chuckled. Though he hated the debacle that brought him here, he didn't have any regret making Eden's acquaintance. He admired her spunk and their spats were becoming a highlight in his day.

She looked up at him, shielding her eyes. "Get to work."

With a salute, he did just that. The task should have been tedious but with Eden by his side and their banter, Mason quite enjoyed it. Plus, they later shared a pizza pie and every now and again, their shoulders touched. She stiffened each time and Mason hoped she would grow less skittish with having him around.

When he pulled up to Lydia's place that night, his muscles were sore from bending over but he felt proud of his efforts and...grounded. Even Eden had praised him for rubbing shoulders with the common folk. Mason checked his cell phone and saw he had missed a call from Lydia. She had even texted him to give her a call.

He tossed the phone on the nightstand. He didn't want to talk shop tonight. Tomorrow. Tomorrow he would return her call. But tonight, he would go to sleep dreaming of a certain small-town girl.

Chapter Five

A week following the slug fiasco, Eden sat cross-legged on her bed and opened her laptop screen. Her roses appeared to be on track to bloom. Hope sprang in her chest about the Rose Fest. She pulled up her online meeting and entered the waiting room. Outside the sun was shining and the temperature was in the eighties but she had stayed in to grade student papers, wash her hair, paint her toes. A few seconds later, her therapist's face filled her screen. Ramona had a buzz cut and wore huge earrings which made her look more like an artist than a therapist.

"I was so glad to get your call," Ramona said once the perfunctory greetings were out the way. Her cheerful voice never failed to calm the quivers in Eden's stomach. "So, catch me up on what's been going on with you since we last met."

"I'm almost done with the spring semester at the university," Eden said. "I've enjoyed it so much, but I don't know if I'll be able to keep working there."

Ramona cocked her head. "What's going on?" For a brief second, Mason's face flashed before her. He had been working sixteen-hour shifts on one of the three master suites on the main floor. After their slug-removal adventure, Eden had kept out of his way, staying in her room and only coming out when he was gone. But she wasn't ready to talk about why she was avoiding the handsome contractor, so she broached her other main concern.

"A student accused me of biased grading," she began. Just saying the words made her fury kindle but she wasn't going to let that anger spread.

Ramona's brows rose. "Oh wow. That sounds serious."

She waved a hand. "I'm trying not to get upset or worry about it. I have enough evidence to support the grade she received. It's the in-person meeting that's making me feel like I'm going to break out in hives."

"Ah!" Ramona moved closer to the screen. "If you think about it, this is the opportunity we have been talking about. One of your goals for this year was to come out of your shell—make a friend or two."

Her heart palpitated. "I know but it's not as easy as I thought. The other day I needed to get some supplies and without thinking I grabbed the keys and started to head out. But I froze. I couldn't even walk through the door." She sniffled from the sudden tears and looked upward. "Like, why am I like this?"

"You are letting your past hold you back inside this house," the therapist said gently. "The guilt from losing your parents has imprisoned you and it's time you put it in its place and set yourself free. You made a mistake, Eden. You were a child, and very much human."

"No, what I did was monstrous. I don't get to have a second chance." She swallowed and wiped her face with the back of her hand. "My parents didn't, so why should I?"

Ramona cocked her head. "If you will excuse me, I am going to have a fierce conversation with you. I'm a mom and I can tell you there isn't a parent alive who would want their child burdened with this shame. I will take the liberty and speak for them and tell you that they have forgiven you. You need to do the same."

How she wished that were true. Eden sobbed. "I don't remember their voices," she admitted. "That's the worst part of all this. I wish I could hear my mother sing again and my father's laugh. I'd give…anything."

"Eden, I'm going to say something, and it might come across as real insensitive, but it has to be said." Ramona rubbed her nose and drew in a deep breath. Then she pinned Eden with a stern look. "You can't change what is. You can only change what will be. Your parents are gone and there is no bringing them back."

Eden reared back, her stomach muscles tight. "Wow. That's kind of harsh. Aren't therapists supposed to be sensitive?"

"But it's your reality and I can't tiptoe around the truth. It's called radical acceptance." Eden wished Ramona would lighten up a bit but her therapist was speaking her mind today. "You have to radically accept the things you don't like because you can't change them. You can fight and fight and try to make things different but there has to be acceptance as well. Now acceptance does not mean you agree with what happened but

since you can't change it, you must learn to accept it."
She pointed a finger at the screen. "Roll up your shirt
and look at your scars."

Eden straightened at Ramona's tone. "I don't know—"

"Go ahead and do it."

She pulled up her sleeves.

"Those scars have been a part of you for thirteen
years. It's time you embrace them and see them for what
they are."

"What are they? Hideous markings?"

"No, child, they are your victory symbols of survival.
You fought life and won."

She looked at the scars lining her neck through her
arms and gulped. All she could see was the raging fire
and her parents' still faces.

Ramona gave her some suggestions and strategies
and at the end of their session, Eden gave a half-hearted
promise to venture to the store before they met again.
Of course, it was easy to do since Eden didn't intend
to schedule another session anytime soon.

Eden trounced down the stairs to see her grandmother, who was up and about, in the kitchen. Grams's
appetite had returned along with her cooking. Eden and
Mason had eaten well the day before. Judging from the
strong scent of cinnamon and vanilla, she would say her
grandmother had baked cinnamon buns. Eden's go-to
when she needed a pick-me-up. Sure enough, the buns
were cooling on the counter.

The tears were immediate. "Grams, how do you always know?"

Grams shrugged. "Intuition." Her lips quirked. "Or
it could be the fact that you've closeted yourself in your
room because of a certain someone?" Eden looked out-

side the window to see that Mason's truck was gone. She buried the pierce of disappointment and continued her conversation.

"I was just talking to Ramona and she said some things that really shook me up."

Grams proceeded to ice the buns. "Oh?"

"Basically she said I should celebrate my scars, calling them victory symbols."

"I always knew that Ramona Giles was a smart one. I knew her when she was a little girl running after dandelions in our garden—well, when we had a garden— and she was precocious and full of life. And so caring. I completely agree with her advice."

Eden wrapped her arms about herself. "You know what else she said? She said Mom and Dad would have forgiven me and how I need to do the same."

"She's right, you know." Grams came over to hug her close. "You're too hard on yourself. And it's time for a mind shift. Change the way you view things." A door slammed, signaling Mason's return, and her grandmother gave her a pointed look. "And, you need to change your attitude about certain people."

Whatever. She stopped short of rolling her eyes. Grams wouldn't go for that. The door creaked and Mason strolled in holding a cardboard box with some containers.

"I brought Chinese for lunch. I ordered a little bit of everything." He sniffed then patted his stomach. "Is that cinnamon I smell? My mouth is already watering." Mason placed the food on the counter.

"Oh, thank you, Mason. How thoughtful. You spared us eating cinnamon buns for dinner," Grams said, reaching for spoons. *As if.* Grams would have whipped up some chili or Eden would have made grits and eggs. "Eden, you want to set the table?" she asked.

"In the dining room?" Eden knew her eyes were wide. They usually ate in their rooms or at the kitchen table. It had been, well, years, since they ate in that space but before she could process how she felt about it, Mason picked up their meal.

"Yes," Grams said with a soft smile.

"O-okay." Yet, Eden hesitated.

"Hang on, let me wipe down the table first," Grams said, grabbing a rag and furniture polish. She said to Mason, "You can get the place mats."

He placed the cardboard container down and picked up the cloth mats. The threading on the edges were frayed and old. She imagined Mason was used to much fancier table settings but he didn't seem to mind.

Eden reached upward to retrieve plates then gasped. She still had her sleeves rolled up. Her scars had been visible this entire time. Had Mason noticed? She bit her lower lip, hating how her eyes misted over. Of course he had. For a second panic coursed through her being and she was tempted to escape to her room, even while her voice within challenged her to be brave. And she wondered if her fear was more about her pride than of people's reactions.

But then he returned and came up behind her. "Eden, can I help you with anything?"

He was acting...normal. Yes, he had glimpsed the wounds to her neck, but the ones on her arms were much worse, a visual memory of the fire licking at her flesh while she attempted to get to her parents on the second floor.

"Eden?" He placed a hand on her shoulder and bent to look into her eyes.

A sob broke free.

"What is it?" he asked, enfolding her in his arms and drawing her close.

"Y-you didn't..." Oh goodness, she was a mess. And...rather dramatic. "You didn't look at me with scorn." She curved into him.

"Wh—" He touched her chin. "Eden, do you think me so...superficial that I would be repulsed by something that must have happened to you as a child?" The wonder in his tone showed he was genuinely surprised at her assumption.

Before she could answer, Grams called out to them to come and eat. She left her sleeves rolled up though she did decide to visit the half bath to wash her face and hands. She opened the door and drew in a sharp breath before looking around. Gone were the pinks and frills. He had replaced the toilet bowl, mounted a circular white ceramic bathroom sink and installed a gold brass waterfall faucet. She stepped onto the new woven marble tiles and turned on the faucet. Eden let it run for a few seconds, admiring the smooth fall, before remembering that Mason and Grams were probably waiting on her to eat.

She dried her hands, then caught up with Mason who was now entering the dining area. "That bathroom looks beyond amazing. It feels so spacious." She rubbed her hands together. "I can't wait to see the rest of your plans."

"Thank you. It took me longer than I anticipated but the end results were worth it." He puffed his chest.

"Wait until you see what I have planned for the kitchen. That's next on my list. But I definitely need some help."

Seated at the head of the table, Grams smiled. "I see you finally enjoyed the fruits of Mason's labor."

"Yes. Oh, my goodness." She slipped in the chair to the left and addressed Mason. "I hope someone answers your ad for help soon. Although I doubt it."

Mason made sure to sit next to her. "Ms. Susan allowed me to post a picture of the bathroom so I might get some takers after that."

"I'll try to help if I can."

"Thanks, I might have to take you up on that." His arm grazed hers and she studied him from under her lashes to see if he was pretending to be unfazed by her scars. But no, he didn't appear to be thinking about any of that. Mason was too busy getting Grams to talk all about Eden's antics as a child. At times, she joined in the conversation, but mostly she reflected on her grandmother's words. She did need a mind shift. Sliding a glance Mason's way, she decided Mason might be willing to help her.

All she had to do was ask.

And that's how they ended up sitting in his pickup outside the flower shop the next morning. Her heart was pounding and her palms sweaty. Now all she had to do was get out of the truck, go inside the store and purchase a bag of fertilizer.

No big whoop.

Except…she knew the person behind the counter. Cadence Witherspoon.

A former best friend who had been especially mean and unkind after her parents' death and her first days back at school. The flower shop had large windows and she had spotted Cadence talking with a customer when they pulled up.

"I can't go in there," she whispered, pulling her hat further down her face.

When she explained why, Mason reminded her, "Sounds like that was years ago, Eden. When you were in high school? Haven't you changed since then?"

"Yes... I have." She gave Cadence a furtive glance and made a confession. "The thing is, we used to be friends." His eyes went wide. "But we were more like frenemies. Mean girls, together." She scoffed. "I don't know why I thought that there would be some loyalty between us."

"Ah... I see. But again, that is in the past. A lot could have happened between then and now. Besides, I'll be right here watching."

Eden squared her shoulders. "You're right. There's only way to find out." She gripped the door handle, pushed the door open and got out. Sweat lined her forehead but knowing Mason was observing everything gave her a small boost of confidence.

Just as she was entering, the customer was coming through the door, so she held the door open and held her breath. The lady barely spared her a glance and went on her way. *So far, so good.* She stepped inside, enjoying the cool blast of air. To her right was the checkout area which had various floral displays and a refrigerator that stored the cut bouquets. Cadence had her head lowered and was cutting a piece of baby blue ribbon for a bouquet she was putting together. To her left were different kinds of plants that needed to be in cooler temperatures as well as an assortment of teddy bears, vases and balloons.

"Welcome to Blue Hen's Garden and Flower Shop," Cadence called out, sounding cheery and welcoming. She had on a green-and-pink shirt which matched the decor of the store.

Eden grunted and sped up her footsteps, almost knocking into the greeting card stand. She headed straight toward the back where she could see a bags of mulch and fertilizer. There were also various kinds of repellants and other gardening supplies. By this time her heartbeat pounded in her ears. *You've got this.*

Ignoring the heat in that section, Eden scurried over and scooped the large bag in her arms then she dashed to checkout. She hoped Cadence would be too preoccupied to pay her any attention. But this was a small town. No one in Blue Hen could resist making small talk. As soon as she rested the bag on the counter, her chest rose and fell in rapid succession.

Cadence put aside her bouquet and gave Eden a wide smile. Eden watched the other woman's mouth drop. "Eden?" Eden froze, her eyes going wide like a deer caught in the road. Cadence narrowed her eyes and leaned forward. "It is you!" She placed a hand on her hip and smirked. "Well, well, well. I didn't know the Beast of Blue Hen would ever show her face in these parts."

Her tone might have been teasing but all Eden heard were the words *the Beast of Blue Hen.* All her confidence deflated. She was foolish to think Cadence would have changed. Spinning around, Eden stormed out of the flower shop, ignoring Cadence yelling, "Wait! Wait!"

Jumping in the vehicle, she ordered Mason to get them out of there, saying she would get the fertilizer online. No matter how much he prodded, Eden refused to tell him what happened. She kept her head trained outside the window and was out of the pickup before he even put the gear in the park. She darted up the stairs then retreated into her room, slamming the door behind her.

She dropped onto her bed. Only then did she allow the tears to fall. As she cried, Cadence's words haunted her. Her body shook as she poured out, her tears soaking her pillow. No matter how much time passed, the people here would only see her as a beast.

Eden would let Dr. Loft know this would be her final semester if they were transitioning to in-person classes, because she was never leaving this house again.

Chapter Six

Someone had finally answered his ad. That very morning at 7:00 a.m. Mason had hired Gabriel Sampson immediately, dispensing with the usual interview, and now Gabriel was on his way. Mason hadn't been so happy to receive a phone call in a long time. He couldn't renovate the house on his own and he needed strong hands. Over the past four days since the disaster at the flower shop, Eden had kept her distance. She stayed in her room, choosing to eat her meals there.

Ms. Susan had asked him to give Eden some time when he inquired about her. All he could do was nod, his chest tight. He missed her. It didn't make any sense because he didn't know her for long, but it was the truth, nonetheless. He liked talking to her and it wasn't like she had a cell phone so he could text her some cute emojis. And even if he could, he didn't dare climb those stairs and enter her private area.

Not seeing her didn't quell this obsession either. His eyes strained for a glimpse of her curls and his ears remained cocked for the sound of her footsteps. But nothing. Mason had no idea when she worked in her garden but it had to be at the crack of dawn because he hadn't spotted her out there and he arrived at six most days. But the rosebuds were about to bloom. Ms. Susan told him they would open in time for Rose Fest on June 20. Mason had already promised to help Ms. Susan carry them to the festival.

Now he stood on the front lawn, beside the huge dumpster he had rented, and waited for his new hire to arrive. Finally, an F-150 pulled in front of the gate. He watched the vehicle stall and prayed that Gabriel hadn't changed his mind. But then the truck turned and trekked slowly down the path, a trailer with various lawn equipment in tow.

Yes! Mason bunched his fists and walked up to the car to greet the other man. Gabriel got out and gave him a firm handshake. Gabe stood a good three inches above Mason's six-one frame, and he was brawny with his hair slicked back in a ponytail. If his former show producers saw Gabe, they would have snapped him up as a cast member.

Mason smiled. "You don't know how you made my day saying you were willing to start today."

"I recently got laid off my landscaping job and I've been doing odd jobs here and there but I can't go long without a solid paycheck, so I decided it wouldn't hurt to answer your ad." Gabe, as he preferred to be called, surveyed the yard and the house. "This here is a major undertaking. I do also have experience in construction, and I've dabbled a little bit in everything, so I can do whatever you need."

"That's good to hear," he said, patting Gabe on the back. "Let me show you what I have done so far." He led Gabe inside, noting how Gabe hesitated before stepping inside the home. Ms. Susan had gone into town to run errands and pick up groceries and Eden, of course, was in her suite.

"I was a teen the last time I came here," Gabe said, his eyes sweeping the kitchen. "Eden used to throw the best parties."

"You know her?"

"Yeah. Not sure she would remember me, though." He chuckled. "I was the class nerd. She used to tease me mercilessly back then."

He defended Eden in her absence. "Oh, really? The woman I know now is really sweet." Well, sort of. Mason led him to the bathroom to take a look.

Gabe stopped. "I do remember her being super smart and helping me out in my computer class." Ducking into the half bath, he whistled. "You did a bang-up job in here."

Mason's chest puffed. "Yes, I got rid of a closet to widen it a little." He pulled up his phone to show Gabe the before-and-after pictures.

"Whoa. The transformation is beyond impressive."

And he had done it all himself. "I'm almost finished with the two master suites down here, but I need to lift up the carpeting and replace some of the flooring. The house is in pretty good shape structurally."

Gabe tapped the wall in different places and then nodded. "Seems like it. That makes your job a little easier."

"I do want to give the kitchen an overhaul. But I'll save that for right before the living and dining areas."

Mason then proceeded to show Gabe his plans. The other man's face lit up. "You have great vision." Then he gave Mason a somber look. "I'm sorry that you lost your television show."

All he could do was nod. "I deserved it."

Gabe cackled. "Well, every now and again, a man's britches get too tight, and he makes a move and splits his pants. It's humbling. You know what I mean?"

Mason straightened. Did he ever. Gabe was obviously someone who spoke his mind. Mason liked that, especially since it was the truth. He had gotten swellheaded and lorded his power over his employees. "I suppose you're right."

"I know I am." Gabe pierced him with a penetrating gaze. "A real man learns from his mistakes and doesn't repeat them."

Hearing the slight warning in Gabe's tone, Mason dipped his head. "Oh, I have learned, and I have every intention of mending my ways."

"Great. Then we will work well together." Without pausing for air, Gabe launched into giving ideas toward the renovation that were sound but cost-effective. Evidently, Gabe was also more than a landscaper, but Mason wouldn't pry. By the end of the day, Gabe had helped him with the flooring, cut the lawn, and was now hacking away at the vines on the house, leaving the area with Eden's rosebushes alone.

At one point, Mason saw the curtains shift on the upper floor and he figured that Eden had peeked out to make sure her flowers remained unscathed. But when he waved, she had skirted away out of sight, the curtains falling back into place.

Ms. Susan came tearing down the driveway. He rushed to help her take the groceries into the house, performing introductions. Gabe came to lend a hand as well, introducing himself to Ms. Susan.

She waved him off and tilted her head back to look at Gabe. "I know who you are, Gabriel Sampson, even though you've lost the thick glasses and fixed that gap between your teeth."

"I'm glad you didn't see me when I was twelve." Mason snorted at that visual image. "Or when I recall myself trying to rock the cornrows." He placed the bags on the counter.

Gabe laughed, putting the rest of the groceries on the counter also. Mason admired how good-natured the younger man appeared to be. "Ms. Susan, I'm glad you're restoring the bed-and-breakfast. I do remember you baked the best pies in town." He rubbed his tummy and licked his lips.

Ms. Susan blushed. "Stop now with all that. Your mother would throw a fit if she heard you say that but I do seem to remember you showing up here—"

"Every Wednesday," Gabe said. "Those were the good old days." Gabe looked over at Mason. "This was the hangout place for us as teens. Not much else to do in town back then besides the movies and bowling. So, we would come out here and kick back, go fishing and play volleyball. Plus, there were always visitors on this end—and occasionally some pretty houseguests our age. But, always, always there was food."

Ms. Susan smiled. "I hope to bring that all back and then some."

"Fishing?" Mason asked.

"Yeah, it's about a five-minute walk from here," Ms. Susan said, "But it's hard to see with all the thicket."

"All that will be gone in a few days," Gabe said, sounding confident.

Mason's brows rose. "That's a lot of trees to trim and weeds to bring down."

"I've got it." Gabe placed a hand to his chin. "Say, I had a small crew I had to release because I couldn't pay them their worth. I can give them a call and see if anybody else would be interested?"

"That would be wonderful," Mason said, and provided an offer of generous compensation.

Ms. Susan beamed. "Tell them there will be food. Lots of food."

"I sure will." Gabe held up a hand. "I'll see you all tomorrow." He left, with his phone cupped to his ear, presumably making his first call.

Mason pointed upward. "Is she going to show her face?" he asked, referring to Eden.

"Give her time," Ms. Susan said, unpacking the groceries. "The other night was a huge deal but if I know my granddaughter, it's a minor setback. She's more ready than she realizes to move on." She gave him a look that could best be described as calculating. "She just needs incentive."

"Humph. Like your playing sick?" He began helping her put items away, taking note of how she had to use a step stool at times. Hmmm...maybe he would tweak his design a bit to make reaching her goods accessible.

Ms. Susan's mouth dropped, and she couldn't meet his eyes. "I have no idea what you're talking about."

"Don't think I didn't notice you made a quick recovery," he said challengingly.

Ms. Susan's shoulders drooped. "What gave me away?" She gave the hallway a furtive glance, probably to see if Eden lurked in the shadows.

"Lucky guess." He shrugged, before adding, "Let's say my stint in reality television has given me an eye to spot the dramatic." He cracked up. "Honestly, I am relieved you are okay, though I wasn't completely sure until you confirmed it just now."

She placed a hand on her hip. "Goodness, you have a good poker face. But yes, I know that's the only way I would get Eden to agree to all of this. She turns thirty on June 26 and I wanted to throw a party here, invite the whole town. I won't be here forever, and I need to know she isn't alone. I had to do something." She spread her hands and gave him a sly look. "And, if I'm not mistaken, she might have found a beau."

He slid his gaze from hers. "I like her. She's remarkable. Unlike anyone I've ever met. But…"

"But what?" she challenged.

"She's too good for me," he confessed.

"Pshaw!" She waved a hand. "That's pure baloney."

This conversation reminded him that he had never told Ms. Susan about his past. "I was fired from my previous job because I was horrible to my staff." He took off his hat and held it in his hands. "I'm not the man you think I am."

"I know all that already. I've seen the video and I hit the delete button." She wiped her apron. "I'm a pretty good judge of character and you're all right by me."

Wow. This was the second time today someone had spoken sincere words of faith about his character. He hadn't expected such grace. Mason swallowed. He hadn't known how important second chances were to him until today. He was beginning to like himself, see himself through their eyes, becoming the man they saw.

"Thank you for that, Ms. Susan," he whispered, somewhat overcome with emotion. He wished his own family would say the same. He knew he had to reach out, fix that.

Ms. Susan asked him to get a couple of glasses and a pitcher while she started cutting lemons. He went to help her with squeezing lemons, after he had washed his hands. She added sugar, ice cubes and water and gave the contents a good stir.

Then she poured some into both their glasses before putting the rest away in the refrigerator.

He took a few gulps. "Oh, this is good." Then he asked, "So…you wouldn't mind if I asked Eden out?" His pulse rate escalated, and hope flickered in his chest. He took a huge gulp to cover his sudden nervousness.

Ms. Susan rolled her eyes. "Of course not. My granddaughter needs what you young folks call a hookup."

He spit some of the juice out of his mouth. "Are you asking me to—to…" He lifted his hands and shook his head. "Um, Ms. Susan, I'm sorry. I can't have this conversation with you. But Eden doesn't strike me as a smash-and-dash kind of girl. Not that I'm looking for that kind of girl…" He mopped his brow and decided to stop talking.

She pulled her lips into her mouth like she was trying hard not to grin. "I'm just messing with you… Sort of." She picked up her glass, her eyes filled with mischief. "I'll see you tomorrow. Lock yourself out."

Mason finished his drink and washed his glass. Then

he went through the door, his steps light as he got into his pickup. He put on some jazz music and whistled along until he was back at Lydia's house. If Gabe's crew started tomorrow, he would be able to get most of the bedrooms finished in about two days. The new furnishings and materials were scheduled to arrive early the next morning.

Trudging up the front steps, Mason couldn't wait to get into the shower. His back ached and his muscles felt tight. He yawned. He sure was going to sleep good tonight. He entered the home and flipped the switch. But nothing happened.

He groaned. The electricity was out and he was covered in darkness. That's when he looked around the neighborhood and saw that the entire area was pitch black. He had been too preoccupied to notice. Mason rubbed his eyes. Maybe a power line went down or something. But whatever it was, it might be hours before the power returned. *Sigh.* It was going to be a long night.

Chapter Seven

Mason was moving in. Mason was *moving* in. Mason was moving *in*. Into her home. Into her space. Ugh. And Grams's firm expression said there was nothing she could do about it.

"I get that you want to help, but he's a distraction I don't need," Eden wailed the next morning. She had been sitting by her computer desk, finalizing the syllabus for the summer course—if she still had a job after today—when Grams came into her room and told her about Mason's plight.

"The power on that side of town will be out for about a week or more due to a power-line issue at the main plant. He had no place to go and we have more than enough room here," Grams said, coming farther into the room to stand by her desk, unmoved by her theatrics. "Both inns are full and I can't have him sleeping in his car like he did last night. Or worse, leaving." *Shoot.* She hadn't considered that. Eden didn't want him *gone* gone. Before she could respond, Grams continued. "Plus, need I remind you that this used to be a functioning bed-and-breakfast? I ran this place with an assistant for years before you moved in."

She swallowed. "I know, Grams. If it wasn't for me, you would still be in business." Guilt felt like bile in her stomach.

"Nonsense, child. I have no regrets." Grams made sure to meet her eyes. "Did you hear me? I have no regrets." Grams had given up the business after Eden's parents' death. Eden had been inconsolable and the first time she ventured back to school, her supposed friends had mocked her behind her back, calling her everything from a beast to a ghoul, while she stood in the bathroom stall, overhearing every word. She avoided them after that, refusing to speak or eat until she became gaunt and thin, collapsing one day on the high school soccer field. That's when Grams pulled her out of school, put her in therapy and allowed her to attend classes online.

Eden gave a jerky nod. "I'm just not mentally prepared to deal with visitors right now." And by visitors, she meant him.

"When have you ever been?" Grams asked wryly. "You'll adapt." She gave Eden's arm a gentle squeeze. "He's what you young girls call *eye candy.*"

Eden definitely agreed with that. It took considerable effort for her to ignore those abs, those taut muscles when she spied on him working outside. But to know he was directly below her, in bed, taking a shower... it was too much. *Whew.* She was feeling warm just thinking about it.

"He's really messing with my equilibrium right now,"

Eden confessed, running her fingers through her hair. "I'm supposed to be meeting with my student and Dr. Loft this afternoon and I don't need the extra stress." Having him here made her ache for things she shouldn't be wanting—like the feel of a man's arms about her; his lips on hers. It was odd but until he came around, she didn't realize how siloed she was. How sequestered. Sheltered.

Grams patted her shoulder. "You might find that you rather like having Mason here. He's great company and quite charming. You can't avoid the man forever," she teased. Well, Eden had planned on it. Then Grams said, "Whatever happened in the flower shop wasn't his fault."

Eden sighed. "I know. I just hate that he was there to witness my mortification. I was a wreck when I came out of the store. The main reason I've been avoiding him is that I am straight-up embarrassed."

"What happened, by the way?" Grams prodded in a gentle tone.

"You remember Cadence? Well, she works in the flower shop. When I went to purchase the fertilizer, she made a nasty comment about me being a beast or something like that. I stormed out of there and I could hear her calling me back but I wasn't going to stay there and have her continue her vitriol."

Grams eyes flashed. "I've a good mind to go down there and give her a thorough tongue-lashing. Cadence is too old for this level of insensitivity. I'm surprised, actually. She's always been sweet to me when I go in." She wagged a finger. "Well, Cadence just lost a customer. I'll drive over to the next town before I step foot in that shop again."

"No, Grams," Eden protested. "I don't need you doing all that. I'm grown and I shouldn't need my grandmother coming to my defense." She sighed and touched her bare arm before walking over to look at herself in the mirror. After working on her plants, Eden had showered and slipped into a sleeveless tank dress as the weather outside would be close to ninety-five degrees. "These scars aren't going anywhere and I've been doing a lot of thinking in here these past few days. Maybe it's time I take both your and Ramona's advice and change my point of view." Her chin wobbled. "I'm closeting myself inside this house, a prisoner of my own making, and..." She gulped. "I hate it. I'm—I'm lonely. I want to make friends and laugh and meet people my age. And..." She sniffled, unable to say the words.

Grams came to stand next to her and gave her hand a squeeze. They stood side by side eyeing each other's reflection. Her eyes were wet. "Fall in love?"

Touching her stomach, she nodded. "But who's going to want me like this?"

Leaning into her, Grams whispered, "Oh, my dear. I want you to have the kind of love I had with your grandfather. That your parents had. A man worthy of you won't be turned off by your victory wounds. He won't place value on superficial things. He'll treasure you. Worship you." She closed her eyes. "There's nothing like being loved by a man who loves you. And, that's what I want for you." She rested her head on Eden's arm and said not too subtly, "Mason's been looking out for you and asking about you, every day."

Eden turned to face her grandmother and spoke her biggest fear. "What if I repulse him?"

"Impossible." Grams rested a hand on Eden's cheek.

"Listen, the world has two kinds of people—those who care and those who don't. We have to share this planet with them but we don't have to live with them. You don't have to take them into your circle. But don't throw the baby out with the bathwater, child."

"What do you mean?"

"Don't let the opinions of people who mean you no good shape your life, your path." She jabbed a finger in Eden's chest. "Take that power from them. You don't have to let them into your circle. You decide. At least if things don't go as you hoped, it was based on your choices."

"Oh, Grams, I love you. I have the best grandmother in the world." Eden snatched her grandmother into a tight embrace. "You are so right."

Grams kissed her cheek. "You are a rosebud and it's time for you to bloom." She pointed to the bookshelf laden with romance novels. "It's time you stop reading them—well, not stop—but take a break from reading romances and actually start living one of your own." She fanned herself. "'Cause honey, you don't know what you're missing."

With a chuckle, Eden gathered her courage, reached for her sweater on the back of her chair then paused. Squaring her shoulders, she scrambled down the stairs to greet the man who occupied her thoughts more often than she would ever admit.

She found him stretched across the bed, shirtless, in a pair of worn blue jeans, his hands tucked behind his head, looking up at the ceiling. A black duffel bag was in the corner and various toiletries sprinkled across the huge chest in the room. The room had been done over in a blue-gray scheme. Eden watched him with her arms wrapped about her, intense hunger swirling on her insides—and it wasn't for food. Although she needed to eat.

He picked up his head and spotted her. His eyes went wide before he sprang off the bed. "Eden, you're here." The wonderment and joy in his voice boosted her confidence. Mason came to stand in front of her with all his male fineness and she had to struggle to keep from dropping her eyes to his chest. Her hands itched to touch his smooth skin and to see if those muscles were as firm as they looked. "Do you want to sit with me a little?" he asked, tentatively reaching for her hand.

All she could do was nod. Because a sudden onset of nerves made her remain frozen in place. Mason steepled his fingers through hers. Quick tears dimmed her eyes. She placed a hand to her chest. This was the first time in thirteen years she had held a man's hand.

"Are you okay?" he asked.

"Yes," she whispered. "I'm more than fine." She cleared her throat. "Just having a moment and snapping a picture in my mind." She was going to replay this action over and over tonight. Her heart soared. They sat side by side on his bed. She looked down at their conjoined hands and fought to hold her smile. "I'm sorry if I've been avoiding you."

"It's all good. You're here now." He shifted his weight, so he was closer to her. Searing heat crackled at the spot where their thighs met.

"I've never had sex before," she blurted out.

Mason's jaw dropped. "Okay... Talk about a conversation shift." He raised a brow. "And, you're telling me this because?"

"I thought you should know that because I'm attracted to you. I tried to fight it but since I learned you're going to be right under me, it's all I can think about. What is it like to have you under me?" Eden was very aware that she was rambling but her mouth was like a waterspout and she couldn't stop talking. "I've read all about the act but having never engaged in it before, I'm unsure of what to expect and if it is as good as I've read about." Then she plopped back on the bed, folded her arms and waited.

He placed a hand to her lips and gave her a tender smile, before trailing a finger to her neck. Scooping his arm under hers, he pulled her back into a sitting position. Eden closed her eyes and puckered her lips... but nothing happened. She popped an eye open to see a small grin on his face, and for a moment wondered if he had been staring at her scars. But when she glanced at him, his eyes—those eyes reflected a hunger that made her squirm. With eagerness.

Mason peered at her for several moments before saying, "First, I'm honored you have chosen me. Second, I'm not going to give a girl her first experience with her grandmother right upstairs—no matter how soundproof this room is. And third, before I make love to you— and believe me, I will—I would like to take you out on a date. On a real date. Out of this house." He lowered his voice to a growl. "I want to get to know Eden Tempest inside and out."

Goodness. She squeezed her knees together. Those words held sexual promise that made her body quiver. "Okay," she breathed out. "How about later tonight? Let's go into town for ice cream. Small steps."

Mason nodded. "You sure? I was going to start with us going on walks and working our way up slowly to venturing back into town."

"Nope. At the rate you're talking about, it will be ages before we make it to the bedroom."

Throwing back his head, Mason laughed. "Eden, I am going to enjoy you."

Eden was glad she had followed her instincts and visited with him. She jumped off the bed and gave him a wink and a wave. "Later."

Chapter Eight

Gabe had been good on his word. Four days after Gabe started, he had recruited more helpers and there were now seven of them. Seven men working in various parts of the main level of the bed-and-breakfast to bring the property back to magnificence. But besides their vehicles, there were two other cars he didn't recognize. Ms. Susan must have visitors.

It was now mid-May. Mason stood outside reviewing the before-and-after shots he had recorded through every part of their labor. He also took daily pictures of Eden's rose garden.

His heart rejoiced that the bed-and-breakfast would be ready before Eden's birthday in about five weeks.

Ms. Susan had already started ordering decorations and had begun preparing handwritten invitations. Since Eden loved historical novels from the Regency era, she was planning a tea party where everyone would dress from that era. Ms. Susan disclosed that Eden loved magenta and she was searching for garb to complement that color. The old him would have scoffed at this idea but Ms. Susan's and Eden's relationship was pure and sweet and warmed his heart. Which is why he had called his brother, Max, when they broke for lunch. Max hadn't answered so he had left a message, pleading with his brother to return the call.

After Eden left his room, he had hurriedly dressed before the men arrived. When the electricity went out, Mason discovered all the lodging in a twenty-five-mile radius had been booked. So, he had spent the night in his car and his lower back pain and sore neck made him ask Ms. Susan for housing suggestions. Mason hadn't expected her to open her home. So fast. So willingly. But that was Ms. Susan. That's why he was willing to do all he could to help her. Including supplement her budget to pay for these workers.

Mason hadn't accepted a salary for himself, having only charged Ms. Susan for labor. Ms. Susan had asked to see the books, but he assured her that the funds were okay.

His cell phone rang. It was Lydia. He slapped his forehead. Had he returned his agent's call that day? He didn't think so. And he needed to tell her that he had moved out of her home. Mason quickly answered. Gabe and one of the men came out toting some rotted drywall to toss in the dumpster.

"Hey, I have the most exciting news!" she boomed. "Someone posted a couple of photos from your current project and your fans are eating it up. They are demanding your return."

"Who?" he bellowed, his chest heaving. "Who posted

the pics? Because I know I sure didn't." The only person besides Ms. Susan he had shown them to was Gabe. Gabe who was out of a job. Desperate, even? Desperate enough to take advantage of Ms. Susan and Eden? Maybe. Mason slid his glance the other man's way and told himself not to presume. Ask.

"Who knows, but that random posting got you the *in* you needed. The producers plan to come out there with a film crew to stream and they are ready to put up some serious bank if you agree."

Mason almost dropped the phone. "What do you mean they are making plans? I didn't give consent."

"Well, I sort of did on your behalf."

He blinked. "You had no right to do that. That is beyond your scope as my agent." Gabe gestured to him. They were getting ready to rewire the plumbing for one of the bathrooms upstairs and he needed to provide oversight. "I've got to go but I'll call you back. In the meantime, please contact them and let them know I'm not interested."

"But—"

"This isn't up for discussion." He drew deep breaths and changed the topic. "There was a power outage in your neighborhood last night so I moved out of your house."

"Oh? I didn't receive any notifications about it… Where are you staying?"

"Here." He lifted a finger to gesture to Gabe that he was on his way and began walking back inside the house.

"Here where?" Then he heard a sharp intake of air. "You're staying at the haunted house?" She cackled. "This gets better and better. Please say you'll reconsider.

Your moving into the house provides better access and even better footage."

"No."

"Fine. Have it your way."

"Great, I hope this is the end of it." Lydia could be tenacious when she wanted something or envisioned something for him. It was what made her a great agent but sometimes not so good a listener. He rushed back inside the house to assist the men.

Ms. Susan stood in the kitchen with two women flanking her sides. They had an assortment of veggies and he saw beef ribs dripping with barbecue sauce and blackened salmon. He could see the steam. And the smell. *Mmm.* The smell made his stomach growl. He sniffed the air and swallowed. "All right now. It looks like some good home cooking in here." The women tittered. "Let me go get the men."

"And Eden," Ms. Susan called out.

He headed upstairs and called out to the guys in the other wing before jogging down to Eden's suite. In the middle of the landing was a small sitting area that had a couch, a coffee table and a small bookshelf holding books and games. He could envision guests using this area to entertain and made a mental note to find more comfortable furnishings that had a pop of color. He continued until he stood outside Eden's room.

Dang it if he's knees didn't wobble. Mason pressed his ear to the wood. He didn't hear even a peep. He rapped on the door, his heart doing a weird sort of flutter.

She opened the door a crack and peered through. "Mason?" She opened the crack wider and stood close to him, propping one leg up on the doorjamb behind her. The tank dress rose high on those tanned legs and his mouth watered now for a different reason.

"Lunch is ready," he said.

She bit back a smile. "Those words are coming off a bit flirty."

He stepped back, his eyes raking her body from head to toe. "Can you blame me? Look at all I'm dealing with here."

Eden's face flushed with pleasure. "Whatever. Tell Grams I'll be down in a minute. I just wanted to prep some things before my call this afternoon."

"Call?"

"Yes, I have to meet with the department chair for the university and a student. I'll tell you all about it later on our date." She blew him a kiss and sashayed back inside her room.

He took the stairs two at a time, anticipation flaring in his chest for their date later. With such good food coming from the kitchen here, Mason thought a trip to the beach to enjoy the sunset would be a good idea. He wanted to hear all about her meeting, anything she had to say really, and he wanted to tell her about the television show offer and the photo someone had shared. The last thing he wanted was for Eden or Ms. Susan to learn about that mishap from anybody but him.

Mason planned to ask Gabe if he had sent the photo.

The men were already huddled around the table, helping themselves to all that food. The dining table could comfortably hold twelve, so there was room enough for everyone. The men were already seated on one end with Ms. Susan at the head, her two friends, whom she introduced as Mona and Pearl, next to her. Mason piled his plate with a sample of everything, then took a seat at the other end, making sure to save a seat next to him for Eden.

There was an air of congeniality and a lot of clinking and scraping of utensils from the men getting their grub on.

"We had another table like this one, but it got damaged," Ms. Susan said. "I'll have to get another one before we reopen." The excitement in her voice was palpable.

"I can build you a new set," Gabe offered, then bit into one of the ribs.

"You're a carpenter as well?" Mason asked. "Why am I not surprised?"

"That's right. Your daddy used to own a furniture store before he..." Ms. Susan didn't finish that thought but everybody at the table nodded then shook their heads.

"This is some good food here," one of the men said, digging in.

Mason supposed that's what it was like being in a small town. Everyone knew everything there was to know about a person. He didn't feel comfortable asking especially since Gabe's face was now centered on his plate. Mason had his own daddy issues so he could respect someone not wanting to talk about theirs.

But what he couldn't respect was someone out for personal gain. He asked for everyone's attention. "I got a call from my agent that someone posted pictures of my gig here and it's going viral."

The room went silent.

"It wasn't me," someone said loudly.

"Me neither."

The men went right back to their meal. Unbothered.

Except for Gabe, who pushed his plate aside. "Why would you even fix your mouth to ask us that?"

"Easy now," Ms. Susan said, putting a hand up.

"Because I didn't send it... How else would it have..." He trailed off, hating to see the hurt mingled with disgust on Gabe's face. "Hey, listen, I had to ask, man."

Gabe stood and bunched his fists. "I thought we were friends. I don't betray my friends. And you good people." Was he though? Good people didn't put others on the spot like that.

Friends? He couldn't tell the last time someone had called him that. But he supposed making enemies and friends came easy in a small town. Mason stood down, walking around the table to talk to the other man. "I'm sorry, bro. I had to ask, you know what I'm saying? I couldn't walk around wondering because I was feeling some type of way when I heard somebody sold me out. Nevertheless, I should have pulled you to the side."

"I'm feeling some sort of way being accused, especially in front of a roomful of people," Gabe said. Then he relaxed his shoulders. "But I do understand. We good, man." The chair scraped as he moved to stand and they hugged it out.

"You good with us, man," another man chimed.

"Good, so we can get back to packing our stomachs because we have work to do,"

The men took their seats. He didn't know who did it but it felt good to settle the squabble instead of letting it fester until he lost his temper. That's what had happened before. The worker had shown up to work late four days in a row—his pet peeve—and then had been on his cell phone when he should have been working. Instead of talking to him about it, Mason had let it pile up until it overflowed. Mason wasn't trying to operate that way anymore.

That's when Eden trounced inside and gave a shy wave. He noticed she had thrown on a sweater over her dress and he rued missing another chance to see those curves. But, if everything went as it should, he would be seeing a lot more of her soon.

Mason took in the interested gazes of all the men in the room but Eden kept her eyes on him. She gave him a bright smile and came to claim her spot. His chest puffed. The men got the message and returned their focus to their food and to each other. Conversation buzzed around them. Ms. Susan was in her element serving everyone.

Eden helped herself to a small portion of salmon and veggies.

"Is that all you're going to have?" he asked under his breath.

"I didn't want to ruin my appetite for later since I wasn't sure where we were going."

He might as well tell her. "I was thinking ice cream by the beach?" Saying it aloud sounded corny. He hoped she didn't get the impression that he didn't think she was worth a five-star date. Or worse, that he had money issues since the loss of his show and couldn't afford it. To cover his embarrassment, he bit into his food.

But to his surprise, she smiled. "I would like that. I haven't been to the beach in years. We could catch a good sunset, listen to the waves and I'll make sure to bring my book with me."

He frowned. "You're bringing a book on our date?" What did that say about his expectations as a conversationalist?

"Good point. I wasn't thinking. The last time I went on a date it was with my mom schlepping us back and forth. I'm rusty." She giggled, then heaped more food on her plate. "Oh snap, I'll have to get a swimsuit."

Ooh, all those curves. All kinds of salacious images raced through his mind. Maybe he needed to take his own book. The Bible. Because Mason didn't know how he was going to keep his hands off her. He gave her the side-eye. Maybe that was her diabolical intention.

And, oh, was he looking forward to it.

Chapter Nine

When Eden entered the online meeting that afternoon, she was surprised to see that her former student, Naomi, and Dr. Loft were already deep in conversation, sharing a laugh.

A measure of unease crawled up her spine at their interaction, but she would not jump to any conclusions nor get upset. She placed a friendly smile on her face and greeted the other two women.

Dr. Loft cleared her throat. "I'm glad you could make it, Professor Tempest." Then she signaled to Naomi to present her concern. Eden folded her lips into her mouth and counted to three.

"I had a lot going on at home and I have to work two jobs but I didn't want to drop the course. I know I missed the last two classes and the review, but I felt confident I could bring my grades up with the research paper. I followed the rubric and made sure I made all the requirements. When I got my paper back, I got a C. I just happened to mention this to another student who received a B and he let me look over his paper and gave me permission to share. We had almost the same things. So, I feel Professor Tempest was being unfair to me because I talk out against a lot of things in class, and she always cut me off."

Eden wiped her brow. "I have no issues with healthy debates. In fact, I encourage it, but I also have course material to cover so I exercise proper time management." She refused to offer any defense about her grading practices and to give credence to Naomi's assumptions. Eden would wait to hear what Dr. Loft had to say.

"I have had a chance to review Professor Tempest's rubric and both of your papers." Eden stomach muscles tensed. "And, Naomi, I find that your concerns are unfounded." The head of the department cleared her throat. "I believe your grade was much more than generous than I personally would have given. The paper was riddled with errors, and you neglected to follow the Chicago Manual of Style when turning in the paper. I won't discuss the other student's paper with you since he is not on the call, but I will say, I concur with both grades assigned."

The tightness in Eden's chest eased.

"Oh… I didn't realize…" Naomi leaned back into her chair. "Are you going to lower my grade?" The cockiness had been replaced by fear.

"No. But I will offer you some advice. Communication is key. If you are unable to attend a session or complete a task, you need to communicate ahead of time, as soon as possible," Eden said.

Naomi gave a nod, thanked her and then left.

Once it was just the two of them, Dr. Loft switched gears. "Great. Now that we have that settled, let's talk about your plans for the fall. We would like to move all our composition classes to in person. We have found that the students make better gains with face-to-face instruction. Our upperclassmen seem to do well with either model, but our freshman classes need that support." She pushed the rim of her glasses up the bridge of her nose. "We want you to take over the bulk of the freshman classes because the student evaluations show that the students love you. They love how you break the content down to them and also prepare them to write college-level papers in their classes moving forward."

Eden's throat constricted. "I'm glad to hear that the students enjoy having me as their instructor, but..." She licked her lips. "If you're moving the freshman classes in person, I would love if you would consider having me teach the sophomore courses?"

The professor released a long plume of air. "I'll talk it through with the dean today and get back to you tomorrow."

"O-okay, thank you." Eden mopped her brow. "I'll remain hopeful until I hear from you."

"Don't get your hopes up," she warned before shaking her head. "You're a perfect fit with the freshman class." Then they ended the meeting. Though she was glad Dr. Loft had been somewhat agreeable with her proposition, Eden didn't feel at ease.

She stood and walked over to the mirror. She slipped off her sweater, then slipped her tank dress over her head and cradled her hands under her breasts. Turning, she took a good look at her scars. Because she had sustained fourth-degree burns, she had lost muscle and tendons in her arms and neck. Restorative surgery had only done so much. So, this was how she would leave the earth. The question was, how long was she going to allow them to dictate her life?

Maybe she should face her fears and teach the in-person courses.

Today when she had went to lunch, none of men at the table had focused on her wounds. Instead, she had seen curiosity in some of the men's eyes about her. The flattering kind of curiosity. It had been a minute since she'd had all eyes on her and though it felt good, she cared most what Mason thought. Watching the banked hunger in his eyes gave her the courage to sit with everyone for lunch. And sitting next to him, knowing he had saved her a seat, made her feel like she was sixteen again.

She inhaled and ran her hands down the side of her body. Closing her eyes, she wondered what it would feel like if it were Mason's hands instead. She moaned, before a realization stopped her cold. If she and Mason got together, he would see her naked.

Flaws and all.

Eden swallowed.

There was a rap on her door. Eden slipped on her dress and opened her door. Her eyes grew wide when she saw who stood outside.

"Your grandmother told me to come right up," Cadence said, her eyes beseeching and...kind? Eden gave her the once over, noting her shorts and T-shirt over a blemish-free skin. Her sandals were cute though.

"What are you doing here?" Eden croaked out, coming outside of her room and closing the door behind her. Simultaneously, she wondered why Grams would allow the very woman who called her a beast to enter their house, much less venture up into her private space. You best believe she was going to get that question answered after she got rid of Cadence.

Cadence couldn't look her in the eyes. "After what happened the other day, I had to come see you. I know you have a lot going on with the renovation right now—it's looking good—but I couldn't go one more night and not try to settle things." She pointed toward the sitting area. "Can we sit and talk for a minute?"

Eden gave a nod before trailing behind the other woman. She could hear the clamor below, signaling the men were back at work. She sat at the end of the couch and wrapped her arms about her, her stomach tense. Cadence clasped her hands in her lap.

For a beat, there was an awkward silence before Cadence chuckled. "Remember how we used to sit in here and sneak popcorn late at night while watching horror movies?"

"Yes…" Eden stood. "I'm sorry, but I can't do this. I don't think you came here to take a trip down memory lane after thirteen years and I can't go there with you. Like everything is all cool between us after the… after the fire." Just uttering the word *fire* made Eden's chest tighten. She took short, raspy breaths. "I think you should leave."

Cadence got to her feet. "I—I don't know where to start." Her lower lip quivered before she cleared her throat and met Eden's gaze. Eden was shocked to see Cadence had tears in her eyes. "Actually, I do know." Stepping close, she reached her hand out to touch Eden's arm. The first thing Eden felt was the warmth.

She hated how she welcomed that feeling. That human touch.

The second thing Eden realized was that Cadence didn't have a look of repulsion, though her fingers were almost touching Eden's warped skin.

She hated how her eyes grew slick from that knowledge.

"We were friends, once," Cadence whispered, giving Eden's arm a squeeze. "Real friends. And when you got…injured… I turned on you. I was mean and harsh." She sniffled and wiped her eyes with the back of her hands. "I was horrible."

"Yes, you were. But what made it worse was how you turned everyone else against me. Teasing me. Ruthlessly," she said, hiccupping, averting her eyes. Waves of humiliation at the memory washed over her. Plump tears trekked down her face but Eden didn't care. Cadence's presence had pierced the sore of the past and now the excretion was seeping out. It wasn't pretty but very necessary if she wanted healing.

"Yes, I know," Cadence sobbed. "When you dropped out of school, so many days I wanted to come and say sorry, but I… I was too ashamed to face you."

"Really?" Eden asked, bitterly. "How ashamed were you the other day when I came into your store?"

Cadence removed her hand off Eden's arm and covered her mouth with her hand. "When you walked through that door, my heart was happy to see you. You see, for years I couldn't face myself in the mirror. I couldn't face the person who had done such abominable things in high school. I blamed myself for your self-imposed isolation but then you strutted in, your head held high, so confident…and I cracked that insensitive joke." She held out a hand. "In a weird way, I wanted to bring up the subject so I could segue into my apology." She sighed. "But as soon as the words left my mouth and I saw how crushed you were, I knew I had done the wrong thing." She sniffled again. "I called after you, but you were too upset to hear me out. Understandably so. Please know that was not my intention."

Eden's heart responded to the sincerity in Cadence's tone. She went with her gut and released all the hurt that had festered on the inside.

"My grandmother raised me right, so I'll accept your explanation, but I want it known that your rationale makes no sense to me. We're not teenagers anymore." Eden shrugged. "A simply apology was the way to go."

"I see that now," Cadence said, sounding grateful. "I'm sorry. I'm sorry. I'm sorry." Then she fell apart. Sank into the couch and sobbed until Eden had to get her a glass of water and a handful of tissues. "Thanks," she said, her eyes and nose reddened. Cadence ran a hand through her long black hair that rested a little above her butt. "I must look a hot mess but I don't care. I was glad I had the courage to come out here and face you."

Wiping her face, Eden didn't voice that she thought Cadence looked beautiful.

"I'm glad, too," Eden replied, realizing she uttered the truth. Then she asked a question to satisfy her curiosity. "I was shocked to see you in the flower shop. If I remember right, I thought you had big plans to go to LA and become the reincarnated Meryl Streep."

Cadence's cheeks reddened. "Well, yes, but plans change. Circumstances change. Like most of our class, I went away to college but…life happened. Something you know more than most." She opened her mouth like she was about to say more before she shook her head. Eden didn't push. They weren't cool like that. "I started working part time the flower shop, but I am mostly in the back or doing deliveries. Two of the workers were graduating so I worked out front a few days."

When they were girls, leaving for Los Angeles to pursue an acting career was all Cadence spoke about, especially when they watched *The Devil Wears Prada*, which they had seen at least twenty times. So, it had to be something major why Cadence returned to Blue Hen.

"You had a birthday, recently," Eden recalled, rubbing her chin. Though she was out of practice, she marveled at how at ease she was engaging in small talk. Small steps.

"Yes, on the eighth," Cadence said, smiling. "I turned thirty last week. I know yours is coming up on the twenty-sixth."

"You remembered?"

"Of course. Hard to forget when our parents would throw us parties in the middle of the month because—"

"That was the only fair thing to do," they said in unison before sharing a laugh.

Cadence grew serious. "Just when I got my big break, my parents were in a serious car accident and I left LA and came back home to take care of them. To be close. I have never been so scared in my life." She gave Eden a quick glance. "I know you understand."

"Yes. Yes, I do." Her breath hitched. Even though Cadence had been terrible, Eden wouldn't wish that kind of loss on anyone. "But at least your parents survived."

"Yes." Cadence breathed out and then shuddered. "For a while, I believed it was karma."

Eden furrowed her brows. "I don't know about all that." Cadence was really hard on herself but who was Eden to argue that point? She had plenty of guilt to take her into more than one lifetime.

"Guilt will make you view things from a whole different perspective." She looked down at her hands.

Looking at her watch, Eden was surprised to see that it was close to 5:00 p.m. She had a date to get ready for. She jumped to her feet. "Cadence, thank you for coming by. For settling things between us."

Cadence shifted from one foot to the next. "I hope we can get together again."

Suddenly, she wasn't ready for their time to conclude just yet. It had been nice to talk with someone her age. Someone who knew her. "I have a—a, um, I have something I have to do. But if you have five minutes, I'll take you out to my rose garden?"

"I'd love to see it," Cadence said, grinning. "I'm entering the Blue Hen Rose Festival this year and I can't wait to beat you."

"I'll be there to see you lose," Eden countered.

The other woman's eyes went wide. "You're coming?"

"Y-yes," she said, wiping her hands on her dress. Then she straightened and said, "I will be there this year."

Cadence mouth stretched into a wide smile. "Let the games begin."

Chapter Ten

Mason's lips twitched. Since Eden and Cadence had come outside to peek at her rosebushes, Gabe had been behaving like a roebuck. He was prancing—yes, prancing around the women—lifting this or that, yakking up a storm, but the funny thing was they weren't paying him any mind.

Well, more specifically, Cadence. The other woman had tried to shoo him away like he was a nuisance but Gabe wasn't having it. Even when Mason called him over to discuss his landscaping plans for the exterior, Gabe wouldn't budge.

As for him, his eyes remained trained on Eden, his heart warming at seeing her interact with her former friend.

But man, did he rag on Gabe when Cadence finally left. "Dude, you were going hard over there. Did you get her number?"

Gabe shook his head. "Not yet. But I will."

Mason cracked up. "I thought everybody knew everybody in this small town. I'm surprised you don't have those digits already."

Scuffing his boot on the freshly paved driveway, Gabe averted his gaze. "I dated her friend for a couple weeks back in the day and that's why Cadence won't give me a chance. Small-town people have a long memory."

"Whoa. That's..." Mason busted out into laughter. Gabe's face turned stony and he tried to compose himself. It was just seeing the antics of this huge man for a woman who barely stood five feet tall was unexpected. "I don't know what to say, man. Maybe she'll change her mind in time. But if not, I'm sure you won't have a problem choosing from your share of single women in this town." Then he patted Gabe on the shoulder. "By the look on your face, I can tell you only want this particular woman."

His face transformed into a smile. "I'm going to win her over too. Just watch me." The crew came outside, all packed and ready to head home.

"That was some good work today, guys," Mason called out. "We start on the upstairs tomorrow." They gave him a friendly wave and went on their way. It was now close to 5:00 p.m. Mason jogged into the house and surveyed the completed rooms on the opposite end of the house from his master suite. One of the bedrooms had been done in shades of brown and gold and the other, which belonged to Ms. Susan, had purple and cream hues. She had gone out with her friends so that they could get the work done.

Ms. Susan was excited with his idea of giving each

room a theme, but she hadn't yet made a decision for each suite.

His cell vibrated, and he pulled his phone out of his pocket and took a look. *Whoa.* It was his brother Maxim. "Hey, Max. I'm glad you called me back." His heart squeezed. It had been a good five years since he had heard his younger brother's voice.

"I almost didn't," Max said, his deep voice a rumble. "But I didn't want you reading about this online because there've been a few reporters hanging around since you got fired from that show."

"What's going on?"

"Dad's sick and according to the doctors there is no cure. It's his kidneys. They gave him six months unless he gets a donor. You know I can't give him one because of my renal agenesis. But if I could I would do it in a heartbeat," Max choked out. "And he's way down on the list and I feel it's because of his past alcoholism, though they say otherwise."

Six months. Wow. Mason felt sucker punched. When he was a child, his father, Alton, had seemed invincible, so hearing news of his demise jarred him. He rocked back on his heels, striving to remain aloof, composed, though his heart grieved for Max. "Thanks for letting me know. If you need anything please reach out."

"If we need anything? If we *need* anything?" Max huffed, his voice raising. "You know what you need to do. You need to make peace with Dad. Forgiveness goes a long way. For once in your life put your own selfish needs aside and think of Dad. Think of me." The line went dead after that. Mason had to get ready for his date and this call had definitely pierced his enthusiasm. However, he didn't want to cancel his plans with

Eden. If he did, she might think it had to do with her. Truthfully, after hearing the news about his father, he needed to be around her right now.

So, he pushed all these conflicting emotions aside, put a basket of goodies and an oversized blanket inside his pickup and then rushed inside to get ready.

When he met Eden by the stairs dressed in a blue shirt, dark blue jeans and blue Timbs for their date, she must have seen something on his face and asked if everything was all right. Eyeing her yellow sundress with the upper body fitted then flaring off at the waist, he nodded, then gave her hand a squeeze. Just that act grounded him.

Mason forced a smile on his face, and they made small talk about the beautiful weather, but Max's words lingered, and he grew quiet with his thoughts. The day Mason turned twenty was the day he left Virginia and he had vowed never to return. He had been generous with his resources but kept his distance, except visiting once a year. But even that ended after his epic falling-out with his father. It had been a volcanic eruption caused by pent-up resentment for most of his life.

Mason's only regret had been leaving Max behind.

A regret that stayed with him to this very day.

Eden dug into her bag for her book and that shook him back into the present. "You really brought reading material for our date? Have you no faith in my ability to keep you entertained?" he teased. He didn't mention that he had seen her white sweater—her crutch—tucked inside as well. Mason hoped he could convince her to leave it inside the vehicle.

She smiled. "Don't take it personal. You've got to understand that books have been my stalwart companions the past thirteen years. I can depend on them. They give me hours of pleasure and they don't laugh at me, or make me feel less than. Books are equal opportunity friends."

"I'm just messing with you," Mason said. "I also love books. My bookshelves at home have the usual renovating and design books but…" He hesitated before dropping his voice to a whisper. "I'm a closet women's fiction reader. Also romance."

She placed a hand over her mouth. "Come again? What do you mean, you're a closet women's fiction reader?"

Mason's face felt hot. "It all started out because of my hormones. Now you won't see these books on my shelves though. You'll see the Harlan Coben, Michael Connelly, James Patterson in my collection. I read the women's fiction and romances on my Kindle or I borrow them from my library."

She raised her brows. "I find this utterly fascinating." Her voice dropped. "And a major turn-on."

"Well, I didn't have the kind of relationship with my father where I could talk to him about girls and dating and…sex. And, I was curious. In high school, I would see all these girls hiding romances between their textbooks, their faces bright and red from whatever they were reading. And then it dawned on me that I could learn about the opposite sex by reading romances. And, let me tell you, those love scenes taught me some stuff."

Eden laughed. Boy, did he love that sound. He must get her to do more of that. "What did you learn?"

"I'll show you soon enough. But let's just say, I've never had any complaints." He slid a quick glance her way, satisfied to see the interest in her eyes. The curiosity. The anticipation.

"Who have you read?" she asked.

"*An American Marriage, Miss Pearly's Girls*...who else?" He drummed his fingers on the steering wheel. "Oh yeah, I read *Lessons in Chemistry* and I just bought *Yellowface*. Basically, if there is buzz about a book, I'm going to read it."

"Wow," she said, "I'm impressed. Mason Powers, you have managed to surprise me. I'm floored. I've read all of those books. I feel like you're talking my love language here."

"As far as romances, I do love me some Emily Henry and Tessa Bailey. But my props go out to LaQuette and Naima Simone. Those ladies know how to write a love scene. They break it down for a brother."

Eden covered her mouth and laughed until her shoulders shook. "You are hilarious. Until recently, I haven't been into romances since I was a teen. It was hard for me to read about people falling in love when I..." She trailed off and looked out the window. "I didn't want to read about something that I didn't ever see happening for me. I also didn't want to be in heat and have no outlet."

"You deserve to be loved and even more." Mason gripped the wheel. His heart hurt thinking of a young Eden grappling with loneliness and the fear that she would remain unloved for the rest of her life. But he couldn't resist adding, "You know they do have toys that could have helped you with your sexual frustration."

Since they were stopped at a light, he peered over at her face which had taken on a rosy hue.

"Ah... Oh... Well, I didn't think about that."

"I can't wait to show you what you've been missing."

"I can't wait either." She tilted her head. "I just started reading some hot romances and so I do have some ideas I want to try out."

The air in the car grew hot and tight as tension rose between them. Mason debated pulling over to the side of the road and satisfying this craving, the potent desire coursing through him. He had read that scene in a romance where the couple got wild on the hood of the car and since then that had become a fantasy, but there was no way he going there with Eden.

At least not yet. He smiled. He was going to relish awakening her inner freak.

Eden must have been watching him. "What put that smile on your face?" she asked.

Nope. He was so not telling her his actual thoughts. Instead, he said, "I was thinking about ice cream." The navigator backed him up by saying he needed to make a turn. "I'm taking us to a creamery I saw that had rave reviews."

That launched a new discussion about ice cream, how it was made, and their favorite flavors. A topic that lasted until they arrived at their destination. He opened her door and helped her out, then they went to purchase their ice creams.

There were a few families out, but they were the last customers of the day. He noticed that Eden received a few curious glances but other than that, no one addressed her wounds. Which was fantastic.

Once they had ordered—he, a double scoop of butter pecan, and she, a single scoop of chocolate chip, they decided to follow one of the trails on the farm. While they enjoyed their treats, Mason reached out to hold her hand. He laced his fingers through hers and turned to make conversation. But at that very moment, she took a lick of her ice-cream cone. And he stopped walking.

Entranced.

She looked delectable and there was nothing more he wanted to do than sample that ice cream right off her tongue.

Chapter Eleven

Dang, his hand was heavy. Eden needed to clench and unclench her fingers a bit but she also wanted to savor the warm feeling coursing through her insides. She was holding hands with Mason.

But she needed to give her hand a rest. Just for a few seconds. And she had thought of the perfect way to distract him. Eden saw how he was looking at her eat her ice-cream cone and a mischievous voice told her to play that up. Since they were alone on the trail, she circled her tongue around the tip of the ice cream, chuckling when she heard Mason's groan.

He released her hand—thank goodness—and snaked his arm around her waist, drawing her close into that broad chest. Much better. "Can I have some?" Mason asked with a low growl. By then, he had already devoured his cone.

She raised a brow. "Some of what?"

"Your ice cream." His breath smelled like butter pecan but she detected a scent of sandalwood and spice which reduced her insides to jelly.

Eden purposely ate another mouthful. She was learning she was quite the tease. A bead of sweat lined his brow. "Nervous?" she asked.

"I want to kiss you so bad." The desperate tone in his confession made her feel sexy and wanton.

"Then kiss me," she breathed out, her chest rising and fall as desire coursed through her. A new kind of frustration was building within, and she needed relief.

"This wasn't how I planned this."

"The best things in life aren't planned."

Mason stepped forward, walking her backward until her back was against a tree. The branches hung low enough to hide them from view. He trailed small kisses behind her ear and she arched her neck to give him access, her hands gripping his back.

Then he kissed her.

And she lost her breath, her balance and her ice-cream cone. He kissed her until she had no air left, squeezing every drop of passion out of her, giving all of himself.

And it was not enough.

As soon as he pulled apart, she grabbed his head and planted her lips to his. Eden lost track of time. All she knew was that when they finally pulled apart, the sun had started to set.

"Let's get to the beach." Mason took her hand, and they ran toward the car, laughing like they were teenagers.

A few minutes later, he parked in a secluded area and retrieved the basket and blanket.

"Oh, you came prepared," Eden said.

"I want tonight to be perfect."

"It already is," she whispered, savoring the taste of him on her lips. She had had her first grown-up kiss and it had been marvelous, exceeding her imagination. Eden didn't know if there was any romance novel that could accurately describe the rightfulness of being in the arms of someone who you clicked with. The sense of belonging.

And that's how it felt when Mason held her close.

He declined her offer to help but set up a romantic spot, sprinkling rose petals and pulling out candle jars, wine glasses, sparkling cider and a charcuterie board. He had ice packs that kept everything chilled. "Wow, you thought of everything." She touched her chest. "Thank you."

"I'm glad you're happy." He snuggled her close to him, her back against his chest and together they watched the sun lower on the horizon, painting streaks of oranges, blues and purples. Oh, there was nothing like it. They ate and kissed and just basked in the moment of being together. Then Mason lit the candles, the scent of cinnamon and apples wafting in the air. A light breeze added to the tender atmosphere.

Mason snapped a few pictures of them and also the sunset on his cell phone. Then he offered to send her the pictures.

"I don't have a cell phone," she said, flicking away some of the sand on her dress. "I never had the need for one." *Until now.*

"I know. We have to remedy that," he said. "I'll email them to you for now, but I want to be able to text my girlfriend some naughty messages." He waggled his brows.

Girlfriend? Her heart did a weird flip-flop. How smooth, how easy that rolled off his tongue. She supposed at their age, it was just understood. Eden didn't want to appear naive by asking, especially since her brain kept zinging on *girlfriend*. She was somebody's *girlfriend*. Specifically, Mason's *girlfriend*. Her inner girl shouted, *Whee!*

"I'll get one tomorrow," she said, trying to sound unaffected by the fact that suddenly, she had a *boyfriend*. She took her *boyfriend's* hands and placed them into her lap, before covering his hands with her smaller ones. They spoon-fed each other between lots of long kisses, her favorite moment when Mason cupped her breasts. She took off her dress to reveal her black bikini—one she had ordered for same-day delivery from Amazon—then held up the blanket so he could change into his colorful trunks. They frolicked by the water, chasing each other and just having fun. The best thing, besides their make-out sessions, was the laughter.

Spent, they returned to recoup on the blanket. As far as first dates went, this was an 11/10. "So, I don't want to ruin our good mood but right before we left the house, you seemed…preoccupied, like something was on your mind. I'm not trying to be nosy but I'm concerned." She played with the hem of her dress. "Did you want to talk about it?"

"I will if you tell me about your meeting."

She touched his cheek. "I guess we're both curious about each other… You've got a deal."

Mason leaned back onto the blanket and looked up at the sky. "I learned today from my brother that my father is dying, and it shook me up a bit. I didn't expect it to as my father engaged in certain lifestyle choices—he was an alcoholic, a heavy smoker and…he was verbally and physically abusive. I had a tough childhood and once I hit twenty, I was out of there. I have only been back a few times."

She stretched out next to him. "I'm so sorry to hear that." This time she reached to hold his hand but she didn't steeple their fingers together. "When are you planning to go see him?" She felt a pang at the thought of him leaving but family was important.

"I'm not," he said, moving onto his side so that he faced her, propping a hand under his head.

"What do you mean you're not?" she blurted out. "I'm sorry, I shouldn't have said that."

"No, it's cool. Your question is only natural. That would be what's expected if I grew up in a normal family." He sat up, as if restless.

She held out a hand and he tugged her to a sitting position. Placing a hand on his arm, she said softly, "Tell me."

"My father worked in a factory and my mother passed when me and my brother were too young to understand fully what that meant. I was seven and Maxim was two and my dad was shattered. Shattered to the point where he started drinking. He drank around the clock, and it started the very night we buried her. Once everyone had left, he sent us to bed, but I wanted to check on him. Now, when he wasn't drunk, my dad was amazing but when he was, he was mean. He was vicious and I got the brunt of it. Of course, in time, he lost his job and we lost everything."

She heard the venom in his tone and wrapped an

arm around his waist. He leaned into her. "You sure you want to hear this?"

Eden nodded. "I want to know everything about you."

He made circles in the sand with his finger. "The only reason we had a roof over our heads was because the house had been paid for by my mother's parents and they had passed it down to my mother. But other than that, I had to cook and clean and take care of Maxim and myself."

"That's a lot of responsibility for a child," she said. "What about your church? Or family? Wasn't there anyone you could call?"

"No, I didn't dare. I knew early on that what happened in our house, stayed in our house." His tone grew bitter. "If I dared open my mouth, my father would backhand me. The only great thing was that Alton Powers never laid a hand on Maxim." Mason reached over to take a sip of sparkling cider. "Maybe it was because he looked like Mom, I don't know, but that was a relief. When I finally got the courage to leave, I wanted to take Maxim with me, but I had scraped enough for only one bus ticket. And I knew he would be okay." He drained the glass. "Turns out that Dad got sober once I was out of the house. Maxim was fifteen and started getting into some trouble and my father got his act together. For him."

Eden could hear the hurt in Mason's voice and she wished she had the right words to comfort him. She gave him a light kiss instead, which he seemed to welcome.

"But all's well that ends well, I guess. Maxim is now a chef at a five-star restaurant and well, you see how

I turned out." He stared out at the ocean. "My brother wants me to go home and mend fences with my father and I admit that when I see you with your grandmother, it makes me tempted to reach out." His lips curled. "But the last time I did that, it did not go well."

"What happened?" She reached for a cheese cube. It was slightly hardened from being exposed to the air but still delicious.

"I was turning thirty and there's something about hitting that milestone that makes you reflect on your life and make changes."

"I get that. I'm turning thirty in a couple weeks and that's all I can think about."

"Yeah, so you get it." He continued. "So, I got on a plane but as I look back, I realize I didn't go back with reconciliation in mind. I was too angry. I was all about confrontation. I was all about making him pay for all the hurt he'd caused. I wanted to battle the demons of the past, not settle them." He shook his head. "Well, that was a bad idea. My father refused to fight with me and Maxim got in my face. Me and my brother got into it real bad. You see, he had a different childhood, a different dad than I did and he wasn't going to sit back and see his father get disrespected. Which though I understood, didn't make it hurt any less."

"But you are allowed to feel how you feel," Eden said, defending him. She knew a thing or two about being angry with your past—only most of her anger was directed at herself.

"Maxim doesn't see it that way." He scoffed, "I don't get how the same man could be two distinctly different people." Then he shook his shoulders like he was shaking off the past. He patted her leg. "But enough about me. Please tell me you had a childhood that was all roses and everything nice." Mason began packing up the basket.

"I thought you wanted to hear about my meeting," she teased, helping him fold the blanket. Or rather, stalled. Her past wasn't all that pleasant, but she found she wanted to open up to Mason the way he had to her.

"That too. But I'm curious as to how you ended up a beautiful girl in a castle." They began walking back to his pickup, her hand in his.

"You're being tactful...you want to know about the fire. I'll tell you on the ride home." Feeling a slight chill, Eden took out her sweater and slipped it over her shoulders. She had shocked herself with how at ease with her body she had been. Maybe it was because of Mason's eyeing her like she was a delectable French treat or maybe it was because the beach was deserted? Eden didn't know for sure, but she did know she had had a beyond amazing time. She told Mason as much when they arrived at his truck.

"I'm so glad you did. This is the best first date I have ever had." Her heart preened at that. Mason was a man of experience, and she wouldn't obsess with wondering if he was just being nice, she was going to take that compliment at face value and squeal on the inside.

He opened the passenger door and helped her up by squeezing her bottom. It would be close to midnight before they made it home. Mason jogged around the front of the truck and slammed the door.

"I'm going to need a good shower once we're back," he commented as the vehicle roared to life.

"Maybe we can shower together," she suggested.

"That's a pretty bold suggestion. Daring even. The shy miss of a few weeks ago is fading," he teased.

She grinned. "I don't believe in half stepping anything I do."

"Well, all right then. I can check to see if the power is back yet at Lydia's place. I was so comfortable with you and Ms. Susan; I didn't even think to check. I don't want to wear out my welcome."

"Nonsense. You don't have to move back there. You're staying with us for as long as you'd like." Forever. For an eternity. Her heart sang.

"Thanks, but I prefer a more intimate setting for our first time."

"The true heart of a romantic." She rolled the window down, enjoying the wind in her hair and the smell of the sea.

"Blame it on the adult novels." He glanced her way before turning back to the road. "How about I book us this weekend at the Bellmore Inn & Spa on Rehoboth Beach? We can enjoy a quiet stroll on the boardwalk and check out the shops on that end."

"Oh, someone has been doing their research. I'd like that a lot."

He backed out of the parking space. "Consider it a date. Now let's get back to my question."

She drew quiet, her shoulders curving. "About the fire…"

"Yes."

"All right." Eden feared she might lose her boyfriend of a few hours when she was done but she knew she needed to be authentic if she wanted to have a real relationship. Though her heart thundered in her chest, she opened her mouth and began.

Chapter Twelve

Mason heard the slight tremor in Eden's voice and tension squeezed his gut.

Maybe asking her about the fire had been poor judgment on his part but this was a life-changing occurrence and he wanted to know everything about her. The absolute high and, in this case, the extreme low. Still, maybe he shouldn't have pushed and should have waited for her to share whenever she was ready.

"You don't have to talk about it if it's going to cause you serious emotional trauma," he offered, giving their joined hands a squeeze.

"No, no. I—I do want to share. I want to open up to you. I just...it's difficult." Eden cleared her throat. "I am an only child and my parents doted on me. They had battled infertility and miscarriages, so I was a miracle baby."

"I bet you were cute as a button," he couldn't resist

adding. "I can just imagine you had a head full of curls with those remarkable eyes. Your parents must have been putty in your fists."

"Probably." She laughed. "I don't know if I would call myself cute with that wrinkly face, but I guess Grams and my mom and dad would agree. I had tons of pictures...before." She straightened, removing her hand from his, and wrapped her arms about her. Mason didn't think she noticed doing so but that indicated to him how stressed she might feel. He pulled over into a parking lot and cut the engine so he could give her his undivided attention.

"So, I guess you could say I had an ideal childhood. This small town is like a village so I had many aunts and uncles and friends. Lots of friends. We all played together, went to each other's houses. You could walk the streets at midnight and be safe—not that I was allowed to. Just saying. It wasn't until high school that there's a great divide—the in-crowd and the others." She scoffed. "Of course, I was in the in-crowd and I let it get to my head. I was ghastly to anybody who wasn't in our little crew. Cadence was the designated leader of the pack. We were smart but we were bored. A boredom that led to trouble."

"What kind of trouble?" Mason asked. "Trouble is relative depending on where you're from."

She lifted her shoulders. "We would skip school, get rides to the beach, sneak a sip of wine here and there."

Mason cracked up. "Sounds like normal teenage stuff to me."

"Well, you couldn't tell our little clique nothing. We thought we were so cool. A few days before my sixteenth birthday, Cadence snuck a pack of cigarettes from her father's pants pocket and we decided to try them."

"Oh no…" Dread set in. He hoped she wasn't about to say what he thought she was.

"My mom caught me smoking behind the bed-and-breakfast and gave me a stern talking-to and I promised not to do it anymore. But back then the voices of my peers held more weight." She fiddled with her skirt. "If only I had listened…"

Mason could hear the regret in her voice. Man, she caused the fire that took her parents' lives. He couldn't comprehend the guilt. "Listen, I get the gist. You don't have to continue."

She faced him, her eyes glistening. "I've got to finish. Please." She wet her lips and continued. "The day of my birthday party, Cadence decided to bring us a pack of smokes so we could party right. So the two of us and a couple of guys went into my bedroom and we started to smoke. We had candles lit and the windows open and our parents were chatting and hamming it with each other so we weren't worried about getting caught. I remember inhaling and my chest getting so tight that I coughed and coughed so hard that Cadence ran to get me water. I kept puffing away though. Then my mother called up the stairs for me to come down to cut the cake.

"I squished the cigarette on a paper plate," she said, her lips quivering. "I'm pretty sure I did. I even checked to see that it was out and I went downstairs. Right as we sang 'Happy Birthday' someone yelled, 'Fire,' and pandemonium ensued."

"That was an accident," Mason said.

Tears spilled down Eden's face and she shook her

head, seemingly caught up in her tale. He wasn't even sure she had heard his defense. "My parents rushed upstairs while everyone else ran out in the yard. I stayed rooted in disbelief, waiting for them to come back down. But the fire caught on quickly, and I heard a loud bang, like the roof had caved in and I rushed up the stairs into the smoke, screaming and calling for them. I called and called but I heard nothing. But the fire was raging at that point, and it was so black and foggy that I think I fell and passed out."

The faraway look in her eyes told him that Eden was back there, seeing everything all over again. Mason drew her into his arms and rocked her back and forth.

She sniffled. "The next thing I know, I was being awakened in the hospital. And that's when I heard the news." She swallowed. "My parents hadn't made it out and some of the ceiling fell on me, giving me these." She lifted her arms. "These are reminders that because of me my parents are dead. If—if I hadn't—" She hiccuped. "Every time I look at them, I remember what I did."

He drew back so she could see his face. "You didn't intend for this to happen. You can't keep blaming yourself. Your parents didn't have to go upstairs. They should have run outside the house."

"The firefighters said they found vestiges of my photo albums, my baby shoes and other memorabilia that my mother was trying to save." Holding her face in her hands, she sobbed and sobbed, as if this had happened yesterday instead of thirteen years ago.

Goodness. That had to cut her to the core knowing that. Mason snatched her close. "They wouldn't want you blaming yourself. I know that."

"That's what Grams says. That's what my therapist says. But my heart says differently." She raised her tearstained face toward him. "Their lives being cut short is strictly because of my rebellion and the very friends I tried to impress turned on me. Treated me like a pariah. That's what hurt the most. I learned too late the true value of my family. I don't even have a proper picture of my parents and me as a teenager. Grams had some but a lot of them are blurred and the professional ones that were on the wall…destroyed. All I have is the one on the staircase that is damaged, but it was a favorite of mine."

"You still have Grams," he said, aching, acutely aware of her loneliness. He wanted to add that she also had him, but it was too soon for that. Plus, he didn't know how long he would be in town, and he had no clue what would happen with their relationship then. But that was a think for another day.

"Yes, it was Grams who got me into planting the roses. They saved me. Before caring for my roses, I didn't do much. Actually, I did nothing."

Mason reached into the glove box to retrieve some napkins he had saved from ordering takeout and gently wiped her face. "You and Cadence seemed to have made up."

"Yeah, she apologized and life is too short to hold on to anger. I know all too well how you can be here one day and gone the next." The knowledge of how she knew that ripped his heart. She gripped the crumbled napkin.

"How long did it take you to rebuild the bed-and-breakfast?" he asked.

She squinted. "We didn't rebuild… I'm not following."

"You said the bed-and-breakfast burned down, so I thought…"

"No. No. We lived behind the bed-and-breakfast in a two-story house."

"Oh, I see," he said. "I would have never known."

Her next words shook him to the core. "Yes, they tore down the entire infrastructure. I would stare at the empty plot for days on end. I stopped eating and communicating. I would just sit in the chair and relive my personal nightmare, every single day."

"Oh, Eden. That was no way to live."

"I know that now. I would have wasted away but Grams dragged me outside and made me start planting. She said a rose's bloom was a sign of a new beginning and that I needed one. So, each morning, we devoted time to tending to the roses on the same plot of land where my house used to be."

It took a minute for him to process her words. Mason drew in a sharp breath. "Your rose garden used to be your home?" Dang it, if his eyes didn't get moist after that. His chest expanded and he placed a hand over his chest. "Your grandmother deserves a medal. She is brilliant and one of a kind."

"I agree." She smiled. "Grams chose roses because she said every year, by my birthday, the roses would be in bloom. A reminder of my parents' love for me. And she was right. I have seen them bloom for the past ten years and every time I win the Blue Hen Rose Festival, I know it's because of my parents. I do it for them. And this year, for the first time, I hope to claim that reward in person."

Mason nodded. He was just the person to help her do it.

Chapter Thirteen

Eden awakened before her five-thirty alarm and stretched. She hadn't gotten home until close to 2:00 a.m. but her body was conditioned to arise at that time. She yawned. Once she was finished with her roses, she would catch a nap. But she had to get to them. The sun peeked over the horizon and she could tell from the mugginess in the air it was going to be a scorcher. She took care of her morning rituals, making sure to apply a generous amount of sunscreen, then dragged on a pair of shorts, a tank top and her hat before shoving her feet into a pair of boots. If she closed her eyes, she could go right back to sleep. But she wanted first prize. Mind on her motivation, Eden bounded down the stairs and stopped short.

Mason.

"What are you doing up?" she asked, her voice sounding groggy from unuse. He was dressed in similar garb, only while she felt like she had been run over by a horse-and-buggy, he appeared rested and camera ready. *Really?*

That fine man gave her a searing kiss that made her toes curl. Oh, she was wide-awake now. "I want to help you with your rose garden. Plus, I get the pleasure of your company all to myself." He walked in step with her toward the kitchen. "Unless… I'm intruding on your quiet time." He paused. "I didn't think about that."

"No, I'm glad for your company. Nothing speeds up work like conversation." Eden strolled toward the kitchen. Grams was already up and working on breakfast. Her grandmother was dressed in a pair of white capris and a colorful top and she had washed and blown out her hair. She was the picture of great health, which made Eden's heart glad. "Something tells me you're making your famous biscuits and omelets this morning," Eden said, eyeing the eggs, veggies, chicken strips and batter.

"You would be correct," Grams said.

"Do you need my help?" Mason asked.

"No, no. You two go on ahead with your plans."

"All right. I'm outside if you need me. Don't overdo it." Ever since Grams got sick, Eden still kept a watchful eye. Her grandmother had looked great the day before she fell terribly ill. Not that Grams was having it.

"Pshaw. I'm fine." Grams shooed them out but not before she and Mason exchanged meaningful glances.

Eden wondered what that was about but her desire to get to her plants exceeded her curiosity. She pushed open the back door and drew in a deep breath. From where she stood, she could already smell the fragrance from the roses, and they hadn't even bloomed yet. She grinned and then addressed Mason. "Let's get to work."

They sat side by side in her rose garden while she taught him how to prune and weed and take care of pesky critters while they yakked away. He about his time on the show and she dished on her job situation. "Dr. Loft should be reaching out today to let me know what's going on..." Eden lifted her hat. "I was thinking of telling her I changed my mind, you know. I really like the freshman classes and I feel I connect with the students. But what if I freeze up?"

Mason wiped his brow. "Eden Tempest, you're the bravest person I know. I think there would be an adjustment, but you have a great support system around you. I believe you'll be just fine. And I think you'll like it."

His optimism pumped up her confidence. "All right. I think I'll do it. I'll email as soon as we're done." She jutted her chin his way. "And what about you?"

He gave her a wary look. "What about me?"

"Your father? Your brother? You've got stuff to settle."

"I think it's best I leave that door closed. I'll send my brother some money." He stomped across the yard to grab a fresh bag of fertilizer delivered the day before. He obviously didn't want to talk about reconciliation, and she knew from experience it wasn't easy. She had had to accept her grandmother's forgiveness and Eden was just now beginning to truly forgive herself. She was a constant work in progress, and she wanted the same for Mason.

When he returned, she gently pressed on. "I lost my parents at a young age and there isn't a day that goes by that I don't think of them. Not a single one that I don't live with this enormous regret. I'd give anything to hear their voices, have them fuss at me. Anything but this silence."

"I get that but you had a loving family. My case was different." He hunched his shoulders and his voice was stern. She had to try a different approach.

Grabbing his arm, she asked, "If the TV station reached out and offered you another chance, wouldn't you take it?"

Mason didn't meet her eyes. "Um, they did offer me something but I turned them down. For now. My agent is on the lookout for other possibilities."

"Oh? I didn't know that." A hollow feeling formed in her gut. "So, you're leaving soon." Of course he would be. He belonged in front of the camera, thrived on the public attention. Eden had watched some of his past shows and Mason was way too talented to hide out in a small town. However, she steeled herself. He was here now, and she was going to cherish all that he had to give her. Then when the time came, she would let him go without a fuss. Eden had known loss before, she would be fine. She hoped. 'Cause just the thought felt like someone was grating her heart.

But she had her rose garden to remind her that life would go on, and in time, she would thrive again.

"I'm here now, with you," he said softly. "And this is where I want to be." He splayed his hand toward the house. "Being in the limelight, you lose a part of yourself. You become more concerned with what your viewers think, what your producers think, that you forget your first love." He lips quirked. "I am loving every moment of this makeover—and I'm not just talking about the B and B."

Her heart soared but she couldn't abandon the conversation around his family just yet. "Have you thought about your brother?"

"What about him?"

"Have you considered that maybe Maxim needs this? His big brother left him to deal with an alcoholic, abusive parent. What kind of trauma do you think he endured? He had to carry that weight on his own, while you pursued your own interests."

Mason placed a hand over his chest. "I did the right thing. Dad never hurt him physically and I did send Max money, like I said. He was well-provided for."

"Money isn't everything. I've never touched my parents' life insurance, and a huge part of that was because of guilt. Grams saved her insurance money from losing the property—I think that's what she's using to fix up the bed-and-breakfast. I worked hard and got a grant to attend college. That insurance money would have made my life easier but I always saw it as stained from the horror of their death."

Mason lifted her chin with his index finger. "It's all about perspective. That money is evidence that your parents loved you enough to secure your future."

She gave him a tender kiss. "I'm going to guess that that's how you were showing your brother your love. But he might see it differently. He's losing the father he loves and he could use your emotional support." She enfolded her arms about him and rested her head against his chest. "Sometimes, a hug is priceless," she choked out, her chin wobbling "What I wouldn't pay to feel my parents' embrace again. I'm discovering that physical touch and quality time are my love languages. Yours might be giving gifts but it doesn't mean your brother feels the same about those monetary favors."

He stiffened. "I think I've been taking my brother for granted, and I didn't realize—until you said it—that he's losing a father who was great to him." Mason's voice was a pleasant low rumble in her ear. "I can't tell you the last time Max and I hugged." He rested a hand on her back. "You're right. I didn't think about the power of human contact. I was so busy thinking about myself and my ordeal that I didn't see that he might just need to see me."

"Go see him then," Eden suggested, tilting her head back. "Now, I'm not an expert but the thing about building bridges is that once you start building one, it might give you the momentum to build another."

"I don't want to desert the crew," he said, rubbing her back. "And I most definitely don't want to leave you."

To her surprise, her lips formed the words "I'll come with you, if you want."

He drew back, his hands on her shoulders. "You would do that? For me?"

Eden swallowed, her heart rate escalating. "Yes. I care about you. I won't lie though. The mere thought of venturing among strangers scares me. Going to the rose festival among people who know me is already terrifying, but I want to be there for you."

"You're right. Some things are priceless. We can make a date of it. If we leave this afternoon, we can have a date night in Virginia. Then we go visit with my family tomorrow before driving back to Blue Hen."

Her brows rose. "An overnight trip…"

His eyes alighted with promise. "Yes, I will reserve our rooms or…one room. It's up to you."

"Make it one." She stood on tiptoes and kissed him long and deep. "I'll let Grams know."

Mason exhaled. "Okay, when Gabe comes, I'll run through what he needs to do until we get back tomorrow." His voice cracked with emotion. "Eden, you make it easy for a man to fall in love with you, if he were so inclined." Mason kissed her with passion, and she was too swept away to mull on what those words signified. It wasn't until she had spoken to Grams that Eden considered his words. Mason had told her clearly that he wasn't about to fall in love with her, or anyone, so she had better not hope for more.

Problem was, she suspected she was already halfway there. She stole a glance his way. But what did she know? She lacked experience and this could be a serious case of infatuation. Still, her gut feared it could be the start of something deeper. Something more.

Chapter Fourteen

Mason knew a tired man working on fumes and sheer will when he saw one. And that was Gabe. Oh, he was doing the work, but the energy level told the truth. Gabe had been crawling up and down the staircase like he had bad knees since he arrived twenty minutes ago.

Mason couldn't have an accident occurring because a man was exhausted or hungover. He pulled Gabe outside to talk before the rest of the crew arrived. "What's going on with you? You good?" The sun was beating on his back but he didn't want to chance anyone overhearing their conversation.

"Yeah. I just had a really good night," Gabe said, waggling his brows. His eyes had dark circles but they were shining. "It's been a long while. I'll get a cup of coffee."

"Really? You had me thinking you were… I didn't

know what to think." Mason was glad he had asked instead of jumping to conclusions like he would have done in the past. He hid a smile. "I'm glad you got lucky. I don't want your silly behind getting injured so make sure you eat and get a couple strong cups in you."

"Ms. Susan's got biscuits warming in the oven and she's working on a fresh batch of chicken fajita omelets." Gabe rubbed his tummy. "I can't wait to dig in. I need to replenish because I had quite a workout last night."

"Wait. What?" Normally, Mason wouldn't pry because he valued his own privacy.

"Yeah a pretty lady needed some company minus the conversation and I was happy to oblige. We're seeing each other again tonight."

"Oh, all right… I'm glad you could be of service." Mason cleared his throat. "I'm going to need you to rest up tonight because I have to go out of town, and I need my best man in charge."

Gabe puffed his chest. "I'm on it. What's going on?"

"I have to go see my father. He isn't doing well."

"Oh, I'm sorry to hear that, bro. Keep your head up and if you need anything, reach out." The genuine concern on Gabe's face gave Mason pause. The other man wasn't just speaking the words, he meant them. Gabe opened his arms, and they shared a brief but awkward hug. It made him feel cared for. Like he had someone besides himself. Eden's words about physical contact came back to him. He was now eager to see his brother.

"Thank you, friend. I'll keep you posted," Mason said. "Since we won't be here, today might be a good day to work on Eden's room."

"So, Eden's going with you?" Gabe stretched the words out, grinning from ear to ear. "You two an item?"

"Yes, she's coming for moral support."

Gabe's face said, *Oh, is that what you're calling it?*
But his words were, "I'm glad she'll be there with you.
Let me go see if Ms. Susan's got any caramel cappuc-
cino to give me a boost." Then he jogged back inside
the house.

Just then a delivery truck pulled up by the gate and
a driver in shorts and a T-shirt jumped out with a box.
"Oh, good. My package is here," Mason said. The young
man started the trek up the driveway. Mason made a
note to talk to Ms. Susan about a potential redesign of
the driveway. Mason decided to meet the delivery driver
halfway, his long strides eating up the length of the path.

After signing for his package, Mason went inside
the house, appreciating the cool temperature. Working
inside during the mornings had been Gabe's suggestion and a really good one. Any work on the exterior—
and there wasn't much left—was just some landscaping
around the premises, and of course, the driveway redesign if Ms. Susan agreed.

Mason sniffed. "Those smell amazing." His stomach grumbled.

"Come on and have one," Ms. Susan said, her face
beaming. Mason had a hard time believing she was
Eden's grandmother. Now that she was "well" again,
Ms. Susan looked at least two decades younger than
she must be based on sheer mathematics of having a
grandchild who was almost thirty.

"How is the surprise birthday party coming?" he
asked, since Eden wasn't lurking about.

"Everything is going according to plan," Ms. Susan
whispered. "I told Eden we're doing a grand reopening
on that day, so she won't be surprised to see the party

truck and all the tables and chairs being set up on the lawn. I also took your advice and decided to have it catered. Momma D's has some of the best barbecue on this side of the Delaware and we're planning for a good three hundred people to turn out."

"I didn't know there were that many people in this town," Mason teased. He was so glad Ms. Susan hadn't taken on everything herself like she had originally planned.

"Whatever." She rolled her eyes.

He sat on one of the stools behind the counter. "I wanted to ask how you would feel if we added paving to the driveway so that we had circular parking. We could put a fountain in the middle and expand the gate, so delivery trucks could get in and out without having to back in."

She tapped her chin. "I like that. It sounds regal and we do have the land space." Her eyes narrowed. "Will we encroach on Eden's garden? We can't take an inch away from it."

"I know what it symbolizes. That won't happen."

"Awesome. Then go for it."

"Great. I'll work out the numbers and get back to you."

Ms. Susan waved a hand. "Just do it. I trust you."

His shoulders lifted at her words. "Consider it done."

The door creaked and the crew came in just in time for breakfast, as was their pattern since they had arrived. Ms. Susan directed them to wash their hands and they all began laying out the meal in the dining hall. Mason loved seeing the diminutive Ms. Susan commandeering the men, who were more than happy to oblige.

One in particular seemed to be a bit chummy but Mason gave him a quelling glare and the other man backed off.

Ms. Susan must have seen their interaction because she sashayed over to him. "I can take care of myself, young man. Been doing it before you were born." He dipped his head and she went to take her usual spot. Gabe strolled in with Eden behind.

His breath caught. She was dressed in a pair of blue shorts, sandals and a yellow shirt, the color of a sunflower. The smile she gave him would melt an icicle. Eden came to sit with him and waited until after Ms. Susan said grace before spilling out, "I just spoke with Dr. Loft, and I told her that I decided to take the position. I didn't expect to feel excited. Thank you for the pep talk."

Mason wished he could kiss her, really kiss her right there, but he didn't want to embarrass her. So he settled for giving her a kiss on the cheek. "I'll give you a proper kiss later," he whispered in her ear. She blushed, the rosy hue spreading across her skin. Tonight, he would see how far that blush went. He exhaled and focused on helping himself to one of the biscuits.

The flaky goodness tasted like heaven in his mouth. "Ms. Susan, you put your *whole* foot in these biscuits. You need to box these and sell them. You would make a fortune. Say the word and I'll make it happen."

"Hush, now. Those are only for family and guests at the bed-and-breakfast," Ms. Susan tittered.

He tapped his head. "I understand. But if you change your mind, I'm here. Just saying."

Ms. Susan pointed to his plate. "Go on now and eat. You have a long journey ahead and I don't want you buying none of that processed food. I'm packing you and Eden a basket."

"Grams, you don't have to do all that," Eden said. "I can do it."

"I've got it." Ms. Susan's warning tone told them arguing with her would be a waste of time, so he didn't bother. Besides, Eden had bitten into her omelet and all that cheese greasing her lips proved to be a scintillating distraction. If she had her phone—

Oh yes. That reminded him. Mason excused himself and returned to the kitchen to retrieve the package he had placed on the counter earlier. He turned around and bumped into Eden. He had to grip the box to keep it from falling out of his hands.

"I came to get that proper kiss you promised me," she said, her arms circling his waist.

Mason took in those full lips and helped himself to a full serving. She kissed him with abandon, like they were alone, instead of in a kitchen where anyone could enter. And Mason returned kiss for kiss, not caring who they gave a show for. A few minutes later, he ended the kiss. Reluctantly. "We'd better get back in there. Our food is getting cold."

She shrugged. "I'll use a microwave."

He remembered he was holding the package and handed it to her.

"What's this?" she asked.

"Open it and see."

"You don't have to buy me anything," she said, opening the box and taking out the small package inside. Then she gasped. "You bought me a phone?"

"Yes." He smiled, then kissed her on the mouth that had popped open, which gave him access into that beautiful cavern. He explored further, gathering her close to his chest and grinding his hips against hers. This time when they both pulled away, they were out of breath.

"You got me all weak-kneed. How am I supposed to walk in there?" Mason scooped her into his arms, and she squealed, kicking her legs. "Put me down, you silly man. I was just joking."

Mason kept walking until they were close to the dining hall. Then he put her to stand and took in her wild hair and reddened lips. "You look like you've been thoroughly kissed," he said, leaving her standing there wide-eyed while he strutted inside and returned to his meal.

It took a minute or two before Eden reentered, looking more composed. She picked up her fork and cut into the rest of her omelet before leaning over to him. "I'm going to make you pay for that later."

"I'm looking forward to it," he shot back, loving their banter. He had a feeling she was going to be all that and then some in the bedroom and he couldn't wait to find out how right he was. Though he didn't like the reason he was driving to Virginia, Mason liked the person who was accompanying him. He liked her a whole lot. Probably too much if he were being honest. But he wouldn't worry about that now. Mason would focus on enjoying Eden and giving her the most pleasurable experience he could, tonight.

Then tomorrow, tomorrow, he would face the man who gave him the most painful memories of his life.

Chapter Fifteen

To prepare for her date that night, Eden gathered her courage and entered the beauty salon and spa. She had reached out to Cadence for beauty tips and the other woman had suggested they get makeovers together.

Cadence had then made them ten o'clock appointments, an hour before the salon actually opened. Grams had dropped her off since Cadence had offered to give her a ride home when they were finished.

She waved at her friend and scurried over to sit next to her. "Thank you for the hookup." There were sounds in the back of the spa and she assumed that was the owner getting ready. She heard the footsteps and saw the shadow before the person turned the corner.

"Raine?" Eden squealed, jumping to her feet. "I didn't know you owned the salon. When did you come back into town?" Raine was a military kid and had been with them in middle school before her father got deployed to Germany. Raine had left at the end of their freshman year of high school. They had tried to stay in touch but lost contact after a while.

Raine came forward with her arms open, a full-figured beauty with sparkling brown eyes. She had on an apron with a scissors and comb embroidered on the front over a pair of black jeans and a purple shirt. Her hair and nails were on point. "I've been back the last two years and Cadence and I reconnected."

"Wow." That was all Eden could say while her brain caught up with the fact that the old crew was now reunited.

"I wanted to come see you, but I heard what happened and I didn't want to intrude," Raine said.

"It's okay. I was curled into myself for a while so I don't think I would have welcomed any reconciliation. But I'm working on that." She reached over to take Cadence's hand and pulled her to her feet.

Then the three women hugged it out. There was some laughter, some tears but much healing. Her soul rejoiced. Time had passed, things were said and done, but life had brought them back together and she was appreciative of that.

Eden then put herself into Raine's care and got herself waxed and plucked and prodded right along with Cadence. When they left, she felt like a new woman. Literally and figuratively.

"Now, let's get you some lingerie for your night with Mason."

Eden lowered her lashes. "Good idea." She had already packed her cotton panties and T-shirt bras but now she giggled. "I want to knock his socks off when he sees me."

Cadence's luxury vehicle purred to life. "I know just the place to go." They then spent the next hour shopping for just the right outfit. She found a fuchsia two-piece ensemble that made her feel sexy and desirable. The top half was a lacy apron with a cage back detail. The matching thong had bows in the back.

"Thank you for your help, Cadence," she said, once they were parked outside the bed-and-breakfast. "You definitely understood the assignment." She giggled. "Mason won't know what to do with himself when he sees me in this."

"I'm pretty sure you're right. You are so welcome." She reached over to hold Eden's hand. "Thank you for giving me a second chance." Her voice broke with emotion.

When Eden turned and looked at Cadence, she was surprised to see that the other woman had tears in her eyes. "No more talk about second chances," Eden said. "The past is the past and all we can do is keep pressing forward."

Cadence wiped her face. "Okay, I'm just happy with our friendship." Eden gripped the door handle to exit the vehicle when she heard Cadence mumble, "Things will work out as they should. I've got to believe that."

Pausing, Eden asked, "Are you okay?"

For a second Cadence looked like she was about to say something but then she shook her head. "I'm fine. I don't want anything sullying your time away with Mason. Have a great time."

"Okay." Eden didn't want to push. They were still in the reconnecting stage of their friendship and she didn't want to intrude by demanding Cadence tell her what was wrong. She pulled out her cell phone and waved it. "You have my number, so reach out if you need."

"I will." Cadence pressed the start button and Eden got out. She stood and watched as Cadence backed her way down the path. There was something weighing the other woman down and it made Eden concerned. But all she could do was be there when Cadence was ready to talk. Cadence had shared that she and Gabe were in an entanglement of sorts. Nothing serious. Maybe she should tell Mason about it. Then she quashed that idea.

No. She couldn't blab about something she didn't know. That would be a violation of the unwritten friend-ship code.

Her cell phone rang so loudly that it echoed. She turned down the volume and tapped on the screen a few times until it answered. She hadn't yet fully mastered the touch screen, but Cadence had shown her how to text at least. She was eager to try all that out on Mason.

"Are you ready?" he asked. "I'd like us to get on the road in the next five minutes."

"Yes. I just have to get my overnight bag." She dashed up the stairs and exchanged her drab under-wear for the lingerie. Eden also dropped in the new perfume and makeup she had purchased from Raine. However, she did leave a comfortable pair of lace un-dies for the next day.

Before she left, she went to check in on her grand-mother. Grams sat in her new white rocking chair with her knitting needles in hand and her cheaters on. "I don't feel right leaving you out here all alone."

Her grandmother placed her handiwork aside. "I've got my shotgun in my nightstand but I'm pretty sure I won't need it. Plus, Mason arranged for Gabe to spend the night here and you know no one's getting through Mr. Beefy Abs."

"Really, Grams? Mr. Beefy Abs?" Eden chuckled, heading farther in the room. "Please don't tell me you've called him that to his face."

"I did more than that. I also said it behind his back."

Eden busted out laughing. "Grams, you must have been a trip back in your heyday."

Grams peered over her cheaters. "My lips are sealed." Then she gave Eden a tender look. "I'm so happy to see you out with friends and just enjoying life. That's all I ever wanted. To see my grandbaby happy again. Your parents weren't all I lost that day."

She rushed over and gave her grandmother a hug before slipping onto the mat and resting her head in her grandmother's lap. "I'm so glad I have you. So glad." The tears came fast.

"There now." Her grandmother patted her on the back. "We've come a long way and there's some ways to go, but at least we're taking steps. That's what matters."

Eden wiped her face and stood, then kissed her grandmother's soft cheek. "I'll text you once we're in Virginia."

"Okay. Now get going."

Mason stood by the door. "Gabe should be here within the hour," he said to the older woman, who opened her arms. Mason took tentative steps before bending over to give her a hug.

"Take care of my baby girl and no speeding," she said.

Eden heard a muffled "I will" before Mason pulled away. He held out a hand toward Eden. With joined hands they left for Virginia. Mason told her it would be one straight path down the US 13 for almost the entire trip to Virginia Beach. He had made reservations at The Cavalier, an oceanfront luxury suite with views of the Atlantic Ocean. Then he gave her a pair of sunglasses before slapping a pair on along with a baseball cap.

Mason tuned the radio to some old jams and she settled back to read her book. They drove in companionable silence until he pulled into a gas station to fill the tank. Eden excused herself to use the restroom and when she came out, he was surrounded by fans, taking selfies and signing a few autographs.

She stopped short. She had forgotten he was a celebrity.

No wonder he had given her the shades. His "cover-up" hadn't stopped him from being recognized. She lowered her head so her hair shielded her face and slipped into the passenger side. The last thing she wanted was to end up with her face all over the internet or in a gossip mag as his current fling.

"Sorry about that," he said once they were on their way.

"We're in such a cocoon out in Blue Hen that I forgot that you have a very recognizable face."

"Being in the spotlight means you sacrifice your privacy. Sometimes people forget you're human. That you need space. You always have to be on. You always have to be nice. This is the trade-off for me being financially secure. You are at the public's whim. You don't get to have a bad day."

"That doesn't sound like fun," Eden said.

"As with any career, there are pluses and minuses. But if you're not careful, it can consume you and you can lose touch with yourself, become someone you never dreamed of becoming." He tapped her on the shoulder. "So, when do your classes start?"

She understood his need for a conversation shift and followed along. "Technically, I begin mid-August since the fall semester begins the last Monday in August. But of course, I'll start prepping way before then. My accepting the position means I'll get a pay hike."

"What about your grandmother's bed-and-breakfast? I thought you would be the one running it."

"No, Grams will still be in charge for now. When I'm not working, I'll assist and learn the ropes. Teaching is my passion though. I feel such joy when I see my students get excited about learning and when I see them put skills I've taught them into practice."

"Wow. You should see how your face is beaming right now." He smiled. "Before coming to Blue Hen, I had lost my passion. But working on Ms. Susan's property has revived my love for what I do. I enjoy working with my hands. It fulfills me. If I ever have the opportunity to do a show again, I would definitely be getting my hands dirty instead of giving orders from the sidelines."

She heard the wistfulness in his voice. It sounded like Mason wanted to be back on the air. "But what if it doesn't happen? What if you're never given that second chance?"

"I can't consider that possibility," he said. "The idea of a second chance is what keeps me going."

"And when that happens, where does that leave us?" she asked.

"We'll figure it out. Find a happy medium between both our worlds." He sounded so confident that she didn't want to ruin the mood with the truth. She couldn't see becoming a part of his world. She couldn't leave her rose garden. She could only savor what they had now and enjoy the ride for as long as it lasts.

Eden looked over at his profile from under her lashes. He was rapping along to a song from way back in the day, spitting out the rhymes and verses like a pro. She could see she surprised him by rapping out the next verse.

"Hey, what you know about that, girl?" he said, eyeing her with admiration.

Chapter Sixteen

Mason couldn't recall a time he had been this nervous. His hand shook while using the key card to enter the Presidential Suite.

Luckily, Eden appeared too awestruck to notice, gaping at the plush surroundings and the view. But the focal point was the king-size bed. It was close to 10:00 p.m. and they had already grabbed dinner. He had asked for a late checkout and had arranged to meet his brother for lunch at his father's house the next day.

Eden placed her overnight bag on the deep red bedroom bench at the edge of the bed. The curtains and headboard were the same luxurious color. He dropped his bag next to hers and moved to close the curtains.

If it were any other woman, he would have already had her out of her clothes. But this was Eden. All innocent yet sweet and naughty at the same time. He didn't want to mess up her first experience.

She fiddled with her shirt, and he put on the television because after nonstop conversation the last three to four hours, he now couldn't think of anything to say. This was so antihero-like. He wasn't accomplishing any romance fantasies standing there all awkward and shy.

So he sat.

Great, now he was sitting all awkward and shy. Good grief. He snuck a glance her way. Unlike him, she seemed calm and assured.

Eden picked up her bag. "I'm going to take a shower. I'll be right back." As soon as the door clicked, he sprung to his feet and called the front desk. A few minutes later, the staff arrived with flowers and rose petals and chocolates. He went to work on setting up a romance-worthy scene. They had also added vanilla-scented candles which he placed in a couple areas of the room. Mason stepped back to view his handiwork and smiled. He didn't know why he hadn't thought of this before. The staff could have had it ready before they checked in.

Oh well. No point in backpedaling now. He could hear Eden humming off-key and grinned. Mason loved hearing her special sounds. He would discover more of them real soon.

When Eden opened the door, the scent of jasmine and something else filled his nostrils. Whatever it was, it was intoxicating. She had donned one of the white hotel robes and Mason wanted to investigate the bare shoulder but he consoled himself with giving her a quick peck on the cheek. Then he headed into the shower. The heat level and the force of the spray on his back had him lingering a little longer than he normally would. He turned off the spigot, then grabbed one of the generously long towels off the rack and dried his upper body, and then wrapped it around his waist. He quickly brushed his teeth, applied deodorant and tiny sprays of his cologne. Mason exited the bathroom, his eyes searching for Eden.

His mouth dropped open. He had found her all right.

All glorious five-feet-eleven inches of her was stretched out across the bed, with one leg propped up and an arm behind her head. She was dressed in a frilly sheer top and a barely there panty, the ultimate definition of seduction. But that color. That pinkish-purple color popped against her skin. Mason feasted on that visual image, pulling his bottom lip into his mouth.

Then she turned over and he lost his breath for a second.

Whew.

"You look... Wow." Dropping the towel to the floor, Mason moved to the foot of the bed and grabbed her feet, pulling her to the edge of the bed. "I am going to sample every part of your body, front and back."

Her eyes darkened, the orbs the color of honeyed liqueur, and she gave herself over to him. And he loved on her. Then when her body was ready, he led her on the age-old path to a scorching climax.

Drenched with sweat and their body perfume, Mason drew her close, cuddling her against him. Sometime during the wee hours of the morning, he awakened to her returning all the pleasurable favors he had bestowed on her. And this time, their joining was furious, frenzied, the resulting orgasm shattering him in a thousand brilliant pieces.

Aww, this woman, this gem he had found in the middle of nowhere was his sexual fantasy come alive. He didn't think he would ever get enough of her.

In her arms, he rested.

Then when dawn loomed, slithers of sunlight coming through the curtains, he awakened and watched her in repose. She had a small smile on her face and he hoped he was a part of the reason for that. Mason allowed his hands to roam her beautiful sun-kissed body before running his fingers through her soft curls. Then he took her gently, their consummation in sync with the sunrise.

In due time, she pinned those cognac orbs on him, and they fed on the last two pieces of chocolates. "This isn't going to hold me," she purred in his ear. "I'm going to need serious sustenance after experiencing the best night of my life."

"I'm happy to hear that." He kissed her forehead. "We're getting room service with a little bit of everything. You'll be well replenished before we leave."

"Let's take a bath together," she said, curling into him, like they had been doing it for years.

Mason kissed her lips and went to get the water ready. He poured in the bath salts and rose petals, making sure the temperature was on the hotter side. After testing the heat level with his toe, Mason got into the tub, and called for her join him.

She came into the bathroom, tall and proud, holding a pink loofah, and without an ounce of shyness, used the restroom before slipping underneath the bubbles. Using Eden's loofah, he gently washed her.

Eden dunked her entire body under the water before popping out and whipping her hair back, mermaid style. He cracked up. "Come here, my little siren." Spooning her against him, at her urging, he entered her, his mind filled with amazement at the number of times he was going to come.

Their breakfast came and they assuaged their hunger, ravenous after all their encounters from the night before. Once they were full, they jumped into the shower, dressed and departed for his father's house which was fifteen minutes away. Reaching over to take her hand, Mason said, "I'm so glad you're here with me. Are you sore?" He had tried to be gentle but a few times she had egged him on past the point of reason.

"I'm glad too. For obvious reasons," she teased. "And I'm a little sore but that's to be expected, considering… but I'm not in pain. It's all good. No worries."

His shoulders relaxed. "I've never taken a girl home," he confessed.

Her brows rose. "Never?"

"Nope. But you're all kinds of special and most of all, a true friend." He kissed the back of her hand. "I'm going to apologize in advance for anything that might go down once I'm at my father's house."

"There's no need to apologize. All will go the way it's supposed to go."

"That sounds like something Ms. Susan would say."

Eden chuckled. "That's because she did."

Chapter Seventeen

Hearing about Mason's terrible childhood, Eden didn't know why she had visualized the house to match. But they pulled into a well-paved driveway of a sprawling home in a cul-de-sac. When they exited his pickup, the lush perennial gardens caught her eyes. "Those are quite lovely." Mason then told her that the five-bedroom, three-bathroom property included a sunroom, an in-ground swimming pool and an oasis in the backyard. Mason even added that they had recently installed solar panels.

"This seems like a nice place to grow up," she said.

Mason gave her a somber look. "On the outside."

"What did your father do?" she asked.

"When he was sober, he was into real estate. Lots of rich clientele who wanted to purchase property on Virginia Beach."

"Ah, I see."

Taking her hand, Mason led Eden toward the door

and rang the doorbell. His hand tightened around hers when the door swung open.

A brown-skinned man with curly hair and light brown eyes, about an inch shorter than Mason, opened the door. Without hesitation, Mason went into his brother's arms. Lots of rocking and back-patting ensued before the brothers pulled apart.

"Bro, it's good to see you here," Maxim said, before turning his gaze on Eden. "And you must be the girlfriend I've heard so much about."

He told his brother about her? "I'm hoping he said good things." Eden extended her hand and smiled.

"He said you had a great sense of humor and I see why." Maxim gently swatted her hand away and gave her a quick hug. Then he invited them inside. They passed through the large sunroom, her eyes taking in a large family picture of two young boys—she figured must be Mason and Maxim—and their parents.

He continued until they were in the dining area but because it was a large, open-concept space, she had a clear view of another family picture on the mantel. Maxim looked a lot like their mother. The woman was standing next to a younger version of Alton, who looked a lot like Mason. Mason and his father shared a strong resemblance, giving Eden a clear picture of what Mason would like in a few years.

She sat next to Mason while Maxim dressed the table. The spread from a five-star chef was picture worthy and by the look of it, he had gone all out. She snapped pictures of balsamic–brown sugar lamb chops, pumpkin risotto, white truffle mac and cheese, crispy potatoes and grilled asparagus.

"Wow, this is quite the feast," Eden said.

"Now you see why my son is in high demand," a new voice said from behind.

Eden spun in her seat as Mason stood, his face stoic. She got to her feet and scooted beside him.

"I'll go get the rolls out of the oven." Maxim departed for the kitchen.

Alton Powers did not look like his diagnosis. Eden had expected to see him frail and bent but he was sprightly and energetic. Alton was shorter than both his sons and was closer to her height.

"Hello, Dad," Mason said, looping his arm through hers. "This is my girlfriend, Eden."

Alton came over to clasp her hand in his briefly. "It's a pleasure to meet you."

"You have a lovely home."

He looked like he would give his son a hug, but Mason's demeanor didn't invite physical contact. Alton rolled back on his heels and dipped his head to his chest before addressing Mason. "You look well."

"Considering I got booted off my own show?" Mason scoffed.

His father gave him a quelling look. "More like I'm proud of you rising above through all this turmoil. Learning and doing better."

"Dad, let's eat before the food gets cold," Maxim said, holding some rolls in his hand.

They all took their seats and Alton led them in prayer, thanking God for bringing Mason home and then blessing the food.

Eden found Mason's father and brother positively darling. She was now rooting for Mason and his family to reconcile, but judging by the brooding expression on Mason's face, she would say that was unlikely to happen during this visit. But good food and full stomachs softened the chill in the room and the brothers entertained Eden by sharing escapades from their childhood.

Alton didn't eat more than a spoonful of his serving of pumpkin risotto, and she could see the corresponding worry etched on Maxim's face.

"You should take Eden on a tour," Maxim said after they were finished with their meal. He had already provided Eden and Mason with to-go containers. Eden had packed an extra one for her grandmother and at Maxim's prodding, Mason would take a tray for Gabe and the rest of the crew.

"Yes, show her your room," Alton said with a charming smile.

"You mean where I spent most of my time licking my wounds," Mason shot back, acid in his tone. Eden slid him a warning glance, but he clamped his jaw.

Maxim looked at him with thunder in his eyes. "You don't let up, do you?"

"Do you want me to pretend that my life was like roses? Well, it wasn't," Mason replied.

"I do expect you to treat our guest with courtesy," his father said with steel in his voice. Both Mason and Maxim straightened.

"Yes, sir," Mason said, getting to his feet before eyeing her with tenderness. "Let's check out the gardens. I do think you'll like them."

Eden stood as well and followed him out the room. As soon as they were out of earshot, she rounded on Mason. "What was that about in there? Did you forget your purpose in coming?"

He spoke through gritted teeth. "I hugged my brother."

"Yes, but you're behaving abominably. It's embarrassing. Not to mention childish."

He cut his eyes at her. "I'm sorry if I'm an embarrassment to you."

"Nope. Not to me. You're an embarrassment to yourself. I get that your father hurt you and it's okay to be an angry about that, because I'm certainly not excusing any abusive behavior of any kind. But if you want a second chance, you've got to be willing to give others a second chance." She placed a hand on her hip. "Has your father ever apologized?"

"He's sent letters and has called and left messages but like I told you, I'm not interested in reconciliation."

"I see. But you're clearly not interested that you're hurting your brother in the process. You were here to be a source of comfort to him, but right now, you're causing him distress."

His shoulders slumped. "That's not my intention." His voice dropping to a whisper. "I'm making a muck of things."

"Until you deal with the anger you have toward your father, you're going to keep lashing out at the wrong people. People like your brother or those who work for you. How does that make you any different from your father? He abused his authority and you're doing the same."

"So, you think I'm a beast. An ogre." He folded his arms.

"No, I see the beauty within you," she said. "I see the generous man helping my grandmother, working without pay. Yes, we know that's what you're doing," she added when his brows rose. "I see your patience toward me when I was afraid to venture out, and your gentleness when you made love to me. That's what I see. And I wish you would give your family the chance to see the man I'm getting to know. The man I'm trying hard not to fall for."

Mason's mouth hung open. "Did you just say what I think you're saying?" All the anger appeared to have seeped out of him.

"Your ears work, correct?" She rolled her eyes. "But your behavior today has given me pause. I'm determined not to fall for your disguise. You are showing me another side to you that I never imagined."

She brushed past him, intending to return to finish the visit with his family but he took her arm. "I'm sorry I'm not the man you think I am. The truth is, I'm not deserving of love, especially not your love. I can't accept that and I can't give it. I'm incapable because I ruin everything I touch. This anger simmers within and it builds and builds until it boils over." He placed a hand under her chin. "What if it boils over and burns you? I could never bear the thought of causing you pain."

Her eyes flew to his. "I'm not the least bit concerned about that happening because I know the man that you are. The problem is, you don't know it. And you're more than capable of loving and accepting love, if you're willing to do the work. I can recommend my therapist, if you'd like. I'm glad to be your friend, your sounding board, but you need someone with the level of expertise to truly help."

"I thought I could pretend that everything was all right and make my brother happy." His lowered his head to his chest. "Maybe we should just go home. I'll take her contact information."

"Nope. You need to make this right. Your father and

brother have been wonderful. I can't say the same for you. But I would like to be able to say that before we leave."

He took her through the house after that, delighting her with his stories. When they approached his bedroom, he tensed up right before he opened the door before admitting, "This is the first time I am actually coming in here since I have left home. I usually get a hotel or sleep on the couch."

"Wow," Eden said.

When they got inside, he gasped. It was the typical room you would expect to see for a young man—posters of his music icons, trophies from playing various sports—but one wall was almost a shrine in Mason's honor. There were framed news articles of his television show and his awards. All the current news about him was there on display.

"I can't believe my brother did all this..." His voice held amazement and his face depicted shock. Eden could see Mason was bowled over. His eyes misted. "You're so right, Eden. I do need to set things right with Maxim."

"All I see is love on this wall," she choked out, overcome.

They rejoined his family, who were now sitting in the living area having a hushed conversation, which ended when Eden and Mason returned.

Mason went over to his brother and snatched him into a tight hug. "I saw the wall in my room. I can't believe you did that. It really touched my heart."

Maxim smiled. "Thanks, but I didn't do that."

Eden watched when the realization of who did hit Mason in the chest. His lower lip quivered, and he turned to face his father. She dropped into the chair, the scene playing out before her like a movie. And this was one she really wanted to see.

Chapter Eighteen

"I'm proud of you, son," Alton said, spreading his arms wide.

For a beat, Mason froze. How he had longed to hear those words as a youth. His heart cracked. That longing hadn't changed as an adult. He just realized that. He looked back at his brother just to make sure he wasn't about to play himself and that his father was talking to him. Maxim was standing there, a goofy grin on his face. Then Mason met Eden's eyes and she was smiling and nodding, as if saying *Yes, he's talking to you*.

Mason turned to face his father, who still had his arms open. "I'm sorry I didn't say that enough to you when you were growing up. I wanted to but the grief of losing your mother was bigger than me and I took that out on you. A child. If I could rewind the past..." Alton shuddered. "I had to hit rock bottom before I joined AA and get into counseling before I lost another son," he choked out.

He heard a sharp intake of breath and realized it came from him. "I—I don't understand."

Maxim walked over to place a hand on his shoulder. "I hated being the middleman between you and Dad. And though Dad was good to me, he was a functional drunk. He would leave in the mornings, slap on the happy face for his clients and then come home and drink himself in a stupor. After I graduated college, I told him I was leaving, and I planned to be done with both of you."

"That's when I knew I had to change. My heart already had a gaping hole when you left but I could live with that because I knew I deserved your contempt. I accepted that you would hate me forever for failing you as a father. And you should."

Goose bumps popped up on Mason's arms. He was more like his father than he realized. Just a few minutes ago, he had pretty much said the same thing—different words, same meaning—that he was undeserving of love. Slaking his eyes over at Eden, he figured she was thinking the same thing because she was sniffling and dabbing at her eyes.

His father wasn't done talking. "But I had been good to Maxim and now even he wanted to leave." Alton pointed to his chest. "That's what told me I was the problem. I was the common denominator."

"But you went into therapy. You got the help you needed," Maxim said, his chest puffed. "And our relationship is better and stronger than it was before. I just wish—" He stopped. "I don't want to ruin the little bit of progress by saying what I want."

"I can fill in the blanks," Mason said with a smile, giving his brother yet another hug. Eden was onto something with that physical contact. Once you started, it was kind of hard to stop. Not that he wanted to. Mason looked at Alton, really looked at him for the first time. All he saw was love, genuine love, reflected in those depths.

Alton lowered his arms. "Even if you hate me forever, I want to advise you to deal with your anger. I don't want you losing time with loved ones the way I did. Don't repeat the same mistake I did."

Wow. His dad sounded like…a father. Mason's eyes blurred and he took a small step and another before falling into his father's arms. "I'll get help too, Dad." He couldn't quite say *I love you* yet, but maybe in time he could? It was worth exploring… He registered a flash of light, and he pulled back to glance behind him.

"Sorry, I had to record this moment to make sure it's not a figment of my imagination," Maxim said, sheepish. "I don't know when I might see this again."

"I did, too," Eden said, her voice sounding stuffy from crying. "You need a keepsake."

A keepsake. That's right. His father was dying. Mason wobbled on his feet. His father's strong grip steadied him. "It's all right, son. I'm ready to go."

Tears streamed down Mason's face as fresh realization hit. "I don't think I am ready for you to go." His chest rose and fell. The words *I'll be your donor* were right there, stuck in his throat, but Mason refused to utter them. He didn't want to go off raw emotion— though losing his father was emotional—but he wanted to make sure he really meant them, and he wouldn't resent doing this in the future.

For the next hour, Mason, his brother and his father talked. Talked without any ill will between them. He had Eden beside him, his hand resting on her thigh. Eden joined in at times, but she also pulled out her Kindle and read, content to allow them to connect as a family. She would have probably gone out to the gardens if he hadn't squeezed her thigh to keep her from leaving.

For some reason, Mason needed her with him. He didn't know what that meant but it was yet another topic worth exploring when he entered counseling.

When they walked out the door of his childhood home, Mason felt light and…happy. He looked over at Eden. This woman had a lot to do with this cheesy grin on his face.

"I had a lovely time," she said.

"I had an enlightening time," he replied. Standing in the driveway, Mason drew her close and kissed the top of her head. He kissed her forehead, her cheeks, behind her ear, her neck and finally, finally, those precious lips. Lips that belonged to a woman who wasn't afraid to speak her mind, to tell him the truth, to say she could fall for him.

And just like that, his eyes popped open and joy filled his chest. Mason stepped back and grinned. Eden's brows furrowed. "What is it?"

Mason placed a finger over his mouth. "It's nothing. I'm just happy, that's all." Well, it was something but he couldn't tell her just yet. He wasn't just happy. He was in love with the woman standing before him. He would laugh but he didn't want Eden wondering if he was okay. Because you don't know how many times in the romance novel where the hero gets slapped with that knowledge that Mason had said, *Yeah, right*, but here he was experiencing the same thing, and yeah, he was now a believer. And yeah, he got why, everyone loved happy endings. 'Cause, shoot, it was bubbling over and threatening to spill.

Mason opened the passenger door, humming under his breath, and settled her inside the pickup before getting in. Excitement thrummed within. He pulled up his playlist and played happy songs. Eden gave him the side-eye. "You're in a good mood."

"I am. I am. And it's because of you."

She cracked up. If only she knew how true that was.

"You're infectious when you're like this," she said while singing along. If only that were true, and she could "catch" some of this love he had, but she pretty much told him she wasn't trying to fall for him. But that's okay, he would work on changing her mind.

If Mason was going to be the hero in this romance that was his life, he was going to show Eden Tempest how much he loved her in a big way, and he was going to get his happy ending. Because that's what he did for a living. Made things happen.

Chapter Nineteen

"What on earth did you do to that man?" Grams asked, pointing at Mason through the kitchen window as she packed away the kitchen goods into boxes. There were about ten men now working on the property if Eden's count was correct. All the clanging and banging was leading to some wonderful makeovers. The kitchen was among the last rooms to get renovated as Mason and the crew planned to start the next day, which was June 7. He was in their yard adding perennial plants to the perimeter of the property and singing at the top of his lungs. "Since you all returned from Virginia Beach, what's it been? Two weeks? He has been humming and singing, and so happy my teeth hurt."

"It's been sixteen days, but who's counting?" Eden giggled as she used the town's old newspapers to wrap the plates. "I don't know what I did, but he has been over-the-top affectionate. Every morning, he waits by the stairs for me, and we go outside to work on the roses. He's been leaving me little gifts everywhere—in the garden, in my bathroom, in my laptop bag—I don't even know when or how he's doing that."

"That the power of the P," Grams said. "That man is sprung wide open."

It took a moment for that to sink in and Eden placed a hand over her mouth. She was sure her cheeks were warm, although they were enjoying quite a robust sex life. She sealed one box with packing tape. "Grams, I can't believe you said that."

Grams rested a hand to her chest. "To clarify, by *P* I meant pheromones."

Eden snorted. *Yeah, right.* The mischief in Grams' eyes told the truth.

Grams's shoulders shook. "Reminds me of your grandfather when he used to come calling for me at my parents' house. He was at my house from sunrise to sunset. It got to the point where my mother said, *Why don't you put this girl on your head and carry her around with you everywhere you go?*" She shook her head. "And you know that man sure did try. I remember kicking and screaming for him to put me down."

"That's hilarious. I love it." Eden loved when her grandmother recounted her and Pop's love story. It wasn't the first she had heard this, but it never failed to make her feel good. Eden's parents had experienced the same kind of loving relationship. It was too bad she wouldn't. She enjoyed Mason's presence, but she wasn't about to tip over into love. The heartache of loving and losing was too real, too crushing. Especially since losing her parents had been her fault. Being with her might cost him her life.

Now rationally, she knew that kind of thinking wasn't true but her heart was afraid to leap, afraid to hope, afraid to accept love.

"His improved disposition probably has to do with the counseling he's been getting."

"Hmm…if that's what you think," Grams replied, with heavy sarcasm. Since Grams finished packing her box, Eden sealed that carton as well and wrote the appropriate label on the top, including the word *fragile*.

The women stood arm in arm and surveyed the area that had been their refuge for much laughter and tears. "In a couple days or so, we will have a brand-new kitchen from top to bottom. Mason has some solid plans. I'm excited but sad about it at the same time," Grams said.

Eden's heart squeezed. "This was the kitchen Mom and Dad knew."

Grams patted her hand. "And this will be the kitchen Mason designs and where you will make new memories. Hopefully, with him."

For a second, Eden allowed herself to imagine the idyllic image of her and Mason and a little girl, a blend of them, sitting at the kitchenette making turkey treats or coloring eggs or decorating gingerbread houses. How wonderful would that be if she took a chance and told him how she felt, only to learn he reciprocated those feelings. But Mason was leaving soon to return to the limelight and she couldn't picture herself anywhere but this small town. So, what was the point? She cared about him enough not to put him in that position to choose.

Ugh, this man had her teeter-tottering all over the place.

The man of her thoughts came inside beaming and swooped her in his arms. "Eden, you've got to see this."

"I can walk on my own two feet," she protested, hearing Grams's cackle behind her. Her grandmother was eating this up.

"Look," he said, placing her at the far end of her rose garden. She inhaled. A single bud had formed, its petals tightly closed, and it was marvelous to see. "It's almost bloom time," she whispered.

"Yes, the festival is in fourteen days."

She scurried into action. "I've got to water them." Mason ran to get the hose.

"They are going to be magnificent," Grams proclaimed, clapping her hands.

Eden could only nod, dabbing at her eyes. Seeing the wonder of the rosebuds open in bloom never got tiring. She could hardly wait. It was a culmination of all her efforts and her yearly reminder of the continuation of life after tragedy. Even those of one's doing. She looked over at Mason, who was now watering the roses and whistling, his eyes bright and filled with hope and her heart expanded.

Maybe after the rose festival, she would have an open and honest conversation with Mason. Suddenly, a splash of water hit the side of her face. And another.

"No! Mason, stop!" she squealed, lifting her hands. Grams took off for the house, moving with speed and dexterity.

Immediately, he stopped and she grabbed the hose from him before proceeding to drench him from head to toe. A fun game of tag ensued coupled with laughter and dirt. He circled the rose garden and came in low toward her, tackling her to the ground, making sure to twist his body and take the brunt of the fall. Thus, she was on top of him and they were laughing like children.

"We're too grown for this," she said, tapping his nose. Something else tapped her midriff and she rolled her eyes. "Really? You're as randy as a jackrabbit."

"Only for you," he said, lifting his head to kiss her. A kiss she gladly returned, the sun beaming down on them. Since they were by the rosebushes, she didn't think her grandmother could see what they were up to. Mason trailed kisses down her neck. "What do you say we take this inside?"

"I need to finish giving the roses a good watering." She sure was tempted though.

He wagged his brows. "Funny, cause that's what I want to do with your garden."

Chuckling, she gave him a gentle shove and stood, holding out her hand. He got to his feet, brushing the mud off his pants. "I've got to shower," Mason said, wiping at the grime. "These wet clothes are uncomfortable."

"Me too. I've got dirt in places I didn't know I had."

"We can shower together to save water," Mason suggested.

"Oh, is that what we're doing?" They joined hands and went inside his suite. It was several hours before she closed his bedroom door, leaving Mason to talk with his physician. He had told her about being tested as a donor for his father and wanted to make sure he was able to do so before telling his family. Since Eden had been spending so much time in Mason's room, she had left clothes in the closet and had pretty much taken over his sock drawer with her undies. Her toiletries were lined up right along with his on the huge chest. She had donned a floral sundress and planned to let her hair air-dry after putting in a curl activator.

Eden went into the kitchen and opened the refrigerator in search of a snack. Seeing a bag of cherry plums, she took three and washed them before taking a bite. Grams had left a note that she had gone into town and would bring back dinner.

Right as Eden bit into one of the plums, there was a rap on the kitchen door.

It was Cadence. Her eyes looked red and puffy, like she had been crying.

"Come in," Eden said invitingly and led her over to the kitchen table to have a seat. "We packed up the kitchen, but I can offer you bottled water?"

Cadence followed her but declined to sit. "No. No. I don't need anything." Fresh tears plopped down her face. "I… I don't know how to tell you this but it's going to eat away at me for the rest of my life if I don't."

For some reason, Eden felt a sense of foreboding. But she couldn't think of any reason to feel that way. They had only just reconnected so she had no clue what this could be about. But Cadence appeared visibly upset, on the verge of falling apart. "What's going on, Cadence?"

"Now that I'm here, I don't know if I can do this." Her chin wobbled, her knuckles turned white gripping her purse. "Give me a minute." She paced across the length of the kitchen, mumbling to herself.

Seeing her in such distress, Eden rushed over and stilled Cadence's movements, holding onto both her arms. "Whatever it is, it can't be that bad. Just spill it out. We will figure it out. We will handle it together."

Cadence wiped her face and sniffled. "You'll hate me."

"Okay, now you're putting me on edge and if I'm going to freak out, I should at least know why." Slouching her shoulders, Cadence walked over to the table and sat, face away from Eden, her body shaking hard enough to rattle the table. "I'm the one who started the fire." Those whispered words threatened to destroy Eden's very soul but she was positive she hadn't heard right.

Eden leaned forward. "I'm sorry. I must have heard you wrong. What did you say?"

Cadence pinned her with a gaze of desolation and repeated, "I started the fire. It was me."

"No! No! You're mistaken." Eden jumped to her feet and rounded on the other woman. "Why would you come here and utter such lies?"

Cadence rushed over to her. "I'm not lying. We were up in your room smoking ciggies, remember? But then you went downstairs to cut your cake. I—I went into the bathroom to finish off my smoke. But I was messing around with the lighter and, I don't even know how, the curtains caught fire. It spread like wildfire. I tried dousing everything with water until I finally had to scream out *Fire!* I screamed, *Fire, Fire,* and raced outside the house." She started to sob in earnest. "I didn't expect your parents would rush up the stairs and get trapped. And I didn't expect you would…go after them."

"All this time…" Eden's knees buckled. She would have fallen if Cadence hadn't caught her. She struggled to catch her breath, inhaling and exhaling but she couldn't get enough air. Cadence bent before her, urging her breath in, breath in, until she calmed somewhat. As soon as she could, Eden lashed out, "All this time I thought I was the one who..." She grabbed her midriff. "How could you make me believe that about myself?" Before Cadence could answer, another memory sliced her to the core and her mouth dropped. "How could you tease me and taunt me, calling me a beast when it was your fault?"

"I—I was a kid myself. I wasn't thinking," Cadence said, wringing her hands.

Rage built and just seeing Cadence's face stoked her anger. "I can't believe you did that. You aren't a friend. You're the one who's actually a monster," she screamed.

"Please, I am so sorry for hurting you," Cadence said, grabbing onto Eden's hand.

"Get out," she commanded through gritted teeth.

Cadence pleaded, "These past few years hasn't been easy for me."

"And you think they have been for me?" Eden held up her hands. "Look at what your careless actions did to my body. This isn't about starting the fire. This is about your allowing me to take the blame and then calling yourself a friend." Her chest rose and fell. "I suggest you get to stepping."

"No, Eden, please. We have been working on our friendship and I can't lose that. Please. I'm sorry." Cadence covered her face in her hands.

"Your apologies are too late and they can't bring my mom and dad back. Get out! Get out before I call the police and don't you dare come back here again. If I see your face, I won't be responsible for my actions."

Mason came bounding into the kitchen just as Cadence flew through the back door. "Are you all right?"

All she could do was shake her head. Eden crumpled to the floor. The tears flowed then, her body wracked with sorrow. Mason scooped her up and cradled her in his arms. She burrowed into him, welcoming the comfort his strong arms provided. He sank onto the living room couch, remained silent and allowed her to cry until she was spent. By then, Grams had returned and when she regained her composure, Eden told them what Cadence had confessed.

Mason was understandably upset, but Grams… Grams shocked her. "Poor girl. To carry that lie for thirteen years was too big a burden for anyone."

Eden rubbed her temples. "How can you have an ounce of compassion after what I just told you?"

"Maybe you should consider pressing charges," Mason added. "I wonder if there is a statute of limitations on arson."

"Yeah. I think that's a good idea," Eden said. "I can do some research. Or we can call the sheriff in the morning. He would know."

"Let's leave the past in the past," Grams replied, sounding weary. "Nothing that is said or done will bring my children back. They need to keep resting in peace."

Eyeing her grandmother's ashen face, Eden didn't know if Grams would survive that kind of ordeal. "Fine, Grams. I'll do as you ask, but I don't want to see Cadence's lying face ever again."

"That will be kind of hard to do, dear," Grams said. "I just hired her to run the bed-and-breakfast."

Chapter Twenty

When his phone rang at 6:00 a.m. the morning of June 10, Mason knew it could only be one person calling.

Lydia.

Gripping the fitted sheet, he groaned and decided to let the call go to voicemail. Again. After Ms. Susan dropped that bombshell, Eden had stormed upstairs into her room. Mason had texted her to see if she wanted to talk but she responded that she would see him tomorrow. So that meant he was sleeping alone. Something he had done for most of thirty-three years. Something he didn't want to do as long as he was here with Eden.

As a result, he hadn't slept well the night before and talking with Lydia wouldn't improve his disposition. Still, he couldn't avoid his agent much longer but—ugh, she was calling again. Reaching over to the nightstand, he grabbed his cell phone and answered the call.

"Thank goodness, you finally answered," she said, worry in her voice. "I thought something happened to you."

Hearing the genuine concern, Mason sat up. "I'm sorry. I didn't mean to freak you out but I had some personal things going on that I had to take care of." He then shared about his reunion with his family.

"Oh, Mason. I'm so happy for you. That would have been a great special to record," she said, giving a shaky laugh. "I'm just joking—" they both knew she wasn't, though "—but don't add years to my life like that again. If I didn't get you today, I was going to be calling nearby hospitals." She cleared her throat. "I know the Blue Hen Rose Festival is coming up on the twentieth, and I wanted to check in to see if you wanted me to send a crew out there. Just to talk with you. Maybe get a few snapshots of you with the members of the community."

"I told you already how I felt about that."

"Yes, but the pictures you've been posting have generated a lot of interest. You're gaining positive attention and doubling your followers."

"Say what?" With a start Mason realized that he hadn't been on social media in a while. There was a time when he monitored his feed after every single post, every interaction, to see what everyone else was saying, to see what they thought about him. Scrolling took up a lot of his time. He frowned. Now he realized that their opinions no longer outweighed his opinion of himself.

Mason liked who he was here in Blue Hen. He liked his friends here—Gabe and Ms. Susan. And he loved, loved, loved Eden Tempest. He just had to find the right time and the best way to tell her. He was pretty sure she knew how he felt but it was important to actually say the words. Give her the fairy-tale reveal she deserved. The usual chocolates and flowers felt…mundane. He believed in bringing it home, going big.

"Are you there?" Lydia asked, breaking into his thoughts.

"Oh yes." He retrieved his laptop from the other side of the bed—a poor substitute for a bed partner—and pulled up his socials. Sure enough, Lydia was right. There were more pictures of him working on the house, smiling and looking as good as he felt. His brows furrowed. "Who's doing this?" He swung his legs off the bed and sprang to his feet, pacing the length of the room.

"It's not you?" Lydia asked.

"No. It isn't."

"Well, whoever it is, tell them your agent said thank you."

He rubbed his head. "This isn't humorous at all. I hope it's not a stalker." When he first started out, Mason had attracted the attention of a real zealous fan. At first, he had found the woman annoying but harmless. Until he woke up one night to see her standing by the foot of his bed. Mason had had to call 911 and keep her entertained until the cops arrived. The thought of someone harming Eden or Ms. Susan gave him pause.

In the short space of time, he had come to love these women.

"I don't think you need to worry about that," Lydia said. "What are the odds of that happening twice?"

"It's not unlikely…"

"I live near that town. I doubt it. Everybody's good people. They look out for each other."

"Really? Lydia, drop the clueless act. You're not naive about the realities of being a celebrity. You just want me to agree to filming. Plus, people move in and out of towns all the time."

Mason wondered if he should tell Lydia his discovery. If he didn't, she might keep pressing to have him do a show. "Um, so, I met a wonderful woman. And she isn't one for the spotlight so we're in the early stages—well, I'm crazy about her—and I don't want to mess this up."

"Wow." Judging by the genuine shock in Lydia's voice, his declaration had caught her by surprise. But this was Lydia, so of course her next question was, "Have you told her how you feel?"

"No. Not yet. I've never said those words to a woman and it might sound corny but I want the moment to be big for her. For the both of us."

"What's bigger than television?" Lydia shot back. "The whole world tuning in to have you put yourself out there, declare your love for the woman of your heart." Okay, so Mason had had no idea that Lydia was such a romantic. She continued; her voice dreamy. "Just thinking about it warms my heart. Love is the biggest comeback of all and your fans would eat this up."

Mason rubbed his chin. "It would be nice to record it. But not for television. I'm thinking more as a personal memento."

"I suppose I understand your need to keep this private. Sentimental," Lydia said. "I tell you what, how about I send a crew down there to get your special moment on film? It will be for your eyes only. And your lady friend's, of course. But if you ever change your mind, we have it on video."

"That could work." His heart pounded. "What if she rejects me?"

"What if she rejects you?" Linda sputtered. "Are you serious? I doubt that very much."

He smiled at his agent's loyalty. "It can happen."

"Don't put that in the atmosphere. Positive vibes only. I'm glad to do this for you. I'll get in touch with your old camera crew and get them to Blue Hen in time for the Rose Festival."

"All right." The line went dead. Anticipation rose in Mason's chest. Especially when he thought of the perfect gift for his beauty. He got dressed quickly and went upstairs to retrieve what he needed, slip it into a bag, then hurried down into the kitchen. Every time he strolled by the finished product, Mason felt a mixture of amazement and pride. The kitchen had been done in all white with sleek accents and pops of color. He had chosen apple green and burnt orange as potholders or kitchen towels. All the appliances were also sleek and white, but his favorite—and Ms. Susan's—was the over-size transparent refrigerator.

Right now, Ms. Susan was using her new marble countertop with a cutting board embedded into it to roll out some dough. "Where are you off to so early?" she asked.

"I've got to get into town to run an errand so I can get back here before the men get here." They were in the planning stages for the living and dining areas and once those were complete, the house would be ready for Eden's birthday party.

Ms. Susan gave him a wide smile. "You have transformed my home into a magazine-worthy showpiece. I've almost finished checking off my to-do list for her party." She trembled with excitement. "I can't wait to see her face."

"I'm eager to see that too. Especially since she has no idea what you have planned." He was bursting to tell Ms. Susan his intentions but he wanted her to be equally bowled over. Her authentic reaction would make for good filming.

Ms. Susan began cutting the dough into small squares. "What are you making?" he asked to distract himself from blabbing.

"Some soda bread to go with the grits and eggs."

His stomach grumbled. "Well, I'll be sure to keep my appetite. I shouldn't be gone long."

"Did you see Eden this morning? She hasn't been down to look about the roses." There was slight worry in her eyes.

"No. I haven't. But I can give the roses a good water. Most are beginning to open and it smells amazing out there. I think Eden has more than enough from what's already there to make her designs."

"Might seem like it, but she is going to need extra in case they don't hold up. These are natural flowers and way more delicate than imitation ones."

"That makes sense."

A thought hit his mind and he gave Ms. Susan a side-glance. "Say, you wouldn't happen to know who is posting pictures of me on the internet, would you?"

She avoided his gaze and basted the dough with butter. "No. No. I don't have any idea," she squeaked out, her pitch at least two octaves higher than before. "But I'm sure whoever did must have their reasons. I don't know—maybe they want others to see you how they see you. I don't know but I wouldn't worry about it too much." She opened the oven and put the dough inside before putting the timer on.

"All right. If you think so." He bit back a smile.

Ms. Susan now stirred her pot of grits, still not meeting his eyes. "You'd best get going."

He glanced at the clock. "Okay. See you soon." He went over to kiss her on the cheek and then he was out the door. All the way there and back Mason kept grinning like a hyena. This was going to be an event to remember.

Chapter Twenty-One

Eden couldn't recall the last time she and Grams had been at odds. But she couldn't agree with Grams's decision to hire Cadence, which was why she was staying upstairs no matter how much her stomach growled. Boy, those sure were some delicious smells coming from the kitchen. Sitting at her desk, she rubbed her tummy. Grams wasn't playing fair. She knew how much Eden loved her grits.

A chat around a bowl of grits could solve anything was one of Grams's mottos. She rolled her eyes. Well, not this time. Cadence worked at the flower shop and drove a fancy car. She didn't need to be in Eden's face. But Grams had only offered a cryptic *Not everything is as it seems* then clammed up. Whatever.

Just then her cell buzzed. It was Mason.

Want me to bring you some food?

Yes. Pls.

Be right up.

Thx. Luv U.

Eden opened up her laptop and clicked on the meeting link that would connect her with Ramona. She had been meaning to connect with her therapist after their last frank discussion. Eden thought she had done tremendous progress and couldn't wait to share that with Ramona. She also needed to talk about these dueling feelings of elation at dating Mason versus the outrage of Cadence's betrayal.

Grams had taught her to practice forgiveness but overlooking Cadence's actions was asking a bit too much. Ramona's smiling face popped up on the screen at the same time that Mason was knocking on her door.

Lifting a finger, she told Ramona, "I'll be just one moment," turned off her camera and microphone then proceeded to open the door. Holding a tray in one hand, Mason used the other to circle her waist then kiss her with the kind of abandon that tempted her to shove him on the bed and try sexual healing.

Breaking the kiss, she took deep breaths and thanked him for the food, which he now rested on the table, before letting him know she was on a video chat with Ramona.

"Oh, okay. I kind of wanted to ask you about…" He paused, then shrugged. "Never mind. Another time. I understand. I'll leave you to it then." He sounded mildly disappointed. "I have a meeting with her later today as well." Throwing her a kiss, he backed out of the room.

"So, how are things going?" Ramona asked once Eden was back on the line.

"I've been seeing someone," she said, giggling when she saw Ramona's eyes go wide. "I'm trying to keep it super casual but I think he's a great guy." And gorgeous. And helpful. And kind. And thoughtful.

"Whoa. Talk about putting yourself out there. I'm happy for you."

"Thanks, I'm happy for me too." She swiveled in her chair. "And I've decided to teach on campus this coming fall."

Ramona moved closer to the screen. "Okay, who are you and what you done with my client?"

Eden laughed. "It's still me. Thanks to you and Grams—" *and Mason* "—I found the courage to put myself out there and when I did, it wasn't as bad as I thought. It wasn't as scary as I imagined. And it was… freeing. I'm actually looking forward to working with the students this fall. I'm going on campus later today to talk with Dr. Loft about their freshman program."

"Look at you." Ramona clapped her hands. "My heart is overflowing for you. I'm proud of you."

Eden leaned in. "So, now that I've gotten the good stuff out of the way. I have something I really need to talk to you about." Her breath hitched. "I'm struggling to navigate through this one."

"What's going on?" Ramona asked.

She then filled Ramona in on Cadence's admission, her grandmother's decision to hire Cadence and how she and Grams were now at odds. "Just when I thought I was at peace and at a good place, Cadence drops all this on me, and I feel betrayed. But on the other hand, I feel like an enormous weight has been lifted off my shoulders knowing I didn't directly cause my parents' deaths."

Ramona exhaled. "Let's talk through that for a minute. Your grandmother forgave you for starting the fire that killed her only child. Why are you surprised she would do the same for Cadence? You guys were sixteen."

Eden didn't have an answer for that. She folded her arms. "Cadence lied to me. That's what I'm most upset about. Made me shoulder the blame when it was her all along." Resentment swept through her body. And hurt. Lots of hurt.

"Yes, that was a horrible thing to do. But what do you think should be done now, thirteen years later?"

"I don't care if it's fifty years later." She slammed a fist on the table. "I want Grams to be upset on my behalf, not offer Cadence a job. All this has just made me miss my parents even more. It stirred up the grief I thought I had finally put to bed for good and then all this happens…" Her voice cracked.

Ramona nodded. "If I know Ms. Susan, she has her reasons." She cocked her head. "Maybe this is her way of coping with her loss. Who knows. But when it comes to death, you will never get to zero. Your parents' deaths will always affect you, though it might vary in intensity. You're always going to have moments of sadness that will come and go." She paused for a beat. "We can't undo the past."

Tears pooled in Eden's eyes. "She hurt me."

"Yes, but for your own healing, you've got to forgive her. Maybe that's what Ms. Susan is doing."

She blinked, allowing the tears to fall. "I don't think I want Cadence to suffer. It was an accident." She touched her chest. "I just wish it didn't feel like my chest was on fire."

"Like you said, your grief is all stirred up right now.

Things will settle soon. You just have to go through the process."

As usual, Ramona had given her sound advice. She just wasn't sure she was ready to take it. She couldn't look at Grams without a sour feeling forming in her stomach. So, she went to seek out Mason, but he was working and she didn't want to disturb him.

Eden took a moment to study him. He was standing with his iPad in hand with Gabe and the others forming a semicircle around him. Whatever he was saying had them animated. Mason was a natural leader and what he had done to the B and B was spectacular. Seeing him eased some of the turmoil raging in her gut and she didn't know why. Warm sensations flooded through her body. Her shoulders slackened and she smiled.

And just like that. She knew.

There was no denying how she felt for this man.

She had found the best aid for grief. Love. The question was, what was the aid for love? Because loving him would be akin to confining an orca to a tiny tank. Mason would constantly yearn for deeper, wider waters and it would pain her to see him limited. Turning, she walked toward Grams's truck to head down to the college. The best thing she could do for Mason was enjoy him while he was here and not stand in his way when it was time for him to leave.

For that reason, Eden would keep what was in her heart to herself. To tell him she loved him might make him feel obligated to stay. And he might end up hating her, resenting her because of it. And that would be a hurt from which she might never recover.

Chapter Twenty-Two

Luv U.

Ugh. Don't read too much into it. Eden could be one of those super casual people who used the L-word for everything. *I love those shoes. I love eggs.* But what if she meant she *loved loved* him and he hadn't replied?

Mason had gone into his room right after lunch on the pretext of using the bathroom. But really it was to reread and analyze this text message until he could decide on his next step.

Pulling up his phone, he read the text message one more time, pacing the length of his room. He rubbed his eyes and decided he was reading way too much into two little words. If she meant more, she would have added a heart emoji or something.

Luv U. Luv U. Luv U. Luv U. Luv U. Luv U. Luv U. Luv U. Luv U.

Ugh. He was officially obsessing. He scrolled through his contacts and tapped on Maxim's phone number. If anyone could answer this question, it would be his brother. Maxim answered and Mason poured out his confusion.

"I just don't know what that means. And how should I answer?" He slipped into the armchair in the corner of his room and waited.

His brother paused for a beat, nodding, his brows furrowed, his lips bunched tight.

"Is everything all right on that end?" Mason finally asked, suddenly realizing he hadn't even inquired about their father. "Is Dad okay? I wanted to tell you that I am looking into being a donor. I have an appointment scheduled for the first week in July."

Maxim shook his head. "Dad is just fine. It's... It's just that..." Then Maxim squinted, his shoulders shaking hard before he busted into laughter. "Yo, If you could only see your face right now." He covered his mouth with his hand and broke into more laughter. "Tell me why that is the funniest thing I ever heard. I was trying to be sensitive but I can't hold it."

Drawing in a deep breath, Mason demanded, "Quit cackling like a hyena and answer me though."

That only made Maxim laugh even more. "You sound like you're fifteen years old." He placed the phone to stand somewhere, bent over, gripping his sides. Mason would have hung up if he didn't need his brother's advice. Then he slapped his forehead. He could have asked Gabe. But in his defense, he wasn't used to having real friends in a long time.

"This is my heart we're talking about. I've never

been in love before." Mason said. Those words sobered Maxim.

"Dang, bro. You really are in love." He cleared his throat. "I don't think she was making a declaration but maybe she's testing the waters, so to speak. Maybe Eden wants to see how you react when she says *Luv U* and then she plans on slipping in the real *I love you* later."

Mason placed a hand to his chin. "Like she wants to see if it's going to scare me off or something."

"Could be, bro." He shrugged. "I don't know. I don't have any experience with love and I don't plan to get caught in that web. If you are looking for me, I'll be swimming in the sea, no strings, no attachments."

Maxim's words succeeded in making Mason focus on something other than himself. "Maxim, I'll admit that falling in love got me a little twisted but there's nothing like it. I feel like I am soaring. Everything is brighter, more beautiful. It's like you're walking around with a ray of sunshine in your chest."

"Whoa." Maxim's brows rose. "That sounds dope." Then he shrugged. "Nope. Still not doing it. The reason why they say *fall in love* is because it's a free fall to certain death." He chuckled. "That's a good one. I'll have to remember that."

"Is it because I left you?" Mason asked, saddened. "Or because Dad is now leaving you? Not everyone who loves you will leave, bro. I'm still here."

Maxim's eyes went wide before they filled with skepticism. "You sound like a therapist. But you're way off base…"

Mason wasn't too convinced but that wasn't a battle he had to win today. "When that time comes, allow yourself to fall, to take a chance." He had a sharp intake of breath and stood. "That's it. Thanks, bro." Renewed energy surged through him. "I'm going to interpret those words the way that I want to and take a chance. Maybe in addition to declaring how I feel at the rose festival, I'll ask her to marry me." As soon as he spoke the words, he felt…settled. A wedding proposal was the ultimate step in the happy-ever-after.

"Wait, what? How did you get to marriage out of a simple *Luv U* text? You need to slow your roll, bro."

But he wasn't about to be deterred. Mason was a man of action. "I admit, it might seem over-the-top, but I'm sure of how I feel. If she thinks those two words are going to send me running back to Ohio, then she has another think coming. I've got to run out to the jewelers."

"You need to run and make another appointment with your therapist," Maxim joked.

Mason froze. "Oh, shoot. I actually have a meeting with Ramona today." He looked at his watch. "But if I leave now, I could make it if I don't dawdle."

Suddenly, he heard his father's voice. "Go for it. I'm rooting for you." Mason didn't realize his father had been in earshot. Maxim handed his father the phone. "This is how I felt with your mother. She was the only love of my life."

"Thanks, Dad," he yelled back, pumping his fists.

"Let's take a road trip," his father said to Maxim. "I need to see how this plays out and I want to cheer for you on the sidelines." He bunched his fists and yelled, "Go big, son."

Dang it, if he didn't get a little misty-eyed. "It would mean a lot to have my family share this moment with me. No matter the outcome."

"It's settled then. See you at the festival."

Mason dashed out of the house and raced to town, his heart light. Thanks to Eden, he now had a relationship with his family again. It felt good knowing they would drive four hours to support him. The old him would have rejected their offer. But this new and improved Mason knew having them there would boost his confidence and also be the firm grip he needed if this didn't work out how he hoped.

Ramona's words came back to him. *Through the trauma, we can find the beauty, we just have to search for it.* Well, that's what he had down. He had found his beauty and he didn't want to ever let her go. For a split second, doubt entered his mind. What if Eden didn't love him in return? But he pushed that out with *What if she did?* He turned into the parking lot of the strip mall. There was only one way to find out and the by the end of the day of the festival, he would find out.

Chapter Twenty-Three

The sun painted gorgeous strokes across the sky when Mason, Eden and Ms. Susan headed to the Blue Hen Rose Festival. The fragrance from the roses stacked in the rear of the pickup filled his nostrils and he kept the windows down so they could enjoy the benefits of a rare eighty-degree day in a summer month.

In contrast to the loveliness of the surroundings, there was a distinct chill in the air with Eden and Ms. Susan still at odds. No matter how Eden pressed, her grandmother refused to explain why she had given Cadence a job. Eden had spent the past few nights in her room and though he had tossed and turned—having gotten used to her presence beside him—Mason had respected her space. However, it troubled him seeing Eden so upset.

But if ever there was a picture of unbothered, it was Ms. Susan.

Dressed in a pair of black jeans, a blue shirt with an embroidered blue hen and a pair of comfortable walking shoes, Ms. Susan sat up front with him and chattered on like a magpie. "You are going to enjoy yourself, Mason," she said. "Not only are there roses, but we have a barbecue contest and our annual pie contest. It's a great day for our town." She patted the oval glass carrier in her lap. "I'm definitely beating Ruthie this year with this recipe."

"It smells good, I can tell you that," Mason said, following the directions on the navigation system. They were now about five minutes away from the fairgrounds. He pointed. "They have a Ferris wheel?"

"Oh yes, plus there's a carousel and a dunk tank. Last year, we had clowns. But they scared the babies, so we're not doing that this year." She twisted in her seat to address Eden. "You used to be afraid of them too. Remember that?"

"Yes," she replied. A one-word answer. No further elaboration. Ms. Susan shrugged, her face serene. Mason eyed Eden through the rearview mirror but she kept her gaze firmly out the window. *Boy.* He wiped his brow. He hoped her mood lifted before his big declaration.

Following the directions of the flaggers, he pulled into a parking spot near the entrance. There were only a handful of cars. Eden jumped out of the pickup before he turned off the engine. He heard the truck bed open and sighed. This was going to be a long day unless Eden and her grandmother resolved things between them.

Ms. Susan tapped his arm. "Don't worry yourself. We'll be like peanut butter and jelly soon."

Chuckling at her analogy, Mason went around the vehicle to hold onto the pie while Ms. Susan exited.

"Thank you. Do you need help with the roses?" she asked Eden.

"No. I've got it."

"Suit yourself," Ms. Susan breezily replied. "Mason, I'm heading out to get a good spot for my pie." She gave him a quick wave and took off with her pie in hand.

Heading to where Eden stood placing roses on the cart they had carried, he snatched her flush against him, spooning her from behind. "I've missed you," he whispered in her ear. He used his nose to play with the blue hen earrings dangling near her neck. "You're looking real cute today." She was wearing a T-shirt that said Queen of the Blue Hen Rose Festival with a pair of white shorts and a tiara made of—no surprise—roses and blue hens. This was her first time wearing one of the shirts she had won and her crown, which had warmed his heart when she told him.

"Thank you." She turned to face him and hugged him tight. "I've just had a lot on my mind as you know. I'll come see you later tonight. I promise."

"I'll hold you to that," he said, giving her a light squeeze and a quick kiss. She tasted so good, he had to get another taste. And another.

"Mason, we've got to go set up," she said between kisses. "I want to get a good location with enough room for my special design and we have to complete before judging at noon."

More cars were pulling in and he could hear the slight panic in her tone. Mason reluctantly pulled away. "I just needed my fix. I think I'm getting addicted to you. Two days and it's like I'm experiencing withdrawal symptoms." She rolled her eyes. "I know it's corny, but it's true," he said.

Together, they continued filling the cart. Eden planned to do a mosaic butterfly using roses of different colors, signifying her personal freedom. Her plans were dope, meaningful and he had gotten emotional seeing them.

"Aww." She placed a hand on his chest. "What a nice thing to say."

"Not so nice to feel."

"You're a big boy. You can handle it," she teased. They began making their way to the grounds, the cart rattling along the pavement. So many roses lined the path—though Eden told him those were fake, including the huge awning at the entrance.

"They look so real," he proclaimed once they had arrived at their designated spot.

"They were all handmade by the ladies of our town," she explained, keeping in step with him. "I couldn't wait to turn eight so I could start making my own. Each year, we add to it, replacing the old ones with new." A family of four passed them. The young girl's dress was made to look like petals, and the little boy had on a green outfit, resembling a stalk. Some families had matching shirts with roses, some with blue hens. He felt underdressed with his T-shirt and jeans until Eden gave him a cap stitched with the town's blue hen.

"Wow. This festival is a big deal." And, very characteristic of a small town. Quite honestly, he had never seen anything like it.

"It's the event of the year," Eden replied, her hands deftly prepping her roses. She stopped to show him how she wanted him to strip the thorns and then wire the roses.

"So, what do the men do?" he asked once they had began setting up the roses on her display.

"Generally, they make the vines, the wire hooks, the stalks and assemble the lighting. Or, some help with the roses. Stuff like that. Wait until you see these roses at night. There's nothing like it." She pointed to her wired butterfly-shaped stand. "Grams had this made for me a couple months ago." He could see the mini lights behind the display.

Beside them, a young woman and a couple other girls put up a wired stand that was shaped like a hen, and they had tons of blue roses and other flowers. Boy, this town sure was proud of its blue hen.

Pointing over at them, he said, "I thought you could only use roses."

"According to the rules, you can supplement with other flowers but the rose has to be the star." Her chest puffed. "Thank goodness, I've never had to supplement except for the usual greens and baby's breath."

He heard her sharp intake of breath and followed her gaze. Cadence was there, right along with Gabe, putting up her design right across from them. He couldn't tell from the wiring but it looked like words. Their bodies blocked him from seeing fully but Eden redirected his attention.

She spoke through gritted teeth. "I didn't see her name on the entrants list, so she must have registered at the last minute. And now she's right in front of me when there are so many other places she could go," Eden said, hurt in her voice, her eyes misty. "It's like she's rubbing it in my face what she did."

Mason cupped her face with his hands. "Don't allow her to distract you off your path." She met his gaze, pinning those cognac eyes on his. "Take deep breaths and focus. You've won the past five years and you will claim that crown again."

"You're right." Grabbing his head, Eden gave him a deep kiss in front of the whole town before squaring her shoulders, then whispered, "Let's get to work." A half hour into their task, she asked, "How is your father doing?"

"He's stable. For now," Mason said, hooking a rose onto the wire. They were one-third of the way finished. His fingers cramped up on him and he opened and closed his hands. "I've set the appointment to get on the donor's list." Maxim had texted that they would arrive within the hour. Good thing too because as each hour went by, nervousness wrapped itself like a vine around his heart.

"That's good to hear. Have you told your dad yet?"

"No, I don't want to get his hopes up until I'm sure it's a done deal." Just then a young teen approached to take a selfie and request his autograph. Mason posed with him before obliging a few others.

"You are wonderful." She gave him a quick kiss on the lips, her eyes warm.

Her praise gave him a shot of confidence. Eden wouldn't look at him that way if she didn't care about him. Caring can grow to love. All will be good. A half hour before noon, they finished her design. Stepping back, Mason said, "This is exquisite."

She beamed. "Thank you." They shared a kiss. "Having you here made it fun."

That's when Mason looked over at Cadence's stand. Both she and Gabe gestured at him to have Eden turned around. He placed a hand on her shoulders and twisted her around. Eden gasped, before covering her mouth.

Cadence and Gabe's display featured the words *I'm Sorry*. He could feel her shoulders shake as she dissolved into fresh tears.

"Let it go, honey," he encouraged, patting her back. "Let it go."

She nodded against his chest. Cadence came over to where Eden was and the two friends embraced. "I know I don't deserve it, but I could use a second chance."

With a nod, Eden said, "I forgive you." She gave Mason a look of tenderness. "I've got too much good happening in my life to keep wading in the past."

To Mason, that was his cue.

From the corner of his eye, Mason saw his crew approaching and his brother and father were a few feet behind. Once they were close, he signaled for them to start recording. Then he took Eden's hand.

Cadence must have caught on what was about to occur because she uttered a quick *We'll catch up later* and scampered out of the way. The townspeople began to gather around. He could feel their excitement and that made his heart gallop in his chest.

"Eden," he began, breathy, nervous. "Since I met you, everything in my life is better."

She nodded, her lashes wet from crying. "I feel the same about you."

"I've never felt this way about anyone before." He moved his gaze away from her to nod at his brother and father, who held up their phones. Come to think of it, there were quite a few people holding up their phones. He spotted Ms. Susan grinning and she signaled to him to continue. And wait, was that Lydia he saw munching on an ice-cream cone?

Meanwhile, Eden faced the crowd. "What the—" She glanced at him with doe eyes. "What's going on?"

Mason spun her around, then gave her a searing kiss. There was a lot of hooting and hollering, which would make for good memories. He couldn't wait to see the tape. Tearing his lips off hers, he said, "I want you to know in front of the entire town, that I love you, Eden Tempest. You are the ultimate woman of my fairy tale."

Her eyes shone. "I love you, too."

The crowd broke into applause. Someone started chanting, "Kiss, Kiss, Kiss," and soon the throng joined in.

Mason and Eden were happy to oblige. His chest puffed at her smiling face. Squaring his shoulders, Mason dropped to his knees. Lowering his head, he reached into his jeans pocket. The crowd stilled to a hush.

"Um, Mason… What are you doing? Is that a camera crew?" she growled out.

"Yes. I'll explain later. Hang on, my love." He dug into his pocket and pulled out the small velvet box. Everyone cheered. Ms. Susan hovered close with Lydia standing beside her. His father wiped his eyes.

"What are you doing?" Eden whispered again. His mind registered that she sounded more frantic than excited, but he pushed on.

With a broad grin, Mason held up the ring and looked at her. He expected to see her smiling. Maybe even crying, overcome with emotion. What he didn't expect to see was the thunderous expression on her face, which brought his marriage request to a grinding halt.

Chapter Twenty-Four

Was he seriously about to propose?

That indicated permanence.

Forever.

Eden was ready for happy-for-now. Not ever after. Mason had read way too many romances to think she would marry him. That would mean leaving the town. Leaving her life. She wasn't cut out for the celebrity life.

Even now, knowing the cameras were on her made her antsy and self-conscious. Why would he put her on blast like this? And how did he expect her to live in the land of the perfect face, booty and hips when she was scarred. She could feel her face burn with mortification. She could feel the crowd's ears cocked listening to their every word but she had to stop him.

"Get up," she urged. Awkwardly, Mason rose to his feet, the box in hand. She eyed it like it was a viper and commanded, "Put that away."

He began to shove it in his pocket but then stopped. "I can't do that." He placed his hands on her shoulders. "I love you and it would be my honor if you would be my wife. For me, marriage is the ultimate indicator of my love. I want to spend the rest of my life with you. Forever." He touched her face and smiled. "I don't want to spend another day without you by my side."

Dropping back to his knees, he opened the box. A large solitaire glistened in the sun and the crowd oohed and aahed. Then he boomed out, "Eden Tempest, will you marry me?" Oh, why did he have to ruin their fling by asking for something permanent?

She placed a hand on her hip. "Is everything a show for you?"

"No, you don't understand. That's for—"

"And where are we spending our days?" she interrupted.

He stepped back. "Huh? What do you mean?" He then beckoned the camera to stop rolling. The crowd began to thin. In that moment, she was grateful for the people of Blue Hen. They knew when to give someone space.

"Where do you see us living in your version of the fairy tale?" she asked when it was just her, Mason and family.

"Well, I—uh—I figure you would live with me." He ran a hand across his scalp. "I have everything you need right there in Ohio."

"Goes to show you don't know me, Mason Powers. You don't know me at all. And that's why I can't marry you." Afraid of falling apart in front of everyone, she dashed off, moving as fast as her feet would take her. She just made it out of the parking lot when she heard a honk behind her. If that was Mason… Cadence pulled up beside her.

"Need a ride?" the other woman asked.

Sweat poured off her from all that adrenaline and she needed to cool down. Plus, she had run off leaving her purse behind. So she didn't have her house keys or her cell phone. With a nod, Eden got inside Cadence's car. "I don't want to talk about what just transpired," she said, slamming the door shut.

"Okay, I hear you. You don't want to talk about the brave man who just poured his heart out to you in front of the whole town. You don't want to talk about how you shot him down, leaving him crushed and dejected. You don't want to talk about how this is about you feeling scared, like you don't deserve to be loved."

Eden gave her a cutting glance.

"Noted." Lifting a hand, Cadence pumped up the air-conditioning and pressed the gas. "Do you want me to give you a ride home?" she offered, her tone gentle.

"N-no. I can't go back there yet. I…just…need…a…minute." Eden broke into heavy sobs. Her heart felt like it was ripping open and that shouldn't be happening. Not when she had done the right thing. The best thing for the both of them.

After driving for a few minutes, Cadence turned into a strip mall and parked. The stores were closed today because everyone was at the rose festival. The area looked as desolate as she felt, which led to fresh tears.

"Why are you crying if you felt turning him down was the best move?" Cadence prodded.

"Because I didn't expect my heart to feel like someone took an axe to it." She slouched over, her pulse rhythm shaky. "Please tell me I did the right thing."

From her peripheral view, Cadence reached behind her and grabbed a bottled water before handing it to Eden. Unscrewing the cap, she guzzled down half of the contents. "Thanks."

"Now to answer your question… Three years ago, I met a man who swept me off my feet. With his southern drawl, cowboy hat and boots, Thad was hard to resist. He was an imaginative lover though a bit possessive, which I didn't like at all. But when he proposed, I said yes, without a care in the world."

Eden took off her seat belt then curved her body to give Cadence her complete attention.

"We moved to this sprawling ranch in Texas. He told me I would never have to work a day in my life again. Now, you know I grew up in a house where I had to get a part-time job at fourteen cleaning houses with my mom. So, imagine how appealing that was for me. I quit my senior year of college, feeding on Thad's bull. As soon as I entered that house, I got a bad vibe but I ignored it."

Cadence picked at an imaginary piece of lint on her blouse. "The first month was marvelous. I was living in newlywed bliss. He even gifted me this car," she said, patting the seat. "Then one night, I was taking a bath, and something caught my eye. I had to get a step stool but what I saw made goose bumps pop up on my flesh. It was a camera. I quickly realized Thad had one in every room, watching my every move."

Eden gasped.

"Yes, girl. That wasn't pretty. I felt like I was a cast member in a psychotic thriller movie. But I confronted Thad. To my surprise, he didn't bother denying any of it. It was like he was proud of what he had done.

When I tried to leave—" she straightened "—he back-handed me."

"Say what?"

"Now you know after that, all I could think about was how he could keep me a prisoner inside his home. As soon as he went to bed that night, I jumped into the car he gave me and hightailed it back to Delaware."

Eden ran a hand through her damp curls. "Where is he now?"

"Same place in Texas, right where I left him. Except he's six feet under."

"Did you…?" Eden trailed off, disgusted for thinking Cadence capable of violence. But still. This was sounding like a thriller so she couldn't rule it out.

Cadence slapped Eden's wrist. "No, girl. The very night I left, someone who Thad owed money to broke into the house and shot him. Now, you know I would have been a chief suspect if it weren't for those doggone cameras." Eden's mouth dropped open for a beat before they started laughing uncontrollably.

When they calmed down, Eden said, "I don't get how that correlates to my situation though. In fact, you seem to be saying the same thing I'm saying."

"The first lesson of the story is that you have to follow your gut. Trust your instincts. If I had listened to my intuition, I wouldn't have dropped out of school. I wouldn't have married Thad and I wouldn't have quit school. Ms. Susan gave me that job so I could quit the flower shop, complete the internship and finish my hospitality degree." That's why Grams had hired Cadence. It all made sense now. It also explained how Cadence was driving this luxury car.

Eden reached over to give Cadence a hug. "I'm glad you got out before it was too late."

"That's the second lesson." Cadence gave her an expectant look but Eden wasn't getting it. "Let me spell it out for you then. Your gut is telling you everything you need to know about Mason. You just have to search deep and listen. And, if you're wrong, trust yourself to know you'll get out of a bad situation." Then she quirked her lips. "Or, at the very least, you'll get a sweet ride out of it. And I mean that in every sense of the word."

"Wow." Eden relaxed against the seat and exhaled. "You went through a lot."

"Mmm-hmm. But now imagine, just imagine, if Thad was wonderful and my gut agreed. I would still be in Texas. Still married. Still happy. And you know what, I would have deserved it. Because every woman deserves to love herself and be loved by a good man."

Several beats went by, the only sound Cadence drumming her fingers on the steering wheel. Eden sank into the seat. "I messed up, didn't I?"

"Yep."

"I can't keep living in fear."

"Nope."

"I deserve to be loved."

"Right."

"I have a gut. I can trust it."

"I agree."

Eden put on her seat belt and tapped her right foot like she was pressing on the gas. "How fast can this thing go?"

Chapter Twenty-Five

Everybody meant well. Mason knew that. But if one more person came up to pat him on the back, he was going to...what? Scream? He sighed. He was going to accept the thoughtful gesture for what it was.

At Ms. Susan's request, Mason had stayed for the judging. Actually, she had guilt-tripped him into staying, saying she would need a ride home. He had kept his head up. His brother and father had left to check into Blue Hen's only hotel. Mason would go hang with them later. And then his personal pity party could begin.

Ms. Susan had gone to check on her pie. Once again, Eden had won first place. And, once again, because of him this time, she had missed hearing her name called. Cadence, who had disappeared as well, had come in second and people had started posing with her sign.

Lydia and the crew had already departed but not before she told him that the execs had okayed a new reality show for him where he would travel to small towns and renovate bed-and-breakfasts and that his name was trending on social media with the hashtag #ManCrush-Mason. Apparently, all these women were posting that they accepted his proposal. And even a few men. A Photoshop guru had already redone the video inserting other celebrities. Everyone was making light of what was the most humiliating act of his life, but he knew that came with his career.

For some reason, people didn't picture a celebrity feeling the same things they did. Like right now, he felt like he had been mauled by a tiger, but people still wanted autographs. He stretched his lips into a semblance of a smile but on the inside, he mulled on Eden's questions.

What had he expected? Eden loved being in a small town. And so did Mason. But he hadn't thought about that when he proposed. His vision was that they would return to his home in Ohio. Then today, when Lydia gave him the news about the series offer, he had skipped on the inside and even a little on the outside.

Meanwhile, Eden had just accepted an offer to teach. Expecting her to give that up was plain…selfish. He could see that now.

He massaged his temples. Happy-ever-after was complicated.

Just then, he spotted Eden running to where he stood. She was probably coming back to see how she had placed and if he cared for her at all, the wisest thing he could do was get out of there. You know what? What he could do was give Ms. Susan the keys to his pickup and ask his brother to come pick him up. He'd sort out getting his belongings shipped to him later. He fired off a text to Max then raced to where Ms. Susan was, claiming her prize. He thought he heard Eden calling his name but he wasn't sure. Probably wishful thinking. He was pretty sure he was the last person she wanted to see right now. If ever again.

He handed Ms. Susan the keys and kept moving. The throng slowed his progress as he had to worm his way past the Ferris wheel queue and then avoid tripping into the barbecue line. A toddler crossed his path which brought him to a screeching halt.

The little boy was crying *Mama* at the top of his lungs. Mason had to pick him up. Panting, Mason looked in all directions, expecting to encounter the worried glances of the tot's parents but he didn't see anyone. "Hush, now," he said, as the youngster was now kicking his legs and trying to wriggle out of Mason's arms.

Seeing that he had attracted speculative glances, Mason bellowed out, "Does anyone know this little boy? He's lost his parents."

Everyone shook their heads. "I thought this was a small town," he mumbled, deciding he would hunt for the sheriff.

That's when he felt a hand snatch his arm in a grip that could best be described as lethal. Holding the toddler against him, Mason stared into the anxious eyes of a beautiful woman.

"My baby. My baby. Thank goodness you found him." She scooped the boy out of his arms, laughing and crying at the same time. She spread kisses across her son's cheek before explaining, "I had to use the bathroom and went into the stall, but while I was going, this little one crawls under the door and leaves. I've never been so scared in all my life."

"It's all right. He's safe. You're safe." He tried to

leave but the woman wouldn't let go of his hand. She kept thanking him and offering him money, which he refused. But she finally loosened her grip and her son's wails had reduced to sniffles.

Then someone tapped him from behind and once again he found his arm snatched. "Thank goodness, I found you." Eden curled over like she was catching her breath. "I haven't run that fast since I tried out for the track team in high school." Then she registered his companion and her mouth dropped open. "Raine? I didn't know you were here."

Cadence strolled up with Gabe in tow.

"Hey, Eden," Raine said, rocking the baby who now had his head on her chest. He had stuck his finger in his mouth and was now studying Mason from under his lashes.

"You have a son?" Eden said. "I didn't know... You never said."

"He is the cutest," Cadence said.

Raine dipped her head. "Yes, I returned home single and pregnant, to my parents' regret, but my hair salon is doing well, and my mom watches Rocky when I work." She cocked her head at Mason. "He's a handful as this man can attest."

"This is Mason," Eden said, pointedly.

"Oh... Mason." Raine gave him the once-over. Mason watched some kind of silent communication pass between the women. Like they had been talking about him. He rocked back on his heels. This was the perfect opportunity for him to leave but now Eden had a hold on him. Seeing Max scanning the crowd, Mason waved with his free arm. His brother jogged over.

"Hey, I parked by the entrance, so we should get

go—" Max stopped midsentence as if mesmerized. His brother scanned Raine's ring finger and seeing nothing there, extended his hand toward her. "Hello, I'm this ugly man's much better looking brother, Max."

Raine batted her lashes and gave him her name.

The two struck up a conversation. Really? Max was supposed to be his escape ride. But even after Mason reminded him about possibly getting a ticket, Max had kept right on talking and flirting. And, Raine had been all with it, the baby now asleep in her arms.

"Gabe, do you think I could hitch a ride with you?" Mason asked.

"No," Eden said, her tone pleading, as if she didn't want him riding with anyone else. But after earlier today, Mason wasn't making any assumptions.

"I gave Ms. Susan the keys, if that's why you're looking for me." He pinned his eyes on Gabe.

"I'm uh—I'm not going out that way," Gabe sputtered out, obviously not about to challenge what Eden said.

Eden led him out of earshot. "Can we talk?" she asked, her voice warm, like she hadn't run like she was being chased to get away from him within the past hour or so.

Mason's brows furrowed. "I'm sorry but am I missing something here?"

"Yes. I mean, no." She released a long plume of air. "I shouldn't have bolted like that. I was wrong. I made a mistake and I'm going to need you to ask me again."

"Wait, what?" Eden had rattled on so fast that he couldn't be sure he had heard what he just heard.

"I said, I'm going to need you to ask me again."

"You want me to get down on my knees a second time in this dirt and ask you to marry me?"

"Yes." She wrung her fingers.

"What about all the concerns you mentioned earlier?" He made a show of peering at his watch. "Nothing has changed in the hour or so that you've turned me down."

"Yes," she breathed out, raising her voice. "Something has changed since you asked me to marry you." Those words made the others around them grow silent. He felt all eyes on them. "My perspective has changed. I want to be with you, and we will work everything else out." She placed a hand on her hip. "Now, unless you've fallen out of love with me in the past hour, are you getting down on one knee or do I have to?"

"Get it done, bro," Max bellowed out.

"Go for it," Gabe yelled.

Another crowd converged. Seeing she had begun to lower herself, Mason lifted a hand. "I've got this. I swear if you make me humiliate myself…" he mumbled under his breath then pulled out the box and got to his knees, noting how this time his hands shook. "Eden, I love you with all my heart. Will you do me the honor of becoming my wife?"

"Yes, yes, I will." She dashed over to him and lunged into his arms. The applause around them was thunderous but couldn't outdo the racing of his heart.

He opened the ring box and slipped the ring on her finger. It was slightly too big. Mason froze. Not one fairy tale ended with where the heroine's ring didn't fit.

But Eden wasn't concerned. Curling her fingers, she cupped his head and smiled. "It's okay. We'll have it sized. Nothing's going to spoil our happy-ever-after." And with a grin, she sealed that promise with a kiss worthy of a fairy-tale ending.

Epilogue

While the guests waltzed on the makeshift dance floor outside the bed-and-breakfast, Eden snuck Mason inside his suite. "This was the best birthday ever. I can't believe Grams managed to surprise me. But now I want to end the night in your arms." She shimmied out of her blue chiffon dress.

"Were you really surprised?" Mason asked.

"Yes, most definitely." He raised a brow. "Okay, maybe I caught a clue when you and Grams would go silent every time that I entered the room." The last week had been a whirlwind and the happiest she had ever been in her life. "Thanks to the both of you, I celebrated my first birthday in fourteen years. I was shocked to see so many people show up."

"The townspeople of Blue Hen love you, Eden."

"Yes. It was either that, or they came for the free food." There was a barbecue station, an Italian station, a dessert station and even a hibachi station. The chef had performed tricks making the crowd break out into applause.

Her engagement ring sparkled in the sliver of moonlight peeking through the curtains. "I'm going to miss this place."

"We don't have to leave," Mason said, kissing the back of her hand. "I haven't signed my contract yet."

She started working on the buttons of his dress shirt. "No, no. I won't change my mind. Dr. Loft has already found my replacement and I'm excited at the idea of exploring different small towns with you and making the wishes of other bed-and-breakfast owners come true. Besides, Cadence has already moved into my bedroom, so I don't have to worry about Grams being alone."

"Okay, but just know you can change your mind at any time."

"I'm not. I am going to enjoy making love to you in all fifty states and the provinces." She pushed him onto the bed. "Our first stop will be Virginia and I've already found us great housing."

"I've got my surgery scheduled for next month so it makes sense to start there. That way we can keep an eye on Dad while he recovers." He gave her a long kiss, his hands roaming her body. "Thank you so much for suggesting it."

"The thing about forever is that when you're with the person you love for life, you can be flexible. What works today might not work tomorrow but if we're navigating together, wherever we end up is where we were meant to go."

"I like the sound of that."

And that was the last thing they uttered for a long time.

* * * * *

A Q&A with Michelle Lindo-Rice

What or who inspired you to write?

Writing for me was therapy. I was a young mother and wife and found myself at home a lot of nights while my husband at that time was off partying with his friends. I was an avid reader and had written songs and, on occasion, a few poems. But writing became "my thing" and my escape. It kept me grounded and it allowed me to channel my emotions into something positive.

What is your daily writing routine?

When I am writing, I use a word-tracking app that tells me exactly how many words I need to complete in order to meet a deadline. I love to compete with myself and beat the daily goal. I also love to snack on fruit, dry cereal and gummies while writing to keep me energized.

Who are your favorite authors?
I have so many! I love Brenda Novak, Nora Roberts and
Sandra Brown. Rhonda McKnight, Vanessa Riley, Belle
Calhoune, Patricia Johns, Toni Shiloh and so many oth-
ers are must-reads for me!

Where do your story ideas come from?
My story ideas come from so many different places and
situations. One story idea came from watching a television show called *9-1-1* where the character said four
words and that inspired a women's fiction novel. I grew
up watching musicals and the movie *Seven Brides for
Seven Brothers* inspired a series. Sometimes, it is a conversation and sometimes it is a situation that inspires
certain plot lines. I also have my husband and sister who
help me with talk-throughs and brainstorming.

Do you have a favorite travel destination?
Most of my traveling of late has been for family functions or circumstances. But I would love to go to Italy.
I would love to venture there and walk the streets, take
in the food and shopping.

What is your favorite movie?
My favorite movie is *The Bridges of Madison County.*
I just loved Meryl Streep and Clint Eastwood and their
unrequited love. I loved the sacrifices she made as a
mother, and the scene where she holds on to the door
handle still makes me cry every time. My favorite line
is when Clint Eastwood says, "This kind of certainty
comes but once in a lifetime." Can you imagine finding
a love like that? Actually, I have. I am now married to
the most wonderful man, who is "when you know, you
know" personified.

When did you read your first Harlequin romance? Do you remember its title?
I was probably about eleven and it was in the library at the Hollis Avenue branch in Jamaica, Queens. I spent hours there, going daily to check out books. I don't remember my first title but my love for Harlequin has never waned.

How did you meet your current love?
My current husband was a reconnection. He was a man I knew years ago that I never saw. Then he reached out to me via email after learning I wrote books from a mutual friend. He designs websites and wanted to give mine a makeover—for free! We exchanged numbers that same day and talked for a good number of hours. Then he called me the next day and we spoke all day. Literally. And then after that, and after that. And, we haven't stopped talking since.

What characteristic do you most value in your friends?
I do value loyalty in my friends. I try to be loyal and trustworthy myself. My friends know that they can come to me with anything and I will be there for them. I value them to tell me the truth but also uplift and encourage me. I am blessed to have the most supportive friends.

How did you celebrate or treat yourself when you got your first book deal?
When I got my first book deal with Harlequin Love Inspired, I remember screaming and hollering. I'm pretty sure I treated myself to ice cream and dinner out with the hubby.

Will you share your favorite reader response?
I appreciate hearing from my readers. Readers have been a strong source of motivation. When I get an email or message from a reader saying that they connected with a character and that they stayed up all night reading, it makes all my time and energy completely worth it. I also do love when a reader reaches out to say that they are going to make a change in their own lives because of a character or storyline in my book. For example, after reading *Tell Me Lies*, a reader contacted me to say she was going to reach out to her father.

What are your favorite character names?
I do love unusual character names. Sometimes, I change my character names several times before it feels like a fit. I have had characters with names such as Sydney, Memphis, Sienna. My male hero, Brigg, in *Twenty-Eight Dates* also has a really cool name.

Other than author, what job would you like to have?
I love my career in education, but I am hoping to build and grow as a literary agent. I hope to help others see their dreams realized of becoming a published author.

Never Tell

Never
Tell

Never Tell

Lisa Gardner

arrow books

1 3 5 7 9 10 8 6 4 2

Arrow Books
20 Vauxhall Bridge Road
London SW1V 2SA

Arrow Books is part of the Penguin Random House group of companies
whose addresses can be found at global.penguinrandomhouse.com

Penguin
Random House
UK

Copyright © Lisa Gardner Inc. 2019

Lisa Gardner has asserted her right to be identified
as the author of this Work in accordance with the Copyright,
Designs and Patents Act 1988.

First published in Great Britain by Century in 2019
(First published in the United States by Grand Central Publishing in 2019)
First published in paperback by Arrow Books in 2019

www.penguin.co.uk

A CIP catalogue record for this book is available from the British Library.

ISBN 9781787466838

Printed and bound in Great Britain by Clays Ltd, Elcograf S.p.A.

Penguin Random House is committed to a sustainable future for
our business, our readers and our planet. This book is made from
Forest Stewardship Council® certified paper.

MIX
Paper from
responsible sources
FSC® C018179

In memory of Wayne Rock,
exceptional detective and human being.
We miss you, my friend.

CHAPTER 1

EVIE

B Y THE TIME I PULL my car into the garage, my hands are shaking on the wheel. I tell myself I have no reason to feel so nervous. I tell myself I've done nothing wrong. I still sit there an extra beat, staring straight ahead, as if some magic answer to the mess that is my life will appear in the windshield.

It doesn't.

With a bit of care, I can still slide out of the driver's seat. I'm bigger, but not that much bigger. I fight more with my bulky coat and the strap of my oversized purse, as I ease out from behind the steering wheel. Conrad bought me the purse as a Christmas gift last year. From Coach. Real leather. At least a couple hundred dollars. At the time, I'd been so excited I'd thrown my arms around him and squealed. He'd laughed, told me he'd seen me eyeing the bag in the store and had just known he had to get it for me.

When I'd hugged him then, he'd hugged me back. When I'd laughed that day, and giddily opened up the huge, gray leather bag to explore all the compartments, he'd laughed with me.

Christmas morning. Nearly one year ago.

Had we hugged since? Laughed since?

The bulge in my belly would argue we'd found some way to connect, and yet, if not for the streams of bright colored lights and gaudy decorations covering my neighborhood, I'm not sure it would feel like the holidays at all. As it is, we're one of the last undecorated houses on the block. A wreath on our door; that's it. Each weekend, we promised to get a tree. Each weekend, we didn't.

I take my time hefting my purse over my shoulder. Then I turn and face the door leading from the garage into the house.

Dead man walking, I think. And something crumples inside me. I don't cry. But I'm not sure why.

The door is open. Cracked slightly. As if on the way out, I didn't pull it hard enough shut. Letting out all the heat, my father would say, which causes me a fresh pang of pain.

I push through the interior door, close it firmly behind me. That's it. I'm home. Standing in the mudroom. Another day done. Another night to begin.

Hang up the purse. Shrug out of the coat. Ease off the boots. Jacket on the coatrack. Shoes on the mat. I fish my cell phone out of my bag and set it up on the side table to charge. Then, I take a final moment.

Breathe in. Breathe out.

Listening for him.

The kitchen? He could be sitting at the table. Waiting in front of a cold dinner. Or pointedly taking the last bite. Or maybe he's moved into the family room, ensconced in his recliner, feet up, beer in hand, eyes glued to ESPN. Sunday is football. Go Patriots. I've lived in Boston long enough to know that much. But Tuesday night? I never got into sports. He'd watch; I'd read. Back in the days when we spent so much time glued together, it seemed natural to also have some time apart.

I don't hear the clinking of silverware from the kitchen. Nor the low rumble of TV from the family room.

Door open, I remember. And my left hand flattens on the relatively small, but noticeable, curve of my belly.

The hall leads me to the kitchen. A spindly table sits in front of the back window. No sign of dinner. But then I notice a rinsed plate lying neatly in the sink.

Breathe in. Breathe out.

I should have a story, I think. An excuse. A lie. Something. But in the growing silence, my thoughts churn more, my brain spinning wildly.

Dead man walking. Dead woman walking?

I'm going to vomit. I can blame it on the baby. You can blame anything on pregnancy. I'm sick, I'm tired, I'm stupid, I lost track of time. Baby brain, pregnancy hormones. For nine whole months, nothing has to be my fault. And yet . . .

Why did I come home tonight? Except, of course, where else do I have to go? Ever since I first met Conrad ten years ago . . . He noticed me. He saw me. He forgave me.

And I loved him.

Ten whole years, I have loved him.

I leave the kitchen. It's small and, like the rest of the 1950s house, still in desperate need of updating. We purchased the place with hope and aspiration. Sure it sat on a postage stamp yard, and each room was tinier than the last, but it was ours. And being young and handy, we'd fix it up, open it up, then sell it for oodles of money.

Now I walk down a narrow hallway where half the wallpaper hangs down in pieces and do my best not to notice.

Family room. Den, really. With Conrad's beloved La-Z-Boy, a modest sofa, and of course, an enormous flat-screen TV. The recliner is empty. The TV is off. The room is empty.

Door open, I remember again.

Our garage fits only a single vehicle, and even that is a perk in a Boston neighborhood. Conrad parks his Jeep on the street. Which I check now. Because I'd spotted it pulling into the driveway and, yes, there it is. Black Jeep. Situated at the curb straight outside. A prime spot I can already imagine he was thrilled to get, as even with parking permits, there's more demand than supply. Hence his kindness in giving me the garage.

It's okay, honey. I don't want you walking down the street alone at night. I like knowing that you're safe.

Dead woman walking. Dead woman walking.

Don't vomit now.

And then . . .

Then . . .

"Door open," I whisper. And I finally notice what I should've noticed from the very beginning.

SMELL. I'D BEEN listening for the sound of my husband. The clatter of silverware in the kitchen. The thump of his recliner banging back in the family room. But there aren't any sounds. No sounds at all.

The house is hushed. Quiet. Still.

As if it were empty.

Smell.

The stairs leading to the second floor are like the rest of the house, narrow, confining, creaky. Conrad tightened the bannister three months ago. When I broke the news. When we both stood in our bedroom and stared at the little stick. My hands had been shaking so hard he'd had to take it from me.

I remember feeling ill then, too. Willing myself not to vomit, though it had been the near-constant queasiness that had led me to take the pregnancy test. A marriage is a mosaic of a thousand moments, a hundred precious memories. That day, watching his hands close around mine. Strong fingers, seamed with calluses. Steady, as they took the pregnancy stick away from me, held it closer to him.

I had that surreal feeling I sometimes get. Where I'm not present in my own life, but even all these years later, standing in my parents' kitchen again. Holding the shotgun. Smelling all that blood.

And Conrad, being Conrad, looked right at me. Looked right *into* me.

"Evie," he said. "You deserve this. *We* deserve this."

I loved him again. Just like that. In that moment, I adored him. We held hands. He cried. Then I had to pull away to vomit for real, but that made us both laugh, and afterward he'd wiped my face with a washcloth and I'd let him.

A thousand moments. A hundred memories.

That pain again, deep inside me, as I lean heavily against the wall, away from the bannister I no longer trust, and work my way up the narrow staircase.

Smell.

The odor hits me hard now. Nothing faint, teasing, ambiguous. This is it. Had I known all along? Turning into the drive? Pulling into the garage? The interior door open, open, open.

What had my subconscious suspected, long before the rest of me had paid attention?

Upstairs, not the bedroom, but the second tiny room, Conrad's office, looms to the left. That door is open, too.

Sounds to go with the smell. Sirens. Down the street. Growing louder. Coming closer. But of course.

My parents' kitchen.

My husband's office.

Blood.

Dark, viscous. A spray. A pool.

I can't help myself. I'm sixteen. I'm thirty-two. I reach out. I touch the spot closest to me. I smear the red across my fingertip. I watch the way it fills in the whorls of my fingerprints.

My father. My husband.

Blood.

More noise. Banging. So far away. Shouts and demands and orders.

But up here, none of it matters. There is just me and this final moment with Conrad. His body fallen back into the desk chair, the back of his head sprayed on the wall behind him.

I fear what I will see on the computer screen before I even look. But I force myself to do it. Take it in. Register the images. This is my husband's computer. This is what my husband was looking at before he died.

Harder banging now. The police. Responding to reports of shots fired. They will not be denied.

"It was an accident," my mother whispers urgently in my ear. *"Nothing but an unfortunate accident."*

I reach over to the computer. I close out the images. Then, because I have enough experience to know it won't be enough, I pick up the gun from my husband's lifeless hand. I curl my palm around the checkered grip. I slip my finger into the cold trigger guard.

And I start shooting.

WHEN THE POLICE finally burst through the door, I stand at the top of the stairs, both hands up, gun in plain view, while turning slightly so that the curve of my stomach can't be denied.

"Drop the weapon, drop the weapon, drop the weapon!" the first officer shouts from the base of the stairs.

I do.

He scrambles up the stairs, cuffs in hands. I hope for his own sake that he doesn't stumble against the bannister.

A marriage is a mosaic. A thousand moments. A hundred memories.

The officer twists my arms behind my back. He cuffs my wrists tight, pats me down as if expecting even more weapons, as more uniforms pour through the door.

"My husband," I hear myself say. "He's been shot. He's dead."

"Ma'am, is there anyone else present?"

"No."

A thousand moments. A hundred memories.

"Ma'am, you have the right to remain silent. Anything you say can and will be used against you in a court of law. You have the right to speak to an attorney, and to have an attorney present during any questioning."

The officer escorts me down the stairs, out of the house, away from my husband's body.

"Do you think I'll be allowed to plan the funeral?" I ask him.

He looks at me funny, then deposits me in the back of the patrol car on a hard plastic bench seat.

More cops. More sirens. The neighbors appearing to watch the show. I know what will come next. The trip to the police station. Where my hands will be swabbed for blood, tested for GSR. Fingerprinting. Processing.

Then, when my past appears on the computer screen . . .

An accident, my mother whispers again in the back of my mind. *Nothing but an unfortunate accident.*

I can't help myself; I shudder.

She will come for me now, I think. And because of that, as much as anything else, I curl my hands around my belly and tell my baby, this fragile, fluttery life that hasn't even had a chance yet, how sorry I truly am.

CHAPTER 2

D.D.

"Okay. Just like we've done before. I'll head straight. Alex will cut left. Jack, you ready?"

Jack nodded. Sergeant Detective D. D. Warren took a steadying breath. Three of them. One target. How badly could things go wrong?

First step forward. Light tread, heel, toe, designed not to make a sound. Alex utilized the same strategy, heading sideways to intercept the line of retreat. They'd done this enough times to know that silence was the key. Alert their opponent too early, and that was it. She was both faster and—D.D. was beginning to suspect—smarter than the three of them put together.

Which made the situation particularly dire, given that it was D.D.'s favorite black leather boot at stake.

She eased into the dining room, where Kiko had wisely retreated beneath the table with her prize. So far, the best spotted dog in all the land was lying contentedly on the rug, chewing on the heel of D.D.'s shoe, as D.D. and Alex made their circular approach.

Five-year-old Jack had taken up position in the family room. His job: catch Kiko when she inevitably bolted from beneath the cherry-wood table. They expected the dog would run toward Jack, her partner in crime. The two adults of the household, on the other hand . . .

A floorboard creaked beneath D.D.'s foot. She froze. Kiko looked up.

Time stood still. Detective and dog locked eyes, D.D. wearing one boot, Kiko holding the second between her paws.

Alex appeared in the left-hand doorway of the dining room. "Kiko! Release! Bad dog!"

Kiko grabbed the boot in her mouth and ran for it.

D.D. lunged to the right. An act of desperation, and she and the dog both knew it. Kiko, a Dalmatian–German shorthaired pointer mix who was all long legs and high energy, dodged the move effortlessly. Alex came charging from behind.

Kiko galloped straight for Jack, who cried out in boyish delight, *"Roo, roo, roo!"* right before he tossed Kiko's favorite toy straight up into the air.

True to form, Kiko dropped the boot and leapt up for her stuffed hippo.

D.D. snatched her boot. Kiko caught her toy. Then Kiko and Jack were off, tearing around the family room in a whirlwind of puppy-boy energy.

"Damage?" Alex asked, coming to a halt beside her. He was still trying to catch his breath. For that matter, so was D.D.

She inspected her boot. The bottom of the heel showed signs of chewing. But the leather upper was still intact.

"You gotta remember to put them in the closet," Alex said, eyeing the teeth marks.

"I know."

"She's going to grow out of it, but not overnight."

"I know!"

"So who do you think is going to take longer to train, her or you?"

D.D. growled at her husband. He grinned back.

"Roo, roo, roo!" Jack added from across the room. He was now standing on the sofa, springing up and down on the cushions, while Kiko matched him jump for jump from the floor. It had been Alex and Jack's idea to adopt a dog from the local Humane Society. D.D., as sergeant detective of Boston homicide, had argued they weren't home enough. To which Alex had ruthlessly replied that *she* wasn't home enough. His job teaching crime scene analysis at the academy had set hours, and Jack's schedule as a kindergartener was hardly grueling. A boy needs a dog, he'd told her.

Which, from what D.D. could tell, seemed to be true. Because God knows Jack and Kiko were already inseparable. The black-and-white-spotted one-year-old pup slept in Jack's bed. Sat next to his feet at the kitchen table. And did everything the boy did, from leaping across the furniture to racing around the yard.

D.D.'s son was happy. Her husband was happy. In the end, a chewed boot heel seemed a small price to pay. That said, Kiko and Jack were now racing laps around the room.

"I gotta get to work," D.D. said.

"Take me with you," Alex tried.

"And rob you of this magic moment?"

"Pretty please?"

"Sorry." D.D. was already sliding on her damaged boot. "Wife shot and killed her husband last night. She's been arrested, but I want to check out the crime scene. Clearly, you'd be biased."

"Woman's already been charged," Alex asked, "and you still need to visit the scene?" Following an on-the-job injury two years ago, D.D. had been moved to a supervisory position in homicide. As her fellow detectives would attest—and Alex would agree—D.D. took a much more hands-on approach with her management style than was strictly necessary.

"I have a personal interest in this one." D.D. made it to the front door, eyed the crystalline sheen to the half-frozen ground outside, and grabbed her black wool coat. A month ago, the air had been crisp but the sun warm. And now this. Welcome to New England.

D.D. spared the twin racing streaks of her son and dog a second glance from the entryway, and despite the chaos—no, because of the chaos—felt the corresponding warmth in her chest. "They really do love each other."

"Heaven help us," Alex agreed. He stood close. They'd just had four whole days off together, a rare treat. As always, they both now felt the pull and pang of D.D.'s demanding job. Alex had always respected D.D.'s workaholic ways. But there were times, even for her, when disappearing down the rabbit hole that was a homicide investigation became difficult. Especially lately.

"Why is this case personal?" Alex asked.

D.D. buttoned her coat. "The woman in question, Evelyn Carter, née Hopkins, I investigated her for murder once before."

"She killed a husband before this one?"

"Nope. She 'accidentally' shot her father. But, seriously, how many shootings can one woman be involved with?"

Alex nodded sagely. "You're going to get her this time."

D.D. smiled, stepped into her husband's embrace for a quick kiss, then waved goodbye to her crazy kid and dog. "Totally."

EVELYN CARTER AND her husband, Conrad, lived in Winthrop, one of the smallest and oldest towns in Massachusetts. Dating back to 1630 and positioned on a peninsula just miles from Logan Airport, the area offered views of the Atlantic for the lucky and up-close-and-personal contact with densely packed homes for everyone else. The Carters' residence was located on a street of modest, distinctly 1950s Colonials that had probably once been strictly working-class.

Now, given property values in Boston, especially this close to the waterfront, God only knew. As it was, D.D. was surprised to see so many of the original homes intact. These days, it felt like every neighborhood in Boston was being gentrified, developers coming in, razing the old, and replacing it with bigger and better. Personally, D.D. preferred a little character in a home, but then again, on a detective's salary she wouldn't be living in any of these neighborhoods anytime soon.

Her former squad mate and onetime mentor Phil had contacted her first thing this morning to fill her in on the shooting. Pretty straightforward case, in his opinion. Neighbors had called in reports of shots fired. Uniformed officers had responded to find the wife standing at the top of the stairs, gun still in hand. She had surrendered without incident and been taken to the South Bay House of Correction.

Pregnant, Phil had added. Far enough along to be noticeable, while not yet huge.

D.D. couldn't yet picture that. The Evie Hopkins she had known had been a sixteen-year-old girl. Thin, dirty-blond hair, huge, doelike brown eyes as she'd sat at the kitchen table, mere feet from her father's blood-soaked body, shaking uncontrollably.

She hadn't cried. D.D., a new detective back then, had thought that odd. But there'd been something to the girl's flat expression, combined with her hard tremors, that had been compelling. Shock. A sort of delayed reaction to grief that made D.D. believe the girl was honestly in pain, only of such an extreme magnitude she couldn't comprehend it.

They hadn't been able to get her out of the kitchen and down to the station for proper processing. At the time, it hadn't seemed such a big deal. Evie, covered in blood, hadn't denied anything. The gun had gone off. Yes, she'd shot and killed her father.

And now her legs didn't seem to work. She couldn't stand, move.

Short of physically picking her up, D.D. and her partner, an older detective, Gary Speirs, couldn't get the girl out of the kitchen. Speirs had made the judgment call not to push it. He'd been afraid the girl would give over to hysterics, ending their interview once and for all.

So they'd all sat feet from the body, the spattered cabinets, the smeared refrigerator.

The mom had stayed in the front room. An actual parlor, which D.D. had found strangely mesmerizing. She'd heard of such things, but to actually see one . . . The Hopkinses lived in a beautiful historic Colonial in Cambridge, as befitting the father's position as a Harvard professor. Perfectly tended, everything in its place. Except, of course, for the crime scene in the kitchen.

Had it biased D.D. at the time? The upper-class home? The well-groomed mom? The obviously shell-shocked sixteen-year-old suspect, her thin shoulders shaking?

The mom, interviewed separately in the front parlor, had corroborated everything her daughter had reported. The shotgun had been a recent purchase given a rash of break-ins in the area. The father had been showing it to his daughter. She'd picked it up, had been trying to figure out how to clear the chamber, when the gun had gone off, blasting her father in the chest from mere inches away. A tragic accident. Follow-up interviews revealed no reports of any ongoing rancor between the father and daughter. In fact, the entire family was described as good people, great neighbors. The daughter a gifted pianist. The wife active with literacy causes and aid for battered women. As cases went, it wasn't even one D.D. had wondered about in all the years since.

Now this.

Yellow crime scene tape roped off the front yard. Several open parking spaces had been secured, probably for the detectives who'd worked most of the night before finally taking off for home in the hours since. Only two official vehicles remained.

All in all, the house appeared quiet. No neighbors lurking outside. No crime scene techs bustling about or uniformed officers working the street. As Phil had said, a straightforward case. A man had been shot and killed. His wife was now sitting in county jail.

D.D. got out of her vehicle. She approached the front door, noting the splintered frame and skewed Christmas wreath. The police had had to force their way in. Interesting.

She entered. Like a lot of the homes hastily constructed postwar to accommodate the boom in young families, the house had a simple layout. Narrow staircase leading straight up against the wall to the left. Front-facing family room to the right. Tight hallway leading to a modest eat-in kitchen. Downstairs bath to the right. Mudroom area and garage access off the kitchen to the left.

The kitchen showed signs of recent updating. Fresh-painted pale-gray cabinets. New, solid-surface dark-flecked countertops. Stainless steel appliances. The hallway, on the other hand, with its ripped yellow wallpaper and scuffed wooden floors, was deeply in need of care.

Clearly a fixer-upper, though given modern tastes for open-area living, a tough one at that. Had the Carters been doing the work themselves?

Had they already started in on the nursery?

D.D. found herself with her hand resting on her belly. Hastily, she dropped it. Lately, she'd been thinking too much about the days she'd been pregnant with Jack. A child she'd never expected to have. Her greatest miracle and deepest love. Usually . . .

"Hey, there you are."

D.D. turned to find Detective Carol Manley standing in the hallway behind her. The petite investigator, just over five feet tall and barely a hundred pounds soaking wet, had taken D.D.'s place on her squad after D.D.'s injury. Manley was a perfectly good detective.

Both Phil and Neil seemed to like her and accept her as part of their three-person team. D.D., on the other hand, still didn't trust any cop named Carol.

Completely unreasonable, but there it was.

Now D.D. carefully schooled her features and reminded herself that part of her job was to play well with others. It was the part of her job she was worst at, but hey.

"Body was found upstairs," Carol was saying now. "Looks like she shot him sitting at his desk. Then shot up his laptop as well."

"Do we know motive?" D.D. fell in step behind Carol as the woman headed for the stairs.

"Wife isn't talking. Phil said you knew her."

"I questioned her regarding another shooting sixteen years ago. That one was ruled accidental. Though now I wonder."

"Watch the bannister," Carol commented as she headed up. "It's pretty loose. One of those things they must not have gotten around to fixing yet."

D.D. gave the wooden bannister an experimental shake; yep, it was definitely less than stable. "Don't suppose murder weapon was a shotgun?" D.D. asked.

"Nah. Sig Sauer P-two-two-six, registered to the vic, Conrad Carter. Looks like he kept the nine-mil in the top drawer of his nightstand."

"Where anyone could grab it."

"Ah, but the ammo was in a shoebox in the closet."

"Because clearly that provides security. Love 'smart' gun owners."

"And yet where would our job be without them?"

D.D. conceded the point. They arrived at the top. The landing was tiny. Only three doors to pick from. Two bedrooms and a bath, most likely. But D.D. didn't need to inspect all three to find the scene of the crime. Smell directed her enough.

Conrad had converted the smaller bedroom into a personal office. Massive executive-style black leather chair, the back now smeared with dark splotches of gore. A wall of waist-high laminate filing cabinets, covered in piles of paperwork and stacks of what appeared to be catalogues. Across from the filing cabinets, the room held a massive oak desk, currently riddled with enough bullet holes and metallic rubble to qualify it as a war vet.

Small space, D.D. thought, huge carnage. Clearly, the wife hadn't been messing around.

"The remains of the laptop?" D.D. asked, gesturing to the debris-strewn desk.

"Yep. Techs have it. Woman closed it up, then emptied her clip into it. Not a huge target, meaning our gal knew what she was doing."

"What do the techs think?"

"They need time to take the laptop apart and inspect the damage. There's a lot going on inside a laptop—battery, RAM, motherboard, Wi-Fi card, hard drive, thin hard drive, et cetera. So lots of things to hit, but in theory, also some things that could've been missed. Unfortunately, a dozen forty-caliber rounds to a target that small . . ."

D.D. arched a brow. "How many bullets to the husband?"

"Three."

The Sig P226 held fifteen rounds. Meaning: "Three to the husband, twelve into the computer? If we view the laptop as a second victim, certainly seems she hated the computer more."

"Or was a woman with something to hide."

"Trying to eradicate something on the laptop," D.D. followed. "Do we know if it was strictly the husband's computer, or did both of them share it?"

"Don't know."

"And she didn't say anything to the police when they arrived? No 'I had to do it,' 'he started it,' 'the voices in my head . . .' Anything?"

"She wanted to know if she could plan her husband's funeral."

D.D. shook her head. "What about her demeanor? Did the arresting officer describe her as appearing shocky, grief-stricken, relieved?"

"Calm and cooperative. Allowed herself to be cuffed and led to the patrol car. Was taken to the station and charged without incident."

D.D. frowned, still not sure what to think. She studied the blood-smeared chair, the spatter across the far wall. "What did the husband do?"

"Sales. Worked for one of those custom window companies." Carol pointed to the pile of catalogues on the filing cabinets. "According to the neighbors, he was on the road a fair amount, speccing out jobs, that sort of thing. But when he wasn't traveling, he worked out of this office."

"The contents of the filing cabinets?"

"Phil went through them. Seem to be customer files. Nothing out of the ordinary."

D.D. nodded, returned to studying the damage. She should've brought Alex, she thought. This was how they'd met, analyzing spatter at the scene of a brutal family annihilation. What did it say about her life that studying a crime scene made her miss her husband?

"And Evie?" D.D. asked. "Her occupation?"

"Evelyn? She teaches algebra at the local high school."

D.D. had to smile. "Her father was a prof at Harvard. Some kind of mathematical genius who taught classes where the names alone hurt my head."

"She's pregnant. Five months along."

"Were they close to their neighbors? Get any good dirt?"

Carol shrugged. "People on the block had nothing bad to report. Couple bought the house four years ago. Been working on fixing it up as time allowed. Apparently in the summer, Evelyn liked to work in the yard. She'd wave when neighbors walked by but wasn't exactly the chatty sort. *Quiet* was the word people used a lot. Conrad, on the other hand, was the social half of the pair. Much more likely to stop, hold court. But then again, uniforms couldn't find any neighbors who'd been invited over for dinners, barbecues, drinks, whatever. Neighbors didn't seem to take it personally as much as there was an assumption the Carters were a young, busy couple."

"So by all appearances, a happy couple?"

"No reports of domestic disturbance calls or loud arguments."

"And Evelyn, when she was arrested, bore no signs of a physical confrontation between her and the husband?"

"Not a mark on her."

"Rules out self-defense."

"But not battered woman's syndrome," Carol pointed out. "Some guys know how to hit where it doesn't show, and if it was ongoing . . ."

"Never know what goes on behind closed doors," D.D. agreed, thinking of that first crime scene, the stately Cambridge Colonial, the impeccably decorated front parlor. Again, had she, a rookie detective, let herself see only what outsiders were meant to see?

She gestured now to the gory wall before her. "Tell me about the husband's body. Three shots fired?"

"Two to the chest, one to the head. Torso shots lodged somewhere inside, probably ricocheted around his ribs. Head shot was a through and through."

Which would explain the far wall and the ongoing stench in the room.

"Close range?" D.D. asked.

"We're still working on the trajectories, but yes, stipling around the entry wounds suggest a distance of less than two feet."

D.D. considered the room, number of feet between the doorway and the desk chair. "Chair had to be facing the door, right?"

"Yep."

"No defensive wounds on his hands, any sign of a previous altercation?"

"Negative."

"Evelyn retrieves the gun from the bedroom," D.D. thought out loud. "Loads it using the ammo from the closet."

"We found the shoe box with ammo open on the bed, loose slugs next to it."

"Walks into the office, maybe calls her husband's name."

"He turns around in his chair," Carol filled in.

"She steps closer, opens fire. Quick. Has to be, for him to never even get a hand up. Just, 'Hey, honey,' then, boom, boom, boom."

"Or, 'You bastard,' boom, boom, boom."

"Something like that," D.D. agreed. "Three shots. Enough to make sure she definitely got the job done, but not so much that it's a crime of passion. That, she saved for the laptop." D.D. frowned. "I'd really like to know what was on that computer."

Carol shrugged. "What would motivate a wife to kill her husband? Porn? E-mails from a girlfriend? Online gambling addiction? Plenty of things out there that would justify shooting up a husband and his laptop. Hell, maybe he was just that into video games, or she was just that hormonal from her pregnancy."

D.D. gave the childless detective a look. "If pregnancy hormones led to homicide, there wouldn't be a husband left alive. Plus, you said it yourself. Evelyn knew what she was doing during the shooting, and she was calm and cooperative afterwards. That's not a woman on a rampage. There's something else going on here. Something more."

"How'd she look sixteen years ago?" Carol asked.

"Young and traumatized. I'm surprised, given that tragedy, she'd allow a gun in her home. You'd think she'd want to stay as far away from firearms as possible. And yet . . ." She glanced at Carol. "Two shots to the torso, one to the head, a dozen straight into the laptop. Even at such a close range, to never miss . . ."

"Sounds like a woman with some training," Carol agreed. "Maybe the ol' face-your-fears sort of thing? After the last shooting, she wanted to make sure she never had an 'accident' ever again. Took some classes, joined a local firing range?"

"Definitely worth pursuing. Her hands were tested for GSR?"

"Absolutely. Tested positive. Not to mention the flecks of blood we found on her clothes, more on her hands."

"She did this," D.D. stated. "Evelyn Carter shot and killed her husband."

"Open-and-shut. Police responded to sound of shots fired. Found her standing at the top of stairs still holding the Sig. Never even denied it."

"The police forced their way into the house. Why?"

"They heard more gunshots."

"But the initial call out was due to neighbors reporting gunfire. How long did it take police to respond?"

"Eight minutes."

D.D. tilted her head. "So fifteen shots were fired over the course of eight minutes?" She eyed the detective.

Carol merely shrugged. "We're still gathering facts. But my guess, first round was Evelyn killing her husband. Second round—when the police arrived—was Evelyn taking out the computer."

"With a gap in between. While she was doing . . . ?"

"Who knows. Closing out files on the computer, maybe? Trying to cover something up? Then, when she heard the sirens, realized the police were closing in . . . she decided on a more definitive approach."

It was possible, D.D. thought, but also a lot of conjecture. "Covering something up?" she murmured, more to herself than anyone. "Or backing something up?"

"What do you mean?"

"Clearly the laptop held something significant. Did she just want it destroyed, or was there also data she wanted to retrieve? E-mail address of her husband's alleged lover, I don't know. But eight minutes . . . It doesn't take eight minutes to close out files or shut down a computer. It could take eight minutes, however, to back up desired data."

Carol nodded slowly. "All right. I'll check on it. If she copied data, it'd have to be to a thumb drive. She didn't have anything on her when she was processed at South Bay. So maybe she stashed it around the house? I'll take a look."

"Something else you should know: Evie's father, the Harvard prof, was known for his photographic memory. It was part of the reason for his success in his field. All he had to do was glance at something once, and he retained the image forever."

"Meaning Evelyn . . . ?"

"Maybe she didn't have to back anything up. Maybe she just had to look."

"Lovely," Carol murmured.

D.D. smiled. "Nothing to worry about, right? Like you said. Open-and-shut."

Carol muttered again. This time, the word was not *lovely*.

D.D. left the detective to take a fresh look at the crime scene. She'd just exited the house when she noticed the person standing across the street. A lone female. Blond hair. Gray eyes. Deceptively slight build.

Flora Dane. Onetime kidnapping victim. Current survivors' advocate/vigilante. Also D.D.'s newest confidential informant. Just a month ago, they'd worked together to find a sixteen-year-old girl who'd disappeared after the murder of her entire family—if *working together* was a phrase that could be used for either D.D. or Flora.

Now D.D. frowned, stared across the street.

"What?" she called out. Because where Flora appeared, trouble usually followed.

Flora didn't approach. She shifted from foot to foot, hunching her shoulders inside her oversized down-filled jacket. If D.D. didn't know any better, she'd say the young woman looked nervous.

Another moment passed. D.D. sighed, crossed the street herself. Flora was staring at the Carters' house as if she were trying dissect all the contents while peering straight through the exterior walls. The girl had many talents—including lock picking and chemical fire—but D.D. didn't think X-ray vision was among them.

"What?" D.D. asked again.

"I saw his picture, on the news."

"You mean the victim? Conrad Carter?"

"His wife shot him?"

"Appears to be the case. Why?" asked D.D. "You know Evie?" Flora ran a support group for survivors. Maybe, after the death of her father at her own hands, that was how Evelyn saw herself. Anything was possible.

"No. Not her. Him. I recognized him." Flora glanced at her, and D.D. knew that her notoriously hard-edged CI was indeed nervous. "I met him before. In a bar. When I was with Jacob."

Jacob Ness was the man who'd kidnapped and raped Flora for four hundred and seventy-two days. He'd died six years ago, during the FBI raid to rescue her.

D.D. had that feeling again. Of knowing only that she didn't know enough. That Evie Carter had reappeared in her life, and it was going to bite her in the ass.

"Flora—"

"Jacob knew him," her CI whispered. Flora stared at D.D. with stark gray eyes. "Conrad Carter. Jacob Ness. I think . . . I'm pretty sure they might have been acquaintances."

CHAPTER 3

FLORA

EVERY DAY, I WORK OUT. I run. I hit various stations set up along the Charles River for fitness enthusiasts such as me. Pull-ups on bars. Triceps dips on wooden benches. Knee tucks, hip twists, calf raises, chest flies, lunges, lunges, lunges. It doesn't matter if it's December and below twenty, or raining, or boiling. I'm a woman who needs her morning serotonin the way others demand a double-foam latte.

The truth is, like a lot of survivors, I've been taught the hard way to ignore physical complaints. Basically, spend enough time starving, beaten, isolated, and you can teach yourself to ignore most anything.

It's true that what doesn't kill you makes you stronger.

But no one says that strength doesn't come at a price.

After my morning endurance event, I return to my tiny one-bedroom apartment with its multiple bolt locks and very kind elderly landlords who charge me only a fraction of the going rent. I make some money working at the pizza parlor down the street, but it isn't much. I have a fund, however, that my mom set up when I first returned home. Filled with checks, some large, some small, sent by total strangers because they felt sorry for me. In the beginning, I hated that money. All these years later, no college degree, no real life plan, it's come in handy. Still, I try to draw from it sparingly. It won't last forever, and so far my only calling—helping other survivors—is more of a volunteer gig. Oh, and now I'm a CI for one Sergeant Detective D. D. Warren, using my street savvy to help solve crimes. Turns out, that pays nada as well. Figures.

I shower. Forever. Cleanliness, after all those months of lying in my own filth, is everything to me. After showering comes coffee.

I turn on my TV. Local news because that's part of my morning routine. Amber Alerts, missing persons, developments on national crime cases, this is what I do—much to my mother's dismay. But six years later, we've agreed to disagree.

I don't look at the TV, the talking heads more of an audio backdrop as I bang around my tiny kitchen, searching for food that still hasn't magically appeared because my mother hasn't driven down from her farm in Maine to bake for me lately. I both dread and long for her visits. My mother fought for me. I went to Florida, a stupid, naïve Boston college student, giddy with the limitless potential of spring break. I got drunk. I got kidnapped. And for the next four hundred and seventy-two days, my mother and my brother went through hell, appearing on national news shows and orchestrating major social media campaigns to beg for my safe return.

Then when it happened . . .

I think we can all agree that the Flora who went down to Florida isn't the same Flora who came back. My brother, Darwin, eventually took off to Europe. It hurt him too much to be around me. My mom is built from sturdier stuff. All these years later, she remains convinced that her sweet little girl who ran around the wilds of Maine and tamed the local foxes is inside me somewhere.

I admire my mother's courage. I'm still never sure what to think of her optimism. Though right now, I really miss her blueberry muffins.

Behind me, the TV is talking about a local murder. Pregnant wife shot and killed her husband last night. Fussing with my coffee maker, I shrug philosophically. Nice to have the pregnant wife come out on top, is my first thought, after all those years when it seemed that every other homicide was some cheating husband murdering his pregnant spouse just to avoid alimony and child support.

It's not until the coffee is percolating that I turn, glance at my tiny flat-screen TV sitting on the far wall cabinet.

And I start to shake. My hands, my shoulders, my entire body. My feet are rooted. I can't move. I stand in the middle of the kitchen. I shake and I shake.

Sheer terror. From a woman who's not supposed to feel such emotions anymore.

Cheap hotel. Too-tight hot-pink tube dress, barely held in place. Jacob smacking me across the face. "Stop fidgeting. For fuck's sake, you look like shit. Is this any way to show some appreciation? Get back into the bathroom and try again."

I do what I'm told, retreating to the dingy bath, where I stare at my reflection in the mirror. My orders are to "look like something worth coming home to." My cheeks are sunken. My eyes bruised. Jacob had left me in the cheap motel days ago, maybe even a week. Nothing to eat. Only tap water to drink. In the beginning I'd expected him to return at any moment. By the end, I was curled up in a ball on the floor, half unconscious from sheer starvation.

Then: Jacob returned. Just like that. No bags of food in his arms. Just this awful dress and instructions that we were going out. Now. Time to clean the fuck up.

I rouse myself long enough to bang on the wobbly faucet. I'm still weak from hunger and definitely not firing on all cylinders, but when it comes to Jacob's demands, failure is not an option.

I shimmy out of the micromini, do my best to rinse my bony arms and sweat-encrusted skin with a wet washcloth. I take a bar of soap to my stringy hair. There's only a hand towel for drying off. Then I pull back on a dress only a hooker would wear.

This time when I exit the bathroom, Jacob grunts his approval. I follow him out the door.

I don't know where we're going, but anyplace has gotta be better than this.

Fresh popcorn. I smell it the moment we walk into the dimly lit bar, and my stomach growls. Fortunately, a jukebox blaring out Montgomery Gentry covers the sound. I'm not sure what town we're in. Maybe someplace in Alabama? I'm only allowed out of my box at night, so I miss long stretches of the road. But we're definitely someplace rural. The locals, clad in tight jeans, worn boots, and way more clothing than me, mill around pool tables, trading shots, guzzling beer, tossing back handfuls of free popcorn.

My stomach growls again. I press a hand to it self-consciously, but Jacob just laughs. His eyes are too bright. He's definitely riding high on something, which only makes him more dangerous.

He didn't bother to clean up. His thin hair is a greasy cap on his too-shiny face. The snaps of his western-style shirt strain around the bulge of his swollen stomach, made more obvious by his skinny arms and legs.

Once, I never knew men like Jacob Ness existed. Once, I thought life was fair and being good meant I would always be safe and secure and loved. Then I went on spring break, had a little too much fun slamming back shots at a Florida bar with my college friends. And now this.

Jacob finds us a spot at the bar, gesturing for me to take the seat, then standing behind me. Protectively, some might think. Possessively. He orders two beers. One for him, one for me. A rare treat.

I pick up my beer, sip nervously.

Popcorn. Delivered in a red-and-white-checkered container. My whole body clenches but I don't make a single move; I glance at Jacob, knowing the rules by now.

He nods. I grab the first few kernels. Warm and salty. I want to devour the entire tray, dump the contents in my mouth. I catch myself just in time. If I act out, if I draw attention . . . I force myself to slow down. Couple of kernels here. Couple of kernels there.

Crunch, crunch. Salty goodness. My eyes close . . .

And for a moment, I could be a little girl again, sitting in my mother's kitchen, swinging my legs, waiting for the air popper to complete our after-school snack: "Darwin, what are we gonna do today . . ."

When I open my eyes again, a guy has appeared beside Jacob, and he's staring straight at me.

Jacob nods at the man, almost . . . congenial. He doesn't even protest when the man pulls up the neighboring barstool and orders a beer.

I grab another handful of popcorn. Have to pace myself. I've learned by now that eating too fast after forced deprivation leads to vomiting. Jacob will kill me if I get sick in public. But the man sitting next to us continues to stare at me.

And Jacob continues to let him.

Something bad is about to happen. I know it, even if I don't understand it.

Sip of beer. But only a sip. I'm on guard now, desperately trying to pay attention.

"Girlfriend's a skinny thing," the man says.

Jacob shrugs. "Chicks these days. Think if they're any bigger than a shadow, they're fat."

Single popcorn kernel. Pick up. Chew, chew, chew.

"Come here often?" the man asks.

"Sure. I'm a regular," Jacob says, and both men laugh, though I don't understand the joke.

"I'm on a business trip," the man offers. *"Sales. Good excuse, you know, to move around."*

"What the wife doesn't know," Jacob suggests.

"Yeah. Sure she doesn't mind?" The guy nods toward me.

My next warning light goes off.

"Nah. My girl's a good girl. She does what she's told." Jacob turns to me abruptly. *"Ain't that right, Molly?"*

I look away. Don't say a word.

I understand then. At least, have an inkling of the threat. Jacob had tried getting me to pick up random men in bars before; testing the level of my obedience. Each time, I'd managed to avoid the situation. Because I understood, somewhere deep inside of me, that while Jacob might make a game of forcing me on someone else, he'd still never take me back. And not because he's big, bad Jacob Ness. But because he's a man. And no man wants used goods.

The part I still don't understand—before, the men had been strangers, maybe a cowboy caught eyeing me from across the room. Whereas this man, he'd come straight over. And the way Jacob is turned toward him, engaging with him . . . It's almost like they'd been expecting each other.

What has Jacob done? What exactly has he promised this not-quite-stranger?

I shake out the last of the popcorn, then grab my beer. No more sipping. Chug, chug, chug. I'm desperate now. Thinking fast, but maybe not fast enough.

The man buys a second round for us. Jacob doesn't protest, though he's eyeing me suspiciously.

Nachos. A plate goes by, heaped high with melted cheese and sour cream. I follow it with huge eyes, never saying a word. The stranger man immediately orders us a platter. Jacob jabs my thigh. I gaze up at him innocently and swallow the last of my second beer.

Then we're off to the races. Food. Drink. Jacob and the man talking in low voices about things I can't hear and don't care about. And maybe Jacob is suspicious, but he's a fast-food addict himself and the nachos, followed shortly by sliders, then chicken wings— all at our newfound companion's expense—are too good for him to pass up.

Except the new man doesn't act that new. And Jacob, who never interacts with anyone, is talking, laughing, slapping the man on the back.

Eat. Drink. Faster, faster, faster. Not much time left. Whatever is going to happen is going to happen soon. The man is staring at me now, his eyes nearly as bright as Jacob's.

The bartender flashes the lights. Closing time. Our new friend pulls out his wallet. Throws down a hundred as casually as a ten. Jacob's smirk grows.

No more beer, nachos, wings, popcorn. My stomach hurts. My legs are wobbly. Jacob grabs my arm, dragging me forcibly off the barstool and toward the door, the man falling in step behind us.

Come on, come on, come on.

I can feel a pale sheen of sweat on my brow. I hesitate, trying to drag my heels even though I know better. Jacob digs his fingers into my bony arm, giving me a stare that promises further pain if I don't knock it off. Right now.

Foxes. Gators. Florida beaches. So far from home. The way Jacob is the evilest person I've ever met. The way all men are the same.

Jacob yanks me into the parking lot, close to a vehicle that isn't his own. The night wind hits my bare arms, my sweaty brow. Then, finally, thankfully, what I've been planning on, waiting for . . .

I turn, and in a move of sheer beauty, projectile vomit all over Jacob's newfound friend.

"Jesus Christ!" The man leaps back.

It doesn't save him. Seven days of starvation followed by three hours of binge eating. I lurch forward and hit him again, a thick stream of barely digested food.

Crowds gather. People gasp. I barely notice, falling to my hands and knees, dry heaving onto the warm asphalt. My stomach cramps painfully, sour bile gathering in the back of my throat. I'll pay for this. Oh, in a million different ways.

But right now, the man's eyes widen with disgust. Then he turns and hastily walks away . . .

Jacob has his games. But I have my rebellion. He might always win in the end. But I'm not completely broken yet.

"All right, all right," Jacob announces to the milling people. "Girl never could hold her beer. Come on, now, not the first time any of you have seen someone puke outside a bar. Move along."

He grips my arm. I'm shaking uncontrollably, too weak to even stand.

But the not-quite-stranger is gone. The immediate threat is over. Which leaves me with just Jacob.

"You did that on purpose!" he growls low in my ear.

"I had to. The thought of leaving you . . . Please. You've been gone for a week. I just want to be with you. Only you."

He narrows his eyes, studies me hard.

"Bitch," he says, but there's no heat left in his voice.

He pulls me to standing. I lean against him heavily. After a moment, his arm goes around me.

And for one more night, I survive.

SIX YEARS LATER, Cambridge, Mass. I'm still standing in the kitchen of my apartment. Images of the murdered husband's face appear, disappear, reappear, on the TV across the room. Followed by snapshots of his wife, the outside of their home, miles of yellow crime scene tape. I'm shaking. As hard as I shook that night, so long ago.

Now, I fist my hand and force myself to focus. Deep breath in, deep breath out. Jacob is gone. Jacob is dead. Jacob can never hurt me again.

The man on TV, Conrad Carter, I never saw him after that night. And now he's dead, too. More power to his wife.

Except that so many thoughts hit me at once, I have to grab a chair for support.

It takes me a bit, but I finally get my legs to move. I retrieve my cell from the coffee table. I make a single call.

"Samuel, it's me. You know how I said I'd tell you about my time with Jacob once and only once, and then I'd never speak of it again? I lied."

CHAPTER 4

EVIE

IT'S AFTER MIDNIGHT WHEN THEY take me to the police headquarters. I have a brief impression of a monstrous glass building; I think I've seen pictures of it on TV. The officer leads me through a vast lobby, then through a warren of hallways. First stop, fingerprints. I was never printed the first time. Ironically enough, it's my job as a schoolteacher that finally put me in the system. I had to have a background check to chaperone field trips, after-school activities. I'd been nervous then. What if they ran my prints and the previous incident—*"nothing but an unfortunate accident,"* my mother whispers—popped up for all to see? You'll be fine, Conrad had kept telling me. You were just a kid; no charges were even filed.

In the end, that's what saved me—no charges were filed, meaning I had no criminal record, versus a sealed juvie record, which could come back to haunt a person later.

After scanning each fingertip into the digital machine, the uniformed officer—Bob, someone calls him—leads me to a clinical-looking room where a woman in a lab coat swabs both my hands with some kind of substance, then uses a metal file to remove scrapings from beneath my nails. "I'm going to require her clothing," she informs the officer, who nods as if this is no surprise.

If they're taking my clothes, what does that leave me with? But no one bothers to tell me, and I can't bring myself to ask.

I'm tired. The shock, adrenaline, something wearing off. Mostly, I feel like a pregnant woman, up way past her bedtime and deeply self-conscious that it's not just me the police are arresting, but my unborn child.

I haven't even met my baby yet, and I'm already filled with so many regrets.

Upstairs. A new floor with miles of blue carpet. I don't get a chance to look around. My escort leads me straight to a small room with two chairs, one table, and a mirrored wall. Interrogation, I realize, and can't help but think it looks much nicer than the rooms you see on TV. Then Officer Bob dumps me in the chair, releases my left wrist from the handcuff, only to attach the bracelet to a ring on the table, and any positive impressions I have of the room are over.

Officer Bob exits. At least I still have my clothes, I think, then move my free hand to rest on my rounded belly. As if that can protect my baby from what will happen next.

The door opens. An older gentleman with thinning brown hair walks in. He's wearing a brown-and-gold-flecked sports jacket over a light-blue shirt. Pleated khakis; the kind that went out of fashion a decade ago, and yet are still favored by people of a certain age. He has a nice face. Serious, but not harsh. Never the bad cop, I think, more like the stern father figure.

I'm grateful I don't recognize him. Then I wonder if they picked him because, given my history, stern father figure is exactly the right approach to take.

"Evelyn Carter?" he asks. "I'm Detective Phil LeBlanc."

I have this ridiculous impulse to wave. Years of social training kicking in. I constrain myself to a short nod.

"I understand you're pregnant?" he says.

I nod again.

"Can I get you anything? A glass of water? Ginger ale? My wife always loved ginger ale."

Definitely the concerned father. I smile at him. I can't help myself. He doesn't understand. They never understood. And now . . . My baby. My poor unborn child.

"I would like my phone call," I say. "And I'm not saying another word until I get it."

THERE ARE TWO people I could call. Option A is the most obvious and the call I can't bring myself to make. Option B will inform Option A of the situation anyway, so it hardly matters. Plus, Option B was my father's best friend. He has plenty of reasons to doubt me, which is why I trust him more.

He doesn't seem to be surprised to receive my call in the middle of the night. Because of his job, or because of how well he knows me? I walk him through the evening's events, at least the bare bones. Conrad shot dead. Me in police custody.

"Have they arrested you?" Dick Delaney, one of Boston's top criminal defense attorneys, asks me over the phone.

"I think so." The events of recent months, let alone the past few hours, are starting to weigh heavily on me, dragging me down till everything has taken on a surreal quality. They never handcuffed me the first time. Never put me in a squad car, never drove me to the station for fingerprinting and processing and interrogation. I don't understand these steps. It's like watching an old movie, except the story line has been changed.

I don't know how this story ends.

"Where are you?" Mr. Delaney asks.

"Police headquarters."

"What did you tell them?"

"Nothing."

"Keep it that way. They're at the house now, working the crime scene?"

I nod into the phone, then remember I have to speak. "Yes. I've been fingerprinted. And my hands were swabbed. Blood. I had blood on my hands."

"Probably testing for blood and GSR—gunshot residue," Mr. Delaney mutters, but he seems to be talking more to himself than to me. "How are you holding up?"

"I'm tired."

"Are you in pain, do you require medical assistance? How is the baby?"

"I'm okay."

"You could be in shock. Perhaps you require medical observation."

"I'm okay," I say again.

Maybe that's not the right answer. Maybe he's trying to tell me something and I'm not getting it, because he falls quiet for a full minute or two.

"Evie—you're going to have to spend at least one night in jail."

I don't know how to process that. Again, the story line is all wrong. I know shootings. I know blood and horror and loss.

The aftermath is not supposed to go like this.

"It's the middle of the night," Mr. Delaney is saying. "Nothing can happen till tomorrow, when the charges against you are formally presented in court. At that time, there'll be an arraignment. I'll be there to represent you, and hopefully get you released on bail. But again, none of this can happen before tomorrow."

"They want my clothes," I hear myself say. "Can they take my clothes?"

"Yes. They're going to try to question you, Evie. Your job is to say nothing. Next, you will be taken to the county jail for overnight admittance. Given the severity of the charge, you'll be held in isolation. But you'll be formally processed. Your personal possessions will be taken and inventoried."

I don't have any. It occurs to me for the first time. I'd taken off my coat, set down my purse. I don't have my cell phone. Not even my wallet. I feel a rising bubble of hysteria.

"They'll take your clothes as evidence," Mr. Delaney continues, "and hand them over to a waiting officer."

My escort, Officer Bob.

"In return, you'll get an orange jumpsuit."

I don't speak, but I feel a giggle rising again in the back of my throat. A prison jumpsuit. Like *Orange Is the New Black*. I'll be the new girl. Fresh meat. Until I win them over with my story of woe. And get a cool new lesbian roommate. Or maybe I'll be the muscle, taking some delicate, fragile thing under my wing. After all, two shootings to my credit. I can get double teardrop tattoos on my cheek, swagger across the prison yard with my soon-to-be enormously pregnant belly. Mess with that, bitches.

I'm not doing well. I'm going to start laughing. And once I do, I'll never stop.

My poor baby, my poor, poor baby.

Conrad.

Mr. Delaney promises to meet me at the courthouse. He reminds me to say nothing. He tells me I have medical rights, as well as the right to speak to my attorney at any time. "You're going to get through this," he says gently. "Hang tough. Be smart."

Like last time?

When the call ends, the older detective returns. He gives me a disappointed look. I've ruined his interrogation, proven that I'm no fun at all.

Then Officer Bob returns, unshackles me from the table, and off we go. Suffolk County Jail.

I sit in the back of the patrol car, my eyes drifting shut with exhaustion. Conrad, face breaking into a smile as he sees me for the first time. Conrad, fingers shaking uncontrollably as he tries to slip the simple gold wedding band on my finger at the courthouse. Conrad, the look on his face as we both stare wide-eyed at the pregnancy stick.

Conrad, collapsed in his desk chair, half his head sprayed across the wall behind him.

A thousand moments. A hundred memories. Some that felt completely right. Some that I know by now were totally wrong. And yet . . .

I loved you, I think, and my hand curls once more around my belly. Not just *my* baby—*our* baby. The best of both of us, at least that's what all parents hope for.

Even my parents, once upon a time.

The patrol car stops, slows, turns, comes to a halt. Outside the windows, I can see nothing but the harsh glare of too many lights. The kind designed to rob even the purest soul of all secrets.

South Bay House of Correction.

This is it.

I GREW UP in a beautiful home in Cambridge. A historic Colonial with dark-stained wood trim, a gorgeous curved bannister, and bull's-eye molding around a matching set of front bay windows. My mother is partial to richly colored oriental rugs, silk-covered wingback chairs, and decorative tables that hold cut-crystal decanters and silver serving trays.

Do not touch was one of the first phrases I ever learned. Followed shortly by: *No running in the house. Comb your hair. Chew with your mouth closed. Sit straighter. Stand taller.*

Do not embarrass your father was never actually said, but always implied.

My father wasn't merely a Harvard professor. By the time I was born, he was already considered one of the greatest mathematical minds of his generation. Bachelor's in psychology, master's in computer science, doctorate in statistics. He held honorary degrees from universities all around the world and his office was wallpapered in various awards. We didn't just have dinners at our house; we had standing Friday night poker games where my father and his fellow geniuses traded discourses on chaos theory, data mining, and string theory, all while vying to see who could count cards.

To the best of my memory, very few women ever attended these nights. There were female mathematicians, of course, as well as physicists, computer scientists, engineers, but not that many. Or maybe my mother didn't go out of her way to include their company. Accomplished, brilliant females rubbing shoulders with her husband . . . ? I don't know. For most of this, I was just a kid.

I understood my father was a great man. I assumed, judging by the quality of our home and the size of my mother's pearl necklace, that we led a life that others envied. Certainly, I spent my days in an elite boarding school where my teachers were suitably impressed by my own intelligence, while having to break the news to my father that I was no mathematical prodigy. Gifted, definitely. I had a fighting chance at understanding a fraction of the conversations I greedily eavesdropped on every Friday night. But my father, his mind, his intellect . . . he was a mystery to me till the bitter end.

He loved me. He took pride in my straight-A schoolwork. And he would sit for hours in the front room, his eyes closed as I ran through Bach, Mozart, Beethoven. He said when I played the piano, he could hear the math pouring out. There is a high degree of correlation between math and music. So maybe for me, math wasn't the classroom. Math was the piano, and the notes, scales, tones I found without even trying, and played obsessively day after day.

My father told me I was brilliant.

Back in those days, sitting at the baby grand in the front parlor, I believed him.

I had my own wing, an only child in a home built for when families had eight kids and three servants. My suite of rooms occupied the front of the second floor, with a pillow-covered seat built into the bank of windows that overlooked the street. I had lavender-painted walls and a wrought-iron canopy bed covered in yards of gauzy fabric. A private bath, of course, not to mention a smaller room, perhaps originally intended as a nursery, that had been converted to a walk-in closet with built-in mirror and makeup table. The adjoining sitting room, however, was my favorite. Bookshelves lined all four walls, filled with everything from Nancy Drew to musical compositions to historical fiction. I loved to read about faraway people living in distant times. Their fathers were never world-renowned geniuses. In fact, in most of these novels, both parents were dead—but no worries; the plucky heroine would make it on her own.

I had more than enough space for slumber parties and playdates. But somehow, other kids didn't want to hang out with a professor's daughter. Especially one more comfortable playing the piano for hours at a time than engaging in common discourse. Fashion, gossip, popular music? I felt like my father in those moments. I wished someone would break out some poker chips and tee off a discussion of the ten most useful mathematical equations (my father loved Euler's identity, but I spent plenty of Friday nights listening to passionate arguments for all ten entries). Sometimes, my mother would set up little mother-and-daughter teas, where she and her cohort-in-crime would cast glances in the direction of me and my obviously unhappy assigned companion, waiting for us to magically hit it off.

What I learned from those teas was that other mothers feared my mom, and that no one really wanted to be friends with a girl as strange as me.

My mother was big on appearances, meaning my bedsheets were of only the finest Egyptian cotton. When not in private school plaid, I could wear Laura Ashley, Laura Ashley, or Laura Ashley. My mother considered me too young for my own pearls, but I was allowed to wear a tasteful heart-shaped silver-and-diamond pendant my father gave me on my thirteenth birthday.

To judge by the look on his face when I opened the Tiffany box, my mother had done the actual picking out of the pendant, but I still hugged my father gratefully, his beard tickling my cheek. And he still hugged me back enthusiastically. Geniuses are geniuses, you know. You can't expect them to waste their brilliance on such trivial matters as a daughter's birthday gift. That's what wives are for, my mother would tell you.

If everything had stayed on track, I would have attended Radcliffe, married some up-and-coming genius, maybe one of my father's own research students, and gotten a string of pearls of my own to wear in a neighboring Cambridge home, where I would teach piano, or something equally respectable.

If everything had stayed on track.

"Squat," the nurse says now.

I am completely naked. My clothes stripped off and taken away as promised, even my underwear. I stand alone with a female nurse, who—given my rounded belly, or maybe the lack of needle tracks on my arms—is doing her best to appear kind.

I still have that surreal feeling. This can't be me; this can't be my life. It's three A.M. I should be home. With Conrad.

I don't know what to do with my hands. Cover my belly, as I've been doing for months now? Or my bare breasts? My exposed pubis? I settle on my stomach. The rest of me already feels too long gone.

"Nothing but an unfortunate accident . . ."

She will come. She will come for me next. Then, the real adventure will begin.

"Honey," the nurse says, snapping the glove on her right hand. "The sooner you do this, the sooner both of us get on with our lives."

I nod. I squat. She inspects. Next order. I bend over, best that I can. She inspects.

I don't cry. I've never been good at tears. My mom, she breaks into hysterics at the drop of a hat. Sixteen years ago, she did enough crying for the both of us. But me—under stress, loss, extreme pain?

I never cry.

I just . . . hollow out. A pit of anguish.

I feel it now, for my baby. Who will never grow up in an impressive Colonial in elite Cambridge, or even a well-intentioned fixer-upper in Winthrop.

Then I take it back. Because if I'm found guilty of shooting Conrad, if I go to jail this time, when my baby is born, they will take him or her from me. And there's only one person they'd give my baby to.

I start shivering then, and I just can't stop.

The nurse thinks I'm cold. Given my unclothed state, I don't blame her. She produces the promised orange jumpsuit, along with voluminous panties. She steps back a few feet as I wrestle the clothing on. The underwear are just plain wrong, like granny panties met men's boxers and tried to mate. The orange jumpsuit is also overly large, and scratchy from harsh chemicals. I can get it over my belly, but it swims around my upper body. The shoulders land somewhere around my ears. The leg length is intended for someone twice my height. The nurse takes pity on me and helps roll up the hems before I trip and fall.

We've already run through all my vitals. Physical description, date of birth, identifying tattoos. Foreplay before this main event.

Now it's done. I'm in the system. Not a prisoner, yet, I'm told, as I'm in jail, which is considered temporary. It all depends on how good my attorney, Dick Delaney, is and what happens at the courthouse a mere few hours from now.

"You'll be in your own cell," the nurse tells me now, throwing away her gloves, picking up her clipboard. "How do you feel?"

She nods toward my rounded belly.

"Tired."

She hesitates. "You're entitled to a medical hold. If you have any concerns about your health, the baby's health."

I have a sense of déjà vu. Mr. Delaney asked me all these questions. I didn't get it then. I don't get it now.

"Your pulse rate is fine," the nurse says now, looking straight at me. "Surprisingly strong, all things considered."

I don't have tears. Just an endless void of anguish.

"Your vitals are stable. In my honest opinion, I would stick to your own cell. But of course, you have rights . . ."

"What happens in medical?" I ask finally.

"The infirmary is a different ward. More like . . . a hospital. You'd get your own room there, as well as access to medical staff, twenty-four seven. Are you depressed?" she asks abruptly.

"I'm tired," I say again.

"If you have concerns, any thoughts of harming yourself, your baby . . ."

"I would never do anything to hurt my child!"

She nods. "This place, it's loud. The pipes, the walls, the inmates in the wards above you. You're going to hear noise, all night long."

I smile; there's not much of night left.

"But the infirmary . . . let's just say, it's its own special kind of shrill. It's not populated by inmates with physical injuries as much as by prisoners with mental ones. The screazies, the other inmates call them—screaming crazies. But again, if you have any concerns for your or the baby's well-being . . ."

I get it now. They all think I'm going to kill myself. Or the baby. Mr. Delaney, this nurse, they don't want me on their conscience. Even if that means assigning me to a night surrounded by frothing lunatics.

"I'm okay," I say again.

That's it. A female CO reappears, leads me out of the medical exam room. I have a little baggie of toiletries; a clear toothbrush the size of a pinky; a small, clear deodorant; clear shampoo; and white toothpaste. On my feet, I wear the world's ugliest pair of flat white sneakers, but at least they're comfortable. Around my wrists, the CO has once again fastened the restraints.

The hall is wide and cold. Cinder block. Thick, but the nurse is right; I already hear the towering prison moaning and groaning around us. Thudding pipes, booming mechanicals, distant murmurs of hundreds, if not thousands, of caged humans, trying to get through another night.

We arrive at a cell. Cream-painted cinder-block walls. A molded stainless steel toilet, no seat. Thin foam mattress with single beige blanket.

I say nothing. Walk inside. Hold out my wrists. The female CO removes the cuffs.

She closes and locks the heavy metal door, with its cutout window so they can monitor me at all times.

I sink onto the hard platform bed. I pull up my legs with my tennis shoes still on. Then I close my eyes and wish it all away.

My father. Conrad. Beautiful Cambridge. Hard-fought Winthrop. Choices made. Cycles repeated. Around and around and around.

And now, growing determinedly in my own womb, the next generation of tragedy.

I need to do better. I have to do better.

Yet, locked inside jail, waiting to be formally charged with murder . . .

I don't have any answers. Just distant notes from piano pieces I haven't played in at least ten years.

Once upon a time, there was a little girl in a big house who loved her father so much she was sure he would never leave her.

But he did.

And now this.

I close my eyes and, curled around my baby, will myself to sleep.

CHAPTER 5

D.D.

FLORA DANE WAS DRIVING D.D. nuts. Which was why, D.D. thought for the umpteenth time, a smart detective should never recruit a wild-card vigilante to be her CI. Because D.D. had to follow rules and procedures, whereas Flora had absolutely no interest.

"You're saying you recognize the victim, Conrad Carter. You spotted him in the company of Jacob Ness during the time of your captivity. Furthermore, you believe they might have had some sort of relationship. At least knew each other."

"I already told you that!" Flora was agitated. Pacing the sidewalk, rubbing her arms. D.D. had never seen the woman so rattled before. All the more reason to get her on the record.

"I need you to come down to the station and make a formal statement."

"No!"

"Flora—"

"I will talk! But we both know it won't be to you."

Which was the other issue. Flora might have been a Boston

college student at the time of her kidnapping, but she'd been on spring break in Florida when Jacob snatched her. Meaning, from the first taunting postcard Jacob had mailed from a small town in the South to Flora's mother in Maine, Flora's abduction had fallen under FBI jurisdiction.

The feds had done right by her. Eventually identifying Jacob as a long-haul trucker. Tracking his rig to a cheap motel. Storming the room with a dozen SWAT team officers and enough bullets and stun grenades to take out a small village. Jacob hadn't survived the raid; Flora had.

To the best of D.D.'s knowledge, it had been at the hospital, still waiting for her mother to fly down, that Flora had given her official statement. She'd made a deal: She'd speak of her kidnapping one time to one person. Then she'd delivered her story, word by painful word, to FBI victim specialist Dr. Samuel Keynes.

The rumor was that Keynes—who had a long history of interviewing international kidnapping victims—had barely made it to the bathroom before vomiting.

Since that day, Keynes and Flora had maintained a relationship that was beyond D.D.'s understanding. She doubted it fell strictly within the guidelines of the FBI's Office for Victim Assistance. Not that it was romantic at all—in fact, last D.D. had heard, the famously reserved psychologist had finally expressed his true feelings for Flora's mom, Rosa, who was an organic-farming, homemade-muffin-baking, free-spirited yogi. What they actually talked about, D.D. had no idea, but having personally seen the spark between them . . .

At least something good had come from Flora and her family's ordeal.

The problem remained; Keynes was Flora's confessor of choice. But he also worked for the FBI. Meaning, the moment Flora started talking to him about seeing D.D.'s murder victim in the company of

Jacob Ness, D.D. now had the FBI involved in her case. Or worse, taking it away.

"How many times did you see Conrad?" D.D. tried now. If Flora wouldn't agree to a formal statement, D.D. would settle for an informal one.

"Just once. At a bar."

"How long ago?"

"I don't know. I'd been with Jacob for a while. Weather was cooler." Flora rubbed her arms. "So maybe it was winter in the South."

D.D. nodded, working some mental arithmetic. Winter of Flora's abduction would mean they were looking back basically seven years. Detective Manley had reported that Conrad had traveled for his job, which could mean he'd had a good cover for many activities.

"What about the wife?" D.D. tried now. "Evelyn Carter look familiar to you?"

"She wasn't there," Flora said. She stopped pacing abruptly. "Was she married to Conrad then? What do you know of their lives?"

"I don't. Not yet."

"She shot him, that seems to signify less than happiness. Could she have been abused? Maybe a victim herself? The news said she was pregnant!"

Flora's voice had grown strident.

"I think we're getting ahead of ourselves. Investigations are a series of steps, and we have many left to take. For the record, the neighbors describe them as a normal, happy couple."

Flora snorted. "Neighbors don't know shit."

D.D. shrugged philosophically. On that, they could agree.

"Do you know what bar you were in? Where Jacob met Conrad?" D.D. tried to refocus her CI.

"I don't . . . Jacob had left me for days." Flora's voice dropped. "I was very, very hungry but I didn't dare leave because Jacob would track me down and kill me. That's what he told me every time he left, and I believed him."

"Okay." D.D. made her voice equally soft. This was the most she'd ever heard Flora say about Jacob. There were questions she'd love to ask, of course, but Flora had never deviated in her onetime, one-telling policy. Mostly, D.D. was left to admire the monster's handiwork, because if Jacob had been the worst of the worst, then the woman who'd survived him was the toughest of the toughest. Whether he'd known it or not, Jacob had served as a particular kind of forge. And the Flora who'd emerged four hundred and seventy-two days later was solid steel.

The detective in D.D. admired the woman's resilience. The mother in her was saddened by the loss.

"You were in the South," D.D. continued now. "Jacob's trucking route?"

"Yes."

"You said he left. You were at a motel."

"Yes."

"Can you think of the name? Letterhead on the stationery in the room?"

"Jacob didn't stay in places that had stationery."

"Okay, flashing neon sign? Work with me here."

"Motel . . . Motel Upland." Flora frowned. "I think. Maybe."

"Motel Upland." D.D. nodded. "Sounds regional. We can work with that."

Flora rubbed her arms and resumed pacing.

D.D. hesitated. In for a penny, in for a pound, she decided. "Flora, I don't think Evelyn was Conrad's victim. She's from around here, has family in Cambridge."

"You know her?"

"Let's just say, I'm not terribly surprised to hear about what happened. When I last spoke to her, it was right after she 'accidentally' shot her father."

Flora's head popped up. D.D. had the woman's full attention now, including a hard gray stare designed to force someone to hand over all their valuables or confess all their sins. D.D. finally got it then—Flora's real fear. That she hadn't talked enough about Jacob. That with her onetime, one-tell policy, she may have left some other victim behind.

As someone who now dedicated her life to helping other survivors, such a thing would devastate her.

"Flora. I think you should come with me. I think there's something you should see."

"What? Where?"

"Come with me to the courthouse. Evelyn Carter is due to be arraigned this morning. I think you should see her in person. I think you should know exactly who it is you're so concerned about."

COURTHOUSES WERE THEIR own special kind of madness. D.D. tried to avoid them as much as possible, though that was difficult in her line of work. Actual trials weren't so bad. They involved a set number of players in a predetermined room—if anything, they were much more boring than anything seen on TV.

The morning arraignment rush, however, was a sea of harried lawyers and wide-eyed—or completely hungover—defendants. The accused piled up, while overworked public defenders tried to identify which handcuffed prisoner would be their date for the party. The front steps were littered with bored reporters waiting for something interesting to happen, small groups of briefcase-wielding lawyers playing let's make a deal, and neck-craning loved ones trying to catch a glimpse of the spouse, kid, friend, whatever, who'd spent the night in the slammer and might not be coming home again.

Inside was worse. D.D. had to shoulder her way through the throngs, reading the signs to determine the proper room. Flora stalked alongside her, head up, gray stare lasering a path forward. At one point, a tattooed and muscle-bound gangbanger paused beside his escorting officer long enough to give Flora a second glance.

Two alphas, sizing each other up? D.D. wondered. Predator to predator? She was never sure with Flora, but half a heartbeat later, the big guy looked away first.

"You like that," D.D. murmured, having finally spotted Phil outside the assigned courtroom.

"Yes," Flora said, no explanation necessary.

"Still working our way through the docket," Phil said by way of greeting. He was the lead detective on the case, which explained why he was in the courthouse. D.D. could already tell from the look on his face that he was exasperated by her presence. Strictly speaking, supervising sergeants didn't need to personally visit crime scenes or arraignment hearings. And having Flora with her hardly helped matters. Both of D.D.'s former squad mates, Phil and Neil, had opinions about the vigilante, much of it having to do with how they'd all first met: Flora, naked, hands bound in front of her, standing over the charred remains of a would-be rapist; Phil and Neil arriving to arrest . . . someone . . . in the case.

Phil, who considered himself the voice of reason to D.D.'s more aggressive ways, hadn't been thrilled when she'd announced she'd recruited Flora to be her new confidential informant. Clearly, his opinion on the matter hadn't changed.

"Flora recognized the victim," D.D. announced bluntly, in order to cut off Phil's arguments at the pass. "She met Conrad Carter at a bar, when she was with Jacob."

Her strategy worked. Phil went from fatherly disapproval to immediate investigative interest.

Flora didn't like Phil any more than Phil liked her. "That's as much as I'm saying on the subject," she said.

Phil returned to fatherly disapproval, for both Flora and D.D.

"I want her to see Evelyn," D.D. said. "Maybe that will jog something. Or help her know what exactly we're dealing with here."

Phil accepted that. "Her mom's here," he said.

"But of course."

"Real lawyer, too. No public defender. Criminal defense attorney Dick Delaney."

"Great." D.D. rolled her eyes. She'd been involved in cases represented by the silver-haired lawyer before. He was very good.

Phil opened the door. They were hit first by a heat wave of humanity, then by the harsh pounding of the judge's gavel as she sought to keep some semblance of order in what was by definition an assembly line of procedures. Already two court officers were leading a young woman, gaunt, stringy hair, wild eyes, from the room, as a door opened to the side and two more officers appeared.

No prison clothes this time. Instead, Evie Carter appeared, pale, slightly trembly, clad in black slacks and a demure cream-colored button-up cardigan that strained slightly over her rounded belly. The Evie D.D. had met sixteen years ago had been a scared teenager. The woman she'd become still had the same dirty-blond hair, but cut short, in a fringed style that emphasized her large brown eyes. The clothes, D.D. was already guessing, had been supplied by Evie's mother, Joyce, who sat in the front row, every frosted blond hair in place as she gazed at her only child.

Evie, D.D. noticed, didn't look at her mother at all, but took her place beside her lawyer at the defense's table. Her hair was mussed, her eyes bruised. For all the dress-up clothes, nothing could change the fact she'd spent the night in the slammer.

"That's her?" Flora whispered in D.D's ear. "She doesn't look anything like I expected."

"Her mother dressed her," D.D. whispered back.

Flora nodded, as if that explained everything.

"Your Honor," the Suffolk County ADA Danielle Fitzpatrick began. "The people are pursuing charges of murder one against the accused, Evelyn Carter, in the shooting death of her husband. We request she be held without bail, given the severity of the charges."

"Your Honor!" Delaney was already on his feet. "That charge is ludicrous. The people lack sufficient evidence for a charge of premeditated murder, let alone given the delicate state of my client—"

"The 'delicate client,'" Fitzpatrick intoned drolly, "shot her husband three times. As for evidence, the police found her at the scene, still holding the murder weapon. In addition, her hands tested positive for GSR as well as human blood. We are confident in our case, Your Honor, and that's without delving into Mrs. Carter's previous history—"

"Objection! Inadmissible and not even relevant. Continue to make such underhanded references"—Delaney glared at Fitzpatrick— "and I'll be forced to demand a change of venue given your deliberate contamination of the jury pool."

The judge banged her gavel again. "Sustained, though I'm not sure what underhanded references you two are bickering about. Feels to me we have enough to discuss with the case at hand."

Flora looked askance at D.D., who murmured in the woman's ears, "Evie shot and killed her father when she was sixteen. It was ruled accidental at the time and no charges were ever filed—I should know, as I was the investigating detective. Delaney's right: Given that, the incident is inadmissible. But Fitzpatrick isn't playing to the judge. She's playing to the press, who I can guarantee you are right now scrambling to figure out what about 'Mrs. Carter's previous history' is worth such a fuss."

"Your Honor," Delaney was saying. "My client does not deny being at the scene of the crime, nor even holding the murder weapon. In fact, she'll even concede she fired the gun. What ADA Fitzpatrick has failed to mention is the slight problem with the police's timeline of events."

The judge turned, regarding ADA Fitzpatrick with interest, while on the other side of D.D., Phil stiffened. D.D. got it a second later. "Oh shit."

"Your Honor," Fitzpatrick began, but Delaney was already on a roll.

"Eight minutes, Your Honor. There's an eight-minute gap between the time neighbors first called in the report of shots fired, and the police arrived on the scene and *also* heard shots fired. That's because there was not one shooting last night but two. The first was the fatal shooting of my client's beloved husband and father of her unborn child. We can prove, in fact, Your Honor, that my client wasn't even home at the time of her husband's death. She arrived minutes later, discovering the dead body. At which point, she did pick up the gun. She fired the weapon.

"She committed the second shooting, Your Honor. Except her victim was a laptop. Which, let's face it, we've all wanted to shoot at one time or another. So, yes, my client handled the murder weapon and, yes, she had GSR on her hands. But she did not kill her husband. We demand the dismissal of all charges as well as my client's immediate release at this time."

The judge regarded Delaney, then the ADA, whose face was now set in a grim line, then Delaney again. "Well," the judge said, "it sounds like we have plenty to discuss at trial. Given there is sufficient evidence worth presenting, charges are not dismissed. However, I will grant bail. Five hundred thousand, cash bond."

The judge banged her gavel. Evie Carter, who'd never looked left or right, was led from the room. A moment later, every reporter in the place had leapt to his or her feet and was racing to the door.

Phil, D.D., and Flora stood to the side to let the rush pass.

"I'll be damned," D.D. murmured. "She's gonna do it." She glanced at Phil, who nodded his agreement.

"Do what?" Flora demanded.

"For the second time in her life, Evie Carter's gonna get away with murder."

CHAPTER 6

FLORA

MY FATHER DIED WHEN I was young. Traffic accident. So long ago, I no longer really remember him. The images in my mind are less from real memories than from the photos my mother still has up around the house.

Jacob, on the other hand, the man who kidnapped me, raped me, tortured me . . . six years later I still dream about him three or four nights a week.

Samuel Keynes, my victim specialist and a trained psychologist, has done his best to explain it to me over the years. Something about the omnipotence of an abductor. It wasn't just that Jacob snatched me off a beach or locked me in a coffin-sized box for days on end. It was his total control over every facet of my life. I ate when he willed it. I drank when he permitted it. I lived, second by second, day by day, because he decided, for that instant, to allow it.

Stockholm syndrome is when a victim starts to bond with her captor, partially due to the captor's role of complete power over her life. Did I bond with Jacob? The question isn't as simple as I'd like it to be. I hated him. I still hate him. I worked hard every day on my own survival. Counting backward and forward in the long hours I was trapped in a box. Wiggling my toes, moving my limbs as the space would allow. Then, when he finally let me out, I observed, I learned, I adapted.

I don't think I ever truly liked Jacob or saw him as a human being. He was a monster, plain and simple. But he was a monster who held the other end of my leash, so I tried to understand him. Anything to survive another day.

But not all days were awful. Not all moments torturous. After weeks turned into months, Jacob would sometimes show up with little surprises. DVDs of a favorite TV show I'd mentioned. Movies for both of us to watch. There's a lot of time to pass in a long-haul rig. We'd look for license plates from all fifty states, play the alphabet game.

I never believed Jacob was human. But sometimes, like a lot of predators, he did a decent impression of one.

And to this day, he remains the single-most powerful relationship of my life.

Which is why I do my best to talk about him as little as possible. But if I'm being totally honest with myself, I'm not angry to finally be breaking my onetime, one-tell policy. I'm simply relieved to finally get the monster out of my head.

SAMUEL AGREES TO meet me after lunch. He's an incredibly busy victim specialist, working for the FBI's Office for Victim Assistance (OVA). A lot of his cases involve high-level executives kidnapped in various far-flung countries. Samuel's job is to help the families understand the process, from the law enforcement steps involved in locating the evildoers to what it might be like when their loved one finally returns home. He also works with the victim him- or herself. Among other things, he generates a "strategy for reentry." It's to help guide both the family and the victim as they transition back to the real world.

Eight years ago, I had no idea such plans existed. Eight years ago, I didn't understand that anyone would need a ten-point plan for re-entering the "real world."

Final step of being a victim specialist: supporting the family and victim through what can be a very long legal process, where they will still be asked to make statements, revisit statements, testify in this hearing, testify in that hearing. Part of the FBI's impetus for creating the OVA is the modern trend of high-profile crimes (say, a five-year abduction case) and mass-casualty events (shootings, bombings, arson) that can take years to wind through the legal system.

See, one day, you're a normal person with an ordinary family. Then, in a single instant, you're not. You're a young girl, waking up in a coffin-sized box. You're a mom, back on her farm in Maine, getting a call from her daughter's friends, asking if maybe her daughter has unexpectedly returned home from Florida.

It begins. The onslaught of local, state, federal investigators. The media camped out in the front yard. Maybe even taunting postcards from the predator himself, stoking fears, inflicting fresh terrors.

My mom had to learn how to work national media. Samuel is one of the people who prepared her. What to wear, what to say, the necessity of humanizing her daughter to an unknown kidnapper in order to increase the chances of his keeping me alive. My brother, Darwin, returned home from college to run the social media campaign. Again, with Samuel's guidance. Posting pictures from my childhood. Quotes from friends. I don't know how they did it, to tell you the truth. It's one of those things we still never discuss. I don't describe my time with Jacob because I don't want to hurt them. And they don't mention the four hundred and seventy-two days they lived in constant fear of letting me down or maybe, through their own inexperience, making it easier for my captor to kill me.

Samuel helped them. I know that. And some kind of relationship was forged between him and my mother. They left it alone for years. Samuel's doing, my guess, given the man has the emotional core of carved granite.

But my own plan for reentry was much shorter than many. Dead Jacob meant no trial. Samuel checked up on me for a good year after I came home. Made sure I understood the resources available to me, prodded me to utilize all my "tools," as he liked to put it. He should've cut me off ages ago. I'm six years back to the real world, hundreds of pages, at least, beyond my "strategy for reentry" plan. But Samuel has always taken my calls, and this morning, when I reached him nearly hysterical, he never even batted an eye.

So here we are again. All these years later, and still about to hash out the same old story.

"Have a seat," Samuel tells me, having met me in the lobby of the FBI building and escorted me upstairs. His office isn't huge, but he does have windows, which I guess makes him a feebie of distinction.

I can't sit. I pace. Five feet this way, three feet that way. He really needs a bigger office.

I left D.D. at the courthouse. She's not happy with me, having wanted to accompany me on this visit. But we both knew that was never going to happen. I might be her CI, but I still live by my rules. Besides, her crankiness is nothing new to me.

"I want to read the file," I say now, cutting straight to the chase. "The FBI must have a file on Jacob. I want to see it. Every word."

"Have a seat," Samuel says again.

"Is he a suspect in other crimes, murders, disappearances? I talked about the things I saw—I told you. But I was only with him for a year. And we both know, there's no way I was his first victim. He'd been busy way before me."

Samuel stands behind his desk. He's known for his wardrobe: Today's perfectly tailored suit appears to be Armani, dark charcoal, and paired with a light gray shirt with white collar and cuffs, topped by a rich blue silk tie. How Samuel pays for his wardrobe, let alone his Lexus, is one of the many things he never discusses. I have my secrets. He has his. It's what I like about him.

Since I won't sit, he joins me, walking with his hands clasped behind him, dark-fringed eyes perfectly serious, black-is-beautiful bald head gleaming beneath the lights. I imagine it takes him serious time to get ready every morning. Trimming his sharply etched goatee. Picking out the suit, the shirt, the tie for the day. Let alone his collection of bespoke shoes and cashmere coats. Samuel is a scarily beautiful man. He uses his wardrobe to further enhance his skills. If others are stupid enough to get distracted by the packaging, that's their problem, not his.

In contrast to my victim specialist, I wear jeans, worn combat boots, and a hoodie, the uniform of disenfranchised urbanites everywhere. When I first returned after my kidnapping, my mother would bring home bright summer dresses, which I never wore. She only recently stopped shopping for me. I wonder now if that's because she finally figured out this is the new me, or if Samuel intervened on my behalf. Either was possible.

"You're sure this Conrad Carter is the same person you saw in a bar?" Samuel asks now, pivoting at the wall, heading back toward me. He goes to one side of the twin chairs; I head for the other.

"Yes."

"And he was there to meet Jacob?"

"Yes! He didn't just sit down next to us; Jacob turned toward him. Jacob, like . . . talked to him. Jacob didn't talk to others."

Samuel tilts his head to the side, regards me steadily, as we reach opposite sides of the tiny office.

"I think they had a deal," I say. "I think Conrad was there for me. Like . . . Jacob offered me to him or something. Some predators do that, you know. Trade around their victims. Or, hell, Jacob sold me for fresh drugs. He'd clearly been on a bender."

Samuel nods. "Had Jacob done such a thing before?"

"No. But sometimes he'd pick out some random guy at a bar, then tell me I had to make the new guy want me."

More nodding. More staring. Samuel has eyes like molten chocolate. When he uses his weapons like this, it always makes me wonder: If Jacob Ness made me, then who made Samuel?

"Some predators talk," I say now. "In chat rooms, on super-encrypted sites, predators have been known to share tips."

Samuel nods.

"So maybe this Conrad guy was another monster. He and Jacob connected somehow—Jacob had his laptop in the rig. And in some chat room, they made arrangements for the evening. Jacob promised me to Conrad. In return for what, I don't know. Drugs, a fresh girl of his own."

"But you didn't go home with Conrad."

"No. I ate and drank till I vomited. That put a damper on the evening."

"You made yourself sick intentionally?"

"Yes."

"Because to directly disobey Jacob would mean punishment, if not death. And to have sex with Conrad would mean punishment, if not death?"

I hadn't thought of it that bluntly, but now I nod.

"You read the situation. You trusted your instincts. You survived."

I sigh, whack the back of the chair. "Samuel! I'm not here for a fucking pep talk. I want the file. You're FBI. The FBI loves files. Give me my fucking file!"

Samuel smiles. It's a devastating look on him. Good luck to my mom, I think, because no man this beautiful can be easy to manage.

"No," he says.

"What do you mean—"

"No. Big *n*. Little *o*. No. I will not give you the file."

"That's total bullshit—"

"That's FBI policy. You're neither an agent nor a member of law enforcement—"

"I'm a CI, working with the Boston police!"

He continues, "You have no right to the file."

"Bullshit! You wouldn't even have Jacob Ness if it weren't for me. Half that file is my life story. Mine!"

"Technically, we wouldn't have Jacob Ness if it weren't for SSA Kimberly Quincy, who tracked him to the motel where he was holed up with you. She put together the data in the file. She organized the SWAT team that rescued you."

I remember her. Not well. Those first few moments, hours, after the hotel room door blew in . . . I think I stood outside my body. I watched it all as a movie, happening to someone else. When she first approached me, asked me my name, I stared at her blankly. My name? It took a shockingly long time to answer that question.

Later, I read accounts of other survivors going through the same thing. First thing any captor does is take away your identity; Jacob forced me to go by Molly. Meaning SSA Quincy wasn't just asking me a question; she was making me take the first step toward the person I used to be.

And have never been again.

"It's my file," I say, and there's a tone of pleading in my voice. I realize I'm on the edge of tears. Me, who never cries. I don't know what's wrong. Since waking up this morning, since turning on the news, seeing the dead man's face . . . I'm not myself. I don't know who I am. I churn, I churn, I churn.

"Flora," Samuel says at last, "please sit down."

This time, I do. I collapse in one of the leather chairs. They're hard and slippery and I hate them. Yet having sat, I feel like I'll never get up again.

This is why D.D. couldn't come. This is what she still doesn't know.

I'm not always Flora Dane.

Sometimes, even all these years later, I'm still Jacob's victim. Now I put my head in my hands and I don't look at Samuel, because I don't want him to see me like this either. Like I've been undone. Turned inside out. And there's no me again, just this terrified girl, desperate Jacob will return at any second, even more terrified he won't and that will be it. I'll die alone in a coffin-sized box and my mom will never find my body.

The way my mom looked on TV. In clothes that weren't her clothes. But her voice, never breaking. So strong. The silver fox charm resting in the hollow of her throat. A fox to show me, hundreds or thousands of miles away, how much she still loved me.

I'm rocking back and forth. Not making a sound, because I can't afford to wake up Jacob. Except he's dead. Except he's still in my head. Except I want it to be over. Except I want it never to have happened. Except I'll never get over him.

Samuel sits down. I'm aware vaguely of his movements. Most likely, he has his elegant fingers steepled in front of him. His position of patience. If I'm a void of darkness, then he has a well of serenity. I hate him for it. But then, I hate everyone right now. Myself most of all.

"There are other victims," I whisper at last, still not looking up.

"Yes."

"Their information, it's in Jacob's file."

"Yes."

"You don't want me to know. You think I'll use it to torture myself more each night."

"Yes."

"How many?"

He won't answer.

"Could I have made a difference? If I'd escaped earlier? Cooperated more with this Quincy agent?" My voice is nearly breaking.

"No."

"Then let me see the file."

"No." He unsteeples his fingers, leans forward. "Because me knowing you couldn't make a difference isn't the same as you *believing* you couldn't have made a difference."

I know what he means. Survivor's guilt. The toughest affliction for people like me.

"I should've told her about Conrad. SSA Quincy. I should've mentioned some of the times Jacob took me out to bars."

"When did he take you out?"

"Nighttime."

"Day, week, month?"

"I don't know. Winter. Someplace in the South."

"What bars? Do you have a list of names?"

I shake my head.

"And the men. Did you know Conrad Carter's name?"

I frown. "I think . . . maybe he mentioned his first name."

"And the others?"

"I don't . . . I don't know."

"So sometimes Jacob took you to some bars in some places to meet some men. Does that about summarize it?"

I flush. "I could've warned her that he was networking with others. She should check his computer."

"You didn't know that much about predators then, Flora. That kind of criminal psychology you only learned after you came home, as part of your coping mechanism. SSA Quincy, on the other hand, happens to be the daughter of one of the FBI's most legendary profilers. She did check Jacob's computer, I assure you."

"What did she find?"

"I don't know. I'm a victim specialist, not a special agent. Her job was to save you then. My job is to save you now."

"Bite me."

He smiles again, and maybe it's just my imagination, but he appears relieved at my returning rancor.

"Flora, what's the biggest enemy for survivors?"

"The coulda, woulda, shouldas," I mumble. We've had this conversation before.

"Whatever happened, happened. You won. Jacob lost. Don't replay the game."

"You're not going to give me the file."

"No."

"But you also know I won't just walk away."

"It's possible I've met you before."

He smiles again, but now it's somber. He and I both know I'll pursue this. I understand that in his professional opinion, this is a bad choice for me. I understand that in his personal opinion, it's also not good for me. Or, for that matter, for my mother. And yet . . .

"I'm sorry," I say. We both know what I'm apologizing for.

Maybe he thinks I'll personally call up SSA Kimberly Quincy. I haven't spoken to her since that day. I barely remember her face. And yet, saving me was probably one of the highlights of her career, meaning she'll more than likely take my call. Maybe even give me a few kernels of information.

But I've spent a lot of time researching both criminals and law enforcement in the years I've been home. The FBI is a stodgy, conservative, rigid institution, where talking out of school is one of the quickest ways to get fired. Whatever SSA Quincy tells me won't be enough for me, while still potentially damaging for her.

Sergeant Detective D. D. Warren recruited me for a reason. Law enforcement officers have their resources. And I have mine.

I know then who I'm going to call. A man who's been waiting six years for this moment. Sending me countless e-mails, from the sweet, to the bragging, to the nagging, to the just plain whining.

I've always ignored him.

Now, thanks to one shooting, I'm going to make his day.

I don't need the FBI after all.

I just need the right true-crime nerd.

I rise to standing. Samuel can tell from the look on my face that I've made a decision. We know each other that well. He cares about me that much.

"Be careful," he says softly.

"Be there for her," I say, because what I'm going to do next will definitely break my mother's heart.

CHAPTER 7

EVIE

D̲O YOU EVER FEEL ALONE in a crowded room? That when other people laugh, you don't get the joke? That everyone knows something—the secret to life, the true meaning of happiness—that you will forever fail to understand?

That is the way I have always felt.

Even when my father was still alive.

MY MOTHER DRIVES me home. She is talking excitedly, completely oblivious to my lack of answers. That's okay. My mother has never required my thoughts or opinions, and most of her questions are rhetorical anyway.

She is nearly sixty years old, I find myself thinking. The age of a grandmother, which makes sense since I'm carrying her first grandchild. She doesn't look a day over fifty. In fact, today I'm willing to bet she looks younger and better than me. The frosted Jane Fonda hair, not a strand out of place. Her signature pearls around her neck. She wears a spring-green cashmere sweater with camel-colored slacks. She looks like Cambridge. She looks like what, in her mind, she'll always be: a professor's wife.

She paid half a million dollars, cash, for the pleasure of my company. I don't ask where she got the money. Mortgaged the house? Probably couldn't do that in a matter of hours. Maybe she extracted it from a Swiss bank account, remains from my father's life insurance. Hell if I know.

We've stayed in touch over the years. Kind of. She'd tell you whatever coldness exists between us is of my making—assuming she admits there's any strain in our relationship. My mother is one of those women who don't have problems. Or really, problems wouldn't dare to bother her.

She's never moved from her and my father's house. She spent a year in black, *widow's weeds*, I believe they used to be called. She played up the tragedy. Her loving husband, killed in the prime of his genius life. Her poor daughter, who would surely never recover from the horror of the experience.

One year. Exactly one year. Then, like some heroine from a Victorian novel, she put away the black Chanel and returned to her signature spring palette. And took up the very important role of preserving her Husband's Legacy.

My father's legacy? Again, hell if I know. He was active in many projects. Most likely, he had unfinished theorems, theories, research projects, research papers. I'm sure his various assistants rushed to fill the gap. What my mother with her cashmere sweaters and Mikimoto pearls had to add to that, I have no idea.

But she continued to be the hostess with the mostest among the Harvard crowd. I think people came in the beginning, attracted to the drama. Unfortunate accidents such as shotgun blasts don't happen much among the academic set. Best I can tell, however, my mother's charm has prevailed. Sixteen years later, she continues to hold court among the intellectual elite.

Only I keep my distance.

Conrad tried to fix us. In the beginning, when he viewed my relationship with my mom as something salvageable. She's such a lovely woman, he'd tell me time and time again. I'd nod, because my mom is a lovely woman. And charming and smart. Can't argue with any of that.

She's also a fucking wack job.

No one wants to hear that sort of thing, but my father got it. During her more trying times or dramatic tirades, he'd offer me a conspiratorial wink. I think, however, that her kind of crazy fit him.

My mother isn't mean, at least not intentionally. She's neither violent nor cruel. She's just—herself. She sees what she sees, she knows what she knows, she believes what she believes, and nothing is going to change that. I think for my father, who lived in the land of the abstract, she was refreshingly tangible. You always knew exactly where you stood with her, which was mostly on the outside, looking in. She also worshipped my father's brilliance, took genuine pride in being the wife of one of the greatest minds in mathematics. Last but not least, I heard some noises as a kid that—later, as an adult—I realized meant my parents had a very robust sex life.

Together, they worked.

Meaning our issues aren't that my mother didn't love my father. Or that that I didn't love my father. It's more like each of us, for various reasons, wanted him all to ourself.

My mother pulls into the drive. Same stately Colonial. Historic gray paint, black-painted shutters, white trim. My mother adheres to a strict maintenance schedule—her hair, her face, her home. I believe the exterior paint is on a five-year plan. Many wait seven to ten, she'd tell you. But why have three to five years of a tired-looking home, when it can appear clean and fresh always?

The front porch has a pair of whitewashed Adirondack chairs framing the huge solid black-painted door and leaded side windows. This time of year, the door is draped with a holiday garland of various greens and festive berries. Beside the Adirondacks sit enormous pots of spruce branches, white-frosted twigs, red bows, and pinecones.

Conrad and I hadn't even gotten to a tree yet.

I feel that pang again. Will myself not to think of the stair bannister, the study, the smell. My husband. My father. Too much blood.

The story of my life: too much blood.

Now this.

My mother turns off her Lexus. Turns to me. And smiles.

"I DID THE best I could without you," she says as we walk into the house. "Of course, since you're here, you can help with the final decisions. When will you find out the sex of the baby? Soon, right? I don't remember exactly when they can tell you that sort of thing, but it seems with today's technology, anything's possible."

I have no idea what she's talking about, only half listening to her prattle as I enter the childhood home I've done my best to avoid for the past sixteen years.

Like many historic homes, the house doesn't have a garage. My mother parks on the driveway; in the winter, some college student will get paid to shovel out and clear her vehicle. As family members, we use the side door off the kitchen. For the full effect, however, my mother prefers to greet even longtime friends at the front door, which better showcases the full impact of the home, including the huge oil portrait of our family. I was four when my mother had it commissioned. Too young to realize no one should ever be painted in a marshmallow-shaped white dress with a giant white bow in her hair. My mother is sitting in a wingback chair, which was custom-upholstered to be nearly the exact same shade of blue as her eyes. My father stands behind both us, his hand on his wife's shoulder, smiling benevolently at the painter. He is wearing a gray tweed jacket over a dark green sweater-vest. His face is slightly rounded, his sandy beard perfectly trim. He looks kind and powerful and maybe just a tad bemused by the whole production.

When I was little, and my father worked late, I used to climb onto the wingback chair just to touch the portrait and my father's curving smile.

I would whisper, "Love you, Papa," then scramble down before anyone (my mother) caught me.

I don't enter the sitting room, though the front parlor, across the way, is just as bad. The baby grand piano, where I used to sit and play for hours while my father relaxed on the settee across from it. The piles of music still sitting on the closed cover. The faint smell of wax and pipe smoke. In the corner sits the octagonal game table that would be dragged out for poker nights.

I imagine given my mother's busy social life, it's still in use, but I don't like to think about it. In my mind, it's my father's table. My mother's house, but my father's table, my piano.

Then there's the kitchen, where my father died.

My mother reaches for my coat, before remembering I don't have one. She hangs up her own in the hall closet. She is still talking. I nod absently.

We pass my father's study, neither one of us looking. I don't have to peek inside to know the walls remain plastered in awards and honorary degrees, that his favorite pens are still scattered across the desktop, along with a yellow legal pad still scribbled with last-minute thoughts. For the first few years after his death, I could smell him every time I walked in. The whisper of his aftershave. Something expensive my mom imported from England just for him. Sandalwood, a hint of lemon, something else.

It used to be how I knew he'd come home. I'd catch a whiff of his aftershave floating through the house.

I don't catch it now. Sixteen years later, scent fades, no matter how much both my mom and I are loath to let it go.

"Your rooms are ready for you, of course."

I nod again. With the exception of the kitchen, my mother hasn't changed anything about the house. *Anything,* which cracked Conrad up the first time he visited.

"Is this, like, your childhood bed?" he said, bouncing up and down on the obviously girlish comforter. *"I feel like I'm corrupting a minor. Maybe I can be the handsome bad boy, sneaking into your room after your parents have gone to bed. Ever fantasize about the local rebel without a cause?"*

I'd merely smiled. The girl I'd been in high school hadn't attracted the attention of boys, bad or otherwise. I'd been quiet and awkward, then after my father's death, just plain freaky.

Meeting Conrad . . . He'd been the first person to truly see me. To tell me I was sexy and attractive and the girl of his dreams. For him, I'd come alive. For him, I'd started believing in second chances.

I should've known better.

There is moisture on my face. Am I crying? I don't want to cry. Mostly, I'd like to shower.

My mom is headed up the vast, sweeping staircase that dominates the center of the house. I follow her up to the second floor, where, yes, my suite of rooms is exactly as I left it.

"This is where the nursery will be," my mom is saying. "I'm sure you want it closest to you. But I didn't want it so far away from me that I couldn't help out."

For the first time, I register where we are standing. In one of the rooms that used to be part of my suite. I believe it had been a sizable dressing room, designed to hold the dozens of dresses my mom had been so sure I'd one day love wearing.

Now the room is devoid of shelving, makeup trays, and shoe trees. Instead, it has been painted a pastel green and contains a lovely white-painted crib and matching diaper table.

I stare at my mother. I'd only called her with the news of my pregnancy a few weeks ago. And not just because I had to gear myself up to make contact, but because Conrad and I had wanted to keep the news to ourselves for the first three months. Our baby. Our family. Our accomplishment.

We would sleep spooned together at night, his hands splayed on my still-flat belly. Everything looking the same but feeling different.

"How did you . . . when did you?" I don't know what to say.

"I don't love the sage green," my mother announces briskly. "It's the top gender-neutral color, but it feels plain to me. The room itself has no imagination, and that won't do. You have to consider that from the very beginning, Evelyn, your baby may have extraordinary intellect. How best to stimulate and nurture such a mind must be integral to the nursery's design. Are you listening to Bach? Reading to the baby in the womb? Better yet, what about playing the piano? That kind of auditory, and yet also kinetic, experience would be deeply beneficial."

My jaw is still hanging open. I don't know what to say, what to do. Even by the standards I've come to expect from my mom, this has caught me off guard.

I find myself already wondering—did she pay bail to get me out of jail, or to save the next family genius? And if I'm found guilty of murder and sent off to prison, leaving her alone to raise the baby, would that even bother her?

"I need to shower," I hear myself say.

"Of course. I took the liberty of stocking up on some maternity clothes for you. You'll find them all hanging in the closet."

Again, when? How? Do I want to know?

I find myself studying my mother. The elegantly coiffed hair, the perfectly made-up face. She really does have beautiful blue eyes. Now, she regards me guilelessly, which makes the hairs rise on the backs of my arms, because nothing about my mother is without guile. As if reading my mind:

"Don't worry about your job," she says. "I already phoned your principal and said you wouldn't be back."

"You *quit* my job?"

"What did you think was going to happen? There's going to be a murder trial, you know. You certainly can't be showing up at a public high school every day through that. And by the time this nonsense has all wrapped up, you'll be ready to have your baby. Might as well let the administrators know now."

She makes it sound so matter-of-fact. The job I loved gone, just like that. Indeed, what did I think was going to happen?

"Do you want to know?" I hear myself whisper.

"Know what, dear?"

"Did I kill him. Did I shoot my own husband."

She pats my arm. "No need to stress yourself out, honey. Other people will judge. Other people will wonder. Which is why family is so important. We understand each other. I know everything I need to know about you and Conrad."

"And what is that?"

She regards me directly with those big blue eyes. "That it was an accident, of course. Nothing but an unfortunate accident."

CHAPTER 8

D.D.

"WE NEED TO FIND OUT everything about this couple, ASAP," D.D. said. She and Phil had returned to BPD headquarters. Phil sat in his office chair, leaning way back, his hands tucked behind his head. D.D. walked small circles. They both had their way of thinking things through.

"Conrad Carter," Phil rattled off now. "Thirty-nine years old. No criminal history. No living family."

"Shit," D.D. said.

"Worked for a major window corporation. Already talked to the head honcho. Guess what?"

"Everyone liked him, no one knew him well," D.D. intoned.

"Exactly. Guy worked out of his home. Had an excellent reputation for sales. Kept up on his quotes, bid sheets, on-site specs. Manager had nothing bad to say about him. Then again, he saw the guy once a month at management meetings. He didn't even know Conrad and his wife were expecting a baby until he heard it on the news."

"Pregnant wife accidentally shoots husband. Three times," D.D. muttered. "Press is going to have a field day with this one."

"So much for open-and-shut," Phil agreed. He yawned.

She glared at him.

He shrugged. "Hey, I was the one working the scene half the night. *Sergeant*."

"And I was fighting an evil canine for the safety of black boots everywhere. We all have our problems."

Phil smiled. He was used to D.D. in this mood, was probably one of the only detectives who could handle her, which is why she liked him so much. And missed her original investigative squad terribly. Managing sergeant her ass. Who wanted to sit at a desk all day anyway?

"Wait, there's more," Phil said now, in his best TV infomercial voice.

"Should I be sitting down?"

"You'd only pop back up and pace. Before moving to Mass., Conrad lived in . . ." Phil dragged it out.

D.D. closed her eyes, already seeing the answer. "Florida."

"Yep."

"Same state as Jacob Ness and where Jacob kidnapped Flora."

"Yep."

"Jacob and Conrad could've known each other prior to meeting with Flora at the bar."

"It's possible," Phil agreed.

D.D. shook her head. She could not believe this case was spinning so far out of hand. "Okay, what do we know of Conrad? Don't suppose techs have anything back on the computer?"

Phil gave her a droll look.

"Cell phone?" she tried.

"Can't find it."

" 'Can't find it'? What does that mean? Everyone has a cell phone, especially a guy in sales."

"Agreed. Except we don't know where his is."

"You ping it?"

"No, we were waiting for it to walk home on its own." Phil gave her that look again. Sometimes, his mood matched her own. "Of course we pinged it. Nothing, nada. Wherever it is, it's shut off. Carol contacted the mobile carrier. Working on getting their copies of texts, voice messages now."

D.D. studied Phil. "You think Conrad hid his own phone? Turned it off, stuck it somewhere before his wife shot him?"

Phil shook his head. "Guy didn't even get his hands up."

"Someone took it," D.D. said.

"That'd be my guess."

"The wife? She hides his phone, shoots up the computer? What exactly is she trying to hide?"

Phil shrugged. "You heard her lawyer. We have an eight-minute gap. It's possible someone else shot him, that person grabbed the phone, that person ran away."

"Please. One shooter runs away just in time for the wife to return home—"

"Or her arrival is what scared him away—"

"At which point, Evelyn enters her own home, discovers her husband's murdered body and . . . doesn't dial nine-one-one, doesn't run to the neighbors for help, doesn't scream for the police. No, she picks up the same gun and fires a dozen rounds into the laptop?"

"The mysterious-first-shooter theory loses something right around this point," Phil agreed.

"We need to know everything there is to know about this couple," D.D. repeated.

Phil shrugged, yawned again. He probably had been up all night. Welcome to homicide.

"Old school," D.D. announced. "If we can't trace Conrad through electronics, then what about personal files, credit card receipts, banking info?"

"Neil's digging through it now," Phil reported. The youngest member of their original three-person squad, Neil had joined the force after serving years as an EMT. He used to be the one in charge of autopsies, but lately he'd been expanding his wings. With D.D.'s promotion out of the unit, and Carol Manley's entry into the squad, he was also no longer the rookie, which seemed to suit him.

"Nothing extravagant has jumped out yet, Neil said. Lotta charges to Lowe's, as you might expect from a couple with a fixer-upper. Between Conrad's sales job and Evelyn's teaching assignment, they pulled in low six figures. Not bad. Course, Boston's an expensive town. Two cars, taxes, mortgage, cable, cell phones. They weren't drowning, nor were they living in the lap of luxury."

"Life insurance policy on the husband?" D.D. asked.

"Hundred grand. That we know of. People have killed for less."

D.D. nodded, but she also registered Phil's lack of enthusiasm on the subject. A hundred grand might be a lot of money to some people, but for Evelyn Conrad, who'd grown up in a multimillion-dollar home in Cambridge while attending the finest private schools and socializing with the city's best and brightest, a hundred thousand wasn't enough.

"What was her father insured for?" D.D. thought out loud.

"Half a mill." Phil spoke up. "Thought you might ask."

"Better motive for shooting him."

"If you're Mrs. Hopkins, sure. You thinking Evelyn didn't do it after all? Her father's death wasn't her fault?"

"I don't know what to think anymore." D.D. gave up on pacing, leaned against the doorjamb. "There are too many strange coincidences here. A woman who may or may not have been involved in two fatal shootings in the past sixteen years. A victim who may or may not have had ties with an infamous serial rapist. It's like this giant Gordian knot. I can't figure out which string to pull first."

"Conrad Carter doesn't have significant ties to this community. No coworkers, no family, no electronic devices. Until the computer geeks can make some progress, there's not enough string there to pull."

"Which leaves us with Evelyn Carter. The quiet one, according to the neighbors."

"She has a mom," Phil said.

"Who just paid half a million cash to get her daughter out of jail. Good luck with that interview."

"Evelyn has a job."

D.D. nodded slowly. "Coworkers. Principal, fellow teachers. All right, let's start there."

"'Let's'?" Phil asked, arching a brow at her use of the contraction.

"Let's," D.D. repeated firmly. "I already worked one shooting case involving this woman. Like hell I'm missing something the second time around."

Phil sighed. "Let's," he agreed.

THE PRINCIPAL OF Evelyn Carter's school was more than happy to speak with them. Unfortunately, Principal Ahearn had nothing useful to say. She'd hired Evie four years ago. The woman was an excellent math teacher—did they know who her father was? The school was lucky to have her; the kids were lucky to have her. Evie was notoriously shy, of course. Pleasant but reserved. Some teachers—especially of the advanced math variety—could be like that.

Yes, Principal Ahearn knew Evie had been expecting. Best she could tell, Evie was very happy. Never in a million years would Principal Ahearn have expected last night's incident. They were making counselors available for the students. Everyone was in a state of shock. There had to be some kind of logical explanation. Or maybe it'd been a terrible accident—

Principal Ahearn caught herself, flushed slightly.

"You mean the way Evie's father died?" D.D. asked helpfully.

The woman turned redder. "Evie's never mentioned it. But of course I had to run a background check before hiring her."

D.D. found this interesting. "She was never charged in her father's death. There wouldn't have been anything in her background reports."

"Well, not hers . . ."

D.D. got it. "Her father. You Googled her father. A famous mathematician, you're looking to hire his daughter. Makes sense. You check out his Wikipedia profile, ending with how he died, accidentally shot by his teenage daughter in his own home."

"Not many Harvard professors come to violent ends." Principal Ahearn shrugged. "And Earl Hopkins was considered to be one of the best minds in his field."

"Did Evie know you knew?" Phil asked.

Principal Ahearn nodded. "It was one of those things. None of us ever spoke of it, but in this day and age of immediate access to information, how could you not? Every now and then, one of the students would figure it out and rumors would start flying. Evie herself . . . She never spoke of it. She showed up. She did her job. And she gave the best of herself as a teacher to her kids. Again, never in a million years . . ."

"Anyone ever threaten her? Try to make a big deal about what happened to her father?" Phil pushed.

"How could they? His cause of death was public knowledge. Tragic, absolutely, but not scandalous. Evie herself had been cleared of all charges. It's a sad family history, one of those things people are bound to whisper about. But other than that?" The principal shrugged.

D.D. nodded. She wondered what it was like for Evie, trying to move forward with her life while being forever shadowed by such a dark past. The principal was right; thanks to the internet, nothing was secret anymore. And having chosen to go into mathematics, even as a high school teacher, Evie Carter was bound to be connected with her father. Did the fact that no one talked to her directly about his death make things easier or worse?

"What did you know of Conrad Carter?" Phil was asking.

"I didn't. I met him once or twice at after-school functions. He traveled a lot. Sales, I believe."

"Any sign of trouble in the marriage?"

"Not that I could see." Principal Ahearn hastily shook her head.

"But you wouldn't know, would you?" D.D. pushed. "You respected Evelyn, but you weren't close to her."

Apologetic shrug. "I wouldn't say we had a connection. But I'll miss her."

"You'll miss her."

"Yes. I got a call, just an hour or two ago, from her mother. She said given the circumstances, Evie wouldn't be returning to work."

D.D. arched a brow. "Her mother quit her job for her? And you accepted that?"

The principal flushed. "Well, given the circumstances . . . At the very least, Evelyn would have to take a leave of absence to handle the legal charges. Then there is the matter of the pregnancy . . ."

D.D. got it: The principal was happy enough not to deal with either situation.

"Did she have a friend among the staff?" Phil spoke up. "A fellow teacher, mentor, someone?"

The principal had to think about it. "Cathy Maxwell," she volunteered at last. "She's one of the science teachers. They often sat together at lunch."

"And where is she now?" Phil asked.

The principal glanced at her watch. "Given that closing bell is in five minutes, finishing up her lecture."

D.D. AND PHIL waited for the students to stream out of the classroom and down the hall. A few of the kids gave them suspicious glances, their gazes going immediately to the gold shields clipped to their belts. Sadly, the presence of two detectives in a Boston public school wasn't that unusual, so most just moved along.

Which sparked a thought. Why public school? Someone with Evelyn's background, not to mention parental legacy, could've most likely written her ticket to a number of the area's prestigious private schools. Better hours, better pay.

But Evelyn had chosen public education. Because she wanted to give something back? Or because she hoped it would keep her one step removed from her past? The more elite the school, the better the odds she'd meet someone who hadn't just Googled her father but had known him personally.

Which led to the next question: Why stay in Boston at all? Her husband was a transplant with a job he could've done from anywhere. Why not move to Florida, or the Midwest, or anyplace where the tragic shooting of a famous Harvard prof didn't still linger in people's memories? Was she that close to her mother? Because Evelyn wouldn't even look at the woman in the courthouse. More and more curious.

D.D. didn't like sitting at her desk in BPD headquarters, but she did like a case where nothing was as it seemed. Meaning she was currently quite happy. Phil, standing beside her, shook his head in exasperation.

Cathy Maxwell was cleaning the dry-erase board when they walked in. The classroom held rows of desks up front and long tables with lab equipment in the back. D.D. recognized Bunsen burners—after that, she gave up. She'd never cared for high school science, though she had no trouble following the latest advancements in forensics. Her educational issues had never had anything to do with her intelligence—it was more her inability to sit still for long periods of time. Much to the chagrin of her academic parents, who were content to sit quietly, discuss politely, and ignore their rambunctious only child pointedly.

D.D.'s parents had retired to Florida. They visited once a year. If D.D. was really lucky, she spent their stay working a major case. They were all happier that way.

"Cathy Maxwell?" Phil spoke up. "We're detectives with the Boston PD. We have some questions regarding Evelyn Carter."

"Oh dear." Immediately Cathy stopped wiping. She clutched the dry eraser with both hands, gazing at them blankly. "Is it true she's not coming back? She really quit?"

"That's not for us to say," D.D. stated.

Phil added: "Would you like to have a seat?"

"Okay." The woman sat at her desk. Stared at them again. Probably around fifty, she was dressed in brown wool slacks and a forest-green sweater. She had long brown hair clipped in a barrette at the back of her neck. Several strands had escaped and were drifting around her face. Between the eraser in her hands, the smudges of ink on her hands and the wire-rimmed glasses perched on the tip of her nose, she looked very much like a teacher to D.D. But a well-put-together one.

"We understand you and Evelyn were friends?" Phil prodded.

"Evie? Sure. We often lunched together. Two females, one math, one science." Cathy Maxwell lifted a single shoulder. "You know, anyone will hang with the lit department, but tell someone you teach math or science, and it's like you're personally reminding them of every test they ever failed. People have a tendency to be intimidated, without ever giving us a chance."

Phil nodded sympathetically. He excelled at the good-cop role. Already, Cathy Maxwell was leaning closer to him.

"How long did you know Evie?" Phil asked. D.D. helped herself to a student desk, willed herself into the background.

"Four years. I was already working here when she was hired."

"And you became friends . . . immediately?"

"Pretty close. Evie's quiet. Keeps to herself. Of course, once you learn what happened to her father . . ." Cathy waited expectantly.

"We know," Phil assured her.

"She was just sixteen." The science teacher sounded genuinely empathetic. "To have something that terrible happen, then have to live forever with the guilt. Of course Evie isn't the most outgoing personality. Who could blame her?"

"Did she ever talk to you about it?" D.D. spoke up.

"Never." Cathy hesitated. "Though she'd mention her father from time to time. Randomly. Something he once said, a piece of advice he gave. She always sounded admiring. I think she loved him very much."

Cathy flushed, shrugged slightly. She set down the dry eraser. "From time to time, someone at the school would figure out Evie's role in her father's death. The whispers would start up again. Evie never said anything. But you could tell it took a toll on her. How could it not?"

"Any one person more vocal than another?"

"No. Evie might not be the warmest person around, but everyone respected her. She's a great teacher. And she supported her fellow educators. Didn't have any Harvard airs or anything like that. Academics"—she leaned forward conspiratorially—"can be the worst kind of snobs."

"What do you know of her husband, Conrad Carter?" Phil asked. "She speak of her home life much?"

"Sure. Their latest house project. And of course, now that they were expecting, she'd speak of the baby. Where would they put the nursery, that sort of thing. She was very excited. At least . . ." That slight hesitation again. "In the past few weeks, I haven't spoken to Evie much. She seemed distant, preoccupied. Morning sickness, holiday stress, I don't know. I didn't worry about it too much in the beginning; everyone gets busy from time to time. But now, in hindsight . . . I wonder if there was something on her mind. Maybe something was bothering her."

"But you don't know what something?" D.D. spoke up.

Cathy shook her head. "She started eating lunch in her own classroom. Catching up on work, she told me. I didn't question it the first few days. But, again, in hindsight, it's been nearly a month. That's a long time to be holed up in a classroom."

"You ever stop in, check up with her?" Phil asked.

"Sure. She'd wave me off and I'd let it go. I mean, this time of year, with the holidays coming, the kids are crazy and we're all losing it a little."

"Do you know how she met Conrad?" D.D. asked.

"Um." Cathy seemed to have to stop and think at this sudden change in topic. "Through a friend, when she worked at her first school. One of the teachers there had a cookout at his house and Conrad was there. They bought their house in Winthrop four years ago. That's what made Evie apply here; it's a much better commute."

"She struggle with her marriage?" Phil asked.

Cathy shook her head. "She wasn't one for that kind of talk."

"What do you mean 'that kind of talk'?"

"Personal. We talked teaching mostly. About being females in our respective fields. About how to get more students excited for two subjects a lot of kids already think they don't like or can't do. We talked shop, I guess. We ate in the teachers' lounge, after all."

"You never went out after work? Ladies' night at the martini bar?" D.D. pressed.

"Evie always went home. Even when Conrad was traveling. I don't know. She seemed the homebody type. Plus, many of the projects going on at their place she did herself. It wasn't that *he* was fixing it up. They both had talents."

Which, again, D.D. found interesting. Where had a rich girl who grew up in Cambridge learned home improvement skills?

"What about her relationship with students?" Phil asked now.

"Her students loved her."

"All of her students?"

Cathy shook her head. "Nothing stands out. We're nearly halfway through the school year now; Evie didn't mention having problems with any particular teen."

"What about a student who might've needed extra attention? Been unusually demanding of her time."

Again, the science teacher shook her head. "You might ask Sharon—Principal Ahearn. I hadn't heard of anything."

Phil and D.D. exchanged glances. The principal already seemed like a dead end when it came to learning more about Evelyn Carter. Asking for detailed information about students probably wasn't going to get them any further; school administrators were naturally disinclined to share those kinds of records.

"Did Evie have a computer?" Phil asked now, nodding to the one on Cathy's desk. "One assigned for her by the school, or she would've used to contact students."

"Sure. We all have school-issued laptops. Though much of what we do is handled by apps now, on our personal cell phones. Attendance, school grades, you name it. The modern era."

In other words, Evie should have a computer in her classroom. Which, once they had the proper warrant, might prove a useful bread crumb given their total lack of a digital trail right now. E-mails with students, other staff, maybe even Google searches Evie had felt safer doing in the relative privacy of her workplace, rather in her own home, just down the hall from her husband . . .

Phil's cell rang. He glanced at the screen, frowned. "Excuse me a moment."

He put the phone to his ear. D.D. could tell it was one of his fellow detectives, probably Neil or Carol, based on the fact that Phil didn't speak as much as grunt. *Uh-huh, uh-huh, uh-huh.* Then, turning toward D.D.: "We gotta go."

Cathy was already rising to standing. Phil handed her a card. "Thank you for your time, we'll be in touch."

He didn't give the bewildered educator time to reply or ask any other questions. Instead, he was already turning on his heel, heading toward the hall with D.D. in his wake.

"What, what, what?" she demanded as she finally reached his side.

"You're never going to believe this. Evie and Conrad's home, *our* crime scene . . ."

D.D.'s heart sank. She didn't need to hear what Phil had to say next.

"It's on fire."

CHAPTER 9

FLORA

THIS IS WHAT I KNOW about Jacob Ness:

He was old and ugly and disgusting, the kind of guy that a pretty blond college girl like me never would've given the time of day. His hair hung in greasy hanks. He had a mouth full of crooked, tobacco-stained teeth. He was built like a scarecrow, all massive belly and four scrawny limbs.

He wasn't partial to showering or any other kind of hygiene. He not only looked repulsive, he smelled that way, too. Every smell that ever made you want to vomit, that was his personal cologne.

He was strong. You wouldn't think it to look at him, with his flabby gut and flaccid limbs. But he had that skinny-guy thing going on—arms like bands of steel. I tried to fight him. As he dragged me back to the coffin-shaped box, as he forced me into various acts of depravity. I'd been a strong, athletic girl in the beginning. But I never won. Not once.

Jacob had a family. Those details are sketchier for me. A father he referred to only as Dickhead or Asshole. The father had been a trucker as well, but Jacob implied that he only came home long enough to smack his kid around. Is he still alive? Did he ever read about what his son did? Mourn his death? Shake his head that Jacob had been stupid enough to get caught? I have no idea.

Jacob was raised by a chain-smoking mother who worked two jobs. When he was little, he talked about a grandmother who helped watch him during the day. According to Jacob, when he was five or six, he found his father's stash of porn, and that's when his obsession with sex began.

Jacob was a sex addict. He was very honest on that subject. He also made it clear he had no intention of reform.

I don't know what happened to the mom. The police or Samuel once mentioned to me that Jacob had been using his mother's address in Florida as his permanent address. That's one of the things that helped them make the connection between him and my disappearance. In the beginning, however, he hadn't kept me in Florida, but in some cabin in the mountains of Georgia. The kind of place with no neighbors and few witnesses.

He was married once. He told me about that. He tried to do the traditional thing. Have a wife, spend night after night in the missionary position. That went so well he beat the crap out of the woman and ended up arrested for domestic abuse after the docs in the ER called it in. He went to jail for a year; he told me about that, too. How prison was no place for a man with his appetites. How when he got out, he vowed he'd never go back. On that, he kept his word.

Jacob raped a girl. That girl had a daughter. The girl died. The daughter, too. This bit of the family tree I know better. Which leaves us with? A father? A mother? Aunts, uncles, cousins? Did any of them care about him, or blame me for what happened?

I have no idea.

What about friends? I considered Jacob to be a loner, and not just because his job was to trawl the highways of the southern United

States, but because I never saw him talk to anyone. Except, of course, that one night in the bar. Conrad.

Jacob spent a lot of time on his laptop. I assumed he was looking up porn, but knowing what I know now, it's also possible he was hanging out with other predators, comparing notes, even bragging. Many perverts do. Is that how he met Conrad? Were there others? I was never granted access to the computer. Maybe Jacob had a whole online community, even a fan club.

I wasn't allowed secrets, but Jacob kept plenty from me. Especially during his benders, the days, entire weeks, he'd disappear, only to return, high, wasted, whatever. He never talked about where he went, what he did. I never bothered to consider, how did he score the drugs? Surely that implies some kind of community right there, a dealer, other addicts, a means of contacting such people. He never mentioned names—and whatever the FBI recovered from his laptop, they never shared with me.

To the best of our knowledge, Jacob never posted my picture online. For that, I'm grateful, as once those images are out, you can't get them back again. Jacob e-mailed some videos and images to my mother; he wasn't beyond taunting. But he seemed to understand that sharing too much might get him caught. Or maybe, in his own Jacob-like way, he didn't want to share.

For the first year we were together, Jacob forced me to call him by my dead father's name, Everett. He referred to me as Molly. We were like characters in a play. Or maybe short-timers in a relationship we both knew would never last. Except one month, two months, twelve months later, Jacob still hadn't gotten around to killing me. And whether I meant it to happen or not, we turned a corner. I stopped fighting. I stopped running. I made myself Jacob's friend and confidante.

A man that lonely certainly wasn't immune to a little female charm.

The last day, SWAT pouring through the door, tear gas exploding everywhere, Jacob crawled to *me*. Jacob draped the water-soaked towels around *my* mouth to block the stinging smoke. Jacob handed *me* the gun.

No one wants to be a monster, Jacob used to tell me. None of this was his fault. Abduction, rape, assault. Four hundred and seventy-two days of hell.

No one wants to be a monster.

It didn't stop him from being my monster. But now I wonder, did my monster know others? Did my monster leave behind other living victims besides me?

I can't ask Jacob these questions anymore. That final day, after he gave me the gun, I did exactly what both of us wanted me to do. At the time I had no doubts.

But welcome to the world of being a survivor. You make it out alive, and yet you spend the rest of your life wondering woulda, coulda, shoulda. I swore I would never look back. Samuel has advised me not to second-guess decisions that can never be changed.

Yet here I am.

KEITH EDGAR FIRST contacted me six years ago. I'd barely returned to my mother's farm, was still trying to get used to the textures and smells of a childhood home that now felt totally alien to me. Keith initially reached out through the Facebook page my brother had set up during my abduction. When that got him nothing, he turned to snail mail. Back in those days, our local postman would deliver mail by the boxload. My mother would stack up all the plastic bins in the kitchen. She never expected me to go through them—no one expected me to do anything but heal, rest, recover. Every night, though, I'd see her sitting at the kitchen table, opening each envelope, skimming the contents, sorting them into piles.

Many of the envelopes contained money. Small checks. Five dollars, ten, twenty. Donations from total strangers who were moved by my story and wanted to help. My mother established a savings account in my name. All deposits went into it. She'd give me updates I refused to hear. I didn't want the donations; they felt like blood money to me. And I definitely didn't want everyone's pity.

My mom wrote a lot of thank-you notes. Diligently, religiously, night after night. My mom is good that way.

But not all letters were nice. Some writers wanted to forgive me. As if getting kidnapped and raped was somehow my fault. In the beginning, my mom dashed off hasty words to correct their misunderstanding. But over time, those notes earned a bin of their own— the trash can. "Can't change narrow minds," she'd mutter.

Forgiveness. My mom is good like that, too.

Then came the other letters. Fan mail, I'd guess you call it. From predominantly male writers. Many with marriage proposals. Some wanted to save me. After all I'd been through, they wanted to sweep me off my feet, promising me I would never suffer again. My mom would set those letters down gingerly. Like she didn't know what to make of such madness, wrapped in good intentions. Pretty soon, they joined the trash pile, too.

Then came the less subtle notes. Men who, having followed every detail of my ordeal, had decided that I'd be perfect for them. Submissive. Pretrained. With tastes as depraved as their own.

My mother didn't throw away those letters. She burned them.

I learned about the various correspondence piles because I didn't sleep much in those days. Meaning that after my mom went to bed, I would take up her position at the table. Driven by morbid curiosity more than anything. Why would any of these strangers want to write to me? What about my terrible story spoke to them? Turns out the answers to those questions are many and varied.

Which brings us to the last category: the Keith Edgars of the world. True-crime buffs. They wrote to request personal interviews. Maybe one-on-one, maybe with their entire Sherlock Holmes geek squad. They wanted to learn from me. Have the opportunity to hear firsthand what a serial predator was really like. The notes were earnest. But again, they essentially wanted me to turn myself inside out, relive my own victimization, so they could indulge their clinical fascination and boost their own stature within the true-crime community. Some offered financial compensation. Some promised to provide me with information in return.

They didn't stop with one letter. They wrote and wrote and wrote. Keith Edgar still delivers a note probably every six months, even though I've never responded. I did look him up. He runs a whole true-crime blog. The group meets in Boston to study a case-of-the-month. Keith lists himself as a specialist in sexual-sadist predators. In fact, according to his blog, even without my help he has managed to become the foremost expert on Jacob Ness.

Why you'd want to be an expert in such a thing, I have no idea. But this is what Keith Edgar supposedly does in his free time. Which makes me wonder just what kind of cave dweller I'm going to meet as I get off the T, make my way up the street to the address I found online. There are no photos of Keith on the site, which I find suspicious in this age of selfies.

My best guess? I'm about to meet a pale, moon-faced geek still living in his parents' basement. Someone who spends all his time hunched in the glow of his computer monitor, surfing crime/horror websites, while chugging Red Bull and plowing through bags of Doritos. Is it really fascination with criminal minds that keeps someone like him coming back for more? Or do the images and stories of such violent acts serve as their own kind of stimulation? I'm suspicious. True-crime geeks can claim all they want that they're attracted to puzzles and driven by the need to find the truth; I still don't believe them.

I climb up the stairs to the Boston brownstone. It's in a nicer neighborhood than I would've thought. A street of well-tended town houses, all nestled shoulder to shoulder with matching wrought-iron railings and freshly painted white- or black-trimmed windows. Wreaths hang on front doors. Many of the porches are decorated with festive ribbons and fresh holiday garlands.

Keith's parents, I decide, must be very successful.

I climb the four steps to the dark-green door, where a huge Christmas wreath encircles an impressive brass knocker.

What the hell. I knock.

It takes a bit before I hear footsteps. Fair enough. I didn't call first. I'm running on adrenaline and shock, same emotional state I've been in since I turned on the news and saw the dead husband's face. I don't want anything like rational thought slowing me down now.

Footsteps drawing closer.

A pause. Someone looking through the peephole no doubt. Life in a big city.

The door opens. I stand face-to-face with a six-foot, thirty-year-old white male, with short-cropped dark hair, startling blue eyes, and definitely a runner's body. He wears a blue Brooks Brothers sweater exactly the same shade as his eyes, coordinated with sharply pressed charcoal slacks and perfectly buffed brown leather shoes. I open my mouth, but no words come out.

On the other hand, his face is already changing, his eyes widening in wonder.

"Flora Dane," he whispers.

"Ted Bundy, I presume?"

His answering smile lights up his entire face. And I realize I've just made a major mistake, as I shoulder my way past Keith Edgar and enter the home of Jacob Ness's biggest fan.

CHAPTER 10

EVIE

MY MOTHER TELLS ME TO REST. I should. For myself. The baby. The days to come. But I can't get comfortable. Everything feels wrong. The too-soft mattress the sheets that aren't my sheets, the pillow that's filled with feathers because my mother loves all things European, whether my dad or I agreed or not. Even as a child, this room was never my room. Just another stage setting for the drama that is my mother's life.

As a grown woman, an adult with her own house, own husband—the pang hits me again—I can't sleep in this place. I just want to go home.

I shower. That at least feels good and allows me to think I'm taking care of myself and, by extension, my unborn child.

Boy or girl. That's what my mother wants to know. I don't have the answer. We were going to be surprised. At least, that's what we'd been thinking. Five months along, still plenty of time to change our minds.

Conrad died never knowing if he was going to have a baby girl or baby boy. Which would he have preferred?

The thought sends a fresh jolt through me, and for a moment, standing under the sting of the shower spray, I can't tell if I'm going to cry or vomit or both.

My hands are shaking so badly, I can barely handle the soap. I move on to shampoo, lathering my hair. I've never seen myself such a mess. Not even the first time. My father splayed back against the refrigerator. The weight of the shotgun. The blood the blood the blood. It had all felt like a terrible, surreal dream. This . . .

This is a judgment I can't escape.

I get out of the shower. Pat dry my swelling abdomen. Do what pregnant women have been doing since time immemorial: I turn sideways and stare at my changing profile in the mirror. In the beginning, being pregnant had felt miraculous, but also not quite real. We'd been trying. Long enough we'd both given up hope, without actually admitting it out loud because that would bring us to discussions on infertility treatments or timing cycles, or some other kind of external intrusion into a relationship that was already fraying.

Except after days of nausea, I gave in to my own curiosity. Peed on a stick, then stared at the results in complete shock.

Conrad's beaming smile. My own lightening chest. For one moment, we were united again. We loved each other. This new life was proof. Despite ourselves, we would do this and live happily ever after.

For six weeks, eight weeks, we floated long, all fresh promise and forgotten regrets. Except I'm not my mom. I don't live in a fantasy world of European pillows and exquisitely cultured pearls. I'm my father's daughter. I see puzzles everywhere. Then I must solve them.

And as any mathematician will tell you, once you've worked the equation, numbers don't lie. What you get is what you get. There's nothing left to do but accept that truth.

And what is a marriage except adding A to B and hoping it equals an amount greater than the sum of its parts?

Briefly, the promise of a new life almost made the math work. Except A was still A, and B was still B. We could create a new life, but we couldn't stop being ourselves.

The bathroom in my mother's house is fully stocked, including a coconut-oil concoction formulated specially for stretch marks. After seeing the nursery, nothing surprises me. I rub the tropical-smelling lotion onto my belly and breasts. I find more products for my face, imported brands way too expensive for a math teacher at a public high school. Generally, I avoid my mother's generosity, as it definitely comes with a price. Given the past twenty-four hours, however, I figure what the hell. If anyone could use some rejuvenation from a five-hundred-dollar French cream, it's gotta be me.

In the closet, I find a full lineup of maternity wear, arranged by size and going all the way up to the final trimester. I have a brief, dizzying thought. I'm trapped now. My mother's going to keep me here, has clearly been planning it all along. I bathed with her soap, used her lotions, and will now put on her clothes. I'll never get out. I'm like that girl in the Greek myth who ate pomegranates in Hades, then could never fully escape.

Except my mother doesn't want me. I already know that.

My child, on the other hand, this final addition to my father's legacy . . .

I lean against the closet door, trying to figure out once more if I'm going to cry or vomit. When I manage to pass a full minute without doing either, I pull on soft gray stretch pants and a matching gray top. Cashmere, probably.

Conrad would laugh if he could see me now. He'd grin and tell me to enjoy the ride. Not having any family left, he couldn't understand my ambivalence about mine. Clearly she loves you, he'd tell me again and again, which only proved he never understood my mother at all.

Downstairs, my mother is in the kitchen. There is a heaping plate of fresh fruit on the kitchen table and she has the Cuisinart whirring away. She turns it off when she sees me.

"High-protein smoothie," she announces cheerfully. "Full of antioxidants and healthy fats for the baby."

Only my mother can work a blender while wearing pearls.

There's no use fighting it. Years of training kick in. I sit at the table. I pick at the fruit. I obediently sip the green sludge.

I don't look at the fridge. I never look at the fridge. Not that it's the same one, of course. After the "tragic incident," my mother had the kitchen gutted. New cabinets, marble countertops, high-end appliances, custom window treatments. It's all creamy and soft and Italian. Not at all like the original dark cherrywood cabinets, green-and-gold granite tops. Meaning nothing in here should remind me of my father or that day.

But it does. It always does. I don't care that the flooring has been ripped out and replaced. Or that the stainless steel refrigerator was exchanged for a wood-paneled model. I see the spot where my father died. I recall the smell. I remember looking at his face, so waxy and still, and thinking it didn't look like him at all.

I don't know how my mom still lives in this house. But I guess I'll get to figure that out for myself now. How to go back to the home Conrad and I shared. How to pick up the pieces of a life, where I'm still not sure where we went wrong.

I notice for the first time that all the lights are on and the curtains drawn, though it's only midday. I don't have to think about it for long.

"The press?" I ask.

"You know how they are." My mother waves an airy hand. At least on this we're united. The media descended the first time, too.

Harvard math professor killed in his own home by his teenage daughter. How could they resist? Initially, my mom had thought she could control the story, the way she controlled every other facet of her highly fictionalized life. Needless to say, the reporters ate her alive.

She retreated. Took up the tactic of letting her grand silence speak for her. As a minor, at least I wasn't subjected to such abuse. But it was weeks, maybe even months, before we could leave our house in peace. I learned to hate the sight of news vans. I learned not to believe anything I saw on TV. At least I got that education early in life, because I'm definitely going to need it now.

Knock on the side door. The one used only by close confidants. My mother bustles over.

Dick Delaney, my lawyer, is standing there, still wearing the same sharply pressed gray suit from the courtroom. He's a handsome man with his silver hair and closely trimmed beard. I have countless memories of him. Poker nights with my father. Laughing indulgently at all the math jokes, as one of the only nonacademics in the room. How did he even know my father? What had earned him a seat at the poker table? I don't know. But he was always part of our household, brilliant and successful in his own right, a fellow Harvard alum, which maybe was all the credentials he needed. I never even thought of him as a defense attorney.

Until, of course, sixteen years ago. Again, the smell, the look on my father's waxy face.

I have this terrible sense of déjà vu. Here we are again, the three of us, this kitchen.

My mom doesn't say a word. She simply steps back, allowing Mr. Delaney to enter. In an echo of my own thoughts, her right hand is already clutched protectively to her chest, fingering her precious pearls.

He looks from her to me to her again. The expression on his face isn't good. "After picking up Evie from the courthouse, where did you go?" he asks my mother.

Her brow furrows. "Here. Straight here, of course. Poor Evie needed to rest."

"No stops along the way?"

"Of course."

"Not even a drive by her old house so she could pick up personal possessions, items of clothing?"

"Absolutely not. Evie has everything she needs right here."

Mr. Delaney stares at me. Slowly, I nod, though I already understand I don't want to hear what he'll say next.

"Your house is on fire." He announces it bluntly.

I try to absorb the statement. I hear the words. I just can't seem to process them. My house. Conrad's and my home. My husband's death scene.

"Total loss," he continues.

The future life I was going to lead. The photos and personal items that tied me to the past.

"I'm sorry," he says. "You're sure you were together all afternoon? Both of you? Right here?"

"Of course!" My mother is outraged.

"The police will be coming," my lawyer says. Then he takes a seat at the table, and together, we wait.

THIS TIME, THE knock comes from the front door. But we were already alerted to the detective's arrival by the sudden spike in noise from across the street—the media spotting the official vehicle and descending with a crescendo of questions. No comment, the police will say. That's what they always say. After all, it's not their lives being torn apart.

Mr. Delaney gets up, does the honors. My mother and I don't

look at each other. We can't. I fix my gaze on my half-finished green smoothie, the piece of uneaten pineapple on my plate. Under the table, my hands are shaking furiously on my lap. Again, I've never felt myself such a mess. Shock? Pregnancy hormones? My heart is racing like a hummingbird's and I suddenly want to blurt out everything, anything. Except I honestly don't know what to say. I just want whatever magic words will give me my life back.

Dead woman walking. If that's what I'd felt like twenty-four hours ago, then what am I now? Corpse walking? The ghost of a never-realized dream?

I recognize the first detective who walks into the kitchen. The father figure who attempted to question me last night. He still wears his very stern, yet somehow equally concerned expression. Standing next to Mr. Delaney, who is wearing a thousand-dollar suit, the detective appears both slightly frumpy and more human.

My mother is already sitting up straighter, her eyes zeroing in on a target. An older male, reasonably attractive and clearly out of his socioeconomic league. She will devour him alive. And relish every bite.

Behind him comes a second detective. Female. Chin-length curly blond hair. Killer cheekbones. Nearly crystalline blue eyes. She's wearing slim-fitting jeans and sleek black leather boots that match her swagger.

I have that sense of déjà vu again. Her gaze goes straight to me, narrowing slightly.

Smell hits me first. The memory of gunpowder and blood. The refrigerator. Don't look at the streaked stainless steel. Don't stare at the wax-doll version of my father on the floor. Sitting at the table. Except not this table. That table. And not in this kitchen, that kitchen.

She'd been the one sitting across from me. Younger. Softer. Kinder, I think. Except maybe because I'd been younger and softer, too. Questions then, questions now.

I look at my mom, Mr. Delaney, the detective, my hands still shaking on my lap. And I can't help but think, the gang's all here.

THE BLONDE, SERGEANT Detective D. D. Warren, doesn't speak right away. She lets the older detective, Call Me Phil, run through the particulars. Warren prowls the kitchen. I wonder if she's noting all the differences—new cabinets, countertops, appliances. Does she think it's strange my mother still lives, cooks, eats, in a crime scene? That we are sitting, even now, mere feet from where my father died?

My mother is talking. With Mr. Delaney's approval. She's also turning her head a certain way—her best side, while periodically fingering a strand of frosted blond hair above her ear, French-manicured nails lingering on the graceful curve of her neck.

I've never seen my mother interact with a man without batting her eyelashes. She remains an attractive woman. Slim, graceful, good bones. Not to mention she's a fanatic for green smoothies and organic this and organic that. In lieu of yoga, she prefers triple-distilled vodka, served straight up. Still seems to work for her.

My father never minded her flirting. He'd watch, a knowing gleam in his eye as she worked the room. I think he liked the way she sparkled. Others admired her. Others wanted her. But she always belonged to him.

I feel like I can't breathe. Time is collapsing. I'm sixteen. I'm thirty-two. My father. My husband.

The same detective. Still prowling the expansive kitchen while most likely thinking, *How many "accidents" can one person have?*

I have a question for her: How many losses can one person take?

My mother is swearing she was with me all afternoon. The detective, politely but forcefully, wants to know if anyone can corroborate. Mr. Delaney intervenes smoothly that if the police don't believe his client's statement, the burden is on them to prove otherwise. Do they have anyone placing my mother or myself at the scene of the fire? For that matter, the city is filled with cameras and prying eyes. Surely, if the police had something more concrete, they wouldn't be wasting everyone's time with these questions.

Mr. Delaney is fishing. Even I can tell that. Do the police have anything substantial? That's what he really wants to know. The older detective doesn't take the bait.

I find it interesting that my own lawyer is curious if the police have evidence that contradicts his clients' statements. Do all lawyers believe their clients are lying to them? Or is it merely because he's been a family friend for decades and knows us that well?

"What caused the fire?" When I finally interrupt, the sound of my own voice startles me. I sound hoarse, like I haven't spoken in years.

The blond detective halts, stares at me. Neither investigator offers an answer.

"You think it was intentional, right?" I continue. "Otherwise, why would you be here? But why would I burn down my own home? I left last night without even a toothbrush. Everything I own . . . everything I had . . ." My voice breaks slightly. I force myself to continue, though I sound hollow even to me. "It's all gone. My entire life . . . it's all gone. Why would I do that?"

The blonde speaks for the first time. "This doesn't look like such a bad place to land."

Just like that, I'm pissed off. I shove back my chair. Rise to standing. "You of all people should know better. You of all people!" I'm almost yelling at her. Why not? I certainly can't yell at my mom.

I stalk out of the kitchen. I can't take the room, with all its creamy wood and expensive marble. A fucking stage setting.

My father was real. His smile, his booming voice, the way he pursed his lips when working a particularly difficult problem, the way he'd sit with his eyes shut and listen to me play the piano for hours.

He loved me. He loved me, he loved me, he loved me.

And Conrad had loved me, too.

The blond detective is following me. Mr. Delaney, too, clearly concerned. Emotional clients are probably a danger to themselves and others. My mother stays behind. With Call Me Phil. She's probably offering him a glass of water, while briefly touching his arm.

I don't know where I'm going. I can't exit the house. Whatever is overwhelming me here is nothing compared to the media that's waiting to pounce outside. I move into the formal room with the baby grand. Black and gleaming. I spent so much of my childhood sitting on that bench, working those keys.

I haven't touched it since.

I can't be in this room. I move into the front parlor instead. I never liked this room. What kid cares about a formal parlor?

"My client needs to rest," Mr. Delaney is informing the detective.

She doesn't listen to him but regards me instead. "You remember me, don't you?" she asks.

I nod. Not sitting, but walking around the small space. It's taken me years to realize that most people do not live like this, with carefully placed silk-covered wingback chairs and antique sideboards and crystalline decanters.

"Yes." I finally glance at her. "You looked nicer then. The sympathetic cop. Not anymore."

The blonde smiles, not offended at all. "I was younger then. Still learning."

"What did you learn?"

"To ask more questions. To accept fewer answers. That even the most honest person will tell a lie."

"My client—" Mr. Delaney tries again.

I hold up a hand. "It's okay. You can go help my mom. Or rather, save the other detective."

Mr. Delaney gives me a stern look. Though he's already torn. He does know my mother, and sometimes her manipulations, even done with the best of intentions, can backfire.

I feel stronger now, more certain. I address Sergeant Warren directly. "You're not going to ask me about Conrad, are you?"

Slowly, she shakes her head.

"Will you tell me about the fire?"

Another pause. She nods. We have a deal. Maybe my lawyer doesn't understand the terms, but we do.

"It's okay," I tell Mr. Delaney again. "Give us a moment, please."

"As your lawyer—"

"I know. A moment."

He's not happy. But I'm the client, he's the lawyer, and he is worried about my mother. As he should be. Finally, he retreats, leaving Sergeant Warren and me alone. Last time, it had been her and me in the kitchen. My mom and the other detective in the parlor. I like this change of venue. I need it.

She does look harder, as if the past sixteen years haven't been entirely kind to her. Or maybe she'd been right before; disillusionment was part of the job. After all, sixteen years ago she'd believed me in the matter of my father's death. And now?

I wonder what she sees when she looks at me. Am I harder? Disillusioned? Angry? I don't think I feel any of those things.

I'm sad. I'm lost. I am my father's daughter, and I always saw the truth even when others didn't. But that doesn't mean I've known what to do with the information. Especially when it involved the ones I loved.

"How are you feeling?" Sergeant Warren asks me. She doesn't take a seat in one of the washed-silk wingbacks. Neither do I.

"I don't know."

She tilts her head to the side. "Are you excited for the baby?"

"Yes."

"Conrad?"

"We'd almost given up hope. We'd been trying for a bit. Nothing, and then . . ." I don't have any more words to say. I place my right hand on the gentle swell of my abdomen. Another silent apology. I already have the same relationship with my child as I do with my mother.

"I have a son," the detective offers. "Five years old. We just got him a puppy. They're both crazy."

I smile. "We were waiting to be surprised. It feels weird now. That Conrad died, never knowing if he was going to have a boy or girl. One of those silly things, because it's terrible enough Conrad will never get to meet his child, what does it matter the gender?" A pause, and then, in the silence, because it's weighing so heavily on my mind I just can't help myself: "I still miss him."

"Conrad?"

I look at her. Shake my head. "Do you think it will be any better for my baby? That maybe by never knowing his or her daddy, she won't miss him as much?"

The sergeant doesn't say anything.

"I didn't shoot him."

"Conrad?" she asks again.

Again, I shake my head.

She doesn't move anymore. Neither do I. We study each other across the small space. Two women who barely know each other and yet are intricately bound by the tangle of so many questions, the weight of too much unfinished business.

"We came home to him," I continue softly, my voice very low, which is the only tone appropriate for confessing sins. "I walked through the back door into the kitchen, and there he was."

"Your mother was with you?" The detective asks, her tone as hushed as my own. She glances at the open doorway. Mr. Delaney will return soon enough. We both know it.

"Yes, standing outside."

"You had blood in your hair," Sergeant Warren states firmly. "Gunpowder on your hands. If you didn't shoot your father, how do you explain that?"

"It rained." I can barely get the words out. Sixteen years later, and still the horror seems fresh. "I walked through the door, and it rained on me." I touch my short hair self-consciously. "Hot blood from the ceiling."

"What did you do?"

"I picked up the shotgun. It was on the floor in front of me. I picked it up. I don't know why. To get it out of the way. Then I saw him. He was half hidden behind the island. But turning the corner I saw . . . all of him."

Another glance toward the foyer. Footsteps, did we hear them in the distance? A tinkle of laughter. My mother flirting with Detective Phil.

"What did your mother do?"

"She screamed."

"What did you do?"

"Nothing. He didn't look real. Not like himself. I kept waiting for him to get up."

"Who called the cops?"

I look at her. "We didn't. I checked the shotgun. Made sure the chamber was empty—"

"You knew how to work it."

"I always knew how to work it. My father wouldn't bring a firearm into the home without teaching us basic safety."

"What did you do, Evie?"

"Whatever my mother told me."

"And she told you to confess to killing him? Not, 'let's call nine-one-one,' 'good God our loved one has just been shot'?"

I know how crazy it sounds. Back then. Today. All the hours in between. I don't have the words.

The sergeant's eyes narrow. "Are you covering for your mom, Evie? She and your father got in a fight. She shot him. You, being a minor with no criminal record, took the blame to save the parent you had left."

"She was with me. She couldn't have killed him."

"Then why such a crazy story? Why not call the police?"

"There would be an investigation. So many questions. The potential for . . ." I couldn't articulate the words back then, but I understand them now. "Scandal. I don't think my mom knows who or why my father was shot. But she didn't want to risk the answer to those questions. Not if they might tarnish his legacy. You have to realize, my father is more than just a man to her. He is . . . everything."

The sergeant eyes me skeptically. "So she threw her sixteen-year-old daughter under the bus rather than seek justice in her husband's murder?" A pause. "Or rather than a risk an investigation into his possible suicide?"

I don't have to answer that question. The sergeant is finally starting to understand. My mother's true fear. The real reason I did what I did. Sometimes, the danger isn't from outside, but from inside ourselves.

"Gonna blame your mom for your husband's death, too," the sergeant asks at last, "or this time did you finally get it right?"

I hesitate. I don't want to. I think of my mother as crazy and manipulative, sure, but not homicidal. And yet the closet bursting with maternity wear, the fully stocked nursery . . . It's almost as if she knew about today. Has been waiting all along.

"What did you think back then?" I ask the sergeant now.

"I thought you were scared. I thought you were in shock. And I thought, based on the physical evidence alone, that you did shoot him, but you were sorry about it."

"And now?"

The detective shrugs. "Looking at your husband's crime scene? I think you're the shooter again. Except this time around, you're not sorry about it."

"It would be stupid math," I say.

She gives me that look.

"Having been involved in a shooting before, to repeat the same equation . . . Stupid math."

"Except the equation worked for you the first time."

"You think so? Sixteen years of murmurs and whispers and innuendos. Sixteen years of loss, and I'm not even allowed to grieve because, supposedly, I'm the one who killed him?"

The sergeant doesn't answer that right away, just continues to study me.

"Besides." I speak more briskly. "I wouldn't burn down my own house. I've now lost everything. My baby has lost everything. No mother would do that."

The sergeant merely shrugs, gestures to our luxurious surroundings.

She leaves me no choice but to play the only card I have left. "I've lied for my mother. Made excuses, enabled her bad behavior, curtailed my own hopes and dreams just to make her happy. But I would never willingly move back in with her. And I would never happily grant her this much access to her first grandchild."

"What are you trying to say?"

I shake my head. This time, I'm the one eyeing the doorway nervously. "I don't know. But don't you think it's curious, a mere twenty-four hours later, how few choices I have left?"

CHAPTER 11

D.D.

"GET ANYTHING OUT OF HER?" Phil asked as they headed back to the car. They'd parked on the family's driveway to get some distance from the reporters yammering on the sidewalk.

"She didn't magically confess to killing her husband," D.D. said as she slid into the passenger side. "But just to make things interesting, she changed her story about shooting her father sixteen years ago."

Phil, firing the engine to life, stared at her. "What would be the point to that?"

"I don't know. Maybe just to muddy the waters? Evie has to know one of the reasons she looks guilty in her husband's death is that she already confessed to accidentally shooting her father. So rather than address her husband's murder now, she's recanting sixteen years ago."

"No statute of limitations on murder," Phil murmured. He twisted around, got to the business of backing down the driveway into the street without taking out any overly aggressive newspeople.

The days were short this time of year; the sun had set while they were inside the house, interviewing the family. Fortunately, the huge spotlights and the blaze of flashing media cameras helped light their way.

"So who shot her father?" Phil asked.

"Evie claims she doesn't know. She and her mother walked into the scene. Her mother convinced her to take the blame, rather than risk an investigation that might tarnish the man's 'legacy.' Still sounds fishy to me. Who discovers their loved one's body and doesn't immediately call nine-one-one? Opts for let's play make-believe instead?"

"The mother's scary," Phil stated. He shuddered slightly.

"Really? Because she seemed quite taken with you. A wealthy widow, and a rather well-preserved model at that."

Phil gave her a look. D.D. already knew the score. Phil was madly in love with his childhood sweetheart and longtime wife, Betsy. Their marriage was one of the few things in life that gave D.D. hope.

"She's scary," Phil said again.

D.D. smiled, turned to studying the view out the window. They'd cleared the reporters now and were cruising through Cambridge, past row after row of gorgeous Victorians and historic Colonials, all decked out for the holidays with shimmering icicle lights, garland-wrapped bannisters, impeccably decorated shrubs. In an enclave this wealthy, D.D. had no doubt the inside matched the outside, towering Christmas trees covered in delicate antique ornaments, decked-out staircases, pots of overflowing greenery. She and Alex were still working on a Christmas tree. Given the modest size of their home compared to the staggering amount of Jack and Kiko's energy, they'd probably have to put up their tree the night before to have any hope for it to still be standing on Christmas morning.

"How much money can one dead math professor be worth?" D.D. muttered. She hadn't really thought about it at the time. Everyone said Earl Hopkins had been a genius, he was also a tenured

Harvard professor. That had seemed worthy of the grand home. But all these years later, he was gone, and to judge by the kitchen renovations alone, the family's lifestyle hadn't suffered. Half a million in life insurance didn't go that far. Did that mean there were other sources of income, more tangible benefits of Hopkins's brilliance his wife hadn't wanted to risk to a murder investigation? Phil was right: There was no statute of limitations on homicide, which meant Evie's changing story line raised all sorts of interesting questions. Though despite what she might have intended, they still centered mostly on her and her mom.

"My partner and I were the first to interview Evie and her mother," D.D. said now, gazing out the window. "At the time, she had blood spatter in her hair and tested positive for GSR on her hands. That kind of physical evidence has gotta mean something."

"Did you ask her?"

"Sure. In her new and improved memory, she walked in when the blood was still fresh. It dripped down on her from the ceiling. Then she picked up the shotgun and checked the chamber, which would contaminate her hands with GSR. The GSR can go either way. But the blood evidence, I'm less convinced."

"I worked a scene once," Phil provided. "Kid was arrested standing in his best friend's apartment, covered in blood, holding a shotgun. His friend's body was slumped in a chair, missing most of its head. Kid was arrested for murder, of course. His story: He'd gotten a call from his friend, claiming he was about to commit suicide. The kid had run right over, heard the shotgun blast, and raced inside just in time to find his friend's body. The blood was from all the spatter dripping down from the ceiling."

"The verdict?" D.D. asked.

"Forensic experts proved the friend was telling the truth. The directionality of the spatter on the ceiling indicated the shotgun blast had blown up, while the directionality of the spatter on the friend revealed the blood had dripped down. Friend was exonerated. And I believe they still cover the case at the academy. You should ask Alex about it."

D.D. nodded. Given that her husband Alex's specialty was blood evidence, she'd definitely run Evie's new and improved story by him. And while suicides by long guns weren't as common as suicides by pistols, they did happen, meaning Evie and her mom might have been right to worry about the results of a full-on death investigation.

"Here's the problem," D.D. said now. "I can pull the file, but my memory of the Hopkins case is that we didn't exactly work it to the letter. We had a body. We had a confession. We had a witness, and we lacked any evidence of motive. Everyone said Evie loved her father, et cetera, et cetera. At the time, all the elements matched the given story line of a terrible family tragedy, versus any whiff of something criminal. Let's just say the senior detective, Speirs, took a more efficiency-based approach to his case management. Close the ones you can, so you have the hours to work the ones you can't."

"Versus your own obsessive, take-no-prisoners approach?" Phil asked.

"How Speirs and I ever survived five years of working together, I'll never know," D.D. agreed. "Except I was the rookie, and in the beginning, everyone gets to do as they're told."

"Did you have doubts about Evie's confession back then?"

"Honestly, no. The way she presented. The physical evidence at the scene. There are cases I still wonder about. But Earl Hopkins's shooting death wasn't one of them."

"And now?"

"I don't like it." D.D. turned away from the window. "I don't like any of it. Evie's husband's death. A fire at their house and our crime scene. Evie's new statement, which frankly makes less sense than her old statement. I mean, who confesses to a shooting just to appease her mom?"

"Scary woman," Phil provided again.

"Questions. I have lots and lots of questions. And you know how I feel about questions."

"I'm never going to see my wife again, am I?"

"I think we have our work cut out for us."

"Making our next stop?"

"Where all confused detectives should go: back to the crime scene. Arson fire and all."

THEY COULD SMELL the charred remains of the scene before they arrived. Phil navigated the narrow street, made tighter by the rows of parked cars on both sides. This time of night, people were home for the evening. The small, boxy homes glowed with cozy kitchen scenes or flashing flat-screens. D.D. thought it interesting that as the homes grew smaller, the outdoor Christmas displays grew larger. Entire rooftops covered in Santa and his sleigh. Blow-up snowmen that ballooned across entire yards. Miles of twinkling lights.

Alex had trimmed their front porch with icicle lights, then wrapped the lone tree in their front yard. Not quite keeping up with the neighbors, but certainly more effort than D.D. had ever made. Then again, they had a kid now, and Jack was obsessed with anything related to Santa.

Phil turned the corner, and the Carters' former home became immediately visible as a black void in the midst of a sea of festivity. Not to mention, the smell of burnt wood and melted plastic grew significantly stronger.

They'd left Evie's school and gone straight to the Carters' residence after receiving news of the blaze. The scene had been too hot to approach, however, with the fire crews still working. In the end, it had made more sense to head directly to the source of their problems—Evie Carter—than wait around.

Now Phil turned in enough to park at the end of the driveway, just beyond the crime scene tape. His headlights illuminated a gutted shell. Collapsed roof. Blown-out windows. While a fair amount of the single-car garage appeared intact, only the front wall of the two-story residence remained, and even that was barely standing.

"All right, this is what we know." Phil pulled out his notebook. Many cops now worked off tablets, or even their smartphones. Phil, however, was a traditionalist. D.D. appreciated that about him.

"According to the arson investigator, Patricia Di Lucca, fire most likely started in the kitchen in the rear of the home. Definitely arson. Looks like a pot was left on the kitchen cooktop, filled with highly flammable materials. Then an accelerant was doused liberally around the house—most likely gasoline—with the largest concentration dumped in the upstairs bedrooms. Range was turned on. Arsonist exited stage right, and once burner achieved proper temperature, poof. Initial spark caught and fire was off and running. These old structures don't take much to burn, but the extensive nature of the damage, particularly given the fire department was here in under six minutes, meant someone really wanted to get the job done."

"Whole house was intended to be a loss," D.D. provided.

"Yep, except the garage, which, as you can see, is relatively intact."

"The arsonist didn't care about the garage."

"Apparently not."

She tilted her head to the side, contemplating. "Seems like a fairly blatant attempt to eliminate the crime scene. Except, if you really wanted to be precise, why not start the fire in the office where Conrad was shot?"

Phil shrugged. "This stove-top system allowed the perpetrator adequate time to get out of the house. Safer than having to outrun a fire, down a flight of stairs you've already covered in gasoline. Di Lucca should have more information on the accelerant and fire-starting device by tomorrow. She'll also run the details through the arson database to see if it matches any established MOs."

D.D. nodded. True arsonists were a lot like serial killers. They didn't—couldn't—deviate from form.

"For now, she'd say it was nothing too sophisticated. Maybe even a single-Google-search-away sort of thing. But Di Lucca is excellent. She'll figure it out."

"Witnesses?"

"Nada. Fire started shortly after two. Not that many people around. Those that were . . . no one saw a car parked in the driveway or anyone dashing from a smoking home. Then again, given the time delay, the person may have exited more like one thirty and simply strolled down the street. This isn't one of those neighborhoods where everyone knows everything and everyone. Too big for that."

"What about cameras?" D.D. asked. Because Evie's lawyer had been right; Boston was a city lousy with surveillance systems, and a good detective knew how to use them.

"Couple of home security systems in the area, but none that capture the Carters' residence. As for traffic cameras, closest one is at the major intersection a mile back, where you make a left onto these side streets. Not terrible, if we knew who we're looking for. But without a target, too many subjects. Plus, there are side roads leading into this neighborhood as well; that traffic cam covers only the main drag."

"Meaning anyone, including Evie and her mom, could've arrived using one of the lesser-known byways?"

"True. Except Dick Delaney came up with quite the alibi for those two."

"When?"

"When you were talking to Evie. It's Joyce Hopkins's custom to park on the driveway."

"I know. We parked behind her."

"Exactly. Meaning her car was in plain sight most of the afternoon. As Delaney pointed out, there are about two dozen rabid reporters who can vouch for it."

"The meddling media as alibis?"

"Told you it was interesting."

"They could've taken an Uber, or a taxi, or whatever."

"Again, without the hordes noticing?"

D.D. scowled. Evie's attorney made a good argument. The media had had the house under constant surveillance pretty much since this morning. The chances of Evie or her mother doing anything without some cameraman or reporter noticing were slim to none.

"I have to admit," she said at last, "I see Evie's point. Why would she burn down her own home, especially without having picked up some personal belongings first?"

"Women are that sentimental about their favorite sweater?"

"I was thinking more along the lines of her baby. Five months along, Evie's probably bought at least one item or two, let alone ultrasound photos, personal snapshots of before and after. I can't see any soon-to-be mom willingly destroying such items. Unless, of course, she removed them before she ever shot Conrad. During the initial crime scene walk-through, did you notice any baby items?"

"I wasn't really looking," Phil confessed. "But we have plenty of photos of the house. Easy enough to look again. I have another thought regarding the fire."

"Which is?"

"Evie shot the computer. Over half a dozen times, right? Seems to me the computer was what she wanted to eliminate. And did. So why risk returning to set a fire?"

"You think she already covered her tracks. The destroyed laptop."

"I think we've established she's partial to firearms."

D.D. couldn't argue with that. She stared at the gutted home again. "Again, from the top. What do we know? Sixteen years ago, Evie's father was shot and killed in his own home."

"Evie now says she didn't do it. But her story is still subject to debate," Phil provided.

"Could it have been suicide?" D.D. postulated. "That would certainly be something the mother might feel compelled to cover up. Evie didn't report seeing anything other than her father's body and the shotgun, however."

"Again, if she's telling the truth." Phil looked at her. "Even if you don't have spatter evidence from Evie, you gotta have crime scene photos of the body. Have the criminalists rework the angle of the blast. That'll tell you where the shooter was standing and whether or not Hopkins could've shot himself."

"Good point. Okay, so one shooting death sixteen years ago that was probably covered up in some manner. Fast-forward to yesterday, when Evie's husband just happens to also meet death by firearm."

"Conrad Carter," Phil intoned. "The kind of guy everyone liked but no one seemed to know. Except maybe your CI, Flora Dane, who claims to have met him in a bar with Jacob Ness."

Phil's tone implied he still had his doubts. D.D. shrugged. With Flora, anything was possible. On the other hand, D.D. had never known the woman to intentionally lie. Omit truth, yes, but deliberately lie . . .

D.D. picked up their story line: "No history of domestic disturbance calls or tension between Conrad and Evie. But according to Evie's fellow teacher, some signs of recent stress in Evie's life."

Phil nodded. "Which brings us to Evie Carter, five months pregnant and tied to one accidental shooting that happened when she was a juvenile. Clean record, however, since then."

"They bought the house together four years ago. Both have day jobs during the week, home renovation projects on the weekends. Ordinary," D.D. said at last, frowning. "By all accounts, a normal if not boring young couple building a life, starting a family. Until last night."

"Three rounds into the husband. Twelve into the computer. Eight minutes in between."

"That time gap is gonna kill us at trial."

"What about your theory Evie used the eight minutes to retrieve something off the computer before destroying it? Which she then must have hidden somewhere in the house, or it would've been recovered from her person during processing."

"And the house was then torched to eliminate whatever she recovered?"

Phil shrugged. "That would imply someone else had to know she hid something. We're still processing phone records for her and him. It's possible something will come up."

"A phone call right after that shooting?"

"Would be pretty damning. And certainly, eight-minute gap or not, we have a tight timeline of the evening. Neighbors called in the first sound of shots fired. Uniformed officers were standing on the front porch for the second. Can't argue with that."

D.D. sighed. "I wish Conrad's laptop was still intact. Seems like the key to this puzzle was on that laptop."

"We know Evie has access to a computer at work. We'll grab that next. Amazing what the browser history can reveal about a person."

"How to burn down a house and still have time to get away?" D.D. intoned dryly.

"Exactly. And we still do have one last item of consideration: if there was . . . is . . . a connection between Conrad Carter and Jacob Ness . . ."

D.D. followed his train of thought perfectly. "Lots of perpetrators use the internet."

Phil sighed heavily. "I can't believe I'm going to say this, but . . . your crazy CI? She may be able to help us yet."

CHAPTER 12

FLORA

THE INSIDE OF KEITH EDGAR'S brownstone is as surprising as the man himself. An open floor plan that yawns way back. Miles of dark wood flooring beneath a stark-white tray ceiling. A slate-covered fireplace that rises like a granite column in the middle of the distinctly modern space. The fireplace boasts gas flames, which dance across highly polished stones. In front of that sits a low-slung turquoise sofa, bookended by orange chairs. Some kind of shag rug covered in bright splashes of color gets the hard job of tying it all together, while above the fireplace, a massive flat-screen TV belches out the evening news, including an update on the fire at the Carters' house. I already caught some details on my phone. Yet more questions about a shooting, a couple, a man, I have yet to understand.

I remain rooted in the entryway of the brownstone, my back to a wall. Now that I'm in the house, actually face-to-face with Keith, I'm not sure what to do.

Keith springs to life first. He darts forward, grabs a remote from the glass coffee table, and turns off the TV. "Sorry, just catching up on the news. Can I get you something? Water? Coffee?" He glances at his watch, notes the hour. "A glass of wine?"

To judge by the furniture, I would've pegged him for a dry martini. And lots of hours spent viewing *Mad Men*. In between his time on the true-crime boards.

"Have a seat," Keith tries now. He gestures to one of the orange chairs. "Umm, welcome, thanks for coming. Is this because of the last letter I sent? I didn't actually think you'd respond. I mean, it's not like the other notes worked. But you can't blame a guy for trying."

He smiles, blushes slightly, and for a moment looks as self-conscious as I feel. I can't decide if this guy is for real or if he's already the most accomplished psychopath I've ever met.

"Is this your place?" I ask at last, moving toward the chair.

He nods.

"Wife? Kids?"

He shakes his head.

"What do you do?"

"I'm a computer analyst. Most of the time I work from home. And don't look anything like this." Again, the charming tinge of color to his cheeks as he gestures to his upscale wardrobe. "But I happened to have a meeting with a client today. You're lucky that I'd just returned home. Or I'm lucky. Something like that."

"I'll take that glass of water now."

He turns immediately, striding past the fireplace and heading to the rear of the house, which must contain the kitchen. I take the moment to compose myself, reassess the space. Front door behind me. Most likely patio doors straight back. An open-bannister staircase to the left. A door at the base of the stairs. Coat closet, most likely. Another door directly across from that. Downstairs powder room.

Otherwise, a very open, expansive space, decorated like a page out of a West Elm catalogue. But in my second survey, I catch what I missed the first time around. No photos. No wall art. Nothing of any personal nature at all.

According to Keith Edgar, he not only owns this house, but also works out of it. And yet this space might as well be a showroom. Perfectly appointed and completely devoid of personality.

We all wear masks. And the more we have to hide, the more accomplished the veneer.

Keith returns with a tall glass of water. I take it from him carefully, not standing too close, making sure our fingers don't touch. Then I do take a seat. My inventory has restored my sense of paranoia. I have all my survivor's instincts kicking in now.

Meaning I'm relaxed for the first time since I knocked on the door.

"Why true crime?" I ask him. I hold my water glass but don't sip it. I notice the glass coffee table has a perfectly clear top. Not a single spec of dust or water ring. I wonder if he cleans it obsessively, or pays someone to do it for him.

"I've always been fascinated by puzzles." He takes the orange chair across from me, leaving the table between us, as if he understands I need the barrier. He leans slightly forward, arms resting loosely on each leg. He's still smiling, clearly delighted by my unexpected presence in his house. I decide then and there that if he takes a selfie, I will kick him in the balls.

"Doesn't explain true crime."

"I particularly enjoy puzzles that haven't been solved. True crime one-oh-one. You start with Jack the Ripper, then the Black Dahlia, and next thing you know, you're reading everything about every notorious homicide, because the only way to get fresh insight into the unsolved murders is to learn from the killers who did get arrested. Why did they do what they did? And how can they be caught?"

"What's the nature of evil?" I ask dryly.

He shrugs slightly. "Most people debate whether evil is born or made. Nature versus nurture. Based on my research, I think of it more as a spectrum. All of the above, but with some predators leaning more one way or another. For example, Ted Bundy—"

"By all means, Ted Bundy."

That quick grin, proving he knows just how much he resembles one of the nation's most feared super-predators. "I think he's an example of evil that's born. Bundy claimed that he was affected by his unconventional upbringing—being raised by his grandparents as his mother's younger brother, versus being acknowledged as her illegitimate child. But I think we can all agree that as traumas go, that doesn't quite rise to the level of spending your adult life hunting and killing young women—particularly given evidence he was playing with knives by the time he was three. Him, Dahmer, they were always going to be killers. Just a matter of when."

I say nothing.

He clasps his hands, continues quickly. "Then you have Edmund Kemper the third. Raised by an abusive, alcoholic mother who was severely critical of him. Forced to live in the basement because she didn't want him near his sisters. Then sent as a teenager to live with his grandparents, whom he hated."

I can't help myself: "He was sent to live with his grandparents because he'd already murdered the family cats."

I earn a quick nod of approval. Whatever game we're playing, I'm at least living up to expectations. Or was just stupid enough to take the bait.

"But here's the deal with Kemper," Keith says now, totally serious. "He shot and killed his grandparents when he was fifteen. That got him sent away to a facility for youthful offenders where he was diagnosed with paranoid schizophrenia. So, sure, you could argue brain chemistry, born bad—"

"He shot his grandmother just to see what it felt like."

"Exactly." Another earnest nod. "And upon getting released, he murdered six young women, even liked to drive by police stations with their bodies stuffed in the trunk of his car. But this is what makes Kemper so fascinating: He was also incredibly intelligent and reflective. Smart enough, he realized one day that the person he really wanted to kill was his mother. So he did. He went to her house, murdered her—"

"Stuck her larynx down the garbage disposal so he'd never have to listen to her again."

"And then he *turned himself in*. That was it. His mother had tormented him most of his life. He'd finally addressed the issue. Then he was done. Compare that to Bundy, who broke out of prison, what—two, three times? Swore each time he'd clean up his act, only to devolve into larger and more horrific crime sprees. Bundy was born evil. Kemper had some of the necessary starting ingredients, don't get me wrong, but his upbringing at the hands of his mother was the deciding factor. So again, there's not one answer to the question of what's the nature of evil, just as there's no one answer that defines anything about human behavior. Evil is a spectrum. And different predators fall in different places along the scale."

"No one wants to be a monster," I murmur.

"What?"

"Nothing."

"You have questions," he says abruptly. He's not smiling anymore. His expression is serious. He steeples his hands, rests his fingertips against his chin. "You didn't come to talk. If you were going to do that, you would've contacted me in advance, made arrangements to meet the group. Asked about the speaker's fee."

"Cashed the check?"

Another nod. "This isn't about what you have to offer us. It's about what we can offer you."

I don't answer right away. I study the glass of water. The way the condensation has beaded up, heated by the flames from the gas fireplace.

"Why don't you have any personal photos in this room?"

"This isn't just my home, it's also a professional space. I don't care to give that much away to clients."

"Your reading has made you that paranoid?"

His turn to fall silent. I know then what I should've suspected from the beginning.

"How old were you?" I ask.

"Six. And it wasn't me who was victimized, but my older cousin in New York. They never caught who killed him; it's one of those open cases. But the details of his murder match four other unsolved homicides from the same time period. My aunt and uncle . . . They've never quite recovered. You grow up seeing the impact such a crime has on a person, a family, a community, it leaves a mark."

"You work his case?"

"I have for the past twenty years. I'm no closer to solving it than the police are."

"A string of related murders that simply ended?" I raise a brow.

"Exactly. Predators don't stop on their own. But sometimes, they get arrested for other crimes. Or change jurisdiction. In this day and age of nationwide law enforcement databases, it's harder for that trick to work. But international travel . . ."

"A killer with means."

"My cousin was strangled with a silk tie. There was evidence of sexual intercourse, but not necessarily assault. He'd told some friends he'd recently met an older, wealthy gentleman. He was excited about the potential for the relationship."

"You think he was seduced, then murdered?"

He nodded.

"I'm sorry," I say at last.

"I was too young to understand the nuances of his death. Later, when I was fifteen, I happened to look it up. Imagine my surprise to find my cousin's murder linked to a series of strangulations on various websites. But it was the true-crime sites, groups like the one I run now, that captured my attention. They'd given it serious thought and in many cases done some real work. We're not all just armchair detectives. Some of our members are retired police, medical professionals, even a coroner."

"And *your* skills?"

"I'm a computer nerd. Trust me, you want to do any kind of meaningful research these days, and you're going to need a geek."

"Why Jacob Ness?"

"Local case. Received a lot of coverage when you were recovered." He pauses slightly and I can tell he's trying to figure out if he should've used such clinical terms. Then he shrugs. It is what is, and we both know it.

"But Jacob's crime is known," I say. "Well documented. Where's the riddle?"

Keith cocks his head to the side. "Do you really call him Jacob?"

"I just did."

"When you were together?"

"Well, 'Rat Bastard' had a tendency to earn me negative consequences."

"You still think about him."

"You're the expert, you tell me."

He shakes his head. "I only know the perpetrators. I don't know . . ."

"Me? Other survivors? The ones who, unlike your cousin, got away?" My words are harsh. Unnecessarily so. I can't seem to help myself. I still can't figure out if this guy is for real. Successful computer analyst by day, brilliant true-crime solver by night. Or something darker, more sinister. Does he study predators because he wants to stop them, or because like always calls to like?

Across from me, Keith has carefully reset his features. He taps his steepled fingertips against his chin, once, twice. Then: "I think Jacob Ness remains an unsolved riddle. I think we know about *a* crime—his abduction of you. But the sophistication of his operation, the box, the sensory deprivation, the brainwashing techniques—"

"I don't need a recap."

"You couldn't have been his first victim. These guys, by definition, they escalate. They build to the kind of premeditated, well-planned, sustainable operation that was your abduction."

"The FBI looked into it. I'm told they couldn't find evidence of other crimes."

Keith regards me intently. "That's not correct, strictly speaking. They found other evidence. Just not enough to build additional cases."

I can't speak. I study my water glass again. I get the distinction he's making. After all my years with Samuel, I know how the FBI thinks. Of course they would make a distinction, and Samuel would split those hairs in delivering that news to me. *We aren't looking at additional cases at this time.* Not because there wasn't any evidence. Just not *enough.*

I can't look at Keith. "How many?" My voice is quiet.

"The group . . . We have been looking at six unsolved missing persons cases. All young women. None of them ever seen again. All during the time Jacob had his truck route in the South. We've been trying to see if we can establish a firm connection. For three of the women, we have been able to place Jacob in the same town as them at the time of their disappearance. The police, of course, want more."

I inhale. Exhale. Six women. I'm waiting for the news to surprise me, but it doesn't. I've always known I couldn't have been Jacob's first. He talked about at least assaulting others. But had he actually kidnapped them? Eventually killed them? I hadn't allowed myself to consider it. That maybe there had been others in the coffin-sized box before me.

"The police would have forensic evidence," I say at last. "From his rig. He had a special compartment. They could study it for DNA."

"The police recovered multiple strands of hair and fibers, as well as additional DNA evidence from Jacob's truck. Most of it, however, was connected to various prostitutes, including two that were murdered in Florida. Gutted after walking off with a beautiful young woman."

I don't say a word.

"With dark hair," he adds.

I still say nothing.

"But there's also evidence that the box where he held you in the truck was new. A recent insert, probably prepared especially for you. Meaning . . ."

"He could've had other inserts for previous girls."

"In your statement, you talked about being held in a basement of some cabin in Georgia. Jacob told you he had to vacate it because the owner died, so he allowed you to join him in his truck."

I shrug. I know this already.

"The police have never been able to locate the cabin. Which is stranger than you might think. While the mountains of Georgia are vast, the number of cabins whose owners died the year you were abducted isn't that big. From there, it's simply a matter of visiting the local community, floating pictures of Jacob and his vehicle, as well as checking Jacob's financials for gas receipts—anything. The FBI should've found a connection between him and one of the towns or cabins easily enough. But they didn't. Haven't. Ever."

I frown. Rub my right thumb along the water glass's condensation. "You think I was wrong? I lied to the police?"

"Actually, I think Jacob lied. To you. He wanted to keep your initial location secret. Even from you. That way, if you did escape, you couldn't give it away."

"His lair," I say the words softly. "That cabin. It was his monster's lair, and he didn't want to give it up."

"I think if we could find it, we'd learn a lot more about Jacob Ness. Maybe even find a link to the other missing girls."

"He's dead. If he did own such a cabin, it would've gone on the auction block by now. Foreclosure, repossessed by the IRS, whatever."

"I tried that. The property can't be in Jacob's name, or listed under any of his known associates because, again, the FBI would've found it already. So periodically, I run a list of all properties up for auction in northern Georgia, with a basement. Unfortunately, that list is longer than I'd like."

"You're serious about this."

"Yes."

"You've been working these other missing girls' cases, for what, six years already?"

"Samantha Mathers, Elaine Waters, Lilah Abenito, Daphne Passero, Rachel Englert, Brenda Solomon."

"Do the police assist you?"

A small pause. "Officially, no. But some of the group's members . . . have connections."

"With the FBI?"

"Not as good as yours," he says bluntly.

"And this is why you wanted to talk to me?"

"Not necessarily. You're a victim. We're the hunters. We don't expect—"

I hold up a hand. "Never call me a victim again. I'm a survivor. There's a difference."

He nods.

"I killed him," I say shortly. The words are hot and fierce. I won't take them back. "Does your group know that?"

"Yes."

"Do you blame me? If I'd let him live, you'd have your answers. These missing girls, their families, they'd have closure."

"Did you ever hear Jacob talk about other girls?"

"Specifically, no. But he was a sex addict, wife beater, and serial rapist. I already knew I wasn't his first. But I assumed that I was the first he'd taken such great lengths to keep."

"Why?"

"Fuck you."

Keith falls silent again.

I can't take it. I'm too agitated. I smack the glass of water on the coffee table. I like the sharp sounds it makes, as brittle as I feel. Water rings. I can already see them forming, and watch as Keith glances helplessly at the growing mess on his precious, shiny table. It gives me a perverse pleasure. Then I'm up, moving, walking, wishing I could shed my own skin.

I don't want to be me anymore. Not today. Not seven years ago. Never every single moment of the four hundred and seventy-two days Jacob kept me his prisoner. I hate to think of him. I loathe remembering what it was like to feel so helpless, so weak.

But I'm further disoriented to be here, in this place, with this man. Somewhere in the back of my mind, I get it. In this room, the two Floras collide.

The teenage girl I used to be. The beautiful blonde who could make any boy look twice. That Flora would've been impressed by Keith Edgar. His dark good looks, a swanky Boston town house. She would've been scintillated to hear of his murdered cousin, his heroic cause to catch other killers out there. She would've been thinking about kissing him.

Then there's the woman I am. Who looks at a handsome, charming man and thinks instantly of Ted Bundy. Who is too skinny and too hard and too tired after seven years without a single good night's sleep. Who doesn't think about dating, or men, or kissing . . . anyone.

I don't have romantic dreams or aspirations anymore. Some survivors do. They figure out how to compartmentalize, that was then, this is now. I can't. I live in a state of lockdown. I spent so long separating my mind from my body in order to survive another day, I can't get it back. My body is merely a tool. Jacob used it for sex. I use it for revenge. Neither of us respects the package.

And now I don't want to be here. I don't want to talk to Keith Edgar. I don't want to think of other missing girls. Whom Jacob might have kidnapped and held in his big rig. Did he keep some longer than me? Did he enjoy their company more? Dear God, is it possible to be jealous of such a thing?

"Flora?" Keith asks quietly. He hasn't moved.

"Did Jacob have a partner?" I say. "In your research, is there any evidence he knew other predators, maybe connected with them online?"

"I'm not sure."

"What does that *mean*?"

"It means I'm not the FBI. I don't have access to his laptop the way they do. Jacob was a loner. Yet, the amount he traveled, his ability to so completely cover his tracks . . . I wouldn't be surprised if he had some friends, associates helping him out. Why are you here, Flora? Why are you asking these questions now?"

"You said you don't have access to the FBI."

"No."

I finally look at him. "I do."

He regards me evenly. "Why here, why now?" he repeats. "What happened?"

"I need to know everything about Jacob Ness before I met him. Help me answer those questions, and eventually, I'll answer yours."

He doesn't even blink. "When do you want to start?"

"Right now. Get your computer. We're going to make a call."

CHAPTER 13

EVIE

WHAT IS THE PERFECT MARRIAGE? When I first met Conrad, I felt like acceptance was the key. I was at a fellow teacher's cookout. A rare public venture, since even back then my past followed me everywhere. But it was May, a beautiful sunny day after another long Boston winter, and I wanted one afternoon of feeling like everyone else. So I showed up, a young teacher, hanging out, eating slightly charred chicken in a colleague's backyard.

I heard his laugh. That's what caught my attention first. Booming. Natural. Unencumbered. In my family, my parents' house . . . I don't remember ever hearing anyone laugh like that.

Conrad was standing in the corner near the fence, sweaty beer in hand, ketchup stain on a blue Hawaiian shirt. He was clearly holding court, regaling the gathering throng. So I drifted closer, still on the outskirts, but listening now.

Windows. He was telling stories of windows. Of five-by-three windows that arrived being fifteen inches by thirteen inches, and custom creams that showed up pine green, which he was then informed was merely a darker shade of cream, and even better the order he placed for a fancy home in Barrington, Rhode Island, that the factory claimed it couldn't deliver because Rhode Island wasn't a state—surely he meant Long Island instead.

More laughter. More swigs of beers. More stories from the road.

I don't know how long I stood off to the side before he noticed me. He glanced over once or twice, taking in the crowd, but surely not zeroing in on a slim woman with dirty-blond hair, still nursing her first beer, which was more of a placeholder than a beverage.

Then, suddenly, he stood before me. The crowd had disappeared and the man himself had appeared. Up close, he was compact, muscularly built, with light brown hair and deep blue eyes. His features were tan, and when he smiled his teeth were a flash of white against his sun-darkened skin.

He looked . . . strong and capable and funny and honest and like all my hopes and dreams rolled up into one package.

Then he shook my hand. Reached over and simply took it, and the feel of his calloused fingers against my skin . . .

I wanted him right then. In a way I'd already taught myself never to want anything. I didn't move. I didn't smile hello. I didn't offer my name. But it didn't matter. He did the talking for both of us. He did the laughing for both of us. Later, he asked for a walk around the block, just so we could get to know each other, and he asked me so many questions, that I found myself answering.

None of my answers fazed him. Not my job as a math teacher (*great, a woman with brains!*), not my legendary father (*that must be interesting, I don't have any family left*), and not what had happened one day when I was sixteen, that still left me gutted and reeling and untethered to real life (*I'm so sorry, I lost both my parents several years ago; you never get over the loss*).

By the time we hit the end of the street and were headed back, I was hooked. I wanted the boom of his laugh, the brightness of his company, the way he looked at me, truly looked at me. As if nothing I could do or say would shock him. Or make him not want me.

That's who I fell in love with in the beginning. A guy who seemed to accept me, unconditionally.

It wasn't until later that I realized that Conrad was also the kind of guy who seemed to get everyone. Strangers gravitated toward him in a crowded bar. Neighbors lingered just to talk to him.

It was his superpower, what made him so good at his job, traveling to job sites, speccing out high-end windows, soothing irate customers.

Everyone loved Conrad. Everyone felt heard and understood and acknowledged by him.

Yet how well did any of us know him? A guy who logged so many hours on the road with little or no accountability? A guy with no family to visit and tell stories about his younger years?

A guy who did all the talking but never really told you anything about himself.

Then there was the locked door.

Innocent enough. I ran out of packing tape in the kitchen. Walked up to Conrad's office, thinking he'd have a fresh roll. He was traveling, his office door shut. No biggie, I thought. I went to turn the knob only to discover that I couldn't.

Confusion. A locked door in my own house? Followed shortly by disbelief. Why would Conrad even bother? There was only me hanging around and it's not like a custom window business involved state secrets. Followed shortly by . . . curiosity.

A locked door is a puzzle. And no self-respecting mathematician can walk away from a puzzle.

It became a game for me. Every time the door was closed, to wander by, test it. Conrad watching TV downstairs at night. Door unlocked. Gone for an afternoon meeting. Locked. Business trips, definitely locked. Two A.M. when I got up just because I had to know, locked again.

I never said a word, of course. That would imply that I didn't trust him—wouldn't it?

Anyway, I grew up with a mom who regularly manipulated reality to best suit her needs. I didn't want to be told an answer. I wanted to learn it for myself.

So I did what any dysfunctional adult who is accustomed to chronic lies would do: I waited till my husband's next business trip; then I picked the lock to his private office.

My hand shook when I first cracked open the door. My heart was pounding. I felt like Bluebeard's wife, stepping into the very room she'd been warned about. The next thing I would see would be the hanging corpses of past wives.

I discovered file cabinets. Stacks of window catalogues. A printer/scanner. And a cleared spot on the desk where Conrad's laptop usually lived. I went through the files. Once you've committed B and E you can't just walk away. I found project files, various blueprints for homes up and down the East Coast. I found vendor files, handwritten notes on upcoming product changes, and new and improved color options.

In the end, I got on my hands and knees. I searched for documents taped under the desk, files slipped behind the cabinets, maybe even a computer code stamped to the bottom of the executive leather chair. I felt crazed. A woman having an out-of-body experience. It struck me that this was exactly what my mother would do. My poor husband was simply in the habit of locking up, and here I was, turning it into sordid drama.

Why couldn't I simply trust him? Or was it me I didn't trust? Did I figure that anyone who loved me the way he loved me had to have something wrong with him?

I crawled around the office on my hands and knees. I went through every single scrap of paper. If Conrad hadn't been out of town, if he'd returned home early, there's no way I would've been able to justify my behavior, the total gutting of his neat and almost hyperorganized professional space.

Except I'm a mathematician, raised by one of the world's best intellects. And part of brilliance isn't just solving a problem; it's seeing a problem no one else realizes is a problem yet.

A locked room, in the privacy of a man's own home, containing only files and not even a computer . . . Why? Why lock it at all?

A puzzle. I needed the solution.

Then I saw the lone piece of semivaluable equipment. The printer/scanner. With a memory cache.

I fell in love with Conrad for his loud laugh, his smile, his personality. And, no, I didn't find any bodies of murdered wives that day. But in the end, I did find a bread crumb. An image of a scanned document, a record of a bank account that I never knew existed.

Not a crime. Not even anything I could mention without having to reveal how I discovered it. But a piece of a puzzle.

Which, of course, I churned and worried and worked. Until I waited for him to go on trips, just so I could once more rip apart his space. Except then he started regarding me through narrowed eyes upon his return, probably because I didn't put everything back perfectly, so he knew something was off even if he didn't quite know what.

I started taking pictures. Of exactly how the office looked upon entry, so I could carefully replace each item. Then, when he still seemed unsettled, I started checking the doorway for tricks I read about online—a piece of hair positioned across the doorway, which would be broken upon entry. Easy enough to replace with one of my own upon exiting. Or lint positioned just so on top of a slightly skewed open drawer. Which I photographed and returned to its exact location.

A duel of sorts. Months, years. A period of strain followed by a period of shame when I swore to myself I'd stop this madness. Conrad was a good guy. Conrad loved me. If he had financials that were his own, frankly, so did I. That made us independent adults, not government spies or nefarious criminals.

But eventually I would break again. And back into the office I would go, tearing apart my marriage in search of answers to a question I couldn't even ask.

What is the perfect marriage? Acceptance, I had thought. But I'd assumed it would be my husband's acceptance of me. I'd never stopped to consider that maybe I'd prove incapable of accepting him. That maybe my mother, via the lie that had become my adult life, had warped me even more than I'd understood.

You can't sneak around in a marriage forever. Sooner or later, no matter how careful you are, you're going to get caught. Yet I couldn't stop. It's almost as if I wanted Conrad to figure out what I was doing. I needed our marriage to fall apart.

Except, suddenly, two made three.

Then my mistakes truly came back to haunt me.

I DON'T KNOW what to do. I can't go outside. Even this late at night, the media vans remain a solid wall of high-powered lights parked just across the street. I'm too keyed up for sleep, my brain jumping between images of Conrad's blood-spattered body and our home's burnt-out shell. I should rest for the baby's sake. I should flee my mother's house for my sake. I should do . . . something.

But I don't know what. Sixteen years ago, confronted by a similar tragedy, I'd simply done what I was told and taken the blame. Now?

I hate the lingering sense of déjà vu. And worse, the feeling of once more being helpless.

I hadn't lied to the detective. I still don't know what happened to my father. One moment, I had a dad, my hero, my rock, the man I could always count on. Then he was dead. Just like that.

My mom's response upon entering the kitchen . . . it wasn't horror; it was outrage mixed with hysteria. That he'd gone and died? Or that he'd gone and killed himself, which is what I've always wondered. At sixteen, shell-shocked and traumatized, I'd never thought to question my mom. If she said we needed to keep what happened between us, then we needed to keep it between us. Denial was what my mother did best.

I followed her lead that afternoon. It wasn't hard. A terrible tragedy had occurred. In my own mind, it was easy enough to substitute myself with the shotgun, maybe even easier than contemplating my beloved father positioning the gun beneath his ribs. Standing grimly in front of the refrigerator, which offered the safest backdrop for gunfire (when cleaning the shotgun, he'd instructed, always aim it at the stainless steel appliance). Then, upon hearing the crunch of my mother's car tires in the driveway, pulling the trigger.

No, it was so much easier to lie than to picture any of that.

For all my father's brilliance, I'd seen the dark shadows that lurked in his eyes. The way he sometimes smiled but still appeared sad. The times he squared his shoulders before walking into his office, appearing less like a gifted mathematician off in search of answers and more like a soldier burdened by a never-ending war.

The truth is, genius and depression have always gone hand in hand. Which was why I spent so many afternoons, sitting at the piano, playing and playing, because my father said my music soothed his spirit and allowed him to rest in a way a truly great mind could never completely be at ease. I did my best to music the sadness out of him.

And that day, walking into the kitchen, my father's hot blood dripping down into my hair, I felt the weight of my failure. That I had loved this man so much, and tried so hard, and it still wasn't enough.

Just like Conrad.

I hope my baby isn't a boy, I think now. Because I just couldn't take another such loss.

I SHOULD MARSHAL my resources, I decide. Money. I'm going to need some. Which is the first time I realize how lost I truly am. My wallet, cell phone, car keys, had all been in the house—which, according to the detectives, is now nothing more than a pile of charred ruins. I have a moment of growing hysteria: Next time you're arrested for the murder of your husband, grab your purse!

But of course, I hadn't, and the police certainly hadn't offered to fetch anything. Meaning I have . . . nothing.

Not completely true. I have a head for figures. Including bank accounts. Just because I don't possess a checkbook or debit card, let alone an unmelted driver's license, doesn't mean I don't know my accounts and their exact balances. The savings account has some money. Not a lot, as neither Conrad nor I had high-paying jobs and it seemed like most of our checks were spent on home renovations.

Then again . . .

My head starts spinning. Suddenly, I'm thinking about a lot of things. Including scraps of documents in a printer/scanner. Conrad's news upon learning we were pregnant. Other forms of photo ID.

The house was burned to the ground. Including Conrad's precious office and all his customer files.

But some things he valued even more than his office. Some things he had made fireproof.

I am not helpless, I tell myself. I'm damaged and incredibly sad. But I'm not helpless.

And now, with a little help from my lawyer, I have a plan.

CHAPTER 14

D.D.

"I THINK I MIGHT HAVE screwed up an investigation."

"You? Never."

It was after nine P.M. Jack nestled in for the night in his red race-car bed, Kiko curled up at his side and taking up nearly as much of the mattress as the boy. Alex had poured himself and D.D. both well-deserved glasses of wine. They sat side by side on the sofa, engaging in their own nightly ritual of catching up and winding down.

"So I'm investigating a pregnant woman who's accused of murdering her husband last night, and who also confessed to accidentally shooting her father with a shotgun sixteen years ago."

"I remember. You handled the father's shooting."

"Exactly. And I believed her. Bought her story, her mom's story, the whole kit and caboodle. This afternoon, she informed me she'd lied."

Alex paused, wineglass halfway to his lips. "Interesting defense strategy."

"According to her revised statement, she and her mother weren't even home at the time of the shooting but must've walked in moments later. The spatter in Evie's hair and clothing was from blood dripping down when she walked through the door. The GSR from her picking up the shotgun."

"Okay. But given that scenario, why confess?"

"Her mother didn't want to risk an investigation that might result in findings that would tarnish her father's intellectual legacy."

It didn't take Alex long. "Suicide. She assumed her husband had shot himself."

D.D. nodded. Took a sip of her own wine. She waited. She did her best thinking out loud. Alex, on the other hand, had a tendency to compose himself. Then, a true teacher, deliver his lecture.

"Suicide by shotgun happens," he said now. "Generally the end of the barrel is positioned under the chin or against the ribs, pressed against the skin in order to help stabilize the long gun while the victim reaches down for the trigger. Though I did read about an enterprising young man who used his toes to pull the trigger. Then there's the Australian case of the triple-shot suicide, where the victim's first attempt ended up being clean through the chest cavity, missing major organs. Then he set up for under the chin but flinched upon pulling the trigger—which happens more than you think—destroying half his jaw, but again, not incapacitating himself. I don't remember his third choice—maybe that was the same guy who finally sat down and used his toes—but the third shot got it done. Now, from an investigative perspective, can you imagine walking into a scene of a man hit by three shotgun blasts and thinking even for a second that it was suicide? In our jobs, anything is possible."

D.D. gave him her best scowl. "I don't want theoretical. I need practical. I'm drowning here in half lies, past assumptions, and a family with a whole new brand of crazy. I think Phil is actually scared of the mom. Probably for good reason."

"Interesting. I like it. And you know you do, too."

She rolled her eyes. Another sip of wine for them both. Then Alex set down his glass on the coffee table and grew serious.

"All right. Let's take it back to the evidence."

"By all means."

"I'm assuming a pump-action shotgun?"

"Yes."

"Contact point?"

"The chest. Evie's official statement was that she'd picked up the shotgun, was trying to figure out how to clear the chamber when it went off mere inches from her father's torso."

"Okay. We can work with that. So the issue with suicide by long gun is trigger access; it's a reach to get it. Given that, like I said, most victims balance the tip of the barrel against their own bodies to help hold it in place. In a head shot, the most common contact point is the underside of the chin. In a chest shot, the ME should have evidence of a contact burn—against the ribs, if not right below the rib cage."

"I'll pull that report."

"Just to play devil's advocate—victims sometimes recoil as they're pulling the trigger, flinching away from the barrel. In which case, you'll get soot markings on the skin, versus an actual sear pattern. Soot means the barrel of the shotgun was held between three-quarters of an inch and a foot from the skin. Unfortunately in your case, such stipling could still go either way, as the girl testified she was standing just inches from her father, right?"

"So searing means the gun was definitely pressed against him—contradicting her statement. Soot means it still could've been suicide but he flinched, or that indeed she shot him from a close distance. I'm going to need more wine for this."

"Ah, but now we need to factor in trajectory. One hallmark of a suicide with a long gun is that there's nearly always a sharply angled trajectory, the bullet having tracked up, with the entrance wound distinctly lower than the exit wound. Think of trying to hold out a loaded shotgun level in front of you with one hand and pull the trigger with the other. It can't be done naturally. I mean maybe if the butt of the weapon was wedged against a wall or some other object, or some machination was in place to hold the barrel level, but you have no sign of that, right?"

"He went down in front of the refrigerator, open space in front of him."

"Toppled chair, by any chance?"

D.D. had to think about it, then shook her head. "I honestly don't remember. I've put in a request to pull the old file, which should have photos."

"If you are thinking suicide, one scenario is that he positioned the butt of the gun on a kitchen chair, placed the tip of the barrel against his torso, and pulled the trigger. Depending on how tall he was—"

"Six feet."

"Then you're still going to have a fairly angled trajectory versus the daughter's scenario, where she's holding the gun up, messing with the chamber, and accidentally pulls the trigger, shooting her father square in the torso."

"Okay."

"Which brings us to the last point of consideration: directionality of spatter."

"Ah yes, what would an evening in our house be without a discussion of spatter?"

Alex picked up his wineglass, clinked it against hers.

"There can be blowback from shooting directly into a torso. But the directionality of that spatter on skin and clothes is not at all the same as what might happen from the suicide scenario, when again, the force of the blast is going to be up and out of the body, distributing a pattern higher up on the wall behind the victim, possibly even on the ceiling."

"She said it dripped down on her when she walked into the room. She could feel the heat of it."

Alex's face was serious. "Wouldn't be the first time. But again, the two scenarios—her shooting her father from mere inches away square in the chest, and her walking in after he's fired an upward shot through his chest cavity—lead to very different blood evidence. Very different."

"So review the photos, and whatever spatter evidence we still have from the scene."

Alex nodded.

"Okay. Got it. Thank you."

"There is a third possibility, you know."

D.D. sighed heavily. Because in this case, why not? "Which is?"

"There is searing on his skin, the trajectory is a steep angle passing through his torso, and the blood pattern from the blast is up and out."

"I thought that meant it was suicide."

"Or someone placed the barrel against his chest and pulled the trigger from a position beneath him. Forensics gives us position and angle, but it still can't tell us everything that might have led up to such a scenario."

D.D. eyed her husband. "As in, there could be other possibilities. Say, a struggle. Two people vying for the shotgun. Other person got it first. Hopkins stood up, tried to step back. Second person jammed the shotgun into his ribs and pulled the trigger. Self-defense. Or possibly murder. Wait a minute! I've lived with you long enough. In that scenario, we'd have a void in the spatter evidence, basically a blank spot where the shooter stood, got hit with blowback, and then exited out the door, removing that piece of the puzzle."

"But didn't you say the girl and her mom walked in right afterwards? Picked up the gun, mostly likely rushed to the body, even fell to their knees beside it?"

"Contaminated the scene," D.D. finished for him.

"I have a feeling your crime scene photos aren't going to be as revealing as you'd like."

"So I'm back where I started. Sixteen-year-old shooting death that could be either suicide or murder."

Alex shrugged. "It can always be murder, D.D. Where would our jobs be without it?"

CHAPTER 15

FLORA

"SSA KIMBERLY QUINCY."

"Hi, um . . . This is Flora Dane."

There's a pause. I'm not surprised. What does catch me off guard is the sound of my own voice, shaky and faint. SSA Quincy and I are hardly BFFs. She organized the raid that eventually led to Jacob's death and my escape. But we haven't exactly spoken since.

Sitting across from me, Keith eyes me uncertainly. Nine P.M., I've just called a federal agent on her personal cell, and she isn't exactly responding with gushing enthusiasm. But I know how these things work. The raid on Jacob's motel room didn't just save me; it also boosted Quincy's career. One way or another, our lives are intertwined. I also know from Samuel that Bureau types don't exactly keep regular hours. This isn't the SSA's first late-night call, just her most unexpected.

"How can I help you, Flora?" Quincy's voice is perfectly neutral. Apparently, she's decided to give me enough rope to hang myself. Fair enough.

Now it's my turn to collect my thoughts. Keith sits up straighter. He has his fingers poised over the keyboard of his laptop as if he's ready to record every word of the call. Maybe he is.

"I need information on Jacob Ness," I finally announce.

"I see."

"It's come to my attention he might be a person of interest in some other missing persons cases."

Another pause. "Flora, it's nine P.M. You're calling me at home. You're going to have to do better than sudden interest in a bunch of cold cases."

"So you *do* think he's connected to other missing women?"

"You have till the count of three, then I'm going to hang up. Future requests can go through official channels. One, two—"

"There's been a development!" I get it out in a rush. "A murder. Here in Boston. I recognized the victim. He met Jacob in a bar. It wasn't random. They knew each other."

Keith's eyes widen. I hadn't told him this part yet, but he doesn't make the mistake of gasping audibly or distracting from the call.

This time, the quiet on the other end of the phone is thoughtful. "Name of the murder victim?" SSA Quincy asks finally.

It occurs to me that Sergeant Warren is probably going to kill me. I decide it's a small price to pay. "Conrad Carter. Now I have questions of my own."

"Of course." Quincy's tone is droll.

"Do you think Jacob kidnapped other women?"

For the first time, there is no hesitation. "Yes."

"Murdered them?"

"Yes."

"How many?"

Cool tone again: "The investigation is ongoing."

"Maybe I can help."

"Can you? Because you never have before."

I wince, the effects of my onetime, one-telling policy coming back to bite me in the ass. She's right. I'd declined all official requests for interviews, debriefing, whatever the agents chose to call it back in the day. I gave my statement to Samuel while still collapsed in a hospital bed. I watched him run off to vomit. Then I never spoke of it again.

"I want to help."

"Does Dr. Keynes know?" SSA Quincy is a clever one.

"Do you know what I do now?" I ask the agent.

"No."

"I work with other survivors. Run a support group of sorts. I'm not qualified, I'm not brilliant, but I am experienced. I teach others to stop surviving and start living again."

SSA Quincy doesn't say anything. Neither does Keith. His fingers are still waiting above the keyboard. He wants details, I realize, not pleasantries.

"I understand I'm late to the party," I say at last. "That by not giving a statement earlier, maybe there were other victims of Jacob's or their families that I've let down. Samuel tells me not to second-guess, but it has been six years. I like to think I'm not the same girl anymore. I like to think . . . I'm stronger now. I want to do better. I can do better."

"I can be on a plane to Boston first thing in the morning," Quincy says.

"I have questions now. Information I need right now."

"Flora, it's late—"

"You really think I sleep at night? You think I care about rest at *all* anymore?" My voice turns hard. Quincy doesn't hang up the phone.

"There has to be quid pro quo," she begins. "Otherwise known as you gotta pay to play. Official department policy."

"I already paid. Conrad Carter. Shot Tuesday night by his wife in Boston. Look it up. Lead detective Sergeant D. D. Warren."

"D. D. Warren?" I can tell by the change in Quincy's voice that she knows the name. "Does she know you're calling me?"

"Not yet. But I'm also her CI, so if she decides on bodily harm, at least she'll feel conflicted about it."

Across from me, Keith's eyes are growing rounder and rounder.

"I want to know what was on Jacob's computer." I plunge ahead. There's no stopping now. "Did you find evidence of e-mail correspondence, chat-room visits, online associates? He spent a lot of time on his computer. In real life, he was a loner. I already know that. But on the internet . . . Some predators network. I know that, too."

Keith is nodding softly, leaning closer to his laptop. Both of us eye the phone positioned on the table between us. This is the heart of the conversation. I paid. Now, would SSA Quincy play?

"Yes and no," she says at last.

My shoulders sag. Keith rolls his eyes. We share an immediate and unplanned moment: feds. Good God.

Then, as if she could see our exasperation: "Ness's computer was curiously clean."

"What does that mean?"

"We know he took photos and videos; we have the images he sent to your mother."

I nod. Keith starts to type.

"But his laptop was clear. Not a single copy existed. And wiping a hard drive is no easy task. Most experienced computer techs can rebuild anything these days. Find ghost images, piece together fragments of a fragment. So how did a long-haul trucker with only a high school–level education know how to clear his entire hard drive?"

Keith opens his mouth. I immediately hold up a hand to silence him, vigorously shaking my head. I probably should've mentioned his presence in the very beginning of the call. Having failed that, I wasn't about to spook a federal agent by mentioning we had company now.

"You think someone must've taught him how to cover his tracks," I say.

Keith is scribbling furiously. He holds up a note.

I continue: "Maybe even told him about particular apps that would assist in clearing his hard drive."

Keith nods.

"What did this Conrad Carter do?" Quincy asks.

"I don't know. He traveled. Spent time in the South, I know that."

"Where did you meet him?"

"A bar. Honky-tonk. He sat down right beside us. After a bit . . . I had the impression Conrad was there for me. Like, maybe Jacob had made a deal with him."

Keith starts typing.

"Did you leave with him?" SSA Quincy asks.

"No. I threw up on him. Then he went away."

There's silence. Keith is no longer typing. I refuse to look at him. I don't want to see what's in his eyes.

"Were there other such instances?" Quincy asks. "Other meetings with other men?"

"No. But soon after that . . . I realized I'd never make it if I kept fighting." I stare at nothing in particular. "I decided to become Jacob's friend. Make him need me a little, as my entire existence depended on him."

"You survived, Flora. That's what matters. You picked a strategy and it enabled you to come home safe to your family."

I smile; I can't help myself. But I know it's a sad expression, because both my mother and brother will tell you that I didn't come home at all. They just got a shell that looks like their beloved daughter and sister, except there's nothing left on the inside.

Keith is scribbling another note. He holds it out to me. I read his question to the agent. "When was the last time the computer was analyzed?"

"Six years ago."

I glance at Keith, already anticipating his next point. "There have been advancements in computer forensics since then," I say.

He nods vigorously.

"Given the new development, I could have the computer reexamined. Did Jacob strike you as techie?"

"No. But—" I catch myself. "He was clever. And mechanical. I mean, he could keep his rig running on his own. And you know, building the pine coffin and all. He prided himself on self-sufficiency. I can't imagine him in a classroom environment. But pursuing something that would help him get something he wanted, yeah, he'd do that."

"He still would've had to utilize resources," Quincy states. "We never recovered any books on computers, web surfing, or programming one-oh-one from his vehicle. On the other hand, he only made contact with your mother through internet cafés, which reveals a certain level of sophistication right there. He knew better than to use his own laptop, which we might have eventually been able to trace back to him via IP address, et cetera."

"You never found the cabin in Georgia."

"We've never found anything resembling a permanent residence for Jacob Ness."

"His lair," I murmur. "What about his mother?"

"He used her address for mail. According to her, she hadn't seen him in years. We did a full sweep of that house, mostly recovering clothing and porn."

"There should've been porn on his computer. He was always watching porn."

"We found DVDs in the front cab; nothing on the computer. Not even a history of porn-site visits or searches."

"That's not right. The guy was a sex addict. His computer should've been ninety percent smut."

Across from me, Keith is nodding. Predator one-oh-one, no level of murder or assault is ever enough for them. They all have to feed their appetites in between, even the ones who travel around the country with their own girls stashed in coffin-sized boxes.

"I'm going to get on a plane in the morning," Quincy says.

I nod, then realize she can't see me. "Okay."

"I want to know everything about Conrad Carter."

"Be sure to use your nice voice," I offer weakly, already picturing D.D.'s face when the federal agent shows up at HQ. Maybe I should warn her in advance. Or call Samuel and beg for safe harbor.

"I'm going to use my bright, shiny federal shield."

Yep, I'm a dead woman. "I want information on the other missing women," I say, because as long as my time on this earth is limited . . .

Keith nods adamantly.

"Flora—"

"I have more to offer."

"Than embroiling me in a pissing match against one of BPD's toughest detectives?"

"I want to find his lair. We need it. If we could find it, think of the evidence."

My voice is soft but certain. Keith regards me curiously. I can't decide if he thinks I'm incredibly brave or truly self-destructive. Quincy must think the same because she doesn't answer for a long time.

"We already checked for cabins in Georgia whose owners died the year you were abducted. We didn't have any luck," she says at last.

"Maybe it wasn't Georgia. Maybe the owner didn't die. Maybe he lied to me, another layer of protection in case I did manage to escape. I mean, if we're now saying Jacob was clever enough to wipe his laptop, what's a few lies to a girl he has locked in a box?"

Again the silence. Then, because I can't help myself: "Was there other forensic evidence in the box? Of, you know, of other girls?"

"We think he built the box for you."

There's something in the way she says it that catches my attention. "But it wasn't his first box," I fill in slowly. "There were others, for . . . other girls."

"An UNSUB doesn't achieve Ness's level of organization and sophistication overnight."

Which is nothing new. Keith had already told me the same. But it's starting to hit me now. Truly register. I might've been Jacob's last girl. Maybe his longest-surviving girl. But there had been others. Ones who, most likely, had been fed to the gators. Ones who'd screamed and begged and still never made it home. Maybe they'd each slivered their fingers on the crudely bored air holes, then sucked their own blood to have something to do. Maybe they'd recited their favorite stories, the names of their childhood pets. Maybe they'd promised anything, everything, if they could just see their mom, brother, boyfriend, ever again.

Except it never happened.

And I'd failed them. Me, the one who did survive. I killed Jacob Ness. I put a gun to his head and pulled the trigger because it had to be done. Then I came home to my family and left all those poor girls behind. Never asked any questions. Never provided any answers. Simply abandoned them, faceless victims whose bones were moldering God knows where, whose own loved ones would never have the closure at least my mom and brother got.

I don't feel guilty. I feel ashamed. I can't look at Keith anymore, because I don't want him to see my eyes filling with tears.

"There are memory techniques," Quincy says at last.

"I know."

"Dr. Keynes," she begins.

"He'll help us," I answer for him.

"And if he recommends against it?"

"He won't. I'm a survivor. Survivors are tough. If I could endure the real thing, then I can handle the memories."

"I'll be on the first flight in the morning," Quincy says.

I nod. A tear splatters down onto the screen of the smartphone. Keith doesn't touch me. But he does reach over and gently wipe the moisture away.

I end the call.

CHAPTER 16

EVIE

THE FIRST THING THAT HITS me when I get out of my lawyer's car is the smell. Charred wood, slightly smoky, and not unpleasant. It brings to mind Sunday afternoons cozied up before a nice fire, sipping tea, listening to the Pats game on TV.

I have to stand perfectly still before I can fully process that it's not a barbecue in front of me, but the remains of my home.

Mr. Delaney lets me be. He answered my call in the middle of the night without hesitation. No doubt used to odd hours, given his job as a defense attorney. And no doubt understanding that it took that long for me to finally be free from my mom, who had to complete her nightly martini ritual before turning in for bed.

It's seven thirty, the sky just starting to lighten given the short days this time of year. The temperature remains below freezing. We are both bundled up in wool coats, hats, and gloves. Half of my neighbors still have their Christmas lights on from the night before, twinkling borders around their roofs, windows, ornamental shrubs.

It gives the whole scene a surreal feel. *Merry Christmas! P.S. All that remains of your life is a charred shell of collapsing wreckage.*

Then the police arrive and it's time to get the party started.

Sergeant Warren climbs out of the car first, bundled up in a puffy blue down coat, embroidered BPD on the chest. She finishes wrapping a lighter blue scarf around her neck, then pulls on black leather gloves and a knitted hat. She still shivers slightly as she waits for the driver, a younger detective with a shock of red hair, to untangle himself from the front seat. He heads straight for the trunk, removes a rake and a shovel before pulling on a pair of heavy workman's gloves. Gotta love the Boston PD. Prepared for anything.

D.D. gives me a look, then heads for my lawyer. She addresses her opening comments to him, as if I'm nothing but a signpost. Posturing. As a high school teacher who spends my days working with teens, I'm unimpressed. She can only *pretend* I don't matter, whereas I have dozens of students who for months at a time honestly *believe* I don't. Till they fail their first test, of course.

"Your client understands that the terms of our initial search warrant still stand, meaning we have the legal right to seize any items relevant to the source of the fire, as well as any additional evidence the fire may have exposed relevant to the shooting which was missed the first time around," D.D. is rattling off.

Mr. Delaney's answer is equally crisp: "I've discussed the matter with my client. She understands that as owner of the property, she is entitled to anything that isn't considered evidence in the case. Furthermore, the police bear the burden of proving an item is evidence. Otherwise, it goes to her."

Mr. Delaney had walked me through it last night. I couldn't just return to my former residence and search for Conrad's firesafe filing box. The police would take exception and seize whatever I discovered as a matter of principle. So invite them over. Make a show of

cooperating fully with the authorities. They would open the SentrySafe box, but the contents should belong to me. Not like the ignition source of the arson fire was in the middle of a fire-resistant safe.

All I wanted was our financial records, including the copy of the
life insurance policy Conrad took out when he learned I was pregnant, as well as our homeowners' policy. The box also contained
our passports, which—in lieu of my now melted driver's license—I
could use as photo ID.

As I told myself last night, I might be sad, but I will not be helpless.
I have my unborn child to consider, and my crazy-as-a-fox mother to
outmaneuver.

The redheaded detective heads for the pile of charred wood, rake
in hand. D.D. refers to him as Neil. He looks like he's about twelve.
Maybe the police are recruiting straight out of elementary school
these days. I often thought about teaching the lower grades. My particular math skills, however, would be lost there. And for all my
moments of sheer exasperation with high schoolers, every semester I
have at least a few students whose potential comes to life. An equation that, for the first time, clicks for them. A test they thought
they'd failed only to find they'd earned the A they always knew they
could achieve.

You don't become a teacher without having some level of optimism. And you don't stay in the field if you don't believe that everyone, from bitter teens to burnt-out administrators, can change.

I used to think that was one of the things Conrad loved about me.

"Fire chief declared the scene safe," D.D. is saying now, taking up
position beside me. "Still"—D.D. gestures to my bulging waist—"I
would recommend you stay clear."

"The fumes?" I ask.

"A lot of nasty stuff burns up in any house fire."

I nod, well aware of the plastic pipes, glued laminates, cheap
stains, fiberglass insulation, and metal appliances that went into home

construction. Yesterday this scene would've been borderline toxic. Now . . . now it held the only hope I had of moving ahead.

"I smell gasoline," I comment.

D.D. eyes me. "So did the arson investigator."

I have to process this. "So someone killed my husband, then the next day, burned down our house?" My voice sounds surprisingly steady. Maybe because even as I say the words, I don't really believe them. Conrad and I . . . A schoolteacher and a window salesman. Surely, this couldn't have happened to us. This couldn't *be* us. "Do you know why?"

"I was hoping you could tell me."

"I didn't do this. I'm not just a wife, I'm a mother." I shake my head. "No mother would do this."

D.D. simply stares at me. I lapse back into silence, but I am shivering slightly. Standing in front of the decimated remains of my life is no longer just sad; it's scary. Because a person who would murder a man, burn down a house . . .

I don't know what happened. Worse, I don't know what will happen next.

The redhead has started working the piles of rubble, using the shovel to lift off charred pieces of sheetrock, collapsed two-by-fours. Mr. Delaney had told them what we were looking for: a fire-rated lockbox for personal papers. It'd been upstairs in our master closet. Given its weight, it had most likely crashed down as the fire devoured the floor from beneath it. The firemen hadn't discovered it yesterday—but then again, they hadn't really been worried about personal possessions.

"Arson investigator will be returning this morning," Sergeant Warren says now, still studying me. "Di Lucca is one of the best. Do you know arsonists generally stick to the same MO? That we have a whole database of local firebugs and their preferred methods? It's only a matter of time before Di Lucca identifies who did this." She pauses, leaving the end of her sentence implied. *And traces that person to you.*

"Why in the world would I arrange to burn down my own home, especially with my cell phone, purse, and all personal possessions inside?"

"People do stupid things."

"Then I must be a real idiot," I finally snap, "to burn down my own home after already being discovered holding the gun that killed my husband."

"Maybe you decided shooting the computer—what was it, twelve times?—wasn't enough."

Standing behind us, Mr. Delaney clears his throat. D.D. isn't supposed to be asking questions about the shooting, and she knows it. She's just trying to rattle me, see what she can shake loose.

"Maybe this isn't about me," I say finally. "Maybe this is about Conrad. All spouses have secrets. Just ask your husband."

The redhead finishes clearing one pile, moves on to the next waist-high collection of rubble. At least the house didn't have a basement, given the high water table in the area. Some of our neighbors did, and the constant flooding drove them insane. Conrad had liked this house particularly for its slab construction, plus the one-car garage. I had liked its cozy size, the charm of the hardwood floors, even if they'd been trashed at the time.

We'd been happy the day we signed the papers on this home. Bought a bottle of champagne, which I'd clutched to my chest as Conrad carried me over the threshold. I'd been laughing, demanding that he put me down. It all seemed so ridiculous and silly and . . . perfect. A great day for a young couple, with so many great days ahead.

D.D. is still watching me. I shouldn't get emotional in front of her. I shouldn't let her know that standing here right now, looking at the destroyed remains of so many dreams, hurts.

The redhead shouts her name. She gives me one last look, then jogs into the debris field toward her fellow detective.

I will have my papers soon enough, I think.

Except a heavy black SentrySafe is not what the redhead has discovered.

THIS LOCK BOX is thin. Maybe an inch tall with roughly the same dimensions as a pad of paper. At first glance, it looks like a tablet computer, which gives me an unsettling thought—I'd shot up a computer, but had I shot up *the* computer? I don't know anymore, and this isn't the time or place to wonder.

The outside of the box is covered in soot and charred along the edges. It doesn't appear heavy-duty enough for a fire-resistant or waterproof rating; then again, I don't recognize the box at all.

The redhead detective clutches it tightly against his stomach. I'd sent the detectives for a file cabinet. They'd discovered a small lock-box. All parties are equally confused—and equally suspicious.

D.D. starts the negotiations: "You got a key?"

"Of course not. I don't even have a fucking cell phone."

If the profanity bothers them, no one says anything. "The key was kept in the lock," I lie eventually. "Dig a layer deeper. You'll find it."

"Neil," D.D. orders, taking the box from him.

The twelve-year-old returns to the blackened debris field, rake in hand.

"You said you were looking for a fireproof safe," D.D. states shrewdly. "You know, like one of heavily reinforced boxes discovered in airplane wreckages."

I ignore her, keep my eyes on the redhead: where he's digging, his approximate location in the house . . . He's standing under Conrad's office, I determine. Which leads me to my next thought: all those wooden filing cabinets, chock-full of boring customer files. What if it wasn't the files that had mattered? What if beneath them had sat this flat, nondescript box?

I want to believe I would've seen it. On my many, many missions, working through the cabinets, shoving manila folder after manila folder aside in sheer frustration. Then again, a container this thin could've been tucked beneath one of the filing cabinets itself; I'd never thought to lift an entire thing. Given the size and weight of the broad, double-drawer units, I'm not even sure I could've. But Conrad, fit and muscular . . .

Would I have noticed the disruption? A slight change in positioning of the cabinet, a fresh scratch on the old hardwood? Or maybe I had, which is why I'd kept coming back. Because just like Conrad had sensed the disturbance in his locked office every time he returned, I'd also sensed something had changed every time I returned. And around and around we'd spun.

Secrets.

Had my husband ever loved me? Or had he married me because once he knew the true story behind my father's death, he'd assumed I would be the type to forgive and forget?

Shouting. The redhead Neil is now attacking a pile of rubble with renewed vigor, clearly having spotted something. Slowly but surely, I make out the compact shape of a fireproof safe. The filing box is not huge, but it is heavy as hell, as I can relate from personal experience. Dragging it out of the master closet was like dragging a boulder, only to stick in a few insurance docs, then—several deep breaths later—heave it back into place.

Neil tosses aside the rake and shovel. He's cleared the area around the box. Now he has both arms around it. Two or three staggering steps later, he's on the move, having to carefully navigate his way through the ruins with the bulky SentrySafe clutched against his chest.

As he approaches, I can tell the fireproof, waterproof safe has lived up to its heavily warrantied reputation. There's barely a scratch on it. In comparison to the flat metal lock box, the SentrySafe still has a key dangling from the front lock. The key is now black and singed, but a key is a key.

Neil drops the box on the driveway in front of us, breathing heavily. D.D. squats down beside it, also out of breath, but in her case, solely from anticipation.

"That looks like a file box," she says, gesturing to the SentrySafe. "So what's this other thing?" She has the charred lockbox at her feet.

"Overflow," I state without hesitation.

She gives me a look. I stare at her right back. This is what happens when you take the blame for your father's death at sixteen. After that, all mistruths are relative. I might have been honest once, even a Goody Two-shoes. But after what I saw, what happened next . . . Really, what's the point?

The SentrySafe has a key, so we start with it first. D.D. does the honors. Strictly speaking, anything recovered at the scene the BPD gets to inspect first, before passing it on to the rightful homeowner. I'm not nervous. I know this box. I've added to it many times. As the wife of a husband who traveled often, the business of personal finances and monthly paperwork was more my bailiwick than his. I'm grateful for that now. I'm not some helpless female who has suddenly lost her husband and has no idea how to hook up cable or find the life insurance policy.

Conrad was equally organized. His parents had died when he was in college, and though he never talked about it much, clearly he'd handled the estate. A family wasn't just a collection of love and well wishes. It was a physical asset to be protected and preserved. Auto insurance, homeowners' insurance, life insurance—he'd believed in all of it.

D.D. turns the key. It's one of those circular ones, distinct for safes. It takes a bit of jiggling, then gives. The lid of the box won't lift, however. The detective frowns, whacks the box, frowns some more. I finally squat impatiently, earning raised eyebrows from all. I grab both sides of the top of the box and shimmy hard, thinking the heat might have warped it. Whether my assumption is valid or not, the technique works. I lift the heavy lid, giving both the detectives a superior stare, before I rise to standing.

D.D. immediately goes to work, flipping through the manila folders labeled Auto Insurance, Property Insurance, Mortgage, Passports, Life Insurance, CDs, Savings Account. All the important papers you'd never want to lose in a fire.

Nothing terribly exciting, and yet my best hope of trying to figure out the next few months of my life. Or how to escape my mother's clinging grasp in the least amount of time possible—depending on your point of view.

D.D. removes each file, flips through the contents—not much, just the latest statements, policies, et cetera—replaces them in the box. When she gets to life insurance, she pauses.

"Million dollars?" She gives me a look. "This appears to be a brand-new policy. Seriously?"

"He took it out when we discovered I was pregnant. According to the insurance rep, it should be enough to pay off the mortgage of the house, cover eighteen years of the average costs of raising a child, plus four years of college."

"In other words, a million motives for shooting your husband."

"If I wanted a million dollars," I inform the detective, "all I have to do is phone home. Or better yet, move in."

She gives me a fresh look. "Which you just did."

"Yeah, and why don't you ask Call Me Phil what that's like?"

The redhead glances up. "'Call Me Phil'?" Abruptly, he breaks into a smile. "*That's* what he was talking about yesterday. We should get him a T-shirt."

Now D.D. and I both scowl at him. He shrinks back, holds up a black, warped object. "I think I found the key to the other lockbox not far from this one."

"Hang on," I say. I look at Mr. Delaney. "I see personal papers and financial files. No source of arson fire. Nothing that rises to the level of evidence."

"Agreed," Mr. Delaney states. He stares hard at D.D.

"I want a copy of the life insurance."

"Snap a photo with your phone," I suggest. Because I'm taking the policy home with me. I need it.

"My client is being more than reasonable," my lawyer seconds.

Clearly, D.D. isn't happy. But she photographs the doc, closes up the file, sticks it back in the box. The SentrySafe has done its job admirably, saving its contents, surviving to tell its tales. Now Mr. Delaney picks it up, grunting slightly from the weight as he carries it to the trunk of his car.

Which leaves us with the thin metal lockbox. I have no idea what it is, but I won't admit to that because I'm dying to see what's inside. It probably doesn't matter anymore, but it might be what I was searching for all along.

The black key is warped. The redhead tries jiggling. D.D. tries jangling. I take it from them both, me, the experienced homeowner who must certainly know the quirks of this lockbox as well as I did the fireproof safe.

It still takes several tries. I coax, beg, plead. Please, after all this time of looking for you, don't you want to talk to me, too?

Then: *click.*

Just like that, the lock gives. The lid doesn't pop open, clearly warped along the edges. But I can feel the box relax, preparing to surrender its secrets.

I place it on the ground before us. I don't know what to expect. Ashes, charred ruins. The heat inside a house fire must be so extreme. And while Conrad clearly meant to keep these contents hidden, he didn't necessarily care if they were safe. An interesting distinction in its own right.

D.D. has to force the lid. Black flakes float down.

Inside the box, the metal is cool and gray, untouched. The first evidence that the contents came through unscathed. Then:

"What the hell?" D.D. stares at me.

The redheaded detective is already digging through the contents, equally mesmerized.

I don't have words. I don't have moisture in my mouth. Of all the things I thought I might see. Of all the secrets I knew Conrad had to have.

I'm staring at bundles of cash. Still in original wrappings, which is suspicious enough. But more than that, I'm staring at piles of plastic cards. Various drivers' licenses, covering half a dozen states.

All with Conrad's photo. All bearing different names.

"You need to start talking and you need to start talking now," D.D. orders intently.

Except I have nothing to say.

CHAPTER 17

D.D.

"YOU NEED TO START TALKING and you need to start talking now." D.D.'s voice was hard.

She regarded the stacks of cash and fake IDs in the soot-blackened box at her feet and ideas raced through her head. Conrad Carter was some kind of secret operative. Except any decent undercover agent would also have a backup piece and ammo stashed with his cash. A criminal mastermind or serial offender? Carter was a man with no family whose job demanded long periods away and who was described as the kind of guy everyone liked but no one knew.

D.D. felt she was standing at a precipice. The next step would take her free-falling over the edge, the answers to dozens of questions roaring past her. Except it would be her job to frantically grab each piece and sort them into a meaningful explanation, all before crashing into the ground below.

In front of her, Evie was shaking her head slightly. The woman appeared shocked, but by what? The contents of the box, or that the police had finally discovered her husband's secret?

Neil, God bless him, did the sensible thing. He snapped several quick pics with his cell phone, showing the box in situ. Then, donning a pair of latex gloves, he started sorting out the contents.

The cash was banded piles of hundreds. Neil organized them in stacks of ten to equal a thousand, then lined up the stacks. D.D. could practically hear Evie work out the math: twenty-five thousand dollars. Not much compared to the solid bricks of Washingtons seized during the average drug raid, but more than enough in a working-class neighborhood where Evie and her husband had probably considered that a solid year's renovation budget. D.D. took several photos of her own, to corroborate Neil's photos. Chain of custody over recovered cash was a big deal in policing. Good cops looked out for each other, dotted all i's, crossed all t's, so neither they nor their squad could face any scrutiny.

Five photo IDs. The first names were a mix of Conrad, Conner, Carter, Conroy—always good to stick with names that sounded similar. The last names repeated the trick. Conrad Carter from Massachusetts became Carter Conrad in Texas or Carter Conner in Florida.

Given the name game, D.D. doubted the IDs were professional grade—the kind of fakes that cost thousands of dollars and involved trolling death certificates for an infant who'd departed thirty-eight years ago, then stealing that identity. Such an alias could conceivably be used for decades, the holder acquiring credit cards, even a passport. This . . . Neil had lined up each slightly warped piece of plastic. These fakes reminded her of the kind underage kids used to talk their way into local bars. Good at a glance, but not great.

She could tell from the look on Neil's face he was thinking the same. Whatever Conrad Carter was doing, he definitely wasn't a pro. Which made him what?

D.D. rose and eyed Evie sternly. Evie was still staring at the cash and cards, but she didn't appear to be looking at them as much as *through* them. Seeing something only she could see.

"My client is tired," the attorney began. "Given her condition—"

"I don't know anything," Evie interrupted. Her voice sounded as far away as her expression.

"You said this lockbox contained the overflow of financial documents."

"I lied. I'd never seen it before. I wanted to know the contents."

"So you admit—"

"All spouses keep secrets, Sergeant. I already told you to ask your husband."

D.D. could feel her temper starting to rise. "Fine. Let's head to HQ, where we can talk about yours."

"Sergeant Warren, my client—"

"Is lying to the police and admitting it? Is possibly leading a double life of her own? Does your baby even belong to Conrad Carter? Or maybe it's"—D.D. nudged the closest driver's license with the tip of her boot—"Carter Conrad's baby? Or Conroy Conrad's?"

"Sergeant Detective!" Attorney Dick Delaney again, all outrage and bluster.

"I don't know anything," Evie repeated quietly. "I thought . . . He locked his office door. A room in his own house. Every time he went away. Except I was the only person around, and his business, selling custom windows . . . Why lock up customer spec sheets? And why protect such documents from your wife? Or was he protecting me from them?"

Evie glanced up. For a moment, she appeared as genuinely confused and puzzled as D.D. felt.

"You suspected something," D.D. stated.

Delaney made another noise in the back of his throat. D.D. nudged Neil with her foot, and he shot immediately to standing.

"We're going to need to see the file box again," Neil said.

Delaney gave them a look, Neil's bid at distraction not fooling him for a moment. "Then you can fetch it from the back of the trunk." He tossed Neil the keys.

D.D. kept her attention on Evie. She was on to something. She could feel it.

"You shot the computer. Why did you shoot the computer?" D.D. moved closer, keeping her voice low. "What did you suspect, Evie? What did you catch the father of your unborn child doing?"

"My client—"

"First your father. You loved him, didn't you? Idolized him. I conducted those neighbor interviews. Everyone talked about what a close bond you and he had."

"Sergeant Detective, I am warning you—"

"You thought he killed himself, didn't you? So acting on your mother's orders, you became the patsy. All these years, carrying that weight alone. Just so you could fall in love and discover . . . what? That your husband's sins were far greater?"

"This conversation is over." Delaney had his hand on Evie's arm. "Take the file box or don't take the file box. Either way my client is coming with me."

"No, she isn't." D.D. was staring directly at Evie. She knew she had the woman's total, undivided attention. She understood then the truth to getting at her prime suspect. Every person had a lever, the button that a good detective learned how to push. Evie had given her the key just yesterday; the woman was her father's daughter. She did work the math. And she couldn't walk away from an unsolved equation.

Curiosity. That was Evie's downfall. Which gave D.D. a slight chill because curiosity had always been her weakness, too.

"Come to HQ. Answer my questions," she told the woman now.

"She's going home!" Delaney snapped.

Evie said, "Why?"

"Because in return, I have photos. From sixteen years ago. Going through them, I can prove to you, your father didn't shoot himself."

EVIE WOULD COME TO HQ. D.D. never doubted it for a second. First her lawyer had to draw her aside and engage in frantic conversation. No doubt informing his client she was being foolish, letting the police get under her skin. If they had any real evidence, they'd be forced to disclose it prior to trial anyway. As for Evie, the woman seemed to have some strong words of her own. D.D. could've sworn she heard the woman state angrily, "I am your client and you will *not* call my mother."

How interesting.

After a few more minutes of terse exchange, Evie climbed into her lawyer's car, file box still planted in the trunk. D.D. couldn't justify seizing the papers as evidence, though she was happy enough to have a photo of Conrad Carter's life insurance for future reference. Neil bagged and tagged the metal lockbox and its contents as the BPD's share of the spoils. They loaded up their car, then led the way to HQ.

BPD's headquarters was an acquired taste. People either were sufficiently impressed by the modern glass monstrosity or, more likely, shook their heads at yet another example of their tax dollars at work. D.D. wasn't into architecture. As a woman who liked to eat, she appreciated the café on the lobby level. And the upstairs homicide suite was far bigger and more useful than the old HQ had been, even if the blue industrial carpet, gray filing cabinets, and collection of cubicles made them look more like an insurance company than an investigative unit. Sometimes, like now, when she had a suspect she didn't want to spook, it was nice to pretend they were just hanging out at an office versus, say, starring in an old episode of *NYPD Blue*.

Given the circumstances, D.D. led Evie and her lawyer to homicide's conference room, something a bit more hospitable than the spartan interrogation rooms. Evie already had her attorney at her elbow. D.D. didn't want to spook her prime suspect before extracting as much information as possible.

After a quick sidebar, Neil disappeared to find Phil. Neil would handle processing the evidence they'd recovered at the arson scene. Phil would resume his role as family man/father figure detective. Again, interviews were strategy and while D.D. liked a good full-court press, that was never going to work with a lawyer in the room. This would be a finesse job. Fortunately, she was a woman of many skills.

And like Evie, of much curiosity.

D.D. played nice. She got Evie and her lawyer situated. Brought them both bottles of water; then, at the request of Delaney, who seemed to enjoy having one of Boston's finest waiting on him, she returned with a cup of coffee. By then, Phil had joined the room, armed with a heavy cardboard box. The outside of the box bore large black numbers: the case number for Evie's father's shooting sixteen years ago.

Phil set the box at the head of the table, away from Evie and Dick Delaney. He and D.D. had been playing this game for so long, they didn't need to speak to know how to proceed. D.D. sat directly across from Evie and her lawyer, engaging them in small talk about best brands of coffee in Boston, black versus cream and sugar, and, oh yeah, having to give up coffee while pregnant, which D.D. had never thought she'd be able to do, but in fact had come quite naturally.

In the meantime, Phil unpacked the box. Slowly. File after file. The murder book. Binders of evidence reports. Stacks of photos. Pile here. Pile there. Pile after pile.

Evie lost focus first. Nodded at whatever asinine comment D.D. was making while her gaze drifted to the head of the table, the growing stack of yellowing papers, frayed photo edges, dirty manila files. Records were all supposed to be scanned and stored electronically these days. And yet, if the average bureaucrat ever walked through the warehouse, saw the full magnitude of the job . . .

Walking the stacks to manually retrieve an evidence box wasn't going away anytime soon.

"That's evidence from my father's case," Evie said suddenly. The woman was agitated. Not even bothering to sip her water but spinning the bottle in her hand.

"That's right."

"You have photos?"

Delaney spoke up. "I would like to go on the record that I don't recommend my client be here today, taking these questions, Sergeant Warren—"

D.D. kept her focus on Evie: "Do you remember your statement from that day?"

"A little."

"Let me read it to you, from my notes: 'sixteen-year-old subject, female, white, appears in state of shock and/or traumatized. Subject states she had been in the kitchen with her father, Earl Hopkins, fifty-five-year-old male, white, after two thirty on Saturday. Father was showing her how to unload a recently purchased Model eighty-seventy Remington pump-action shotgun. Father was standing in front of refrigerator when female subject, in her own words, picked up shotgun off the kitchen table and attempted to clear the chamber. According to female, shotgun discharged into her father's torso from a distance of mere inches. Female states father fell back against the refrigerator, then sank to the floor. Female claims she set down gun and attempted to rouse her father without success. Female further claims she then heard screaming from the doorway, where her mother, Joyce Hopkins, forty-three-year-old female, white, stood. Mother claimed she'd witnessed the shooting. Detective Speirs interviewed independently.'"

Evie didn't say anything while D.D. read, just kept staring at the box. D.D. set down her notepad. "Does that fit your memory?"

Evie finally looked at her. "What do the photos say?"

"Phil?"

Phil stepped forward with the first set. They were gruesome. A shotgun blast at close range did a tremendous amount of damage. Evie had sat through the real event. In theory, there was nothing here she hadn't seen before, though in D.D.'s experience, memory had its way with things over time. Meaning the photos could look far worse than Evie had allowed herself to remember, or more likely, given the woman's burden of guilt, far less awful than the images that replayed in her head night after night.

D.D. spread out the first three photos in front of Evie and her lawyer. Delaney inhaled sharply but didn't look away. He'd been there that day, too. A friend of the family, summoned by Evie's mom, who hadn't thought to call 911 but knew immediately to dial the family lawyer. Said something about the woman's mental state right there.

"Long guns are used in suicides more often than people think," D.D. stated now. She kept her voice even but soft. No need to play hardball just yet; that would come later. "This particular shotgun, the Model eight-seventy Remington, comes in two different barrel lengths for the twelve-gauge. Your father had purchased the slightly shorter version, but even then, the barrel length is twenty-six inches, the full length of the shotgun forty-six and a half inches. In instances of suicide, the victim will generally press the tip of the barrel against his own body to stabilize the weapon while he reaches for the trigger. Hence, one of the most common indicators of suicide by long gun is a clear burn pattern against the victim's skin from the heat of the barrel."

Evie glanced up at her. "I don't see a burn mark. It would be on his stomach, yes? I just see . . . soot."

"Scorch marks," D.D. provided, "indicating the shotgun was in close proximity to the victim at the time of discharge, but not actually touching the victim's skin. In fact, the scorch marks are consistent with your initial statement, a scenario of someone standing mere inches away from the victim, pulling the trigger."

"I don't understand."

"The second indicator of suicide by long gun is trajectory. It's nearly impossible to hold a long gun level and pull the trigger, meaning inevitably the impact of the blast should be up and out. The projectiles enter lower on the body, travel in an upward diagonal until exiting higher on the body. In this case"—D.D. tapped a photo—"we can see the entrance wound was beneath your father's lower ribs. But according to the ME, the shotgun pellets didn't follow any diagonal path. Instead, they traveled nearly straight through the body, shredding his organs and intestines along the way."

"Sergeant!" Delaney objected.

Evie, however, did not look away. "The gun was fired level. From someone standing directly in front of my father."

"Which, again, would be consistent with the story you provided. You picked up the shotgun. You were trying to inspect the chamber, and instead, you pulled the trigger while standing directly in front of your father. Hence no burn marks, no upward trajectory."

"Except I didn't! We'd been out. Myself and my mother. We parked on the driveway. I'd just opened the car door and I heard a noise. We entered the kitchen. And there . . . I saw . . . There was my father."

"The third thing we'd look at for a suicide," D.D. continued relentlessly, "is the blood spatter. If someone else was in the room, if someone else pulled the trigger, that person would be subject to blow-back, or spray from the impact of the shotgun pellets entering the body. Meaning we should have at least one person covered in spatter."

She stared hard at Evie, who sputtered: "I walked in . . . the blood . . . it dripped down on me . . ."

"We'd also have a void in the spatter. A clean spot in, say, the floor or countertop, where the shooter's body blocked any droplets from landing." D.D. tapped a third photo, where, sure enough, bloody spray appeared above and to the sides of Hopkins's body, but directly in front . . .

"Your father didn't commit suicide," D.D. stated firmly. "The evidence has now been reviewed several times by several different experts. There was someone else in the room, and that person shot him."

Evie opened her mouth, shut her mouth. "You think I'm lying now," she whispered at last.

"I think your story sixteen years ago is a better fit with the evidence than the line of bull you tried to feed me yesterday."

"Sergeant," Delaney started again.

"Why would I lie? I only did it back then to protect my father."

"Your father, or your mother?"

"My mother was with me! We'd gone out shopping. Surely, you can find a witness, pull store security tapes. A credit card receipt. Something that proves we were together."

"From sixteen years ago?"

"I thought he'd killed himself! He'd been . . . off. Not himself. And genius and suicide . . ." Evie shrugged, sounding genuinely distressed.

"Your father did not commit suicide."

"I didn't shoot him!"

"So you're a liar, but not a killer. And Friday night, with your husband?"

"Sergeant! This line of questioning is over!"

"Not so fast, Counselor. Your client came to me yesterday, recanting her story from sixteen years ago. She's the one who reopened this can of worms. Based on her new statement, the case of Earl Hopkins is no longer being considered accidental. We're now treating it as an active homicide, and you know the statute of limitations on homicide—there isn't one."

"I didn't do it!" Evie, still aghast, pounded her water bottle against the table. "I would never harm my father!"

"But your husband? The guy with rolls of cash and nearly half a dozen fake IDs?"

"We're out of here." Delaney was already on his feet, pulling at Evie's arm. The woman, however, continued to resist. And it wasn't the allegations about her husband that had her agitated. Clearly, she was still distressed about her father. Even sixteen years later, it was all about her father.

She was gazing at D.D. wildly now. "My hair. You took photos of my hair. Samples. I remember that!"

D.D. nodded slowly.

"Test it. Have it reexamined. You can, can't you? I don't understand it all, but I watch crime shows. You can prove directionality from blood spatter, right? Say, the difference between this blowback you're talking about, versus contact smear from someone entering the room right afterwards."

"I don't know if we have enough evidence," D.D. said, which wasn't entirely untrue.

"Test it. Do whatever you have to do. I didn't kill my father. *I didn't!* All these years." Her voice broke off. "I assumed the worst about him."

"Him, or your mother?"

"*She was with me.* I'm telling you the truth. My mom is crazy, I know, but she loved him. They loved each other. I don't know. Not all relationships are meant to be understood by outsiders—"

"Talking about your husband again?"

"My mom didn't do this," Evie repeated more firmly. She seemed to be pulling herself together now, allowing her lawyer to guide her to standing. "She, me, we didn't do this. All these years, we thought he shot himself. That's why we lied. Not to protect ourselves. But to protect him. If you'd met him, if you'd talked to him . . . My father was a great man. He deserved better than to go down in the history books as one more depressed genius."

"Then who, Evie?" D.D. rose to standing. "Who would have motive to shoot your father? Did he have professional rivals? Failing students? Jealous husbands? Someone pulled that trigger. If not you, then who?"

"I . . . I have no idea." Evie glanced helplessly at her lawyer. It was all he needed.

"This interview is over. You asked for answers from my client and she provided them. You want to learn anything else, Officers, I suggest you go out and—here's a thought—do some detecting."

Delaney guided his client around the table. But Evie's gaze was still glued to the photos as she walked by. Fascinated. Fixated. Frustrated.

That she finally realized all these years later she'd lied for nothing? Or because she'd just discovered yesterday's attempt at changing her story was never going to work?

D.D. still couldn't figure it. But there was something about the way Evie looked at the photos that tugged at her, made her wonder if that woman hadn't told her the truth yesterday after all.

Longing, she finally decided. Evie Carter looked at those photos like a woman who, sixteen years later, just wanted her father back.

It made D.D. wonder what other regrets the woman had, and how many might involve her husband and his own death just two nights ago.

Knock on the door. Neil poked his head in. He appeared nervous.

"Got something on the fake IDs?" she asked immediately, collecting her notes.

"Ah, no. You got a visitor."

"I have a visitor?"

"A fed. SSA Kimberly Quincy from the Atlanta office. She's here with Flora Dane and some other guy. Says she needs to talk."

"No," D.D. said.

"Too late," a female voice drawled from behind Neil.

D.D. sighed. "Shit."

CHAPTER 18

FLORA

MEMORY IS A FUNNY THING. There are moments that sear into our minds. If we're lucky, it's because we're happy—first kiss, wedding day, birth of a child. The kind of experience where you both have it and stand outside of it because your brain recognizes this is something so special that you're going to want to relive it.

I have some of those memories. Being asked to prom by the cutest boy in high school, practically floating home to share the news with my mom. The first time I got a baby fox to eat a piece of hot dog out of my hand. A particular bedtime ritual my mom used to have when I couldn't get to sleep. And the nights my brother and I turned it on her, giggling hysterically as we pretended to tuck her into bed, but really ended up in a giant mosh pile of limbs in the middle of her mattress, a tangle of family.

I have other memories, too.

The moment I woke up in a coffin-sized box. The sound the first woman made, when Jacob stuck in the knife, followed by the look in her eyes as she stared right into me, knowing he was killing her, knowing she was dying, knowing I was doing nothing to stop him.

Now I have to face the fact there could be six more of her out there, six more girls who never made it home. Maybe Jacob made good on his promise and fed them to the gators. Maybe they're buried on his property, if I could just help figure out where that is.

Memory. Such a fickle tool. And for better or worse, the best option I have left.

I DON'T SLEEP. After leaving Keith Edgar's house, I return to Cambridge, then pace my tiny apartment until my elderly landlords politely knock on the door and ask me if I'm all right. After assuring them I'm just dandy, I give up on walking continuous circles and debate calling Sarah. She's a fellow survivor who once held off a murderer by using the severed arm of her just-butchered roommate. She's also the closest thing I have to a friend.

She understood bad nights. How the brain could spin for days, weeks, months at a time, an endless cycle of remembered traumas from falling off your bike at seven to being attacked by a knife-wielding maniac at twenty. Trying to sort out the experiences, Samuel had explained to me once. It felt like my brain was racing wildly, but really, it was searching for patterns, matches, order. Something that would give it context, so my mind could go, *Aha—that's what happened*. Then, presumably, people like Sarah and me would sleep again. Except some experiences defied definition. So our brains kept spinning long after the horror had ended.

If not Sarah, then I could call Samuel, who most likely was expecting to hear from me after this afternoon's discussion. Or my mother, who would be simultaneously honored and stricken to have me finally open up about what it's like to be me.

But I don't feel like talking. I pick up the clothes in my bedroom. I wipe down kitchen counters. I rearrange the four things I have in the fridge. Then, in a burst of inspiration, I try on my own to recall the original place Jacob had held me. The first coffin-sized box in a dingy basement of some house. Small windows, up high. Shit-brown carpet that I used to comb through with my fingers, marveling at how many shades of brown it took to make carpet the same color as dirt. I jot down notes. Ugly carpet. Moldy sofa. Stairs leading up. Pine trees. When he finally led me out of the house, I remember pine trees.

But my mind keeps ping-ponging, until I can't be sure anymore if I was remembering the first place, or that second motel, or what about that place in Florida? I grow light-headed, can feel the edges of the panic attack start to build, when it's been years since I've been humbled by such a thing.

Four A.M., sweaty, panting, and borderline feral, I opt for a different memory. The day I was rescued, an image that should be higher on the happiness scale. I force myself to sit calmly on the floor of my apartment, recall exactly the crash of the motel window. The canister of tear gas bouncing into the room, then releasing an ominous hiss. My eyes welling, my nose running. Then the front door blowing open, and a horde of heavily armored men pouring into the tiny room. They scream at me, yell at Jacob. Scream louder when I pick up the gun. Fall silent when I've done what I had to do.

Then, Kimberly Quincy. The fed. She'd been the first to greet me outside the room, her arm around my shoulders, telling me over and over again I'd be all right. Everything was okay now. I was safe.

I remember her voice clearly. Clipped, firm, in control. The kind of voice that inspired confidence.

But what does SSA Kimberly Quincy look like? For some reason, that piece of the puzzle keeps escaping from me. I work on it for an hour. The sound of her voice. The feel of her arm around my shoulders. Me, turning my head, looking straight at her.

I had to have seen her. My eyes had been red and swollen, my nose a snotty mess, but still . . . No matter how much I try, I still can't bring her face to mind. She remains a voice in the dark. Clipped. Firm. In control.

The kind of woman I'm going to need for the day ahead.

Five A.M., I give up on sleep completely and go for a run in the ice-cold dark, neon vest glowing, headlamp beaming. Then shower. Bagel. Black coffee. Still hours to kill.

I boot up my computer, check in on my new friend Keith Edgar, who, interestingly enough, has posted nothing from yesterday on his true-crime blog site. Trying to impress me with his restraint? Or just waiting for something more significant to share?

I decide not to worry about it for now. Instead, I cycle back to where I'd started my evening. Memory. Such a fickle tool.

I read anything and everything about how to handle traumatized minds, from EMDR to virtual reality simulations to old-fashioned hypnosis. Ten A.M., my phone finally rings. That familiar clipped voice: "My plane has landed."

I'm not nervous anymore. I'm ready.

ARRIVING AT BPD headquarters, I spot Keith first. He is standing awkwardly to the side, gazing up at the glass structure as if he's not sure its existence is such a good idea. When he sees me walking toward him, his face immediately brightens and I feel an unexpected tug inside my chest.

He's dressed upscale metrosexual. Open dark wool coat. Black skinny jeans topped with a deep purple sweater over a lavender-and-pink-checked shirt. He looks like an Abercrombie model. Which is to say, an updated Ted Bundy. I wonder what SSA Kimberly Quincy will make of him.

Then I see her. Stepping out of an Uber vehicle. Long camel-colored coat to fight off New England temps that must feel shocking after Atlanta. A dark leather shoulder bag slung across her body. Nice brown boots, currently getting ruined by the wintry mix of salt and sludge.

I don't even have to hear her voice to know it's her. Something about the line of her body as she leans down to retrieve a smaller overnight bag. Then she straightens, turns.

And I realize why I blocked her face from my mind. Because for all intents and purposes, SSA Quincy looks almost exactly like me. Same lean profile, gray-blue eyes, dusty-blond hair, hard stare. Except she's a slightly older, wiser version of myself. No dark shadows under her eyes. Real muscle mass lining her frame. A woman who sleeps at night, eats three to five healthy meals a day, and knows exactly who she is and where she's going.

"Damn," Keith says, taking in the two of us, and I realize I'm not ready for the day after all.

KEITH AND I let Quincy take the lead. She shakes my hand, then his. If she wonders about his presence, she doesn't say anything. Maybe she thinks he's my boyfriend. Maybe I don't mind that impression.

She leads us into BPD, slaps down her credentials to announce her arrival, and crisply requests to see Sergeant D. D. Warren. Keith is looking all around the vast glass and steel lobby. I can already feel myself shrinking inside my down coat. As I'm a woman who'd once been confined to a box, you'd think I'd like large open spaces. But this kind of space makes me nervous.

A redheaded detective appears. I've met him before, Neil something or other. He chirps about do we need breakfast, coffee, anything? Quincy stares at him. He stops talking, leads the way up to the homicide unit.

Along the way, we pass an older man in a suit and a woman I

recognize instantly from the news—Conrad Carter's wife. The woman who supposedly shot and killed her husband. My feet slow on instinct. I open my mouth, feel like I should say something, anything. How well did you know your husband? Would it surprise you to know he was hanging out with a known rapist in a honky-tonk in the South? But Keith suddenly has a grip on my arm. He drives me forward, till she's gone, and I'm left with a last impression of a woman who's as anxious and exhausted as I am.

D.D. greets us with her normal chipper self. "What the hell?"

Quincy smiles. "Sergeant Warren. Nice to speak with you again. Shall we?" Quincy gestures to the conference room behind D.D. D.D. looks like she's on the verge of arguing, probably on principle, but Quincy smiles again, says, "Not in front of the children," and that does the trick.

The two female investigators enter the conference room, closing the door firmly behind them. Keith and I remain in the hallway, still in the company of the redhead, who's fidgeting.

"Coffee?" he asks again. Most likely to have something to do.

Keith and I exchange a glance. "No," we state in unison. Which makes me feel warm all over.

From inside the room: "A Boston shooting is a Boston case!"

"I'm not interested in your murder. I'm interested in the victim's possible connection to Jacob Ness."

"This has nothing to do with Ness. We've already charged the wife in the shooting."

"Then my angle of inquiry won't conflict with your own."

"Like hell! You start digging in Conrad's past, raise the specter of some serial killer bestie, and you've just handed the defense reasonable doubt. Evie Carter didn't kill her husband. Clearly the ghost of Jacob Ness did it."

"Do you know for sure someone else didn't do it? Because a man who was known to go on frequent business trips, and at least spent part of them in the company of a serial rapist . . . As an investigator, these are questions I'd like to answer."

"Me too. Which brings us back to the wife. Who in addition to shooting her husband, plugged even more bullets into his computer."

"Anything recoverable?"

"Not yet."

"The FBI forensic techs are the best in the industry—"

"Bite me."

"Sergeant Warren, your case intersects with an ongoing FBI investigation. Period. You can invite me to assist gracefully. Or I can commandeer your case forcefully."

"What ongoing investigation?"

"The disappearance of six women believed to be additional victims of Jacob Ness. With his death, we've lacked investigative avenues. However, this new information, that he might have met with other predators, could prove promising."

"Conrad Carter can't help you, he's dead. And so is his computer."

"Jacob Ness's computer isn't."

For the first time, quiet. A long pause, where Keith and I lean forward. The redheaded detective as well.

"You have Ness's computer?" D.D. asks.

"In all its mysterious glory."

"What does that mean?"

"Invite me to play and I'll be happy to share."

"And Flora?" D.D. asks abruptly. "Why is she here?"

"She's also agreed to help."

"How?"

"A trip down memory lane. We've never found the house where Jacob originally held her. We have reason to believe it might be more significant than he let on. And that he took steps to mask its location."

"You think Jacob Ness still has property out there? A personal cabin, residence?"

"I think finding such a thing could provide a great deal of information regarding six missing women, and, who knows, one recently deceased husband. Do you have all the answers for your case, Sergeant Warren?"

"No."

"Neither do I. So, shall we?"

Heavy sigh. "You did help me with Charlene Grant."

"And you did keep her alive."

A change in tone. "How are the girls?"

"Amazing. Ten and seven. Ready to take over the world. Yours?"

"Jack is five. Has a new dog. They spring around the house going 'roo, roo, roo.'"

"Never a dull moment."

"Wouldn't change it for the world."

"Me neither."

"Fine. You want in. Let's do this. But I'm telling you now, there's more about this case that doesn't make sense than does."

"My favorite kind."

Just like that, the deal is struck, the hunt is on.

Quincy turns back toward us, motioning through the window for us to enter.

"Holy shit," Keith whispers under his breath.

I don't stop. I don't think. I simply squeeze his hand.

Then we enter the conference room and the real work begins.

CHAPTER 19

EVIE

"YOU HONESTLY BELIEVED YOUR FATHER killed himself?"

After sitting in silence in the car for so long, the sound of my lawyer's voice startles me. I've been staring out the window, watching perfectly normal people walk down the snowy streets of Boston, continuing on with their perfectly normal lives. I wonder if that's how I look to others; like I'm normal and functional, too, when in fact, I feel completely emptied out. Stacks of money. Fake IDs. Not exactly a treasure trove of dead wives, and yet, I'd been right: Conrad had been hiding secrets from me.

Which I want to think is only fair, because I hid my secrets from him. Except it doesn't feel okay at all. It feels awful and unjust, a final act of betrayal by a man I'd genuinely loved. True, I had my own suspicions. But then, maybe that's what love was for me. An exercise in mistrust.

"Evie?" Mr. Delaney prods again, his voice gentle.

I pull my attention from the window.

"My mom never told you?"

"All I've ever known is what she said that afternoon. That your father had been showing you how to handle the shotgun. There was an accidental discharge. She saw the whole thing from the kitchen doorway."

I nod. That was our story, and for sixteen years we'd been sticking to it.

"Do you think my parents loved each other?" I hear myself ask.

He doesn't answer right away, tapping his finger on the steering wheel. I always thought of Mr. Delaney as one of my father's friends. But all these years later, he continues to come around the house. Unmarried. Attentive to my mother's moods. Now I can't help but wonder.

"I met both your parents in college," he says now, surprising me. I'd known that he and my father went way back, but I hadn't realized it included my mother as well. "From the very beginning, their relationship was . . . volatile. And yet, the more they collided, blew apart, collapsed back, the more it seemed to work for them. You know your father genuinely loved math?"

I nod.

"Well, over the years, I've come to think of his relationship with your mom as his exercise in physics. She challenged him, in a wholly different way, and your father liked a good challenge. As for her . . . Your mother was never meant to live an ordinary life. Your father, in his overly intellectual, unquestionably brilliant, completely indulgent way, was perfect for her."

"The cocktail parties. University functions. Build the legacy. Protect the legacy."

Mr. Delaney smiles. "They fit together, Evie. Whether it made sense to outsiders or not, they were meant to be. And they both loved you."

I return to the window. My father loved me. I know that. My mom, on the other hand, is a different story. A genius husband had fit the exotic story line of her life. A daughter of slightly above-average intelligence, who taught math at public high school, not so much.

"You can talk to me," Mr. Delaney is saying now. "You're my client. Our conversations are protected by privilege. Whatever you say stays with me."

"And not my mom?" I can't help it; I sound bitter, maybe even petulant.

"Mum's the word," he says so quietly, I almost miss the pun. When I catch it, I smile, and he smiles back. It occurs to me that Mr. Delaney has been one of the few adult fixtures in my life. First as my parents' close friend and confidant, then as a substitute father figure, coming by the house regularly to check up on us in the months following the shooting. He'd been holding my mother together, though I hadn't thought about it back then. But Mr. Delaney had been the one who'd appear three or four nights a week, quietly making sure food appeared in the fridge, vodka bottles disappeared from the cabinets. He'd tried to get my mom to sell the house, then failing that, at least remodel. For me, he always said. She should do these things to ease her daughter's stress, help in my recovery.

She'd listened to him, certainly in a way she never would've listened to me. My father had been her world. Whereas she and I could never even agree on much of anything.

"We found him . . . dead, when we first arrived home," I murmur now. "Clearly, it had just happened. You could smell the gunpowder. And the blood . . . it was hot on my hair."

"I'm sorry, Evie."

"There was no sign of anyone else. No cars on the drive, no one in the home. And my father, those past few months, his mood had grown darker."

"On occasion, the genius in your father got the better of him. But he always came out the other side. He told me once, that was the power of fatherhood. Even when he felt he was failing at solving the great mysteries of the universe, he knew he would never fail you."

"I thought he had." Suddenly, I'm crying. I hadn't expected to. But all these years later . . . I haven't been carrying around just the shame of my secret, but the pain that my father chose to end his own life rather than stay with us. The father I loved so much. The father I would've done anything to make happy.

I turn back to the window, wipe hastily at my cheeks.

"You didn't pull the trigger," Delaney states now.

"No. He'd already shown me how to load and unload the Remington. I wouldn't have made such a stupid mistake. But as it was, Mom and I weren't even home."

"Was he expecting anyone? A TA, a fellow professor?"

"Not that he told us. When we left, he was holed up in his study, standing at a whiteboard, muttering away. You know how he could be. We called out to him that we were off to run errands. I don't even remember if he answered. We drove away. When we came back . . ."

Mr. Delaney nods. "You walked into the kitchen first," he fills in quietly. "Then came your mother, who took one look and fell apart."

"She told me what to say. She told me what had to be done. In the moment, I never questioned it. Maybe . . ."

"It's okay, Evie. I understand. You'd just lost one parent. Of course you went out of your way to make your surviving parent happy."

I'd never thought of it that way, but it made sense.

"You and your mother were together?"

"Yes."

"But according to what we just heard from the police, your father didn't commit suicide. There had to be another person in the house. Was the door open when you walked in?"

"The back door was always unlocked during daylight hours. Often because so many students were coming and going."

"I think you should prepare a statement. Write down in your own words what you can remember from that day. Then give it to me for proofing. Ultimately, we'll deliver it to the police."

"So they can charge me in my father's murder as well?"

"Did you shoot your father, Evie? Remember, anything you tell me is protected."

"No."

"Did you shoot your husband? Again, anything you tell me is protected."

"No."

"But you pulled the trigger."

"I shot my husband's computer."

Delaney takes his eyes off the wheel long enough to give me a look. "Interesting. Well then, sounds to me like we have some work ahead of us."

"Why do I only love men who leave me?" I whisper.

"I don't know, honey. Some of us just aren't lucky in love."

MR. DELANEY TAKES me to lunch. A sandwich place he knows downtown. He doesn't fuss over me as openly as my mother, but he adds orange juice to my salad order and refuses to utter a word until at least a quarter of my food is consumed. His own choice is a rare roast beef sandwich with horseradish mayo. Once, I would've ordered the same. Now, in my delicate state, the sight of the bloody beef makes me nauseous. I do my best to focus on my lunch, take small bites, chew thoroughly. Even if I have no interest in sustenance, the baby does. Everything I do next, the whole rest of my life, this is what—this is who—my life will be about.

Again, I wonder if my mom ever felt that way about me.

"Why didn't my parents have more children?" I ask Mr. Delaney halfway through my salad. If my question surprises him, he's an experienced enough lawyer to hide it.

"I don't know. Have you ever asked?"

I give him a look. He grins back. The silver fox can be charming when he wants. Already, I'd noticed several female heads turning to admire the new lunch addition. Then they scowled at me, no doubt thinking I was his much-too-young trophy wife, because handsome men are never allowed to be merely friends with other women.

"Your father was nervous," he says at last, picking up a napkin, dabbing at his meticulously trimmed mustache. "When your mother found out she was pregnant, he was excited, but concerned. As he put it, no genius in history has been noted for their parenting skills."

"Was I a surprise?"

"Always."

I roll my eyes at him again. "I mean, did they want to have children?"

"I don't think they would've actively sought it out," Mr. Delaney allows after a minute, "but I would also say, you were the light of your father's life. Your turn." He looks at me. "Is your baby a surprise?"

"Yes. No. Kind of. We'd been trying once. But had mostly given up. And then . . ."

"I've heard that. Sometimes, not trying is exactly what a new life-form needs most. Did you love Conrad?" he asks me softly.

"Yes. No. Kind of."

That smile again, but a bit sad this time, as if he knows exactly what I mean.

"In the beginning," I hear myself say. "I thought he was everything I could ever want. Outgoing, funny, compassionate. He sought me out. He looked at me. He wanted to talk to me. He wanted to be with *me*. I know it sounds awful. Like an exercise in narcissism. But in my whole life, it never felt like anyone wanted me. Then, after my father died—"

"And you took the blame."

"Let's just say if I was the quiet weird kid before, I was the scary weird kid after." I shrug.

"You know, your father worried you'd be gifted like him."

"He *worried*?"

"It's a lonely life, in case you didn't notice. His brain was exceptional because it didn't work like anyone else's. But it put him forever out of step with others. Even in elite math circles, he stood out."

"One of the greatest minds of his generation," I intoned. And suddenly, I feel like crying again, because I'd never wanted the genius, just the father, and I still missed him so much.

"If you loved Conrad," Mr. Delaney asks softly, "what do you think happened to your relationship?"

I can't answer right away. When I do, the words are hard to say. "I don't think I'm good at marriage."

"How so?"

"I don't know how to trust. I don't know how to . . . believe. The kinder Conrad was to me . . . the more I grew suspicious. I'd wonder what he wanted, what he wasn't saying."

"You thought he was being unfaithful?"

"I don't know. He was gone so often on business trips, but when he came home, he didn't want to talk about it. Life on the road is boring, he'd tell me. Let's hear about your week. Except I didn't believe he really wanted to learn about my week. He just didn't want to talk about his."

"You grew up in a household with adults who generally had an agenda."

I have to smile because I know exactly whom he's talking about. "My mom."

"Some men do like to hear from the women they love."

"I know. And I'd tell myself that. The problem is me. I believed my husband had secrets because, of course, I have this huge secret. But then, I'd notice little things, see little things . . ."

"Such as?"

"Conrad knew everyone. Every neighbor who stopped by, every fellow teacher of mine. He was a walking encyclopedia of names, faces, vital statistics. Except . . . no one knew Conrad. Where were his colleagues, family, friends? He'd told me his parents had died in an accident years ago. Our marriage was very small, at the courthouse because Mom—"

"Didn't approve."

"But month after month, year after year . . . All these people Conrad could tell you so much about, and yet no dinner with the neighbors, no guys' night out. He always had an excuse. For someone who appeared so outgoing, if you stepped back, peered at him from a distance, he was a loner. Separate from all of us. Even with me."

"Did you ever ask him about it?"

"He said he had me, he didn't need anything more."

"Romantic."

I look Mr. Delaney in the eye. "Is it? Because my knee-jerk reaction was that he was lying. So again, was the problem him or me?"

"Do you have close friends?"

I shrug, uncomfortable. "I have a colleague, another teacher at the school. She and I often have lunch together. But see, I know I'm antisocial. And frankly, given that I've spent my adult life being the woman who killed her own father, I have good reasons for being reserved. I admit to these things. Conrad . . . He came across one way, but over time if you paid attention . . ." I shake my head. "I felt sometimes he was less a person, and more a character in a play. He said the right things, but were they things he really meant, or just the next lines of dialogue?"

"You didn't trust him."

"I worried about it," I say carefully. "The inconsistencies between what he said and what he actually did. Add to that the whole locked office in the privacy of his own home. Yet, when I tried to bring it up . . . he'd make me feel petty. Like I was being paranoid. I really couldn't argue with that. They say liars are always the first to think others are lying. And let's face it, for sixteen years now, I've been one helluva liar."

"But you got pregnant."

I smile roughly. "Ever hear of desperately-trying-to-save-your-marriage sex? We got pretty good at it."

"All marriages are hard," Mr. Delaney tells me. I know what he means, but I'm not sure all marriages are the constant exercise in suspicion that mine was.

"By the end," I say softly, "I didn't believe Conrad anymore. He was lying. Maybe not about his love for me, which he promised was true. Maybe not about the baby, which he wanted so badly. He swore he'd be the best dad in the whole world. But he was also almost frantic on the subject. Something was up. I could feel it. Something was going to happen. The past few weeks, the tension in our home, all the things we suspected but couldn't say. I still don't understand it all. My husband was a liar I couldn't catch in a lie. And our marriage was on a collision course with something terrible I just couldn't see."

"The fake IDs?"

"I don't know anything about them."

"But you shot up the computer."

"One day, I found a document in the memory cache of the printer. Financial records regarding a great deal of money. More than even the cash Conrad had in that lockbox."

Mr. Delaney waits patiently.

"There were also monthly withdrawals. For what? What was this account? What was he funding on all those business trips?"

"Prostitutes? Drugs?"

"Maybe worse. I saw . . ." I can't bring myself to say it. I can't bring myself to see it again. I shake my head.

"You understand, Evie, the police are going to figure this out. When they do, they're going to say that Conrad's misdeeds are your motive for murder. Shooting the computer proves it—you were trying to cover your tracks."

"But I wasn't. At the time . . ." I shrug, feeling again the crushing weight of my dysfunctional childhood, followed by an equally dysfunctional marriage. "He's the father of my child," I say at last.

Mr. Delany doesn't need me to explain any more. "Still protecting the legacy," he murmurs.

"Some habits are hard to break."

"Do you have any idea who might have burned down your house?"

I shake my head. Which, now that I'm truly considering, sends a trickle of unease down my spine. In the shock of everything that's happened over the past forty-eight hours, the loss of my house has felt mostly like that—a loss. But after visiting the scene and talking to Sergeant Warren I'm starting to realize it's also a threat. Someone out there murdered my husband. Some unknown person torched my home to cover his or her tracks.

And for all my searching, all my questioning about the man I married, I have no idea who that person might be. Or if they're finished yet.

"Have you felt watched, threatened, in the past few weeks?" Mr. Delaney asks, as if reading my mind. "What about Conrad? You said it felt like something was up."

"He was tense. I wondered . . ." I can't put into words yet what I thought. The increasingly silent meals. The way I'd wake up some nights and find Conrad staring at me. The reason I had come home late from work that night, because if I arrived at the house any earlier . . .

I haven't been worried about some mysterious stranger out there.

But increasingly, I had started to wonder about the man sharing my bed.

I shrug. Everyone wants answers. My lawyer. The police. I only wish I had some.

"Evie, whatever your husband did, it's not your fault."

"I'm a liar. I married another liar. And now, my baby . . ." My throat closes up. I can't speak anymore. Whether it makes any sense at all, at one time I did love Conrad. Then I lost him. And like my father, Conrad remains a mystery; there are so many things now I'll never know about him. I feel tired of it all. The pattern of my life is wrong, and yet I can't seem to break it.

"I want to know the truth," I whisper. "I want to know one thing to be true."

"About your husband or your father?"

"I'll settle for either."

Mr. Delaney regards me for a long time. "Then I think you're going to have to start asking more questions."

"How? Who? I don't know anyone to talk to Conrad about. And my father, that was sixteen years ago. You were his closest friend. If you don't know who might've shot him, how am I supposed to figure it out?"

"There is another person."

I have a sudden sinking feeling. "No!"

"Yes. If you really want to understand what happened sixteen years ago, you should talk to your mom."

CHAPTER 20

D.D.

FROM THE BEGINNING, PHIL HAD warned D.D. that she'd regret making Flora Dane a CI. The woman was a known vigilante, an avowed loner, and just plain reckless. D.D. always hated it when her mentor was right.

"So to recap," she said briskly now, sitting at the head of the table, "you"—she skewered Flora with a glance—"took it upon yourself to call an Atlanta FBI agent and invite her into my investigation."

"Technically, I invited her to assist in *my* investigation," Flora said.

Yep, D.D.'s confidential informant had definitely gone rogue.

Flora continued. "I have an interest in all this, too, you know. What was Conrad Carter's association with Jacob? Were there other men or predators he was meeting? Does this mean he was part of some larger network of sociopaths and I missed it? Then, talking to SSA Quincy and hearing about other missing women—"

D.D. held up a hand. She pointed at the other newcomer in the room, who appeared to be around thirty years of age, could've passed for a Tom Ford model, and was sitting a lot closer to Flora than strictly necessary.

"And you? What's your role in all this?"

Kimberly Quincy was already smiling, which meant this was going to be good.

To the man's credit, he planted both elbows on the table, leaned forward, and met D.D.'s stare. "My name is Keith Edgar. I'm a computer analyst, and, um . . . I run a forum for true-crime enthusiasts. In particular, we've been working the Jacob Ness case for the past six years."

"*You've* been working the Jacob Ness case?"

Kimberly Quincy's smile was growing.

"We've always suspected there were other victims. The degree of sophistication and planning that went into Flora's abduction . . . no predator gets that smart overnight."

If Flora was offended to be discussed as little more than a case study, she didn't show it.

"And you know this because you're a computer analyst?" D.D. pressed.

"No, I know this because I've done a great deal of reading on the subject—"

"Internet true-crime porn."

"And I work with a group of talented experts, which included retired BPD detective Wayne Rock."

That caught D.D.'s attention. She'd known Wayne before his retirement five years ago. Great man, brilliant detective, who had lost his battle with cancer just a few months ago. The whole department had grieved, herself included.

"Wayne also believed there were other victims?"

"Absolutely. Most predators follow a pattern of escalation. With a self-proclaimed sex addict such as Ness, he probably started young as a voyeur, then evolved to inappropriate touching, before engaging in full-fledged sexual assault, and finally, ultimately . . ."

Edgar gestured awkwardly toward Flora, who still remained completely expressionless. Briefly, D.D. felt her heart soften. This was Flora's life. To be forever defined by a monster, whether she wanted to be or not. For the two years D.D. had known Flora, the woman had always refused to discuss her past. So to be part of this conversation now, to have invited a feebie no less, was an act in courage, whether D.D. liked it or not.

"Which brings us to you." She switched her attention to SSA Quincy. "The agent who actually figured out Ness was a long-haul trucker and organized the SWAT raid. You must've recovered a helluva lot of evidence."

"Yes and no, that's the problem. Ness's rig offered up some hair, other DNA samples. But his computer—which, according to Flora, he logged on to daily—"

Flora nodded.

"—was suspiciously lacking in content. Not even porn."

"He always watched porn." Flora spoke up.

"Completely wiping a hard drive is nearly impossible," the computer analyst spoke up. "He must have used a tool or app. Let's see, we're talking 2010." Edgar paused, seemed to be considering. "I'm guessing SteadyState, which was a free Microsoft app that worked with all XP operating systems. Microsoft offered it as a home computer safety system. It basically reverted the computer to a prior clean slate every time the laptop was rebooted, effectively deleting any malware or viruses kids might have inadvertently downloaded while playing online. The app worked so well, many computer professionals used it as well, myself included."

Edgar regarded Quincy with open curiosity.

"Ness's laptop did indeed contain SteadyState," she volunteered tersely.

"Interesting. Because it takes some time and capability to set up the app. To pick which items on the hard drive should be cleared and which should be left alone each time the system is rebooted. That alone proves an interesting level of computer sophistication for a man who didn't even graduate high school. And you're saying you didn't recover a single book in Ness's truck on computer programming, Windows operating systems, anything?"

"Nada."

Edgar and Flora Dane exchanged a look. D.D. wasn't sure she liked it.

"Ness's cell phone?" D.D. interrupted now.

"No smartphone," Quincy supplied. "We recovered a cheap, prepaid flip with hardly any usage. Certainly no texts or anything useful."

"I don't remember him ever using a cell," Flora said. "I would've guessed he had no one to call."

"Meaning the lack of evidence *is* the evidence," D.D. filled in. "Someone must've taught Ness how to cover his tracks, both with this computer app, and the prepaid flip." She glanced at Flora. "But the only time you remember him meeting up with another person was the one time you saw Conrad at the bar?"

"That's the only person I saw. But Jacob would disappear for days, sometimes even a week at a time. I always assumed he went on drug binges. But he could've been meeting up with other buddies. Maybe he was going on mini crime sprees, I don't know."

"Don't you think he'd brag to you?" Quincy spoke up. "He spoke to you about a great many things. And wasn't above threatening you with replacement."

Flora shrugged. "Jacob bragged. If he'd spent days with another woman, whether victim or prostitute, he might say something. But . . ." Flora took a deep breath. "Jacob was clever. He knew who he was.

From a very young age, he told me, he knew he was different from others. And he knew he had to hide it. He was very adept at self-preservation. If he'd found some group, started networking with other predators, even met them from time to time, no, I don't think he'd tell me. He liked his secrets, too. And it amused him when others underestimated him. Saw just a white-trash trucker, when he knew himself to be more."

"What about a Tor browser?" Edgar spoke up.

Quincy regarded the computer analyst coolly. "As a matter of fact, in addition to SteadyState, Ness's laptop also had the Tor browser."

"What does that mean?" Flora spoke up.

"Tor, a.k.a. 'the Onion Router,' is a browser that uses a peer-to-peer network that intentionally obfuscates source IP addresses," Edgar explained. He looked at D.D. "It's perfectly safe and legal. It also happens to be the primary browser used to access the dark web."

D.D. got it. "Where Jacob could very well have trolled chat rooms filled with other perverts such as himself, picking up all sorts of new tricks and forensic dodges, while rebooting his laptop each night, allowing this SteadyState to automatically clear all record of such site visits and chat-room logs." She glanced at Quincy. "And knowing all this, the FBI can't magically do anything to rebuild the computer's history?"

"The FBI has tried its magic," Quincy drawled drily, then turned to Keith Edgar. "Don't even think about it. No matter how brilliant a geek you are, I assure you, my geeks are better. Nor is the FBI in the business of sharing evidence."

Edgar sank down. D.D. started to remember how much she liked Kimberly Quincy.

"What about his trucking log?" asked D.D. "Don't long-haul truckers have GPS and computer monitoring and that kind of thing? Seems like that should be a significant source of data."

"Once again, the answer is yes and no," Quincy said. "The

company Jacob worked for only kept the backup data for three months. So we know his last three months of movement, give or take, but as for the time he had his rig at his safe house to first load up Flora, nada. Likewise, even if we had a specific time period—say, Flora could pinpoint the week or month Jacob met your murder victim at the bar—we can't look it up. What we did find . . . Jacob drove the highways of the South with some side trips to cheap motels, et cetera. We also discovered gaps in the data, which leads us to believe Jacob may have figured out how to turn off his GPS and computer monitoring—and that's not easy to do. These systems are required by law and designed to track how many consecutive hours a trucker has traveled and basically demand driving breaks. You can't just turn them off with a flick of a switch, or all drivers under a tough deadline would do it. Again, a surprising level of electronic sophistication from a man with a ninth-grade education."

Quincy tilted her head toward Edgar, who'd first made the point.

"So what exactly is the plan here?" D.D. asked. "Go after Jacob Ness's principal hideaway? See if we can find new evidence there?"

Quincy and Flora nodded.

"And to do that, Flora has volunteered herself as what, a hypnosis subject? Because you know experts still don't agree on the validity of recovered memories, and juries just plain hate that crap."

"There are other techniques." Flora spoke up first. "I've done some research. The human brain works a lot like a computer. First, there's the matter of what data is recorded in the moment. Particularly in traumatic situations, some people's senses heighten and they see all. But most people actually shut down. They squeeze their eyes shut, cover their ears, try to block what's happening. They don't want to know. Meaning the data is incomplete."

D.D. arched a brow at her CI.

"I was a long-term victim," Flora supplied in response to the next logical question. "In the beginning, maybe I did try to shut it out. I certainly don't remember many specific details of the first . . . assault. But over time, the . . . continuity"—Flora picked the word carefully—"made the events less traumatic and more normal. At which point, I had plenty of opportunities to note and record more . . . data. So it's not like I'm trying to recover one memory, which might be suspect, but a string of impressions I had months to form."

On the table, Edgar's hand moved closer to Flora's. Still not touching, D.D. noticed, but closer. In return, Flora's hand drifted slightly toward his. Fascinating. D.D. had never known the woman to even look at a member of the opposite sex. Now this: a true-crime buff. She hoped Flora knew what she was doing. And she hoped like hell Keith Edgar saw Flora as a person, and not just the object of a macabre criminal case.

"But there are other issues with memory recovery techniques," D.D. stated now. "To keep with your analogy, it's not enough for the data to be present. There's the small matter of extracting it without corrupting it with other information—the power of suggestion."

"I wouldn't do hypnosis," Flora said immediately. "I've been doing some research and that's my least favorite option."

D.D. and Quincy both eyed the woman.

"I would prefer a visualization exercise, grounded in known triggers."

"I'll bite," D.D. said. "What?"

"Smell is the strongest known trigger for memory. Therefore, some experts suggest starting a visualization exercise with what the subject knows to be true about the episode: say, the smell of urine-soaked pine wood." Again, the woman didn't flinch. "The taste of blood on my tongue. The feel of a sliver in my finger."

It took D.D. a moment to get it; then she wished she hadn't.

"You're talking about sticking yourself back in the coffin? Re-creating your own captivity, for the sake of a memory?"

Flora stared at her. Very gaunt now, D.D. saw. Very dark shadows under her eyes. "I think it's worth trying."

"And Dr. Keynes—"

"It's my decision!"

"I'll take that to be a no." D.D. turned to Quincy. "Did you know about this?"

"No," the agent said immediately. "And to be honest, I don't agree with it. Re-creating trauma, particularly of that nature, risks sending you down the rabbit hole all over again. The psychological impact on you, where this might lead. It's not a good idea."

"We need to find where Jacob lived—"

"Not at the expense of your mental health," D.D. snapped. "He took enough from you. Don't give him any more."

"This is my choice. This is me fighting back!"

"This is you sacrificing yourself. First you wouldn't talk about anything, now you're risking a complete meltdown. You do realize there are options in between, don't you?"

"Such as?"

"Forget coffins for a second. For the sake of argument, we can try out your technique but go after a memory that's much less traumatic. How about the night Jacob met Conrad? You described it as a dive bar. You said you ate and ate. Nachos, chicken wings, beer? Country music on the radio, maybe you know a particular song? If you're going to use your five senses to attempt to trigger a memory, I think beer, hot wings, and country songs are a much safer place to start. With the assistance of Dr. Keynes, of course. Because this is way out of my league, and yours, too." D.D. gestured to SSA Quincy.

"You want more information on Conrad Carter," the federal agent filled in.

"That is the point of my investigation. But for the record, we made an interesting discovery today: Conrad Carter had hidden away half a dozen fake IDs. Not great ones, but good enough to get into a bar."

"You think he used the IDs as an alias when he traveled," Quincy stated. "Including when he met up with Jacob Ness."

"If Flora could remember what name Jacob called him, that would confirm our suspicions. But also, what exactly did they talk about, did any other names come up? You want to find Jacob's secret clubhouse—fair enough. But maybe the other way of coming after Jacob Ness is to identify the other members of the club. Especially if some of them are still alive . . ."

"They might be able to provide information on Ness, including his cabin hideaway." Keith Edgar spoke up.

"Based on what SSA Quincy is saying, they were probably the ones who gave Jacob the pointers on how to keep it hidden." D.D. looked at Flora. "What do you think?"

The woman frowned. "I don't know. I was drinking heavily that night. Meaning, the quality of the data recorded . . ."

"At a certain point you were drunk. Drunks have notoriously lousy memories."

"But I don't remember Jacob calling him Conrad. I think it might have been another name. And that was in the beginning. Maybe there is more I saw, or noticed, than I think. If Jacob had help—and it seems like he must've—then, yes, I'd like to go after those men, too."

"Not just one predator, but a whole network of them." Keith Edgar sounded slightly breathless.

D.D. frowned at him. "Not so fast, big boy. This is an active criminal case. Civilians need not apply."

"He's not just a civilian." Flora spoke up quickly. "He's an expert on Jacob in his own right."

"Hey." Quincy tapped the table. "I believe the FBI wears that crown."

"I'm not doing it," Flora said, "if he's not around."

D.D. stared at her CI. Yep, Flora had definitely gone rogue. And was possibly love-struck? Except that didn't fit with the Flora she knew at all. Meaning . . .

More and more questions. Where would D.D.'s case be without them?

"He signs a nondisclosure."

"Done." Edgar spoke up immediately.

"We talk to Dr. Keynes and get his agreement."

"I'll do it." Flora already had out her phone.

"You should tell your mother," D.D. said, mostly because she was a mom and she just couldn't help herself.

She got back the answer she expected: a mutinous stare.

D.D. sighed. She didn't know if this was the best idea or worst idea she'd ever had. She respected Flora's strength but worried about her self-destructive streak. D.D. needed some kind of fresh approach to get her investigation going, but a "recovered memory" from a night spent binge drinking definitely felt like a stretch.

And yet, for the first time since D.D. had known Flora, the woman was willing to talk about Jacob. She was willing to look backward, at four hundred and seventy-two days of absolutely horrifying memories. There was a determination and resilience in evidence that D.D. had to admire.

If Dr. Keynes helped them, if they started with something easier than Flora climbing back into a pine coffin . . .

Maybe Flora could get the answers she now so desperately wanted. While Kimberly Quincy caught a new lead on six missing women, and D.D. found out what Conrad Carter had been doing on all his business trips and who, other than his wife, might want him dead.

It sounded simple enough. Which probably explained the sinking feeling in D.D.'s stomach. The best-laid plans . . .

Flora was still staring at her. SSA Quincy, too. Flora was going to do it one way or another, D.D. realized. She'd made up her mind sometime in the middle of the night. And once set on a course, she wasn't the type of person to let anything stop her.

"Fine," D.D. announced. "A trip down memory lane it is."

Flora hit dial.

CHAPTER 21

FLORA

WHEN I WALK INTO FBI headquarters two hours later with a bag of takeout nachos and chicken wings, no one gives me a second glance. Wearing my usual uniform of worn cargo pants and a baggy sweatshirt beneath a bulky down coat, I probably look like a delivery person. Keith, trailing behind me with a six-pack of Bud cans, earns several startled looks, but that's nothing compared to the attention Samuel gets just by waiting for us. My victim specialist, Dr. Keynes, has features that stand out in a crowd.

Compared to Sergeant Warren, Samuel was surprisingly agreeable to my plan. If anything, I had the feeling he'd been waiting for such a call. He probably recognized my refusal to talk about Jacob was a form of denial that couldn't go on forever.

Now Samuel moves forward. I get a clasp on the shoulder, a show of warmth from a man who knows everything awful there is to know about me, including the fact I don't do hugs. He shakes Keith's hand, and the two take a moment to size up each other. Neither says anything, but Keith still appears a little starstruck.

Samuel never initiates a conversation. His job is listening, not talking, as he once explained to me, but he's also intensely private. If he knows every terrible thing about me, it took me five years to figure out he was secretly in love with my mom. Even then, I didn't actually deduce anything; my mom had to announce they'd decided to start dating, but only if I was okay with it.

I'm not sure I ever gave permission. I think I was too busy standing before her with my jaw hanging open. I still can't picture my mom, in her free-spirit yoga clothes, driving a tractor around her organic potato farm, with a man addicted to Armani—but then, no kid wants to imagine her mom dating. I think they're happy. I guess I even hope so. But mostly, I don't want to know.

Federal buildings have a lot of security. Samuel is meeting us because of the beer, which the guards either don't like or surreptitiously hope to confiscate for later. Samuel takes one of them aside, murmurs a few words, and just like that, we're through. Keith continues his wide-eyed stare. I roll my eyes at Samuel and don't even bother to ask what he said. I've never seen Samuel not get his way. That and his cheekbones are like his superpowers.

Upstairs, Sergeant Warren and SSA Quincy are already waiting. They both have cups of coffee and are chatting away like old friends. Territorial pissing match aside, they seem to have mutual respect for each other, which makes my life easier. Individually, they are solid investigators. Together, I should have double the chance of getting answers.

I'm still very curious about D.D.'s earlier meeting with Conrad Carter's wife. Did the woman really shoot her own husband? Because D.D. implied the case wasn't as clear-cut as the news reported. I'm trying out some strategy of my own: assist with D.D.'s investigation now with this little trip down memory lane, then interrogate the detective on what she knows about Conrad Carter later.

Samuel has booked a meeting room. Much like the one at BPD

headquarters, it has a wall of windows, which will allow the others to observe from the hall. For the "visualization" exercise, Samuel has already said it should be only him and me in the room. I'm supposed to relax, which is already nearly impossible. Having other people around won't help.

Now I open up the takeout and arrange the nachos and chicken wings in the middle of the table. Already, the smell wafts across the room. I wait for scent alone to transport me. I mostly feel like I'm standing in the middle of a federal building with soggy tortilla chips.

Samuel produces a glass. Keith does the honor of pouring out a beer. Again, we're trying to be as specific as possible. Jacob always ordered Bud, always in a glass. Final touch, country music. I have a vague memory of it playing in the background. I'm less sure about the song. Keith already Googled country's greatest hits from seven years ago and, while we were waiting for the food, compiled a playlist. He sets his phone on the table now and gets the party started.

Again, I wait to feel . . . something. Mostly, I'm self-conscious and awkward.

"We're missing something."

Four pairs of eyes stare at me. Not helping.

"Popcorn. There was popcorn in little red-and-white-checkered containers. And it shouldn't be this bright. No honky-tonk is this bright."

Keith heads for the panel of light switches. Samuel disappears without ever saying a word, meaning he must know how to get popcorn.

That leaves me with the two investigators. D.D. is eyeing the food in the middle of the table.

"I'm hungry," she says.

"You're always hungry," Quincy replies.

It's like they've suddenly become besties. This, I have a feeling, will not be as good for me.

Keith can't figure out how to dim the overhead bulbs. In the end, he shuts them off. Given all the light still pouring in through the glass windows, the effect works out nicely. At least it takes the edge off the room, makes it feel less sterile.

Samuel returns with a bag of microwave popcorn. He opens the bag, the smell hits, and for the first time I feel it. Like a door opening in my mind. I can smell the bar, the beer, popcorn, melted cheese. I pick up the glass, take a small sip, and then I can taste it, too. I'd been so thirsty, so hungry, so scared.

Fake-Everett. That's what I'd called him back then. Because he'd started my programming by taking away my name. No more Flora, just Molly. Molly in a hot-pink dress only a hooker would wear. And I was to call him by my father's name. I didn't even remember my father, but I had to believe he had loved me, so to call this beast by his name had hurt.

Everett, which I said out loud. Fake-Everett, which I used in my head, because silent rebellions were all I had left.

"Have a seat," Samuel tells me, and I realize for the first time the others have already left. It's just Samuel and me and beer and country music and the smell of popcorn and a memory of one evening, already trying to claw out of my head.

"Where are you, Flora?"

"Molly."

"Molly," he amends.

"I'm hungry. So, so hungry." I press a hand to my stomach. Then I pick up the first kernel of popcorn, tasting the saltiness of it against my tongue. Another small sip of beer. "He left me for the whole week," I murmur. "Each day hungrier and hungrier. But I couldn't leave the motel. If I did, he'd find me. He'd kill me. He told me so. And then he'd head north and kill my whole family. So I waited. Starving and starving. I waited."

Sweatshirt is all wrong. Too warm, too comforting. I should be overexposed and shivering from the AC that always blasted away in the South.

No thinking. Doing. Shed the sweatshirt, followed by my long-sleeve top, until my arms are exposed in my gray tank top. Goose bumps ripple up across my flesh. Better.

"Where are you, Molly?" Samuel asks again. His voice is deep and rich. Hypnotic. It gives me a moment of uneasiness. I don't want to be under anyone's thrall. I don't want to surrender control. Not when I've spent all these years fighting to get it back.

My choice, my choice. Another kernel of popcorn, concentrating on the buttery goodness.

Hungry. I'd been so desperately, acutely, stomach-growlingly hungry. And that, as much as anything, takes me back.

"TWO BUDS," I whisper. "Fake-Everett lets me have a beer. He hardly ever orders me food or alcohol. Waste of money, he'd say. The beer is nice. I'm grateful to him."

"Are you sitting or standing?"

"I'm sitting. On a barstool. Fake-Everett stands behind me. Like he's protecting me. I'm his girl."

"What do you smell?"

"Popcorn. Oh my God, it smells so good! The bartender brings us some. Happy hour perk. I know the rules. I look at Fake-Everett. He nods. He's going to let me eat free food. My hand is shaking so hard I can barely raise it. One kernel. One single kernel."

On the table, my hand rises. Takes one single kernel.

"When you haven't eaten in a while," I whisper, "you have to pace yourself. Otherwise, you'll get sick. And I can't afford to get sick. Not when I never know when I'll get to eat again."

Another single kernel.

"Tell me about the bar," Samuel intones. "The bartender?"

"Umm, white guy. Red flannel shirt over a black T-shirt. Busy. Nods at Fake-Everett once. Won't look at me at all. Glasses above his head. Pulling them down, pouring beers from the tap, sliding them down the bar. Scooping out more popcorn. Moving, moving, moving, always in motion."

"Name tag?"

"No."

"What does the bar look like?"

"Dark wood. Very shellacked. Shiny. But sticky. Popcorn all over the floor. Pool tables behind me. Clink, clink, clink. Lots of people sitting around the bar. Guys in cowboy hats, women in tight jeans. I keep tugging my dress up. I feel ashamed. I don't look at the bartender anymore. I don't want to know what he thinks of me."

"Is the beer sitting on a coaster? A napkin? Directly on the bar?"

I frown, squeeze my eyes shut, focus harder. "Coaster."

"What does it say?"

"Bud Light."

"Are there any lights behind the bar? Glowing signs?"

"Amber. Um . . . Abita Amber, glowing in orange and red."

"How's the popcorn?"

"Good! God, I'm hungry."

"Look around the room. What do you see?"

"I can't. Eyes straight ahead. Or Fake-Everett will get mad and I don't want him to be mad. Not till I've gotten to eat more popcorn."

"What about beside you? Can you see anyone beside you?"

"A man. He sits down. He looks at Fake-Everett and nods. Fake-Everett nods back. The man comments that I'm skinny. Fake-Everett says it's my own fault. I eat more popcorn. I don't look at either of them, but I'm confused that Fake-Everett is talking to a stranger. He never talks to anyone."

"Can you describe the man to me?"

"Umm, younger. Early thirties, maybe? Fit. Not tall, but muscular.

Dark hair, smooth shaven. He's wearing a blue T-shirt and jeans and I can smell him—soap and aftershave. Fake-Everett only ever smells like sweat and dirty clothes. The man stares at my chest. I pull up the top of my dress again. I hate the dress. Fake-Everett tells me I should be grateful when he gives me clothes. I'm not."

"What happens next?"

"A tray of nachos goes by. All chips and melted cheese piled with salsa and sour cream. Oh my God, they smell so good! The man sees me eyeing them and asks the bartender to bring us some. I'm pretty sure to share, but I don't dare ask. Fake-Everett has a hand on my shoulder. He's squeezing very hard. He's on something. His eyes are too bright. In this mood, Fake-Everett is very danger-ous. I don't feel so good anymore. I'm nervous. Very nervous."

"Are the man and Fake-Everett talking?"

"The man is tapping the bar." My fingers move. There is a pattern. Same rhythm, over and over again. I can hear it in my mind. My fin-gers play it out on the table. *Tap, tap, tap, tappity tap.* "I think he's nervous, too," I whisper. "But I don't know why. He keeps staring at me. I just wish he'd look away."

"And then?"

"Nachos. They arrive. The man says we can share. I look at Fake-Everett. I'm trying to understand. He never talks to others, he never shares. He tells me to show the man some respect, be more apprecia-tive. I don't understand that. Something is wrong. This whole . . . sce-nario. Something is going on. The strange man, Fake-Everett, it's like they know one another. And the man keeps tapping, tapping, tapping. I wish he would go away."

"What does Fake-Everett do next?"

"Eats nachos. Scoops up big mouthfuls. Smears sour cream and salsa on his face. He doesn't care. He's a pig."

"What do you do?"

"I eat, too. Quickly. Drink more beer. Something is going to happen. I don't know what."

"And the man?"

"He doesn't eat. He ordered the nachos but takes only a single chip. He just keeps looking at me, and fidgeting. He orders more food, but again, for Fake-Everett and me, not for himself."

"What do you hear, Molly?"

The change in focus startles me. I return to tapping the table. The man's restless beat. Then, I'm humming, too. A Kenny Chesney song playing from the jukebox behind us. *Clink, clink* of pool balls.

And voices. Fake-Everett and the man. Heads closer together, murmuring while I grab another chicken wing and hastily gnaw away. I have a suspicion now. A growing feeling of dread over what's going to happen next. Must eat. Must eat as much as possible as fast as possible.

"Conner. Fake-Everett calls the man Conner.

"*'Told you she was pretty,'* Fake-Everett says.

"*'Too skinny,'* Conner says.

"*'Not at the rate she's eating now. Trust me, trained her myself.'*

"*'You're sure?'*

"*'Course. Deal's a deal.'*

"*'And the return?'*

"*'Same place tomorrow night. Parking lot. Don't want to make too big an impression, hanging out at the same bar twice.'*

"*'And she's agreed?'*

"*'Course. Girl knows better than to make fuss. You'll see.'*

"The bar lights flicker." Seeing it abruptly in my mind, I report the memory out loud. "Closing time. We have to leave." My hand presses against my stomach. "I'm scared."

"What happens next, Molly?"

"The man, Conner, he pays the bill. Throws down a hundred

without even blinking. When the man turns away, Fake-Everett grabs the money for himself. So fast, like a snake. I don't feel good. I stumble, walking out. The beer, the food, what I'm now sure is going to happen next."

"What's going to happen?"

"Fake-Everett . . . he sold me. Or rented me? But what they were whispering . . . Fake-Everett is going to tell me to go home with this man. I should be grateful. He's cleaner, younger, better-looking. But I think that's the problem. I know Fake-Everett. He doesn't share his toys. And I can already tell you, he doesn't like this guy. He doesn't like any man better-looking than him. He's playing some game. This Conner, myself, we'll both pay for it in the end."

"What do you mean?"

"Fake-Everett's already told me he's going to kill me and feed me to the gators. Conner touches me, Fake-Everett will kill him, too. Both of us. And take all the money, drugs, whatever it was Conner promised. Fake-Everett doesn't negotiate. He steals. He hoards. He is awful, but he's consistent. Conner doesn't understand yet. He's as dead as I am."

"Where is Conner?"

"Walking ahead of us. Straight into the parking lot. He has square shoulders. Strong, fit. Fake-Everett's fingers are digging into my arm. He's dragging me out of the bar. I can feel the rage coming off him in waves. I think he would like to kill me right now. Or maybe it's Conner that he hates so much."

"How do you feel?"

"Like I'm going to vomit. But I have to hold it in, time it right."

"For what?"

"Parking lot. The air is warm, humid. For the first time, I'm not chilled. Except now I'm breaking into a sweat. But it's okay. I know what I'm doing. I got this.

"People disappear, climb into their pickup trucks. Conner stops.

Looks back at us. And then—I vomit. All over his shoes. He jumps back. Swears. Yells. Others turn, start to pay attention. Fake-Everett waves them off. I can still feel his anger, but it's softer. Conner is backing up. No one wants a puker.

"Conner turns away," I whisper. "He leaves without me. And I know Fake-Everett isn't happy, but then I also know exactly what to say. *You've been gone for a week. I just want to be with you. Only you.* Fake-Everett thinks he's so smart. He thinks he's the one in control. But I have my tricks, too.

"Fake-Everett isn't angry anymore. Fake-Everett takes me back to the motel. And I survive another day."

I'm tired suddenly. So exhausted my head slumps forward. I'm not thinking of popcorn or beer or country music. I'm thinking of the intense fatigue of all those minutes, hours, days. Never knowing if I would make it. Hating my life, but still not quite able to give it up. Eking out each moment because the will to live makes it harder than you think to simply let go.

Samuel's hand, solid on my shoulder. "Flora, open your eyes."

I do, but I still feel blurry, out of it.

"It's okay. Take a moment. You did good."

A bottle of water appears before me. I drink it gratefully, washing the aftertaste of beer from my mouth. I hardly ever drink, and certainly not Jacob's favorite beer. I'm shivering slightly. I realize I'm barely dressed and find my pile of clothes, pulling each layer back on.

The others are behind me, murmuring in low voices.

"Conner was one of Conrad's fake IDs," D.D. is saying.

"Abita Select Amber is one of the top-selling beers in Mississippi," Quincy supplies.

Keith says nothing. Comes to sit beside me. Remains silent, for which I'm grateful.

"The tapping," Samuel says. He rests his dark hand on the table, finds the pattern. It jars me a little, the sound from my head playing out in real life.

He regards all of us expectantly. "No military backgrounds?" he presses.

Keith suddenly lights up. "Oh my God. He was tapping in Morse code!"

"Exactly."

"What was he saying?" D.D. asks.

"He wasn't. He was asking a question, the same question, over and over. He was asking, 'Are you okay?' But Flora never answered him."

CHAPTER 22

EVIE

BEFORE RETURNING HOME, I CONVINCE Mr. Delaney to swing by CVS for some basic supplies. I find a gigantic purse. Cheap brown leather, covered in miscellaneous pockets and snap detailing meant to make it look urban cool. Definitely not my classic Coach Christmas gift from Conrad. My mom will hate it. I smile as I sling it over my shoulder.

I pick out a toothbrush, toothpaste, deodorant, light makeup. My mother has the bathroom fully stocked but I want my own toiletries. Brands I prefer.

I find myself in front of hair dye for a long time. Mr. Delaney has wandered off. No doubt trying to give me space. Alone in the pharmacy store aisle, I find myself thinking like the murder suspect I truly am. Maybe I should think beyond my preferred hair gel. What about a bug-out kit? New hair color, new hairstyle? Sunglasses, hat? If I ever want to leave my mother's house, it will require some subterfuge.

So I do it. A rich brunette to cover my ash blond. Then, while I'm at it, a cheap purple scarf, oversized sunglasses. Then I go a little nuts in the hair accessory section, from scissors to hair extensions to flowered barrettes. I don't know why I pick the things I pick, and yet it all makes perfect sense. Next up, pen and notepad. Then, even better, I stumble across a rack of prepaid cells. I select three. Again, not sure why. It feels right.

I need money. But my ATM card melted in the house fire. Maybe Mr. Delaney will take me to my local bank, where I can withdraw in person. Or loan me money? I feel uncomfortable, like I'm crossing some line; then I order myself to get over it. I can't be dependent on my mom and helpless in the face of whatever is going to happen next. Between retrieving my passport and financial documents from the safe, and now this little shopping expedition, I'm going to make it.

I head back to the checkout line. Mr. Delaney magically reappears. He already has a credit card in hand, which makes me feel self-conscious again. Then he spots the prepaid cells. Without a word, he returns his credit card to his wallet, extracts cash instead.

I think I get it. He doesn't want there to be evidence he bought the phones. In case they are recovered later at . . . what? The scene of a shooting? Another house fire? He doesn't ask. I don't tell.

"Nice purse," he says finally when we emerge from the store and I start transferring over my supplies.

"I need cash," I say. "And a new ATM card."

He drives me to the bank.

There, things get more interesting. I walk in, and the first teller across from me, some woman I've never met, immediately gasps. I actually stop and glance behind me, wondering what the fuss is about. Did someone famous walk in behind me? Nope. Next, I look down. Are my clothes covered in lunch? No. Then, finally I get it. She's gasping at me. A woman whose picture has been all over the news as a murderer.

I feel a lot better about my decision to buy hair dye. I only wish I'd bought more.

I square my shoulders, produce my passport, and get to work.

I know my accounts. I know what Conrad and I have and don't have in our joint savings. I'm not sure if the police can freeze the funds as part of their investigation—sounds like a logical enough thing for them to do—so I make a large withdrawal now. The woman fusses, says she needs her manager. I play it cool, officially having an out-of-body experience where I'm no longer a shy mathematician's daughter whose been shunning the limelight for her entire life but a regular La Femme Nikita. Yeah, that was me on the news. And if I was willing to shoot my own husband, just think of what I might do to you.

Then I wise up enough to turn sideways and show off my rounded belly. By the time the manager returns, I have the full pregnancy profile going on. She softens almost immediately. At least my future stretch marks have come in handy.

She tries to tell me there's a limit on what I can withdraw. Which is partly true, but not the paltry amount she's conceding to me. I keep my voice firm and polite as I walk her through it. This account is in my name. My passport verifies my identity. I am entitled to withdraw what I want to withdraw. Any questions, my lawyer is sitting in the car.

In the end, the manager counts out five thousand dollars. Stacks of hundreds. I find myself thinking of the metal box again, Conrad's own stash of IDs and cash. It both confuses and saddens me. What was he really doing on all those business trips?

And why marry me? Why acquire a wife, then a child, if his whole life was just a lie?

As long as I'm in the bank, I order a new debit card to be sent to my mother's address. That customer service person is equally skittish to be around me. I keep my chin up, but on my lap my hands start to shake. I'm an introvert. This level of attention is difficult for me. Especially the way people look, whisper.

Forget Conrad. I feel like a sixteen-year-old girl who just shot and killed her father all over again.

I get my money. I get promises of a new card. Then I clutch my bag to my shoulder and flee the premises.

THE MOMENT MR. Delaney turns down my mother's street, reporters rush forward. He is patient and firm. One slow, steady speed. The reporters quickly start giving way because he will not. It occurs to me that he's probably driven this gauntlet before, both given his line of work and given what happened sixteen years ago.

Did I come out of the house back then? I don't remember. I was so lost in my own grief. While I'm sure the media was terrible to my mother, asking for the gory details again and again, I'm also sure she got to vamp up her role of heartbroken widow. While I, the strange quiet kid, was let off the hook as a minor.

What did I do after my father's death? Sat in my room and stared at a wall, trying not to see his shattered chest. Sat in his office and stared at his whiteboard, trying to capture his last bit of genius. Then one day my mother said I was going to school, so I did. Because that's how it works in my family. We don't talk. We don't resolve. We just . . . move on.

Mr. Delaney turns into the driveway. Once we're on private ground, the reporters have to give up. I notice signs staked in the lawn: No Trespassing. Probably Mr. Delaney's handiwork from when he first arrived this morning. It makes an interesting counterpart to all the neighborhood Christmas decorations.

Mr. Delaney parks the car and looks at me.

"I'll be okay," I tell him.

"Two vodkas are okay," he says. "Five are too many." He's

referring to my mother, who probably is a functioning alcoholic. Take away her vodka and she's unworkable. Too much vodka and she's overly dramatic.

Conrad rarely drank, only the occasional beer. I realize now that's one of the things I liked about him. Growing up in a household where alcohol felt like a necessary evil, I barely touched it myself, and was happy my husband didn't either.

"Will you tell her about the lockbox discovery?" Mr. Delaney asks me.

"No. She already hates him enough."

"Do you know why?"

"A window salesman isn't worthy of Earl Hopkins's daughter."

Mr. Delaney smiles. "I don't think that's the case."

"Then why?"

"You should ask her yourself."

My turn to give him a look. But I'd told him I'd be okay and I can't make a liar out of myself now, so I pop open the door and step resolutely out of the car. Across the street, the reporters shout questions, hoping to get lucky. In front of me, my mother appears at the side door, vodka martini already in hand, though it's only three in the afternoon.

Last glance at Mr. Delaney.

Then, ready or not, here I come.

MY FIRST ORDER of business is trying to gauge how much my mother has already consumed. A jug of Ketel One sits on the kitchen island, a peeled lemon beside it. She follows my gaze, then raises her martini glass in open defiance. Normally, my mother waits till five o'clock sharp for her daily habit, but she's never been great under pressure.

As usual she is impeccably garbed. Dark-green wool slacks, a cashmere turtleneck the color of oatmeal, a beautifully pleated chocolate-brown vest. Given her beverage and the waiting media, I doubt she's planning on going out, but in my mother's world, there's no excuse for ever looking other than your best.

Now she spies my new chunky, clunky purse. Immediately, her brow furrows. "What is *that*?"

"My new bag. Old one burned up in the fire."

"Evie, if you needed a purse why didn't you just say so? I have a number of Chanels that would be perfect for you."

I don't answer the question, simply set my purse on the kitchen chair closest to me. Then I cross to the bottle of vodka, screw back on the cap, put it away. In my world, this passes for conversation.

"Did you eat lunch?" she tries now, going on the attack as a concerned mom.

"Mr. Delaney took me for lunch."

"Did you eat? It's very important that you eat. The baby—"

"I had a very healthy, fulfilling lunch, thank you. Including OJ, hold the vodka."

She flushes, frowns at me again. "Did you find what you needed at your house?"

"I learned enough."

"Is it a total loss?"

I hate to say this. "Yes."

"Then, that's it; you'll stay here. Your rooms are ready to go, the nursery is nearly done. A woman in your condition can't be subject to undue stress. Frankly, all this nonsense about the shooting is enough."

For a moment, I think she's referring to my father, then realize she means Conrad.

"The police say Dad didn't kill himself." I don't mean to utter the words so baldly, but I don't know how else to deliver them.

My mom freezes. There's some kind of look on her face, but I can't read it. Horror, sorrow, confusion. All three.

"Why are the police talking about your father's death?"

"Because I told them the truth: I didn't do it."

"Evie Hopkins—"

Not my married name, I notice. Even half drunk and caught off guard, my mom can still get her digs in.

"I didn't shoot him. We both know it. We lied to protect him sixteen years ago, Mom. Because we loved him. Because we couldn't bear to think he killed himself. But it's been sixteen years, and given what happened with Conrad . . . If we lied to protect Dad all those years ago, then I need us to find out the truth now, in order to save me."

My mom sits. Hard. Just collapses in the chair, vodka sloshing against the sides of her glass. For a moment, she looks lost, almost childlike, and it unnerves me. Then she takes a fortifying sip.

"I don't understand," she says.

"According to the police, someone else shot Dad. Someone had to be here in the house."

"But we didn't see anyone."

"Then the person left right before we entered."

"Are they sure? How can they know these things?"

"You watch TV—"

"I don't watch those shows—"

"Of course you watch those shows! Everyone watches *those* shows. Plus, I've seen them in your Netflix queue. This isn't the time for posturing, Mom. Now is the time for truth."

She glares at me. It makes her look more like herself. We both relax. She takes another sip of her martini.

"They're sure?"

"Yes, Mom. Dad didn't commit suicide." The words are harder to say than I thought. Again, my family has always been defined by the things unspoken. And *suicide* is such a sad, terrible word. We never talked about it. Just like myself at lunch, my mother gets a sudden sheen in her eyes. The weight of her own burden lifting after all these years. What could've been a shared burden, if only we'd been the type of people to share such things.

She looks away, drains her glass. Then, without another glance at me, gets up, crosses to the cabinet, and gets the vodka back down. I don't try to stop her. Some battles are too hard to fight.

"Everyone loved your father," she says at last, peeling off a curl of lemon rind. "He was a genius. Who doesn't love a genius?"

"Other geniuses," I answer. "Jealous professors, overworked TAs, flunked students."

She frowns again but, focusing on the preparation of a perfect martini, at least doesn't immediately dismiss my ideas.

"It's why your father threw the poker parties," she says abruptly.

I shake my head, not following.

"The academic world is competitive. For ideas, grants, students, funding. Your father didn't love that aspect. Especially in math, he saw everyone working alone. He thought ideas would be better if people shared their ideas and opinions. The university environment wasn't conducive to such things, he said. So, poker nights. Invite other professors, doctorate students, et cetera. Get everyone relaxed, having fun. Collaboration would naturally follow."

I nod. I never heard my father dismiss another colleague's ideas or talk down to a student. As professors went, I always thought he was ahead of his time. Or maybe, simply that secure in his own brilliance. But I hadn't known this aspect of the poker nights and it only makes me miss him more.

"There was a TA," she says abruptly. "Aarav Patil. Very promising, your father said. But a loner. He rarely attended the poker nights, no matter how many times your father invited him. And while your father wasn't one to go into detail with me, I could tell he was getting frustrated with Patil. I'm not sure the boy would've been his TA much longer."

"Okay." Belatedly, I realize I should be writing this down. Ugly purse to the rescue. I have my pad and paper. "Did this Patil know where we lived?"

"They all did. Your father was just as likely to have students over to his home office as the one on campus."

"What about professors?"

She takes her first sip of her martini but is contemplative now, less emotional. "I'm not sure. I never heard your father say a bad word, but that didn't mean others weren't jealous. There were things your father could just . . . comprehend. His mind . . ." She looks as me abruptly. "There was no else in the world like your father," she whispers. "No one else."

For the first time I get it, truly get it. She loved him. Probably as much as I did. We both loved him. And neither one of us has been the same since.

"I miss him, too," I say.

She just smiles, but there are tears on her cheeks now. I think I should stand up, give my mom a hug. But I'm too afraid she'll turn away. So I remain seated. She drinks her vodka. We both wait.

"You should talk to Dr. Martin Hoffman," she says abruptly, "the department chair. He's retired now, but sixteen years ago, he would've known everyone and what personalities might have had issues with others." She pauses a moment, then concedes: "And who might've been more ambitious. When your father died, that left a vacancy, of course, which had to be filled."

"Who got his job?"

"Katarina Ivanova."

"A woman?" It shouldn't surprise me but still catches me off guard. "Did my father know her?"

"Yes. He'd been mentoring her for the past year. He was . . . impressed." My mother's face shutters up, and in her expression, I learn a few more things about Katarina Ivanova: She was very beautiful and my mother hated her.

"I don't remember her from poker night."

"Not everyone could always make it." Or my mother hadn't wanted her around.

"But she'd been to Dad's home office?"

"Of course. That was how he worked."

"Thank you."

My mother looks at me. She still has tear tracks on her cheeks, and her fingers on the stem of her martini glass are trembling. "What good will come of this?" she asks me softly.

"I don't know."

"He's dead. We both paid the price. And as for what happened Tuesday night . . . How can the circumstances of your father's death matter? You were a child. The records were sealed."

"The police are reopening the case."

"Because you stirred the pot."

"I have to know, Mom. I can't keep . . . being the same person, telling the same lies. Just once, I want to know the truth."

My mother smiles sadly. "You know what they say, dear: Be careful what you wish for."

CHAPTER 23

D.D.

"SO WHAT DO WE ACTUALLY know about this guy?" D.D. asked.

They'd taken over the FBI's meeting room. Not D.D.'s favorite location, as she felt she was ceding more and more of her homicide investigation to the feds. Then again, she had two feebies at the table to her one BPD self. Add to that a rogue CI and a civilian true-crime buff, and this was getting to be the craziest investigative team she'd ever seen.

She didn't approve of crazy. Or the fact that she didn't know what to do next. She *always* knew what to do next.

Dr. Keynes did the honors: "Flora, did you ever see the man—Conrad or, I suppose, Conner—at another bar? Or perhaps meeting up with Jacob at one of the truck stops?"

"No. But Jacob would often take off on his own . . ."

There was a slight hesitation and D.D. caught it.

"What?" she demanded.

Flora wouldn't make eye contact with any of them. "It was shortly after that, Jacob returned to Florida with me. Where he became . . .

involved in other business. Whatever he may have been doing previously, I think once he hit Florida, that became his full-time focus."

D.D. understood what Flora wasn't saying. Dr. Keynes and Kimberly Quincy should as well, meaning Flora's oblique reference had to do with the new guy in the room. Fair enough. Everyone was entitled to their privacy, and God knows a survivor of a sensational kidnapping case had to fight to keep hers.

"So Jacob had definitely made a connection with Conrad. Everything about what you described was hardly a coincidental meeting," D.D. stated.

"But Conrad's own intentions are unclear." Quincy spoke up. The FBI agent wore a frown similar to D.D.'s own. Clearly, she didn't approve of crazy either. "Was he there as a second perpetrator, or as some kind of self-appointed savior? Do you think he recognized you from TV?" she asked Flora.

Flora shrugged. "I doubt it. By that point, I'd lost a lot of weight. My hair was hacked off. Most of the time I didn't recognize myself in the mirror. Jacob had been taking me out in public for months, and no one ever looked at me twice."

"Did Conrad try to make eye contact, send you any other signals?" D.D. tried again. "Morse code isn't exactly the easiest way to establish contact. And risky, given Jacob was a long-haul trucker and had experience on the radio."

"I kept my gaze down. Jacob didn't like it when I looked up. Conrad might have tried something. I wouldn't have known. And Jacob never left us alone. He had his hand on my shoulder the whole time."

"When did you leave the town?" Quincy asked now.

"The next day. Up and out. Jacob was hardy. He could drink all night, still get up at four and start driving. He'd been off the road for a week. I imagine he had to get back to work."

"Motel Upland," D.D. provided. "Last time we talked, you thought you recalled a flashing motel sign that read Motel Upland. Something more for us to check out. Maybe we can even find a record of Conrad Carter or one of his aliases staying there or nearby. Of course, it would help if we had a state and not just 'someplace in the South.' "

"Try Mississippi," Quincy suggested. "Given the Abita beer."

"I think Jacob promised Flora to Conrad, made some kind of deal." D.D. noticed Keith didn't look directly at Flora as he said this. He spoke evenly, his tone strictly professional. It made D.D. wonder if Flora would hurt him now or later.

"I don't think that's much of a stretch," Quincy said drily.

While Flora added, "You think Conrad intended to take me away. Jacob would've thought it was to abuse me. But maybe Conrad was really trying to rescue me."

"Interesting thought," Dr. Samuel mused. He nodded toward D.D. "Does Conrad have any history in law enforcement, military service? Time with at-risk kids?"

"Not even a volunteer at a soup kitchen," she assured him. "Which makes this all stranger still. But he did have a box of fake IDs. Meaning whatever he was doing in that bar, he was working 'undercover,' so to speak. The question remains, to what end? One predator networking with another? Or some lone gunman trying to save the day? But how would he know about Flora? And if this is really what he did, shouldn't there be some record of other girls he rescued, or crimes stopped? Certainly, his wife doesn't know about any of this. She appeared as shocked by the fake IDs and cash stash as anyone. Though again, she shot up his computer, which may prove his travel activities weren't altruistic after all."

"What do you know about his other aliases, the names on the IDs?" Quincy asked.

"Nothing yet. One of my fellow detectives, Neil, has been working on them. He's running each name through state databases with the license number, but given how common the aliases are, he's getting too much information. The few he's managed to whittle down to the 'right' Conner or Carter or whatnot, there's no attached credit history, criminal records, anything. He suspects the IDs are hollow— not representative of whole new lives, just literally a piece of plastic procured for getting into a club."

"But didn't you say Conrad had a connection to Florida?" Quincy pressed. "And Jacob was from Florida. Surely that can't be coincidence."

"I don't like coincidences any more than the next person," D.D. assured her. "But Florida is a big state. Conrad's family lived in Jacksonville. Jacob Ness's mother lived on the west coast, north of Tampa. They were hardly neighbors. On the other hand, Jacob drove all around on his job and Conrad traveled all around on his, so anything is possible. Neil will keep searching. But we just learned about the aliases today, so it'll take a bit more digging.

"I don't think we should worry about Conrad's reasons for meeting Jacob and Flora." Keith spoke up. "We can speculate about why Conrad came to the bar all we want, but at this time we lack adequate data."

An IT geek through and through, D.D. noted.

"The real question is: How did Conrad and Jacob make contact? You said Jacob had a cheap burner phone. Did you see him call anyone before you entered the bar?" Keith asked Flora.

"No. But he could've done it while I was in the bathroom cleaning up."

"But Conrad knew exactly how to find you. Walked straight over to you."

"I guess."

"Clearly the meet was planned in advance. By a guy who didn't really use his cell but had the Tor browser on his laptop."

Once again, Flora shrugged. The rest of them simply waited.

"All the more reason to suspect that Jacob was active on the dark web and networking with other predators there. Now, Tor works to obscure a user's IP address by encrypting internet traffic while bouncing it through odd routes. However, it's not as anonymous as people think. A user's information is briefly unencrypted when entering and exiting the dark web, meaning there should be some recoverable information."

Quincy shook her head. "I already told you, the FBI turned the computer inside and out. Nothing."

But Keith wouldn't be denied. "To access anything, dark web, deep web—"

"What's deep web?" D.D. interrupted.

"Any site you need to log in to—banks, e-mail, e-commerce. Social networks, too, such as Facebook or Twitter. But there are members-only forums for just about anything and everything these days.

"Most people start on the deep web—visiting sites where they feel they're safe—then move on to the dark web. But either way, Jacob would have to have a username and password for some of these online accounts, which would be stored in his hard drive's SAM— Security Account Manager. Unless, of course, he remembered to remove that data. The Tor browser, for example, includes a screen asking the user if he really wants to save the information, as a way of prompting him *not* to store the info. Not all accounts are as helpful, however, and it's not uncommon for even the savviest IT guru to miss a stored password here or there." Keith stared at Quincy.

"I already said," the FBI agent bit out tightly, "our computer techs are the best in the business. As a matter of protocol, we ran the password cracker against the computer's SAM file and, yes, we discovered stored credentials for a single Gmail account, JNess. Except none of the recovered e-mails revealed anything of a criminal nature. Certainly nothing related to the dark web."

"What about a domain name? Most bad guys love to register vanity domains, BadAssDude.com, whatever."

"No."

"Then he had another e-mail account," Keith stated. "He left the first as a reward for prying eyes, better hid the second. There are plenty of ways."

"Not that someone with Jacob's background should know about." Quincy clearly wasn't convinced. "You're giving him too much credit."

"But again, once on the dark web, the experts he could've met, the lessons he could've learned. Flora said he was clever and driven when it came to hiding his habits. And we're not talking about complicated programming. Get one tech nerd in a chat room, and the rest becomes paint-by-numbers security steps. Jacob would just need to do what he was told."

Keith spoke matter-of-factly. Flora looked interested, while Kimberly appeared even more pissed. At least D.D. was now having some fun.

"What would you suggest trying next?" D.D. asked Keith. The man did seem to know his stuff, and as long as the "best in the business" FBI techs were coming up empty . . .

"Work on figuring out a second username. Just because there's no record of one on his laptop doesn't mean we can't use old-fashioned deductive reasoning to come up with some possibilities. We could then plug and play those options on known websites till we get a hit."

"You mean given Jacob's own background and history." Dr. Keynes spoke up. "We determine what online identity would appeal to him?"

"We did every version of Jacob Ness possible," Quincy argued. "JNess Jacnes. NJacob, et cetera. Hell, one of our techs wrote an algorithm just to run all possible name combos."

"He'd never use his own name to access the dark web," Flora stated immediately. "Too obvious."

"We tried Everett, too," Quincy reported. "Fake Everett. Any detail we could glean from your interview with Dr. Keynes. Including your name, your father's name, even your brother's name. Jacob had a sly and cruel sense of humor. We all can agree on that."

"Hang on." D.D. raised a hand. "Forget username for a minute. Given this Tor browser, we can be sure Jacob was accessing the dark web?"

Quincy and Keith nodded.

"Meaning if Conrad was connecting with the likes of Jacob Ness or other predators—either as a fellow abuser or a naïve avenger—he'd have to be part of the dark web as well."

More nodding.

D.D. smiled. First real break all day. "Meaning, Conrad's wife may have destroyed his computer, but there should still be traces of his activities on the dark web, right? You said every time a user logged in and out, there's a moment when their data is unencrypted. Meaning, we figure out Conrad's username, log on through Tor, and . . ."

"We should be able to identity frequently visited sites, maybe even some chat rooms," Keith supplied. "Basically, identify this Conrad guy's username, or Ness's evildoer username, and the amount of data we could suddenly recover . . . Contacts, activities, identities of other predators."

D.D. started nodding. "I like it. Two subjects, two usernames, two bites at the same dark web apple."

Quincy had stopped frowning. "But do we have ideas for Conrad's username?" she asked.

"His wife might."

"Is she cooperating?"

"Not yet, but I have some ideas on that subject." D.D. eyed Flora.

"Monster," Flora stated.

"What?" D.D. didn't follow the transition.

"Jacob always referred to himself as a monster. *No one wants to be a monster.*"

D.D. was still confused, but Keith was suddenly nodding. "Loch Ness Monster," he murmured.

Quincy immediately sat up, expression intent. "Could it be that simple? His username is some play on Loch Ness? Jacob Ness the monster, Nessie the monster?"

"I don't think he'd use Ness." Flora again. "Too direct a tie. But that kind of sly inference he'd like."

"There are other creatures," Dr. Keynes provided. "Ogopogo, for instance. It would appear random, while having a secret meaning to Jacob that would fulfill his need to be silently superior."

"The sightings of the monster took place in Inverness-shire in Scotland," Keith rattled off. He turned toward Quincy. "Correct me if I'm wrong, but didn't Jacob's mom live in Inverness, Florida? A city named by a Scotsman who said the lakes in the area reminded him of the lochs of his homeland?"

Quincy nodded. "Jacob's mailing address was his mother's home in Inverness, Florida."

"There's a connection there." Flora again, looking convinced. "Inverness, loch Florida, L Inverness, something like that."

Quincy started to scribble on her notepad.

"There are some algorithms which could blow out all possible combinations," Keith began.

Quincy's turn to hold up a hand. "Quit while you're ahead. All right, I got this. I'll get in touch with the techs, see what we can do."

"The office next to mine is empty," Dr. Keynes offered. "You can set up shop there."

The agent nodded her appreciation.

Flora looked at D.D. "What next?"

"Boyfriend goes home."

"He is not—"

"Civilian goes home," D.D. reiterated firmly. "You can catch him up later. But you and I have business. You're still my CI. Time to earn your keep."

"What do you mean?"

D.D. was already rising to standing. "Come on, you're with me."

"Where are we going?"

"I'll explain along the way."

D.D. headed for the door. Flora scrambled after.

CHAPTER 24

FLORA

"WHAT DO YOU KNOW ABOUT arson?" D.D. asks me ten minutes later. I'm sitting in her car as she navigates through the snarl of downtown traffic. I'm not sure where we're headed yet but figure she'll tell me soon enough.

Boston is beautiful at Christmastime. The buildings decked out in huge holiday displays, streets lined with festive trees, poles covered in twinkling white lights. My mom loves this time of year. She's probably already planned the entire meal down to reserving some organic turkey named Fred who'd grown up free-range and was now completing the farm-to-table cycle of life. She's hoping Darwin will fly in from London to join us. While I don't say as much out loud, I hope he does, too. Otherwise it'll be myself, my mom, Samuel, I guess, and maybe a neighbor or two. Maybe I could ask Keith. Would that be too weird? That's probably too weird.

"Earth to Flora. Arson?"

I belatedly pull my gaze from the giant tinsel snowflakes hanging from the streetlights. "I don't know anything about arson."

"Perfect. Then this will be a growth experience for you. Manila folder tucked next to your seat. Open it."

"Wait a minute. Is this about the Carters' house burning down? You want me to investigate their house fire?"

"Yes."

"This is stupid. I *don't* know arson. My time would be better spent chasing down more connections between Jacob and Conrad."

"I think we've already made progress on that front today."

I stare at her, closed file on my lap. "What the hell is going on here?"

"You're a CI. I'm giving you a job. Stop whining."

"I'm not whining, I'm telling you no."

D.D. takes her eyes off the endless row of brake lights in front of us long enough to arch a brow. "Conrad is connected to Jacob. Meaning whoever torched Conrad's house, possibly with the intent to cover up that connection or other significant information, might be yet another means of learning more about Jacob."

"Bullshit. You just want me out of the way."

"No. I want Jacob out of your head. Personally, I think you've given him enough real estate today. Don't you?"

The sharpness of her tone sets me back. I retreat in the passenger's seat. Whether I like it or not, I get her point. Ever since turning on the news yesterday morning, I've done nothing but obsess about Jacob. D.D. has a point; I could use a break.

Arson it is.

I open the file, peruse the contents.

"That's the report from the arson investigator, Patricia Di Lucca," D.D. provides. "Cause of the fire was a homemade ignition system prepped on the stove top, involving cooking oil and cotton, which then set ablaze the copious amounts of gasoline poured all over the house. Real low-end job. Materials all readily available. Cooking oil and cotton could've come from the house itself. Gasoline, given the amount used, probably was brought with the arsonist, as we're talking several gallons."

"When did this happen?"

"Fire was reported around two in the afternoon. Could've been set up earlier, say, one thirty, given the cooking oil needed time to heat up."

I start flipping through the papers. In addition to a formal write-up and a list of materials, the arson report includes detailed sketches of the home, the path of the fire, all sorts of visual aids. More photos and diagrams show the area of heaviest damage—where the arsonist clearly had poured a small lake of accelerant.

The office. Whoever the arsonist was, he, she, or it definitely had something against the office.

"Is that where Conrad was shot?" I ask D.D., pointing at the photo.

"Yes."

"You think the wife did it?"

She frowned, worried her lower lip. "I'm not sure. Maybe. Between you and me, detective to CI?"

This is a new conversation for us. I nod eagerly.

"There's an eight-minute gap. Reports of shots fired, then an eight-minute gap before more shots are fired. The police showed up for round two and discovered Evie holding the gun. She hardly protested when they arrested her, but was that shock from discovering her husband dead, or from pulling the trigger?"

"Clearly, she had the gun."

"According to her, she shot the laptop. Twelve times, to be precise."

"Why would she destroy the computer?"

"Wouldn't I love to know."

"She's not saying?"

"Not as long as she keeps hanging out with her lawyer. Damn defense attorneys."

"You think she was covering something up."

D.D. glances over. "I think you and I will be chatting with her sooner versus later on that subject."

"I get to meet her?"

"I think you *have* to. It may be the only way to get the truth out of her. Now, *you* tell *me*: If she shot up the computer, who burned the house?"

"I don't know."

"And *why* burn the house?"

"To cover tracks . . . destroy evidence, like you said."

"Evidence above and beyond the computer, which was already destroyed?"

"Did the arsonist know that?"

D.D. actually smiles at me. "Now you're thinking like a real detective. Okay, so you're looking at the report on burn patterns, right? Most concentrated area of damage was the office?"

"Yes."

"As of this morning, we know the office held two things: one, the computer; but, two, a metal lockbox filled with Conrad's fake IDs."

"You think that's what the arsonist was trying to destroy." I pause. "Why not just steal them?"

"Again, good question. My theory, the person couldn't find them. Remember, an entire forensic team swept through that house Tuesday night after the shooting without ever stumbling across the lockbox. In hindsight, I'm wondering if Conrad had a fake bottom in one of his desk drawers or filing cabinets. Those IDs mattered to him. Keeping that secret mattered to him."

"But someone else had to know," I counter immediately. "Otherwise, why burn down that house in an attempt to destroy them?"

Once again, D.D. smiles. "Flora, you just might be good at this. Someone else did have to know. And that person . . ."

"Might be another connection to Jacob Ness."

"Last page of the report," she orders now.

"It's a picture. Some skinny kid."

"Read."

"Rocket Langley. Twenty-year-old African American male. Really? Because he looks like he's fourteen. Okay, he's a person of interest in several fires in abandoned buildings, the warehouse district of Boston," I summarize. I skim farther down. All three fires involved gasoline as the accelerant, and the second was started by a cheap camp stove, which had a soup can filled with kerosene and a cotton wick.

"Arsonists are like serial killers," D.D. explains as she finally eases her car onto Storrow. "They have signatures, preferred methodology. Once they find their identity as firebugs, they don't deviate. Investigator Di Lucca put the elements of the Carters' house fire through the arson database and Rocket's name was what it immediately spit out."

"So we're going to arrest him?"

"Based on what? Being a 'person of interest' in an arson database? Without a history of prior arrests, an eyewitness report, or physical evidence that directly ties Rocket to the Carters' home, we have no grounds for an arrest. I could, of course, drag the kid down to HQ for questioning, but Di Lucca has already tried that. Rocket clams up tight, which is probably why he's never been charged with a crime. Just because he loves fire doesn't mean he's stupid.

"I'm going with a different strategy. I'm going to drop you off in his neighborhood. Where you're going to track him down and talk to him. Shady character to shady character."

"I'm a shady character?"

"We both know you don't like to color inside the lines."

I consider the matter. "I'm going to have to kick his ass, aren't I?"

"See, you sound happier already."

D.D. DROPS ME off a few blocks from Rocket's last known address. It's dark this early in December, and let's just say Rocket's neighborhood is a long way from the dazzling Christmas lights covering the Boston Commons. These row houses appear hunkered down in the winter gloom, half the windows boarded up, the rest covered in security bars. A lot of the poor neighborhoods in Boston have been bought up and renovated in the past few years. Rocket's isn't one of them.

D.D.'s right: This is my kind of place.

With my bulky coat over my equally shapeless sweatshirt, I blend right in. It's tempting to pull on my hood against the chill, but I don't want to reduce my peripheral gaze or muffle my hearing.

I stroll around the neighborhood for a bit, getting my bearings. There are no lights on at Rocket's address, which doesn't surprise me. If I lived here, I certainly wouldn't hang out any more than I had to. Then again, I doubt the kid's out holiday shopping, so then what?

I consider my play as I roam from block to block. D.D. already revealed something interesting: no witnesses. If memory serves, the Carters' neighborhood is mostly white. Meaning some black teen was sniffing around their house and no one noticed it? I doubt that already. At least in his mug shot Rocket had aspiring hoodlum written all over him. Most people living in an urban environment are hardwired to pay attention to such things.

Meaning . . .

I try on various theories and ideas. One appeals to me the most. I tuck it away, just as I notice a neighborhood hardware store. Not many such places left, but this one gives me an idea.

Ten minutes later I'm walking around with a bag in my hand and new, local knowledge courtesy of the checkout clerk. Where do the local teens hang out? Again, in an urban environment, people know these things.

It's dark. Some ambient lighting here and there from random windows where people are tucked in for the evening. There's a strange mix of both closeness and isolation in such densely packed areas. So many people, crammed together. And yet each in his or her own little world.

I don't envy their battles ahead. But I have my own.

I cross to the left, rounding the corner, and a gap appears in the building ahead. An awkward space wedged between two tenement housing buildings, like the hollow left from a lost tooth. Once, it had probably been a basketball court, or some kind of common ground. Now I behold the glow of what appears to be quite the fire roaring away in a centrally placed trash can. Around it, the flash of movement, glint of metal. Kids, on skateboards maybe. Or just hanging out. Way more of them than me.

At the same time, I become aware of a new presence behind me. I've picked up a shadow. Maybe D.D., who told me she'd be around, but I doubt I'm that lucky. I'd guess I have a new friend, someone cuing in on a lone white girl stupidly walking around his neighborhood.

I can't help myself: I smile. D.D. was right. My night is looking up.

I WALK STRAIGHT to the trash can. The kids don't scatter. Why would they, when there's at least a dozen of them and only one of me? I don't make individual eye contact. More like a quick head scan. There, to the left, features hard to make out beneath a gray hoodie, is a long, thin face that matches the photo of my guy.

Perfect.

I don't speak. I don't pause. I reach into my bag, pull out the first item, and toss it into the fire.

Boom! The fire roars up, spitting flames and showers of deep red sparks. Now the kids scatter.

"Jesus Christ!"

"She's fucking crazy!"

But not my guy, of course. My guy remains standing right there, looking at the new and improved fire with total fixation.

"Want one?" I ask. I hold out my bag.

"What is it?"

"Kerosene-dipped pinecones. Basically a fire-starter kit from the hardware store. They come in several colors."

Rocket curls his lip at me. I can tell he's tempted, but a premanufactured fire starter? Where's the fun in that?

"I also have bottles of vegetable oil."

Now I have his interest.

"Sure," he says, though I can tell he remains wary. But I'm thinking of the other thing D.D. said: Arsonists are like serial killers. Once they find their true selves, they can't go back. As Keith Edgar and his true-crime buddies would tell you, there's no serial killer out there who's ever been able to quit. What starts as a horrific crime becomes a terrible compulsion. And compulsions can be used against you by law enforcement—and by people like me.

I heft a small bottle of vegetable oil in his direction. He catches it effortlessly.

We both take a small step back. Then he oil-bombs the fire. More boom, now accompanied by a splatter and hiss. Whatever kids stayed earlier officially retreat. Fire might be cool, but hot oil is just plain dangerous.

Rocket smiles. I understand his grin. I've worn it enough times on my face.

"I'm trying to figure out how you did it," I say at last, voice conversational. There's still a presence behind me. I drift left, trying to get the form into my side view. Meanwhile, I help myself to another kerosene-dipped pinecone and add to the festivities. Rocket holds up a hand. I toss one in his direction.

His flares blue. I like it better than the red. Who needs Christmas lights when you can be doing this?

"I'm thinking pest control," I continue now, Rocket still staring at the flickering flames. "I mean, you walk into a neighborhood like the Carters', people are gonna notice. Especially lugging a few gas cans. But a young guy in a pest control uniform, walking the property with spray cans . . . People see what they want to see. Which is good for the likes of you and me."

My turn. I go with another small bottle of veggie oil. No cool colors, but I like the sizzle sound. This is fun. Maybe I should try for arson next.

Rocket still isn't speaking.

"You pick the back lock. No one to watch. Easy to do. Set up your stove-top ignition. Spray the 'pesticide' all around. Hell, if a neighbor saw you through the window, they wouldn't think twice. Very clever, I gotta say."

He holds up a hand. I toss two pinecones. This time, green and blue flames. We're both impressed.

"Too clever," I say, "for the likes of you."

Shadow behind me has drawn closer. I slowly but surely unzip my jacket. I want ease of movement for what comes next. Not to mention, I never leave the house with empty pockets. Even now, I'm pulling out a small canister of my homemade pepper spray. Now, what *this* stuff could do to that fire . . .

Rocket finally looks at me. He's clearly reluctant to leave the flames. "I don't know what you're talking about."

"You did good work. The burn patterns, total destruction of the second floor, the way it collapsed onto the first . . . a thing of beauty."

"You a cop?"

"Nope. Just an interested party."

"Interested in what?"

"Hiring you. That's how it works, right? Your age, where you live, your world . . ." I gesture to the burning trash can. "This is what you're about. There's no way you and Conrad crossed paths—"

"Conrad?"

"The guy whose house you burned down."

"Who?"

"Exactly. You didn't care about him or his wife or their unborn baby. You cared about the fire. You were there for the burn, and how much better that someone paid you to do it?"

He frowns for the first time. As if finally seeing the trap. I don't give him a chance, though. I toss another bottle of vegetable oil in his direction and, of course, he has to catch it. Of course he has to throw it on the blaze.

"I'm not a cop," I say now. "But I saw a bunch of them pulled up in front of your house. Bet they're ripping apart your room now. Finding the uniform, the 'pest control' cans. Then, wow, you're going to have some explaining to do."

But I made a misstep because immediately Rocket shrugs, then returns pointedly to staring at the fire. The uniform, I realize, was probably soaked in gasoline and used to start this blaze, because what kind of self-respecting arsonist wouldn't burn up the evidence?

"I want to hire you. One grand."

He frowns, staring at the flames. I find one of the last pinecones, toss it in. Red. We both nod in fascination.

"Five," he says. "Cash."

"Don't got it on me."

"I'll tell you where to leave it. You drop off half, with the address. Afterwards, other half."

"Trusting of you."

He finally stares at me. In his dark eyes all I can see are the dancing flames. "I like to burn things. All kinds of things. No one messes with that."

Good point. "It has to be discreet. You come up with the pest-control uniform, or did your last client provide it?"

"What do you care?"

"Has to be discreet," I repeat, voice steady.

He shrugs. "Depends on what I'm burning. Abandoned is easy

access. Residential work, yeah, you can provide the props. Or, I've figured out what works over the years. Whatever."

So maybe his client had provided the pest uniform, or maybe Rocket is that clever. He certainly loves fire, and anyone who loves his job is bound to get better and better at it.

I still don't think this kid knew Conrad Carter or Jacob Ness. He was strictly the hired help. But he's also our first link to whoever it was who shot Conrad and then felt compelled to further cover his tracks by totally eradicating the house. My next step is clear:

"Give me the address to the drop site," I say. "I'll get you the money."

"Tomorrow," he says. "Already got plans for tonight."

"Which are?"

"Right behind you."

I don't turn my head. Rookie move, especially as I've been tracking my shadow for the past ten minutes. Instead, I plant my feet wide for better balance, whirl my entire torso, and whip the plastic bag with its remaining two bottles of vegetable oil at my attacker's head. Solid *thwack* as I connect.

The form, face hidden in the shadows of another hoodie, staggers back, grabs his head, clearly dazed. I dance forward three steps. I kick to the side of his knee, then snap the heel of my hand straight into his nose. He goes down, clutching his face, moaning.

I step back. I don't need to do anything more, prove anything more. I turn to Rocket. "I'm not a fucking cop. Now, give me the address."

Rocket appears stunned. Exactly where I want him.

From my pocket, I pull the burn phone I always carry on me. "Text now."

I'm not surprised when he produces a matching prepaid cell. His fingers fly across the surface. Buzz as the address is delivered.

I smile. "Pleasure doing business with you."

Then I toss my bag with the two remaining bottles of oil straight into the burning barrel.

Another roar and sizzle. When I walk away, Rocket is still staring at the flames, his friend moaning behind him.

D.D. PICKS ME up four blocks later. I don't ask where she's been or how she found me. She has her skills, I have mine.

"Well," she demands.

"Hired firebug, definitely. Didn't even respond to Conrad Carter's name, and frankly, too much of a burn freak to have pulled this off without help. Canvass the Carters' neighborhood again, except this time ask about pest control. That's how he did it. Uniform, or what's left of it, is at the bottom of that burn barrel. If you look around, the pressurized spray canisters he used have to be around somewhere."

"Who hired him?"

"He wasn't *that* forthcoming. But"—I hold up my phone—"I have the address where I'm supposed to leave money for my future transaction. I'm guessing it's the same drop spot as Rocket used last time, given he appears to be a creature of habit."

"We can pull videos of the area from Tuesday night, Wednesday morning," D.D. fills in thoughtfully.

"Which should give you the client, caught on candid camera."

"Nicely done," D.D. informs me.

I just smile.

CHAPTER 25

EVIE

MY MOM MAKES SOME KIND of French stew for dinner. Filled with lentils and greens and all sorts of things perfect for a growing baby, she informs me. Never mind that with every comment she makes me feel more and more like a broodmare.

I set the table. Three martinis in, my mother shouldn't be handling breakables. And it's only six P.M.

I need to get out of here, I think again. But how? Whom to call? Mr. Delaney? A teacher I sometimes sit with at lunch? I never realized how small my world is until now. How in keeping everyone out, I'd also shut myself in.

A knock on the side door. I'm so grateful for the interruption, I nearly knock over my chair standing up. "I'll get it!" I announce.

My mom appears mildly annoyed. I notice she's not eating her stew, just pushing lentils around in the bowl. This is what happens, I think, when you spend your afternoon filling up on vodka.

I head for the door. Sergeant D. D. Warren stands on the other side. She flashes her badge. Next to her is a younger woman in an oversized down coat and a gray hoodie. She looks like she'd be more comfortable on the mean streets of any major city than hanging out at an impeccably decorated Colonial in Cambridge.

I let them in.

"Evie Carter, Flora Dane. Flora, Evie." D.D. makes the introductions. I shake hands with the woman, who looks like she could benefit from my mother's stew even more than I. Her face is vaguely familiar but I can't place it. Someone who knew Conrad? Or one of his half a dozen aliases?

I feel the first trickle of unease.

In for a penny, in for a pound. I lead them to the table and introduce my mother.

In response, my mother scowls, reaches an unsteady hand for her martini. "Really, Sergeant, couldn't this wait? It's dinnertime, and meals are very important for a woman in Evie's condition."

Yep, nothing but a broodmare.

The Flora woman eyes me with renewed interest.

"Please have some stew," I mutter. *Please save me from this meal.*

"Actually, we have a few things to discuss. Perhaps we could move into the front?" D.D. suggests. Works for me.

"I'll do dishes," I inform my mother because, again, she shouldn't be touching plastic plates, let alone Waterford crystal.

She only scowls, pushes more lentils around her bowl. She's depressed, I think. About our conversation earlier? The news her husband didn't kill himself? Or is this simply what midday martinis do to you? I've never known how to talk to my mom. I certainly don't have any answers now.

I direct D.D. and Flora to the side sitting room, with its greenery-swathed mantel and professionally decorated Christmas tree. My mom likes to have a theme for each tree. This one is Hark the Herald Angels Sing, meaning there is a lot of gold and, yes, a lot of angels.

As for actual sitting space, the room has a silk-covered love seat in stripes of pale green and pink. We all stare at it. It looks like something out of a dollhouse. The pile of matching throw pillows doesn't help.

I have to get out of this house.

"Can I take your coats?" I ask belatedly, because the sofa barely looks capable of holding two women, let alone their heavy winter coats. D.D. shrugs, unbuttons her long black wool coat. I notice the other woman follows more reluctantly. She's been taking in the room. Assessing. Again, the pinprick of unease. What is she doing here?

I don't know what to do with the coats. Walking to the coat closet in the main foyer will expose me to the reporters across the street. This is the problem with a nighttime siege—the house is nothing but a glowing fishbowl, putting both my mom and me on display. No doubt why D.D. used the side entrance. And why we're not seated near any windows now.

Finally, I pile the coats on the back of a wingback chair. I should sit, but I don't want to. In fact, I suddenly don't want to hear what they have to say.

"How are you feeling?" D.D. asks quietly.

"Like a bird in a gilded cage."

"Your mother brought you clothes for your arraignment." The woman speaks. She glances around the room. "I get it now."

"You were at my arraignment? Why? Who are you?" My tone is sharp.

"My name is Flora Dane—"

"She already told me your damn name!"

The woman regards me evenly. "It doesn't ring any bells for you?"

"Why would it? I've never met you before in my life. Now, what the hell is this all about—" I break off. My eyes widen. The sense of déjà vu, that I'd seen this woman before. Flora Dane. Six years ago.

Oh my God, I know who she is. And I no longer feel a tinge of unease. I want to vomit. Hurl my mother's good-for-the-baby stew all over this fine silk-covered furniture. Because I'm sure I don't want to hear what she's going to say next.

"Sit," D.D. is murmuring in my ear, her hands on my shoulders. "Just like that. Head between your knees. Deep breaths. In, out, exhale all the way. Now deep in, hold, hold, hold, exhale. Two more times. You got this."

When I finally stop hyperventilating, I'm collapsed in the wing-back chair with the coats. Both D.D. and Flora are now kneeling on the floor in front of me.

"What did he do? Those fake IDs, all his secrets. What did Conrad do?" I stare straight at Flora Dane.

"Don't you know?" D.D. asks me. "You're the one who shot up the computer."

"I had to."

"Why?"

"Protect the legacy." I'm not crying. I sound like a rote imitation of my mother, which is worse.

"You wanted to protect Conrad." D.D. eyes me. "The father of your child. From what, Evie? From what?"

"I don't know." That's the truth. He had secrets, I knew. And at least in my family, secrets can only cause pain. But that doesn't mean I know what his secret was.

Both women are eyeing me. I take a deep, shuddering breath, soldier on: "Have either of you been in a relationship with someone who travels a lot?"

They shake their heads.

"I loved Conrad. When we bought our house together, of course we each had to adapt. He snored. Left his shoes in the middle of the floor. Would enter a room chattering away, even when it was clear I was grading papers and needed to think. But you get used to those things.

"Except then he'd leave again. And I would sleep better without him. Appreciate being able to walk down the hall, get my work done faster. Then he'd return, and I'd have to reorient. You can't help yourself—inevitably, you're only in the relationship halfway, because it's only a marriage half the time."

D.D. and Flora wait patiently.

"It makes you look at your spouse more objectively than maybe the average married person. Analyzing things, noticing things. Like the way Conrad asked so many questions about my life, but never answered any of mine. The way he'd shut down sometimes, and I could tell something was bothering him, but he wouldn't say what. The hours he logged in his office. A window salesman? Still working at midnight? Then locking up the door to his own study when he left?

"I . . . I began to wonder. So I started snooping, which then gave him doubts. One day I found a page of a financial statement for a Carter Conner in Conrad's printer. At first I thought it was a mistake. But the account was from a bank in Florida, and I just . . . knew. He had a secret life. That's why he was always on the business trips. Why he never wanted to talk about them afterward. Why he was always locking up after himself. It's bad, isn't it?" I stare at Flora. "Is he . . . a predator, too?"

"I met Conrad," Flora says at last. "In a bar in the South. He was using the name Conner when he approached my kidnapper, Jacob Ness. It was clear they were expecting one another."

"Oh." I can't think of anything else to say. Instead, I clutch my stomach, as if covering my unborn child's ears, trying to block him or her from this terrible information. I'd known. Especially in the past year or so, I'd looked at my husband with a growing sense of dread.

"Conrad's a predator?" I whisper. "But he was so excited for our baby. He seemed genuinely happy." I don't know what it is I'm trying to say. "Do evil people love their children, too?"

"Did you know about the lockbox of IDs?" D.D. asks.

"No. And I tore that office apart trying to figure out what he was hiding. I never saw it."

"Conrad never talked about his trips?"

"No."

"How often was he gone? How long did he go?"

"One or two trips a month, usually three to five days. But not just to Florida. He traveled all over New England. I saw some of his tickets. He flew to Philadelphia, Virginia, Georgia. Some of his business travel was real. But I don't think all of it was."

"Did Conrad watch the news a lot?" Flora spoke up. "Say, follow national cases, maybe even watch a lot of true-crime shows on TV."

"He liked *Forensic Detectives*." That sinking feeling again, except how could this get any worse?

"Why did you shoot the computer?" D.D. asks again.

"I had to."

"Where did you find the gun?"

"On his lap. I took it. From . . . him."

"He was holding the gun when you found him?"

"Yes."

"What did you think, Evie, when you walked into the study and found your husband's dead body? What was the first thought that crossed your mind?"

"That he shot himself. That all these years later, I still wasn't enough."

"What was on the computer, Evie? What was Conrad looking at when he died?"

"Pictures." I squeeze my eyes shut. I don't want to see them again. It was so much easier to forget, pretend it never happened. Maybe I am my mother, after all.

"What was on the computer?"

"Girls. Photos. Terrible photos. They look thin and horrified.

Beaten. Young. Why would he be looking at something like that?" I shake my head. "He's the father of my child. And even knowing he had secrets . . . couldn't it have just been another woman? Maybe a gay lover? Even knowing something was wrong, even knowing I would regret digging, I never suspected what was on his computer." My voice is hoarse, hard to hear. I finally look at them. "I loved him. How could I love a man like that?"

"What did you do next, Evie?"

"I closed up the laptop. But the police were there. Already banging at the front door. There wasn't enough time to clear the hard drive, not properly. I couldn't . . . He's the father of my child," I say again.

"Protect the legacy." D.D. nods, as if she understands. Maybe, being the one who was here sixteen years ago, she does.

"I destroyed the laptop. Kept shooting until there were no bullets left."

"That was some good shooting."

I nod. "My father taught me."

"And you're not afraid of guns, are you, Evie, because you didn't shoot your father?"

"I didn't shoot my father. Or Conrad. I just . . . loved them both." I feel it now. The horrible weight of it all. To love so much, and it still wasn't enough. Was never enough. Seeing those images on the computer screen. *Horror* was not a strong enough word. It was like a knife to the heart. Not just because of what it said about him and how well he'd played me for ten years, but because of what it said about me, who'd had doubts, had known he was hiding things, and had stayed anyway.

"I knew he was a loser." A voice spoke up. My mother, standing in the arched entranceway, where she'd clearly been eavesdropping for a while. Her words were slurred. I stare at her dully.

"I know you hated him, Mom," I say tiredly. "I just assumed it was because he was stupid enough to want me."

"Window salesman," she grunts.

"Good news. Turns out he was a bit more than that."

She has her vodka; I have my bitterness. Maybe we deserve each other.

"You should know something," Flora says quietly.

She's still kneeling on the floor, clearly not the type to take a seat on a silk-covered settee. It makes me feel bad, to have a woman who's been through so much feel uncomfortable in my home. That this is that kind of place. That myself, my family, we are those kinds of people.

"When Conrad was at the bar, he tried to signal me. Using Morse code. Unfortunately, I didn't catch on and never answered him."

"What do you mean?"

"He was asking if I was okay. Tapping it out on the bar top."

I shake my head slightly, very confused now. "Why? I don't . . . Why would he do that?"

"I don't know. I was hoping you could tell me."

"When was this?"

"Probably seven years ago."

"Conrad and I were together. He went on his business trips. But that's all I knew. Often, I wasn't even sure where."

"Do you remember anything about the website he had pulled up on his computer? URL, anything?" D.D.'s turn.

"It was weird. Not a dot-com or dot-net, but dot-onion. I didn't know what that meant; I had to look it up. Apparently, it's a site on the Onion Browser; the dark web." My voice cracks slightly. I hear myself say, as if understanding for the first time: "My husband was surfing the dark web."

Flora and D.D. exchange a look.

"You never saw any other records bearing the names from his fake IDs? Just that one financial statement from the printer?" D.D. asks.

I shake my head.

"I don't suppose you kept a copy of that statement?"

"No. I didn't have to."

"What do you mean?"

I shrug. "I'm a numbers person. I don't need a statement in front of me. I can write out the account number off the top of my head. Including bank, address, and at that time, its balance of two hundred and forty-three thousand dollars and twenty-two cents."

D.D. whirls to my drunken mom in the doorway. "Get a pen," she orders sharply.

And I finally get to feel good about myself for the first time in days.

CHAPTER 26

D.D.

"ALL RIGHT. IT'S LATE, IT'S nearly the holidays, and I still have shopping to do. Let's get this done." D.D. had assembled her team back at BPD headquarters. Boxes of pizza sat in the middle of the table, surrounded by pots of coffee. At this time of night, comfort food and caffeine were two of the best investigative tools available.

Seated at the conference room table was the three-person detective squad who'd landed the initial shooting case: Phil, Neil, and their newest partner, Carol. In addition, D.D. was proud owner of one feebie, SSA Kimberly Quincy, and two wild cards, Flora Dane and—heaven help her—Keith Edgar, who had a laptop fired up and was clacking away wildly.

Odd team for an odd investigation. Yet, D.D. had that tingle in the base of her spine: They were on the verge of a breakthrough. Between Flora's conversation with the firebug and their candid face-to-face with Evie Carter, they were getting somewhere.

"Phil." D.D. nodded to the oldest and probably wisest detective in the room. "Tell us what you got on Conrad Carter's alias bank account."

"The account was opened eighteen years ago in the name Carter Conner at a local credit union in Jacksonville, Florida. Carter Conner matches the name on the Florida driver's license discovered in Conrad Carter's charred lockbox. The starting balance of the account was four hundred and fifty thousand—"

"Lot of money." Quincy spoke up.

"Yep. One initial deposit, which I'll get to in a second. Otherwise, Conrad, Carter, whoever we call him—"

"What do you mean whoever we call him?" Flora's turn. "Is Conrad or Carter or Conner his real name?"

Phil sighed heavily. "Everyone," he said. "Eat some pizza. And shut up."

They did.

"So, Carter Conner has an active account at the Florida First Credit Union. Since the initial deposit, he's been slowly but surely drawing down the balance. Cash withdrawals, always under ten thousand dollars."

D.D. nodded, understanding the reasoning behind that.

"Several withdrawals a year. So not a lot of money, but if you figure he was always taking it out in cash, a solid slush fund. Then three years ago, a new transaction shows up: monthly transfers of five hundred dollars to a separate account."

"Under one of his other aliases?" D.D. asked.

"Don't know yet. I entered the account info into our electronic tracing system but got back an error message. I'll have to call the bank manager in the morning."

"So what do you think he was doing with this money?" D.D. pressed.

"Good question. Neil, Carol"—Phil nodded to his two squad mates—"you're up."

Neil did the honors. "In answer to Flora's question, we asked the coroner to run prints, but we're pretty sure Conrad Carter is actually Carter Conner. That's his real name, real driver's license. The rest are fakes."

"Your murder victim," said Quincy, "was living under an assumed name? Good God."

"It's the money trail, the onetime significant deposit," Carol took over the story. "It got Neil and me thinking, where did that money come from? Sale of an asset, settlement check, lottery winnings? Because Conrad never deposited again. Just that one check."

D.D. made a motion with her hand. "I'm assuming you have an answer."

"Life insurance," Carol announced. "He received a death benefit twelve years ago when both his parents were killed in a hit-and-run outside of Jacksonville, Florida."

"Evie said his parents had died," Flora murmured. Beside her, Keith frowned, clicked away at his computer, frowned again.

"Which is what got us looking," Neil said. "We couldn't find any death records for surname Carter. But we knew the aliases from the other driver's licenses. So we ran those last names. And sure enough, William and Jennifer Conner died in an MVA three months before Conrad opened the bank account."

"His parents are killed, Conrad receives the life insurance money, then uses it to open an account at a Florida credit union." D.D. stared at her detectives.

"We're just getting started," said Carol. She leaned forward. "William Conner, the dad, was with the JSO."

"Jacksonville Sheriff's Office," Quincy provided for the civilians' benefit.

"He worked in Major Cases, including homicides, missing persons, assaults. And get this, the MVA that killed him and his wife wasn't an accident. Someone ran Detective Bill Conner off the road, knowingly targeting an officer and his wife."

D.D. was still having to process the details. "Conrad's parents were murdered?"

"Yes."

"At which time, Conrad deposited the life insurance payout from his parents' deaths, then headed north to live under an assumed name? Until someone gunned him down in his own home two nights ago?"

"Exactly." Carol beamed.

"That's it," D.D. said. "I'm having more pizza."

"I DON'T GET it." Flora spoke up a minute later. Which was fair enough because D.D. wasn't convinced she understood everything either. "Why the alias? Did Conrad think he was a target? Like, whoever killed his parents was coming for him next?"

"Unknown," Neil said.

"Or," Flora continued now, "was Conrad a suspect in his parents' death? Was he running away from the police?"

"I doubt that," Quincy answered immediately. "He kept both an active bank account and a valid driver's license from Florida. That's no way to hide from cops. Not much of a way to hide from a determined killer either."

The entire team was frowning.

"Conrad appeared in the bar with Jacob Ness seven years ago." Keith spoke up. "Conrad and his family are from Florida. Jacob and his family are from Florida. I still think there has to be a connection."

"The FBI has made some progress on that front," Quincy reported. "After our little powwow this morning, we started running

Google searches based on some of the username ideas we discussed, across some of the online platforms we believe Ness would've frequented. In the end, we discovered an identical username on several social media sites as well as some more . . . specific . . . sexual fantasy forums. We're still building the user profile, but we believe Jacob's username is most likely I. N. Verness. Capital *I,* period, capital *N,* period, capital *V,* Verness. So it looks like first two initials, followed by a last name. But it's actually a shout-out to Jacob's hometown."

"And a county associated with another legendary monster." Flora was nodding. "That sounds exactly like him."

"Our experts will now flesh out a full online profile of I.N.Verness, including specific site visits and website details. In turn, this will allow us to subpoena information from these sites. We're also running codebreaker software as we speak. I'm told within twelve to fourteen hours, we may finally have the answers to Jacob's online activities."

The FBI agent sounded triumphant. D.D. couldn't blame her.

"You said Conrad's father worked Major Cases for the Jacksonville Sheriff's Office." Keith again. "Is it possible he'd been investigating Jacob Ness?"

"Twelve years ago?" Neil shrugged. "Was Ness even on anyone's radar screen?"

"We didn't know about him till Flora's abduction," Quincy said. "At least not as a serial predator. Prior to that, he had a criminal record for assault. Upon release from prison, however, he disappeared from law enforcement radar screens."

"He was never going back," Flora murmured. "A man with his appetites didn't belong behind bars." She looked up at Quincy. "He didn't stop attacking women after prison. He just got smarter about it."

"Meaning a JSO detective might have been looking into him," Keith pressed.

"I'll call the Investigations Division chief," Neil conceded. "Given how far back we're looking, it might take them a bit, but there's gotta be a record of Detective Bill Conner's active cases at the time of his death."

"I'm thinking a big rig could certainly run a car off the road," Keith said. "That's all."

Personally, D.D. thought Keith Edgar saw Jacob Ness everywhere. Which was the problem with amateur sleuths—they often started with a theory of the case, then worked backward to justify their suspicions, versus letting the evidence do the talking. However . . . She leaned forward to address Neil. "When you're talking to the Jax commander, ask him if Conrad ever called with the same request. Or has made any follow-up inquiries about his father's work. It would help tell us where his head was at—searching for his parents' killer, trying to finish what his father started. I don't know. But we need to figure it out."

"If only his wife hadn't shot up the computer," Phil said now.

"She claimed she did it to protect her husband's reputation," D.D. provided. "When she walked in on the scene, Conrad was already dead, and the laptop was open with photos of . . . victimized girls on the screen."

"Sounds like motive for her to kill him right there," Phil countered.

"Sure. But . . ." D.D. frowned. "I don't think she did it. The story she told Flora and me, coming home to the scene in the office, her instinctive need to cover for her future child's father . . ."

"Ah, but didn't you believe her story last time? Which turned out to be just that, a complete fabrication concocted by her and her mother?"

D.D. scowled at her former mentor. "I'm not saying we take her off our radar screen. Clearly, there was a lot going on in this marriage. But she did give us the financial lead . . ."

"All the better to direct you away from her."

"And there was an eight-minute gap between shots fired." D.D.

skewered Phil with a look. "Say, the gap that would occur if a wife had come home right after the killer had fled, stumbled upon the scene, and for reasons of her own, took action against the laptop."

"You mean a mysterious killer who fled through a heavily populated neighborhood and left no trace, no witnesses behind?"

"You're a pain in the ass," D.D. informed Phil.

"Thank you." He helped himself to a fresh slice, no doubt thinking he'd earned it.

"Which brings us to the arsonist." Flora spoke up, redirecting them. The woman looked tired, D.D. thought. She probably hadn't slept since first seeing Conrad's picture on TV. But she had acquitted herself well today.

"The suspected arsonist is a firebug. Obsessed with one thing only."

"He's not the shooter," Quincy filled in.

"If it doesn't involve flame, it would never hold his attention. His services are for hire, however."

"The shooter employed the firebug to burn down the house in order to cover up any evidence he might have left behind," Quincy said.

Flora nodded. Keith looked impressed by her new leading role. "Now, this arsonist, Rocket, isn't exactly big-time muscle. More like a local kid with a reputation for playing with matches. He's smart, though. Smarter than I originally gave him credit for. He's never been caught or charged with a crime, so while his services are available for hire, how you learn about him . . ." Flora's voice trailed off. She looked at Keith. "I was wondering about the dark web again. Earlier, you and SSA Quincy were discussing that Jacob was definitely using it. Evie says the images her husband had loaded up on his laptop were on an Onion site. This Rocket kid, how would someone know enough to hire him unless his . . . interests . . . appeared somewhere?"

"Entirely possible," Keith said. "The dark web is a known clearinghouse for everything from drugs to weapons to, yes, illegal services.

For that matter"—he addressed the group—"you can also find a gun for hire on the dark web."

"Great," D.D. muttered. Most major criminal enterprises had moved online. A good detective adjusted. She still missed the good old days, however, when the felons were up close and personal, versus a computer screen away.

Flora was shrugging. "Since I located Rocket in his own backyard, we conducted our business mano-a-mano. I got him to give me the location of the money exchange. I leave an initial deposit and target address. He picks up, then goes forth in fiery bliss."

"You're going to hire the arsonist?" Quincy asked with a frown. "Shouldn't you just have arrested him and be grilling him for a description of his previous employer?"

D.D.'s turn: "Given his drop-box method, Rocket probably doesn't know who hired him. Safer for him that way. What matters is the handoff location. Assuming it's the same one he used last time, I've assigned two detectives to start tracking down all video surveillance in the area. Traffic cams, security systems, ATMs. If we're lucky, the drop box itself is covered by a camera. If not, we know the same person has to visit the area twice—first time for deposit, then final payment, within a short span of time. Not the easiest parameters for ID'ing a potential suspect, but we've worked with less."

"All right." D.D. looked around the room. "Phil, you're on deck to follow up with the bank. Neil, Carol, the Jax sheriff's department. Kimberly, you'll keep us in the loop regarding codebreaker progress. Flora, your job is to get a good night's sleep. Keith, I don't actually know what the hell you're doing, but the Inverness thing was good enough for now."

"I'm still chasing some leads," Keith said, completely straight-faced.

D.D. had nothing to say to that. She rose to standing. "Kimberly, you headed back to Atlanta?" Because the FBI agent could phone in any new findings.

But Quincy was already shaking her head. "Oh no. I'm staying. From what I can tell, this party is just getting started. And I'm not going to miss whatever happens next."

CHAPTER 27

FLORA

KEITH AND I WALK OUT of HQ together. The sky above is pitch black, the horizon around us aglow with city lights. I have no sense of time. It feels like this night has been going on forever, but dark comes early in December, so it might be only eight or nine P.M.

Keith has his computer bag slung over his shoulder, his hands in his pockets against the cold. I like to exhale and watch the cloud of steam. I don't have a hat or gloves. I should be freezing, but I rarely notice such things. Sometimes I think rage is like a furnace, and I've been angry for so many years now, I'm perpetually heated from the inside out.

"I. N. Verness," Keith states finally. He smiles, and I realize he's happy. I've spent the day battling with demons from my past. But for Keith, this is simply a six-year-old puzzle that he's finally cracked. I decide to be happy for him.

"What happens now?" he asks me.

I shrug. "We do what the sergeant recommended. Go home, get some sleep, see what tomorrow brings."

"Do you sleep?" he asks, his voice genuinely curious.

"Not much."

"Night terrors?"

"I don't relax well."

"Do they pay you to be a CI?"

I frown. "No. Should I be paid?" I never thought to ask, and now I wonder if I missed something obvious.

"I don't know," he says. "But . . . do you have a job?"

"This and that."

"Focus issues?"

I sigh. He's pissing me off. I'm sure he doesn't mean it. People rarely meet survivors of major crimes, so of course they have a million questions, combined with an equal number of misperceptions. They assume I flinch at firecrackers or that I'm terrified of closed-in spaces. Or they once heard that I have a million dollars secreted away from a wealthy benefactor (maybe Oprah or Dr. Phil!) who was moved by my story.

I don't have or do any of those things. Nor am I the type who wants to talk about it.

"What did you think of the day?" I ask him instead.

"Got off to a rough start—"

"Sergeant Warren doesn't like anyone."

"Good to know. But by the end, the breakthrough with the username . . ." He bounced up and down on his toes. "I'm excited. We're going to solve this one. All these years later, we're going to locate Jacob Ness's lair and, hopefully, evidence of six missing women. Amazing."

"Gonna tell your true-crime group?"

He appears offended. "I signed a nondisclosure."

"Make them pinky promise to keep the news to themselves."

"I signed a nondisclosure," he repeats, his tone firm.

"What will you do now?" I ask.

"I don't want to go home," he says. "I'm too wired. There are a few things I could research, of course. That this Conrad Carter is actually Carter Conner and his father a murdered cop . . ." He's nodding to himself. "Have some digging to do there."

I study him for a long moment. "Want to get a drink?" I hear myself say.

My newest admirer and/or possible serial killer breaks into a smile. "I thought you'd never ask."

KEITH HAS AN app for one of the ride-sharing services. He also claims to know a bar. I know plenty of bars myself, but probably not the type he'd feel comfortable frequenting. Not to mention that at quite a few of them, his computer would be stolen in minutes.

If I chased down the robber, took him out with a flying tackle and gallantly returned to Keith with his computer bag, would that earn me a look of adoration, or end the evening abruptly? In movies, everyone loves the kickass heroine. I'm less convinced the average man wants one in real life. Keith looks like he works out, but at the end of the day he's a tech guy. And I'm, well . . . me.

Keith takes me to Boylston Street. This is pretty Boston. With high-end boutiques nestled in between historic churches, the architecturally significant public library, and of course, dozens of restaurants and bars. Each window is framed in twinkling Christmas lights, while the ornate streetlamps are capped with glittering wreaths and the row of trees wrapped in dazzling holiday cheer. Keith leads me up four steps to an old stone building, very dark and subdued compared to its neighbors. Which should be my first hint.

We are greeted by a man in a tuxedo who could be anywhere between forty and a hundred. He nods at both of us, his face perfectly impassive. I note two things at once. Keith, in his cashmere sweater and finely tailored slacks, blends perfectly with the wood-paneled foyer. I do not.

Keith is already shedding his outerwear. I remove my ratty down jacket with more reluctance. I like my coat. It has many pockets, each a treasure trove of tools and resources for the vigilante on the go.

The maître d' holds out his hand. At the last minute, I can't do it. I clutch my coat to my chest. "I get cold easily," I say, to justify my decision.

Tuxedo man says nothing, merely turns, hangs up Keith's coat. Then he leads us into a much larger room, also covered in exquisitely carved walnut panels, and dominated by a gorgeous curved bar bearing a gold-flecked marble top. Around us is a collection of seating areas, some white-draped tables, some antique furniture pulled close for a more intimate feel. A fire crackles impressively from a massive fireplace against the far wall. Our host walks straight toward it, indicates a private arrangement of a single love seat with a spindly coffee table, then stares pointedly at my coat again.

If anything, I clutch it tighter.

"Thank you," Keith says. Our silent guide nods in acknowledgment, then disappears.

"What is this place?"

Keith has already taken a seat. His legs are so long he has to stretch them out at an angle to avoid the coffee table. I perch awkwardly on the other corner, not liking this seating arrangement at all.

"It's a private club. There are many of them around the city. Representing various Ivy League universities, special groups—"

"*Elite* groups."

"My father's a member. I picked this bar because I thought it would be quieter, a more private place for us to talk."

I'm not sure what I think of that. Private is good. But this . . . This isn't me. And if he was paying attention at all, surely he recognized that. Meaning this place was what? His way of showing off? Look at my success? Look at what I can buy you?

Mostly, I feel very uncomfortable and wish I'd gone hunting instead.

"What would you like to drink?" he asks.

"Seltzer water."

He doesn't comment, just flags down another man in a white tuxedo jacket, this one bearing a silver tray. Keith orders seltzer for me, a single malt for him. I wonder if this is the kind of place women aren't allowed to order for themselves, or again, if this is Keith's idea of making a great first impression.

"Do you know the others in the room?" I ask.

Keith looks around. I've already taken inventory. The only obvious egress is the arched doorway through which we entered. I would guess the wood paneling on the surrounding walls disguises other options, and I have to fight the temptation to circle the room and feel out all the seams for myself.

"No," he says at last.

"Come here often?"

"No."

"But tonight, hanging out with a girl dressed like me"—I gaze down at my gray sweatshirt, worn cargo pants—"this seemed like a good idea?"

"No one cares," he tells me.

Which makes me scowl because, of course, I care, but like hell I'm going to admit that.

"If someone came up to you, how would you introduce me?" I press.

"Given you're someone who appreciates your privacy, I would say you were a visiting friend."

"No name?"

"Only if you want me to."

I give him slightly more credit for this answer, then resume my working theory that he's a serial killer, and this is how he lures future victims back to his place. By pretending to be courteous and charming and sensitive. Ted Bundy with access to an elitist club.

"I'm not claustrophobic," I say abruptly.

He seems to consider the statement, and the second tuxedo man returns with a tray bearing our drinks. He also has a small bowl of what appear to be wasabi-coated nuts. After the pizza, I'm happy with my seltzer, lime wedge perched artistically on the rim.

Keith holds up a heavy crystal tumbler of amber liquid. We toast, not saying a word.

"People always assume I'm claustrophobic. You know, all that time in the coffin. Except that's the point. I spent so many days, weeks, in a pine box, I had no choice but to grow comfortable with it. Make it my home."

"I still wear scarves," he says at last.

It takes me a moment; then I get it. His cousin was strangled with a silk scarf. Touché.

I raise my seltzer in acknowledgment, allow myself to relax a fraction on the too-low, too-small love seat.

"Bring any of your true-crime buddies here?"

"No."

"Why not?"

"We generally meet at someone's house. When you're spreading out crime scene photos, it tends to disturb others."

"I think Jeeves could take it."

"Jeeves?"

"The guy who greeted us."

"His name is Tony."

"Really? That doesn't seem right at all."

He shrugs, takes a sip of his scotch. "Now who's typecasting?"

I almost stick my tongue out him. At the last minute, it occurs to me that would be childish, and I'm supposed to be the serious avenger sort.

"I think you can fit in this room," he says shortly, his gaze directly on mine. "I think you're strong and smart and can go anywhere you want to go and be anything you want to be."

"No."

The word comes out hard and matter-of-fact. Keith doesn't push it, just waits.

"I work at a pizza shop. Which, oh shit, I was supposed to be at this afternoon. So from that alone, I'm not even a good pizza employee. I never finished college. I'll never get a degree."

"In the tech world, you'd be amazed how many business owners don't have them."

"But I'm not a techie either. I'm just . . . me."

Again, he waits.

"People think trauma is mental," I say abruptly. "I'm mentally scarred, damaged, take your pick. And with enough therapy, time, my mind will heal and, ta-da, one day I'll be all better again. But trauma isn't just mental. It's physiological. It's an adrenal system that's totally burnt out, so that I spend days at a time in fight mode." I realize as I'm describing this that one of my knees is bouncing uncontrollably. "Followed by crashes where I can barely get out of bed.

"I can't function in crowded rooms. I never take the T during rush hour. I can't stand the stench of other bodies. I'm hypervigilant to the point there's no way I could pay attention to a lecturer in a classroom environment, let alone start and finish an assignment. It's not in me."

"You stayed on track today."

"We moved around today. From idea to idea and building to building. I need that kind of action. Plus, I'm better when I'm with Samuel." I pause. "And I almost like D.D. Almost."

"So, the right people, the right mix of activities, and you can function. Ever thought of becoming a cop?"

"No way. Real policing requires a degree, for one. So that whole college thing is an issue. Plus, ask Sergeant Warren, the paperwork alone would kill mere mortals. It's the whole advantage of being a CI. I get all the fun, none of the legal responsibility. Besides, why should I become a detective, when it's only a matter of time before I convince D.D. to join me on the dark side?"

Keith nods. "Based on what I know from my detective friends, you have a valid point. Are you happy?" he asks me abruptly.

"I don't aspire to happiness."

"Why not?"

"It's just not something I feel."

"Survivor's guilt?"

"Maybe. Or again, burnt-out adrenals. Highs are hard to come by."

"Your family?"

"Love me despite me."

"Mine, too."

"You're an obviously successful computer guru. What's not to love?"

"My blog. My intense interest in violent crime. They find it . . . distasteful. So do a lot of women, I might add. In the beginning, when I first mention my true-crime club, it sounds like a cool hobby. But then when they start to understand that it's real work, with photos of corpses and sketches of crime scenes and analysis of blood spatter . . . I enjoyed today," he says suddenly. "Today, for the first time in a long time, I didn't feel alone in a crowded room."

The way he says the statement, so quiet, so matter-of-fact, makes me catch my breath. Then, in the next instant, the alarms start ringing in my mind. It's too perfect. It's too exactly the right kind of thing to say to a woman like me. Almost as if he's been studying me. Which we both know, for the past six years, he has.

"I have to go." I put down the seltzer. My hand is shaking. I hate that. But then I snatch up my jacket and immediately feel better. The inside left pocket contains my homemade pepper-spray concoction. I reach for it without even thinking, let my fist close around it.

Keith is blinking, as if I've confused him. But I don't buy the act anymore. At least, I think it's an act. I don't know. I wish he didn't look the way he looked. I wish I didn't know the things I know.

The worst part of being a survivor: There's no security blanket anymore. You can't assume the worst won't happen, because it did. And none of your screaming changed that. Meaning that just because I don't want to believe this handsome, smart guy has nefarious intentions doesn't mean for a second that I'm safe.

"I'll walk you home," Keith is saying, climbing awkwardly to his feet.

"No, thank you."

"At least let me call you a Lyft."

"I'll be fine."

"Flora—"

I don't wait for him. I'm already weaving my way out of the room. In the dark foyer, the greeter, Tony, I guess, snaps to attention. "Nice digs," I inform him, before pushing through the heavy wooden door.

Keith catches up with me outside. Did he even stop to pay the bill? Maybe elite clubs don't bother with things as common as money. They just run a tab into perpetuity.

He grabs my arm. I whirl sharply, pepper spray out.

He immediately drops his hand, steps back. "I don't understand," he says at last.

"I'm not your puzzle to solve."

But I can already see in his face that I'm exactly that. His riddle to answer. His trophy to win. His prey to snare.

The look on my face makes him take a second step back.

"I just want to help," he states carefully.

"Why Jacob Ness?"

"The other missing girls, I already explained . . ."

"Not really."

"I. N. Verness. If my intentions were evil, would I have given you that?"

"Yes."

"Why?"

"Because all good predators bait the trap."

"I'm not—"

"Good night." Then, before this conversation can drag out any longer, before he can talk me into doing things I know I shouldn't do, I turn and race up the block. At the last minute, I turn back. I shouldn't. But I do.

He's standing exactly where I left him on the sidewalk. Staring straight at me.

He doesn't look angry. He doesn't appear frustrated.

He looks . . . lonely.

It's too much for me. I take off running again and, this time, keep on trucking.

CHAPTER 28

EVIE

I KNOW IT'S MORNING WHEN I wake up to the sound of the Cuisinart whirring away downstairs in the kitchen. Probably more green goo supplemented with flaxseed, coconut oil, probiotics, antibiotics, maybe a horse salve or two. All the better to grow the little genius that had better be occupying my womb.

I roll onto my side, already feeling sulky and rebellious. What is it about returning to my mother's house that immediately turns me into a five-year-old?

The clock next to the bed glows seven A.M. The sky is just beginning to lighten. I don't know how my mother can do it, knock back so many vodka martinis the night before and still be the first one up in the morning. It occurs to me, there's a lot of things I don't know how she does. Such as roll around this huge, empty house, day after day. Like find the energy to decorate each room with its own Christmas theme, when her only family, Conrad and me, hadn't even committed to coming over for the holidays. We probably would've. Arriving late and leaving early and clenching our jaws in between.

I'm going to have to learn this. How to live in a house all by myself. How to get up day after day, just me and my soon-to-be-born child. Does my mom think about my father every day? Does she still picture him in his study, which remains largely untouched? Or lounging in the front parlor, waiting for me to take up position at the piano? Or sitting on the front porch, puffing away on the occasional cigar?

I miss my house. Yet I don't know if I could've continued living there without seeing Conrad in every room. And I don't know what would've hurt more. Memories of Conrad laughing at his first attempt at laying floor tiles, which didn't go anything like the video showed, or dead Conrad, brains on the wall, gun in his lap in the upstairs office?

What was my husband doing? And what kind of woman marries a man like that?

I imagine I'll get another visit from the police today, and that as much as anything motivates me to roll out of bed.

I shower, taking my time because I'm in no hurry to face my mother or start the day. I don't have the answers when it comes to Conrad. Flora Dane met him in a bar. A kidnapping victim and my husband, meeting up in the South. I can't wrap my mind around it. Crazier, Flora thought he might have been trying to send her a message in Morse code. How did Conrad even know Morse code?

I feel like I've spent years trying to unravel the riddle of my husband. If I haven't figured it out by now, it's not going to happen. Instead, I have a different target in mind. My father. Maybe the first step to understanding what my life has become is to go backward, to try to solve the question of what happened sixteen years ago, when everything first went so wrong.

My mother gave me names of some of my father's colleagues from that time. I think it's time I give them a call.

I complete my shower, getting to use the toiletries I purchased yesterday, my own brands versus my mother's, and that minor show of strength bolsters me until I open the closet and contemplate the full lineup of brand-new maternity clothes, all in tasteful pale shades and in order from barely pregnant to hot-air balloon.

That's right, my mother is batshit crazy.

But also clever. The perfectly appointed house. The meticulously outfitted nursery. Just how far would she go to get her daughter back—or really, to get her future grandchild all to herself?

I never saw who shot Conrad. I have no idea who might have been in the house before me. I can't picture my mom opening fire on my husband any more than I could picture her aiming a shotgun at my father. But then, my mother has never been one to do her own work. That's what underlings are for. Particularly men, whom, from my earliest memory, she's been able to manipulate with a single crook of her finger.

I always thought my parents loved each other. But did they? All marriages have ups and downs. If she thought for a moment that my father was losing interest, might even leave her . . . Who was the female professor my mother mentioned?

I pick a heavy cable-knit sweater in a light caramel, because I'm suddenly chilled and not liking at all where my thoughts have taken me.

WHEN I GET downstairs, I discover Mr. Delaney at the kitchen island. He has already shed his wool coat, revealing a deep-blue sweater that is stunning with his silver beard and hair. My mom doesn't seem to notice, throwing what appear to be fistfuls of kale into the Cuisinart.

Mr. Delaney eyes me ruefully. "Breakfast of champions," he says. "Please tell me you have Pop-Tarts somewhere on your person."

My mom pauses right before hitting the grind button to stare at us in horror.

"Never mind," I tell her. "Green is beautiful."

She smiles, returns to pulverizing.

I take the seat next to Mr. Delaney. "What brings you here this morning?"

"Just wanted to see how you were doing." But he's looking at my mom as he says this. I take in his sweater again, a color that he must know is flattering. Mr. Delaney has a bit of a reputation with the ladies, enough of one that he always jokes he's too busy to settle down. But is that true? He's never had one significant relationship that I know of. And yet he returns here, again and again, to the widow of his best friend.

And my mother? To the best of my knowledge, she's never dated since my father died. Sixteen years later, surely she's entitled to move on. Maybe the beautifully decorated house isn't for my benefit after all.

Do I mind? My mother, Mr. Delaney?

I can't wrap my mind around it. I'm adult enough to know my mom is self-absorbed, vain, and probably a functional alcoholic. I still can't view her as a woman who might be lonely, a woman with needs.

I'm never getting through liquefied vegetables now. I get up and make some toast. My mother frowns at me, then throws an entire cucumber into the Cuisinart. Does she think I'm giving birth to a rabbit?

I make three pieces of toast, butter them, slice them in half, then bring them to the table. My mother has finished with the Cuisinart and has moved on to furiously slicing fruit. She has yet to pause since I entered the kitchen, or even say good morning. There's something manic about her efforts. She's not just preparing breakfast. She's on a mission. I feel my uneasiness grow and look at Mr. Delaney again. I suddenly have a feeling I'm not going to like why he's really here.

Sure enough, once the fruit's been savaged and tossed on a serving platter, liquefied vegetables poured out for all, my mother arrives at the table, pulls out her own chair, folds her hands, stares at me.

"You have a trust," she says.

I stare at her blankly.

"Your father was a very successful man."

I nod, vaguely understanding this. "You once said he contributed to some major projects."

"He still receives royalties," my mother states. "Significant royalties."

I guess that explains the house, the clothes, my mother's lifestyle, which has never changed.

I'm still confused. "So you're setting up a trust for me?"

"We set it up when you were eight."

"Excuse me? I've *had* a trust? Since I was *eight*?"

I stare at Mr. Delaney because, of course, this has something to do with him. "I assisted your parents in finding the best attorney for establishing the trust," he says now. "As a criminal defense lawyer, it's not my area of expertise. At your parents' request, however, I agreed to be executor of the funds."

"So . . . you're the one who never told me I had a trust?"

"Actually, I assumed they had informed you." The look he gives me is faintly apologizing. I'm not buying it.

"They didn't."

"Well," my mother interjects, "like most trusts set up for second-generation wealth—"

I'm second-generation wealth?

"—you don't come into the money all at once. Eligibility occurs in stages, as you turn certain ages. And given that we already had college resources set aside for you, and that we didn't want you inheriting too much money when you were still young and stupid, the first-stage gate . . . Well, you'd just met that Conrad. It hardly seemed the time to turn you into an heiress. How would you know what his true intentions were? Then, of course, you had to go and marry him."

I open my mouth. I close my mouth. I don't know what to say. My mom gives me a little shrug—as if to say, *So that's that*—and picks up a piece of cantaloupe.

I can't decide if I want to scream or throw things. So I settle for sitting perfectly still. I have money. Apparently, a great deal of it. And no one bothered to tell me. Forget Conrad. She just didn't want me to know. My mother, that selfish bitch, wanted to remain in control.

I turn to Mr. Delaney. "You figured it out. Yesterday, when I asked to go to the bank, you realized I had no idea."

He nods.

"You're the one who confronted her." I point at my mom. "You're the one who ordered her to tell me. Otherwise, I'd probably still be in the dark. Because if I have money, then I have independence. And heaven forbid"—my voice grows low and forbidding—"that I be able to take care of myself and my child."

My mother looks right at me. Takes a bite of toast.

"How much vodka do you have in that orange juice, Mom?"

"I did what I thought best. No need to be nasty about it."

I give up on her completely. She's never going to apologize or reconsider her actions. She doesn't have it in her. I target Mr. Delaney instead. "How much?"

"Roughly eight million dollars."

"Eight million dollars?"

"You can't take it out all at once," he warns. "There are some provisions in place. I can go over it with you later today."

"How successful was my father?"

"Your father was brilliant," Mr. Delaney says simply, as if that explains everything.

"But being a math genius doesn't necessarily translate to financial gain. Lots of geniuses die poor."

"Let me put it another way. Your father's genius translated nicely to the expansion of computing power and a couple of Department of Defense encryption programs."

I feel like a gaping fish again. I had no idea. My dad was just my dad. The father I loved, standing at a whiteboard, dry-erase marker in hand, muttering under his breath.

There was applied mathematics, and there was theoretical mathematics. My father had been the theoretical kind, which my mother used to say proved he was a true genius. As if the applied kind were secretly selling out their intelligence for capital gain. But no, my father had ended up profiting. A lot.

I wondered what the applied mathematicians had thought of that. I wonder what his TAs and research assistants who probably helped develop some of the theories that then ended up being worth so much money thought of that. Let alone work that went to the Department of Defense.

I have so many things to consider. My mind feels overfull, near bursting. I'm sitting in my childhood home and yet it's like I've never been here. Never truly looked at my family, never seen any of us at all.

"I have some calls to make."

"You haven't eaten breakfast." My mother sulks.

I pick up the glass of green juice, which has separated into silvery green at the top, swampy green at the bottom. I chug it down. Then, just because I am feeling childish and petty and pissed off, I wipe my mouth with the back of my hand.

My mother glares at me.

I turn to Mr. Delaney. "I need to speak to some of my father's former colleagues. I want to meet with them, today, in person. Can you help me?"

"Of course."

"You should know, the police came by yesterday. I spoke with them—"

"Told you!" my mother bursts out, eyes on fire now as she turns for Mr. Delaney. "I told you she met them without your permission!"

"As your lawyer," Mr. Delaney begins, his voice clearly placating as he attempts to split his attention between the two of us, "I advise against talking to the police. Or, if you feel compelled, let me set it up and be in the room. My job is to protect you, Evie. I can't do it if you won't let me."

"They talked to me, too. Sergeant Warren learned some things about Conrad."

"Such as?"

"He definitely had secrets and aliases. But maybe they weren't all bad." I stare at my mother. "Maybe, some lies are for good."

She sips her orange juice, which I'm now convinced is half vodka.

"I'm sure they'll get back to me today with more information," I continue. "Till then, I want to learn more about my father. Exactly who he trusted, what he was working on, sixteen years ago."

Mr. Delaney doesn't seem surprised. Following in my footsteps, he picks up his own glass of liquefied veggies and quaffs it down. "When do you want to start?"

"Right now."

I leave the room to finish getting ready. As I exit, I can see Mr. Delaney cross to where my mother is sitting, a hard set to her face.

"She does love you," I hear him murmur in my mother's ear, his hand familiar upon her shoulder. "Unfortunately, neither one of you is any good at saying it."

For a moment, I think she's going to shut him down. Then, briefly, she reaches up, enfolds her hand around his own. They stand there, a second, two, three.

When my mother looks up again, sees me watching them, her hand falls away. She glares at me, her gaze as hard as ever, till I give up and walk away.

CHAPTER 29

D.D.

D.D. AWOKE TO THE THUNDER of footsteps. She just had time to brace herself before the bedroom door burst open and Jack came plowing into the room, Kiko hot on his heels. Boy and dog hit the bed in a single flying leap.

"Two weeks till Christmas!" Jack roared. "Daddy says we can get a tree this weekend!"

Next to D.D., Alex groaned. Jack found the space between them and started his favorite morning ritual of bouncing. Kiko, on her spindly black-and-white legs, did her best to dance around her favorite boy, while tripping over Alex's and D.D.'s prone forms.

D.D. managed to turn her head toward her husband. "We're getting a tree this weekend?"

"Seemed like a good idea at the time."

"We are going to find a real grown tree and cut it down!" Jack fairly screamed. "With a chain saw and everything. Then we're going to drink hot cocoa with whipped cream and marshmallows!"

"When he discovers coffee," D.D. said, "we're in real trouble."

She managed to unpin her arms from the covers and hold them out to her very exuberant child. In response, Jack collapsed to his knees, then pitched forward into her arms. He was still vibrating. He smelled of grubby hands, syrupy pancakes, and little-boy sweat. God, she loved him.

"Will a Christmas tree survive in our house?" she asked him.

"Of course! Kiko and I will take very good care of it."

"You can't leap on the Christmas tree."

"No!"

"You can't jump around the Christmas tree."

"Never."

"No throwing ornaments. And absolutely, positively, no *peeing on branches*."

Jack stared at her indignantly.

"That last instruction was for Kiko," D.D. informed Jack. Since Jack was on top of her, Kiko had moved on to Alex and was attempting to lick his face, whether Alex wanted his face licked or not.

"What time is it?" Alex mumbled around dog tongue.

"Round bottom six," Jack supplied.

"Oh dear." D.D. moaned. "I gotta get to work."

"No work!" Jack ordered. "Let's go get the tree."

"How about work and school today, tree tomorrow?"

Alex, one hand blocking his cheek from Kiko, arched a brow at her. First rule of thumb for a kid Jack's age was not to make promises you can't keep. Given the demands of D.D.'s job, that was easier said than done.

"I can figure it out," she assured him. "For that matter, I have a new fed playmate. Maybe I can make her work tomorrow."

"You have a playmate?" Jack asked. He'd calmed down slightly, curling up in her arms, head pressed against her shoulder. Kiko gave up on Alex, licked Jack's face instead. The dog was very gentle about it, as if she was grooming her puppy. Kiko loved Jack, too.

"A fed playmate?" Alex asked.

"SSA Kimberly Quincy. She has an interest in my victim, who we're pretty sure has been living under a false identity."

"What about the wife?" Alex asked.

"I still don't know. But I'm thinking that whatever happened Tuesday night was more than a domestic situation. Which is why"— she flipped abruptly, catching Jack beside her and tickling his sides while he giggled hysterically—"I gotta get to work."

"Gonna catch bad guys?" Jack asked. It was his favorite question.

"Oh yeah. And lock up a few from Santa's naughty list as well. We all gotta do what we can to help the big guy this time of year. Speaking of which, where's the elf?"

The Elf on the Shelf, which Alex had sagely brought home a few weeks ago and started moving around the house, was supposedly the eyes and ears of Santa. Reported all naughty, noticed all nice. Personally, D.D. thought a spying house elf was a little creepy. But Jack was all about keeping the elf happy, given that his future supply of Christmas LEGO bricks depended on it. Oh, the power of the holidays.

Not to mention, D.D. herself had taken up Googling photos of Felonious Elf on the Shelf, posed in various criminal acts, and/or at various crime scenes. Some of them made her laugh hysterically, which was probably inappropriate. Then again, she knew for a fact that Alex had already looked up how to make elf blood spatter. What either one of them was doing raising a child was the real question. And yet, here they were.

At the mention of Elf on the Shelf, Jack untangled himself from D.D.'s embrace and went tearing out of the room, Kiko in immediate pursuit.

"Does he ever walk?" D.D. asked.

"Not that I've seen."

"I could use that kind of energy on my case team."

"What do you think?" Alex said, referring to her case now that Jack was out of the room.

"I have no idea. You know how at the academy you're always talking about the importance of victimology?"

He nodded.

"This is one of those cases. Turns out Conrad Carter wasn't Conrad Carter at all. He's been living for years under an assumed name. Even met Jacob Ness in a bar in the South under an alias."

"The Jacob Ness?"

"Which is why I got a visit from the SSA Quincy. Then, just to make it really interesting, Conrad's father was a detective in Florida who died under mysterious circumstances."

Alex's eyes had widened. "That's one of the crazier victim backgrounds I've ever encountered."

"Hah. Wait till you meet my case team."

"You love this case, don't you?" He knew as well as anyone, the larger the riddle, the bigger D.D.'s fascination.

Now, she broke into a wide smile. "Honest to God, it's like Christmas has come early."

D.D. ARRIVED TEN minutes late to work. Supervisor's privilege, she decided. But in consideration of the fact that several of her detectives had no doubt pulled all-nighters, she arrived bearing gifts: a tray of four fancy coffee drinks with whipped cream and chocolate drizzles and peppermint pieces. Not just caffeine, but caffeine and intense amounts of sugar married together in a concoction designed to cause an immediate jolt to the central nervous system.

She set down her shoulder bag. Ditched her coat. Switched from her thick winter boots to her much sleeker black leather boots, which she'd decided to keep at the office and away from Kiko's evil clutches. Then, picking up the tray of chocolate minty goodness, she went in search of her detectives.

She found Phil first and presented beverages. He selected the cup closest to him and, without a word, took a hit, smearing whipped cream across his upper lip.

"When I'm done with Betsy, I'm gonna marry you," he said.

"Oh, you adore her, you big softy."

"I adore coffee. Whipped cream. Chocolate. What is this, a liquefied brownie?"

"Entirely possible. What do I need to know?"

"Video surveillance sucks."

"Fair enough. Walk me through it."

Phil caught her up on the techs' attempts to find footage of the arsonist Rocket Langley's designated drop site. As it was located in a major urban environment, the issue wasn't whether there were cameras, but how many cameras, where were they positioned, and were any of the captured images any good?

"Patrol collected the tapes," Phil explained. "Tech support started skimming for content. We have a photo of Rocket, so our first goal was to see if we could capture a shot of him in the general area. Which we did."

"Sounds promising."

"Yes and no. Drop site is a loose brick on the side of a building. Pull brick out, leave behind money, instructions, replace brick. There's only one camera angle that's any good for that side of the building, however. We caught Rocket walking up the street. Full on, there's his face square in the lens, so that was excellent. But then that camera loses him. Security footage from a local business picks him up again, standing at the wall, but from that angle we can only see the back of his head. Rocket stood there so long we honestly thought the dude was urinating. I finally drove out there at four A.M., which is how I discovered the loose brick."

"Anything there now?"

"No."

"Okay. So you've located the drop site and at least spotted Rocket in action. What time and day?"

"Wednesday morning, seven A.M."

"And the fire was Wednesday afternoon?"

"Yeah. I think we caught him picking up the target address and down payment. So now we're going forward to late Wednesday evening/early Thursday morning to see when he picks up his final payment. Once we have that, we have two opportunities to catch Rocket's client—either when the suspect first leaves the address or when he drops off the final payment. It's taking a bit, though. Footage is dark and grainy. Combine that with random people bumbling about, and there are a lot of visuals to sort through. Hell, I think I've already ID'd several drug buys. It's not a quiet area."

"Smart thinking on Rocket's part. That much activity, his own comings and goings hardly matter."

"The kid's been a known firebug for most of his life. I doubt anyone in the neighborhood messes with him. Anyone who likes to burn things for sport is best left alone."

"He's got a reputation."

"He has a reputation *in certain circles*. Word-on-the-street sort of thing. Your CI might have been on to something last night. Rocket's hardly big-time. Meaning our shooter is either local, or Rocket already knows enough to advertise on places like the big bad web. Hell, even the mob has gone cyber. It's sad, really. Pretty soon, the department will be staffed by virtual cops programmed to ID virtual criminals. Where's the fun in that?"

D.D. rolled her eyes. "Given that we're not computer programs just yet, find me video of whoever hired Rocket the arsonist. A drop box is an old-fashioned system that will hopefully get us old-fashioned results. Sooner versus later, I might add. Now, Carol and Neil?"

"In the conference room. They've been working on Conrad Carter's background all night." Phil eyed her remaining coffee. "Make sure you keep one of those for yourself. By the time they're done, you're gonna need it."

WHEN D.D. WALKED into the room, Neil and Carol were just hanging up the department's speakerphone. They both appeared jazzed.

D.D. handed over coffees and took a seat. "All right, what'dya got?"

"Homicide, definitely. Conrad's parents' vehicle was run off the road shortly after eight P.M. One moment they're driving home from a local restaurant along a well-known route, next their car is rolling down an embankment into a canal. They were dead upon impact." Carol shook her head.

"Witnesses? Leads?" D.D. asked.

"Nada," Neil supplied. "We just spoke to Detective Russ Ange from the JSO; he personally worked with Bill Conner and has been investigating the MVA on and off for years. Road was rural, no cameras, but Ange is sure it was foul play due to damage on the rear fender consistent with impact. Height of the damage indicates a large vehicle, say, a truck or SUV. No paint, however, so maybe a chrome bumper. Unfortunately, there are a lotta trucks and SUVs in Jacksonville; without any witnesses, it's been difficult to get any traction in the case."

"Surely he's looked at Conner's active investigations? Suspects, criminals the detective has come into contact with over the years and had reason to hold a grudge."

"Detective Conner had a couple dozen open cases at the time," Carol reported. "Two are worth noting: First, a significant domestic abuse case. Asshole husband, rich, entitled, kept beating up his wife and, given that he was rich and entitled, didn't think her restraining order should apply to him. Situation had been going on for months. Detective Conner had taken a personal interest, meeting with the wife several times. Week prior to the accident, asshole husband showed up again, drunk, enraged, tried to break into the house. Detective Conner arrived at the scene. He and asshole had an exchange. Asshole ended up in the slammer for the night, with a black eye, and none too happy about it."

"Detective Conner punched the man?" D.D. asked in surprise.

"In self-defense," Neil clarified. "Husband took a swing at Detective Conner first."

"Okay," D.D. said. "But one way or another, I'm taking it the rich husband didn't care for some local cop's intervention into his self-perceived right to beat his wife?"

"Exactly." Carol this time. "Apparently, the husband, Jules La-Page, yelled some pretty nasty threats at Detective Conner during his arrest. Unfortunately, LaPage owned a Porsche, not a truck. Jacksonville detectives couldn't find any evidence he borrowed or rented a second vehicle. On the other hand, LaPage had no alibi either, so he hasn't been ruled out as a person of interest in the Conners' murders."

"What happened to LaPage?" D.D. asked.

"He violated the restraining order two weeks after Detective Conner's death. Shot his wife in the face. She lived. Barely. LaPage is now a long-term resident of the state. Still a smug bastard, though. According to Detective Ange, LaPage spends his days filing appeal after appeal. Ange believes it's only a matter of time before LaPage finds the loophole or uncovers the technicality necessary to overturn his conviction. LaPage has unlimited time and resources. Not like the JSO can say the same."

"What happened to the wife?" Because Detective Ange was right, anyone with enough determination and money could often beat the system. If Jules LaPage had been angry and arrogant enough to take out the cop standing in his way, there was no telling what he might do upon discovering the detective's son was still investigating the case all these years later. Which also made her more and more curious about what exactly Conrad Carter had been doing in his free time.

"Courtesy of the gunshot to her left jaw, Monica LaPage had to undergo several rounds of reconstructive surgery. She testified with the bandages still on, then took her new face and fled the state. General consensus is, the moment LaPage gets out of prison he'll go after her again."

D.D. made several notes. "Is anyone from the sheriff's office still in contact with her?"

Neil shook his head. "No, but according to Detective Ange, if she'd stayed in touch with anyone, it would've been Detective Conner."

"Does Ange know where she is?"

Neil shook his head again. "No, and Ange was pretty blunt that it was in Monica's own best interest to keep it that way. A man with LaPage's money can buy a lot of information, including from underpaid public servants."

"Meaning the sheriff's office itself could become the weak link. Has Ange heard from Conrad about the case?"

"According to Ange, immediately after his parents' death, Conrad spent a lot of time at the JSO, talking to various detectives who'd worked with his father. He asked about all his father's active cases. Basically, like we just did."

"And presumably got the same answers?"

Neil cleared his throat. "Detective to detective, Ange let it slip they may have made some copies of . . . pertinent details . . . for Conrad. Bill Conner was the kid's dad after all."

D.D. arched a brow. In other words, the detectives at the JSO had duplicated case files for their friend's son. A definite procedural no-no and yet . . . Detectives were people, too. And sometimes, particularly after a hard loss, the rules mattered less than justice. Detective Conner's fellow investigators wanted it, and by the sound of it, his son, too. "So Conrad was actively investigating his parents' deaths?"

"Definitely."

"To the extent he took on an alias and ran away to Massachusetts?" D.D. murmured, then corrected herself. "Or discovered something dangerous enough, he had no choice but to get out of town?"

"Detective Ange had no idea Conrad was living under an assumed name in Massachusetts," Carol reported. "He says he heard from Conrad often in the beginning, but it's now been years. He assumed Conrad had moved on with his life. Ange also thought that was healthy and exactly what his parents would've wanted."

"So if Conrad was still investigating his parents' deaths, he was doing it on his own?" D.D. frowned. "But how did that bring him to a bar with Jacob Ness?"

"Second case of note," Carol spoke up.

"Two missing persons cases. Both female, white. One eighteen, in Florida visiting friends when she never made it home from the local bar. That girl, Tina Maracle, liked to party, so some debate whether she was truly missing or had just chosen to move on. Maracle had family in Georgia, however, and none of them had heard from her. While they may not have been the closest family in the world, three months without contact was unusual and they firmly believed something bad had happened."

"And the second girl?" D.D. asked, because this was interesting. Keith Edgar might have been on to something yesterday when he'd asked if Conrad's father had crossed paths with Jacob Ness. As Flora had pointed out, just because Ness hadn't made the FBI's radar screen didn't mean he was on good behavior. He probably had been actively abducting and raping young women. As someone who grew up in Florida, he would've been familiar with Jacksonville, and many predators started out close to home, before venturing farther afield.

"Second missing woman is Sandi Clipfell, age nineteen, who waitressed at McGoo's Tavern. Her shift ended at two A.M. Her habit was to walk home to her apartment just down the road. But that night, she never made it. According to her roommates, she was the steady type. Didn't necessarily love being a waitress but was saving up her money to go to school to become a dental hygienist. Sandi Clipfell didn't have local family but had worked at McGoo's for an entire year. Always on time, very reliable. She'd recently broken up with a short-term boyfriend but didn't sound like there was much drama there, plus, he had an alibi for the night in question. He also said she wasn't the type to simply cut and run. If she'd tired of her job, she would've given notice and settled up with her roommates before moving on."

"Any leads?" D.D. asked.

"At the time, Detective Conner was investigating regulars at both bars—looking for overlap between people who frequented McGoo's, where Sandi worked, and guys at the White Dog Tavern, where Tina Maracle was last seen. Detective Ange has continued to work the case since, and finally got a hit: A registered sex offender was in McGoo's the night Sandi disappeared, by the name of Mitchell Paulson. When Ange went to bring him in for questioning, however, the apartment was cleared out, and Paulson long gone. Ange put out an APB, but trail's been cold ever since."

"Did Paulson own a vehicle?" D.D. asked.

"A late-model Dodge Ram truck," Neil answered. "Bit of a beater. Could've had damage to the front bumper. No one would notice."

D.D. frowned. "Does Ange think he's the one who ran Detective Conner off the road?"

Neil and Carol both shrugged. "According to Detective Ange"—Carol spoke up first—"he's always suspected the abusive husband, LaPage. The accident seemed low-down and sneaky, exactly the kind of thing LaPage would do, plus, he definitely had a personal grudge against Detective Conner. Then again, something had to spook sex offender Paulson to make him violate his parole and split town. Meaning maybe he caught wind of Conner's investigation. And maybe that scared him enough to take the extra step of eliminating the detective working the case."

"Does Paulson have a history of violence?" D.D. asked.

Neil shook his head. "Just a thing for sixteen-year-old girls."

"The missing women are eighteen and nineteen. That's not exactly sixteen," D.D. pointed out.

"Ange doesn't claim to have all the answers; just a lot of questions, which apparently he shared with Conrad shortly after his parents' deaths."

"But he hasn't been in contact with Conrad in the past few years?" D.D. eyed her detectives. "Do you believe him?"

"Ange claims he wasn't that close to Conrad," Carol offered. "There was another detective, Dan Cain, who'd worked with Conrad's father for years, came over regularly for cookouts, that kind of thing. Ange's guess is that if Conrad was still in touch with anyone in the department, it would be Cain. He retired shortly after Detective Conner's death, but he's still around. Ange will track him down, then get us his contact info."

D.D. regarded both of her detectives for a moment. "So what do you think?" she asked them.

Neil answered immediately. "I think Conrad was investigating his parents' death. Meaning he was pursuing an incarcerated criminal with a lot of resources at his disposal, as well as a registered sex offender who may have been involved in the disappearance of two women."

"Not work for the faint of heart," D.D. said.

Carol took over. "LaPage, the asshole ex, knew Detective Conrad had a son. Apparently Conrad's real name was included in newspaper articles covering his parents' deaths. Given LaPage's threats against his father . . ."

"Conrad may have felt he needed to leave the area, even change his name?"

"All the better to protect himself while launching his own inquiry," Neil commented.

"But he never told his wife?" D.D. asked.

Carol shrugged. "Maybe he thought he was protecting her. According to Ange, LaPage is still working on his release and is still a rich asshole. Let alone, prison isn't exactly a stopgap. If anything, think of all the violent offenders LaPage has probably met over the past decade and offered money to, if only they'll do him one little favor upon their release . . ."

D.D. nodded. Somehow, prison seemed to be a breeding ground for criminal enterprise. Ironically enough, the county had probably increased LaPage's access to illicit resources.

Conrad's decision to move north and live under an assumed name was starting to make more sense to her. But it still didn't tell any of them what had led to his murder Tuesday night.

Photos of abused girls on his computer screen. The last thing Conrad had been looking at before being shot. Like Conrad's meeting with Jacob Ness, possession of such images could go either way. Conrad was either part of the problem, a sexual predator himself, or some lone-wolf operative, trying to make a difference.

D.D. knew who she wanted him to be, especially for his wife and unborn child's sake, but that didn't make it so.

"You think whoever shot Carter three nights ago might be the same person who ran his parents off the road?" Carol asked now.

D.D. shrugged. "We don't know what we don't know. We're just going to have to keep following the questions wherever they take us."

"Pretty damn scary ride," Neil murmured.

"Which apparently Conrad had been living for a long, long time. Find this retired JSO detective Dan Cain."

Both detectives nodded.

"And let's start digging into the missing sex offender, and what the hell, LaPage's terrified wife. But that inquiry—"

"Strictly on the QT," Neil filled in for her.

"Our best assumption: Conrad's father once got too close. Then, years later, his son, going down the same path . . ."

"Met the same fate. We need to find this bastard," Carol said.

"Agreed. Because whoever it is, the guy figured out Conrad's alias. Meaning he also knows about Conrad's wife and unborn child. And once you've killed three, what are two more?"

CHAPTER 30

FLORA

CAN'T SLEEP. ALL NIGHT long I'm plagued by terrible dreams where I'm running frantically down long corridors, only to turn the corner and find Jacob standing there. Except it's not Jacob, it's Keith Edgar, and he's telling me he'll take care of everything, which sends me careening away, running even faster.

I never make it to bed. I collapse on my sofa, where my legs twitch and my eyes keep flying open and I bolt upright like some demented jack-in-the-box.

My past and present have collided. I honestly can't figure out where old ghosts end and new demons begin. Is Keith Edgar just some computer genius who, due to a family tragedy, has a true-crime obsession similar to my own? Or is he too good to be true? The handsome guy who's been writing to me continuously since the day I came home, studying and perfecting the right thing to say so that one day, when we finally meet in person . . .

How many true-crime aficionados would love to brag they have Flora Dane as their girlfriend? Or maybe he is something darker, more sinister? The guy who got into studying killers because everything about murder fascinates him? In which case, could there be any bigger coup than claiming Flora Dane as his first victim?

I'm being selfish, arrogant. Assuming I'm worth so much. Yet, total strangers stop me on the street to say, *Hey, aren't you that girl,* and, *Why didn't you run away the first time he left you alone,* and, *Doesn't that mean you must've liked him at least a little bit?* Sicko men write marriage proposals. Others think I'm the only one who can truly understand them.

Just because you're paranoid doesn't mean they're not out to get you.

At six A.M. I give up. Shower. Leave a message for my boss at the pizza parlor, claiming to be deathly ill and apologizing for missing my shift yesterday. Given how I feel, I'm not totally lying. This is the other thing I resent about Keith Edgar. Him and his whole *you can be anything.* What a load of shit.

If I could do better, don't you think I would've by now? Instead of hanging out in a triple-locked apartment plastered with articles about missing persons cases. I'm not even a good pizza employee. And I don't want to write a tell-all novel or sell the movie rights or exploit my situation to make a quick buck.

Sure, I help other survivors. I assist the police. But six years later, I'm mostly still me, seeing monsters everywhere, and training every day to kill them.

I hate Keith Edgar all over again. Him and his elitist club and his quiet competence, which seems to argue you can fight predators and still lead an almost-normal-looking life.

I decide we need to talk. Which is why I grab my favorite down jacket, fill the pockets with all my latest tricks, then, hunching my shoulders against the cold, trudge down to the T station in Harvard Square.

It all seems like a very good plan. Till I knock hard on Keith Edgar's door. And SSA Kimberly Quincy opens it.

I FEEL IMMEDIATELY like I'm intruding on something, but I don't know what. Quincy doesn't say a word, merely opens the door wider. She doesn't seem surprised to see me. Maybe after yesterday's display, she thinks Keith and I are friends. Or more than friends.

She's wearing a pantsuit very similar to yesterday's ensemble, except today she has a dark-green fitted top beneath the short black blazer. Sensible heels, I notice, as she leads the way to the back of Keith's town house and I reluctantly follow.

They are set up in the dining room at a sleek, dark wood table. I note Quincy's long coat slung over the back of a chair, her computer bag occupying the seat. On the table, her computer is up and running, while across from her, Keith's hunched over a laptop. It doesn't look like his computer from yesterday. This machine is both larger and older-looking. I'm confused for a moment, then . . .

"Is that?" I ask Quincy, staring at the computer in rapt fascination. Keith still doesn't look up. He seems intent on avoiding me. That pleases me.

"Ness's actual computer? No. First rule of forensic analysis, you clone the hard drive so you're never working on the original. Granted, we made this replicate six years ago, so some of the external scarring is authentic by now."

"You brought the machine to Keith?" I leave my next question hanging in the air. Why?

"He seems to know a great deal about Jacob Ness, as well as computers. I have profilers who can give me the first half of that equation and geeks who can give me the second half, but as for one person with insight into both psychology and technology . . ."

Quincy's voice trails off. I scowl. I don't want Keith to be that valuable to this investigation, never mind that I'm the one who involved him in the beginning.

"The geeks cracked the password?"

"We think. But that's only a piece of the puzzle. Are you familiar with the dark web?"

Quincy pulls out a chair, takes a seat without asking. Clearly it's up to me to follow if I feel so inclined. Across from us, Keith continues to type furiously, scowling at the monitor. Briefly, the FBI agent's gaze goes from me to him and back to me again. I don't think much gets by her.

"The evil underbelly of the internet," I say. "Its haunted house."

"Good analogy. The typical online experience, or open web, features legitimate businesses, interests, services. The dark web . . . the less reputable sort. Illicit drugs. Firearms. Assassinations. And, yes, human trafficking."

I take a seat.

Quincy leans forward. "One of our issues with Ness's computer was how clean it initially appeared. His use of SteadyState meant that every time he rebooted his computer, it automatically deleted any traces of websites he may have visited or content he downloaded."

I nod.

"Even knowing he must've been visiting the dark web—given the Tor browser—we couldn't make any headway with the one username we had. Keith and you, however, cracked that nut for us yesterday when you helped determine Jacob's 'real' username, so to speak."

"I. N. Verness," I fill in. "But you still need a password."

"To access sites on the dark web, absolutely. Which meant we were thrilled at four this morning when codebreaking software finally churned out the magic answer. Better yet, like a lot of people,

Jacob seems to have reused the same password over and over again. Meaning now, a mere six years later, that computer right there, our Ness clone, is currently logged in to several markets and forums on the dark web. Hallelujah!"

Keith looks up briefly at Quincy, nodding in acknowledgment. The glance he throws my way is harder to interpret. Sullen? Hurt?

"But here's where it gets tricky," Quincy continues. "Even if we could re-create every IP address Ness ever visited six years ago, the internet—open or dark—changes all the time. Basically, we've finally arrived in the right country. But all the roads and landmarks are different. We have no idea where to go or what to do next."

"So what's he doing?" I ask, gesturing to Keith. "Learning the landscape?"

"Actually, I have other techs mapping out the terrain; one of them is an expert on the dark web and is continuing to cross-check Jacob's username with all the pages we know would appeal to a subject with his tastes."

"Porn, prostitution, human trafficking," I provide.

"Keith, on the other hand, I gave a different task. He's basically . . . wandering around. Seeing if he can get anyone else to approach with directions."

I don't understand right away; then it comes to me. "This is the first time I. N. Verness has been logged on in six years," I say slowly. "You're waiting to see if someone who used to do business with him, or hang out in a chat room with him, recognizes the name and initiates contact."

"Precisely. To the best of our knowledge, Ness kept his online identity secret, even from his fellow surfers. Meaning they don't know I. N. Verness was Jacob Ness or that Jacob is dead. They're simply seeing a visit from a long-lost guest."

"Won't the six-year gap scare them off? I mean, why now?"

"Fortunately, given that a lot of the activity on the dark web is illegal, it's easy to imply Verness spent the last few years in prison. Just got out. Not a new or interesting story, given the company. And of course, as someone who's been incarcerated, he's trying to get his bearings again."

I can't help myself. I move around the table and peer over Keith's shoulder. Up close, I can smell the scent of Keith's shampoo, see the ends of his hair still damp from his morning shower. I also sense the tension through his shoulders. My own stomach has tightened, as if readying for a blow.

I turn my attention to the screen. I'm not sure what I expected, but this appears so . . . banal.

"There are hundreds, if not thousands, of portals within the dark web," Keith says now, his fingers still moving as he scrolls down a screen too fast for my eyes to follow all the content. "One of the most famous, the Silk Road, was run by the Dread Pirate Roberts."

"*Princess Bride*," I murmur.

"Jacob Ness wasn't the only felon who prided himself on being clever."

"This page," I say, "it looks so boring." White background, menu items running down the side, with innocuous-sounding labels. Small photos of goods I have to squint to see, paired with brief descriptions. Frankly, it reminds me of scrolling through any old e-commerce site.

Keith has already moved on to another page, is scrolling rapidly. I don't know how he can take in data that fast. But then, my skill sets have always been more hands-on. And while I had a passing knowledge of things like the dark web, I'd never tried to visit or analyze it myself. I didn't have the computer expertise. Plus, I genuinely worried the stark reality of such a platform would completely overwhelm me. I had enough sleepless nights patrolling Boston. An entire virtual world of predators . . . Even I knew I couldn't take it.

"Post–Silk Road, these sites had to learn to be more careful. Many now appear exactly like a normal retail page."

"Obviously."

"There are backdoor portals that get you to the real page. Even then, sales items often appear under clever labels—hardware for guns, or you may have a prescription meds site that at first blush is completely legit, except if you click on the photo of aspirin, the jpeg file is much larger than it should be."

"Data is hidden in the photo. There's a term for that . . ." I search my mind.

"Steganography. Not all dark websites bother. But marketplaces dealing with child porn, human trafficking—"

"Jacob's kind of places," I fill in.

Keith looks at me. "They have the highest security features in place. They have to. They're hated even by other criminals who'd turn on them in a hot second. Which, of course, makes our job of retracing Jacob's virtual footprints that much more challenging. It's not just that he was walking around in bad neighborhoods, so to speak; he was touring the most sordid, dangerous back alleys possible, where everyone is suspicious and taking extra precautions."

I'm confused. "Given all that, how would Jacob even learn of such marketplaces? Know that clicking on this photo actually gets him that pornographic image? Is there like a web version of street smarts?"

"Welcome to forums—or chat rooms as some people call them. Ness had to belong to at least one to learn all the things he learned. Unfortunately, given the paranoia of the members of the more twisted forums, learning who, what, when, where, how, and why is that much more difficult."

"So what are you doing?"

"The dark web is a competitive marketplace, right? Illegal or not, the goal is still to make money. Hence customer reviews, rating systems, everything."

"Okay."

"I'm hoping one of Jacob's past business associates will find us. Start a private chat in a pop-up window, hey we haven't seen you in ninety days, welcome back with a free thirty-day trial . . ."

"Business is business," I murmur. I nod slowly. "You don't know all the forums Jacob visited or the members he might've 'chatted' with. So if you can't go to them, you're hoping one of them will come to you."

"Exactly. You said Jacob used a lot of drugs."

I nod.

"Those e-commerce sites have less security, believe it or not, so might be one place to start. But I think those deals had to be local, because to order off the dark web Jacob would need a PO box for delivery. Given his life on the road, always going from state to state . . ."

"He had mail sent to his mom's house."

"Exactly. Meaning he'd have to return there every time he needed a fix; and we know he didn't go there that often. As an illegal consumer, what other items would Jacob have been into?"

"Porn. And not child porn. But more like everyday porn." I grimace in distaste at the distinction. I tap the screen, where new images have appeared. "Wait. Is that what this is? But it looks like a gardening catalogue? Aren't those photos of different kinds of daffodils?"

Keith glances up. His expression is faintly apologetic.

"It's awful," he says.

I stare at the screen. "You said only the really terrible sites relied on steganography. The ones even other predators hate."

"It's awful," he repeats.

Meaning those daffodils aren't really daffodils. Young girls? Images of children for sale? He's right; the possibilities are too awful to consider. I sink down into the chair beside him. Just as a pop-up window appears on the screen.

Keith straightens, looks over the laptop monitor to Quincy. "We have contact."

The FBI agent marches over, takes up a position behind Keith's shoulder.

She reads the message, nods in grim satisfaction, then takes out her iPhone. She aims it at the screen and hits video.

"All right," she says. "Let's play."

CHAPTER 31

EVIE

M R. DELANEY INSISTED UPON DRIVING. I couldn't decide if he thought a woman in my delicate condition shouldn't be allowed behind the wheel of a car, or if he was just one of those guys who had to be in control.

I had wanted to meet with Dr. Martin Hoffman, the department chair during my father's tenure at Harvard. My mother had implied he'd know all my father's associates, so I thought he'd be the best place to start. Unfortunately, he hadn't answered his phone. I'd left a message but then decided I was too antsy to wait. I'd dialed Katarina Ivanova next, locating her office number on the department website. Interestingly enough, she'd answered and, after a moment's hesitation, had agreed—rather coolly, I thought—to meet with me.

I had looked up her photo online. She was indeed beautiful, thick, wavy locks of hair, darkly lashed eyes, golden skin. Everything my platinum-blond mother wasn't.

Personally, Katarina's photo sparked few reactions for me. Vaguely familiar. I probably had met her at one of the Friday poker parties.

But I couldn't bring any specific memory to mind. Just the mildly shocked reaction that such a gorgeous woman was a Harvard math professor, an ironic generalization from a fellow female math geek who should know better. Just because I complain about the system doesn't mean I'm immune to it.

Now Mr. Delaney and I drive through Cambridge in comfortable silence. The Harvard campus isn't far at all, a matter of miles. Given the narrow, congested streets of Cambridge, it's probably a faster walk than a drive. But this time of year, with the frigid temps and slushy sidewalks, driving it is.

We make it another creeping half a mile; then I just can't help myself:

"Are you and my mom seeing each other?"

Mr. Delaney takes his eyes off the road long enough to give me an arched brow. The car in front of him stops short for a pedestrian darting across the street. Mr. Delaney slams on his brakes, then throws up an arm as if to keep me from flying through the windshield. I'm wearing my seat belt, not to mention we're barely moving, but I appreciate the protective instinct.

"Why do you ask?" he finally says.

"Why don't you answer?" I counter, having seen the lawyer at work before. "I'm not saying I care. I just want to know."

"Your mother's a beautiful woman," he concedes at last.

I nod in encouragement. Mr. Delaney and my mother. The more I think about it, the more I don't mind. It's good for my mother to have someone in her life. I know better than anyone that my father had been her entire world. The years since have been rough for her. I'm glad she has someone like Mr. Delaney in her life.

"I would be honored to be in a relationship with her," Mr. Delaney continues now, "if I was the kind of guy interested in a relationship with a beautiful woman."

It takes a moment for me to register what he has just said. The car ahead of us begins to move again. We edge forward. I feel like my head is in spin cycle, my brain the image of the whirling symbol on a smartphone as it struggles to load content. Wait a minute. Does that mean?

Suddenly, with a little click, I get everything I never truly noticed before. The incredibly handsome man beside me who never married, never had children of his own. Flirted shamelessly with every female in the room but never arrived or left with any one woman on his arm. I had watched ladies' interest in him and, given his charming smiles, assumed he was a player of the highest order. But again, for my entire childhood, then adulthood, no girlfriend, no serious relationship.

I feel ridiculously stupid.

"I'm sorry," I say.

He smiles gently. "It's not something I talk about. My parents weren't exactly open-minded on the subject."

"Haven't they passed away?"

"Old habits die hard. Close friends and associates know my preferences, but it's not something I advertise."

"I'm sorry," I say again.

"Whatever for?"

"Because . . . Because you shouldn't have to say who you are. You shouldn't have to feel self-conscious. And you shouldn't have to explain yourself to an idiot like me. Not that I care," I hasten to add, then realize that came out wrong. "I care about you," I correct. "I don't care about who you date."

"As long as it's not your mother?" he asks slyly.

"Ha. Please tell me I don't have to ask about my father." I roll my eyes, clearly joking.

The look he gives me has me going wide-eyed.

"What? Wait! No way."

He starts to laugh, and just like that, I know he's played me.

Good God, I have to start sleeping more, because every time I think I'm starting to understand my family, my worldview gets turned upside down again.

"Both my parents knew?" I ask, trying to regain my bearings.

"I understood who I was by the time I got to college. Your father figured it out first. As I said, it wasn't something I advertised. His complete and total acceptance was very dear to me, at a time in my life when I was still struggling to be comfortable with myself."

I almost say I'm sorry again, then catch myself.

"Your mother . . . She toyed with me for months. Had eyes only for your father, of course, but felt a need to keep me in the mix, most likely in an attempt to make him jealous. We didn't bother to correct her. It was too much fun to watch her work. I believe when I finally broke the news, she slapped me—for lying—then hugged me in sheer relief that there was a good reason I hadn't yet succumbed to her charms. Your mother is a complicated woman."

"Tell me about it," I mutter.

"She does love you."

I shrug. "She is the sun. She will always be the sun. I can only orbit around her, and sometimes, that's really draining."

"She is who she is, just as I am who I am."

"Is that what the three of you had in common? My mother, who needs what she needs, whether she wants to or not. My father, whose brain worked the way it worked whether he wanted it to or not. And you, who preferred who you preferred, whether you wanted to or not."

"The three misfits," Mr. Delaney concedes.

It's hard for me to think of my parents that way. My father had always been the genius, while my mother has always been the gorgeous hostess, every frosted strand of hair. Add to that Mr. Delaney, the silver fox himself, one of the best criminal defense attorneys in Boston . . .

But before all of that, they were kids. Given my own awkward years, is it really so strange to think they had their own?

"Do you want to know another secret?" Mr. Delaney asks me.

"Yes!"

"Back in those days, I was a complete reprobate."

"A wild child?"

"They say inside every criminal defense lawyer is an excellent criminal, hence our ability to be so good at our jobs. I met your father outside a bar, brawling with another student."

"You were fighting? Like punching and hitting?" I take in his three-hundred-dollar cashmere sweater and can't picture it.

"Please, I was winning." His tone turns dry. "You don't have to look so surprised."

"Umm . . . Why were you fighting?"

"I don't even remember. Back then, I didn't need much of an excuse. Hot Irish temper. A great deal of misplaced rage. A need, I think, to prove myself a man in the more elemental ways, since there was one fundamental way I could not."

I can't help myself. "I'm sorry."

"All before your time. And everyone has to spend their days young and stupid. Otherwise we'd never figure out how to grow up."

"My father didn't mind you beating up the other kid?"

"The other student had been heckling him in the bar. Your father was so awkwardly cute about trying to thank me for taking down his tormentor, how could I resist when he offered to buy me a beer?"

Now I'm not so certain about Mr. Delaney and my father anymore, and I'm not sure just how many new visions of my childhood I can take.

He smiles at me. We are at the campus, looping around it. From here we'll have no choice but to park and walk our way to Dr. Ivanova's office.

"I did have a crush on your father. In the very beginning. He may have known it, too. It was always hard to tell with him. Your father came across as socially awkward, disconnected. But later, if you asked him questions about an evening, a person, a situation . . . The things he saw. I used to catch my breath at the sheer stunning clarity of his insights. And I would wonder what a burden it had to be to see everyone, everything, so exactly."

"He saw me," I hear myself whisper. I look down at my lap. "He knew I was an awkward child, and no matter how many forced tea parties my mother arranged, I'd never belong with my own peers. He knew how much I needed the piano, something that was mine. He knew how much I needed him."

"Earl loved you very much."

"My father loved all of us very much."

Mr. Delaney smiles sadly, turns into the parking garage. "I can honestly say, he was one of the great loves of my life. And there isn't a day that goes by that I don't miss him."

Looking at his face, I believe him.

DR. KATARINA IVANOVA glances up from her desk as I walk into her office. She looks older than in her website photo. Thicker around the face. She also doesn't look happy to see me. Her expression sours further when Mr. Delaney appears behind me.

Her office is small, nothing special. Linoleum floors, no windows, fluorescent lights.

She rises from behind her desk. She's wearing a dark cranberry-colored wool wrap dress that flatters her lush figure and rich hair. Clearly, Dr. Ivanova feels no need to apologize for being one of the only female professors in the math department. I want to like her for that, but her wariness has set me on edge. I'm already not sure I want to learn more about her—her and my father.

"Evelyn Hopkins?" she says, calling me by my maiden name.

I don't correct her. I'm here about my father, so when I'd called, using the name Hopkins had made more sense.

"Dick," she says, nodding toward Mr. Delaney. If I hadn't just had such a revealing conversation with my father's closest friend, I'd be forming assumptions about how well Dr. Ivanova and Mr. Delaney are acquainted. Now I have no idea.

I take a seat. After a moment, Mr. Delaney joins me. Then the three of us stare at one another. Now that I'm here, I don't know what I'm trying to ask. What I need to learn.

"I have some questions about my father," I say at last.

"You said as much by phone." Dr. Ivanova has resumed her place behind the desk. She leans forward and plants both elbows on the clear surface. It thrusts her chest forward and, given the line of her dress, reveals quite a bit of cleavage. I wonder if this is to distract Mr. Delaney, or if Dr. Ivanova is one of those women who's used her looks as a weapon for so long, she's not even aware she's doing it.

I open my mouth to tell her the police have reopened his death investigation, then, at the last moment, change my mind. I'm not an expert in police work, but I know from watching countless cop shows that I shouldn't give too much away. If this woman did have something to do with my father's death, the fresh investigation into his murder would put her on guard. No need to go there just yet.

Then again, the real killer knows I didn't shoot my father. The real killer knows I've been lying for sixteen years. Is there something I can do with that?

Suddenly, I have a plan.

"You've seen me on the news?" I ask now, keeping my voice deliberately calm.

"You were arrested for shooting your husband."

"I didn't do it. Mr. Delaney, my lawyer." I nod in his direction. Dr. Ivanova sneers slightly. Definitely no love lost there.

"He will have this cleared up soon enough," I continue. "In the meantime, I'm pregnant. Homeless."

She arches a brow.

"Oh, didn't you hear? My house burned down the other night."

Slowly, she shakes her head. Her expression remains shuttered. I'm not surprising her, and yet she's clearly feeling defensive.

"I'm suffering a reversal of financial fortune," I say, leaving out this morning's abrupt news about the trust fund. "I would like to remedy that situation."

She stares at me long and hard. She really is stunning. I could see my father finding her attractive. Her choice of dress alone hinted at an adventurousness no one would ever accuse my mother of. But would he stray? I always thought of my mother and him as being so much in love. Yet, like all couples, they had their differences. Then I have another, stranger thought.

If Conrad had met this woman, would he have strayed? Did he stray? Fake IDs, bricks of cash. How would infidelity even rate after that level of betrayal? But just the thought of it leaves me feeling slightly breathless.

Something must have shown in my eyes because Dr. Ivanova frowns at me. "I do not know what you are implying."

"He loved you." I keep it simple.

I score a hit. There, in her eyes. The words she wanted to hear. What all women want to hear.

"He never would've left my mother for you, but he loved you."

She glances away, but not before I see the sheen of emotion in her eyes. Beside me, Mr. Delaney says nothing. He's letting me run the show, unspooling secrets no doubt he already knows.

Sure enough: "Did you tell her?" She turns on him abruptly.

"She was a child. Of course not."

"Then how—"

"I'm not a child anymore. I'm a grown woman. Married. Widowed. I don't need to be told how the world works."

"What do you want?" she repeats.

"I know what you did. I covered for you all these years. The least you could do is repay the favor."

She scowls at me. "I don't know—"

"The police are reopening the investigation into my father's death."

Her eyes grow wide.

"In light of my husband's death, they have new suspicions they want to pursue."

"You didn't shoot your father accidentally."

"I didn't shoot him at all. And we both know it."

"What?" She sits backs from her desk abruptly. She appears genuinely shocked, which gives me pause. So far, I've been reenacting my own episode of *Law & Order*. Except in my script, now was the moment she confessed. Not stared at me in confusion.

"I know what really happened in the kitchen that day," I double down. "My mother was distraught. The truth would've further destroyed her. So I lied to protect her. But that doesn't mean I didn't keep some evidence of my own."

"You are ridiculous."

"Hair often gets left behind at crime scenes. Especially long dark strands. Embedded in so much blood."

She pales. Beside me, Mr. Delaney flinches slightly.

"The police can still run them."

"They won't believe you. You shot your husband. They know you for who you are."

"I didn't shoot my husband. I shot the computer. And the police believe me."

Now she's just plain confused. I don't blame her. I'm trying to keep her off balance. Turns out, I'm pretty good at this.

"Who shot your husband?" she asks bluntly.

"Who burned down my house?" I ask back.

She shakes her head, clearly starting to think I'm losing it. I need to wrap this up before she finds all the holes in the tale I'm haphazardly weaving.

"I know what you did," I state again. "I have evidence. But I'm also a woman down on her luck. Meaning, for the right price, I can make it all go away."

Now Mr. Delaney does turn and stare at me. Is he impressed or appalled? I don't have the courage to glance at him to find out.

"I do not know what you think you know." Dr. Ivanova scowls at me. "But I did not shoot your father. Yes, I slept with the man. He was handsome and brilliant. But I did not expect him to leave your mother. Nor did I want him to. He was much too old for me, and I have no need for marriage. I much prefer my life this way."

"But you two fought."

"We did not. We were two grown adults. We had appetites. We were greedy and then it was done. Well, except, of course, your mother found out. She was not happy with him. Though clearly it was not the first time she had learned such things. Your father worried for a bit. She was angrier than usual. What did he call it? 'The straw that broke the donkey's back.'"

"The straw that broke the camel's back."

"Yes, that. When I heard Earl had been shot, I assumed his wife had done it."

"My mother was with me."

For the first time, Dr. Ivanova smiles. It is a feline expression. "Please, your mother would never dirty her hands like that. And I've always thought she is much smarter than your father gave her credit for." Ivanova waves a hand at me, gesturing that she is done with me. "You do not have anything. If the police come, I will tell them the truth. Your father and I were lovers, a very long time ago. Then we were not, also a very long time ago. I do not shoot my exes. Frankly, I couldn't afford that many bullets."

She gives me a blatant stare. And just like that, my crime solving is done. She's won. I've lost. Game over.

I rise to standing, surprised to find that my legs are shaky. To be honest, I believe Katarina's claim that she had no reason to kill my father. Now I have doubts about my mother instead, which is worse.

I want to get as far away from here as possible. This morning has been disorienting. Maybe children aren't meant to know their parents this well. Maybe no one should look too hard at their childhood memories.

Mr. Delaney also rises to his feet. As I head for the door, he hesitates. I hear him murmur something to Dr. Ivanova. Maybe a final, parting barb. Whatever it is, she hisses in response, clearly unhappy with him.

I don't care anymore. I just want to get back to the car. And then what? Return to my mother's house? Watch her mix more martinis in the kitchen? Or ask her, finally, point-blank after all these years: Did you arrange for Dad to die?

I'm doubting things I don't want to doubt. And seeing things I don't want to see.

As we step outside the building, into the harsh chill of mid-December, Mr. Delaney's cell phone rings. He answers it crisply. "Delaney. Yes. Excuse me? What did you say?"

His footsteps immediately pick up. I'm rushing to keep up with him when he ends the call, pockets his phone.

"There's a fire," he says, his voice hard.

"Where?" Then, before I can help myself, "Mom?"

"She's fine. It's not your mother's house, Evie. It's mine."

CHAPTER 32

D.D.

D.D. WRAPPED UP HER MEETING with Neil and Carol. Based on everything they had learned, it seemed logical that Conrad Carter had continued investigating his father's cases after his parents' deaths. That meant he'd been covering everything from how to hide Monica LaPage from her incarcerated-and-yet-still-vengeful ex-husband to pursuing the disappearance of at least two missing girls in Florida. Also, based on Evie's account of spotting a dot-onion site on her husband's laptop, Conrad had been using the dark web to do it. Which was where he'd encountered Jacob Ness, and arranged a meeting in a bar? Or where he'd met all sorts of predators, one of whom had ultimately figured out Conrad's true good intentions and felt compelled to kill the man? Or Conrad had simply learned something he shouldn't have?

They knew more, but they still didn't know enough. Neil and Carol were to contact retired Jacksonville detective Dan Cain, who presumably had kept in touch with Conrad. They were also to make discreet inquiries into Monica LaPage's whereabouts. D.D. was already wondering—the monthly withdrawals from Conrad's account. Had he been sending financial support to the beleaguered woman, again, taking up where his father had left off in trying to help her?

So many questions.

In the meantime, D.D. headed back up to her office, where she could call arson investigator Patti Di Lucca. She wanted more information on Rocket, who appeared to be their prime suspect for burning down the Carters' home. Not to mention this whole firebug-for-hire gig. Had Di Lucca heard of such a thing before? Did it fit with her impressions of the scrawny kid? And how exactly would prospective clients learn of such services?

Clever in his own way, Flora had said about Rocket. In D.D.'s world, nothing good came from that.

She was just reaching for her cell phone when it rang. She took one look at the caller ID and smiled.

"Great minds think alike," she said, as she took Patti Di Lucca's call.

"Though fools seldom differ," Di Lucca finished the proverb.

"Uh-oh. Does that mean I'm not going to like this call?"

"That depends. What are your feelings on a second fire?"

"Where?"

"Defense attorney Dick Delaney's town house. Reeks of gasoline—and I'm told the first firefighters on the scene discovered a burnt-out pot on the stove and thick smoke from cooking oil."

"Rocket Langley," D.D. breathed.

"I'm already on scene," Di Lucca reported.

"Any injuries?

"Nope. Residence was empty at the time the fire was started."

"Meet you there."

PHIL HAD TO park several blocks back from the scene of the blaze. Thick smoke drifted up in a dark column ahead, and D.D. found herself coughing the minute she stepped out of the car. The street near Dick Delaney's Back Bay town house was already choked with fire engines and emergency responders. Given the brownstones nestled shoulder to shoulder down the stately block, the BFD hadn't wasted any time knocking down the flames.

Phil and D.D. flashed their credentials, then ducked under the crime scene tape. D.D. found Di Lucca tucked behind one of the fire engines, taking refuge from the heat of the blaze. The sharply dressed arson investigator nodded at their approach.

"I still don't know anything more than I told you by phone. Scene's way too hot to enter. But the first responders all reported the smell of gasoline. Also, they spotted a clear burn pattern, which would be consistent with the use of an accelerant."

D.D. nodded while slowly turning in place. As befitting a notoriously successful defense attorney, Dick Delaney lived on one hell of an expensive block. The street was lined with imported automobiles, and every expensively restored town house appeared slightly grander than the one before. Huge wreaths decorated dark-painted doors. Pots of fresh Christmas greenery flanked front stoops, while the precisely manicured bushes were decked out in sparkling white lights.

"He's gotta be watching," D.D. murmured.

"Firebugs love to admire their own work," Di Lucca agreed.

"Any empty buildings in the area?" D.D. asked Phil, studying the row of windows across from them. This time of day, it was impossible to see inside. The windows merely reflected back the smoky sky. It was possible Rocket was standing at one of those windows now, the young kid staring down at them. Or he was hunkered on a fire escape, or tucked in the crowd of gawkers. So many possibilities. And yet she swore she could feel his eyes on her.

"Witnesses?" D.D. asked Di Lucca as Phil went to make some inquiries.

"Nothing. But not many people home this time of day."

"He blends in," D.D. said. "We have reason to believe he might have dressed up as pest control for approaching the Carters' residence. No one thinks twice about service people. Plus, gave him an excuse to walk around with giant spray cans."

"Smarter than I would've thought for a kid who's only ever been known to have an interest in abandoned real estate."

"We think he's expanding his skills—arson for hire. Getting paid for doing what he loves best."

Di Lucca sighed heavily. "Great, gangster turned entrepreneur. Just what this city needed."

A commotion in the crowd. D.D. and Di Lucca turned to see Delaney walking quickly up the street toward them. Evie trailed behind him, talking on her phone. Delaney came to a halt in front of the patrol officer working the perimeter. The patrol officer put up a hand to block his progress. Delaney uttered something sharp and the younger man nearly leapt out of way to let him through.

Evie looked up, spotted D.D. waiting for them. Something flitted across the woman's face. Guilt? Whomever she was talking to, Evie ended the call abruptly, stuck her phone in the folds of her coat.

"Mr. Delaney," D.D. called out, summoning them both over. She peered into the crowd as she waited for their approach. Again, nothing. But Rocket had to be around. She knew it.

"I'm sorry for your loss," D.D. said as Delaney and Evie halted before her.

"Was anyone hurt?" Delaney asked immediately.

"No," Di Lucca did the honors of answering. "A neighbor spotted smoke almost immediately; BFD was on-site in a matter of minutes. Unfortunately, it appears the damage to the structure is substantial."

Delaney shrugged unhappily. "Smoke damage. Water damage. Forget the fire. I doubt anything is salvageable."

D.D. didn't say anything, just watched the criminal attorney.

He was staring at his home, but it was impossible to read his expression. Sad? Angry? Surprised? All three?

"May I ask where you were this morning?" She spoke up.

"Tending to my client." He gestured to Evie, who was gazing at the smoking building with open regret.

"And what were you up to this morning?" D.D. asked Evie. The silence dragged on for so long, D.D. didn't think the woman was going to answer. Then:

"Is it the same as my house? Arson?"

"We have reason to believe so," Di Lucca answered

Evie gazed at the woman. "Did you investigate my house? The Carter residence?"

"Yes."

"Do you think it's the same person?"

"I can't comment on an active investigation."

"In other words, yes." Evie shook her head. "But why? Why burn down my house? Why burn down my lawyer's house? Why, why, why?"

"I was hoping you could tell me." D.D. this time, regarding both Delaney and Evie frankly.

"I have no idea," Evie said, and she sounded so distressed, D.D. nearly believed her.

"Did you take anything from your house after the shooting?" D.D. asked her now.

"Of course not. The police arrested me. I didn't even grab my purse or cell phone."

"Eight minutes," D.D. said softly. "Eight minutes between the first round of shots and the second. Plenty of time to grab something and tuck it away."

"But I wasn't there during the first round of shots. I already told you; that wasn't me. I was just there for the end, to destroy the computer and try to save my future child more grief."

"Anything she would've taken"—Delaney spoke up abruptly—"would've been seized during intake at the county jail." He eyed Evie. "You were searched, I presume?"

She blushed, looked down. "Yes."

"Then she couldn't have had anything," Delaney informed D.D.

"What about you?" D.D. turned on him. "Did you meet her at intake?"

"No, we only spoke by phone. Our first contact was the next morning at the courthouse."

"Someone must think you have something. Come on. First her house is burned to the ground"—D.D. pointed at Evie—"then yours. That's not a coincidence."

Delaney's tone remained clipped. "I'm sure it's not. But the connection . . . Honestly, Sergeant, I have no idea."

"Where were you this morning?" she tried again, this time going after Evie, who seemed the more cooperative of the two. Di Lucca was watching the show with obvious interest, but then her cell rang. With clear regret, she stepped away to take the call.

"We met with an old friend of my father's," Evie told D.D.

"Why?"

"I've been thinking. I know I didn't kill my father. Based on what you said, I also now realize he didn't kill himself. Which begs the question . . ."

"Good God, you're investigating your father's murder? What is it with everyone these days? Doesn't anyone understand that policing is real work?"

Evie stared at her slightly wide-eyed.

"Your husband was conducting an investigation, too. Did you know that?" D.D. pressed.

Evie shook her head.

"His parents' accident wasn't an accident. They were run off the road. Possibly in connection with one of the two cases Conrad's father, a Jacksonville detective, was working at the time."

"He never said . . . He never told me—"

"He lived under an assumed name. He was hiding, Evie. Your husband was hiding. Do you know from whom?"

Now the woman was positively pale. "No."

"Did you ever talk to him about your father? Say you didn't shoot him?"

"No! Remember, I thought my father killed himself. So, no, I never brought it up."

"But Conrad was tense. You said you thought something bad was going to happen. You just assumed it had something to do with your marriage."

"He *was* tense."

"Did you ever notice anyone watching the house?"

"No."

"Strange phone calls, strings of hang-ups?"

"No, but Conrad was in sales. He was always on his cell phone."

"He was digging into something, Evie. He was on to something. I need you to think."

"I don't know! Just the computer. The images of those girls. Oh God, I thought he was a predator. I was so sure. But instead . . . His father was a cop?"

"Did you know anything about this?" D.D. whirled on Delaney abruptly.

"Absolutely not," he said stiffly. But her tactic had worked. She caught a flicker in his gaze before he had time to cover it up. Then, she got it:

"You ran a background. When Evie first met Conrad. The daughter of your deceased best friend meets a new man . . . Of course you did. And in doing so, you figured out Conrad wasn't his real name."

Now Evie was staring at Delaney.

The lawyer opened his mouth, looked like he was going to deny it all. Then, abruptly: "Yes. I ran his name. Evie's safety and well-being are my responsibility. I take my responsibilities seriously."

"What did you do?" Evie breathed.

Delaney sighed heavily. The jig was up and he knew it. "I confronted Conrad. I told him I knew his identity was a lie. At which point, he told me about his parents, his father's work. And we reached the mutual conclusion that it was in your best interest"—Delaney regarded Evie—"that Conrad continue to live under an alias."

"Who was he investigating?" D.D. demanded to know.

"He had two lines of inquiry. The first into some missing girls. But he wasn't as concerned about that as he was the status of one Jules LaPage. According to Conrad, if LaPage ever got out of prison, he'd come for him. Hence the assumed name."

"Why would LaPage come for Conrad?"

"Because Conrad's father helped LaPage's ex-wife escape. He knew her location, and going through his father's papers, Conrad discovered her new identity as well. LaPage wasn't stupid. If he got out, the most direct line to his ex-wife would be through Conrad."

"He never said anything," Evie murmured. She was shaking her head slightly. "Never. Not once."

"It was his burden to bear. He didn't want you to worry. As the years went by and he never said anything more, I honestly thought the situation had worked itself out. LaPage was still incarcerated, so no news was good news. Perhaps Conrad was just being paranoid. It happens." Delaney turned to D.D. "When I heard the news about Conrad, the first thing I did was check on LaPage's status. He's still in prison, I assure you."

"But something had changed," D.D. said. "Evie already told us that. Conrad had become tense. Something was worrying him."

"I got pregnant." Evie shrugged. "If one of these guys he was investigating found him . . . there would be greater consequences."

D.D. shook her head. "It had to be something more direct than that. He found something. Serious enough someone didn't just kill him, but burned down your home. Except they're still worried. Why would they still be worried? So they went after your place next." She looked at Delaney. "Because you're Evie's lawyer, or because this person knows you learned the truth about Conrad?"

"I have no idea," Delaney answered coolly.

"Who did you speak with this morning?"

"Just a former friend of my father's," Evie volunteered. "Dr. Katarina Ivanova. She and my father were involved once. I thought maybe . . . maybe she'd grown jealous. She'd shot him."

D.D. couldn't help herself. "And?"

"I don't think Dr. Ivanova gets jealous. She just moves on to bigger prey."

D.D. frowned again. The more information she got, the less anything made sense. Evie's father's death. Evie's husband's death. Evie investigating her father. Evie's husband, investigating two different major cases.

A lot of stirring the pot of past secrets and current crimes. Any number of things could've risen to the surface. But what tied it all together? Two shootings. Two house fires. There had to be one connection.

Phil appeared beside her. "We have a sighting."

She didn't need to ask of whom. "Where?"

"Boarded the T three blocks from here. Green Line."

"Get MBTA on it," she ordered, referring to the Massachusetts Bay Transportation Authority police.

"Already done."

"You two"—she skewered Delaney and Evie—"sit tight. No more running around asking dangerous questions. We've got enough going on."

Then D.D. was on the move, phone in hand. She had one last tool to deploy. Someone who already knew Rocket Langley, who was intimately familiar with the city's subway system, and who could move faster and hit harder than any police officer could.

She called Flora.

CHAPTER 33

FLORA

KEITH IS TYPING FURIOUSLY. FROM my angle behind Quincy's shoulder—the FBI agent is still videoing the computer screen—it's harder for me to make out all the words. Not to mention Keith seems to be using some kind of shorthand known by computer geeks and cybercriminals.

I catch snippets of the exchange. The usual long time, no see. Keith answering he's been on an extended getaway, which seems to serve as a euphemism for prison. Which is then followed by a stream of questions I don't get at all.

When Quincy murmurs some of the answers, I start to understand. The online target is trying to establish that Keith really has been incarcerated. Which prison, block, hey what'd you think of the corned beef? A level of specificity that never would've occurred to me, and without Quincy standing there, I'm not sure Keith could've handled. He's sweating profusely. But he resolutely clacks away, building I. N. Verness's story of being gone from the game for a bit, but now out and ready for some action.

"Don't go to him," Quincy murmurs, placing a steadying hand on Keith's shoulder. Keith had just typed, *I'm interested in* . . .

"Make him come to you," Quincy continues.

My phone rings. I check the screen, see it's D.D., and take a step away from the table.

"Flora," I answer.

"Rocket Langley is back in action. Just torched Dick Delaney's house. No one was hurt, but uniforms caught sight of Rocket leaving the area. Hopped on the Green Line, headed in the direction of Lechmere."

I frown. "Do you have eyes on him now? Green Line is a major subway vein. Plenty of places for him to get off or switch lines."

"We have transit authority searching. But you've met him. You know how he thinks. I thought you might want to help."

I nod. So far, fighting cybercrime consists mostly of sitting around watching Keith type. I should be more patient. But I'm not. I prefer my action face-to-face.

"Why do you think he burned Delaney's place?" I ask now. "Isn't that Evie's defense attorney?"

"According to Delaney and Evie, they have no idea." D.D.'s tone is droll.

"First Evie's house, then her attorney's." I try to follow the thought. "Someone's trying to destroy something, but what?"

"Oh, it gets weirder. We're now relatively sure Conrad Carter was investigating two different Florida cases, one of which probably got his parents killed."

"Conrad is Batman? Turned into a lone crime fighter to avenge his parents' death?"

"I'm surrounded by nutjobs with no respect for law enforcement," D.D. agrees. "One of the cases involved two missing women, which may be what put Jacob Ness on Conrad's radar screen. Oh, and Dick

Delaney, Evie's attorney, knew Conrad's true identity. Delaney ran a background check on Conrad when he and Evie started dating."

"Did Evie know about Batman, or did she just think she was married to Bruce Wayne?"

"I hate you," D.D. informs me.

But I have a thought now. I have no idea if it's any good or not, but I lower my cell briefly and check back in with Keith and Quincy.

"Hey, I have Sergeant Warren on the phone. We have a question. Has I. N. Verness gotten this dude to talk . . . product"—I hate the word even as I use it—"yet?"

"Getting there," Keith mutters.

"Can you ask about a mutual friend?"

Both Keith and Quincy stare at me. "Who?" Quincy asks.

"Conrad Carter. He's been using the dark web to conduct his own investigation into missing women. If this is all about human trafficking, and Jacob was using his name—I. N. Verness—to make connections on the web, then chances are he crossed paths with Conrad, right? That's why Conrad was in the bar meeting Jacob. Because his username—um, Jacob called him Conner at the bar—and Jacob's username had made arrangements."

Keith nods.

"I. N. Verness hasn't been logged on in six years. But Conrad was probably active right up till his death Tuesday night. So if we can establish what he was doing, who he last was in contact with, that may give us a bead on his killer, and maybe another connection with Jacob."

Keith looks up at Quincy. She nods. He starts typing again.

"I think it's the dark web," I tell D.D. by phone.

"*What's* the dark web?"

"Your connection. Jacob used it to perfect his crimes. Conrad used it to investigate crimes. Even Rocket Langley—I bet he's on it, as well. Services for hire, right? He's exactly the kind of vendor people on the dark web are looking for."

"Rocket has some loose-brick drop-box system for making contact."

"No," I correct the detective. "That's for getting payment. He's not sophisticated enough for Bitcoin. But he has a smartphone, and he's gotta get clients somehow, right? Why not have a local flyer, so to speak, on the world's most invisible want ads?"

"It's possible," D.D. muttered. "Used to be the local hoodlum was just the local hoodlum. But for a kid Rocket's age, the internet is simply one more tool in his pocket. Why not use it to find new and improved ways to make fire?"

I turn my attention to Keith again. "How hard would it be for an arsonist for hire to set up an account on the dark web?" I ask him. "I mean is it just like preparing a business ad, but . . . well, secret?"

"Getting established as a vendor would take some doing," Keith reports from his seat at the dining room table. "For starters, there's a wait list."

This shocks me. "There's a *wait list* on the dark web?"

"Absolutely. And quite a few hoops a buyer or seller must jump through. Remember, the goal is to be anonymous, but at the same time, vendors have to establish credit and credibility. You don't want any idiot making promises they can't deliver. Or conversely, buying services they can't pay for."

"How is this done?" I ask Keith.

"New buyers must establish escrow accounts to guarantee ability to pay. And references are used to guarantee a seller's ability to provide services."

"Criminal vendors vouch for other criminal vendors?" The dark web sounds stranger and stranger to me.

"Something like that."

"Which means," I say, "someone else must be checking these references, verifying the escrow accounts?"

"All websites have administrators, even illegal ones. For that matter, these encrypted forums where Jacob would've met other predators—each have two or three moderators who know one another in real life. They trust each other, which forms the heart of the chat room. They then network and mine prospective new members, demanding evidence of illegal behavior such as a digital copy of child porn, snuff films, et cetera. This makes all site members equally guilty and therefore equally protected. For all the cyber in cyberspace, it's still a human system. You can't just hang out, chat, or trade on the dark web. A real person has to vouch for you. A real-life administrator has to grant you access."

I nod and feel it again—a tenuous connection forming, as delicate as the web I'm learning so much about. Conrad, spending year after year, hunkered over his laptop, dredging through the internet's worst of the worst. A particular kind of cat-and-mouse game with multiple targets. He was investigating two different cases. Missing women . . .

"What was his other case?" I ask D.D. now, my voice urgent. "Conrad's second investigation. You said missing women and . . . ?"

"A disgruntled ex-husband who shot his wife in the face. She lived. He went to prison. He's on the record for just waiting till he can get out and finish what he started. We think Conrad knew where the ex was hiding. Might've even been sending her some money to help out."

"Ex is behind bars?"

"Yes."

"So, evil ex can't look for the wife himself?"

"No."

"Vendors," I state. "Jacob used them. Conrad must've been exploring many of them. Pimps, predators, hired guns. Kidnappers.

Hell, maybe even an arsonist or two. Like you said, behind every transaction is a real person, buying or selling. Now consider that Conrad has spent years on the dark web."

"A good ten to fifteen," D.D. supplied.

"Think of the network he himself must've started building under his various aliases. Providers of services who knew and trusted him, allowing him to dig deeper and deeper. Except he's not just looking at one crime. He's looking at all sorts of criminal enterprises. What if he figured something out? What if he figured *someone* out? Because as Keith is saying, none of the dark web can exist without actual people managing the works."

Long pause. "You mean like Ulbricht from the Silk Road."

"Maybe. But it doesn't have to be he identified some huge mastermind. It would be enough to reveal the principal at the local high school is actually the person running the child porn forum, or the nice lady up the block is a secret assassin for hire. It would explain the arson angle as well. If Conrad figured out an identity, the person in question might be worried Conrad documented it somehow. A notebook tucked in a drawer. A journal he gave to a known criminal defense attorney who's close personal friends with his wife."

A pause as D.D. considers the idea. "Not a bad theory," she says at last. "But given that it's also pure conjecture, it doesn't help us."

"Not yet. But give Keith some time. He can approach it from the dark web itself, using Conrad's various aliases to identify connections. He'll figure it out." I look at Keith squarely for the first time all morning. He arches a brow at the huge promises I just made in his name. But he doesn't shake his head. He'll do it. Meaning maybe I was wrong about him after all. Maybe there is hope for us. Maybe there is hope for me.

"We know Conrad knew Jacob," Quincy murmurs from behind Keith's shoulder. "If we use I. N. Verness to vouch for Conrad, and Conrad to vouch for I. N. Verness . . ."

Keith starts to nod. Quincy peers down closer at the screen. They are on it. Meaning my work here is done. I end the call with D.D., head for the door.

"Where are you going?" Keith calls out.

"I'm gonna catch myself a firebug."

I START WITH a map of the Green Line pulled up on my phone. It's a major artery, but then the Boston T system has many of them. Unfortunately, based on where Rocket entered the system, he would've passed through several major hubs where he could've exited the Green Line and entered any number of other ones. It takes me about thirty seconds to realize the possibilities are endless and I'm not going to get anywhere staring at a color-coded mass-transit map.

Instead, I start plotting points. Rocket's neighborhood. Where I'd think, having conducted his business, he'd head back to. A comfort-zone sort of thing, till the dust settled. Add to that, the location of his drop box. Having performed a major job, he'd also want to collect his fee.

Both of these points are in the exact opposite direction of Rocket's Lechmere-bound subway. Was he trying to be clever? Knew the police might be watching so deliberately tried to mislead them? Except if he's that smart, he'd know they'd be waiting for him at home, too. So maybe, in fact, he can't go back to the hood. He needs a safer place to hang for a while.

I decide to be brave. I dial not D.D. but her second-in-command, Phil, the detective voted most likely to be Father of the Year. He doesn't like me. I'm never sure what to make of him. I didn't grow up with a father, so I'm never sure if his perpetual scowl of disapproval is the real thing or a show of affection.

"Does Rocket Langley have a list of known associates?" I ask without preamble. "I'm staring at the T map, and he headed directly away from his neighborhood, which makes me think he may have another place to hang out."

"D.D. asked you to chase Rocket?" Yep, definite disapproval.

"I've met him before."

"And if you catch him?"

"I pinky promise I'll only talk to him. Unless, of course, he starts playing with matches. Then all bets are off."

"Rocket has an older brother and a friend from high school. Both live on the same block, however."

So much for that theory. "Do you know when he got the gig to burn Dick Delaney's town house?"

"Actually, we have two detectives reviewing every second of video footage, and the only activity we can find at his drop box is Wednesday morning before the first fire. If he was contracted to do a second job at Delaney's, we haven't picked up any contact yet."

I frown. Rocket had a system. Why deviate from it now? I'd made contact with him last night, but he had no reason to think of me as a legal threat. Instead, I'm his somewhat scary future client. So again . . .

I get an uncomfortable feeling. Lechmere. Headed toward Cambridge. Where Evie lived with her mother.

Her house.

Her lawyer's house.

Her mother's house.

"It wasn't one target," I hear myself whisper.

"Excuse me?"

"The initial drop. Rocket wasn't contracted to burn *just* Evie's house. He was contracted to torch three homes, the three places Conrad could've hidden a secret. His home, the attorney's home, his mother-in-law's home. Rocket is headed to Cambridge, where he'll hit Evie's mother's house next."

CHAPTER 34

EVIE

"YOU HAD NO RIGHT!"

Mr. Delaney trails after me, holding out a hand in reconciliation. I'm not interested. I come up against a wall of gawking people, staring at the still smoking building, and feel my frustration double. I'm sick of crowds and media vans and people who treat my life like entertainment. I'm equally sick of my mother and Mr. Delaney, the two people who claim to love me but never tell me the truth.

I veer from the crowd, then think, *Fuck it*. I duck under the yellow perimeter tape. People part instantly as I shove my way through. I assume Mr. Delaney will stay behind. Instead, he plunges into the throng of people behind me.

"Just give me a minute."

"I don't want to hear it!"

"One minute!"

"No!"

But now we've burst through the sea of people. The sudden onslaught of fresh air stops me. Mr. Delaney grabs my arm.

"I'm not going to apologize," he says sharply. Which catches me off guard. "Your father was my best friend. When he died, I took it as my personal responsibility to look after you. I'll never apologize for that."

"You *lied* to me!"

"When?"

"That's lawyer-speak and you know it. Lies by omission. You never mentioned that I have my own money—"

"I thought your mother had told you."

"Really? As evidenced by my big house, my shiny car, my new clothes?"

"You were never into those things, Evie. Your mom is the one who needs appearances. You took a job at public high school where you could use your gifts to make a difference. I didn't *question* your lifestyle; I *admired* it."

I scowl at him. I want to hate this man. How dare he be nice to me now.

"You never told me my husband had an assumed name."

"It wasn't my story to tell."

"Bullshit! You want to keep me safe? I was living with an impostor and didn't even know it!"

"Conrad told me his reasons. In addition, I looked it up. His parents' deaths. His father's work. It all checked out. If he felt it was safer for you to continue to know him as Conrad—again, not my story to tell."

"I sat with you just yesterday. I cried about my marriage. I told you I thought the problems were all my fault. *I* had secrets, so I assumed my *husband* had secrets. *And you never corrected me!*"

There, the true source of my rage. That I really hadn't been wrong. That Conrad really had lied to me. And even if he claimed he had good reason—well, so did Mr. Delaney, and my mother, and once upon a time my father. Everyone had their reasons for lying to poor little old me. And I hated all of them right now.

Except I also wanted Conrad back, so I could throw my arms around him and tell him how sorry I was to hear of his parents. What a terrible burden that must have been to bear. I would've shared it with him. I would've helped him. We could've grown closer, dealt with it together.

Instead, we lived in a house full of secrets. Both of us fearing the other. Neither of us able to confess.

We loved each other. We hurt each other. And now Conrad is gone, and neither one of us will ever be able to make it right.

I wipe at the tears on my face. Mr. Delaney uses the opportunity to pull me in his arms and hug me hard.

"I hate you," I say, my words muffled against his heavy wool coat.

"I'm so sorry, Evie. If I could turn back the clock. If I could make things better for you."

"I am sick to death of regret."

"I know, honey. I know. Shh . . ."

I finally stand still, accepting his fatherly embrace. It occurs to me that I haven't been hugged in a very long time. Have had no one offer me comfort in what felt like forever. Our marriage had grown that strained. I've been that lonely.

"Did Conrad love me?" I hear myself ask, though I'm not sure I want the answer.

"Very much. He told me so himself. Before you, Conrad was totally fixated on the past. With you, he had a future."

Which had to terrify him as much as it terrified me. All the years of undercover work—I don't know what else to call it—digging into his father's past cases, taking on new identities to approach criminals such as Jacob Ness. How awful it must've been to dive into that world, seeing such horrors and depravity. Then come home and have to pretend everything was all right, he'd merely been out quoting custom window designs, nothing to talk about here. And all the while, still not finding whatever he was seeking, and still having to worry that one day, his other work might follow him home.

He'd been so tense these past few weeks. What had he finally discovered—and, dear God, how much had it cost him? His life, our house, now Mr. Delaney's house.

But it occurs to me just how dangerous my life has become. My husband shot. My home burned to the ground. My attorney's home incinerated. Conrad must've finally learned something, and just because I have no idea what that was doesn't mean it won't cost me and my baby everything.

I need to focus. I do still have work to do today. While Delaney was distracted with the fire, I'd made a second call regarding my father's death. And this time, I got results.

"I need to go," I say now, pulling away from Mr. Delaney.

"Are you okay?" he asks me quietly. He wipes at the moisture on my cheeks.

"You're the one who lost your town house."

He shrugs. "I'm also the one with two vacation homes. Guess I'll be working on the Cape for a bit. Or maybe Florida."

I have to laugh. "Well, it doesn't totally suck to be you," I say. "As for me, I'll check in on Mom. If she sees this on the news . . ."

Mr. Delaney immediately tenses. "Go. Keep her company. And, of course, limit the vodka." He sighs. "Tell her everything is fine here. Just some property damage, nothing more. I'll come by first chance I get."

"Okay. I have a couple of errands I have to run first," I hedge. "But I'll call her, definitely. And if you get to the house before I do . . ."

Delaney looks at me funny. "What are you doing, Evie?"

"Nothing. Baby stuff. Just . . . maybe I don't want go straight from this to my mother and a bottle of vodka."

Mr. Delaney thins his lips, looks like he's about to argue. And he probably should, given that I'm lying through my teeth. But given all the lies that people have told me lately . . .

I wave goodbye. Then, before he has a chance to say anything more, I turn on my heels and head for my own little dance with danger.

THIS TIME KATARINA is clearly annoyed when I walk in. Not her office—for this conversation, we needed a less conspicuous location, hence a local coffee shop popular with Harvard students and jam-packed this close to finals. No one pays me any attention as I wedge my way through the door, then work my way to the back of the overheated, overpopulated space. Katrina is perched at a table in the rear corner. With her long black coat belted around her waist, she looks like a character out of a spy movie. Which makes me?

"I already told you," she starts stiffly.

I hold up a silencing hand. "You already told me what you thought would make me go away. Now I want the real story. The one you and obviously Mr. Delaney know, but I don't."

She scowls. In my mind, I've already turned over our earlier conversation several times. In particular, the end, when Mr. Delaney leaned down to whisper something in her ear. Maybe it was paranoia, but it felt to me that all the adults in my life were keeping secrets. I didn't want secrets anymore. I wanted the truth, even if it hurt.

So I'd called Katarina again. Except this time, I told her I'd make her and my father's affair public knowledge, if she didn't talk to me again. I understood academia. Whether Katarina had done something inappropriate or not, she still couldn't withstand the whiff of impropriety. Especially given the reopening of the investigation into my father's death, which would immediately shroud her in scandal.

"You didn't kill my father." My anger has made me bold. I like it.

She ceases scowling, appears more puzzled.

"You really didn't care that the affair ended."

I earn a single Slavic shrug.

"What about him? Did he care?" This is what I'd started wondering about after talking to her. So what if the affair hadn't been an issue for Katarina? That didn't mean it hadn't mattered to my father. Or my mother.

What was it Mr. Delaney, my parents' closest friend and confidant, had told Katarina? What did he know that I didn't?

"Your father had many affairs," Katarina said at last. That shrug again. "It was common knowledge. He was not a man who felt a need to follow rules. A mind as great as his own . . ."

"Did he love you?"

Her expression is surprisingly candid. "Men will say anything to get a woman into bed. As to what they actually mean . . . The other woman is always the last to know, hey?"

I can't decide what I think of her. "Do you think he would've left my mother for you?"

"No."

This time her answer is immediate and firm.

"That didn't bother you."

"No." Same tone.

"I don't get it."

She seems as genuinely confused by me as I am by her. "What is there to get? We met, there was a physical attraction. We scratched the itch. And the world moved on, as it always does. I am not a woman who wants forever. And your father was not the kind of man to leave his wife."

"He loved her?"

For the first time, Katarina purses her lips, appears thoughtful. "I believe so. Their relationship was . . . different. But again, Earl was not one to live by traditional rules. Your mother suited him. For that matter, he loved you, as well." Now she shrugs both shoulders. "A genius and a family man. They are not so easy to find."

"But you didn't want him."

"I always knew he was already taken."

"My mother."

Katarina doesn't answer as much as she regards me steadily. And in that look, I know what I was afraid to hear. The doubt that had been growing for hours now. My mom had been with me that day. But as Katarina said, my mother wasn't one to do her own dirty work. My volatile, reckless, overdramatic mom . . .

"She knew about the affair," I whisper. "You said my father told you as much. It was the straw that broke the camel's back."

"She came to see me."

I don't speak. Now that the moment has arrived, I am genuinely frightened by what I'll hear next.

"She told me to stay away from her husband. The whole 'how dare you' speech." Katarina sounds bored. "Followed by the 'if I can't have him, no one will.'"

"What did she mean?"

Katarina arches a brow. "What do you think she meant?"

I can't breathe. I think the coffee shop is too hot, too crowded. My mother, famous for her rages. If she really thought my father was going to leave her for another woman—especially one as beautiful and gifted as Katarina Ivanova. My mother, whose entire world had revolved around her husband, nurturing his genius, protecting his legacy. A widow was well respected. A jilted ex-wife, on the other hand . . .

"She couldn't have done it herself."

That steady stare.

"Who would she . . . How would she . . . I mean, this is my mom. It's not like she has a number for some hired shooter next to home repair."

Katarina finally smiles. "She does not need such a number."

"What do you mean?"

"She already knows who to call. Don't you?"

I can only stare at her in confusion. The gorgeous professor finally shakes her head. "You really do not know your family, do you?"

"I guess not."

"Do you still want to know the truth?"

"Yes."

"Then I'm not the one to talk to, for I honestly do not have the answers. Suspicions, yes. Answers, no."

I understand. Where I need to go next. Whom I must see next.

Katarina rises to standing. She is done with me. And most likely, based on my washed-out, shell-shocked features, she assumes I really will take it no further. People think they want knowledge. Until they have it, of course.

I watch her weave her way through the crowded room. The way certain men glance up, then look again. The smile she has for each and every one of them. She is beautiful, beguiling, and brilliant.

If I see that, my mother saw that, too. This new and unexpected danger to her heart, her family, her very identity.

I finally rise to standing. What I need to learn next can't happen here.

I'm just leaving the coffee shop when I first hear the sound of sirens.

CHAPTER 35

D.D.

"WE GOT A PROBLEM." PHIL hung up his phone, turned to D.D., who was just now climbing into the vehicle.

"Talk," D.D. demanded. They'd wrapped up the scene at the Delaney fire and were now headed for Cambridge, given Flora's suspicion that their arsonist, Rocket Langley, was headed for Evie's mother's house next.

"A series of fires have erupted in Cambridge."

"Rocket is already at Evie's mother's house?"

"No. Harvard campus. Trash-can fires. Three, four, five. I'm not sure. Calls are still pouring into the fire department. Details are sketchy, but it sounds like there's a series of fires all over campus."

D.D. didn't know what to say. "What are the odds our firebug was last seen headed for Cambridge, and now there's a string of fires on the Harvard campus? Except"—she glanced at Phil in confusion—"Rocket is known for structural fires. Why the hell would he suddenly be messing around with something as petty as trash-can fires."

Phil shrugged. "Got bored? Killing time? I don't know. I'm still not sure why anyone likes fire so much. But I'm with you—Rocket was last seen headed toward Cambridge. These new fires must be his handiwork. Too coincidental to be anything else."

D.D. shook her head. "As soon as this case almost makes sense, it runs away from us again. Burning Evie's house I can get. Torch Evie's lawyer's house, sure. But trash-can fires on a campus where Evie's father worked sixteen years ago? That defies all logic." She scowled, whacked the dashboard of Phil's car, scowled again. "Any sightings of Rocket?"

"Not yet. But the fire department is just now arriving on-site. And given it's a college campus right before Christmas break . . ."

"Tons of panicked students milling about."

"I'll let Flora know," Phil said.

"Really? You're in charge of my CI now? I thought you didn't even like her."

"She's had a couple of good points on this case. Plus, she's already headed to Cambridge. Given the traffic we're about to hit, she'll be there way before us. And as you said"—Phil shrugged uncomfortably—"she knows what Rocket looks like. That helps."

"Fine. Manage my CI. See if I care." But D.D. was frowning again. They were chasing their tails. Worse, they were chasing a firebug's arson spree. A good investigator didn't just react to all the crimes going on around her. She got ahead of the game.

Three fire events. Evie's home. Dick Delaney's town house. And now a spree at the Harvard campus where Evie's father had once worked.

What the hell had Conrad stumbled upon? Because of all their avenues of investigation, the angle that made the most sense was Conrad's involvement with the dark web. All those years he'd spent running his own undercover operations. The level of trust and access he would've gained over time. The secrets he might have learned . . .

Since Phil was dialing Flora, D.D. did the next best thing: called Quincy. The fed picked up at the first ring.

"SSA Quincy."

"We got more fires—a string of trash cans all over the Harvard campus."

"That doesn't make any sense."

"Exactly. What have you and Keith learned?"

"Flora recommended we switch gears, see if we could use Jacob's username, I. N. Verness, to pick up traces of Conrad's activities on the dark web."

"Any luck?"

"Kind of. Conrad appeared to be shopping for an assassin."

"What?" That caught D.D. off guard.

"On the dark web, you really can buy just about anything. From human trafficking to murder for hire."

"Conrad was taking out a hit on someone?"

"Given the depths of Conrad's online activities, our preliminary theory is that he's spent years posing as a 'criminal of all trades.' Kind of a shadowy underworld figure, dabbling in drugs, women, all sorts of unsavory activities. Leading up to his death, where he talked about having some kind of serious threat that required a serious solution. He was looking for recommendations for wet work."

"He wanted to identify possible assassins," D.D. said.

"Clearly."

"Because he realized he was in trouble? That maybe someone had finally figured things out and was coming for him? Or"—she had a second idea—"the missing ex-wife. If Jules LaPage had found her, his next move would be to hire an executioner. Maybe this was Conrad's way of trying to be one step ahead. Identify the major players, so he'd know if any of them got assigned that kind of hit."

"Either way, Conrad was researching hired guns. Then Conrad himself was gunned down."

"He got too close. Flora was right; he discovered something he shouldn't have. Dammit, if Evie hadn't shot up the laptop . . ." D.D. was frustrated again. She forcefully exhaled, got herself back on track.

"From a federal perspective," Quincy began.

"By all means."

"This is a cleanup operation. First the shooting, now all the fires. Someone is aggressively removing any and all traces of Conrad Carter and what he may have discovered."

"But why trash-can fires?"

"I have no idea. Except firebugs are like serial killers—they can't always control their impulses. Maybe your Rocket guy has gone from controlled burn to arson spree."

"Meaning he won't stop," D.D. began.

"Until someone stops him," Quincy finished for her.

D.D. shook her head. Just what they needed, an out-of-control fire-happy kid to go with their already-too-complicated investigation. Focus, she thought. Forget Rocket and trash-can fires. Think motive. Conrad, who'd spent years surfing the dark web. Meeting in person the people behind the cybermasks. Gaining trust. Building relationships. Year after year. What was it Keith had told Flora—the dark web was still a fundamentally human system? Real administrators who knew each other, forum managers who personally vouched for one another. And the assassin he'd been trying to hire? Maybe he'd also arranged to meet face-to-face?

"Gotta go," D.D. announced.

"We'll continue our work here," Quincy said.

"Keith any good?"

"Better than I expected. Interesting."

D.D. didn't have a reply for that. She ended the call, nodded once at Phil, and he roared away from the curb, hurtling toward Cambridge and the next danger to the city.

CHAPTER 36

FLORA

I HAVE JUST EXITED THE T stop, climbing up into the slushy sidewalks and cold air of Harvard Square, when the first fire truck roars by. I track it instantly. Except the fire engine barely makes it three blocks before coming to a screeching halt, and I realize belatedly the sky is gray not from low-hanging clouds, but from plumes of smoke.

The sidewalks are a crush of activity. Groups of students moving away from the fire in an organized fashion, intermingled with lone gawkers who want to see what's going on. I decide to play gawker, too, pulling the hood of my gray sweatshirt over my head and burying my hands deep in the pockets of my down jacket as I shoulder my way toward the bustling firemen, already pulling hoses and shouting orders.

I had assumed Rocket was headed toward Evie's mother's stately Colonial in the residential part of Cambridge. But given the kid's penchant for burning things, I have to figure he's behind this latest danger, even if I don't understand why.

Which means he's around, somewhere. Watching.

Except then I identify the firemen's target and draw up short. I'm not looking at a building fire. Something big and ominous and impressive. I'm looking at a narrow cloud of smoke, followed by a sudden skinny burst of flame. Except there's another and another and another. Trash cans. I'm looking at four trash cans, spaced at random intervals, all on fire.

What the hell?

I think back to the first night I met Rocket, that particular trash can. And almost on cue, a new line of smoke rises in the distance . . .

I don't yell at the firemen. I burst into a run. It's Rocket. I know it. Working his way across campus, dropping firebombs as he goes. Why, I have no idea. But I've met the boy and this . . . this is exactly his style. Fire, beautiful and mysterious and everywhere.

Screaming. Chaos. None of the fires are big; it's the sheer number and randomness that are leading to panic. Trash cans bursting aflame here and then there and here again. Students are trying to scurry off campus as fast as I and various firemen try to push through. The firefighters need to hose down each trash can and stomp out embers. Me, I need to get to the head of the line, spot the source.

How is Rocket pulling this off? No way he boarded the subway with canisters of gasoline or a backpack of Molotov cocktails. Had he already stashed supplies nearby? A first stockpile for the lawyer's town house? A second buried behind a dumpster on campus? Is there another target?

I spy a figure moving ahead. Not running, but definitely moving in a brisk, direct fashion. Dark hoodie—not dissimilar to mine—pulled over his face. I don't stop to think if this is wise, or what I'm going to do if I draw too close and Rocket notices me. I trust in my training and the low buzz of adrenaline that's jolting through my entire system.

As I'd explained to Keith, it's hard for a girl like me to experience an up.

But this . . . this does it for me every time.

Rocket. Right in front of me. He turns just as I start to close the gap. For one moment we're eye to eye. He has a backpack slung over one arm. As I watch, he pulls out a small clear bottle. Alcohol. With a rag stuffed into its neck. A Molotov cocktail, just as I had expected, in a bag he must've stashed somewhere nearby. Meaning he knew he was coming here. All part of his plan. Burn down a lawyer's tony brownstone in downtown Boston, then head to Cambridge and light up a college campus.

Why?

My time for thinking is up. Rocket is no longer holding the Molotov cocktail; he's lit the fuse and is hurtling it straight at me. I yelp, dive left. The flaming alcohol hits the ground to my right, where lucky for me, it sputters out against the winter mush. I don't bother checking it. There are enough professionals on-site and my mission is clear. I clamber to my feet and start running. There, up ahead. I spot the dark hoodie again. Rocket, running pell-mell through a startled crowd of bundled-up students. The kid is crazy fast. In a straight-out sprint, I'm never gonna take him. Instead, I do my best to guess his direction, then race a diagonal intercept.

I'm just starting to gain on him, when he glances over his shoulder and realizes my strategy. Just like that, he veers left, farther away from me. I redouble my efforts, plowing through a huddle of students, leaping over a bench.

I land wrong, my right foot sliding out on the slushy ground. My shoulder hits hard, and briefly, I lose my breath.

"Are you okay?" someone asks.

Another: "What happened?"

I just shake my head, stagger to my feet, and take off again. Except

I no longer see my target. Maybe there, around that corner. Wait, that coffee shop. That entrance to the subway.

I rattle down the steps as fast as I can, but belowground, on the waiting platform, I encounter a sheer wall of people. Heavy coats, obscuring hats, strangling scarfs.

I look all around, but it doesn't matter.

I've lost him.

CHAPTER 37

EVIE

WHEN I FIRST ARRIVE AT my mother's house and discover the media gone, I'm nearly disoriented. Where are the flashing bulbs, the screaming questions? Three days later, the silence is almost disturbing. What did I do to deserve this?

Then I remember the fire trucks in Harvard Square. Of course, a local fire. The media have moved on to bigger news. How kind of them.

I walked home from my meeting with Katarina. Only a mile and a half, and the kind of brisk trek I needed to put my thoughts in order. Still, when I reach the side door of the kitchen, place my hand on the knob, I can see my gloved hand is shaking.

All these years. All these years I considered my parents a great love story. And now this? My father had been cheating on my mom. Worse, she had known about it, and probably taken extreme measures to secure her own future.

Is that how she's lived in this house all these years? Because coming home that day to my father's body wasn't some terrible, shocking tragedy? Just a well-executed plan? That she then conned her own daughter to take the blame for?

I feel like such a fool. I've spent most of my life as nothing but a pawn for my mother. I was never strong or clever enough to have helped my father. Then I went on to marry a man who also kept me entirely in the dark.

All these years, I thought I was the one carrying around secrets. Instead, it's the people I love who've never trusted me with the truth. Who've manipulated me, over and over again.

I open the door and march right in.

My mother isn't in the kitchen. The vodka bottle is out, though, a fresh lemon peeled on the cutting board, meaning she couldn't have gone far. I pull off my gloves, hang up my coat, begin the search.

The sitting room with the impeccably decorated mantel: nothing. The ridiculous parlor with all its silk sofas: not there either.

Then I know.

I walk to my father's office. My mother is sitting, quiet and still, behind his desk. To judge by the empty state of her martini glass, she's been there a bit.

And she looks, at this moment, so small, so lost, so alone in the world, I lose my head of steam, just like that.

"This is where I feel him the most," she says quietly, not looking at me, but clearly knowing I'm in the doorway. "It's why I could never bring myself to change it. The kitchen was mine. But this room . . . Sometimes, I swear I can still smell him, his aftershave, the whiff of chalk from his fingers, the shampoo I bought him from Italy because it really did help thicken his hair. He swore only I cared about things like that, yet he smiled every time I got him a new bottle. Silly, all the ways we knew each other. Awful, to still miss him so much after all these years."

"You had him killed."

She finally glances up. Her expression is unfathomably sad. Again, not my mother at all. "What are you talking about?"

"Stop lying to me! I spoke to Katarina Ivanova."

Just like that, she deflates. "I was stupid," she mutters at last. "Vain and silly and upset. Your father knew that about me. He understood."

"Understood what? That given a choice between him leaving you and him dead, you wanted him dead?"

"I didn't want him dead. I loved him! It was her. She was the problem. She needed to go!"

I'm so confused it takes me a moment. Then I get it. The whole *if I can't have him, no one will* didn't necessarily mean my mom had gone after my father, but after Katarina, the other woman. Who, being dead, still wouldn't have him.

"You hired someone to kill Katarina Ivanova? You tried to take out Dad's mistress?"

"I didn't go through with it. I just . . . had a weak moment. I was angry. Hurt. These things happen."

"Mom, you hired a hit man to murder a woman, and you call that a *weak moment*?"

"You don't understand! He was my world. My entire world! If he left me . . . I couldn't have lived with it. I'm not like you, Evie. I've never been like you."

"What did you do, Mom?" Because I'm still so confused. If she'd tried to kill Katarina, then why was that woman still alive and my father the one who was dead? And where in the hell had my mom found a hired gun? Who in the hell?

"I was upset. I'd read your father's e-mails and it sounded like he was going to leave me. I became emotional. That woman . . . she had to go. But I don't know how to do such things. I don't even like guns. So I went to a . . . friend. Explained the situation. He tried to talk me out of it but when he wasn't looking, I swiped his Rolodex. Discovered what I needed for myself and made the call. Except then your father came home. He'd heard all about my confrontation with Katarina. He assured me he'd never for a moment been tempted to leave our marriage. He loved me and only me. I was the great love of his life. And then . . . things were good."

I struggle to grasp what she's saying. "So Dad plans to leave you, you plan to kill his mistress, but both of you decide you're perfectly happy together instead?"

"You've never known great passion, Evie. It's the real reason I didn't like Conrad for you. Oh, he was nice enough. But the way you looked at him . . . You were playing it safe. Again."

"Wow, I'm so sorry. My husband didn't cheat on me and I didn't try to assassinate the other woman, so clearly we had a boring marriage. I'll bear that in mind for the future."

"You don't have to sound so sarcastic, Evie. I'm merely being honest. Frankly, I've never understood where you get all this anxiety from."

I stare at her empty martini glass and think that's an ironic statement.

"For a man like your father, with his ability to see what no one else could see . . ." My mother shrugs. "What are rules for a man whose own intellect exists outside of all preconceived notions? He wasn't just an extraordinary thinker; he was an extraordinary person. He didn't accept limits, and he didn't see how societal norms should apply to him. I loved him for that, just as he loved me. We were made for each other. And you"—she frowns at me slightly—"were our strange, introverted child, who never would've even made a friend if I hadn't forced you."

"I hated those damn tea parties!"

"Tough love, my dear. Isn't that what everyone calls it these days?" My mom lifts her martini glass, realizes belatedly that it's empty.

"Who killed Dad?" I grind out.

"I don't know. I'd made that silly call. So once your father and I patched things up, I had no choice but to contact the man again and say I'd changed my mind about Katarina. He just laughed at me. Said there was no such thing as a renege clause. Really? All contracts can be voided. It's just a matter of negotiation. He was rather stubborn on the subject, though, even when I promised him twice the money not to do anything. So that was it. I went back to our . . . mutual acquaintance, told him what had happened, and made him swear he'd make it right. I assumed that was the end of the matter."

"Except Katarina Ivanova is very much alive, Mom, and Dad isn't. Didn't you think it was strange? Didn't you wonder at all when you then came home and discovered your own husband shot to death on the kitchen floor!" I'm not asking the questions as much as I'm shouting them. I can't help myself. All the anger, rage, helplessness.

My mother simply stares at me. "I don't know what happened," she states. "I didn't know then. I don't know now."

"Who was your friend? How did you get the contact information for a hired killer?" Except in the next moment, I don't need her to answer. I know. I've always known. He told me so himself. A man with a violent past. Who then went on to represent most of the major criminals in Boston. Oh, the names he would have in his Rolodex. "Mr. Delaney," I whisper.

My mom acknowledges the name with a small nod.

"Dick had assured me everything was handled. He'd called the person directly, agreed on a payoff to go away. Of course he lectured me on being so stupid. But in the end, nothing happened, all was made right. So that day . . . Walking through the door . . ." My mother's voice trails off. She's no longer looking at me, but I know what she's seeing. My father's body, splayed against the fridge. Such a great man, brought so low. And the blood, so much blood. When she speaks again, her voice is so soft I can barely hear her. "Walking into the house . . . I honestly thought your father had had one of his bad days. We'd been fighting, obviously. Maybe it had become too much for him and, well, he did what geniuses often do. I'd worried about him in the past. Done my best to keep his world right. It's not easy, though, being brilliant. Nor being married to one."

I don't believe her for a moment. Her words are too glib. Too casual. And her hand, still wrapped around the stem of the martini glass, is shaking.

"Did you ask Mr. Delaney about it? Had he really reached your hired gun? Made the payoff? Maybe your hired killer really was unhappy about you terminating his services. I mean, seriously, a hired gun? Who believes they can truly negotiate with someone like that?"

My mother thins her lips. She appears less tragic, more mutinous. "For your information, I did talk to Dick about what happened. And he assured me everything had been taken care of. Besides, I hired the person to harm that witch, not my husband!"

"Did you pay the 'kill fee'?" I use the term ironically.

"No. Dick handled it."

"In other words, you don't know what happened next."

"I know my husband was alive! I know my husband said he loved me. I know everything was good again. And then . . . it wasn't."

I shake my head. I still can't believe my mother's naïveté, or that she'd be so foolish as to contact some professional killer to handle her marital problems. Then believe a second call would make it all go away. But I'm also confused about Mr. Delaney. What he'd done, or maybe, not done, sixteen years ago. Except he was my father's best friend. His first instinct should've been to help my father. Right?

I cough, feeling a tickle in the back of my throat. I try to turn all the pieces of the puzzle around in my head. Cough again.

Then, for the first time, it comes to me. What I should've realized before, but I'd been too intent on my mother and her ridiculous story.

"Mom," I say, as my eyes begin to water. "Do you smell smoke?"

CHAPTER 38

D.D.

"THAT WAS FLORA," D.D. SAID to Phil, hanging up her phone. "She spotted Rocket running across the Harvard campus with a bag full of Molotov cocktails and gave chase. She lost him."

"So this is definitely his handiwork." Phil regarded the firefighters marching through the snowy grounds, hitting first this trash can, then that trash can. In the chaos of students stampeding across the grounds, a few bins had toppled. Fortunately, the wintry conditions made short work of any errant flames. "Is it just me, or does this seem haphazard?" Phil continued now. "I mean, for a kid known for taking down entire buildings with gasoline-soaked structural fires, this seems more . . . child's play?"

D.D. nodded. She was struggling with the same thought. This hardly seemed up to Rocket's established standards.

Phil's phone rang. D.D. let him answer the call while she stared at the various plumes of smoke wafting across campus. To give Rocket credit, he'd covered a lot of ground. Seemed like everywhere she looked there was some sort of small fire. Add to that, building evacuations, panicking pedestrians, and sorting out this scene would take the fire department the rest of the day.

"That was Neil and Carol," Phil reported in. "They just found Jules LaPage's ex-wife. Or rather, she found them."

D.D. waited expectantly.

"Carol reached out to Bill Conner's retired partner, Dan Cain. As Detective Ange had theorized, Conrad went underground almost immediately after his parents' death, keeping in contact with Cain while he worked his father's old cases."

"Batman," D.D. muttered.

"What?"

"Nothing."

"Of the leads Conrad was pursuing, he felt it was most likely that Jules LaPage had engineered his parents' MVA. Not that LaPage had personally done it. But using his considerable financial resources had hired it out. It was one of the reasons Conrad became fascinated by the dark web. He felt whatever happened to his parents, finding the actual driver would never be enough—the person would just be one more cog in the wheel. Whereas Conrad wanted to understand the entire system, so he could use it to trace all activities to LaPage, whom Conrad continued to believe was operating a criminal empire while behind bars."

"Wouldn't be the first time."

"As we suspected, Conrad was helping out LaPage's ex, Monica. Sending her money. He and Cain both must have a way to contact her because, after Cain got off the phone with Carol, he dialed Monica direct, and she called Carol in minutes. Conrad had reached her about a week, maybe ten days ago. He believed LaPage had not only discovered her new identity, but had taken out a hit. She's been on the run ever since, living with a burner phone, waiting to hear more from Conrad."

"Except he never called her back." D.D. sighed heavily. "Okay.

Let's take it from the top. Conrad has a whole second life on the internet, where he has spent more than a decade establishing himself as some shadowy figure. He spends his time working his way through the dark web, learning a little bit of this, a little bit of that. Comes across a Jacob Ness or two. Maybe has been getting to know various guns for hire, because those would be the kinds of contacts LaPage would tap from prison. Till one day Conrad learns what he's been waiting to hear: A contract has been taken out on poor terrified Monica. LaPage is once again in motion, his ex-wife in his sight."

"He calls Monica directly, warns her." Phil picked up the story.

"Then sits around at home?" D.D. frowned.

"Maybe he was working contacts of his own. Is knowing there's been a transaction the same as knowing who's going to carry out the hit?"

"He needed more information," D.D. agreed.

"Except the hired gun must've found him first."

"And what? Walked into Conrad's own home and shot him three times with his own gun? That doesn't sound like any professional hit I've ever heard of. Hang on. Conrad isn't the only one who needed more information. We do, too."

D.D. pulled back out her phone, dialed SSA Kimberly Quincy. She walked down the block, away from the noisy din of the firefighters. Phil followed in her wake. The air smelled acrid. Later, she figured, she'd blow soot straight out of her nose. So many fires in a single afternoon. And somehow, she had the unsettling feeling they weren't done yet.

"Quincy," Kimberly answered her cell.

"D.D. here. Have a question for you and Keith. Okay, you're Conrad Carter. You're investigating an evil son of a bitch, Jules La-Page, who's currently locked behind bars, but who you're pretty sure engineered the death of your parents, and given the first opportunity will strike again to take out his ex-wife. So you set yourself up on the dark web, you learn the lay of the land."

"Does this story have a happy ending?" Quincy asked.

"I don't know yet. Conrad finally finds what he's been looking for: whispers of a hit being taken out. A connection to one of the hired guns bragging about a new job. I don't know. But Conrad called Monica LaPage over a week ago. He warned her to be on the lookout. Something tipped him off."

"Okay," Quincy said more thoughtfully. She was following the conversation now.

"So, what would be Conrad's next play? The whole point of the dark web is to be anonymous, right? Except it can't be completely anonymous. Flora was talking about escrow accounts, vendor reviews. At the end of the day, it's still people, offering services to other people. And someone has to know what's going on. At least one real person."

D.D. heard a muffled sound as Quincy lowered her phone, then a distant exchange of voices. The fed was obviously hashing something out with Keith.

"So," Quincy came back over the line. "You're on the right track. The dark web is really just technology connecting real people to other real people. And, yes, it takes many key players to make that happen. IT gurus, for one—though, according to Keith, they spend more time coding than worrying about vendors. You'd have a management team. Who are actually funding individual sites, keeping their infrastructure running and paying the IT guys while coming up with new services, new payment opportunities, and more importantly, new security guarantees, which is the primary attraction of the dark web. And you'd have sales, I guess, for lack of a better term. Real people working from their own shadowy desks to recruit new shadowy vendors. It's a marketplace. You always have to be offering the latest and greatest."

"So if Conrad had learned a hired gun had recently taken on a new job, he could take steps to learn the hit man's identity. Starting with the site manager?"

More muted talking.

Quincy returned: "Conrad would probably want to make a financial offer of his own. For example, I'll pay you twice that amount to do a job for me right now. But if that failed, his next—and I gotta admit, it's a pretty clever play—would be to lodge a complaint against the vendor."

"Excuse me?"

"Keith just came up with it," Quincy said. "Remember, reviews matter. So if Conrad wanted to mess someone up, he could file a formal complaint against the hit man. I paid Vendor X and they didn't deliver. Or better yet, Vendor X is a cop. Now the site administrator has to investigate Vendor X. The site's credibility is shot until the matter is resolved."

"So Conrad contacts the site administrator. Vendor X cheated me or is a rat," D.D. filled in.

"The web manager will then have to open up a case review, just like in the real business world. Talk to Conrad. Talk to the hired gun. Sort things out."

"You've got to be kidding me," D.D. murmured. Forget the criminals on the dark web, what Quincy had just described was pretty much the same way complaints were handled at BPD. "In the course of this interaction, Conrad might've learned the hired gun's real identity," she guessed.

"Keith and I are only now retracing Conrad's virtual footsteps, but from what we can tell he'd established about as deep a cover as I've ever seen. Honestly, a professional agent couldn't have done as well. Ten years of lurking, Conrad didn't just visit the dark web. He became part of the landscape."

"Until he learned too much," D.D. said.

"Which cut both ways," Quincy amended. "Conrad didn't just learn a vendor's identity. A vendor, a manager, a customer—someone learned his."

And just like that, D.D. got it. The piece of the puzzle they'd been missing. She clicked off her phone. She stopped walking, stared Phil in the eye. Delivered the hard truth: "Phil. We've been idiots."

"Again?" he asked with a sigh.

"Investigative one-oh-one. Don't forget what you already know. We've gotten so caught up in the dark web and Conrad's mysterious double life, we forgot to factor in the basics: our crime scene."

"You were just talking about it. Conrad was shot in his own home with his own handgun."

"Exactly. Yet we've spent the past twenty-four hours spinning our wheels over hired assassins and dark-web vendors and shadowy criminals that go bump in the night. Really? How would a hit man know that Conrad kept his gun stashed in his own bedroom? How would a hit man gain access to Conrad's house, given that Conrad lives under an alias and has been on hyperalert for nearly a decade? Then, having accessed the house, and crept up the stairs and retrieved the hidden handgun, how does this ninja simply stand in the doorway of the study and shoot Conrad three times without Conrad ever putting up a hand in self-defense?"

"Conrad would've been on guard."

"Meaning Conrad never saw the threat coming," D.D. concluded for both of them. "He let his killer into his home. He thought nothing of it when his killer joined him upstairs in his study. He knew the person, Phil. Conrad had to have known and *trusted* his shooter; it's the only explanation."

Phil stared at her. "He finally identified the gun for hire contracted by Jules LaPage, and it turned out to be someone he personally knew? That seems far-fetched."

"Because I don't think it's the contract killer he identified. Or who identified him. I think Conrad stumbled upon a bigger fish. Not the vendor. The site manager. A person with a double life worth burning down the entire city to protect."

"Who—" Phil started, then stopped. "We *are* idiots," he said.

"Yep. We need to get to Evie's mother's house. Now!"

CHAPTER 39

FLORA

I CAN'T KEEP ROAMING HARVARD Square in hopes of spying an arsonist. For one thing, being the heart of a college campus, the area is swarming with kids in hoodies. Rocket blends right in. Also, with emergency response vehicles and news vans piling up, it's getting hard to move.

I don't like crowds. I don't like the feeling of bodies bumping, jostling, hemming me in. My heart rate is too high and that's not simply from chasing Rocket.

I discover a little side street and exit the teeming masses. I take a moment to breathe more easily, exhaling little puffs of steamy air. Shouldn't all these kids be on Christmas break? It's been too long for me; I don't remember how my own college calendar worked, let alone what a place like Harvard does. It makes me feel old—and, for a moment, adrift. The life I used to lead. The dreams I never returned to.

Okay, time to think like an arsonist. If I can't follow Rocket, how can I out-anticipate him?

He'll want money. Two big jobs in one day, he'll return to his neighborhood to pick up his cash. Phil told me the police had it under surveillance, however, so that doesn't feel like a good use of my time.

But wait—is Rocket done for the day? The criminal attorney's stately brownstone must have taken some finesse. No way a fancy lawyer didn't have a state-of-the-art security system—and no way a kid like Rocket didn't stand out in a neighborhood that upscale. So, a finesse job. Like disguising himself as pest control for the Carters' residence. He could've used the same ruse for Delaney, except the police sightings of him afterward didn't reveal any uniform.

Maybe a delivery boy? Pizza? He'd just need a cap to pull that off. In a city of twenty-four-hour takeout, no one notices delivery people either. He could've stashed the gasoline earlier, as many of those town houses have patios in the back. A kid as athletic as Rocket could definitely scale a fence.

Then exit the same way. Watch his handiwork. Bolt when the police presence got too high or he needed to get moving to his next job. Which took him to the T stop. A simple transfer to the Red Line and Harvard Square it is.

Where he must've stashed his Molotov cocktail backpack somewhere out of site. In this day and age of constant vigilance, no unattended bag could've been left sitting at a T stop or, for that matter, near a college campus. So he would've had to have scoped out everything first. Prepared his supplies, identified key drop sites. Then once the first fire started in Delaney's house, it was all go, go, go. Moving fast, leaving a trail of fire and chaos in his wake.

Which left me with the lingering feeling that he still wasn't done.

Then something came to me. Like a whisper in the back of my mind. The media craning for a closer look of the Harvard fire.

The media that used to be camped out in front of Evie's mother's house. Documenting everyone coming and going. Making approaching that house nearly impossible.

The media, now drawn away to a string of fires on a college campus that was clearly more exciting than curb patrol.

My first instinct had been correct. Rocket Langley is still after Evie Carter. And he set the fires around the Harvard campus to lure away the media and expose his true target. Molotov cocktails for the foreplay. No doubt a fresh stash of gasoline for the main event.

I start to run.

CHAPTER 40

EVIE, D.D., AND FLORA

B Y THE TIME I PULL my dazed mother out from behind my father's massive desk, then convince her to leave her martini glass behind, the smoke is noticeable. We pass through the doorway, then draw up short.

Thick black plumes roll out of the kitchen.

I remember what I'd heard about the fire that took out my own home. It had most likely started on the stove top, some kind of homemade trigger system utilizing cooking oil, which had flared up, igniting a trail of gasoline . . .

I eye the edge of the open parlor in front of us, and almost as if I've willed it a thread of flame appears in front of my eyes and darts along the perimeter straight to the front door, where—*whoosh*—it hits the mother lode of accelerant.

My mother and I both stagger back, trying to shield our faces from the sudden heat. The entryway is gone, consumed in a wall of flame, while to our right the kitchen flares with fresh heat while belching out black soot.

My mother moves first. She tugs at my hand, moving in the direction of the stairs. I try to resist. We go up, and then what? Fire climbs, heat rises. We will only be trapping ourselves on a different level. But on the other hand, both first-floor exits are now blocked. I give up and follow.

My mother doesn't talk. I can hear her ragged breathing as she hits the stairs, still holding my hand, still pulling insistently.

"Fire extinguisher?" I manage to gasp.

"In the kitchen."

Which certainly isn't going to help us. "We should . . . call . . . nine-one-one," I try next.

"How can they not know?"

Indeed, a fire already this big in a neighborhood with houses this close together, half of Cambridge has probably dialed by now. Given the intensity of the flames, however, the fire engines need to get here miraculously fast.

Keep climbing. Help is coming. I have to believe it.

I choke on more fumes, use my free hand to cover my mouth, and think immediately, *This can't be good for the baby.*

We make it to the second floor. My bedroom suite is to the right, but given how greedily the fire is burning in the entryway beneath it, we don't dare risk it. We head toward my mother's rooms instead, which are positioned over the kitchen. Halfway there, we pass the guest bath. I stop abruptly. My turn to tug at my mother's hand.

"Wet towels," I manage to choke out, the smoke growing heavier. "Wet towels . . . wrap around . . . our faces."

She gets it. For once in our lives, we move together. I'm throwing bath towels in the tub, she throws hand towels in the sink, and we're both running cold water, soaking through our piles. No more words. Working as quickly as we can. I throw the first dripping bath towel around my mother's shoulders to try to block the heat, as she pretty much slaps the smaller version on my face.

It takes a few minutes to come up with our new ensembles of cold, wet white; then we brave the hallway once again. Only to find the shadow of a man standing right in front of us.

My mother screams.

Me, I simply stare at what the man has cradled in his arm: my father's shotgun.

"THERE!" D.D. YELLED, hitting the dash with her hand, just before Phil hit the brakes. "Rocket Langley. Just took off through that yard."

Phil didn't even get the vehicle pulled over. She already had the door open, was tumbling out into the snowy bank. Her phone was buzzing away in her pocket. She grabbed it out of habit, taking off in pursuit even as she heard Phil on the radio, calling for backup behind her.

"Rocket Langley torched the Harvard campus as a distraction," D.D. heard Flora exhale in a rush. "Evie's mother's house is his real target."

"I'm on Langley. In pursuit now."

"Okay. I'm almost at the house—shit! House is on fire. Repeat. Front windows totally engulfed. He got here first. Goddammit!"

"Are Evie and her mother inside?" D.D. demanded. There, Rocket's black hoodie, disappearing around the corner. She attempted to put on a fresh burst of speed, slid in the slush, and forced herself to move more lightly. This is why a Boston detective wore decent boots even in December.

"Car's in the drive," Flora said tensely. "A second car, too. Uh . . . luxury SUV. Lexus."

"Dick Delaney," D.D. muttered. "Listen to me, Flora. He's our shooter. He set this all up. If he's in that house, they're in double trouble."

"That's how Rocket did it!" Flora snapped. "I was trying to figure out how he could access such a prime target. Delaney set it all up for him!"

Up ahead, the firebug in question was gaining ground. The kid was young, fast, and all limbs. Just for a moment, D.D. really hated being a middle-aged woman who was none of those things.

But you didn't have to be fresher. Just smarter.

"Phil's called for backup," she gasped, watching the kid dart forward, working the next line of angles, preparing her play.

"I'm on it," Flora said.

D.D. clicked off, jammed her phone back into her pocket. Knowing it was her job to nab the arsonist.

And that she'd just sent her CI—a woman she respected, and even worried about—into the flames.

IT OCCURS TO me again that I don't know fire. For all my training, preparations, dangerous scenarios, this isn't something I know. How to *start* a fire in survival conditions, sure. But I studied fire as a tool, not as a threat for me to survive.

I shudder at the irony. I never worried about fire, because Jacob didn't like fire. Further proof that all these years later that motherfucker is still running my life.

I seize my rage. Good things can be forged from bone-deep fury.

The front of Evie's mom's stately Colonial is an inferno. Porch windows shattering, flames roaring up in response to the fresh influx of oxygen, dancing around what has to be some kind of fire-rated front door in pure frustration.

Fire is a greedy bitch, I decide. But like all beasts, it's a slave to its appetites.

With that in mind, I work on a strategy. Rear fire escape. Building has to have one. Cambridge loves its fire codes. Rooms must have a duel egress, meaning if there are bedrooms at the rear of the house, there must be a second way out.

Another glass window explodes. I reflexively throw up an arm as I dash around the side of the house. Out of the corner of my eye, I realize the neighbors are outside, watching the fire in horror.

"Call nine-one-one," I call out reflexively.

"Someone's in the second-story bathroom," the woman screams back. "I saw someone through the window!"

"Thanks!"

Then I spot it, a rickety metal fire escape. I hit the bottom rung and start to climb.

CHAPTER 41

EVIE, D.D., AND FLORA

I DON'T SPEAK RIGHT AWAY. Beside me, my mother stands perfectly still.

As Mr. Delaney steps through the smoke, heading straight for us. He's holding a handgun, I realize now. My eyes had been playing a trick on me, seeing the past when I need to be focused on the present. I'm not sure what kind of gun he currently has, but his grip is steady, his aim true.

"You're not supposed to be here," he tells me tightly, his voice already raspy from the smoke. "You said you had a meeting."

"I finished early." My voice sounds strange to me. Too normal. Too polite. Like this is any other conversation we've ever had. Like we're not standing in the middle of the conflagration, and that his comments alone didn't just reveal that while I wasn't supposed to be here, he assumed my mother would be.

"You killed my dad," I say.

Watching him now, the way he holds the gun, the way he moves comfortably through the house—how had I not seen it before? That day, I hadn't seen anyone leaving the house or scuttling down the sidewalk—all the more reason to think my father had possibly shot himself. Except, of course, there was another option—the shooter hadn't left the house. Maybe Dick Delaney had seen our car pull up and had simply moved to the front of the building, or even walked upstairs. He knew our house that well, my parents' oldest and dearest friend. He could've cleaned up in one of the upstairs baths while my mother was screaming, I was sobbing. Then once my mother had called him, he could've used the ongoing chaos to walk out the front door and walk back in the side door. Neither one of us had been paying attention.

But now . . . Now I feel like I'm seeing everything.

"My mom told you what she'd done. She admitted that much to me."

Delaney frowns. He seems agitated, but his grip on the gun is certain. The smoke is building around us, the fire growing closer. It occurs to me, he may have a pistol, but Mom and I have wet towels. Fire doesn't care about bullets, but it does hate getting wet.

"You always were impetuous," he snarls at my mother now. She still stands stiffly beside me. She's thinking something, but I can't tell what.

"You can't just call off a hit," Delaney says impatiently. "Good God, only you would be stupid enough to take one out in the first place, then honestly believe you could change your mind. That's not how things work with these people."

"You were one of them," I fill in now, speaking my suspicions out loud. "That's how you knew who to call. You were one of them."

"I did my best," Delaney says tersely. "I even paid the goddamn bill, once your mother saw the light, told the man it was for his trouble and he'd best go away. But I saw the look in his eyes. Hired killers don't simply quit jobs. I actually came here that afternoon to warn your father." Delaney glances at my mother. "Trying to kill off his mistress? Good God, you were always dramatic, but that was just plain crazy. Unstable. I tried to tell him. Because we all knew he wasn't going to change his ways." Delaney stares hard at my mother again. "Meaning what about the next mistress? Or the one after that?"

Now he positively glares at my mother.

"You tried to warn my father?" I ask, starting to inch backward, away from him, away from the blaze.

"He was cleaning his shotgun. Said Joyce had already confessed to it all. He was sorry for the trouble and expected there was some kind of reasonable solution that could be reached. When I tried to explain the severity of the situation, that you can't just hire a professional assassin then simply walk away, that it was one thing for Joyce to be possessive, quite another for her to be homicidal. Good God . . ." Delaney stops. Coughs raggedly. I glance quickly at his gun, but he still has it pointed at my mother's chest.

"He didn't believe you?" I ask. Because I didn't understand this either. My father was a very rational man. And there was nothing rational about a wife who tried to resolve marital disputes through contract killers.

For the first time, Mr. Delaney looks at me. What he says next comes out flat and hard: "He accused me of being jealous."

In that moment, I get it. Mr. Delaney. His close relationship with my father. But always as a friend, the outsider looking in, because my father had my mother, not to mention so many other women.

"He knew how you felt about him. How you really felt about him," I say. I'm saddened for this man and how much that had to hurt.

"He always saw everything," Mr. Delaney muttered roughly, which is answer enough.

"You loved him."

"It didn't matter! He had her. For your father it was always about her!" He jabs the gun toward my mother's chest. "So much so, that even when her actions threatened him, his reputation, his own mistress, for the love of God, even when I, as a good friend, tried to warn him no good would come of their increasingly volatile marriage, he didn't hear me. He laughed. He . . . He . . ."

"He rejected you." I can see it clearly. My father, who could be arrogant, who hadn't wanted to hear how his relationship with his wife might be wrong. Easier for him to turn on the messenger instead. Dismiss a legitimate warning as nothing more than the jealous ramblings from a friend he'd always known had more than friendly feelings for him. And Delaney, standing there, having come in good faith to talk about something he was the expert on . . . Delaney, who had loved my father, respectfully, from a distance, only to have his closest friend turn on him.

I can see it. I can see all of it. And it hurts so much.

"I picked up the shotgun," Delaney says now, as if watching the movie in my mind. "At the last minute, Earl realized what I was going to do. We struggled. It went off." Delaney's voice falters. He and I both know no shotgun just "went off." It had to be pumped. It had to be fired. Into the torso of his best friend.

"He fell down. And I heard a car. Your vehicle in the driveway." He glances at my mother. "I wiped down the shotgun. Took off my shoes and tiptoed out of the kitchen. Upstairs, in Earl's bathroom, I rinsed my hair, hands, and face. Then I balled up my bloody clothes to be retrieved later and re-dressed in items from Earl's closet. You never even noticed."

My mother still isn't talking or moving. But I feel it now, a subtle pressure from her hand, tugging me closer to her. For a moment, I resist. Because I have to know the rest.

"Then I said I shot him, and you were home free," I provide now.

"I thought you knew." Delaney stares at my mother. "I thought you knew and asked Evie to confess to protect me. I kept waiting for you to approach me, make some kind of demand in return. But you never did. Then one day I realized, my best friend was dead." Delaney took a shuddering breath, coughed again from the rapidly thickening smoke now. "And I got away with it."

"And Conrad?" I whisper because there's more to this story; I know that now. More things I don't want to hear but have to know. I press the wet towel closer to my lips and nose. I can feel the heat growing. The fire is coming for us.

In fact, that's what I'm hoping for.

"You're on the dark web, aren't you?" I hear myself now. "A man with your past experiences, current contacts. What do you do? Run a site, a forum, something?"

"Even on the internet, it takes personal connections to vouch for, say, certain professionals." Mr. Delaney shrugs, as if this is the most obvious thing in the world. Maybe for him, it is. Maybe for my husband, all those years, all those aliases, logged online, it was as well. I know too much, I think, and yet still feel like I know nothing at all.

"Conrad figured you out," I venture. "Surfing the dark web, he came upon something."

"Ironically enough, he lodged a complaint against a particular gun for hire. When I went to mediate . . . I realized from Conrad's e-mail who'd sent it. I knew then, it was only a matter of time before Conrad realized my role as site manager as well."

I stare at him. I don't care anymore about the smoke stinging my eyes, the intensity of the nearing flames, the feel of my mom tugging my hand. "Tell me," I order, my voice so thick I barely recognize it. "I want to hear it. Straight from you. Tell me exactly how you killed my husband."

"I didn't have a choice—"

"Tell me!"

"I waited till you were out," Mr. Delaney says slowly. "I went into the master bedroom and retrieved Conrad's gun, which both of you had mentioned before. Eventually he came home, went to work in his study. I appeared in the doorway. 'I never heard you knock,' he said. Then I . . . Then I did what I had to do. Then it was done."

"You killed my husband. You burned down my house."

"I did what I had to do."

"You burned your own house. Then this house? My mother's house?" I'm practically screaming. At least I think I am. It's hard to hear over the flames.

"She knows," he said. "And now you do, too." He stares hard at my mother again. "Sixteen years ago, you didn't suspect?"

My mother doesn't say a word.

"But when Evie told the police the truth, you started thinking about that day again, too. If Earl hadn't shot himself, then there were only two logical solutions: The hired gun had come to the house, maybe to see you, and got in a confrontation with Earl instead. Or the only other person who knew everything that was going on had done it—namely, me. Of those two choices, who do you think you were going to turn on first?"

"You killed your best friend," my mother finally snaps. "He loved you!"

"You hired a contract killer to take out the competition. And he loved you still!"

"He was going to leave me!"

"No! You should've just been patient, Joyce. For the love of God, you weren't going to lose him."

"No. You took him from me instead."

Suddenly, my mom's grip on my hand tightens. Except this time, she doesn't tug. She yanks me backward. I stumble, falling halfway through the open bathroom doorway. Just as my mother, my platinum-and-pearls mother, ducks her head and charges.

She plows straight into Delaney, his pistol, the black smoke.

"Run, Evie, run!" my mother cries.

Then she and Delaney disappear into the flames.

YOU SPEND ENOUGH time chasing a dog to get back a precious black boot, you start to think like a dog. Spend the rest of your time chasing criminals, and you learn to think like a criminal.

Rocket was going over the wooden privacy fence across the street. D.D. knew it. He was counting on his youth and athleticism to launch himself up and over and leave his chaser in the dust.

D.D. couldn't beat him to the fence. Nor was she swinging over tall wooden structures anytime soon. Ten years ago, maybe, but now she'd be kidding herself.

What she could do was tap him, just enough. Vaulting took timing, balance, and a proper launch. Rocket knew how to start a fire; D.D. knew how to take someone out.

A last burst of speed on her part. Her lungs did not appreciate it and she made a mental note to get back to morning runs, even if it was snowy and cold and she hated winter. Sound of a vehicle up ahead. Rocket heard it the second she did. He made his move, a mad dash in front of the vehicle, which he most likely assumed would slam on its brakes—or, better yet, swerve and hit D.D. instead.

D.D. smiled.

Just as Phil turned right into Rocket's path, the kid slammed into the side of the hood. Then D.D. was on him, yanking both arms behind his back, as Phil flew out of the front and, weapon drawn, covered her.

"Just like old times," she gasped as she cuffed her prey. Being an administrative sergeant, this was her first takedown in a bit. It felt good, even if she couldn't catch her breath and was dangerously close to ruining the moment by vomiting.

"Anything for my partner."

Carol who? D.D. thought. She and Phil shared a smile. Then both of their attentions turned to Rocket, facedown against the hood.

"Who hired you?" D.D. demanded to know.

"Man, I don't know what you're talking about—"

"Yes, you do. And if you want any help saving yourself after today's fire show, you'd better start talking."

"I don't know his name," Rocket hedged.

"Sure you do." She leaned closer. "We know, Rocket. We know everything. Now the question is, who makes the deal first? You? Or some criminal lawyer who played you from the very beginning and won't hesitate to throw you under the bus? Talk."

Rocket's eyes widened. "You know about Mr. Delaney?"

"Mr. Delaney? That's interesting. Keep going."

Rocket did. About burning a crime scene, then about the attorney who deactivated his own security system so Rocket could have access. Followed by the distraction fires to pull everyone into Harvard Square. Exposing his real target. A fucking awesome Colonial in Cambridge.

"Those old homes," Rocket said with a gleam in his eyes. "Man, do they burn."

Phil and D.D. exchanged a glance. They could hear sirens in the distance.

"Flora's already there," D.D. said.

Phil didn't need her to explain anything more. He threw Rocket in the back of his car, and they headed for the fire.

I REACH THE second platform of the fire escape easily enough. The metal is already heating up from the flames inside the home. Smoke pours up from the windows below me and I can smell the undertones of grease, like that night Rocket and I tossed bottles of vegetable oil into the fire drum.

The fire escape on this level leads to an old double-hung window. The neighbor had said she saw someone in the second-story bath. I'm tempted to shatter a pane of glass, reach through to unlatch the window and open it up. But at the last second I hesitate.

I'm not an expert, but I know fire likes oxygen. If I burst open a window and introduce a huge gulp of fresh air into an inferno, I'm pretty sure something bad happens.

I don't know if this is my best idea or worst, but I keep climbing. Third level of the fire escape. Much smaller window. A tight squeeze—but not a problem for a woman whose nervous energy keeps her on the emaciated side of skinny.

I have some experience smashing windows. Briefly, I think of another time, another place, another girl dying in front of my eyes as I desperately try to break us both out of a house. Then I force it from my mind. Elbow is your best tool. If you're a female in a hand-to-hand combat situation, an elbow is better than your fist any day of the week. Let alone what you can do with your knee, or the heel of your foot.

I turn my head away, count on my heavy coat for protection as I jab my elbow into the middle of the pane. Glass rains down. Quickly, I shrug out of my down coat, wrap it around my forearms, and use it to clear the rest of the glass from the pane. Then, for good measure, I lay my jacket over the bottom sill as I shimmy headfirst through the narrow space.

I land with a thud. No graceful tuck and roll, more like ass over teakettle. But I'm in. I cough instantly, smelling the smoke.

Okay, now I just have to make it down a level, find Evie, her mother, whomever, and watch out for a homicidal defense attorney. I tell myself I've been in worse situations. But the fire still makes me uneasy. Rocket Langley is right: Flames have a lethal sort of magic all their own.

The door of the room is closed. I have a vague memory from

childhood fire safety drills that I should touch the door with the back of my hand first before tugging it open. It's warm, not hot. I stand behind the door, then yank it open.

Nothing. But beneath me I hear an ominous sound. Sort of a scary cackle, like a witch, or blades of flame, sensing the fresh input of oxygen from above, and greedily changing course.

Quick, I realize. Whatever happens next, it'd better be quick. The fire will give me one shot at this. Then it's coming up these stairs one way or another. I'll be out first with whomever I can find, or that will be that.

If I survive this, I find myself thinking, *I really should call my mom.*

I head down the stairs, keeping my head down as the smoke builds. I'm not even at the bottom before my eyes sting and the smoke feels like a crushing weight against my chest. I rip off my hoodie and tie it around my mouth and nose, though I'm not sure that will help. I just hit the second-story landing when I hear coughing that's not my own.

My steps quicken, but again, I'm very aware of what D.D. said: If Dick Delaney is in this house, he's a threat as big as the fire.

Then, before I can move, a person emerges from the smoke down the hall and nearly crashes into me. She is weeping and coughing and . . . wet. Wet towels, I realize. Her head, her shoulders.

"Evie?" I ask.

"My mom," she gasps, heaves. "She went after him. Shoved him down the stairs I think."

"Your lawyer?"

"He killed my father. He killed my husband. Please"—*cough cough*—"find my mom."

"Okay, we're getting you"—short pause for my own hacking fit—"out of here—"

"My mom!"

"Evie! Listen to me. *You're* a mom!"

My statement startles her. Immediately her hands drop down to her belly, and I can tell with everything going on, she'd forgotten that fact.

"Your mom did what she had to do for you." *Rasp, wheeze, hack.* "Now you're going to do . . . what you have to do . . . for your baby."

"My mom hates me."

"No mom hates her daughter, Evie. Some of us just don't understand one another." I'm tugging her down the hall. Prattling a little because I need her to be moving and moving fast. I don't want her to look behind her. I don't want her to see the column of flame that just figured out there's an open window upstairs.

I don't want her to realize that if her mother really ran backward into that . . . there is nothing Evie or I can do for her now.

"You should meet . . . my mom," I rasp out. We can't go up. Pregnant Evie will never fit through that window. Which leaves us the second-story egress. A room at the end of the hall, I'm guessing. It's one thing to study a house from the outside. Another to be inside a smoke-filled abyss and still keep a sense of direction.

"She would love you," I continue. I pass a doorway on the right. Jerk it open. Discover a linen closet. Keep us moving.

"My mom's a farmer." I adjust my hoodie over my mouth. The smoke is so thick, cloying, stinging. "Her happy place is . . . nurturing a daughter who continuously puts herself in harm's way . . . bane of her existence. You . . . she could feed. Me. So sorry."

New doorway. Please let this be the one, because I hear a roaring sound now. Nothing good comes from that sound. Not to mention, my eyes are tearing so hard I can't really see. And the pressure on my lungs . . .

I falter, go down.

Oxygen. The greedy fire has consumed all the oxygen. We think we have air, but we don't.

Evie is tugging at me. She still has her wet cloth around her head. Smart girl.

I find myself wondering what it would be like to be an expectant mother. Have a baby to take care of. A life to grow, versus my daily mission of obliteration.

I think I'm going to pass out.

She slaps me. Actually slaps me. I sputter. Try to get myself up. I can't seem to do it.

"Fire escape," I manage. "Last bedroom. Window."

She nods. Then, she looks up, past my shoulder, and I see fear widen her eyes.

It's coming now, for both of us. But she can still make it.

I think my mother will like her very much.

They will be happy together.

She's gone. I don't see her leave as much as I feel her absence. But it's okay. Because the heat is fierce now. Like a lover, licking at my face.

I think I hear laughing. And I know who is in those flames. Jacob. Walking through the fires of hell himself. Having the time of his afterlife. He always did love pain and suffering.

That, as much as anything, makes me start crawling again. Because I know in my heart of all hearts, no amount of good I've done in the past six years will ever be enough. The real reason I don't sleep, I don't eat. Because those flames of hell, they are waiting for me, too. Someday, I will join Jacob there. Just as he promised.

But not yet. Not yet.

Then, fresh air. I feel it, gulp it greedily. Evie, she's opened the window. She's found the fire escape. She and her baby are going to make it.

I have a sudden terrible premonition of what's going to happen next. Fresh air, hitting those flames.

I flatten on the floor, throw my hands over my head as if that will make a difference. Just as something flat and wet smacks against my arms.

"Run," Evie screams hoarsely in front of me. "Goddammit, move!"

She stumbles for the far window. I'm up, making a crooked dash. The roar the roar the roar. The searing heat against my back.

She dives awkwardly through the window. I think she's screaming. I think I'm screaming. But all I hear is the howl of racing fire.

I throw myself at the opening, falling against the frame.

Just as a hand snaps through the opening, grabs my wrist, and pulls hard.

"You will not fucking die on me!" D. D. Warren growls as she drags me through the window. The upper glass shatters. We flatten against the metal platform as flames explode above, and a spray of shockingly cold water shoots us from below, blasting back my hair. Firemen to the rescue.

I'm clutching D.D. Or maybe she is clutching me.

I think we are both now laughing.

But then we are both crazy.

"Evie?" I manage to ask.

"Phil's got her."

I don't talk anymore. We wait till the firemen beat back the flames enough for us to slide down to the ground. Then we lie in a puddled mess for a long time.

I look up at the sky. I think of so many things. Jacob, being sent back to the hell he came from. Keith, who is maybe more dangerous than I originally thought, but for entirely different reasons.

Evie. Motherhood. Mothers.

I make a decision. Then I close my eyes, because I'm simply too exhausted to think anymore.

Jacob is laughing again. But this time, I'm the one who lets him go.

CHAPTER 42

EVIE

When flora said her mother lived on a farm in the wilds of Maine, she wasn't kidding. We have been driving forever. A good four hours at least, heading farther and farther north out of Boston.

Flora is at the wheel. It's my car, as she doesn't own a vehicle—but she's the pilot, as I don't know where we're going. Getting out of the city had been . . . interesting. Flora drives the same way she moves: quickly, impulsively, aggressively. I might have actually let the older couple cross the street, but hey.

Flora doesn't talk much. It's okay. These days, I don't often feel like talking.

Once Boston was behind us, she headed for Route 1 up the coast. Longer drive, but more scenic. It had been nice, watching the quaint towns and ocean views pass before us. Lobster rolls for lunch. She knew a place, total dive, which of course meant it had the best lobster in New England.

I settled for a simple garden salad. One month after our fiery experience, we are both recovering. Flora's throat still holds a rasp. I cough up black soot that makes me fear for my baby. Medically, however, we've both been checked up, down, and sideways. My health is good, my baby amazing. No more gentle swelling; I now have a firmly established baby bump and I couldn't be more grateful. Every day I start the morning talking to my baby. Letting him or her know how happy I am to be a mom. How I can't wait to finally meet in person. How much I'm already totally in love.

"And your daddy loves you, too," I always whisper. Because in my heart, I know that is true. Conrad had his secrets. But they were merely painful, not sordid. My husband was a good man. A great man, many might say, working quietly and discreetly for others.

Sergeant Warren tells me they're still piecing it all together, but with information from the Jacksonville Sheriff's Office and testimony from the ex-wife Conrad was helping keep hidden, the Boston PD had been able to track down several other women Conrad had assisted over the years. Flora could've been one of them. She doesn't talk about it. And I don't pry. We are both women who understand there's no point to the coulda, woulda, shouldas of life.

Flora makes the transition from Route 1 to another windy rural road, then another and another. She is humming slightly, her fingers tapping the wheel.

We've spent some time together these past few weeks, first at the hospital, then being debriefed by the police, then just . . . because. The day I was discharged from the hospital, she and D.D. seemed to have already worked out a plan: a month-to-month rental of a cute little home in Waltham. Maybe not the best location ultimately, given my job, but then again, I haven't been to work in months and, with the baby coming and no family of my own to say *do this, stay there, think about that,* the rental was as good a start as any.

Who knew there'd come a time when I'd miss my mother's overbearing ways?

I had lunch with the school principal and my friend Cathy Maxwell last week. It was awkward, as I expected. And yet . . . They were both so kind. *We're so sorry we didn't know. What can we do? How can we help?*

I feel like I've spent my life putting up walls, hiding behind my preconceptions while judging people for their own. I'm too shy to have real friends. And who would like some awkward woman most notorious for having shot her own father?

I told them the truth at lunch. About all of it. My dad. Conrad. The men I loved. The people I lost. The mother who died for me even though I'd gone most of my life feeling as though she didn't even like me.

They cried. They got up, gave me hugs. They asked about what I wanted to do with my future and, of course, I needed to think about my baby, but bear in mind I'm a gifted teacher and the students love me and they both hoped I'd come back to work, even if it wasn't until the fall.

I cried. I hugged them back. We scheduled a time to get together again, and it occurred to me, this could be my life. This could've always been my life. I just have to reach out. I have to keep some doors open.

Especially after losing so much.

Now, Flora. She's been working on me for weeks. I need to meet her mother. Her mother needs to meet me. We will love each other.

My first instinct, of course, was to decline. I don't want to be a bother, I've already taken up so much of Flora's time . . . So of course I forced myself to say yes. I'm not trying to replace my mother, I remind myself firmly. Because to picture her at all, her last determined rush into the flames, taking Mr. Delaney with her . . .

I still can't think about it. On my bad days, I'm angry. The whole thing was her fault anyway. The selfish, narcissistic witch, plotting Katarina Ivanova's murder in a fit of envy, then letting me carry the burden of my father's death for the sake of his legacy. Myself, even my baby—we were merely stage pieces in the theater that was her life. She dashed into those flames, I tell myself, because that was the dramatic thing to do, and she always loved a good drama.

My mother died. The police recovered her and Mr. Delaney's bodies at the foot of the stairs. Still tangled together. Completely and totally burnt to a crisp.

My mother died.

My mother told me to run. My mother charged Mr. Delaney and plunged them both into the inferno.

My mother died.

I just can't process it.

I'm rich. This is a different thought for me, too. A good one, because God knows my baby and I need the money. I've been working on finding a lawyer. Not a criminal defense attorney this time. Right after the fire, I didn't know what would happen: Mr. Delaney had confessed to me that he'd killed Conrad, not to mention my father, but then he'd also gone and died, which made it my word against whatever the police believed to be the case.

Sergeant Warren told me not to worry. Delaney might have arranged to burn down his own town house, but not before removing his computer, valuables, and personal papers. The detectives found a treasure trove of information in his office. Including a confession he'd written years ago, then locked in his personal safe. Maybe an attempt to purge his sins, sleep better at night? I don't know.

Apparently, the computer experts would be tearing apart his hard drive for months to come, and with my help figuring out all of Conrad's usernames, they could now rebuild his own activities online, uncovering the very dangerous dance that Conrad had started, thinking he was thwarting a hired assassin, but instead unwittingly exposing himself and his activities to Mr. Delaney, who then decided Conrad had grown too dangerous to live.

I don't get to hear about it as much, but I've caught snippets of conversation between Flora and D.D.—the feds are reworking Jacob Ness's computer. In fact, they are using some of Conrad's usernames to track Ness's online activities during Flora's abduction. A local expert, Keith Edgar, is helping. I only know this because D.D. likes to say Keith's name to watch Flora blush. Interesting.

Flora is waiting for something. Wants something. From time to time she snaps at D.D., have you heard anything new, what the hell is Quincy doing anyway? D.D. counsels patience. She is clearly waiting for information, too. But I can tell she's much more worried about what the information will mean.

The truth hurts. I know that. Sergeant Warren knows that. Flora will figure out it, all in good time. And when she does, D.D. and I and maybe this Keith guy will be there for her.

My husband is gone.

We loved each other. We created a home together. We made a life together. And we lied and we lied and we lied.

I miss his smile. I miss the solid strength of his arms. I miss the look of wonder on his face when he contemplated the swell of my stomach, the mystery of our unborn child.

And now I will raise our baby alone.

I think I will teach. Return to my classroom and my brilliant, lazy, frustrating, hormonal, but never boring students. I feel like if I don't put one stake in the ground, one piece of something familiar, I will become completely untethered and float away.

Too much of my life has been lies. I get to own that. Too much of my life has been isolating. I get to own that, too. And too much of my life has been spent running away instead of running toward. I want something to run toward. My child. A community. Friends.

I think Flora and I are friends. She doesn't know it yet, but once my lawyer sorts everything out, Flora will be coming into an inheritance of her own. I'll disguise it somehow. Anonymous gift, legacy from a long-last aunt. There's always a way.

But she saved me. I wouldn't have gotten out of the burning house without her. She saved me and she saved my unborn child.

My baby lives.

This, I can process. I can feel him or her each night, a swelling of my own body, making way for this new, incredible force. I can close my eyes and see each little finger and toe, resiliently forming, then growing, growing, growing. Arms, legs, nose, mouth, delicately curving ears.

My baby lives. We talk. We love. We share. No more lies. No more walls. My father was brilliant, my mother was melodramatic, my husband was a hero and a liar, my family was complicated.

No more.

I want to buy a cute town house in a normal neighborhood. Maybe one with a park nearby. And given my improved fortunes, I will have a nanny for the early years, then day care when my child is older. Or maybe I'll meet a nice older woman who'd love to help out a single mom living on the same block. I will host barbecues where I can get to know my neighbors' names, and let them learn a little bit about me.

And I won't stand in a corner anymore. I will step up. I will become part of the world I live in, even when it's scary. Because life is scary, but it still beats the alternative.

Flora turns down another road, then another.

She's not humming anymore, but her finger is tapping impatiently on the wheel. We're getting close, I think. I wonder if Flora knows that she is smiling.

Then a house bursts into view. Two stories, painted a charming yellow with slightly eccentric lavender shutters. The wraparound farmer's porch offers an array of benches, and rocking chairs with all sorts of brilliantly colored pillows, while the front door is a bright cherry red.

The car hasn't even parked when the front door bursts open and a woman I can only presume is Flora's mom comes hopping out, still pulling on her second boot. Half her hair is on top of her head, half is trailing down her back, and she is wearing so many different tops I give up sorting it out. She's grabbed some kind of man's checkered blue flannel shirt as her outer layer and is dusting what appears to be flour from her hands.

The parking area has been shoveled for our visit. Now Flora brings my car to a jerking halt.

"My mother, Rosa," she says, her voice still slightly hoarse. Time, the doctors had told her, had told me. We all need time.

But it's not her voice that matters. I'm looking at her face, and this is a Flora I've never seen. Younger. Lit up. Happy, I think again. But more than that, home.

This is Flora at home.

She already has the car door open, flying across the yard. In the passenger's seat, I slow, struggling with my seat belt. An inner instinct tells me not to rush. I don't want to miss what's going to happen next.

A pause. At the last minute, Flora's mom draws up short. I would swear she'd been about to fling her arms around her daughter, but then caught herself, as if knowing better.

For one moment, Flora's mother appears awkward, less certain. Yearning. She is staring at her child with clear, deep longing.

My own breath catches in my throat. I wonder if my mother ever looked at me like that. I'm already promising my baby I will always look at him or her with such love.

Then . . .

Flora closes the distance. Flora throws her arms around her mother and hugs her so hard, so tight. On and on and on.

Rosa closes her eyes. She squeezes back. Even from this distance, I know she is crying. And laughing and crying some more. I blame the baby hormones, but I'm crying, too.

I take my time easing out of the car. I cross the yard more carefully, aware of the snowy footing.

Flora has finally stepped back from her mom.

Rosa is teary-eyed but beaming. She looks at me. She smells of molasses and cinnamon and brown sugar, which are things I've been told mothers smell like, but I have never experienced it for myself.

"You," she says, "must be Evie."

ACKNOWLEDGMENTS

This book has been such an adventure! First off, my deepest appreciation to my editor, Mark Tavani, for keeping me focused and at the computer, even when the book was evil and all my characters hated me (which happens more than you think!). Not just anyone is cut out to deal with the cranky authors of the world. Thank you, Mark, for being the voice of wisdom for me.

On the investigative details front, a big shout-out once again to Lieutenant Michael Santuccio of the Carroll County Sheriff's Department for educating me on cold cases, prior shootings, and proper procedures for current arrests. Given this book also delves into the nefarious world of the dark web, thank you, Robin Stuart, for helping me understand all the cool ways to scrub a computer, and all the cooler methods forensic techs will use to rebuild a hard drive in the end. Rob Casella from Northledge Technologies also educated me on cloud technology and multifactor identification. In the war of cops versus criminals, I'm happy there are such brilliant people on our side. Oh, please bear in mind that any mistakes in this novel are mine and mine alone. My sources may be experts, but I am just me.

Under the care and feeding of authors, the list is very long this year. First and foremost, thank you, Laurie Gabriel, for the warm reception from yourself and your family. Thank you to my posse, who always have my back: Michelle, Kerry, Genn, and Sarah. My deepest appreciation to my local family, Pam and Glenda, Bob and Carol, for taking such good care of me, especially this past year. And of course, love and affection for my real family, including my ninety-nine-year-old grandmother, who e-mails me weekly to make sure the book is getting done, and my teenage daughter who questions anything and everything but also makes me real chocolate cream pie so at least I have hope of surviving another day.

To my pub team, you are extraordinary. For my agent, Meg, thank you for all the extra guidance and heartfelt support. Finally, I couldn't have done this without the constant presence of my snoring elderly terrier, Ruby, or the youngsters, Bowie and Annabelle, crashing around the living room. Certainly, life is never boring.

Along those lines, several people joined the bookmaking fun by winning naming rights in this novel. Patty DiPiero won the right to a character of her choice, coming up with Patricia Di Lucca, arsonist investigator extraordinaire. Rhonda Collins won the annual Kill a Friend, Maim a Buddy Sweepstakes, nominating her friend Sandi Clipfell as the missing woman, presumed dead. Tina Maracle won the international edition, Kill a Friend, Maim a Mate, naming herself as missing, presumed dead. There are more books to write; who knows what will happen next? But thank you all for your generous support and I hope you enjoy your literary immortality.

To all my readers out there, thank you for your warm embrace of Flora and her particular journey. There is more to come. Hope you enjoy the ride.

INTRODUCING
FLORA DANE

I am Flora Dane

My name is Flora Dane. Once I was an ordinary teen. I grew up on my mother's organic farm in the wilds of Maine, racing through the woods with my older brother Darwin while trying to tame foxes. My mother named me in honor of Florence Nightingale; she wanted my brother and me to dream big.

When I first disappeared, my brother Darwin left college to run the social media campaign pleading for my safe return. He posted candid photos, childhood stories, anything to humanize me so my unknown kidnapper would be less likely to kill me. My mother, in her mismatched flannels, appeared on national news programs begging for my life. She wore a silver fox charm around her throat, and in seedy hotel rooms I would watch the interviews and cry, because whether she or my brother knew it, the girl they once loved was already gone.

My name is Flora Dane. Once I was a kidnap victim.

Jacob Ness held me for four hundred and seventy-two days. He was a monster, a beast, who'd lock me in a coffin-sized box for days on end, then show up with my favorite TV show to prove he cared. He'd starve me, then suddenly return with piles of food, new clothes, a special trinket. Jacob broke me. Then he rebuilt me into the playmate he'd always wanted. He told me during all our hours and days together that he would be the most powerful relationship I ever had. He wasn't wrong.

My name is Flora Dane. I am a vigilante.

I killed Jacob Ness. I put a bullet through his brain as a SWAT team stormed the hotel room and men in black armor screamed at me to put the gun down. I did. Eventually. But every night, I still dream of Jacob. The terrible smell of his breath. The feel of the blood I'll never get off my hands. The sound of his mocking laugh ringing in my ears. So I took up self-defense. Then firearms training. Then all sorts of things you can do with chemical fire, or plastic straws, or metal bobby pins. It's been five years now. Some people sleep at night. Personally, I hunt the streets of Boston. I look for the girl I once was—wild, trusting, naïve—and I save her. While I grow leaner and harder and colder.

My brother left the country because the sight of me hurts too much. My mother refuses to give up, even though I flinch at physical contact and no longer return her hugs. She still believes one day her little girl will return to her. She doesn't know how much I long for the same; I simply know better.

My name is Flora Dane. Once I was a plaything for a monster. Now, I am a hunter of predators. I am a victim. I am a vigilante. But mostly . . .

I am Flora Dane and I am a survivor.

ABOUT THE AUTHOR

LISA GARDNER is the number one *New York Times* best-selling author of twenty previous novels, including her most recent, *Look for Me*. Her Detective D. D. Warren novels include *Find Her, Fear Nothing, Catch Me, Love You More,* and *The Neighbor,* which won the International Thriller of the Year Award. She lives with her family in New England.

Keep in touch
with
Lisa

WWW. lisagardner.com

 @lisagardnerbks

 @LisaGardnerbks